South Africa a Personal Perspective

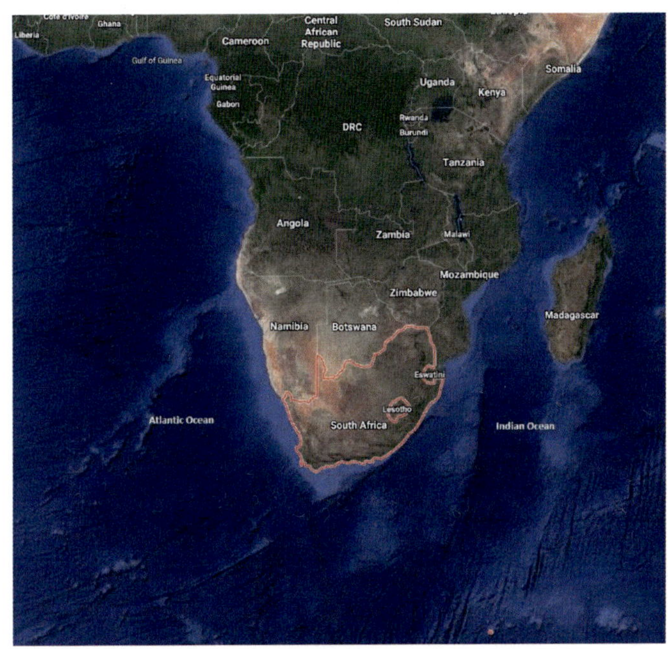

AN ABSTRACT REVIEW OF THE EVOLUTION OF SOUTHERN AFRICA FROM DISCOVERY TO FIRST WORLD DEVELOPMENT AND BACK TO THIRD WORLD

by

Steve Coetzee

Introduction

AN ABSTACT REVIEW

Steve Coetzee

An overview of the misconceptions of Southern Africa through the eyes of one who lived, believed and followed tradition to make it happen. Through these eyes many misconceptions will be explored and hopefully a clearer understanding into the woes of Africa will be communicated during daily discussions by those who never knew or really understood. A brief introduction into Southern Africa followed by the life, dreams, patriotism, and eventual resignation of one who left what was his heritage, culture and history.

Between 1962 and 1972 the UN paid out $298 Million dollars to underdeveloped countries.

In the same period South Africa spent $558 Million dollars on the development of the traditional tribal homelands for Self Rule

The Communist ANC deliberately destroyed any chances these 10 Tribes had of Sovereign Independence...

"The Plot Against South Africa" (Klaus D Vaque 1989) BondStaat.com

CONTENTS

ACKNOWLEDGMENTS

The author wishes to thank his darling wife Annie for the comfort, support and partnership that has been moulded into a wonderful marriage. To all the SADF friends, comrades and acquaintances, this writing is in essence the untold stories of all our sacrifices, celebrations, trials and tribulations through a very turbulent period in Southern Africa. I am truly blessed to have had the opportunity to serve with you.

To my fellow Flight Engineers, you are a breed that stands apart from the rest and I am truly proud to have been part of the fraternity.

Military Veterans.

You can quote us, disagree with us,
glorify or vilify us.
The only thing you can't do
is ignore us.

It really doesn't matter whether you like
our opinions on Facebook or not.

For those who had to fight for it,
life has a flavour the sheltered
would never know

GLOSSARY

- Bantu - An ancient group of people from Africa, whose origins are unclear. Some of the people from West Africa traversed from the Congo or Niger Delta Basin to become the main inhabitants of East and South Africa. They migrated slowly, such as in small groups and in the process of traveling they became known no longer as West Africans, but rather the Bantu, which translates as "The People." They migrated within the years of 1000-1800 AD.
- Bittereinders – A "war party" is a faction within a political or military group favouring the waging of war or for any group which does not wish to diminish its "fighting spirit" wanting to fight it out to the "bitter end".
- Bomb Shell – Terrorists escaping in different directions to attempt confusion in tracking.
- Braai – "Barbecue" A fireplace or pit for grilling food, typically used outdoors and traditionally employing hot charcoal or wood as the heating medium.
- Cape Province - The Province of the Cape of Good Hope, commonly referred to as the Cape Province was a province in the Union of South Africa and subsequently the Republic of South Africa. It encompassed the old Cape Colony and had Cape Town as its capital.
- Casevac - Casualty evacuation is a military term for the emergency patient evacuation of casualties from a combat zone.
- C of G – The center of gravity of an aircraft is the point over which the aircraft would balance. Its position is calculated after supporting the aircraft on at least two sets of weighing scales or load cells and noting the weight shown on each set of scales or load cells. The center of gravity affects the stability of the aircraft. To ensure the aircraft is safe to fly, the center of gravity must fall within specified limits established by the aircraft manufacturer.
- Contact – Military term defining that there is enemy fire received and returned. When enemy fire is detected a radio call from the receiving unit will be "Contact, Contact", meaning that a firefight is in progress.
- Cuca Shop - A Cuca shop is a Southern African term for a "Shebeen", an unlicensed house selling alcoholic liquor. The term is used in Namibia and Angola and is derived from a Portuguese make of Cuca beer, which was available in Angola.
- Eastern Cape – A province of South Africa. Its capital is Bhisho, but its two largest cities are Port Elizabeth and East London. It was formed in 1994 out of the Xhosa homelands of Transkei and Ciskei, together with the eastern portion of the Cape Province.
- Esbits - Unique fuel system to cook food and heat beverages. Also helps start a fire at camp, for the grill, or in a fireplace. Burn time is approximately 12 minutes per tablet.
- F/E – Flight Engineer, Technical Air Crew for South African Air Force Aircraft equipped to have a station for the position.
- Giant – Acronym for the Puma AS330 Medium Lift Helicopter as utilized in the South African Air Force from 1969 to 1989.
- Gogga – SAAF Officers Course phrase for extended period of exercise.
- Gook - Refers particularly to communist soldiers. The term has been used, notably by the Rhodesian forces during the Rhodesian and South African Bush Wars, where it was used interchangeably with Terr and Terrorist to describe the Guerrillas.
- Gunship – Acronym for the armed Alouette III Light Helicopter as utilized in the South African Air Force from 1960 to 2006.
- Highveld – The Highveld is the portion of the South African inland plateau which has an altitude between 4000 and 6000 Ft.

- IF and IFR – Instrument Flying and Instrument Flight Rules, when operation of an aircraft under VFR is not safe, due to visual cues outside the aircraft being obscured by weather or darkness, instrument flight rules must be used instead.
- Impi - Zulu word meaning war or combat, and by association a body of men gathered for war, for example impi ya mashosha is a term denoting 'an army'.
- Kopje - An inselberg or monadnock is an isolated rock hill, knob, ridge, or small mountain that rises abruptly from a gently sloping or virtually level surrounding plain. In southern and south-central Africa, a similar formation of granite is known as a koppie, an Afrikaans word ("little head") from the Dutch word kopje.
- Koppie – See Kopje.
- Kraal - An Afrikaans and Dutch word for an enclosure for cattle or other livestock, located within an African settlement or village surrounded by a fence of thorn-bush branches, a palisade, mud wall, or other fencing, roughly circular in form. It is similar to a boma in eastern or central Africa.
- Lapa - An open structure in South Africa, typically a thatched roof supported by wooden poles.
- Lowveld - The Lowveld is the name given to two areas that lie at an elevation of between 500 and 2,000 feet above sea level, in the North Eastern Part of Southern Africa.
- Lubango - Lubango is the capital city of the Angolan province of Huíla. It is the main Military Headquarters for FAPLA (The People's Armed Forces of Liberation of Angola - Portuguese: Forças Armadas Populares de Libertação de Angola) and was one of the most well defended Cities in the Southern Hemisphere during the Border War.
- MAUW – Maximum All Up Weight. The Gross weight of an aircraft.
- Met Kassie – Meteorologist.
- Natal – A region in South Africa stretching between the Indian Ocean in the south and east, the Drakensburg in the west, and the Lebombo Mountains in the north. The main cities are Pietermaritzburg and Durban. Today, it is administered as the Province of KwaZulu-Natal.
- Necklacing - The practice of summary execution and torture carried out by forcing a rubber tire, filled with gasoline, around a victim's chest and arms, and setting it on fire. The victim may take up to 20 minutes to die, suffering severe burns in the process.
- Nguni - The Nguni, Ndebele, Swazi, Xhosa and Zulu tribes, diverged from the Sotho-Tswana and Tsonga within the past 1,000 to 2,000 years. At some point along their southward journey, they came in contact with San hunters, which is why they now produce the "click" sounds that characterize their languages today.
- NVG – Night Vision Goggles as utilized by helicopter crews in the South African Air Force.
- Orange Free State - The Orange Free State was an independent Boer sovereign republic in southern Africa during the second half of the 19th century, and later a British colony and a province of the Union of South Africa. It is the historical precursor to the present-day Free State province. Extending between the Orange and Vaal rivers, its borders were determined by the United Kingdom of Great Britain and Ireland in 1848 when the region was proclaimed as the Orange River Sovereignty, with a seat of a British Resident in Bloemfontein.
- Ops – Acronym for Military Operations.
- Rat Pack – South African Defense Force Acronym for Dry Ration Pack.
- Rondawels - An African-style hut known in literature as cone on cylinder or cone on drum, but popularly referred to simply as Rondawel from the Afrikaans word Rondawel.
- SAAF – South African Air Force.
- SADFI – South African Defense Force Institute, a military run shopping store for enlisted personnel.

- SAR – Search for and provision of aid to people who are in distress or imminent danger. SAR in various fields include mountain rescue; ground search and rescue, urban and cities rescue; combat search and rescue on the battlefield and air-sea rescue over water.
- San - Indigenous people of southern Africa for the last 70,000 years, also referred to as Bushmen. The San people, or Saan, also known as Bushmen or Basarwa, are members of various indigenous hunter-gatherer people of Southern Africa, whose territories span Botswana, Namibia, Angola, Zambia, Zimbabwe, Lesotho and South Africa.
- Snag – Acronym for a technical defect on an aircraft.
- Spoor - Track or scent of an animal or person.
- SWAPO - South West Africa People's Organization, officially known as SWAPO Party of Namibia, is a political party and former national liberation movement in the former South West Africa, now known as Namibia. It has been the governing party in Namibia since achieving independence in 1990.
- Telstar – Light aircraft with Army Commander on board to control and direct a ground attack from the air.
- Transkei – A significant precedent and historic turning point in South Africa's policy of apartheid and "separate development", it was the first of four territories to be declared independent of South Africa. Throughout its existence, it remained an internationally unrecognized, diplomatically isolated, politically unstable de facto one-party state, which at one point broke relations with South Africa, the only country that acknowledged it as a legal entity. In 1994, it was reintegrated into its larger neighbour and became part of the Eastern Cape Province.
- Transvaal - Transvaal is a geographic term associated with land north of (i.e., beyond) the Vaal River in modern-day South Africa. Many states and administrative divisions have carried the name Transvaal.
- UDF - The United Democratic Front was a major anti-apartheid organization of the 1980s. The non-racial coalition of about 400 civic, church, students', workers' and other organizations was formed in 1983, initially to fight the new Tricameral Parliament. The UDF's goal was to establish a "non-racial, united South Africa in which segregation is abolished and in which society is freed from institutional and systematic racism, "Its slogan was "UDF Unites, Apartheid Divides."
- MK - Umkhonto we Sizwe, Xhosa pronunciation, uˈmkʰonto we ˈsizwe, meaning "Spear of the Nation", was the armed wing of the African National Congress (ANC), co-founded by Nelson Mandela. Its mission was to fight against the South African government.
- U/T F/E – Under Training Flight Engineer at 87 Helicopter Flight School, located at Air Force Base Bloemspruit on the outskirts of Bloemfontein in the Province of the Orange Free State.
- Veldt - A type of wide open rural landscape in Southern Africa. Particularly, it is a flat area covered in grass or low scrub.
- Veldskoen or vellie - walking shoes made from vegetable-tanned leather or soft rawhide uppers attached to a leather foot bed and rubber sole without tacks or nails.
- VERTREP – Vertical Ship Replenishment conducted via helicopters with Naval ships at sea.
- VFR – Visual Flight Rules, flying solely by reference to outside visual cues, such as the horizon to maintain orientation, nearby buildings and terrain features for navigation, and other aircraft to maintain separation.
- VIP – Very Important Person.

Chapter 1 - A HISTORY LESSON

First Nations

The Middle Stone Age covers the period from 300,000 to 50,000 years ago. The hunter-gatherers of Southern Africa, named San by their pastoral neighbours, the Khoikhoi, and Bushmen, are direct descendants of the first anatomically modern humans to migrate to Southern Africa more than 130,000 years ago. The term Khoisan groups the pre-Bantu populations of South Africa.

The San were much more widespread than today, their modern habitat being reduced due to their decimation during the Bantu expansion. They were dispersed throughout much of Southern and Southeastern Africa. During the Middle Stone Age, the climate fluctuated between glacial, rainy, and increasingly humid causing the early hunter-gatherers of South Africa to adapt their technological advancements, movements, and foraging strategies.

The San and related peoples, a nomadic people with great understanding and respect for nature originally inhabited South Africa. They roamed most of Southern Africa, and even today evidence of their visitations can be seen in many cave drawings all over the region. Blombos Cave contains personal ornaments and what are presumed to be the tools used to produce artistic imagery, as well as bone tools. Still Bay and Howieson's Poort contain variable tool technologies. The San were a very shy nation and kept their distance from any larger settlements. With no understanding of war, greed or aggression, they were easy targets for any infiltrators. The Khoisanid populations ancestral to the Khoisan were spread throughout much of Southern and Eastern Africa throughout the Late Stone Age, about 75,000 years ago. A further expansion into Africa, dated to about 20,000 years ago, is evident with the spread of click consonants to eastern African languages. The Middle Stone Age Sangoan industry occupied southern Africa in areas where annual rainfall is less than a 1000mm. The contemporary San and Khoi peoples resemble those represented by the ancient Sangoan skeletal remains.

First Contact

European exploration of Sub-Saharan Africa begins with the Age of Discovery in the 15th century, pioneered by Portugal under Henry the Navigator. The Cape of Good Hope was first reached by Bartolomeu Dias on 12 March 1488, opening the important sea route to India and the Far East.

Bartolomeu Dias discovers the Cape

The European powers were content to establish trading posts along the coast while they were actively exploring and colonizing the New World. Exploration of the interior of Africa was thus mostly left to the Arab slave traders, who in tandem with the

Muslim conquest of the Sudan established far-reaching networks and supported the economy of a number of Sahelian kingdoms.

Jan van Riebeeck, a Dutch navigator and colonial administrator joined the Vereenigde Oost-Indische Compagnie (VOC), Dutch East India Company, in 1639, he served in a number of posts, including that of an assistant surgeon in the Batavia in the East Indies. He was head of the VOC trading post in Tonkin, Indochina. After being dismissed from that position in 1645, he began to advocate a refreshment station in the Cape of Good Hope after staying 18 days there during his return voyage. Two years later, support increased after a marooned VOC ship was able to survive in a temporary fortress. The Heeren XVII requested a report from Leendert Jansz and Mathys Proot, which recommended a Dutch presence. The Dutch Cape Colony of the Dutch East India Company was to be formed and commanded by van Riebeeck. He volunteered to undertake the command of the initial Dutch settlement in the future South Africa and departed from Texel on 24 December 1651. He landed two ships, the Drommedaris and Goede Hoope, at the future Cape Town site on 6 April 1652 and the Reijger on 7 April 1652 and then commenced to fortify it as a way station for the VOC trade route between the Netherlands and the East Indies. The primary purpose of this way station was to provide fresh provisions for the VOC fleets sailing between the Dutch Republic and Batavia, as deaths en route were very high. The Walvisch and the Oliphant arrived on 7 May 1652, having had 130 burials at sea.

Jan van Riebeeck arrives

Van Riebeeck was Commander of the Cape from 1652 to 1662, where he was charged with building a fort, with improving the natural anchorage at Table Bay, planting cereals, fruit, and vegetables, and obtaining livestock from the indigenous Khoi people. In the Kirstenbosch National Botanical Garden in Cape Town, a few wild almond trees still survive. The initial fort, named Fort de Goede Hoop, 'Fort of Good Hope', was made of mud, clay, and timber, and had four corners or bastions. This fort was replaced by the Castle of Good Hope, built between 1666 and 1679 after van Riebeeck had left the Cape. Van Riebeeck reported the first comet discovered from South Africa, which was spotted on 17 December 1652.

In his time at the Cape, Van Riebeeck oversaw a sustained, systematic effort to establish an impressive range of useful plants in the novel conditions on the Cape Peninsula, in the process changing the natural environment forever. Some of these, including grapes, cereals, ground nuts, potatoes, apples, and citrus, had an important and lasting influence on the societies and economies of the region. The daily diary entries kept throughout his time at the Cape provided the basis for future exploration of the natural environment and its natural resources. Careful reading of his diaries indicates that some of his knowledge was learned from the indigenous peoples inhabiting the region, the San.

The coat of arms of the city of Cape Town is based on the Van Riebeeck family coat of arms. Many South African towns and villages have streets named after him. Riebeek-Kasteel is one of the oldest towns in South Africa, situated 75 km from Cape Town in the Riebeek Valley together with its sister town Riebeek West.

While the new settlement traded out of necessity with the neighbouring Khoikhoi the authorities made deliberate attempts to restrict contact. As a consequence, VOC employees found themselves faced with a labour shortage. To remedy this, they released a small number of Dutch from their contracts and permitted them to establish farms, with which they would supply the great VOC settlement from their harvests. This arrangement proved highly successful, producing abundant supplies of fruit, vegetables, wheat, and wine; they later raised livestock. The small initial group of free burghers, as these farmers were known, steadily increased and began to expand their farms further north and east into the territory of the Khoikhoi.

The majority of burghers had Dutch ancestry and belonged to the Calvinist Reformed Church of the Netherlands, but there were also numerous Germans as well as some Scandinavians. In 1688 the Dutch and the Germans were joined by the French Huguenots, also Calvinists, who were fleeing religious persecution under King Louis XIV. In addition to establishing the free burgher system, van Riebeeck and the VOC began to make indentured servants out of the Khoikhoi and the San. They additionally began to import large numbers of slaves, primarily from Madagascar and Indonesia. These slaves often married Dutch settlers, and their descendants became known as the Cape Coloureds and the Cape Malays. A significant number of the offspring from the White and slave unions were absorbed into the local proto Afrikaans speaking White population. With this additional labour, the areas occupied by the VOC expanded further to the north and east, with inevitable clashes with the Khoikhoi. The newcomers drove the beleaguered Khoikhoi from their traditional lands. Europeans also brought diseases which had devastating effects against people whose immune system was not adapted to them. Most survivors were left with no option but to work for the Europeans. Over time, the Khoisan, their European overseers, and the imported slaves mixed, with the offspring of these unions forming the basis for today's Coloured population.

The best-known Khoikhoi groups included the Griqua, who had originally lived on the western coast between St Helena Bay and the Cederberg Range. In the late 18th century, they managed to acquire guns and horses and began trekking northeast. On route other groups of Khoisan, Coloureds, and even white adventurers joined them, and they rapidly gained a reputation as a formidable military force. Ultimately, the Griquas reached the Highveld around present-day Kimberley, where they carved out territory that came to be known as Griqualand.

Burgher expansion

As the burghers, too, continued to expand into the rugged hinterlands of the north and east, many began to take up a semi-nomadic pastoralist lifestyle, in some ways not far removed from that of the Khoikhoi they displaced. In addition to its herds, a family might have a wagon, a tent, a Bible, and a few guns.

Trekboere

As they became more settled, they would build a mud-walled cottage, frequently located, by choice, days of travel from the nearest European. These were the first of the Trekboere, Wandering Farmers, later shortened to Boers, completely independent of official controls, extraordinarily self-sufficient, and isolated. Their harsh lifestyle produced individualists who were well acquainted with the land. Like many pioneers with Christian backgrounds, the burghers attempted to live their lives based on teachings from the Bible.

Migrating South

The Nguni peoples migrated from the North and West Africa in the middle of the 15th Century, just before the Portuguese circumnavigated Southern Africa. According to archeology they migrated from what is now Cameroon. Some groups split off and settled along the way, while others kept going. Thus, the following settlement pattern formed, the southern Ndebele in the north, the Swazi in the north east, the Zulu towards the east and the Xhosa in the south. Owing to the fact that these people had a common origin, their languages and cultures show marked similarities.

The remaining Nguni nation moved further south, with those who moved south west ended calling themselves Xhosas, and those who moved south east remained calling themselves Zulus.

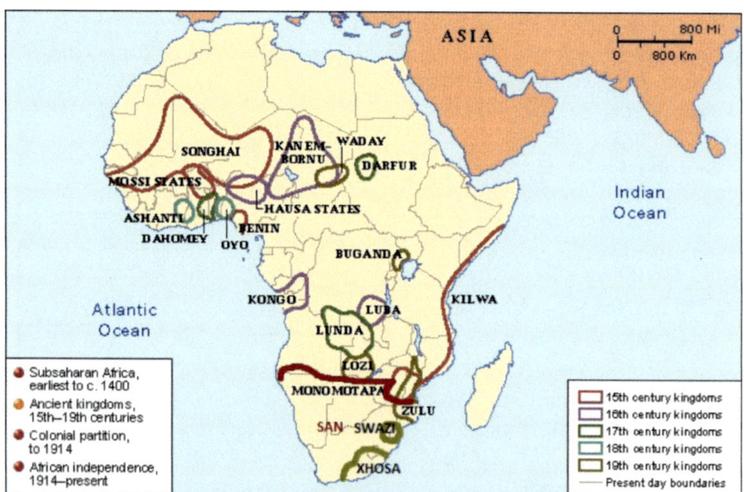

In 1818 the then Zulu King, Dingiswayo was captured and killed. Shaka stepped into the vacuum with his small but very disciplined and effective Zulu army. Many tribes and clans are said to have been forcibly united under Shaka Zulu. Shaka Zulu's political organization was efficient in integrating "conquered" tribes, partly by the age regiments, where men from different villages bonded with each other. The Nguni are divided into 3 groups, the Northern Nguni, Bantu-speaking peoples in modern Kwazulu Natal and now almost all called Zulu, the Southern Nguni, all in the Transkei and Cape and all now grouped together as Xhosa, and the Swazi.

Initially, Shaka avoided direct battles with the main Ndwandwe armies, but he would harry smaller units or retreating forces. He began to rally the smaller groups and rapidly incorporated them into his Zulu army. In a short time, his growing army began to be successful. Eventually, he defeated most of the tribes in the region, who were either killed, incorporated into the Zulu or were driven out with a couple of bands fleeing into Mozambique. In fact, Shaka was soon engaged in a massive program of conquest and incorporation of all peoples. Shaka's methods were brutal, but effective. People who submitted were incorporated into the Zulu kingdom, in some cases in the early days they even retained their leaders. Those who resisted were smashed. In battle, the Zulu did not take prisoners, old people were killed, and the young incorporated into Zulu society. Young men and women were incorporated into regimental systems. People from many different political entities had been moulded into one. Moreover, the identity as Zulu was very strong and there was no possibility of breaking down. Previous identities had been submerged and all thought of themselves as Zulu. The Zulu by their depredations had become enormously wealthy in cattle and this added to the pride in being Zulu.

Under Shaka, Zulu society was intense and violent. Political, social and economic aspects were arranged to support the militarization of society. It was often compared to ancient Sparta, but in fact, the proportion of the male population involved full-time as warriors was substantially higher than in Sparta. Terror was an important aspect of Shaka's rule. Executions were frequent for a wide variety of offences and often were capricious. If a person angered Shaka for any reason, he might simply order them to be killed; a frequent form of execution was impaling. Shaka insisted that all trade remain a royal monopoly. Trade was never a huge element, but there was certainly some limited trade with Mozambique and later with a small group of Englishmen who established a small trading post on the coast at present day Durban in the early 1820s. Shaka succeeded in building a large kingdom and a powerful sense of identity that has remained, in spite of a number of disasters, down to the present. The effects of its creation and its predatory character resulted in the devastation of huge areas and populations. Its creation initiated a period of turmoil and trouble in Southern Africa which came to be known as the 'mfecane' or 'difaqane', time of troubles.

Like the epicenter of an earthquake, the creation of the Zulu Kingdom and the militarism upon which it was based sent shock waves throughout Southern Africa. Its effects and ramifications were felt much farther afield up into Central Africa as far as modern Tanzania and lasted for decades. By the end of the process, the surviving Northern Nguni had either been incorporated into the Zulu State or had been driven out. Refugees and smashed chieftaincies were set in motion. Some groups were small and not well organized, although they were often desperate and starving. Other groups were organized and powerful fighting units. The Southern Nguni along the coast, Transkei, were subjected to successive waves. Many of the refugees were taken in by the Xhosa as dependent clients where they became known as Mfengu.

In the turmoil, an outstanding man, Moshoeshoe, was able to use two hilltop fortresses to provide an island of refuge and relative safety. There he collected and received refugees of many peoples and welded them into a kingdom known as Basutoland.

A breakaway group from the Zulu led by Mzilikazi began to establish the Ndebele kingdom in the Orange Free State / Transvaal area. When white trekboers in the Great Trek moved into the area in 1837, defeats in several clashes convinced Mzilikazi to move north of the Limpopo River and establish his kingdom there.

Another manifestation was a group known as the Kololo. It was formed from fragments of Sotho and Tswana peoples in the Highveld. They attacked and disrupted peoples in modern Botswana and eventually, pushed by attacks of Mzilikazi's Ndebele, moved north to settle in the upper Zambesi River. There, they helped to form the Rozwi kingdom and became known as the Barotzi.

Other refugee groups fled from Northern Natal. Around 1820, a group led by Soshangane devastated the area around Lourenço Marques. The Portuguese had to flee to ships and watch as the town was looted and burned. Eventually, they settled down, becoming known as the Shangaan, and created a large chiefdom in Mozambique.

Another band left Zululand in the 1820s led by Zwangandaba. The history of this group shows the amazing durability of a social, military system. After harrying people in Mozambique, the group moved into Zimbabwe where it finished the Shona culture and society that had originally centered on Great Zimbabwe. The group crossed the Zambezi River in 1835. There was some fragmentation in the next decades as some elements attacked and then settled down in a number of places around Lake Nyasa; sometime during this period, they became known as Ngoni. Others, however, continued north and eventually were brought to a halt in southern Tanzania just south of Lake Tanganyika in the late 1860s. When the Germans arrived in the area in the late 1880s, the process was still going on as the Hehe and other peoples in the area were copying and adopting the military formations of the Ngoni as a means of surviving.

The secret of this durability was the regimental system which could continually incorporate new recruits to replace those who died off or who dropped out to settle down. The system also provided very substantial military advantages over the organization and fighting tactics that were commonly used. Even where peoples managed to avoid being smashed, they did so only by adopting the same innovations as their attackers. Thus, there was a reorganization and militarization of societies in all areas affected either from elements that dropped out and used the system or by forcing people to adopt the same innovations in order to survive.

With Zwangandaba's Nguni / Ngoni, it was conquest and incorporation. In the course of their wanderings, the personality was completely changed as the original Nguni members from Natal were killed, died or dropped out. By the time they reached central Africa, the language had changed along with the name. Also, the Swazi were forced to move North-Westward from Natal and managed to hold their own despite some Zulu attacks in what became Swaziland.

The results of all this were enormous losses of life and massive disruptions of many societies. Even cannibalism broke out as disruptions led to famines; however, cannibalism was no more common among Africans than among Europeans.

The Zulu used spears to make holes in the abdomens of their slain enemies. Europeans reacted with horror at these 'mutilations'. The Zulu regarded the taking of a human life as an 'awful' act. The Zulu made the hole to 'let the spirit of the dead person out'. Otherwise, they thought that the spirit would haunt and harm them. The idea of a trapped spirit probably arose from the bloating of corpses in the hot sun. After killing someone, the person was ritually impure and in great danger until purification and strengthening ceremonies could be performed.

Large areas in South Africa were depopulated, or at least were left with small groups of people hiding out in inaccessible areas. In Natal, it was even more so the case. The Zulu were North of the Tugela River, but Zulu impis were sent South frequently. The rest of Natal had only small, isolated and very insecure little bands left in remote, out of the way places. Thus, it seemed relatively vacant and empty when the Trekboer 'spies' visited in the early 1830s. Thus, the mfecane helped to facilitate penetration of the Highveld and Natal by white settlers, moving up from the Cape region. These Settlers initially arrived in the Cape in around 60 different parties between April and June 1820. The 1820 Settlers were granted farms near the village of Bathurst and supplied equipment and food against their deposits, but their lack of agricultural experience led many of them to abandon agriculture and withdraw to Bathurst and other settlements like Grahamstown, East London and Port Elizabeth, where they typically reverted to their trades.

The Bantu peoples, including the Zulu and Xhosa, migrated to the region beginning around the 15th century and established large native kingdoms. These nations were driven by Tribal power and on their trek down South from Central Africa, they took what they needed and moved on. This was not unlike the practice of the Holy Wars during the Middle Ages. As a warrior nation the Zulu Impi's needed to hone their skills in constant preparation for war and accomplished this by hunt and slaughter the SAN like animals, until they fled to the far Western regions of Africa, where pockets of them still survive today in the Kalahari Desert.

British colonization

Like the Dutch before them, the British initially had little interest in the Cape Colony, other than as a strategically located port. As one of their first tasks they tried to resolve a troublesome border dispute between the Boers and the Xhosa on the colony's eastern frontier. In 1820 the British authorities persuaded about 5,000 middle-class British immigrants, mostly tradesman, to leave England behind and settle on tracts of land between the feuding groups with the idea of providing a buffer zone. The plan was singularly unsuccessful, within three years, almost half of these 1820 Settlers had retreated to the towns, notably Grahamstown and Port Elizabeth, to pursue the jobs they had held in Britain.

British 1820 Settlers arrive

While doing nothing to resolve the border dispute, this influx of settlers solidified the British presence in the area, thus fracturing the relative unity of white South Africa. Where the Boers and their ideas had before gone largely unchallenged, European Southern Africa now had two language groups and two cultures. A pattern soon emerged whereby English speakers became highly urbanized, and dominated politics, trade, finance, mining, and manufacturing, while the largely uneducated Boers were relegated to their farms.

The gap between the British settlers and the Boers further widened with the abolition of slavery in 1833, not because the slaves were freed, but the way in which they were freed, compensation for freed slaves, for example, had to be fetched personally in London. Yet the British settlers' conservatism and sense of racial superiority stopped any radical social reforms, and in 1841 the authorities passed a Masters and Servants Ordinance, which perpetuated white control. Meanwhile, British numbers increased rapidly in Cape Town, in the area east of the Cape Colony, present day Eastern Cape Province, in Natal and, after the discovery of gold and diamonds, in parts of the Transvaal, mainly around present-day Gauteng.

Difaqane and destruction

The early 19th century saw a time of immense upheaval relating to the military expansion of the Zulu kingdom. Sotho-speakers know this period as the difaqane, "forced migration", while Zulu speakers call it the mfecane, "crushing". The full causes of the difaqane resulted in the rise of a unified Zulu kingdom. In the early 19th century, Nguni tribes in KwaZulu-Natal began to shift from a loosely organized collection of kingdoms into a centralized, militaristic state. Shaka Zulu, son of the chief of the small Zulu clan, became the driving force behind this shift. At first something of an outcast, Shaka proved himself in battle and gradually succeeded in consolidating power in his own hands. He built large armies, breaking from clan tradition by placing the armies under the control of his own officers rather than of the hereditary chiefs. Shaka then set out on a massive program of expansion, killing or enslaving those who resisted in the territories he conquered. His impis, warrior regiments were rigorously disciplined: failure in battle meant death. People in the path of Shaka's armies moved out of his way, becoming in their turn aggressors against their neighbours. This wave of displacement spread throughout Southern Africa and beyond. It also accelerated the formation of several states, notably those of the Sotho, present-day Lesotho and of the Swazi, now Swaziland. In 1828 Shaka was killed by his half-brothers Dingaan and Umthlangana. The weaker and less-skilled Dingaan became king, relaxing military discipline while continuing the despotism. Dingaan also attempted to establish relations with the British traders on the Natal coast, but events had started to unfold that would see the demise of Zulu independence.

Mfecane

The Great Trek

Meanwhile, the Boers had started to grow increasingly dissatisfied with British rule in the Cape Colony. Various factors contributed to the migration, including Anglicization policies and restrictive laws on slavery. Beginning in 1835, several groups of Boers, together with large numbers of Khoikhoi and black servants, decided to trek off into the interior in search of greater independence. North and east of the Orange River, which formed the Cape Colony's frontier, these Boers or Voortrekkers, "Pioneers", found vast tracts of apparently uninhabited grazing lands. They had, it seemed, entered their promised land, with space enough for their cattle to graze and their culture of anti-urban independence to flourish. Little did they know that what they found deserted pasture lands, disorganized bands of refugees, and tales of brutality resulted from the difaqane, rather than representing the normal state of affairs.

The Great Trek

With the exception of the more powerful Ndebele, the Voortrekkers encountered little resistance among the scattered peoples of the plains. The difaqane had dispersed them, and the remnants lacked horses and firearms. Their weakened condition also solidified the Boers' belief that European occupation meant the coming of civilization to a savage land. However, the mountains where King Moshoeshoe had started to forge the Basotho nation that would later become Lesotho and the wooded valleys of Zululand proved a more difficult proposition. Here the Boers met strong resistance, and their incursions set off a series of skirmishes, squabbles, and flimsy treaties that would litter the next 50 years.

First Indians

The Great Trek first halted at Thaba Nchu, near present-day Bloemfontein, where the trekkers established a republic. Following disagreements among their leadership, the various Voortrekker groups split apart. While some headed north, most crossed the Drakensberg into Natal with the idea of establishing a republic there.

Since the Zulus controlled this territory, the Voortrekker leader Piet Retief paid a visit to King Dingaan, where the suspicious Zulu promptly killed him. This killing triggered other attacks by Zulus on the Boer population, and a revenge attack by the Boers.

The culmination came on 16 December 1838, in the Battle of Blood River, fought at the Ncome River in Natal. Though several Boers suffered injuries, they managed to overcome the Zulus without suffering a single death. They killed several thousand Zulus, reportedly causing the Ncome's waters to run red.

After this victory, which resulted from the possession of superior weapons, the Boers felt that their expansion really did have a long-suspected stamp of divine approval. Yet their hopes for establishing a Natal republic remained short lived. The British annexed the area in 1843 and founded their new Natal colony at present-day Durban.

Most of the Boers, feeling increasingly squeezed between the British on one side and the native African populations on the other, headed north. The British set about establishing large sugar plantations in Natal but found few inhabitants of the neighbouring Zulu areas willing to provide labour. The British confronted stiff resistance to their encroachments from the Zulus, a nation with well-established traditions of waging war, who inflicted one of the most humiliating defeats on the British army at the Battle of Isandlwana in 1879, where over 1400 British soldiers were killed. During the ongoing Anglo-Zulu Wars, the British eventually established their control over what was then named Zululand and is today known as KwaZulu-Natal.

First Indians Arrive

The British turned to India to resolve their labour shortage, as Zulu men refused to adopt the servile position of labourers and in 1860 the SS Truro arrived in Durban harbour with over 300 people on board. Over the next 50 years, 150,000 more indentured Indians arrived, as well as numerous free "passenger Indians", building the base for what would become the largest Indian community outside of India. As early as 1893, when Mahatma Gandhi arrived in Durban, Indians outnumbered whites in Natal.

Anglo Zulu War

The Anglo-Zulu War was fought in 1879 between the British Empire and the Zulu Kingdom. Following Lord Carnarvon's successful introduction of federation in Canada, it was thought that similar political effort, coupled with military campaigns, might succeed with the African kingdoms, tribal areas and Boer republics in South Africa. In 1874, Sir Henry Bartle Frere was sent to South Africa as High Commissioner for the British Empire to bring such plans into being. Among the obstacles were the presence of the independent states of the South African Republic and the Kingdom of Zululand and its army.

Frere, on his own initiative, without the approval of the British government and with the intent of instigating a war with the Zulu, had presented an ultimatum on 11th December 1878, to the Zulu king Cetshwayo with which the Zulu king could not comply, including disbanding his army and abandoning key cultural traditions. Bartle Frere then sent Lord Chelmsford to invade Zululand after this ultimatum was not met. The war is notable for several particularly bloody battles, including an opening victory of the Zulu at the Battle of Isandlwana, followed by the defeat of a large Zulu army at Rorke's Drift by a small force of British troops. The war eventually resulted in a British victory and the end of the Zulu nation's dominance of the region. In 1878 the Zulu Kingdom under its last great king, Cetewayo, rebelled against British rule in Natal. British troops attacked Zululand in 1878 and crushed the rebellion in 1879.

Zulu War

The Boer Republics

The Boers meanwhile persevered with their search for land and freedom, ultimately establishing themselves in various Boer Republics, the Transvaal or South African Republic and the Orange Free State. For a while it seemed that these republics would develop into stable states, despite having thinly spread populations of fiercely independent Boers, no industry, and minimal agriculture. The discovery of diamonds in 1869, near Kimberley turned the Boers' world on its head. The first diamonds came from land belonging to the Griqua, but to which both the Transvaal and Orange Free State laid claim. Britain quickly stepped in and annexed the area for itself.

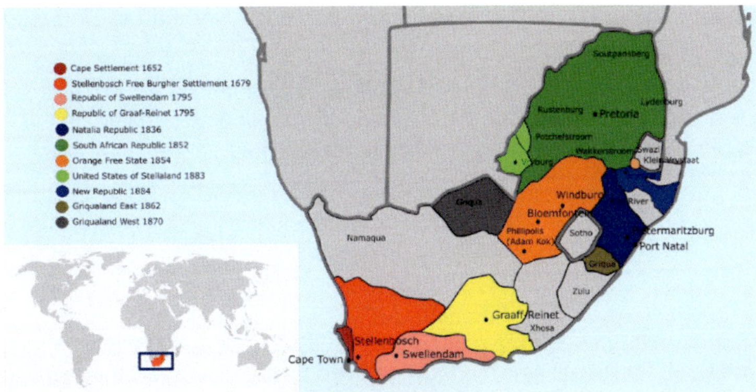

Boer Republics

The discovery of the Kimberley diamond-mines unleashed a flood of European and black labourers into the area. Towns sprang up in which the inhabitants ignored the "proper" separation of whites and blacks, and the Boers expressed anger that their impoverished republics had missed out on the economic benefits of the mines.

The Anglo-Boer Wars

Long-standing Boer resentment turned into full-blown rebellion in the Transvaal, under British control from 1877, and the first Anglo-Boer War, known to Afrikaners as the "War of Independence", broke out in 1880. The conflict ended almost as soon as it began with a crushing Boer victory at Battle of Majuba Hill on the 27th February 1881.

The republic regained its independence as the Zuid-Afrikaansche Republiek, "South African Republic", or ZAR. Paul Kruger, one of the leaders of the uprising, became President of the ZAR in 1883.

Long Tom Cannon used by Boers during siege of Mafeking

Meanwhile, the British, who viewed their defeat at Majuba as an aberration, forged ahead with their desire to federate the Southern African colonies and republics. They saw this as the best way to come to terms with the fact of a white Afrikaner majority, as well as to promote their larger strategic interests in the area.

Inter-war period

In 1879, Zululand came under British control. Then in 1886, an Australian prospector discovered gold in the Witwatersrand, accelerating the federation process and dealing the Boers yet another blow. Johannesburg's population exploded to about 100,000 by the mid-1890s, and the ZAR suddenly found itself hosting thousands of uitlanders, both black and white, with the Boers squeezed to the sidelines. The influx of English labour in particular worried the Boers, many of whom resented the English miners.

The enormous wealth of the mines soon became irresistible for British imperialists. In 1895, a group of renegades led by Captain Leander Starr Jameson entered the ZAR with the intention of sparking an uprising on the Witwatersrand and installing a British administration. This incursion became known as the Jameson Raid.

The scheme ended in fiasco, but it seemed obvious to Kruger that it had at least the tacit approval of the Cape Colony government, and that his republic faced danger. He reacted by forming an alliance with Orange Free State.

Second Anglo-Boer War

The Second Boer War 11th October 1899 to 31st May 1902, was fought between the British Empire and two Boer states, the South African Republic, Republic of Transvaal and the Orange Free State, over the Empire's influence in South Africa, also known variously as the Boer War, Anglo-Boer War, or South African War. Initial Boer attacks were successful, and although British reinforcements later reversed these, the war continued for years with Boer guerrilla warfare, until harsh British countermeasures brought the Boers to terms.

The war started with the British overconfident and underprepared. The Boers were well armed and struck first, besieging Ladysmith, Kimberley, and Mafeking in early 1900, and winning important battles at Colenso, Magersfontein and Stormberg. Staggered, the British brought in large numbers of soldiers and fought back.

General Redvers Buller was replaced by Lord Roberts and Lord Kitchener. They relieved the three besieged cities and invaded the two Boer republics in late 1900. The onward marches of the British Army, well over 400,000 men, were so overwhelming that the Boers did not fight staged battles in defense of their homeland.

The British army seized control of all of the Orange Free State and Transvaal, as the civilian leadership went into hiding or exile. In conventional terms, the war was over. The British officially annexed the two countries in 1900. Back home, Britain's Conservative government wanted to capitalize on this success and use it to maneuver an early general election, dubbed a "khaki election", to give the government another six years of power in London.

British military efforts were aided by Cape Colony, the Colony of Natal and some native African allies, and further supported by volunteers from the British Empire, including southern Africa, the Australian colonies, Canada, India and New Zealand. All other nations were neutral, but international opinion was largely hostile to the British. Inside the British Empire there also was significant opposition to the Second Boer War.

The Boers refused to surrender. They reverted to guerrilla warfare under new generals Louis Botha, Jan Smuts, Christiaan de Wet and Koos de la Rey. Two years of surprise attacks and quick escapes followed. As guerrillas without uniforms, the Boer fighters easily blended into the farmlands, which provided hiding places, supplies, and horses.

The British response to guerrilla warfare was to set up complex nets of blockhouses, strongpoints, and barbed wire fences, partitioning off the entire conquered territory. In addition, civilian farms and livestock were destroyed as part of a scorched earth policy. Survivors were forced into concentration camps. Very large proportions of these civilians died of hunger and disease, especially the children.

British mounted infantry units systematically tracked down the highly mobile Boer guerrilla units. The battles at this stage were small operations. Few died during combat, though many of disease. The war ended when the Boer leadership surrendered and accepted British terms with the Treaty of Vereeniging in May 1902. Both former republics were incorporated into the Union of South Africa in 1910, as part of the British Empire.

The eventual British victory led to the establishment of British rule in all of South Africa and to the formation of the Union of South Africa in 1910. The union became a self-governing state within the British Empire in 1934.

Boer War

The situation peaked in 1899, when the British demanded voting rights for the 60,000 foreign whites on the Witwatersrand. Until that point, Kruger's government had excluded all foreigners from the franchise. Kruger rejected the British demand and called for the withdrawal of British troops from the ZAR's borders. When the British refused, Kruger declared war.

This Second Anglo-Boer War lasted longer, and the British preparedness surpassed that of Majuba Hill. By June 1900, Pretoria, the last of the major Boer towns, had surrendered. Yet resistance by Boer bittereinders continued for two more years with guerrilla-style battles, which the British met in turn with scorched earth tactics. By 1902, 26,000 Boers, mainly women and children had died of disease, hunger and neglect in concentration camps.

Concentration Camps

Scorched Earth Policy

On 31st May 1902 a superficial peace came with the signing of the Treaty of Vereeniging. Under its terms, the Boer republics acknowledged British sovereignty, while the British in turn committed themselves to reconstruction of the areas under their control.

Roots of union

During the immediate post-war years, the British focused their attention on rebuilding the country, in particular the mining industry. By 1907 the mines of the Witwatersrand produced almost one-third of the world's annual gold production. But the peace brought by the treaty remained fragile and challenged on all sides. The Afrikaners found themselves in the position of poor farmers in a country where big mining ventures and foreign capital rendered them irrelevant. Britain's unsuccessful attempts to anglicize them, and to impose English as the official language in schools and the workplace particularly incensed them. Partly as a backlash to this, the Boers came to see Afrikaans as the volkstaal, "people's language", and as a symbol of Afrikaner nationhood. Several nationalist organizations sprang up.

Blacks and Coloureds remained marginalized in society. After much negotiation with the Boers a form of "segregation" was introduced. The authorities imposed unpopular taxes, while the British caretaker administrator encouraged the immigration of thousands of Chinese that undercut wages. Resentment exploded in the Bambatha Rebellion of 1906, in which 4,000 Zulus lost their lives after rebelling due to onerous tax legislation.

The British meanwhile moved ahead with their plans for union. After several years of negotiations, the South Africa Act 1909 brought the colonies and republics, Cape Colony, Natal, Transvaal, and Orange Free State, together as the Union of South Africa. Under the provisions of the act, the Union remained British territory, but with home-rule for Afrikaners. The British High Commission territories of Basutoland, now Lesotho, Bechuanaland, now Botswana, Swaziland, and Rhodesia, now Zambia and Zimbabwe, continued under direct rule from Britain.

English and Dutch became the official languages. Afrikaans did not gain recognition as an official language until 1925. Despite a major campaign by Blacks and Coloureds, the voter franchise remained as in the pre-Union republics and colonies, and only whites could gain election to Parliament.

1910 Union of South Africa

In 1910 the Union of South Africa was created by the unification of four areas, by joining the two former independent Boer republics of the South African Republic, Zuid-Afrikaansche Republiek, and the Orange Free State, Oranje Vrystaat, with the British dominated Cape Province and Natal. Most significantly, the new self-governing Union of South Africa gained international respect with British Dominion status putting it on par with three other important British dominions and allies, Canada, Australia, and New Zealand.

South Africa United

South African politics became dominated by friction between British and Afrikaner whites; no effective black participation in government was permitted. The United South African party, led by Jan Christiaan Smuts, advocated cooperation between the two groups and led South Africa to join World War II on the Allied side, over the opposition of the pro-Afrikaner Nationalist party.

After the war the Nationalists prevailed and won control of the government in 1948. Racial politics became the country's paramount concern, and the Nationalists introduced the policy of "apartheid" (segregation), under which racial groups were rigidly defined as White, Black, Asian (primarily Indian), and Coloured (mixed ancestry). Each group was to be kept physically separate and develop its own political institutions within defined areas of residence; mixed neighborhoods, intermarriage, and other relations were prohibited. Blacks, in particular, were restricted by "pass laws" that allowed them only temporary access to white areas for employment.

International condemnation of these policies began almost immediately, as India broke relations with South Africa in 1946 over discrimination against Asians, and South Africa became the focus of mounting protest, U.N. resolutions, and international sanctions beginning in the 1960's.

Jan C. Smuts

On May 31, 1961, South Africa gave up its dominion status and became a republic; its application for membership in the British Commonwealth was withdrawn in the face of strong opposition by most of the Commonwealth Countries. The African National Congress (ANC), organized in 1912, was banned by South African authorities.

The South African general election was held on 26 May 1948 and saw the Nationalist Party together with the Afrikaner Party winning the general elections. They won the elections with a very narrow majority of five seats in Parliament, although they only got 40 percent of the voter support. This was due to the loaded constituencies in cities, which was to the advantage of rural constituencies. The nine Afrikaner Party MPs thus made it possible for Malan's HNP to form a coalition government with the Afrikaner Party of Klasie Havenga.

H.F. Verwoerd was elected to the South African Senate later that year and became the minister of native affairs under Prime Minister Malan in 1950. In that position, he helped to implement the Nationalist Party's program. The Bantu Education Act ensured that black South Africans had access to education.

In June 1954, Verwoerd in a speech stated: "The Bantu must be guided to serve his own community in all respects. There is no place for him in the European community above the level of certain forms of labour. Within his own community, however, all doors are open".

In December 1956, Nelson Mandela, leader of the ANC, was arrested alongside most of the ANC national executive, and accused of "high treason" against the state. Held in Johannesburg Prison amid mass protests, they underwent a preparatory examination before being granted bail. The defense's refutation began in January 1957, overseen by defense lawyer Vernon Berrangé, and continued until the case was adjourned in September. In January 1958, Oswald Pirow was appointed to prosecute the case, and in February the judge ruled that there was "sufficient reason" for the defendants to go on trial in the Transvaal Supreme Court. The formal Treason Trial began in Pretoria in August 1958, with the defendants successfully applying to have the three judges all linked to the governing National Party replaced. In August, one charge was dropped, and in October the prosecution withdrew its indictment, submitting a reformulated version in November which argued that the ANC leadership committed high treason by advocating violent revolution, a charge the defendants denied.

In the 1958 election and the death shortly thereafter of Prime Minister J.G. Strijdom, Verwoerd was nominated together with Eben Dönges and C. R. Swart from the Free State as candidates to head the party. Verwoerd got the most votes in the second round and thus succeeded Strijdom as Prime Minister. Verwoerd's vision of a South Africa divided into multiple ethno-states appealed to the reform-minded Afrikaner intelligentsia, and it provided a more coherent philosophical and moral framework for the National Party's racist policies. Verwoerd felt that the political situation, that had evolved over the previous century under British rule in South Africa, called for reform. Under the Premiership of Verwoerd, the following legislative acts relating to apartheid were introduced:

- Promotion of Bantu Self-government Act, 1959
- Bantu Investment Corporation Act, 1959
- Extension of University Education Act, 1959

In April 1959, Africanists dissatisfied with the ANC's united front approach founded the Pan Africanist Congress Mandela disagreed with the PAC's racially exclusionary views, describing them as "immature" and "naïve". Both parties took part in an anti-pass campaign, in which Africans burned the passes that they were legally obliged to carry. One of the PAC organized demonstrations was fired upon by police, resulting in the deaths of 69 protesters in the Sharpeville massacre. The incident brought international condemnation of the government and resulted in rioting throughout South Africa, with Mandela publicly burning his pass in solidarity.

Homelands were established under the Promotion of Bantu Self-Government Act of 1959 to further the policy of apartheid by creating separate, but dependent, states for South Africa's blacks. Their form of government was set up in the Black Constitution Act of 1971. The South African government intended that the homelands be regarded as separate nations, but none was ever internationally recognized.

In January 1960, Verwoerd announced that a referendum would be called to determine the republican issue, the objective being a republic within the Commonwealth. Two weeks later, Harold Macmillan, then British Prime Minister, visited South Africa. In an address to both Houses of Parliament, Macmillan gave his famous Winds of Change speech, which was interpreted as an end to British support for white rule. This speech, which implicitly criticized apartheid together with the worldwide criticism following the Sharpeville massacre, created a "siege mentality" in South Africa, which Verwoerd seized upon to booster his case for a republic, presenting Elizabeth II as the ruler of a hostile power. Verwoerd also ensured that South African media gave generous coverage of the breakdown of society in the Congo in the summer of 1960 following independence from Belgium as an example of the sort of "horrors" that allegedly would ensure in South Africa if apartheid was ended, which he then linked to the criticism of apartheid in Britain, arguing the Congolese "horrors" were what people in Britain were intent upon inflicting on white South Africans, fanning the flames of Anglophobia. The 1960 South Africa referendum was accepted by Parliament.

On 9 April 1960, Verwoerd opened the Union Exposition in Milner Park, Johannesburg, to mark the jubilee of the Union of South Africa. After Verwoerd delivered his opening address, David Pratt, a rich English businessman and farmer from the Magaliesberg, near Pretoria, attempted to assassinate Verwoerd, firing two shots from a .22 pistol at point-blank range, one bullet perforating Verwoerd's right cheek and the second his right ear. Colonel G.M. Harrison, president of the Witwatersrand Agricultural Society, leapt up and knocked the pistol from the gunman's hand. After the pistol fell to the floor, Harrison, with the help of Major Carl Richter, the Prime Minister's personal bodyguard, civilians and another policeman overpowered the gunman. He was taken to the Marshall Square police station and later transferred to the Forensic Medical Laboratory due to his peculiar behaviour. Within minutes of the assassination attempt, Verwoerd still conscious and blood gushing from his face was rushed to the nearby Johannesburg Hospital. Two days later, the hospital issued a statement which described his condition as 'indeed satisfactory further examinations were carried out today and they confirm good expectations. Dr. Verwoerd at present is restful. There is no need for any immediate operation.' Once his condition stabilized, Verwoerd was transferred to a Pretoria Hospital. The neurologists who treated Verwoerd later stated that his escape had been 'absolutely miraculous'. Specialist surgeons were called in to remove the bullets. At first, there was speculation that Verwoerd would lose his hearing and sense of balance, but this was to prove groundless. He returned to public life on 29 May, less than two months after the shooting. David Pratt was initially held under the emergency regulations, declared on 30 March 1960, nine days after the Sharpeville massacre and shortly after Verwoerd received a death threat with a red note reading, "Today we kill Verwoerd". Pratt appeared for a preliminary hearing in the Johannesburg Magistrates' Court on 20 and 21 July 1960, once it was clear that the attempt was not fatal. Pratt claimed he had been shooting 'the epitome of apartheid'. However, in his defense, he stated he only wanted to injure, not kill, Verwoerd. The court accepted the medical reports submitted to it by five different psychiatrists, all of which confirmed that Pratt lacked legal capacity and could not be held criminally liable for having shot the prime minister. On 26 September 1960, he was committed to a mental hospital in Bloemfontein. On 1 October 1961, his 53rd birthday, he committed suicide, shortly before parole was to be considered.

In March 1961 at a conference of Commonwealth prime ministers in London, Verwoerd abandoned an attempt to rejoin the Commonwealth, which was necessary given the intention to declare a republic following a resolution jointly sponsored by Jawaharlal Nehru of India and John Diefenbaker of Canada declaring that racism was incompatible with Commonwealth membership. Verwoerd abandoned the application to rejoin the Commonwealth after the Indo-Canadian resolution was accepted mostly by votes from non-white nations, Canada was the only majority white country to vote for the resolution and stormed out of the conference. For many white South Africans, especially those of British extraction, leaving the Commonwealth imposed a certain psychological sense of isolation as South Africa had left a club that it belonged to since 1910 and had been a prominent member of. The Republic of South Africa came into existence on 31 May 1961, the anniversary of the signing of the Treaty of Vereeniging that had brought the Second Boer War to an end in 1902, and the establishment of the Union of South Africa in 1910. The Anglophobic Verwoerd timed the declaration of a republic with the anniversary of the Treaty of Vereeniging as a form of revenge for the defeat of the Transvaal Republic and the Orange Free State in the Boer War. The last Governor-General, Charles Robberts Swart, took office as the first State President.

In 1961, UN Secretary General Dag Hammarskjöld visited South Africa where he could not reach an agreement with Prime Minister Verwoerd.

In 1962, the UN General Assembly requested that its members sever political, fiscal and transportation ties with South Africa. On 6 November 1962, the United Nations General Assembly passed Resolution 1761, condemning South African apartheid policies. On 7 August 1963, the United Nations Security Council passed Resolution 181 calling for a voluntary arms embargo against South Africa, and in the same year, a Special Committee Against Apartheid was established to encourage and oversee plans of action against the authorities. From 1964, the US and UK discontinued their arms trade with South Africa. Economic sanctions against South Africa were also frequently debated in the UN as an effective way of putting pressure on the apartheid government.

The National Party under Verwoerd won the 1966 general election. During this period, the National Party government continued to foster the development of a military industrial complex, that successfully pioneered developments in native armaments manufacturing, including aircraft, small arms, armoured vehicles, and even nuclear and biological weapons. Three days before his death, Verwoerd had held talks with the Prime Minister of Lesotho, Chief Leabua Jonathan, at the Union Buildings in Pretoria. Following the meeting, a joint communique was issued by the two governments with special emphasis on "co-operation without interference in each other's internal affairs".

On 6 September 1966, Verwoerd was assassinated in Cape Town, shortly after entering the House of Assembly. A uniformed parliamentary messenger named Dimitri Tsafendas stabbed Verwoerd in the neck and chest four times before being subdued by other members of the Assembly. Four members of Parliament who were also trained doctors rushed to the aid of Verwoerd and started administering cardiopulmonary resuscitation. Verwoerd was rushed to Groote Schuur Hospital, but was pronounced dead upon arrival. Tsafendas escaped the death penalty on the grounds of insanity. Judge Andries Beyers ordered Tsafendas to be imprisoned indefinitely at the "State President's pleasure"; in 1999 he died aged 81 still in detention. Verwoerd's state funeral, attended by a quarter of a million people, was held in Pretoria on 10 September 1966, during which his South African flag draped casket was laid on an artillery carriage towed by a military truck. He was buried in the Heroes' Acre.

An uprising in Soweto in 1976 was put down by South African police and armed forces with the loss of hundreds of lives, providing a further focus of black protest. Pieter Willem Botha was elected president in 1978, pledging to uphold apartheid while seeking solutions to racial problems.

In the early 1970's, South African troops intervened in civil wars in Angola and Mozambique and were deployed to counteract growing pro-independence rebellions in SWA.

South African troops conducted raids against ANC bases in Zambia, Rhodesia, and Botswana. A new national state of emergency was declared as strikes and riots marked the 10th anniversary of the Soweto uprising.

Chapter 2 - PANDORA'S BOX

What "diversity" means in South Africa: Nobody can understand "Apartheid" (Segregation) unless they understand the diversity of the people of South Africa. Let us start with the whites, in South Africa there are several groups of whites; the two main groups are the Afrikaans speaking and the English speaking. The Afrikaners are the descendants from mainly Dutch, Flemish, French, German and some other Western European backgrounds. The Afrikaners have a unique culture, their own language and they are mostly protestant.

The English-speaking whites of South Africa are from mostly British background. They are made up of English, Scots, Welsh and Irish descendants as well as a large contingent of ex Rhodesians. These English-speaking Whites of South Africa can today not be referred to as British anymore. Very few hold British passports. They developed a unique accent and culture in South Africa and are fully South African today. Their forefathers came to South Africa long before there were any Whites in Australia or New Zealand.

South Africa also has other large white communities such as the Portuguese, the Greek and the Jewish communities. They all have their own religions and cultures. The Portuguese are mostly Catholic, the Greeks are orthodox Christians and the Jews are mostly orthodox Jewish. Further, South Africa has a Chinese population who arrived around 1870 to work in the gold mines until Chinese immigration was stopped by an exclusion act in 1904.

The Cape coloureds are also diverse and complex from a wide variety of backgrounds. Today there are the two main groups, Christians and Muslims. There are about 4 million coloureds in total. It is commonly understood by most foreigners and also amongst many South Africans, that the coloureds are a mixture of Black and White ancestors. This is false, the coloureds as a group existed long before the Whites saw any Blacks for the first time around 1770 in the Eastern Cape about 1000km from Cape Town. This was 120 years after the Dutch settled at the Cape (1652).

The indigenous people of the Cape were the Khoi Khoi, also known as Hottentots. They were almost 90% annihilated by a smallpox epidemic at the Cape in 1703. The Dutch also imported artisans such as bricklayers, carpenters, etc. from Malaysia and Indonesia. These were the Muslims or Cape Malay people. The Khoi Khoi and the Cape Malay also intermarried and interbred. A small percentage of Whites also married coloureds, but it was actually very rare. A large amount of the passing sailors frequented coloured prostitutes. Today the Cape Coloured features vary from dark brown to almost White or yellow and their hair vary from peppercorn curly to straight black. Some have Khoi Khoi features and some Arabic or Malaysian. Today the Muslim and Christian coloureds have distinct and different cultures. Some speak a dialect of Afrikaans and some English.

In Natal we find most of South Africa's Indian population. They total about one million and are descendants of indentured labourers, for the sugar cane plantations, and traders from India and Sri Lanka. They speak mostly English, but many still speak Tamil, Hindi or Urdu. Their religion is mostly Hindu, but many are Muslim. So far, I have not even started with the blacks yet.

Most foreigners believe that South Africa has one group of Blacks that speak one language and have one culture. Nothing could be further from the truth. South Africa's Black population is not homogenous. There are several different tribes who all speak different languages and who have distinct and hugely different cultures. There are main tribes such as the Zulu, Xhosa, Tswana, Venda, Ndebele, Sotho, Swazi and the Shangaan / Tsonga people. But it does not stop there, because these main tribes consist of smaller tribes. For instance, the Xhosas are made up of Mpondo, Fingo, Thembu, Bhaca, Nhlangwini and Xesibe tribes. The Sothos are made up of North Sotho (Bapedi) and South Sotho (Basotho) tribes. The Tswanas are only a part of the main tribe known as the West Sotho. Other tribes that make up the West Sotho are the Kwena, Kgatla, Tlhaping, Tlharo, Rolong and Ngwato. The Venda tribe is made up of mainly the Mphephu and the Lemba, but in total the Vavenda can be bordered off into 27 clearly distinguishable tribes. The Zulus are made up of about 200 smaller tribes. The Swazis are made up from the Nkosi, Shongwe, Khumalo and Hhlatyawako tribes. The Northern Sothos are made up from the Pedi, Koni, Phalaborwa, Lobedu and Kutswe tribes, and so on and so on. All in all, South Africa has nine official Black languages, with 23 sub categories and innumerable dialects. Yes, these different tribes of South Africa all have different languages, cultures and belief systems. The Vendas for instance have a special affinity to crocodiles. The Zulus consider themselves as a warrior tribe and they do not circumcise their boys when they are initiated into manhood, they have to kill a bull with their bare hands. The Xhosas on the other hand do circumcise their boys and therefore Xhosas consider Zulus as mere boys regardless of their age. When a Xhosa and a Zulu work together and they have words, the Xhosa will first and always accuse a Zulu of being a boy, thus not a man.

Another remarkable piece of information that very few people know about is that the Lemba people who form part of the Venda tribe are JEWISH. No! They did not convert to Judaism after meeting some Jewish immigrants to South Africa. President Kruger found them already with their Jewish belief system going back more than two thousand years. They migrated from the Kenya or Ethiopian regions, South Africa's black Jews.

With this clarification, South Africa is a palette of people, cultures and religions, but also note that it is the white people who were leading in the atomic age into Africa and the Blacks who are for all intents and purposes still nomadic Negro tribes stuck in the stone-age. With this background, is it really so unimaginable and difficult to understand that the way of "Separate development" (Apartheid) was the best and fairest solution for the problems of South Africa?

The violent nature of Blacks is first rationale for Apartheid. Many white South Africans feel guilty about Apartheid, they feel as if they actually did something evil or bad, but that is totally wrong. Anyone who knows the history of South Africa will know that nobody suffered more on the soil of South Africa, no one has bled as much as the Afrikaners and their descendants the Boers. The Whites of South Africa and specifically the Afrikaners have nothing to be sorry for. In fact, the Blacks owe them a tremendous gratitude and a gigantic apology for the way they treated Whites in the last 350 plus years.

It records the brutality of the Xhosas who would indiscriminately kill white women and white babies during the nine Kaffir wars. Black men are mostly cowards who are only brave when in packs. They actually seldom engage in head on confrontation with White men. When they attack it is always in groups, while people are asleep. Their preferred targets are the elderly, women and children.

Myth of Southern Africa

A common myth amongst foreigners and South Africans alike is that they think that before the White man came to Africa, Blacks lived in peace and harmony with nature and with each other. This harmony with nature is not entirely wrong. It is the perception of "In harmony with nature" that is misunderstood. Nature amongst African blacks has always been very cruel. Blacks who supposedly lived in tune with nature were regularly eaten by lions, crocodiles, bitten by snakes, stung by scorpions and their numbers controlled by insects like the mosquito (Malaria) or the Tsetse fly (sleeping sickness). Yellow fever and Cholera were other forms of nature to control the numbers of Blacks.

But it has to be said that before the white people came to Africa, the most effective way Blacks controlled their own populations were with genocidal tribal wars and cannibalism. Amongst the Black communities it is not allowed for individuals to show ingenuity or individualistic prosperity. The moment one Black person starts to rise a little above the others; he will be the first one to be hammered down by the community like a nail in a wooden floor. Those who do prosper are ostracized by their black tribes and it will be said of them that they are not real blacks that they are whites with a black skin. That mentality still persists to this day, but this petty envy is accompanied with an inbred, inextinguishable, brutality that the whites of Africa came face to face with and learned about the hard way.

Ever since the white man set foot on South African soil, he has been shocked and horrified at the brutality of the tribal blacks. No matter how much the whites wanted to believe in the "equality of man", they were sadly confronted only with the brutality and reality of Stone Age savages. Not unlike the Vikings, Huns and Mongols of a few hundred years before, the Black Tribes of Africa practiced the same rape, pillage and plunder tactics to gain power and ownership of regions in the continent. Cannibalism, brutality and extermination were the order of the day. In Southern Africa the Zulu were the most notable and vicious of the tribes.

Blacks of central Africa sold other blacks they have conquered, into slavery to Arabs, other black tribes and also to whites. The moment one tribe had a bit more than the others, they would be prone to a nocturnal raid by neighbouring tribes who would kill all the men, rape the women and children, steal the cattle and incorporate the women and children into their own tribes. Tribes who were not strong enough would flee the area. In sub Saharan Africa it meant that nobody wanted to flee north, because they knew it was a desert where they could not survive. So, the only way was to flee south. The weakest of the weakest tribes were right in the front, followed by a slightly stronger tribe, followed by ever increasing stronger tribes further north, driving the weaker one's south.

Chapter 3 - SOUND OF FREEDOM

It's a hot summer's day of 1969 in Malelane, Eastern Transvaal Lowveld, and the Primary School children in class are more interested in getting out of school to get to the local swimming hole. In the standard five class, Steve and his classmates are enjoying the spectacle of Miss Penelope sitting upright in the straight-backed chair with her hair tied back and her wrinkled face caked with face powder. In front of her is a battery powered fan, blowing the already hot air straight into her face and lifting a cloud of powder dust. Giggling hysterically the class whispers back and forth, when suddenly there is a strange sound in the distance. Something vaguely familiar to the children is a high-pitched whine with the occasional slapping of blades in the air. Almost immediately the recognition lights up in the boys as they identify the sound of a helicopter coming towards the small town.

The sound grows closer and soon they can hear the helicopter settling to land in the direction of the local Police Station. Steve and his friends cannot wait for school to finish and the minutes of the next hour drag by ever so slowly. Eventually the bell sounds and the excited boy's race towards the Police Station to catch a glimpse of this flying wonder from close up.

As they round the corner they spot the French built Alouette III Helicopter standing in the veldt, just across the road from the Police Station. Wild with excitement the boys race closer. Inside the Chopper is the Pilot and next to him a Police Officer. Walking around the Chopper is another person with a flying helmet on looking into the panels and checking all the doors. The next moment the man outside gives the pilot a thumb's up, and a high whining sound starts up. A deep grumbling sound follows and then the heat waves float up at the exhaust section of the strange looking engine. The man outside gives another thumb's up, and the high-pitched whine picks up until the blades start to turn. They increase in speed and the man outside gets into the left-hand seat of the chopper.

Alouette III

A couple more minutes of checks and then the blades, looking like a disc at the speed of rotation, cone up. The shock struts extend, and the downwash starts gushing dust and dirt outward from the chopper as it slowly lifts off the ground. The man on the left is checking the back of the helicopter while the pilot continues to edge it higher into the sky. At rooftop level the nose suddenly nods down, and the helicopter picks up speed and clears the trees in the distance.

The boys stand and stare in awe and amazement, for this is the first time that any of them had ever been so close to a helicopter. The sounds of the blades and the high whine of the engine could be heard for some time until the helicopter is but a speck in the distance.

It was at this point that Steve decided that he would join the Air Force, like his father before him, a veteran of World War II. This would be the end of his Primary School career after which a new chapter was about to start. Steve would be leaving home to go to school in Nelspruit and a new English Medium High School. As Malelane was quite a distance from Nelspruit Steve would take up residence at the Hostel, and only visit home over weekends.

It is 1969, Steve is 13 years old, and Hostel life is great. Soon after being dropped off at the new school, Steve settles into meeting new friends and planning his future in the Air Force. Steve has a short stocky build and an attitude to suite. Rugby, running, swimming are sports he excels at, but with a toned voice takes part in school operetta's and plays as well. One of the predominant characteristics that Steve has is the love of the Bush. It's not very long before he joins the Scouting movement and excels in most of the disciplines. Scouting teaches him that he has natural leadership abilities and can correct problems far quicker than the average person would. His Schooling career is more a growth period for him at this time.

South Africa being an ex-member of the Commonwealth, opposes communism. Terrorism however is rife and due to the increase of terror attacks in the country, South Africa decides to quench it at the roots, and starts an all-out campaign in the early 1970's.

Steve finishes his High School career by 1974 and as South Africa has conscription, he is destined to join the Signal Corps in Heidelberg, Transvaal. Steve however, has other plans, as his call up papers require him to report on the 2nd June 1975, he immediately applies to the South African Air Force for permanent employ. Steve is accepted and has to report to 68 Air School in Verwoerdburg, Pretoria.

Chapter 4 - START OF THE DREAM

Steve takes up a part time job in Johannesburg to help the time pass before he would join the Air Force. He packs his car and leaves home to start his life away from home. The journey is uneventful, and it takes him four hours to travel from White River in the Lowveld area, to Johannesburg in Transvaal, where he will rent a room from an old friend of his mother.

The weeks turn into months and Steve works hard to keep the time moving on. All the time he has not cut his hair. His mother comes to visit and immediately escourts him to the local barber to have the record set straight.

The summer months quickly go by and very soon it's autumn and time to get ready for his new career in the Air Force. Steve heads home one last time to his parents in preparation for his new life. There is not much time to get all the preparations complete, and he also has no idea what he was heading into.

It's almost two months after his 18th birthday on a cold winter's morning, 2nd June 1975 when Steve reports to 68 Air School in Vervoerdburg, Pretoria. There are approximately 100 recruits milling around the parade ground and there is a lot of nervous banter and trepidation on what was about to happen. A smartly dressed corporal, in what was to become familiar in the very near future as "Half Blues", has a clip board and yells out at the group to form up as he shouts out their names.

68 Air School

Very soon the motley groups are divided up into Flights to form a Squadron on the parade ground. First stop is haircut, next clothing, then food and accommodation. Walking around from this point is taboo; every movement between locations is in a flight and at a jog. The day becomes incredibly long and soon the exhausted men have their sleeping quarters, haircuts per military specification and clothing to meet all requirements. Next step is three months of hell with early morning inspections, physical training in shorts and vests during winter, and lots of running around, marching and drilling.

Before the young men have time to mourn their situation it's time to complete combat training, including very long route marches by day and at night. Weapons drill is practiced over and over until it becomes second nature to them. Route marches always include additional packages of 2 or 3 bricks or rocks. Within a very short period the young men are fit and completing the various physical tasks within the allotted time or less.

Every time a new milestone would be set and off they go to break yet another record. The tree at the corner of the parade ground is visited on many occasions and if the troops don't ask the tree for permission to pick one of its leaves, then it's another trip back to the tree to apologize for defacing the poor tree. The tree never accepted the apologies.

Before long, three months has passed, and the new recruits are allowed a weekend pass for the first time. Smartly dressed in the blue Battle Dress uniforms, the men form up and await their pass slips from their Flight Leaders. The Corporal comes out of the office and at the top of his voice yell out "tree aan", translated to English as "fall in".

Battle Dress

Steve and his group form up in a Flight and right dress quickly to space themselves and eyes front to await the next command. Roll call is screamed out, and if the trooper did not respond timely or loud enough, there would be consequences.

The Corporal shouts out in Afrikaans "Labeskagnie" and gets no response.

He repeats the name, to which an English trooper shouts back, "its Labuschagne Corporal".

To which the Corporal responds, "Jy is in Suid Afrika, Troop, en hier is jy Labeskagnie, het jy my?" (You are in South Africa, and here you are Labeskagnie, have you got me?)

To which Labuschagne responds "Yes Corporal".

The Corporal once again reiterates, "As ek Afrikaans praat, dan antwoord jy in Afrikaans Troop, het jy my?" (If I speak in Afrikaans then you answer in Afrikaans Trooper, have you got me?)

Once again poor Labuschange responds "Ja Korporaal" (Yes Corporal).

The entertainment comes to an end and the weekend passes are handed out. Dressed in his Blue Battle Dress, Steve and his new-found friends make a beeline for the Main Gate and head out to the main road for the long trek home. With no vehicles available, the young men find their own way home.

Steve uses the old thumbing a ride version, and very soon is on his way to White River 320 kilometers away. People would easily pickup members in uniform, and often give them a meal to tide them over to the next pickup. The Government has also approved signposts on the road where serviceman could wait at for pickup by passing vehicles. It is close to midnight when Steve arrives home.

Serviceman Pickup Point

The very next day, Steve's Mother insists that he wear his uniform to Nelspruit where they are going to do some monthly shopping. Embarrassed Steve complies, but pretty soon changes his mind when girls from his old school recognize him and are full of praise for his new look.

A good weekend is enjoyed and very soon it's time to head back to camp. As he has to thumb ride all the way to Pretoria and be there before curfew time, he is on the road by midday. Steve is fortunate with his rides and is in camp by early evening. The Barracks have to be ship shape for morning inspection, so its floor wash, polish, packing of clothing, cupboard tidying, dusting and polishing of windows and brass handles. This has now become a daily routine. Before bedtime the troops give the whole Barracks a final once over, so that a few extra winks can be stolen the next morning.

Aviation Training

Aviation training is a compacted cramming process to ensure that the new recruits are appropriately prepared for the disciplines that they will be trained into. There is very little time for play and long hours are spent completing tasks. The next Block to start is the Practical Learning phase, commonly known as "Tech Block".

Every morning after the parade ground ceremony, the various Flights are marched off to their respective areas for further tutoring. Steve and his group clamber into the back of waiting Bedford Troop Transporters for the short ride to "Tech Block" for the workshop phase. Here the recruits are put through workshops and taught the skills of sheet-metal working, welding, machining, and workshop practices.

To pass each phase a project has to be completed, in the Sheet Metal Shop manufacturing a Tool Box, the Machine Shop on the Lathe a Jack, and Metal Clamp, In the Welding Shop a Brass Vase, and many more. Steve excels in these tasks and is awarded with a commendation for his efforts.

Very soon the first School Block session is in process to further the academics of the young students, and the favourite subjects like Science, Math, Strength of Materials, Design, Metal and Properties of Materials become the banter of the day. To Steve's amazement, Math becomes a subject he thoroughly enjoys and is soon obtaining distinction worthy marks in tests and exams. The three-month School Block is the first of three to supply the future Technical recruits with the knowledge to qualify as Aircraft Maintenance Engineers.

As duly oriented Apprentices, the young men are transferred to Units in various parts of the Country. The transfers as all Military Orders are an authorized movement of personnel. Each recruit has to have the authority to move from one location to another by means of a Route Form.

To obtain a Route Form, one first has to "Clear Out" from the location you are resident at. "Clearing In" or "Clearing Out" is personnel transferring process, whereby a form listing each and every section of the Base or Unit, whereby the person in charge authorizes that all borrowed items are returned and that the recruit was cleared out from the Base or Unit's accountability. Only now are the recruits allowed to move to the next location where the reversal process of "Clearing In" would be completed.

Steve is fortunate to end up at 1 Air Depot where there is a large manufacturing, maintenance and overhaul unit. Here Steve and his mates hone their skills on various parts of an aircraft. Steve spends three months in the Propeller shop, three months in the Engine Shop and another short period in the Carburetion Shop. All the while they are learning the technical knowhow and discipline of how to work in aviation.

As apprentices all the dirty and laborious work is delegated to them. Being on an Air Force Depot for Steve is no different from being at a Hostel as he was during his High School career. The only addition was that at 18 years of age, he could now legally enter the Military Bar and with the cheap prices of Alcohol was soon partaking in many drunken discussions.

This is followed by the second three-month School Block at the Air Force's Technical College in Verwoerdburg. Every third or fourth weekend Steve would take time to visit his parents, who have now relocated to Marivale, a Gold Mine, near Nigel in the Transvaal, a mere hour drive away.

Next Steve and a few of his friends are transferred to Central Flying School (CFS) Dunnottar, only 5 kilometers from Marivale, where all the Air Force's initial flight training takes place. Steve requests a Sleep Out Pass and does not take a room at the Air Force Base but goes home to his parents every evening.

As apprentices, Steve and his group are taught the basics of minor servicing and repair on the Harvard Trainer Aircraft. This six-month period teaches the young men a lot about the operations of Air Force workings and all too soon it's over and they are once again transferred, this time to Air Force Base Ysterplaat in Cape Town, in the Cape Province.

CFS Dunnottar

Early the next morning Steve reports to Air Force Base Waterkloof, Movement Control to catch a flight to Cape Town. This is Steve's first trip to the fairest Cape, and also his first trip in a military transport aircraft, namely the C130 Hercules. Once again winter is in full swing.

Unlike the rest of South Africa, the Southern Cape region has winter rainfall and dry summers. Steve and his group arrive for the first torrential winter rains coupled with high winds. The final three months of School Block at Maitland Technical College, further adding to honing him in preparation to qualify as an Aircraft Maintenance Engineer.

The group of Students has to clamber into the back of a tarpaulin covered troop carrier every morning after breakfast to head out to the Maitland Technical College, where they are schooled alongside other civilian students. Once again three months is a short period to cram in a lot of studies and the students don't have much free time.

On Weekends Steve breaks away and tries to see as much of Cape Town as he can. Steve loves Cape Town and decides that he would love to get posted here in the future.

Back in Pretoria, Transvaal at 68 Air School, the last Phase of orientation is the preparation for deployment to the field as a qualified Aircraft Maintenance Engineer. This session for the next three months, focuses around aviation and aircraft orientation.

Tests are a daily occurrence, and very soon the young men can quote aerodynamics, airflow, engine types, airframes, hydraulic systems, airfoil design and so on, starting to sound like well-educated engineers. They receive file, upon file, of data, schematics, drawings, and figures. Once the examinations are concluded it's time to define which aircraft type each person is going to qualify on.

"Semper Pugnans" - Always Hostile

Those with higher score cards are selected for postings to the latest aircraft that the Air Force had just obtained from France, namely the Mirage F1 fighters. Steve is amongst this fortunate group and is therefore transferred to 1 and 3 Squadron based locally at Air Force Base Waterkloof, a few kilometers away. But before this, he must complete the Mirage F1 orientation at 68 Air School. More books, data, schematics, drawings, and figures to learn. As the technology is new, it's very interesting and Steve thoroughly enjoys his conversion to the F1.

Mirage F1

It's early in 1978 when a freshly qualified Aircraft Maintenance Engineer and newly promoted Corporal, Clears In at Air Force Base Waterkloof, to be stationed at 1 and 3 Squadron for his permanent posting. Steve takes up residence at the Air Force Base in a Barrack with one of his new-found friends Michael Freer, whose parents live in Springs about an hour's drive away.

At the Squadron, Steve settles into the daily routine of preparing aircraft for daily flights, maintaining them after completion of all sorties, and deploying away with the Squadron on weapons camps or operations. All this time Steve still has the image of the Alouette III helicopter in the back of his mind, and every time one of them flies by he would look up and wonder.

Steve walks past the hangar where the Buccaneer Bombers are stationed on his way to 1 and 3 Squadron, and ends up chatting to one of the Sergeants, also an Aircraft Maintenance Engineer. Keith duly asks Steve if he is going to apply for Flight Engineer Training. Steve's eyes light up and he starts asking questions. At Tea Break, Steve quickly reports to the Duty Room to check for any Signals that reference Flight Engineer Training. He gets what he needs and races back to the Squadron to complete the required applications. This must be approved by his Superior and then the Officer Commanding 1 and 3 Squadron.

Hawker Siddeley Buccaneer

With the application submitted there is nothing more Steve can do but wait. The months fly by and one day without warning, Steve is summoned to the Officer Commanding. A very nervous Corporal Coetzee reports to the office where the Commandant congratulates him on being accepted for Flight Engineer Training.

Steve is ordered to 1 Military Hospital to conduct Flying Medical Examinations, to ensure his medical acceptability for flight training. The Flying Medical Exams are long and exhausting, X-rays, Lung Functions ECG's, Ear Nose and Throat, Physical and Stress Testing. Eventually it's over and Steve has the green light to proceed.

New era of Politics

When Vorster resigned following allegations of his involvement in the Muldergate Scandal in 1978, P.W. Botha was elected as his successor by the National Party caucus, besting the electorate's favourite, 45-year-old Foreign Minister Pik Botha. In the final internal ballot, he beat Connie Mulder, the scandal's namesake, in a 78 to 72 vote.

Botha is keen to promote constitutional reform and hopes to implement a form of federal system in South Africa that would allow for greater "self-rule" for black homelands (or Bantustans), while still retaining the supremacy of a white central government, and foremost expand the rights of Coloureds (South Africans of mixed ancestry) and Asians in order to widen support for the government. Upon enacting the reforms, he remarks in the House of Assembly; "We must adapt or die."

Upon becoming Prime Minister, Botha retains the defense portfolio until he appoints SADF Chief General Magnus Malan, his successor. From his ascension to the cabinet, Botha pursues an ambitious military policy designed to increase South Africa's military capability. He seeks to improve relations with the West especially the United States but with mixed results. He argues that the preservation of the apartheid government, though unpopular, is crucial to stemming the tide of African Communism, which has made in-roads into neighbouring Angola and Mozambique after these two former Portuguese colonies obtain independence.

In 1977, as Minister of Defense he began a secret nuclear weapons program, which culminated in the production of six nuclear bombs. He remained steadfast in South Africa's administration of the neighbouring territory South-West Africa, particularly while there was a presence of Cuban troops in Angola to the north. Botha was responsible for introducing the notorious police counter-insurgency unit, Koevoet. He was also instrumental in building the SADF's strength. Adding momentum to establishing units such as 32 Battalion. South African intervention, with support of the rebel movement, UNITA, Dr. Jonas Savimbi, a personal friend, in the Angolan Civil War. To maintain the nation's military strength, a very strict draft was implemented to enforce compulsory military service for white South African men.

Flight Engineering

It's the beginning of another winter when Steve and the new U/T (Under Training) F/E's, (Flight Engineer), "Clear In" at Air Force Base Bloemspruit, located in the Orange Free State, just outside of Bloemfontein. Once again, it's back to Basic Training with early morning inspections, physical training, and marching to and from the living quarters and the hangars at 87 Helicopter Flight School. Many hours of lectures involving all aspects of technical knowledge, navigation, regulations, safety and operations are concluded. An average pass mark of 80% has to be achieved or the recruit would be sent packing back to his Unit. Next, the Flying Phase starts. All the U/T F/E's have to be accompanied by an Instructor F/E or Instructor Pilot. 87 HFS (Helicopter Flight School) is a Flight Engineer and Helicopter Pilot Training School. Bloemfontein has some of the coldest winter temperatures in South Africa, and early mornings always have a sheet of ice in front of the hangar doors. This leads to interesting movement of aircraft and personnel, sometimes in hysterically funny scenarios. On one occasion a U/T F/E comes racing up with a bicycle until he hits the ice in front of the hangar door, with a loud bang he comes to an abrupt stop with a look of confusion on his face. The onlookers howl with laughter at the spectacle.

One fine Sunday evening Steve and his mate from Johannesburg, Ian Nicholson end up at a party in Bloemfontein on the way back after a weekend pass. After a bottle of Brandy and some more go-go juice, both Steve and Ian are much the better for wear at the early morning parade the next day. For punishment, they both must complete a circuit. A circuit consists of carrying an Alouette Jack in each hand and running a lap around the helipads, close to 200 meters. With a Hang Over this is no fun at all. Next both are assigned 3 hours of Cargo Sling exercises each. Not a very good exercise with a Hang Over. Flat on his stomach pattering the pilot into Cargo drops in the practice area Steve is taking a lot of strain. In the second sortie as he is guiding the pilot into the drop, he feels the nausea building up. He quickly moves the microphone from his mouth leans out and barfs his lungs out. Just as quickly the downwash sprays his deposit back in his face. Fortunately, he has the helmets visor down, without missing a blink he lifts the Helmet and can see again. Steve continues pattering until the next wave, clears the mic away again, leans out and let's go. The same thing once more, but this time the barf flies up into his face and glasses. He pulls the glasses off and can see once more. Gratefully the sortie comes to an end, and he can escape to the washroom after landing, to clean up before the final sortie of the day.

The next phase will be the Mountain Flying Phase in the Drakensburg, bordering on Natal. These mountains range in altitude from 4,000 to 14,000 ft. above sea level, and are the most difficult mountains to complete all the required training in. Once crews have mastered the art of Drakensburg Mountain Flying, they would be able to fly anywhere. The Unit deploys en-mass to the Drakensburg Camp near Bergville, in Natal, where a local farmer has made his farm, Kelvin Grove, accessible to the

Air Force for the purpose of training. Tents are setup including a kitchen, dining area and pub. All the required nourishment is transported by Bedford Trucks driven by the crews from 87 HFS. The Mountain Flying Phase is the Crème De La Crème of flying, and although very stressful, it is also very beautiful. The weather changes in a matter of minutes and if caught unaware, a helicopter could easily be trapped above the clouds and must shut down on the top range in very cold conditions.

Although the training is intense, and the hours are long, Steve and his fellow U/T F/E's are having the time of their life. There are only a privileged few who have the opportunity to explore the might and beauty of the Drakensburg so close up. The mornings start off early with aircraft preparation and the U/T F/E's are very busy performing Pre-Flight Inspections and then updating the aircraft Logs to declare the aircraft serviceable for flight. Then it's a quick breakfast, cup of coffee and morning briefing with the Instructor for the days sorties.

After the briefing, it's an entry into the Squadron Flight Authorization Book, where the crew now accepts the assignment per signature, both Pilot and Flight Engineer. Next the crew steps towards the aircraft to perform a team Pre-Flight walk around. Helmut's on and pilot strapped in, the start-up is initiated. The pilot gets clearance from the Flight Engineer to initiate start who verifies area clear and start is initialized.

The Flight Engineer then inspects the engine and transmission bays for leaks or problems and then indicates to the pilot that it's clear to engage rotors. The pilot slowly advances the fuel flow and the crescendo of the Artouste IIIB engine climbs as the RPM increases from 16,500 RPM to around 20,000 RPM for rotor engagement. Once the rotors are engaged the pilot advances the fuel flow to flight idle position which is at 33,500 RPM.

1978 Course 2 U/T Flight Engineers and Instructors

Students: Steve, Ollie, Pielle, Mannetjies, Gert, Johnny, Geysie, Ian, Klein Piet,
Instructors: Salies, Frik, Mike, Lange, Danie

The Flight Engineer has now strapped in and counter checks engine gauges to ensure all are in the green. The After-Start Checklist is verified and Pre-Take Off completed. The Pilot now obtains take-off clearance from the Ops Tent and the take-off is initiated. The take-off is spectacular as the morning mist is still covering the lower mountain peaks.

For today's exercise Steve and his pilot will be honing their pinnacle landing skills on the Pinnacle. There is a sheer drop of 5000 ft around the Pinnacle and it can be quite a daunting task. They are at maximum climb rate, and slowly as they climb up the might of the 14,000 ft Drakensburg peaks come into view. Steve and his pilot are in awe and there is a silence in the cockpit to reflect the beauty unfolding in front of them.

Gatberg (Hole in the Wall)

All too soon they are at 1,000 ft. above the Pinnacle in an orbit assessing wind direction, updrafts and downdrafts. The landscape offers many clues of wind direction but at this altitude, roughly 8000 ft., they must be sure there are no anomalies. As they circle the Pinnacle the rate of climb indicator quickly reflects where the downdraft or updraft areas are. Once satisfied of the wind direction Steve and his Pilot prepare their approach on the Pinnacle to attempt a touchdown. The approach will be kept with the aircraft always facing into wind and utilizing the maximum updraft for the landing. The more the updraft, the less power is required. At the same time there always must be an escape route, should the landing attempt fail. In the approach they have chosen they will be breaking to the right and then descend to gain speed before leveling off to climb away. The approach is text book and with Steve hanging out of the left-hand door, he patters the pilot onto the Pinnacle for the landing. The landing is carried out, and only then do they look around at where they are. With seemingly nothing below them in 360 degrees, it is a very sobering feeling at how small they are in the midst of the Mighty Drakensburg.

The Pinnacle

To end off their period in Natal, a coastal flying phase is to be completed as well. This exercise is more to get the crews used to the increased effect of denser air on the performance of the aircraft, and of course to review the entertainment of Durban. The crews prepare for an early morning en-mass lift off to Air Force Base Durban where they will be hosted by 15 Squadron. Bags are packed, and aircraft prepared. Aircraft are refueled from 44 Gallon drums with small gas powered refueling pumps known by the slang name of "Putt Putt's". These pumps are notoriously difficult to start, and many of the Flight Engineers have backup systems of spray that they use for quick starting.

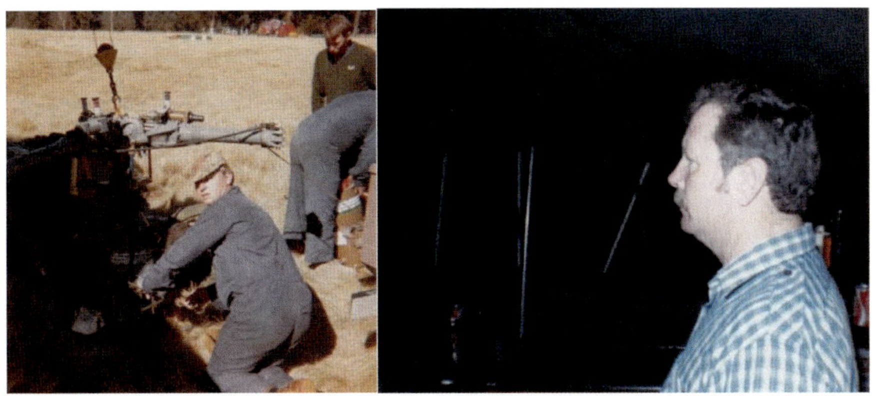

Maintenance at Kelvin Grove and the Barman in the Pub

Eventually all the Aircraft Logs are signed, Authorization Books approved and after the debriefing they all depart to the field where all the aircraft are waiting. A short time later the field is drowned out by high pitched engine noise and rotor blades slapping. Slowly each aircraft stretches its oleo struts and lifts into the air. Soon all aircraft are airborne and a loose formation heading towards Durban 200 km to the South East.

All too soon the Indian Ocean is visible on the horizon, and the formation breaks up to spread out for landing. The Air Traffic Controller at Durban International controls the gaggle of helicopters to the landing approach and then landing on the taxi way closest to Air Force Base Durban's entry gates. Once the aircraft have landed and taxied into the Base, they line up to their designated flight line positions per the Marshaller's for shut down. Steve and his pilot sign off the Travel Log of the aircraft and prepare to unpack their belongings. These will be stored in the crew room while they conduct the Coastal Flying phase of the sortie. Steve refuels his aircraft and completes the Travel Log entries for the next flight. All the crews are then mustered to the Operations Room at the Air Force Base Command Post for a briefing on Coastal Flying and the route that will be followed. With the briefing completed all crews move off to their aircraft in preparation for their sortie. There will be delayed take-offs to stagger the traffic out of Durban International. Steve and his pilot are second to depart, with their route taking them down the South Coast of Natal for about 45 minutes and then returning the same way. The plan is to remain landward on the out sortie and seaward on the return sortie, at the extremely high altitude of 50 ft. above the ground. This is awesome flying for chopper guys, and the South Coast of Natal does not disappoint with scantily clad young ladies all along the beaches. This is just what the crews needed and with wolf whistles and shouts of delight they continue their Southerly trip. The Natal coast is known for its lovely beaches and amazing scenery and is really a treat from the air. Steve and his pilot are having the time of their life. Quite a contrast from the stressful mountain flying phase they had just completed. Both, however, are looking forward to the weekend in Durban with its amazing night life and entertainment.

Durban after Drakensburg

On return to AFB Durban the aircraft is refueled and serviced for its return flight to Bloemfontein next week. It's Friday afternoon and the crews are raring to go to the Durban Central area for well-earned period of R&R (Rest and Recuperation). They have all been booked into a local Hotel and it's a quick rush to deposit their belongings, change into civvies (Civilian Clothing) and then off to start the weekend. Steve and a couple of his U/T F/E's are off to a local pub for a few beers. With Steve is Ian, a tall well-built man who obviously does weightlifting, and Johnny, an all smiling happy go lucky Afrikaner.

Walking along the Durban Esplanade, Steve and his two friends are confronted with a group of young East Indians walking toward them. It is quite evident that the one chap had no intention of stepping aside as they continued walking three abreast towards the Air Force contingent.

The young man shoulders Steve, who immediately turns around and shouts "What is your problem?"

To which the young man screams at his friends, "Hold me back, hold me back, I am going to kill this Whitey!"

The young man's friends immediately grab hold of him to restrain him.

Steve beckons to them and says, "Let him go", which they immediately do.

The young man turns around in fear and screams at his friends, "What are you doing man?" and runs off into the distance like a rabbit being chased by a fox.

Steve and his mates burst out laughing at the scene and walk away slapping each other's back at the spectacle they had just experienced. The fun in Durban has just started off on a high note.

Later that evening, Steve, Ian and Johnny have visited several watering holes and start sauntering back towards the Hotel. On the way is a famous Pub called the Fathers Moustache. Inside is a gathering of Chopper Pilots and Flight Engineers, already quite intoxicated and singing all the Air Force songs. Beers in hand Steve, Ian and Johnny join the group and with arms around shoulders they all erupt into the "Chopper Song".

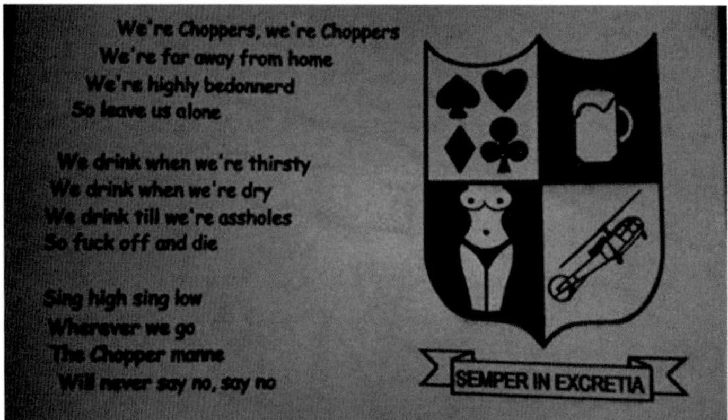

Chopper Song

Sometime later Steve, Ian and Johnny make their way out of the pub and are confronted with a very amusing spectacle. To the right of the Pub entrance is a Mercedes parked alongside the curb. On the roof of the car is a lady's handbag and standing next to the car is a Chopper Pilot peeping in the window. Curious to the spectacle, Steve and his mates move in to see what's going on. As they get closer they hear the obviously intoxicated Pilot mumbling into the window "Can I watch?"

As they get there Steve and his mates can make out a woman and man busy doing the deed. The woman was obviously too far along to care and continued as if no one was there. The guy is already oblivious to everything around him. It did not take Steve and his Mates long to join in the chant and urging the couple along. A free blue movie in real life! Once the couple completes their business, the woman calmly opens the window to retrieve her bag, which is now being offered to her by the Chopper Jock.

Just before she closes the window again, the Chopper Jock asks innocently, "Can I join?"

The guy jumps into the front seat, starts the car and drives off. At this point everyone has tears running down their faces from laughter.

Saturday night turns into Sunday morning and a very late morning Steve, Ian and Johnny make it back to the Hotel for some shut eye. All too soon the weekend is over, and the Squadron is back at AFB Durban preparing for the return flight to Bloemfontein. There will be one refueling stop near Ladysmith at an Army camp. Back at 87 HFS, Steve and the remaining U/T F/E's are in the final stages of qualifying for their half wings. Another three weeks of flying, couple of exams and then individual interviews would conclude their 10-month journey to qualified Flight Engineers. Included in the daily routine now was parade practice for the Wings Parade.

Its early morning while Steve and his roommate, Mannetjies (Mah ne kees) Wilken, are preparing for the weekly inspection by the Regimental Sergeant Major (RSM). The floor is shining spotlessly, cupboards packed per military standard, beds made up per specification, uniforms and shoes spotless. Mannetjies and Steve are a very mischievous combination, and it just takes one look from Steve and suddenly, they are play wrestling all over the room. Beds in disarray, floor marked with black shoe marks, uniforms untidy. 10 Minutes before the RSM would arrive; they quickly straighten everything out and jump to attention next to their beds.

The RSM, knowing these two, has silently sneaked in and caught them in the final throws of tidying up.

In a bellowing voice he yells, "Wat de fok maak julle troepe? Is julle nie reg vir inspeksie?" (What the fuck are you doing Troops? Are you not ready for inspection?)

Both Steve and Mannetjies stare straight ahead and answer crisply, "Reg vir inspeksie Samjoor!" (Ready for inspection Sarmajor).

The RSM just smiles and says, "Thank God you are nearly finished, I don't think 87 HFS can survive you any longer".

With that he looks around the room, scowls, turns on his heel and leaves the room. Steve and Mannetjies are grinning as they gather their items for the day's events.

Ready for Inspection

Only one more item on the training schedule required to complete, weapons training. The Alouette in the South African Air Force can be fitted with a multitude of weapons, but the training that Steve and his fellow students are to receive will be the most common configurations namely, MG151 20mm Cannon, Twin .505 Browning, and single .303 Browning System. All the weapons are side facing and therefore the aircraft must be flown at the appropriate height and speed for the sight harmonization to be effective. At between 500 to 800 feet above ground and between 50 and 70 knots forward speed, the target aimed at will be struck. Steve turns out to be quite the marksman and passes his gunnery phase with flying colours.

All too soon the day, 23rd November 1978 arrives, for Steve and his U/T F/E's to get their wings. Mannetjies makes a quick pit stop at the toilet and comes running out just in time to see the U/T F/E's falling in for the parade. The next moment there is dust flying and Mannetjies is sprawled out on the parade ground. He is up quicker than he fell and frantically brushing the dust off his Full Blue uniform. His palms are bleeding but no serious injuries. A bit of spit in a handkerchief and a dab here and there and he is good to go. Eventually everyone is formed up in a flight, and together with other flights from the Air Force Base, creating a Squadron they smartly march up with the Air Force Band. The Chief of the Air Force (CAF) is presenting the wings. All the families of the recipients are seated on the bleachers either side of the podium. VIP guests are also in attendance and waiting in anticipation for the presentation.

The Chief of the Air Force accepts the salute and then the parade comes to a halt for the presentation. The CAF then delivers a motivating speech on the role of the Flight Engineer and welcomes the newly qualified group to the fraternity. Each qualified Flight Engineer is individually presented with a half wing with the crest and letters FEBT on it. Covering both official languages, it stands for “Flight Engineer” in English, and “Boord Tegnikus” in Afrikaans. Next the CAF awards the Monster Wilkens best Student of the course award. The parade concludes with a march past by the Flights and then off the parade ground to be dismissed.

Flight Engineer Wing

Flight Sergeant (FSgt) Mike Web, the course lead instructor then gathers everyone around to hand out their postings. Steve and Ian are transferred to 22 Squadron, at AFB Ysterplaat in Cape Town. They will have a couple of days off and then on the 27th November 1978 they must report to AFB Ysterplaat. The long trek to Cape Town will start on Saturday 25th November 1978 on their way to begin their careers as Flight Engineers.

Chapter 5 - MARITIME ISOLATION

It is end of the year 1978, when Steve and Ian partner up to travel to Cape Town in Steve's new Citroen GS1220. Steve decides to leave home early on the Saturday morning to make his way to Johannesburg where Ian lives. The two will then take the 1500 km drive down to Cape Town through the night and arrive the next day. The car packed and the two in possession of their legal route forms, transferring them from 87 HFS to 22 Squadron. Both men are excited and looking forward to their new life away from where they grew up.

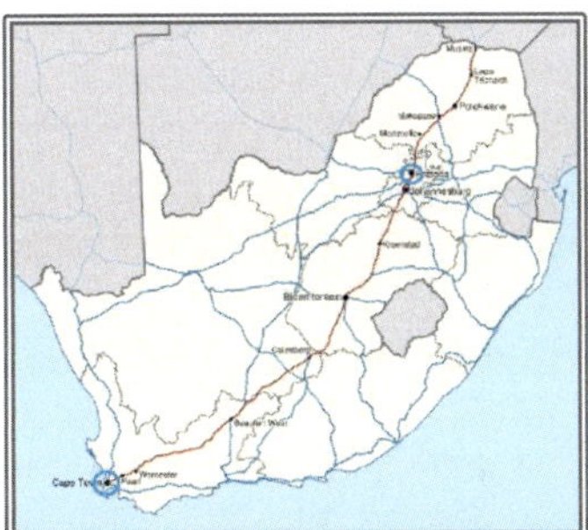

The beginning of the trip goes by uneventful, and four hours later they arrive on the outskirts of Bloemfontein with a vivid reminder of the year they had just spent there, qualifying as Flight engineers. The little Citroen had a range of approximately 450 km, and after 18:00 on the weekend there would be no Fuel available as all the Pump Stations would close. There are fuel restrictions limiting sale of fuel during daylight hours from 07:00 to 18:00 Mondays to Saturdays with no fuel on Sundays. They are still 1,100 km from Cape Town and would have to refuel at least once more to make the trip. Steve stops at the first Pump Station and refuels to the brim, with a little pressure refueling; he holds his hand below the nozzle to prevent the fuel from spilling out and overfills the tank. This would give them an extra 20 km or so. Their next target is Three Sisters, and then Laingsburg and finally the last stretch would be Cape Town.

All was going well until they hit the Nuweveld Mountain Range on the border of the Orange Free State. The little Citroen did not comply and started to guzzle fuel, they needed to make Three Sisters which was 629 km from Bloemfontein, if they wanted a shot at making Cape Town. Steve uses every hill to coast and extend their range. Eventually with huge relief and very tired they make it to the Pump Station at Three Sisters. After a quick refuel, and bite to eat, it's back on the road. The shadows are long on the road and the Swartberg Mountain Range looking eerie in the twilight. Both men are silent in their own thoughts as the kilometers wear on, only the stereo system in the car is blaring in the background to the sound of Pink Floyd's Dark Side of the Moon. The journey ahead is going to be through some of the most spectacular areas in Southern Africa, through the semi desert of the Great Karoo and fertile farmlands of the Klein Karoo. But first they must cross the large expanse of the Great Karoo. In the distance is Beaufort West and along the roadside evidence of the Boer War in the late 1890's still visible by the huge Block Houses at strategic intervals.

English Block House

Ahead of them the Langeberg Mountain Range starts to unfold and seems to start channeling them towards a narrow funnel, which is the descent down to Laingsburg. Laingsburg is an old "Boer" City and the architecture of all these towns will now mostly resemble what is known as the Cape Dutch style. Once through Laingsburg their next stop would be the last city in the Great Karoo, Touwsriver. Touwsriver is an awesome place and one is reminded of the age and rich culture of the country by looking out over the vast expanse of farmland. The world famous Merino sheep are also farmed here and are harvested for their high-quality wool.

Their next target is the Hex River Pass and onto De Doorns. As they drop down into the Hex River Valley the vegetation immediately changes, with citrus, grape, apple, and many other farms visible along the valley. Known worldwide for the export quality fruit and wine, the Hex River Valley occupation goes as far back to 1700AD. They still have a long way to go and stop off at for a break and a cup of coffee. They follow the Hex River all the way through the Klein Karoo, until they reach the Du Toitskloof Pass, and then on down to the city of Worcester.

Cape Town is now only 112 km away, and the fuel gauge is almost reading empty. Steve goes into preservation mode, as it is very early Sunday morning, and nothing is open. To be stuck on the side of the road at this time would be defeat. They have come so far, all he must do is squeeze out the last drops to get them to AFB Ysterplaat.

Coasting every hill and then gently applying accelerator on uphill's without laboring the engine Steve keeps plugging away. All too soon the lights of Paarl loom into sight, and on the highway, they continue, both anxiously wishing the car on. Next in the predawn they see the outline of Table Mountain, and the lights of the City at its foothills. They may make it yet. The road just never seems to end and kilometer after kilometer they expect to see the off ramp to Milnerton, which will take them to Ysterplaat where the Air Force Base is located.

Down the long winding hill Steve coasts and right there in front of them in the distance to the right they can make out the runway lights of AFB Ysterplaat. Not yet ready to breathe a sigh of relief, as the fuel low level light had been on for quite some time now, they plod on.

Eventually the off ramp comes into view and Steve gingerly urges the little Citroen up towards Ysterplaat and Milnerton. A short while later, they turn down the access road to AFB Ysterplaat, and at last are challenged at the Security Gate by the Guard on Duty.

It is the 27th November 1978, Steve and Ian with Route Forms in hand, report for duty at AFB Ysterplaat's Duty Room. First port of call after the Duty Room is 22 Squadron Technical Control. 22 Squadron was the only Maritime Helicopter Squadron in the Air Force and operated the Westland Wasp Anti-Submarine Helicopters.

These aircraft were procured before the Arms Embargo from the United Kingdom. They had already been in service for many years and the South African's have become very knowledgeable on the Operation, Maintenance, Repair and Overhaul of the aircraft type. It is both Steve and Ian's first close up view of the Wasp, which looks like a Tea Trolley with Rotor Blades.

Westland Wasp

The Squadron is well organized and within the first few days both Steve and Ian, are put to work. The Alouette's just recently transferred to 22 Squadron has different markings for easier identification when flying over the sea and additional Floatation Gear should there be and emergency at sea.

Steve wastes no time in familiarizing himself with Squadron SOP's (Special Operating Procedures) and is soon looking over the Wasp with the aim of qualifying on the type as soon as possible.

Alouette III with Floatation Gear

SAR Diver

Steve has joined the Squadron just in time to participate in the upcoming Naval Swimmers and Diving course. As a Flight Engineer at 22 Squadron the duties involved standby for both Flight Engineer and Diver.

The Diver would be suited up with wet suite, snorkel, fins and goggles, ready to be lowered into the sea for rescue recovery missions. As Steve is an outstanding swimmer he was looking forward to the challenge.

It's early Monday morning, Steve and the rest of the trainee's report at the Squadron for pickup. A minibus driven by one of the students is to take them through to Simonstown Naval Base.

The drive to Simonstown is spectacular and the route they follow takes them over the Cape Flats and then past Muizemberg, over Ou Kaapse Weg (Old Cape Road) mountain pass, through Fish Hoek and then round the bend Simonstown comes into view.

At the Main Gate, everyone clambers out with Route Forms in hand to get security badges for entrance into the Naval Diving School.

A small dockyard facility was first established in Simon's Town by the Dutch East India Company in 1743; 275 years ago. This was taken over by the British Royal Navy in the 1790s, under whom the facility was further developed over the following century and a half.

A pair of handsome stone storehouses dating from the 1740s stand on the seafront where they were built by the Dutch East India Company, marking the initial location of the Yard. Immediately adjacent is the earliest Royal Naval building on the site is a combined mast-house, boathouse and sail loft, dating from 1815, now serving as the South African Naval Museum.

Over the next few decades, the site was developed gradually, with steam engineering and coaling facilities being added mid-century. In 1885, the government of the Cape Colony transferred the assets of the Simon's Bay Dock and Patent Slip Company to the British Admiralty.

By the close of the century, however, it became clear that more space would be needed to accommodate the requirements of a modern Navy.

In 1898, a large site was acquired to the east of the original Yard for a dockyard extension. Sir John Jackson and Co Ltd. was chosen to do the work. Construction began in 1900. The new harbour encompassed an area of 11 hectares, with a breakwater of 914 meters in length.

It also contained a dry-dock 240 meters long and 29 meters wide, with a sizeable steam factory constructed alongside.

The dry-dock was named the Selborne Graving Dock after the Earl of Selborne, the High Commissioner of the Cape. Work on the Simon's Town dockyard was completed in 1910.

The naval base was handed over to South Africa in 1957 under the Simonstown Agreement. The Dockyard was expanded in 1975, a large area of land was reclaimed and the harbour walls were extended to form a new Tidal Basin.

18th Century Dockyard ***Navy Docks*** ***Selbourn Graving Dock***

Naval Base Simon's Town

For the Navy there is no love lost of the Air Force, and they look down at the sorry bunch with grins, knowing that there is going to be pain and fear ahead. The morning starts off with lectures and issuing of diving gear. By midmorning everyone is ready, and the instructor cannot wait to issue the order. The guys are still milling around, adjusting the tightness of the wet suite around their necks and battling to get the booties and fins on, when all of a sudden, the Instructor bellows.

"To the Rock and back, move!"

The rock is an actual rock in the sea about 200 meters from shore. The water of the Cape's Western Coastline is cold, very cold, and Steve's breath is taken away as he hits the water. Once settled in Steve sets his hands behind his back and starts kicking, keeping his head submerged enough so that the snorkel just breaks surface. This position affords him maximum forward movement with the least effort. On his return Steve is overtaken by Kenny Dalgleish, a strong swimmer, and he obviously is very comfortable in the water. As they get closer to the shore the instructor is already shouting back at them to continue, this was round one of five. Although he is tiring, Steve keeps going and just when he thought he was about to run out of steam, the last round is finished. All is not over yet; the group has 10 minutes to race to the change rooms, strip off the wet suites and other gear, back into their uniforms to report back to the classroom. Steve, Kenny and Nic make it, but there are stragglers, and therefore the next morning they would be surprised with an additional task for their tardiness. Not just the late comers but the whole group. The next day and additional lap was added to ensure no more tardiness would follow. It works; nobody would be late for the rest of the training.

The training continues and every morning the group starts with a rock swim, followed by rescue techniques and recoveries, saving of a person drowning, and first aid for all types of recovery situations. The day would then end off with another rock swim, and then classroom in preparation for the next day. All too soon the course is in the final phase with qualification tests consisting of 70-foot jumps from the SAS Tafelberg's flight deck, timed rock swim, and jumping from a Helicopter at 50 feet. Steve enjoys every second of the tests and requests a second Helicopter jump. Once in the aircraft Steve asks the Flight Engineer to check with the pilot if they could attempt 100-foot jump. With grins all around, the aircraft is lined up and the next second Steve gets the tap on his shoulder to exit the aircraft. Keeping his site on the horizon to keep himself upright and adjusting his arms close to his side to keep him level, he falls, falls and falls some more. Breaking the urge to look down, which would most certainly change his attitude and cause him to fall flat on his face, he waits. The next minute he hits the water cleanly and goes down deep. As the wet suite is an awesome floatation device, Steve is not too concerned. When he bottoms out and starts ascending, Steve soon realizes that he will have to swim or else he will run out of air. He breaks the surface to cheers from all around. The course completed, and everyone congratulated, no failures and 22 Squadron have a new batch of qualified Divers for Rescue Standby.

Diver's course completed, Steve now focuses on getting his Wasp Certification, and discusses getting assigned to the next conversion course. It's at this point that Steve and Ian find out that 22 Squadron does not perform Operational Tours to Rhodesia and Angola. Both are very disappointed, as the purpose of all the training they had completed was in preparation for deployment operationally.

Steve is assigned to the next Wasp conversion and knuckles down to get qualified, taking his mind off the disappointment. He passes the Technical Phase and is assigned to the Flying Phase. The Wasp has a Rolls Royce Nimbus engine which unlike the Alouette has a Free Turbine Engine. The Free Turbine drives the Gearbox which in turn drives the Rotor system.

The Rolls Royce Nimbus gas turbine engine is related to a family of Turbomeca units which all adopt the same combustion chamber design. The core Nimbus is almost identical to the Alouette's Artouste Engine. The Nimbus differs with the addition of a free power turbine and a two-stage axial compressor which precedes the centrifugal impeller. Dating from the 1960s this engine was used to power the Westland Wasp and Scout Helicopters, a few of which are still flying today. The Nimbus features a fully mechanical fuel control system with a compressor and power turbine governor. This mechanical fuel system allows the engine to be safely operated at idle speed when not connected to a load.

Ian Nicholson has at this point contacted a local Helicopter Company "Court" and is made a job offer which he could not refuse. Ian submits his Buy Out option and prepares to leave the Air Force. Steve would not see Ian again for many years to come.

Steve has requested some vacation to visit the family and weigh up his options. 22 Squadron personnel are proving to be a very close nit bunch and not easy to break into the inner circles. With the rank of Corporal, Steve is at the bottom of the Totem Pole and therefore not included in the larger picture.

Steve arrives home after a lengthy absence and finds out that one of his friends, Nico Beets, who had been on many courses with him in the past years, has also left the Air Force. Nico encourages Steve to join him; the money is good, and double what he was earning as a Qualified Flight Engineer. This is a trying time for Steve, as he really enjoys the Air Force way of life. He returns to 22 Squadron with the thoughts of leaving weighing heavily on his mind. Steve approaches the Technical Officer at the Squadron to discuss his predicament but unfortunately is not hearing what he wanted. The decision is made, Steve submits his Buy Out request to the Air Force and a month later is on his way back to Transvaal to join Nico at Fields Aviation in Germiston. It is March 1979 and a new life was about to begin.

Chapter 6 - ANOTHER LIFE

Reporting to Fields Aviation, Steve is immediately hired and put to work. Fortunately, Nico has given Steve the rundown on what's required, so he comes prepared with coveralls, tools and knowledge. Steve soon knuckles down to the daily work routine and is up to speed with all the tasks within the week.

Fields Aviation is located at Rand Airport in Germiston and caters to many contracts. One of these contracts is complete Overhaul, Repair and Heavy Maintenance on the Air Forces aging older aircraft, namely the Harvard, Dakota, Sky Master and Viscounts. Steve is working on Air Force aircraft again. The work is dirty and hours long. There is also a bunch of Portuguese ex Mozambique Air Force AME's working at Fields. These gents are a different breed and did not mix well with others. It does not take long before Steve has a tête–à–tête with one of them. The line is drawn and from this day on it would be your side and my side.

Steve's hair grows quickly and soon is on his shoulders, he did not even notice as he is working a lot of overtime and very rarely goes anywhere. One morning Steve awakes with an incredible tooth ache. Nico and Steve share rides from Brakpan to Germiston, and when Nico sees what pain Steve is in, he offers to drop him off at a local dentist. The Dentist takes one look and tells Steve that he has an abscess in the wisdom tooth and that it must come out. With no choice Steve sits back and lets the Dentist have his way. After the extraction the dentist gives Steve a prescription and instructs him to go and lie down for the rest of the day. Nico collects Steve at the dentist, and takes one look at his face and said, "You are going to my house, my Mom will look after you". Steve does not argue. Nico gets the pills and feeds Steve his ration for the day. By the next morning Steve feels like death, vomiting, dizzy, headache and weak. Nico takes him straight to the Dentist once more. The Dentist takes a look and informs Steve that the abscess has drained into the socket of the extracted tooth and had caused the infection. The Dentist then prescribes a series of Antibiotics' to clear the infection. Three days later Steve gets home for the first time. The lady where Steve rents a room from, Auntie Rassie, is beside herself out of concern.

During his recovery period Steve manages to have a haircut but chooses to keep his beard. He has just recently acquired an Alf Romeo 2000, and it is the era of CB Radios. Steve gets one and his mates dub him as "Red Beard" for a call sign. It's a Friday evening and time for some drinks and a chat on the CB. Steve drives through to Springs to meet up with his roommate from a couple of years back at AFB Waterkloof, Mike Freer. Mike and Steve spend the evening touring from one party to the next, and in the early hours of the morning, Steve makes CB friends with what sounds like a delightful, cheerful, and available young lady.

There is a lot of joking, when Steve throws out a proposal. "Will you marry me?" questions Steve.

Almost immediately she comes back' "Most certainly, get a Minister on the air!"

Next second, an Afrikaans sounding deep voice booms over the CB, "Do you Red Beard, take Angel to be your lawful wedded wife?"

"I do", responds Steve.

"And do you Angel, take Red Beard as your lawful wedded husband?"

"I do", responds Angel.

"I now pronounce you husband and wife".

To this day Steve has never met Angel and has no idea where she is or was that night. Steve and Mike then proceed to the local watering Hole in Springs for celebrations.

Still Airborne

Steve's love of flying leads him to stop off at Brakpan Airfield on the way home from work. He enquires about flying lessons and is introduced to the chief flight instructor "Sluggy". Sluggy fills in part time at the Flying School as he is a South African Airways Boeing 747 Captain. Steve and Sluggy hit it off and set up an introductory flight immediately. Sluggy briefs Steve on the process and soon finds out that Steve actually knows how to do it. Sluggy stands back and instructs Steve to complete the Walk Around Pre-Flight inspection. Steve is allocated a seat in the left-hand side and Sluggy reads through the check list. Steve looks at Sluggy waiting for him to proceed, but he just nods his head.

“Continue, you know your stuff”, says Sluggy.

Steve starts up and continues down the check list. Sluggy briefs him on how to taxi and then instructs Steve to proceed. Steve makes a blind radio call, as Brakpan does not have and ATC, informing any traffic in the area of his intentions. He taxi’s out to the runway holding area and completes a run-up check for take-off. Sluggy corrects a few errors for Steve and shows him improved methods of completing check list items.

Sluggy gives Steve the thumbs up and they proceed to the runway for take-off. Steve completes another radio transmission informing traffic that he is about to take off from the runway and head out to the general flying area. Steve pushes the throttle in and monitors Engine RPM, Oil Pressure, and keeps the little Piper 140 straight on the runway while they build up speed. At 50 Kts Steve starts to apply a little back pressure on the yoke, and at 60 Kts he lifts the aircraft into the air. The aircraft climbs away and Sluggy directs Steve towards the general flying area, while briefing him on the requirements to qualify as a private pilot.

As they arrive in the general flying area, Sluggy instructs Steve to climb to 3,000 ft. above ground level. Steve now has to remember that on the Transvaal Highveld he is already at 5,300 ft. on the ground which means he has to climb to 8,300 ft on the aircraft’s altimeter. At 8,300 ft Steve levels off, and Sluggy briefs him on the exercises he is going to demonstrate.

Sluggy retards the throttle completely while keep the aircrafts nose on the horizon and the wings level. The aircrafts speed drops off quickly until the stall warning horn goes off. The next instant the nose dips suddenly and the aircraft wants to fall away to the port side. Sluggy demonstrates to Steve how to counter and then let the speed build up while at the same time adding power to slowly climb away safely. Sluggy lets Steve try a stall which seems quite the challenge for the aspiring pilot. Steve takes the controls and Sluggy retards the throttle. Steve concentrates and keeps the aircraft level with the nose on the horizon. The stall warning sounds loudly in the confined space of the cockpit, and Steve is about to overreact when he remembers Sluggy’s instructions. He concentrates lets the aircraft fall into a gentle dive, adds power and then levels out to climb away. Steve impresses himself at the ability to read the aircraft.

“Wow that was awesome,” says Steve.

“Good job Steve you have a natural ability to feel the aircraft. Keep it up, next we will do a spin”, says Sluggy.

Sluggy takes control of the aircraft and sets it up for another stall. This time though, he allows the aircraft to dip a wing which automatically puts it into a spin. The attitude is quite scary, and Steve is not very comfortable. Sluggy however allows the aircraft to dive and then levels the wings off while countering the spin with rudder and then gently adding power in the same process as for the stall, climbing the aircraft away.

“There you go Steve, piece of old Tackie”, says Sluggy. (Tackie - A canvas shoe with a rubber sole).

Sluggy hands over to Steve and instructs him to complete the exercise. Steve sets the wings level with nose on the horizon. Sluggy retards the power and then instructs Steve not to counter the wing drop. It is a very unnerving position for Steve, as nerve wants desperately to correct the situation.

Steve pulls the nose up, unfortunately a bit too much and almost completes a wing over maneuver. He manages to level the aircraft off and then counter with the rudder and remembers to add power climbing away in recovery. Sluggy is impressed but warns Steve.

“That was almost a wing over Steve and placing the aircraft out of its limits. Be careful on being aggressive on the spin entry. Your recovery, although a bit low, was perfect. I predict you will be solo within the next 5 hours”, Says Sluggy.

Steve starts a regular session in flight training with Sluggy, and true to his word, lets Steve Solo 5 hours later. Steve is excited yet fearful that he may just “Fuck Up”. The sortie of circuits and bumps goes off flawlessly and it is a smiling Steve that emerges from the aircraft to shake Sluggy’s hand.

“Well done young man, from here you looked pretty professional. How did it feel?” asks Sluggy.

“That was great thanks Sluggy, can’t wait to get the rest under the belt and build my flight hours,” says Steve.

Steve’s flying career has once again taken off, and he climbs happily into his car to head home for the evening. Pretty pleased with himself Steve keeps reliving the freedom of being solely in charge of an aircraft for the first time. Something has been awakened in Steve and he is driven to get back into flying.

Love is in the Air

Steve's land lady has a friend whose is disabled and has problems with her car. The clutch lever has become very difficult to operate with her arm. Steve immediately offers to have a look at the problem and see if he can rectify the issue. Steve arrives at the address and is introduced to Naomi, and she is delighted that he is willing to assist. The car is an older model Ford Escort and the disabled modification is a homemade installation. A lever with a handle on the end had been fixed to the underside of the dashboard and then connected to the clutch lever with a fork and clevis pin. The mechanism had become worn and was difficult to move. Steve quickly identifies that he could readjust the lever's position, rotate the handle and set the clutch lever to make the assembly work much easier. Steve is buried in the driver's side underneath the dash finishing off; when a different younger voice tells him that his coffee is ready. Steve squints up and sees an attractive Strawberry Blonde young woman standing beside the car door. Suitably impressed with what he sees, Steve quickly finishes off and slips out of the car to take the coffee.

"Hi, I am Steve".

"I know, nice to meet you" says Zella-Lynne.

Zella-Lynne Botes is a nursing Student, home for the weekend from University in Johannesburg. Steve wastes no time in asking her out on a date. In a very short time Steve has met the parents and the two seem to be heading down the path to marriage. It's at this time that Steve realizes he needs to forgo his ideas of insecure jobs and goes on the hunt for a path similar to the one he had started in the Air Force. If he is thinking marriage, then he needs to have a means of supporting a family. Steve approaches South African Airways (SAA) for a position as a Flight Engineer. After a mountain of paperwork, he is finally granted an interview.

Back at Fields Aviation, there are a number of Air Force personnel working in the Stores and Project Office. Steve has built up friendship with most of them. It is a sunny day and coffee break time, when Steve sets down his tools and wanders up to the Project Office. Immediately Steve recognizes Warrant Officer (WO) Rivers from Air Force Headquarters. WO Rivers is in charge of the Technical Qualifications of the Air Force and as such manages the Trade Test for all Technical Personnel.

WO Rivers shakes Steve's hand and says, "What the hell are you doing here?"

Steve laughs and shakes the old man's hand.

"I am thinking of joining SAA", says Steve.

"Hmm, why don't you come back to the Air Force?" asks WO Rivers.

"There is an urgent need for people of your caliber, and the war in Rhodesia and Angola is heating up"

"Oh! And where would I be stationed then?" asks Steve.

"Well I can only offer you 87 HFS at Bloemfontein, but they are actively involved in the Ops Tours", Says WO Rivers.

And so, Steve is back on the dream path he had started so many years ago. Steve contacts SAA and finds out that he is on the short list for selection. Reluctantly he turns down the opportunity and sets his sights on the future in the Air Force.

Steve has proposed to Zella and also been approved for reinstatement into the Air Force. It's May 1980 when he resigns from Fields Aviation and travels down to Bloemfontein to restart his Flight Engineer career. As he has been out of the Air Force for two years, Steve has to redo his basic training in a shortened version named Air Force Orientation. While he is waiting for the orientation to start, Steve works in civilian clothing at 87 HFS, completing major maintenance servicing on the Alouette Helicopters. He still has long hair and a full beard. Lt. Fluffy Dempers, an ex-Flight Engineer, is the Technical Officer at 87 HFS, and very soon he takes Steve under his wing to guide and mold him. The weeks fly by and then on the 2nd June 1980, Steve reports to Valhalla in Pretoria where his orientation is to take place. It's back to parade groundwork, physical training, route marches and weapons training. Somewhere through the ordeal Steve had gotten a beard pass and therefore no longer needed to shave. Zella did not approve of his clean-shaven face and preferred his beard. All too soon the orientation is over and with Steve back in full blue uniform proudly wearing his FE Badge, at the passing out parade, bringing this milestone to a close.

"Take a community of Dutchman of the type of those who defended themselves for fifty years against all the power of Spain at a time when Spain was the greatest power in the world.
Intermix with them a strain of those inflexible French Huguenots, who gave up their name and left their country forever at the time of the revocation of the Edict of Nantes.
The product must obviously be one of the most rugged, virile, unconquerable races ever seen upon the face of the earth.
Take these formidable people and train them for seven generations in constant warfare against savage men and ferocious beasts, in circumstances in which no weakling could survive; place them so that they acquire skill with weapons and in horsemanship, give them a country which is immanently suited to the tactics of the huntsman, the marksman and the rider.
Then, finally, put a fine temper upon their military qualities by a dour fatalistic Old Testament religion and an ardent and consuming patriotism.
Combine all these qualities and all these impulses in one individual and you have the modern Boer."

Sir Arthur Conan Doyle

"Docemus" – We Teach

Back at 87 HFS and new flying kit received, Steve is put on a refresher course to bring him back up to speed as a Flight Engineer. Steve is also delighted to see his old roommate from AFB Waterkloof; Mike Freer is on the present U/T F/E course. Steve and Zella have planned their marriage and at the same time Steve also applied for married accommodation at AFB Bloemspruit. These are old Barracks that had been cordoned off with fences to create living quarters for married personnel. The Potlucks, as they are known, can be modified to accommodate a family. The Potluck assigned to Steve requires some major alterations and Steve invites Zella to join him during her vacation to assist in the rework. Steve had bought Zella a Triumph Spitfire Sports Car and she arrives early the Monday morning. They both knuckle down to fix the Potluck up. Steve is breaking through walls and installing doors, while Zella, the artist, completes the painting projects.

A very sad day for the Air Force had happened the week prior, with an Alouette being shot down in Southern Angola. The Pilot managed to flee and make his way back to friendly troops, but Koos Cilliers, the Flight Engineer, took a round through the neck, and his body was taken by the terrorists. Early Tuesday Morning a Super Frelon Helicopter carrying 25 of the 87 HFS personnel, including Steve, takes off to Rustenburg, where an empty Grave for Koos would be the ceremonial burial for a fallen comrade. A very moving ceremony takes place, with every member marching up to the grave and saluting a fallen comrade. "We will remember them".

Koos's Photo in Luanda War Museum

It was a very somber return flight to AFB Bloemspruit that afternoon. When Steve arrives back at the Potluck, he is amazed to see that Zella is still there. The car's battery had frozen and Zella could not leave. Steve calls in the local AFB Bloemspruit Mechanics who keenly assist and very soon the car is started, and Zella can leave for Brakpan. The winters in Bloemfontein are very cold and easily dip far below freezing.

Zella in the meantime has given up on Nursing and changed careers to Dental. She is in the process of qualifying as a Dental Assistant and had already been offered a position in Bloemfontein when she moves down. With the wedding plans progressing well, Steve gets into the daily routine of a Squadron Flight Engineer and assists in the training of the U/T's. In the evenings he continues to ready the Potluck, and when Zella returns for a visit, they both plan to buy some furniture.

All too soon the wedding day 4th July 1980 arrives. Steve together with Krimpy Coetzee, a new friend from 87 HFS, and his wife, travel to Brakpan for the big day. As Zella is Catholic, the wedding would be performed by the Priest with the Reception in the Community Hall next to the Church. The reception is full of people, many of which Steve has only met once or twice. Steve's Father and Mother are at the Main Table together with Zella's parents and Grand Parents. The reception continues into the night, but Steve and Zella have a short Honeymoon hotel booking on the way back to Bloemfontein. Steve has not much vacation from just rejoining the Air Force and is scheduled to accompany the Squadron to Bergville for the current student's mountain flying training phase at Kelvin Grove in the Drakensburg.

As a Base F/E Steve now accompanies the U/T F/E's on sorties and evaluates their performance. The majestic Drakensburg is also the best opportunity to ensure that the U/T's have the right stuff as there are numerous dangers in flying through these mountains. In the evenings Steve is free to accompany the rest of the instructors on outings to the local towns. The U/T's must prepare for the next day's flying. Tonight, the group is taking one of the Bedford Troop Carriers into the local town of Bergville. The group saunter into the local Pub and are soon Air Force loud and the party starts. Initially the locals are not impressed but soon start enjoying the banter and songs that the group are singing. It is at one of the crescendo moments that Steve gets the idea and at the top of his voice shouts out.

"Dead Ants!"

The whole Air Force contingent falls to the ground on their backs with legs and arms in the air. Each one still holding his drinks. The Barman slowly looks over the counter and asks Steve.

"What's happening?"

"Did anyone spill a drink?" Asks Steve.

The Barman nods and points to a pilot who is still struggling to keep his arms and legs up.

"Your round Sir!" Laughs Steve.

Steve turns to the Barman and describes the rules. Upon the instruction "Dead Ants" everyone must fall on their back with arms and legs in the air while holding their drink aloft. Anyone who spills or is last down must buy a round for all.

"Awesome, can I also play?" Requests the Barman.

The evening gets progressively rowdier, attracting more locals. One couple enter and are about to approach the bar when the Barman yells out.

"Dead Ants!" and proceeds to fall behind the bar on his back with arms and legs in the air.

The couple take one look at the sight and turn on their heel to disappear quickly out of the Pub. It is a very inebriated group that eventually clamber into the Bedford for the return trip to Kelvin Grove.

The months fly by and suddenly Steve has his turn for operational deployment. It's the 14th October 1980, Tuesday morning and Steve has cleared out, packed his duffle bag, checked his survival and flying kit, and verified his documentation. Zella drops Steve off at the Bloemfontein Railway Station for his overnight trip to Pretoria, where he is to take the C130 Hercules flight from AFB Waterkloof to the operational area at AFB Ondangwa. The trip is uneventful, but Steve struggles to sleep, as he plays all the scenarios in his mind of what he is about to experience. All his training was now going to be put to the test.

The War in Angola

Founded in 1966, Unita fought alongside the Popular Movement for the Liberation of Angola (MPLA) in the Angolan War for Independence from 1961–1975, and then against the MPLA in the ensuing civil war from 1975 onward. The war was one of the most prominent Cold War proxy wars, with Unita receiving military aid from the United States and South Africa while the MPLA received support from the Soviet Union and its allies.

In the early 1960s the MPLA named its guerrilla forces the "People's Army for the Liberation of Angola" (Exército Popular de Libertação de Angola - EPLA). Many of its first cadres had received training in Morocco and Algeria. In January 1963, in one of its early operations, the EPLA attacked a Portuguese military post in Cabinda, killing a number of troops. During the mid-

1960s and early 1970s, the EPLA operated very successfully from bases in Zambia against the Portuguese in eastern Angola. After 1972, however, the EPLA's effectiveness declined following several Portuguese victories, disputes with National Liberation Front of Angola (FNLA) forces, and the movement of about 800 guerrillas from Zambia to the Republic of Congo.

The 1970s in Angola, a time of political and military turbulence, saw the end of Angola's War of Independence that spanned 1961–1975, and the outbreak of civil war. Agostinho Neto, the leader of the People's Movement for the Liberation of Angola (MPLA), declared the independence of the People's Republic of Angola on November 11, 1975, in accordance with the Alvor Accords. UNITA and the FNLA also declared Angolan independence as the Social Democratic Republic of Angola based in Huambo and the Democratic Republic of Angola based in Ambriz. FLEC, armed and backed by the French government, declared the independence of the Republic of Cabinda from Paris. The National Liberation Front of Angola (FNLA) and the National Union for the Total Independence of Angola (UNITA) forged an alliance on November 23, proclaiming their own coalition government based in Huambo with Holden Roberto and Jonas Savimbi as co-presidents and José Ndelé and Johnny Pinnock Eduardo as co-Prime Ministers.

Angolan Flag

The South African government told Savimbi and Roberto in early November that the South African Defense Force would soon end operations in Angola despite the coalition's failure to capture Luanda and therefore secure international recognition at independence. Savimbi, desperate to avoid the withdrawal of the largest, friendly, military force in Angola, asked General Constand Viljoen to arrange a meeting for him with South African Prime Minister John Vorster, Savimbi's ally since October 1974. On the night of November 10th, the day before independence, Savimbi secretly flew to Pretoria, South Africa and the meeting took place. In a remarkable reversal of policy, Vorster not only agreed to keep troops through November but promised to withdraw the SADF troops only after the OAU meeting on December 9th. The Soviets, well aware of South African activity in southern Angola, flew Cuban soldiers into Luanda the week before independence. While Cuban officers led the mission and provided the bulk of the troop force, 60 Soviet officers in the Congo joined the Cubans on November 12th. The Soviet leadership expressly forbade the Cubans from intervening in Angola's civil war, focusing the mission on containing South Africa.

In 1975 and 1976 most foreign forces, with the exception of Cuba, withdrew. The last elements of the Portuguese military withdrew in 1975 and the South African military withdrew in February 1976. On the other hand, Cuba's troop force in Angola increased from 5,500 in December 1975 to 11,000 in February 1976. FNLA forces were crushed by Operation Carlota, a joint Cuban-Angolan attack on Huambo on January 30, 1976. By mid-November, the Huambo government had gained control over southern Angola and began pushing north.

On August 1st, 1974 a few months after a military coup d'état had overthrown the Lisbon regime and proclaimed its intention of granting independence to Angola, the MPLA announced the formation of FAPLA, which replaced the EPLA. Moscow started to arm Neto's faction exclusively and the Soviet Union supplied the MPLA with $300 million worth of materiel as compared to $54 million over the previous fourteen years. The weapons that went to MPLA included AK-47 assault rifles, 120-mm mortars, 82-mm and 107-mm recoilless rifles, 37-mm and 14.5 mm anti-aircraft guns, and T-34, T-54, and PT-76 tanks.

By 1976 FAPLA had been transformed from lightly armed guerrilla units into a national army capable of sustained field operations. This transformation was gradual until the Soviet-Cuban intervention and ensuing National Union for the Total Independence of Angola (UNITA) insurgency, when the sudden and large-scale inflow of heavy weapons and accompanying technicians and advisers quickened the pace of institutional change.

Beginning in 1978, periodic South African incursions into southern Angola, coupled with UNITA's northward expansion in the east, forced the Angolan government to increase expenditures on Soviet military aid. Dependence also increased on military personnel from the Soviet Union, the German Democratic Republic (East Germany), and Cuba.

Unlike African states that acceded to independence by an orderly and peaceful process of institutional transfer, Angola inherited a disintegrating colonial state whose army was in retreat. The confluence of civil war, foreign intervention, and large-scale insurgency made Angola's experience unique. After independence, FAPLA had to reorganize for conventional war and counterinsurgency simultaneously and immediately to continue the new war with South Africa and UNITA. Ironically, a guerrilla army that conducted a successful insurgency for more than a decade came to endure the same kind of exhausting struggle for a similar period.

UNITA Flag

Unita was led by Jonas Savimbi. Jonas Savimbi and Antonio da Costa Fernandes founded Unita on March 13th, 1966 in Muangai in Moxico province in Portuguese Angola (during the Estado Novo regime). Unita launched its first attack on Portuguese colonial authorities on December 25th, 1966.

UNITA Jonas Savimbi

The People's Armed Forces of Liberation of Angola (Portuguese: Forças Armadas Populares de Libertação de Angola) or FAPLA was originally the armed wing of the People's Movement for the Liberation of Angola (MPLA) but later in 1975, became Angola's official armed forces when the MPLA took control of the government.

Savimbi was originally affiliated with Holden Roberto's National Liberation Front of Angola (FNLA). Unita later moved to Jamba in Angola's south-eastern province of Cuando Cubango. Unita's leadership was drawn heavily from Angola's majority Ovimbundu ethnic group and its policies were originally Maoist, perhaps influenced by Savimbi's early training in China. They aimed at rural rights and recognized ethnic divisions. In later years, however, Unita became more aligned with the United States, espousing support for capitalism in Angola.

In the 1980s, Savimbi sought out vastly expanded relations with the U.S. He received considerable guidance from The Heritage Foundation, an influential conservative research institute in Washington, D.C. that maintained strong relations with both the Reagan administration and the U.S. Congress. Michael Johns, the Heritage Foundation's leading expert on Africa and Third World Affairs issues, visited Savimbi in his clandestine southern Angolan base camps, offering the Unita leader both tactical military and political advice.

Under Savimbi's leadership, Unita proved especially effective militarily, becoming one of the world's most effective armed resistance movements of the late 20th century. According to the U.S. State Department, Unita came to control vast swaths of the interior of Angola. Savimbi's very survival in Angola in and of itself was viewed as an incredible accomplishment, and he came to be known as "Africa's most enduring bush fighter" given assassination attempts, aided by extensive Soviet, Cuban, and East German military troops, advisors and support, that he survived.

After World War I the League of Nations gave South West Africa, formerly a German colony, to the United Kingdom as a mandate under the administration of South Africa. When the National Party won the 1948 election in South Africa and subsequently introduced apartheid legislation, these laws were applied as well to South West Africa. It was considered the de facto fifth province of South Africa.

SWAPO (South West Africa People's Organization)

SWAPO was founded on 19th April 1960 as the successor of the Ovamboland People's Organization. Leaders renamed the party to show that it represented all SWA. But the organization had its base among the Ovambo people of northern South West Africa, who constituted nearly half the total population.

During 1962 SWAPO had emerged as the dominant nationalist organization for the South West African people. It co-opted other groups such as the South West Africa National Union (SWANU), and later in 1976 the South West African People's Democratic Organization. SWAPO used guerrilla tactics to fight the South African Defense Force. On 26th August 1966, the first major clash of the conflict took place, when a unit of the South African Police, supported by the South African Air Force, exchanged fire with SWAPO forces.

This date is generally regarded as the start of what became known in South Africa as the Border War. In 1972 the United Nations General Assembly recognized SWAPO as the 'sole legitimate representative' of South West Africa's people. The Norwegian government began giving aid directly to SWAPO in 1974.

The country of Angola gained its independence on 11th November 1975 following its war for independence. The leftist Popular Movement for the Liberation of Angola (MPLA), supported by Cuba and the Soviet Union, came to power. In March 1976, the MPLA offered SWAPO bases in Angola for launching attacks against the South African military.

First Bush Tour

The operational area in South West Africa (SWA) comprises of many different Arms of Service Units and spread out along the northern border. The strategy is to form a line of defense against infiltration and attack from Angola, Zambia, and Zimbabwe.

SWA Sectors

The South West Africa Sectors:

- Sector 10 - (Kaokoland and Owambo) - HQ Oshikati.
- Sector 20 - (Kavango and Western Caprivi) - HQ Rundu.
- Sector 30 - HQ Otjiwarongo (Citadel).
- Sector 40 - HQ Windhoek.

- Sector 50 - HQ Gobabis.
- Sector 60 - HQ Keetmanshoop.
- Sector 70 - (Eastern Caprivi) - HQ Mpacha

It is the 15th October 1980 and the flight to AFB Ondangwa is uneventful, at the Estimate Time of Arrival (ETA) for the C130, fondly called the "Flossie" by the troops, enters a steep descending turn to the right and continues to spiral down until it is at 1000 ft. above the ground. The big aircraft levels off when flaps and undercarriage are lowered in preparation for landing. The quick spiral descent is to evade the possibility of Surface to Air Missile (SAM) attacks. The big aircraft lines up on the runway, and all to soon the reverse pitch engaged and it slows down to turn off onto the taxi way. While taxiing to the Movement Control area the Load Master opens the rear ramp, exposing the passengers to the heat and glare of the Ovamboland sun and sand.

The word "Flossie" used for the transport aircraft from 28 Squadron' history started after the arrival of the C130B's onto the SAAF register. As South Africa became embroiled in a Border War along the South West African / Angolan border the C130's were used on a daily basis to convey Troops and Material to and from the border. In later years SAFAIR, operating L100's were contracted to assist in the air transport effort. To the casual observer the C130 and L100 look so much alike that one could be forgiven for thinking they were the same.

At 28 Squadron, the operators of the SAAF C130's, was a Flight Engineer named Phil or "Flippie". He was a most dedicated man who ate, slept and dreamt C130. In his private life he was a most disciplined man, real old school, soldier, who never did a half job of anything. The type, "if it's worth doing, do it properly or don't do it at all".

Phil was married to a lady named Florence. In her family she was called Flo, and among her siblings she was called Flossie. Being the consummate professional Phil would always walk out, long before the rest of the crew, to the aircraft he was scheduled to fly in and do a proper pre-flight inspection.

A few of his fellow flight engineers would pull his leg and tell him the aircraft was only due for a major technical inspection at a future date. His standard reply was "Chaps, if you treat and look after your Aircraft like you look after your wife, she will never let you down". This comment always gave all of his Squadron mates a smile. Over the months, whenever his crew were due to walk out to the Aircraft they would ask "Where is Flippie, is he at Flossie?" or "Come guys we shouldn't keep Flossie waiting!"

In time the reference to Flossie was made more often at the movement control section at Air Force Base Waterkloof and more and more people became attuned to this reference and this then morphed into, all troop transport aircraft, becoming known as "FLOSSIE".

C130 Hercules (Flossie)

Steve disembarks with the rest of the passengers (PAX) and is met by the chap he will be replacing on this tour, Sergeant (Sgt) Piet van der Berg. Piet helps Steve with his kit and takes him to the Nissan Truck, assigned to the F/E crew for use at the base. With the Truck, and Piet's help, clearing in is a breeze.

With his kit dropped off at the Chopper Air Crew revetment, Steve and Piet go over the Alouette Gunship he will take over. Steve's aircraft has a MG151 20mm cannon fitted, loaded with ball and high explosive (HE) rounds. Steve checks the

Technical Logs and verifies all data accurate and up to date. Next, it's time to drop Piet off at Movement Control for his flight back to the States (South Africa).

MG151 20mm Cannon

The first night is Steve's initiation into Bush War life, and it's down to the Tree Pub for some wet ones, and then the Mess for sustenance, followed by more wet ones, before heading back to the Chopper Corner.

"The Pub" at AFB Ondangwa

At the Chopper Corner, Steve and the remaining F/E's have stocks of beer, brandy and coke to last them through a card game called "Black Bitch", Air Force's version of Hearts. Or as the Air Force boys call it "Hunt the Cunt". Steve quickly picks up the game and is soon racking up the wins, the lowest score wins. All the while Andre' Geyser is getting drunker and drunker as the game continues and has a very comical process of shrinking in size the drunker, he gets. It's as if he forms a natural crouching position to prove he can still stand.

Early the next morning, everyone is up and about, off to breakfast, followed by daily Intelligence Briefing at the Command Post. After the briefing the daily identification and recognition session takes place to ensure that crews can identify friend or foe in the air and on the ground. After these briefings one of the Flight Commanders would give a briefing of the previous day's events.

Today it was the Impala Flight Commander's turn.

Impala Ground Attack Aircraft

The Impala is a South African built ground attack strike aircraft and has to date been very effective in the Bush War efforts against SWAPO. The Flight Commander moves to the front of the Briefing Room and starts his Brief.

"At 10h00 yesterday, two aircraft were dispatched to the Techamutete area to complete a reconnaissance mission. Flying at 200ft agl (Above Ground Level), at 350 Kts (Knots) in battle formo (Formation), the lead pilot identified some vehicle spoor (Tracks) heading in a Southerly direction. The tracks looked fresh and the vehicles seemed to have been heavily laden due to the depth of the spoor. It is estimated that the spoor was no older than 24 hours".

The briefing ended, and everyone dispersed for task allocation by their respective Flight Commanders. Steve and his pilot Lt. Mike Hill are assigned to Top Cover. Top Cover is a Gunship flying the Air Force Base's perimeter along the flight path of incoming and outgoing aircraft, thus ensuring that an opportunity of a ground attack on these aircraft is prevented. Steve and Mike immediately bond, and Mike updates Steve on all the pointers necessary to be effective and efficient in the Bush War. On one sortie, Mike gets clearance from the ATC (Air Traffic Controller) to test the Cannon. Steve cocks the Cannon and awaits Mike's authorization to fire. Mike sets the aircraft up in an orbit around an Old Russian Truck in a Shona (Dry Pan) and tells Steve to fire when ready. Steve takes aim through the Cannon sight and gently squeezes the trigger releasing three quick rounds, perfectly on target. The HE (High Explosive) rounds exploding like grenades on impact. Steve and Mike log 5 hours Top Cover for the day and its last light when Steve gets the Ground Crew to assist him in getting the Gunship into the hangar for a quick maintenance check. Steve spends the next hour greasing and oiling the transmission system, then cleaning the engine and transmission platforms, before completing a most important check on the cannon. Steve sees that the canon's dampers are worn and jogs over to the Armoury to get some spares to replace them. Aircraft serviced and covered, Steve tows it out onto the Flight Line for the night. Then it's off to the mess for food and pub for liquid replenishment.

Early the next morning it's a repetition of the previous day's events at the Command Post, with the exception that the Puma Flight Commander jumped up to give a briefing.

Puma Helicopter (Giant)

"At 14h00 yesterday two "Giants" were dispatched for a Casevac (Casualty Evacuation) north of Xangongo. Both aircraft followed a flight path to the west around the city to avoid detection and called for smoke (Smoke Grenade) at 5 minutes out. The LZ (Landing Zone) was immediately identified and the Casevac picked up.

The onboard Medical team then did an excellent job of addressing the wounded. After Take Off, the Giants set heading on a different return route to avoid being detected. On route both aircraft, were flying in loose battle formo, at 50 ft. agl and 135 Kts, when the co-pilot of the lead aircraft noticed some foot spoor on the ground. He immediately identified that it must have been a pregnant woman, as the toe prints were deeper than the heels prints. The spoor was also very fresh, between 2 to 3 hours old, and it was heading in an easterly direction".

By this time there was so much sniggering and giggling from the chopper crews, and the fighter boys were red in the face, realizing that the piss was being taken out of them for yesterday's briefing. Without breaking a smile, the Puma Flight Commander looked over everyone and calmly said, "That's all, any questions? Do the Imp Guys need some lessons in spoor identification?" With that he turned on his heel and sat down. By this time the laughter had reached a crescendo and lasted a very long time.

Steve and Mike are assigned First Standby together with Andre Geyser and Heinz Katzke. Steve and Andre prepare the aircraft for pre-flight inspection and sign the Flight Logs. Then they settle into a day of waiting for a call out. It is just after Steve has made them a cup of coffee when call for the standby crew is made over the Public Address. Steve and Andre race to the Command Post to see what the briefing is.

Recce Success

The Recce (Reconnaissance) Teams had been following up on a lead where Gooks (Terrorists) had entered SWA and were tasked to capture young men for training as SWAPO Terrorists. They had just picked up a fresh spoor and needed Gunship Top Cover to assist in the hunt. Within 30 minutes both crews have briefed, got navigation, weapons, and kit and head off in the direction of the Recce's. Both Steve and Andre test their weapons on take-off, so that they would be ready upon arrival on target. It's a quick 30-minute flight when they spot the yellow smoke indicating the LZ. Mike makes contact with the Recce Commander and gets debriefed on what is transpiring. Mike then decides that Heinz would refuel first after another 30 minutes of flying. The refuel would take 15 minutes and the refuel truck is 10 minutes away, so by the time Heinz and Andre' get back Steve and Mike would head in for fuel.

Follow Up

The idea then is to circle ahead of the trackers to keep the Gooks head down while the Recce's catch up with them. By circling back every now and then Mike could pick up the general direction that the spoor is going and then heads out in that direction once more.

Heinz and Andre' peel off and leave to refuel. Steve and Mike continue to orbit above and ahead of the trackers while keeping a lookout for the Gooks. Steve is straining his eyes but cannot pick out a thing. Exactly 30 minutes later, Heinz radios that he is on his way back and would be on target in 5 minutes.

Just then Mike throws the aircraft into a left bank and shouts at Steve, "There they are, shoot them".

Steve looks down and sees nothing, but pulls off a shot, asking Mike to guide him from where the round hit. Mike shouts lift the cannon up a little, now shoot. Steve pulls of another round, and as if by magic the shape of a camouflaged human form jumps out at him, then another, and another. Suddenly Steve can make out 5 shapes lying on the ground. He takes careful aim and 15 rounds round later there is dust everywhere. As Steve stops firing, Andre' lets loose with his cannon, but it's too late, all five have been eliminated. The Recce trackers quickly catch up after the dust settles and confirm 100% kill. Steve's actions are methodical, and he reacts as he was trained to do. He is excited but emotionless at the same time. Mike is babbling about what a good shot Steve is, but Steve just grins and is left to his own thoughts over what had just transpired.

A quick survey of the area by the trackers confirms that there were no more Gooks around, and the tracks that they had been following are the confirmed kills. Both Gunships space for landing near the contact area and shut down. A quick debrief is conducted with the Recce's and with smiles all around another group of terrorists has been eliminated, ensuring the safety of the local children that had been earmarked for abduction. Steve and Mike get airborne first to get a quick top up from the fuel truck, before returning to form up with the other Gunship, and head back to AFB Ondangwa.

Steve and Andre' are still servicing the aircraft when one of the Recce troops rolls up the hangar door and states that he had been given instructions to fetch the Gunship crews who has been at the contact today. Steve and Andre' quickly complete signing up the aircraft logs and jump into the truck. Next, they picked up Heinz and Mike and head toward Fort Rev, strategically located off the main runway at AFB Ondangwa.

Recce Base Fort Rev

The chopper crews are challenged at the gate, granted access and escorted to the recreation area. At the Pub they meet up with the Recce Team of the days contact. A quick tour of the Recce Camp is conducted followed by some liquid refreshments and then supper. This contact had been a major achievement for the teams, as SWAPO was stepping up the infiltration and abduction of children at an alarming rate. With this quick follow up and clean up, the Gooks main plan had failed. The evening takes on a different tune and lifelong friendships are being kindled, as the men start finding out more about each other, and how similar they all are. It is in the wee hours of the morning when the last notes of "Oh Chopper" is sung by the Chopper Crews, before being ceremoniously removed from the Fort and told to go to bed.

<u>Old Chopper Song</u>

Oh, Chopper we fly the sky together,

Oh, Chopper in any kind of weather,

When you're flying days are over,

And your blades are folding over,

Good old Chopper Friend of Mine.

Keep your revs up fellows; the moon is yellow tonight,

Keep your revs up fellows; the moon is yellow tonight.

When you're flying days are over,

And your blades are folding over,

Good old chopper friend of mine.

Early the next morning Steve has time to reflect on the past day's events and realizes that he had crossed the line in the sand and was now a trained killing machine. Understanding the threat against the Southern Region of Africa and having witnessed the demise of first Rhodesia and then Mozambique, Steve is comforted by the fact that South Africa is far better prepared for an onslaught and have extremely well-trained personnel to complete the tasks at hand. He gets satisfaction in knowing that what he has been trained to do will ensure safety for the citizens of South Africa. A true patriot Steve is afraid yet excited about continuing the process of war in Angola. With the political situation as it was currently, and the cold war utilizing Africa as its scapegoat, there would still be many situations arising which are going to make Steve question the decisions made and going to be made to control this region of Africa. Right now, the Cold War is in full swing and Communism is the threat and very real. Africa has been armed to the tooth by Russia and supported with Equipment, Manpower and Training to control this region of the world. With Cuba, East Germany, and other Eastern Bloc Countries supporting Russia, this conflict was going to escalate.

The next few days are uneventful, and Steve volunteers Top Cover often, as he wants to ensure that he is well versed with the operations and procedures he now finds himself in. While on standby the aircrew relax next to the pool that they constructed.

Aircrew Pool AFB Ondangwa

Two weeks of his tour have come and gone and every evening he sees the line up at the party telephone for chaps booking calls back home. A call is made by turning the handle and waiting for the operator to answer, then you state the number you want to call, the operator puts you on hold and you hear them connecting with your loved ones. The operator asks if they accept the reverse charge from you, and only then is the connection made. Each person is given 5 to 10 minutes on a call. Steve connects with Zella but cannot share much with her, except that he misses her and can't wait to get back. Zella tells Steve that she is enjoying the Dental Practice where she is working and is thinking of Studying to become an Oral Hygienist. Happy for her, and pondering over his own situation, Steve says his goodbye's and says he will see her in two weeks.

Marienfluss round One

Steve and his fellow F/E's are all lounging around the pool when an announcement to all Chopper Crews goes out. Grabbing their kit, they all sprint to the Base Command Post. Once everyone has settled, Colonel (Col) Ollie Holmes steps in from the Sector Command Post "Oshikati" and starts the briefing. Intelligence has been gathered about a large contingent of SWAPO in the South Western part of Angola, near the town of Iona. There will be four Gunships and four Giants operating from the Marienfluss in the Kaokoveld region of SWA. Take off will be at 05h00 the next morning, an hour before sunrise.

Very early the next morning Steve and the rest of the F/E's are already on the flight line preparing for the mission, they will be deploying for at least four days. Night stop kits packed, aircraft prepared, and rations loaded, the heavily laden aircraft are to first fly to Ruacana for refueling, then on to the desert runway in Marienfluss. Mike comes out while Steve is removing covers and gets ready to start the Gunship. Steve rushes round to check area clear and too late notices that the one main rotor blade is directly over the Strella modification jet pipe. Within a couple of seconds Steve reacts, but it's too late the blade has already sustained damage and is already bending down where the heat had been too much for the materials. Steve indicates to Mike to cut the engine and then shares the bad news with him. While Mike retreats to the Base Command Post, Steve rushes off to the hangar to get the ground crew to assist him in changing the whole set of blades. The Alouette has a balanced set of blades and therefore you had to change the complete set and not only one blade. Fortunately, there are sufficient sets of blades available, so Steve gets to work. Luckily one of the F/E's on Top Cover for the day has a Thimble Rigging tool, which enables one to simply take the difference between the removed blade angle and the new blade angle and adjusts the control rod accordingly. After setting the control rods, a quick ground run to set the fine tracking of the blades is completed. Next Steve completes the documentation updates and clears the snag in the Technical Log entered by Mike. All that is required now is a quick power and autorotation check after take-off, and then Steve and Mike can make their way west to the Marienfluss.

Mike and Steve once again sign all the required documents, double check the aircraft and then are on their way to Ruacana for a refuel followed by the final stop at the Marienfluss.

Mountainous Area en-route to Marienfluss

The flight is uneventful and the lonely little Gunship, fully loaded makes its way from Ondangwa to Ruacana. Steve and Mike are left to their own thoughts with the occasional radio chatter or validation of check list items. 45 Minutes later they are on final approach to the Ruacana runway. Mike lines up a roll-on landing onto the taxi way, and then turns off to the refueling bladders. After shutting down Steve quickly refuels the aircraft and completes a visual walk round inspection of the aircraft to confirm that everything is still in order. A short while later the Gunship starts up, taxis out and takes off down the taxi way, setting heading for Marienfluss. The country side changes quickly and soon they are in very mountainous terrain and climbing to cross over the Zebra Mountains through a saddle to drop down 5000 ft into the Marienfluss.

In the country's far north, is the Kunene River, and the only permanent source of water in the region on the border between SWA and Angola, is lined with a narrow belt of riverine vegetation and palm trees. Perpendicular to this northern border lays the enormous Hartmann's and Marienfluss Valleys. These valleys run for miles between the Hartmann and Otjihipa Mountains, largely folded, dark metamorphic rock which, when exposed over time to the sun, wind and temperature extremes, cracks and rusts into reddish-brown gravel plains. In rainy years, the enormous Marienfluss and Hartmann's valleys become grassy expanses, but generally their flat topographies are covered by sand broken only by a few tough grasses, toxic euphorbias, mysterious 'fairy circles' and sheer granite inselbergs.

The principal, albeit minimal, source of water comes from the famous South West African early morning mists, generated when the icy water of the Atlantic Ocean meets the hot desert air of the Skeleton Coast. This daily cycle of airborne moisture rolls inland along the various depressions and canyons formed by ancient rivers. As the dew settles, it is eagerly harvested by plants, animals and insects before the sun burns it off.

Wildlife such as Gemsbok (Oryx), Springbok, Brown Hyena, Hartmann's Mountain Zebra and Cape Fox occur sporadically, while smaller creatures abound in this surreal setting. The Kunene River also harbors a large population of Nile Crocodile and vibrant birdlife. Desert Plated Lizard, Kunene Racer, Namaqua Chameleon and Horned Adder are some of the reptiles to be seen here. Burchell's Courser, Bokmakierie, Pririt Batis, Stark's Lark, Rüppell's Korhaan and Benguela Long-Billed Lark are among the characteristic bird species to be found in this area.

In the distance they can make out the Heli Admin Group (HAG) with Giants and Gunships parked strategically around a small tent city. The descent seems extraordinarily long, as they follow the valley down to the Fluss.

<u>Marienfluss HAG</u>

Eventually they are on final approach, and Mike deftly puts the Gunship down next to the rest of the aircraft. After Shut Down, Steve completes the maintenance actions while Mike heads over to the HAG to check in with Col Holmes. With the aircraft serviced and covered, it's time for food, drink and bed. Soutie Sowden an old Armourer, who changed his trade to AME for qualification as F/E, was there as well. Steve and Soutie have become good friends. Soutie's nickname for Steve is "Rooi Baard" (Red Beard) and with Soutie is Andre' Geyser and Boats Botes, as the other Gunship F/E's.

Col Holmes has requested that all members attend a briefing after supper at the Ops Tent, which included the Infantry Troops from 32 Battalion, aircrew from the Giants and Gunships, and the Intelligence officers. Col Holmes, an ex-fighter pilot, is a no-nonsense type of guy and shoots straight from the hip. After the attack plan is shared, with the Gunships taking station over target first over the town of Iona, the Giants will drop their forces north and west of target to form an attack pattern. The Giants will return to the Fluss to pick up 200 Lt Drums of Jet A1 and fly them closer to a safe refueling point from the target. With the Giants there is to be a small defense team to guard the refueling point. This is also to be the holding point for the Giants until called.

Next Col Holmes reiterates, "Gents we know there is AA (Anti-Aircraft Guns), and SAM's (Surface to Air Missiles) stationed in Iona so be aware. We will lose a crew if you do not pay attention to the dangers."

With that sobering thought the briefing is closed and everyone saunters off to their respective groups to deal with their thoughts. Steve, Soutie, Andre' and Boats decide it's time to play "Proppie" (Cap of Bottle). Soutie brings out a bottle of Vodka and starts topping up the Proppie for each one. This continues until the bottle is finished. The same process is then initiated once more with a bottle of Whisky. The discussion has taken on a serious note with the guys elaborating what to look for in AA and how to detect SAM's. AA is normally stationed in three batteries around a town in the form of a triangle and can be identified from the air with the round base plates and barrels pointing upward. SAM's on the other hand, are the hand carry versions, namely the SAM 7 and 9 shoulder fired versions. These are lethal weapons to the Puma's as they don't have any heat dispensing Strella modifications to the jet pipes making them susceptible to infra-red lock from the missile. The Alouette Gunships on the other hand, have Strella Mods fitted and are not as vulnerable. They are however very susceptible to RPG7 (Rocket Propelled Grenade) fire, and there are many of them all over SWA and Angola.

<u>Alouette Gunship with Stella Mod</u>

Each SAM launcher has a crew of two, and they have two missiles they can launch. When a SAM is launched, there is a huge plume of white smoke emitting from the location, and if a Gunship reacts quickly, the launcher and loader can be taken out, and therefore stopping any future launches. The RPG-7 and small arms fire are a different problem entirely, and there is no way of detecting where these will be coming from. With this knowledge shared amongst the group of pretty inebriated group of F/E's, Soutie turns and disappears between the rocky outcrops. The next minute there is a terrible sound of someone hurling. Steve goes running after Soutie and sees him hurling once more. In front of Soutie on the rocks is a heap of his deposit.

Steve asks, "Soutie, you alright Boet?"

Soutie blinks, looks at Steve and reaches into the pile, grabbing a handful and pops into his mouth, asking Steve, "You want some?"

Steve turns on his heel and pukes a straight burst at the opposite rock.

Soutie bursts out laughing and says, "Man this Mixed Veg is lekker man."

Soutie had emptied a can of Mixed Vegetables on the rocks and had just caught Steve for a sucker. Slightly sobered and giggling the group disperses to their sleeping bags for the night.

Early the next morning all the F/E's have already started pre-flight inspections and are preparing for the days contact. The 32 Battalion troops are all hunched around the campfire and cleaning their weapons in preparation for the days battle. The Gunships start-up and disperse to the target area with authorization to proceed after a final briefing. The Giants, with their troops onboard, will follow in 15 minutes, making the time over target the same as the Gunships. Steve and Mike discuss the approach to the target and what to expect. Steve and Mike, Andre' and Heinz will be first over Target with Soutie and Boats and their pilots taking up defensive station north and west of target. The plan is to come in low and fast, then pitch up and pick AA targets for aiming at. The flight seems long, and Steve is nervous, this will be his first experience across the border attacking an enemy camp.

Both Gunships arrive on target and at the arranged signal both pitch up and veer left and right to choose targets. Gooks are running everywhere and as the two Gunships climb into a 600 ft. orbit, there is no evidence of AA fire. There is however small arms fire from everywhere and within 30 seconds Steve and Mike are hit all over the aircraft. Mike breaks away from the target area while Steve leans out the aircraft to see what damage has been inflicted. Immediately Steve notices a huge fuel leak and mentions to Mike that he must land immediately. Mike finds a spot to the south of the target on a hill and puts the aircraft down quickly. While Mike completes shutdown, Steve is under the aircraft inspecting the damage. Mike radios for a Giant to bring in protection troops. With the aircraft shutdown Steve sees that the most damage had been caused by a bullet that had hit the main frame just forward of the fuel tank. The bullet had then tumbled and torn up the side of the tank, destroying the self-sealing material and leaving a large tear which then allowed the fuel to pour out. Steve goes to his toolkit and starts looking for items to plug the tear. Mike, still with helmet on, has his AK47 aimed in the direction of the target and is lying down next to a rock for protection. Even in this dangerous situation this is a very comical sight.

Steve screams at Mike while laughing loudly, "What the fuck dude, take your Bonedome off man."

Mike grins sheepishly and removes his helmet and continues to keep guard. Steve grabs his survival knife and starts to shape a wedge from a branch he has just chopped off a small bush.

In the distance they can hear a Giant approaching. Very soon the huge chopper drops down and four troops run to form a protection defense around the Gunship. The Giant F/E then rolls out two drums of fuel for Steve, and then they take off and leave the way they had come. Steve gives each troop a handful of chewing gum to chew on, before wrapping all of it around the wedge he has made and places the whole conglomeration into the tear of the fuel tank. Next, he takes all the soap he has on board and smoothes this over the wedge. Steve then removes the refueling hoses from the Gunship and connects them up to the electric pump and starts to refuel the aircraft. The leak is still evident, but acceptable to fly the aircraft out. Steve briefs Mike on the damage and reminds him not to take too much power and keep the attitude changes slow and calculated, as the main frame has been badly damaged by the bullet. The rest of the damage was through the fuselage and all superficial. With that said, they bid farewell to their defense support and get airborne for the Fluss. After a ten-minute flight four Giants form up around the Gunship, as if protecting their little brother. Another 10 minutes later and Steve is watching the fuel gauge like a hawk when one of the Giants radios that the fuel leak has gotten much worse. Steve looks out the door to the rear and cannot even make out the tail rotor in the mist of fuel leaking out. Both Mike and Steve are in real panic mode, as this could turn bad quickly if the fuel mist ignited from the engine heat. Fortunately, the Fluss is visible and the minutes feel like hours till they eventually touchdown, both breathing a huge sigh of relief.

Col Holmes comes straight to the aircraft and asks Steve, "What is the damage, can you make it to Ondangwa?"

To which Steve responds, "No Sir, the frame is badly damaged, and I cannot seal the fuel leak."

Col Holmes then says, "Ok no problem I already have a Transall on route to collect your aircraft".

The C160 Transall, is the French two engine version of the C130 Hercules and is very capable of landing in the desert.

Steve starts the preparation for loading the Gunship into the Transall. Four hours later the Giants return with their troops onboard. The feedback was one hell of a fight that had taken place. It had been a very successful operation. The Gunships come in last and settle down in their spots. Steve is questioned by everyone on the damage to his aircraft and a lot of oohs and aahs over what had taken place.

In the distance Andre' crawls out from underneath his aircraft with an ashen face.

Steve asks him, "What's wrong Geysie?"

Andre' shakes his head and says, "Fok Tjom, my aircraft is fucked."

An AK47 round had clipped the main control rod for the Collective Pitch, tearing the material that houses the bearing. The only part holding the bearing in place is a small piece of metal that could break off any second. It was indeed a very close call, and the Gunship Gods had definitely been in their favour this day. The Transall now has two Gunships to take back to Ondangwa.

While the crews await the arrival of the Transall, Soutie feels the need for relief, and picks up his shovel, toilet paper and heads over the dunes for a shit parade. Steve sees Soutie sauntering off and grabs his own shovel with a length of branch he found, together with some stainless-steel safety wire. Moving quickly but silently behind Soutie, Steve fashions a long-handled Poop Scoop. Soutie has reached his point of no return and prepares a hole in the sand for his deposit. Next, he unzips his flight suite and drops them together with his shorts to his knees and flicks the whole lot forward away from his now very exposed butt. He now positions himself to do the dirty. At this point Steve is moving in with the Poop Scoop and is trying desperately not to laugh as the shovel waves within millimeters of Soutie's exposed butt. Just in time Steve catches the deposit, waits a couple of seconds to confirm there is no more, and quickly withdraws to bury the evidence. Soutie continues his post poop cleanup process with toilet paper and then stands up while at the same time pulling his shorts and flight suite into position. Soutie turns around with shovel in hand to bury his deposit, when to his surprise there is only toilet paper. Soutie drops the shovel and slowly reaches up to his neck to feel in the collar of his flight suite. Nothing there, so he slowly steps out of the flight suite and shakes it down. Also, nothing there, and as a last resort he gingerly steps out of his shorts to check them for evidence. Also, nothing there and shaking his head he bends down to pick up the shovel, flight suite and shorts.

Steve has at this point tried very hard not to give the game away but smiling broadly he indicates to the rest the arrival of a very comical site into the camp. Soutie with flight suite and shorts over one arm and spade with toilet paper in the other, and a pair of well descended balls hanging almost down to his knees with an expression of disbelief on his face.

Soutie comes in muttering, "I just had a phantom shit. I felt it, I heard it drop, but when I turned around it was gone!"

At this point Steve could not hold any longer and collapses in gut wrenching laughter. The rest of the audience joins in and very soon all of them are speechless and breathless from all the laughter. Steve had just got Soutie back big time for last night's puke story.

An hour later the Transall comes into view, rumbling along overhead the runway, and makes a tight circuit over the HAG to line up for a downwind leg. The troops had already walked the length of the runway to make sure there is no debris or items that could damage the aircraft on landing. The Transall makes a long flat final approach and then touches down gently on the desert runway. In a huge cloud of red dust, the reverse pitch is engaged to bring the huge aircraft to a standstill.

C160 Transall at Marienfluss

The aircraft is then turned around and positioned for takeoff before they shut down. Mike and Steve, Andre' and Heinz start up their Gunships and position them in line astern behind the large cargo aircraft. Then both aircraft are defueled completely, and main rotor blades removed. Next the aircraft are loaded into the Transall, the first Gunship facing forward and the second facing backward with their tailboom's placed next to each other. The Load Master then secures both aircraft, while the Gunship crews say good bye to their friends, collect their kit and head to the Transall to hitch a ride back to Ondangwa.

The sun is setting over the desert when the big aircraft rumbles down the runway and lifts off into the desert twilight. Steve, Mike, Andre' and Heinz are sitting in the hammock seats in the middle of the aircraft below the mainplane. The required bottle appears from nowhere and the "Proppie" is passed around. It had been a very close call for both crews.

The guys are joshing each other and joking about reactions when Heinz jumps and says, "I just shat myself!"

With screams of laughter everyone bombshells away from Heinz. Andre' rushes up to the Cockpit to get a roll of toilet paper for Heinz. Mike dives into the Gunship and slams the door to get away from the shit. Steve is laughing uncontrollably at the spectacle. Andre' brings Heinz a roll of toilet paper and he disappears behind the onboard toilet curtain. Next minute he sticks his head out and asks if anyone has some shorts for him. Steve rummages through his kit and throws a pair at Heinz. Now Steve is 5'4" and Heinz is close to 5'10", it is going to be a tight squeeze. Heinz emerges from behind the screen with a black garbage bag over his shoulder and wearing Steve's shorts with his flying boots still on. It was a back slapping hysterically comical sight.

The gents are still jostling poor Heinz when they feel the Transall making an attitude change for landing at AFB Ondangwa. The aircraft taxis to the Movement Control area for the offload. As the ramp opens up, the two Gunship crews are amazed to see a large crowd gathered round to see what is being offloaded. Word had gotten out that two aircraft have been damaged in the contact and concerned members are there to see firsthand what has happened. Unfortunately, all the wives and children from the base have also gathered to see, and at the top of the ramp is Sir Heinz in tight shorts, flying boots and shit bag over his shoulder. It's a very comical situation.

The next morning Steve and Soutie have the day off. Steve is waiting for the ground crew to complete a major servicing on an aircraft he is to take over while his previous aircraft is being prepared for shipment back to the States to undergo repairs at Atlas Aircraft Corporation.

Loading Gunship for Repair

Soutie wants to build rockets and asks Steve to find masking tape and straws. Soutie grabs a couple of .303 rounds from the Trooper Alouette's machine gun and pulls the bullets off the cartridge. He pours the stick cordite out in a pile. Steve tears off a few strips of masking tape and forms a square sheet. Soutie places some of the stick cordite in the centre of the sheet and then rolls the masking tape up as if he is fashioning a smoke. Just before he folds the last piece over, Soutie adds the straw to the roll and places it upright in a Coke bottle. Next, he pulls out his Zippo Lighter and holds it at the base of the fashioned rocket. The next minute there is a whoosh and the home-made rocket flies off into the sky.

"Nice" the two say simultaneously.

"Get a Smoke Grenade", says Soutie.

Steve gets to work on filing the base of an Orange Smoke Grenade. He now extracts the compacted smoke capsule and grinds off some slivers to the next masking tape square. With straw fixed the same procedure is repeated, and the rocket whooshes off with a trail of Orange Smoke belching out behind.

"Now that's mooi man", says Soutie, "but check this one"!

Soutie has pulled out a thousand-foot flare and tears off the plastic coating, exposing the aluminium casing. He removes the top parachute and detonator, cuts the base into four fins and fashions a true rocket. Soutie places the rocket on its fashioned fins and once again with the Zippo Lighter the launch is celebrated. The rocket speeds up to a thousand feet as advertised and then falls back to earth. It travelled to fast to see how high it actually went. So Soutie comes up with an alternative detection method.

A second thousand-foot flare is similarly prepared, but this time the parachute detonator is left intact. Soutie wanders over to the Armoury and in a little while returns with a ball of PE4. He fashions a ball and places it on top of the parachute detonator of the rocket. Count down initiated and Zippo exposed, the faultless launch takes place and the rocket whooshes towards the heavens. The next instant there is an almighty bang at around 1000 ft. with a telltale ball of black smoke. The two rocket men are overjoyed at the success.

Across the flight line is the Control Tower, which is located next to the Taxi Strip. The ATC comes running out of the Tower, jumps into his car and with the Orange Light on the roof rotating, he speeds in the direction of the Ops Room. Soutie and Steve are laughing hysterically at the sight and still sniggering when they see the Officer Commanding pull up in his vehicle.

"Wat de fok maak julle twee?" (What the fuck are you doing) asks the Colonel.

"Ons speel so bietjie Kolonel!" (We are playing a little Colonel) says Soutie.

Soutie and Steve are marched off to the HQ Building where they both receive an appropriate amount of tongue lashing. They both promise never to do it again and are dismissed. As the grinning duo step off the HQ Building's veranda, they can hear the Colonel bellowing with laughter that he could no longer withhold.

The rest of Steve's Bush Tour he shares with two more pilots and a new aircraft, as Gunship number 57 has to be returned to Atlas Aviation for repair. Lindsay Crawford and Steve partner up for a day and then Paul Downer is assigned to Steve and Gunship 67. A lot of Top Cover is carried out followed up by a few call outs from Koetvoet.

Koevoet

Koevoet, created by South African Police Brigadier Hans Dreyer, a veteran of the Rhodesian Special Air Service, the unit's initial directive was to conduct internal reconnaissance. Koevoet quickly becomes one of the most effective combat forces deployed against the South West African People's Organization (SWAPO) during the war, consisting of some 250 white and 800 black Ovambo operators.

Steve is assigned another Gunship and Pilot for deployment to Opuwa to the west. Capt. Ricky Vergotinni knows Steve well from his time completing Chopper conversion in Bloemfontein a couple of years ago. Together with another Gunship they pack, brief and get airborne for Opuwo. The route will be Ruacana for a fuel top up and then Opuwa direct.

Opuwo is considered a desert climate with virtually no rainfall. The name Opuwo was given by the commissioner of Ondangwa, Mr. Hugo Hahn, who came in search of land to build an office. Upon his arrival, he asked local headmen for land where he could build an office.

The headmen gave him a small plot, and when the headmen tried to give him more land, Mr. Hahn responded saying "Opuwo (it's enough for me). I don't want any more land". That is how Opuwo got its name. The local residents of Opuwo called it Otjihinamaparero at the time, and some still call it that.

Hugo Hahn called the land "Ohopoho Otjitopora" which means "they see the bore hole and their water comes out". The name Otjihinamaparero was changed to Opuwo in 1974 due to orthographic reform.

The first office to be established in the Kaokoland area was the colonial administrator in Swartbooisdrift on the banks of the Kunene River. This was the administrative center of the area from 1925 to 1939. Afterwards, administrative control of the area shifted to Ohopoho, later called Opuwo.

The police station in Swartbooisdrift was run by Sergeant Herbert, and his aim was to receive the Angola Boers who had trekked to Angola out of refusal to accept the British government in South Africa. Sergeant Basson took over the office at Swartbooisdrift, and excavated Opuwo's first bore hole. Basson had the nickname "Katjiriamakaja" (a person who eats tobacco).

The two Gunships approach from the east into the flat open expanse where Opuwo is located. At first sight the isolated town looks deserted. The runway looks like a very straight road carved out of the dirt close to the town. In the distance is a truck on the road with a huge cloud of dust bellowing out behind it. Ricky looks at Steve.

"Where the fuck are we now"? exclaims Ricky.

"Looks like a shithole to me", replies Steve.

Ricky radios to the other Gunship to space for landing. Ricky slows the Chopper down and flares to bring it into the hover. The next minute they are in a brown out. Dust is blowing everywhere and there is no way to see where the ground is. Ricky pulls power and climbs away, while he radios a warning to the other Gunship.

Ricky then plans an assault landing which means they will roll on instead of hovering, a faster but safer approach. Both Choppers touch down without further incident. After shut-down the crews get out and inspect the ground they have landed on.

The fine dust is very much like dry cement powder and dust clouds puff up by just placing your foot on the ground. Both aircraft are covered in a fine layer of dust. Steve has his work cut out to keep the dust out of critical areas. A quick debrief and all agree the best thing for operating from here would be roll off take-off's and roll on landings to protect the aircraft.

Opuwa Desert Town

The crews unpack in the stifling heat and make their way up to the Air Force Ops Tent where they will be housed for the next week. Their tasking is stand-by for potential SWAPO Special forces infiltrating from the south west region of Angola.

After a quick brunch they debrief with the Army Int officer. They will be on call for teams that are currently deployed in the field. Steve takes a sip of the muddy coloured water to quench his thirst and gets his first taste of the brackish Opuwo water. Water is scarce and any well that produces water is very brackish. To kill the taste there is an abundance of battery acid available to dilute the taste and make the mixture more drinkable. Battery acid is the name given by the Air Force Chopper Crews to the standard issue Concentrated Orange Juice that is mixed 1-part juice to 5-parts water.

The days are long and heat intense. Steve rigs up a sprinkler on top of the tent, from the brackish waterhole, and lets the water spray over the tent to run down the roof. The light breeze then creates evaporation cooling the inside of the tent. Everyone is just settling into the daily routine when the Int Officer comes running, calling for take-off, as the troops have an imminent attack. The Chopper crews scramble down to the Gunships and are airborne in 15 minutes. Ricky updates the target location over the radio with the Int Officer and sets heading. 15 Minutes later Ricky calls for smoke, and almost immediately 3 km ahead, Steve picks up yellow smoke.

The two Gunships split up to form an orbit around the Caspirs and Troops on the ground and pick up the general direction. Once Ricky identifies the route, he sets out to form a larger elliptical orbit in the hopes of forcing the Gooks to ground. Both Choppers spaced at 180 degrees apart keep moving in the anticipated direction. Steve leans out and sees movement and points is out to Ricky.

"Don't fire yet Steve, let's get the troops closer so that none of the fuckers get away"' says Ricky.

Steve relaxes his grip on the cannon and keeps a close eye on the movement below them. The Gooks have taken to ground and are trying to camouflage themselves. The Caspirs seem to have missed the direction so Ricky decides to get Steve to throw a smoke grenade to indicate the direction. Steve pulls the pin and turns the smoke grenade upside down so that the release handle flings downward away from the aircraft. The grenade firing pin pops and flies downward, but unfortunately the handle flings back upward and contacts the main rotor blade of the aircraft.

"What the hell was that Steve?" asks Ricky.

"The smoke grenade handle flew up into the rotors", says Steve.

"Oh shit, is there damage?" asks Ricky.

"There is no vibration, so we should be fine", says Steve.

Just then the Caspirs arrive, racing into the scene. Ricky orders Steve to fire and within 3 minutes the contact is over. A mop up operation is initiated, and no further Gooks are found. Steve proposes that they do not land as Opuwo is only 15 minutes away where there is fuel and then he can inspect the aircraft for damage.

Back at Opuwo Steve discovers that the smoke grenade handle had ripped one of the blades from behind the main spar. Steve decides that the set of blades has to be replaced and requests Ricky to arrange this through the Ops Room. A Puma is going to be bringing in a set of blades from Ondangwa that afternoon with one of the Atlas Personnel to assist in changing and rigging the rotor system.

The Puma arrives and Steve together with the crew unloads the set of blades. The Puma Crew joins Ricky at the Ops Tent while Steve and the Ground Crew complete the maintenance and conduct the blade track ground runs. Chris Schutte from Atlas is helping Steve and within the hour the set of main rotor blades are changed, and thimble rigging completed. Steve then briefs Chris on the blade tracking. He first runs the Engine at 28,000 RPM, Chris brings the tracking flag in and just clips the blade tips that have been colour coded with wax crayons. Chris checks the track and indicates to Steve to raise the RPM. Steve increases Engine RPM to 33,500 and gives Chris the thumbs up. Chris tracks the blades once more and shows Steve to shut down. After shutting down, Steve and Chris measure the split in the blade track and decide to raise the red blade and drop the blue. Chris makes the adjustments and Steve restarts the engine to complete the process once more. At full Engine RPM Chris completes the track and shows Steve a thumbs up. Steve pulls 0.02 degrees pitch on the collective lever and shows Chris to check the track once more. The reason is to ensure that with power the blades don't spread as this will induce a vibration. The track is clean. The marked track is one single line of red, blue and yellow. The only thing to do now is complete the technical log entries and conduct a 15-minute test flight to verify vibration and rigging. Steve and Chris load the damaged blades into the Puma and watch as the Giant takes off back to Ondangwa.

<u>Main Rotor Blade change</u>

Steve summons Ricky for the test flight and soon they are airborne over Opuwo. Ricky banks left and right and then enters VNE (Velocity Never Exceeded) envelope to check for vibration. Satisfied that the blades are behaving as advertised the only item left on the check list is an autorotation. At low pitch stop setting from an altitude of 3000 ft above ground, the aircraft needs to have sufficient rotor RPM build up for a safe landing. Ricky places the aircraft into an auto rotation and the rotor RPM builds up satisfactorily. Steve shows Ricky thumbs up and they break away to land at the runway.

Steve is completing the servicing on the aircraft when a crowd of locals arrive and beg a ride. Steve gets a "brain fart" and tells the group that the aircrafts battery is low, and they will need to push start. The excited group is all keen to shove the aircraft up and down the runway. Steve instructs them on where they can push and where not to push. Next minute the Gunship is being wheeled along the dirt while Steve selects the start button to vent and shows the group to push faster. Just as they start a run Steve let's go the starter switch and indicates for the group to stop. Steve gets out, tinkers in the rear and then helps to turn the aircraft around. He jumps back in the aircraft and indicates the group to push again. As the speed build up Steve vents the engine once more and leaves it a bit longer this time before once again shutting down. Steve gets out, shrugs and indicates that it won't start. The excited group is disappointed but still had a lot of fun as they saunter off still excited at having pushed a helicopter. Needless to say, there is no connection between the wheels of a helicopter and the engine. All Steve had been doing was venting the engine, a standard procedure to clear residual fuel before starting. The rest of the stay at Opuwo remains excruciatingly hot but all too soon, their time is up, and they head back to Ondangwa.

Steve clears out from AFB Ondangwa and is awaiting his replacement at Movement Control. The morning goes by in a blur and very soon Steve is settled into the hammock seating of the C130, heading back to AFB Waterkloof in Pretoria South Africa.

The War Continues

It's the first week of May 1980, 9 days before Steve's 23rd birthday and he is back at 87 HFS, settling back into Squadron life, and assigned to the daily flying program for the next conversion course currently being trained to be Helicopter Pilots and Flight Engineers. In a few short months the year comes to an end, but Squadron life continues, and Steve is racking up the hours. Steve and Zella have made many improvements to their Potluck. Weekends are spent exploring the area around Bloemfontein and they soon make friends with other young married couples at the base. Zella has settled into her new position as Dental Assistant and has made a number of friends. This gives Steve solace, as now he knows that she will be keeping herself entertained and not worrying over what was happening on the Border.

Once again, the next Bush Tour looms up and it's mid-February 1981 as he heads north to AFB Ondangwa. In the next four weeks Steve racks up 60 flight hours with Gunship 621 and Nellis as his pilot. Steve and Nellis are deployed with another Gunship at Eenhana, located just south of the Angolan Border. The Air Force contingent at Eenhana consists of the Intelligence and Ops Officer plus the Gunship Crews. They are guests of the Army Contingent that run the base.

__Eenhana refueling point__

At Eenhana is a brand-new program, still top secret in prototype phase. South Africa's Unmanned Aerial Vehicle (UAV) is being put through its paces. Steve wanders over to the SAMIL with the mounted control room and is surprised to bump into one of his former school mates from Lowveld High.

Neville Ansel is working on the Seeker, as it has been named and is one of the team trialing the UAV across the border. Neville gives Steve a rundown on the system and shows him the control room and how they fly the UAV. Steve is suitable impressed. Seeker is going to be deployed across the border to monitor enemy movement so that future operations can be initiated.

__Seeker UAV__

Nellis and Steve spend lazy days in the Operations Room checking in to see if there are any leads for call out. On four occasions they do get called out but don't manage to engage in a firefight or contact. On their last few days the two Gunships are scrambled to a Koevoet chase about 30 minutes south east of Eenhana. Steve and Nellis enter the orbit with the other Gunship over the Koevoet Kaspir's (Armed Troop Carrier)

Trackers ahead of Kaspir

The two Gunships flying lazy orbits approximately 5 kilometers ahead of the advancing Kaspir's, and every couple of orbits then Nellis would head back to the Kaspir's and fly directly overhead to pick up a new heading of the spoor that the trackers are following. All of a sudden, the chatter on the radio reaches a crescendo, as the Gooks have Bomb Shelled (Split off in different directions), meaning that the trackers are closing in on them. Steve has lowered his yellow visor to accentuate shadows, making it easier for him to pick out a camouflaged Gook.

As if by magic, Steve quickly picks out a Gook standing next to a tree and tells Nellis to bank left. Nellis adjusts his orbit and Steve takes aim and quickly fires three shots off, hitting the target directly. Almost immediately two other Gooks scatter from cover trying to make a break for it. At this time both Gunships are in the same orbit 180° apart and with each other in view they are picking the targets off one at a time. The next minute a Kaspir races into view directly underneath the Gunship firing line.

Nellis screams on the radio, "One Zero, Gunship, you are in our direct line of fire!"

The Kaspir's ignore the warning and with canons blazing they attack the rest of the Gooks. Within a minute orders to cease fire are being shouted out to all. Amongst all the chaos the two Gunships have widened their orbit and are now waiting for order to establish and see if there are still any Gooks left. Another minute goes by and slowly the Kaspir's are getting back in line and all come to a stop. The trackers are feverishly checking for any tracks outside of the contact area.

Another ten minutes goes by when the lead Kaspir radios the Gunships, "Gunship one zero, confirm 100% kill no targets left! Do you chaps want to land?"

Nellis responds, "One Zero, Gunship, we will land in the Shona to your west".

After conferring with the other Gunship, Nellis and Steve make an approach and land in the area. The second Gunship follows close after, and then both aircraft shut down. A lot of very tired but excited faces are milling around and jabbering continuously about the contact. The Gunship crews debrief with the Koevoet Commander and with back slaps and thumbs up, the two Gunships get airborne for Eenhana.

Upon arrival at Eenhana the Commanding Officer had already been relayed the news and greeted the Gunship crews with a huge grin.

"Guys the Braai (Barbecue) and Beers are on me tonight, good job".

That evening the Chopper Crews are enjoying plenty brown bottles and Braai, when 32 Battalion comes straggling into camp from an extended period in Angola. Lt. Jim Savory is the officer in charge of 32, and requests permission to join. The Major in charge of Eenhana knows of 32 Battalion and warns Jim that his soldiers can set up camp next to the runway. Jim is angry, but instructs his troops to set up camp, as they are exhausted after the long hike out of Angola. Nellis tries to reason with the Major but to no avail. The Major pulls rank on Nellis and tells him to ship up or ship out. Nellis storms out and informs the rest of the crew. Everyone packs up and heads out to the choppers. In a few hours it will be light enough to fly. Nellis gets on the radio and informs Oshikati of the Air Force contingent's intentions.

At first light Nellis briefs the crews and contacts Oshikati for flight authorization. The two aircraft are airborne 30 minutes later and on route to AFB Ondangwa. It's an uneventful flight and Steve mulls over the last couple of weeks of action. It feels like there is tension in the air and that the war effort is escalating.

Back at AFB Ondangwa Steve washes the dirt off his Gunship and gives the whole aircraft a thorough inspection to ensure that there will be no surprises. Tonight, he will be joining the rest of the F/E gang left at the base for a Steak Night down at the Pub. There will be a long night of drinking, cards and stories to be shared for sure.

At the early morning briefing in the Ops Room Neil Reid and Steve learn that they will be dispatched to Ruacana for the remainder of their tours. Two Gunships will be placed at Ruacana to assist in the follow up operations that have detected that the Ruacana Dam was being targeted for attack by SWAPO.

The Ruacana Power Station is a hydroelectric power plant near Ruacana in northwest SWA, close to the Angolan border. Water for the power station is stored in a dam just above the Ruacana Falls along the Cunene River in Angola. Several dams upstream help regulate the Cunene River to help the power station operate more efficiently. The power station is operated by SWA's national power utility company. The first three 80 MW Francis turbine-generators were commissioned in 1978. The Ruacana Power Station feeds into the Southern African power grid which provides the whole Southern African region with power, making it an important target to enemies.

Ruacana Dam

The two Gunships allocated, leave an hour later from AFB Ondangwa. It will take them just on an hour to make the trip to the town of Ruacana where they will be landing at the runway for fuel and then move over to the military camp. Their tasking is standby for call out should any of the units in the veldt require Top Cover follow up action.

Ruacana and the Heli Pad

The next two weeks the two Gunships are only called out on few occasions and all these end up being lemons. Neil has a daily discussion with the Army Ops Officer and then a Radio Call discussion with Sector Command at Oshikati. Two days before the end of Neil and Steve's Bush Tour, they are recalled to AFB Ondangwa to prepare for the handover to their replacements.

Dancing Alouette's

It's the end of March 1981 when Steve returns to 87 HFS and is immediately included in the air show that will be touring the Province of the Orange Free State to celebrate 20 years of South Africa as a Republic.

In 1961 South Africa left the Commonwealth to form the Republic and every ten years the Government arranges for celebrations accordingly. To practice for the Air Shows a team of four Alouette's would perform a formation act together requiring timed precision and disciplined flying.

Fortunately, 87 HFS has the best helicopter instructors in South Africa and within a very short period the dancing Alouette's are touring all over the Orange Free State and delighting the crowds with a spectacular show.

It is 1st May 1981 and Steve is summoned to the Officer Commanding 87 HFS. Steve quickly cleans up and hurries over to the Office Building. Cmdt Van Rooyen beckons Steve to come. Steve salutes smartly and greets the Cmdt.

"Hi Steve, and how are you enjoying Bloemfontein? I see you have done quite a number of Bush Tours already!"

"Hello Cmdt, the wife and I have settled in well and we are comfortable. The Bush Tours have certainly come fast and furious Sir".

"Well Steve, let me be the first to congratulate you on your promotion, Sergeant Coetzee".

With that Cmdt van Rooyen stands up and shakes Steve's hand. He hands Steve the signal authorizing him to obtain his new rank from the Base Stores. With a grin on his face, Steve thanks Cmdt Van Rooyen, salutes and withdraws. He retrieves his bicycle from the squadron and cycles down to Stores to collect his new rank. Upon his return to the Squadron, FSgt Mike Webb congratulates Steve on his promotion and invites him for a beer at the pub after work.

At 16:30 the AFB Closes for the day and the 87 HFS Flight Engineers are headed in mass to the pub for a celebrity drink on Steve and his promotion to Sergeant. Many rounds are enjoyed and it's not very long when the group breaks out into the "Chopper Song" and various other Air Force songs.

George Avis, Ben Lötter and Steve are the last to leave the pub and will all be in matrimonial trouble when they get home. As they get outside Johnny Beukes and DJ de Kok are lighting a smoke on Johnny's Suzuki 1000 motorcycles four into one exhaust. Johnny has the throttle wide open to get the exhaust hot enough for lighting the cigarettes.

It is late and dark the evening when Steve stumbles home to the Potluck, where Zella is not in the mood for his drunkenness, she locks him out and refuses to answer the door. Steve is in a jovial mood and decides to mow the lawn.

He has no sooner started the lawn mower when Zella grabs his arm and leads him inside. As angry as she was, she had to giggle at the stupid look on his face and insistent mumbling to the tune of "Angel of the morning".

"Just call me Sergeant, Sergeant of the morning".

At the Squadron Steve settles back into the daily general flying routine, with daily flights involving test flights, general flying, confined area landings, cargo slinging and navigation. As there is an F/E and Pilot Course underway, all the qualified F/E's and Pilots take turns at honing their skills during the gunnery phase, which is currently underway at the De Brug Military Shooting Range.

Steve has his turn and is overjoyed at the fact that he now can fire one round at a time with the MG151 20mm Cannon, making it more accurate to place a round directly where he needs it to be.

The twin .505 Browning Machine Guns prove to be effective but difficult to control. They do however have destructive fire power and it is amazing to see the damage that the wave of projectiles can produce.

A new platform is also being trialed, four hydraulically mounted .303 Browning Machine Guns, controlled by a remote site and trigger mechanism, commonly known as the 4x4 Binocular System.

With a fire power of 4,400 rounds per minute, there was an awful amount of lead flying around. The system is very effective, and Steve enjoys the sortie immensely.

4x4 Binocular .303 Browning System

On the 21st May 1981 Steve is assigned to ferry Alouette 52 to Atlas Aviation for a repair action that can only be performed at Atlas Aviation. The Atlas Aircraft Corporation of South Africa (also known as Atlas Aviation) was established in 1965 to manufacture a number of sophisticated military aircraft and avionics equipment for the South African Air Force, as well as for export. It was established primarily to circumvent the international arms embargo (United Nations Security Council Resolution 418) which commenced in 1963 against the South African government because of its Apartheid policies. With the establishment in 1968 of the South African government owned conglomerate named Armscor (Armaments Corporation of South Africa), the Atlas Aircraft Corporation was also brought under Armscor's control.

Major Venter and Steve take off at 06:30 the morning for the 2 hour and 15-minute flight to Kempton Park where Atlas Aviation is located next to Jan Smuts International Airport. Atlas shares the runways with Jan Smuts International but is totally isolated on the northern side of the large airport. The flight is long and Major Venter allows Steve to take the controls. They chit chat about squadron life and the Bush Tours that are increasing, as well as the number of operations currently being planned. Both agree that the war against terror is still going to be a huge factor to deal with on the northern borders. The rest of the flight is uneventful, as they leave the undulating farmlands of the Orange Free State and enter into the large Metropolis of Transvaal with its multitude of Mine Dumps dotting the horizon. Some of the World's deepest Gold Mines can be found here.

Transvaal is a province of South Africa from as far back as 1910. The name "Transvaal" refers to the province's geographical location to the north of the Vaal River. Its capital is Pretoria, which is also the country's administrative capital, while its largest city is Johannesburg. In 1910, four British colonies united to form the Union of South Africa. The Transvaal Colony, which had been formed out of the bulk of the old South African Republic after the Second Boer War, became the Transvaal Province in the new union. Half a century later, in 1961, the union ceased to be part of the Commonwealth of Nations and became the Republic of South Africa. The PWV (Pretoria-Witwatersrand / Vereeniging) conurbation in the Transvaal, centered on Pretoria and Johannesburg, became South Africa's economic powerhouse.

Waterberg Massif

The Transvaal Province lies between the Vaal River in the south, and the Limpopo River in the north. To its south it bordered with the Orange Free State and Natal Provinces, to its west are the Cape Province and Botswana, to its north Rhodesia, and to its east Mozambique and Swaziland. Except on the south-west, these borders are well defined by natural features. Within the Transvaal lies the Waterberg Massif, a prominent ancient geological feature of the South African landscape.

Major Venter radios Johannesburg Information for clearance and control. Very soon they are handed over to Jan Smuts Tower and then cleared over to Atlas Aviation for landing at the Heli Pad. While Major Venter and Steve are entertained by the Management of Atlas Helicopter Division, and enjoy a cafeteria luncheon, while the aircraft is being maintained. After lunch Steve makes his way down to the workshop floor to review the actions being taken to correct the issues with the aircraft. Steve then verifies that the documents are correctly completed and begins his Pre-Flight inspection for the return flight to AFB Bloemspruit.

Its early afternoon when Major Venter and Steve get airborne off the Heli Pad at Atlas and under Jan Smuts control set heading for Bloemfontein. The flight will take just over two hours, and once again Major Venter invites Steve to take the controls. The conversation is a continuation of the morning's discussion and very soon they are flying over the Vaal River, the border between Transvaal and Orange Free State Provinces. The landscape quickly changes from the large metropolis they had been flying over to undulating farmlands.

The Orange Free State (Afrikaans, Oranje Vrystaat) was an independent Boer sovereign republic in Southern Africa during the second half of the 19th century, and later a British colony and a Province of the Union of South Africa. It is the historical precursor to the present-day Free State Province. Extending between the Orange and Vaal rivers, its borders were determined by the United Kingdom of Great Britain and Ireland in 1848 when the region was proclaimed as the Orange River Sovereignty, with a seat of a British Resident in Bloemfontein. In the northern part of the territory a Voortrekker Republic was established at Winburg in 1837. This state merged with the Republic of Potchefstroom which later formed part of the South African Republic (Transvaal).

Following the granting of sovereignty to the Transvaal Republic, the British recognized the independence of the Orange River Sovereignty on 17 February 1854 and the country officially became independent as the Orange Free State on 23 February 1854, with the signing of the Orange River Convention. The new republic incorporated both the Orange River Sovereignty and the traditions of the Winburg / Potchefstroom Republic.

Although the Orange Free State developed into a politically and economically successful republic, it experienced chronic conflict with the British until it was finally annexed as the Orange River Colony in 1900. It ceased to exist as an independent Boer republic on 31 May 1902 with the signing of the Treaty of Vereeniging at the conclusion of the Second Anglo-Boer War. Following a period of direct rule by the British, it joined the Union of South Africa in 1910 (becoming the Republic of South Africa in 1961) as a Province under its former name, along with the Cape Province, Natal, and the Transvaal.

The Free State is situated on a succession of flat grassy plains sprinkled with pastureland, resting on a general elevation of 3,800 feet only broken by the occasional hill or kopje. The rich soil and pleasant climate allow for a thriving agricultural industry. With more than 30,000 farms, which produce over 70% of the country's grain, it is known locally as South Africa's breadbasket.

The Province is high lying, with almost all land being 1,000 meters above sea level. The Drakensberg and Maluti Mountains foothills raise the terrain to over 2,000 meters in the east. The Free State lies in the heart of the Karoo Sequence of rocks, containing shale, mudstone, sandstone and the Drakensberg Basalt forming the youngest capping rocks. Mineral deposits are plentiful, with gold and diamonds being of particular importance, mostly found in the north and west of the Province.

The flats in the south of the reserve provide ideal conditions for large herds of plain game such as black wildebeest and springbok. The ridges, koppies and plains typical of the northern section are home to Kudu, Red Hartebeest, Southern White Rhinoceros and Buffalo. The African Wildcat, Black Wildebeest, Zebra, Eland, White Rhinoceros and Wild Dog can be seen at the Soetdoring Nature Reserve near Bloemfontein.

The Free State experiences a continental climate, characterized by warm to hot summers and cool to cold winters. Areas in the east experience frequent snowfalls, especially on the higher ranges, whilst the west can be extremely hot in summer. Almost all precipitation falls in the summer months as brief afternoon thunderstorms, with aridity increasing towards the west. Areas in the east around Harrismith, Bethlehem and Ficksburg are well watered. The capital, Bloemfontein, experiences hot, moist summers and cold, dry winters frequented by severe frost.

Very soon Naval Hill at Bloemfontein becomes visible and Major Venter selects the frequency for the International Airport. After obtaining clearance Major Venter takes over from Steve and completes the approach and landing at AFB Bloemspruit. While Major Venter retires to the Flight Office, Steve assists the Ground Crew in getting the aircraft secured in the Hangar. Steve quickly completes an After-Flight Inspection on the aircraft and then signs up the Technical Log, making the aircraft available for the next day's flying program.

Naval Hill Bloemfontein

It's the beginning of June 1981 when Steve is approached by FSgt Mike Webb, the Chief F/E at 87 HFS. The increased effort to combating terrorism that Major Venter and Steve had been discussing was starting. There had been a request to send additional resources to the Border for a Secret Operation to be clarified only upon arrival at AFB Ondangwa.

Steve did not hesitate and accepts the offer immediately. As he walks away, he is excited but also concerned about Zella. How was she going to handle the situation? The last time that things had turned bad during contact, news had leaked down to the States, and Zella had feared the worst. Steve is in a pensive mood when he gets home and decides to sit Zella down straight away and discuss the situation.

Zella is very quiet during the discussion and Steve can see she is close to tears. He hugs her and reiterates that the chances of something bad happening are always there but that the South African Defense Force always ensures that the intelligence they obtain is the best and allowing the Operation Commanders to utilize the best equipment for neutralizing the threat.

The previous situation was an unknown and unfortunately things had gone wrong. Steve then tells Zella that he was not prepared previously and did not know what to look out for. Now with a couple of tours under his belt he is much more comfortable and knows where to find the danger. Zella is not convinced but puts up a brave smile. The two of them enjoy a lovely bottle of Cabernet Sauvignon with supper. Steve will be leaving very soon, and they make the best of the time together.

Wings Parade

At the respective Air Force Flying Schools another batch of students have made the grade and will receive their wings to be baptized into the elite fraternity of Air Force aviators. The Group from 87 HFS are flying to CFS Dunnottor to support their students in the ceremony. A DC3 has been tasked from 86 Multi Engine Flying School at AFB Bloemspruit, to transport the instructors and Base Flight Engineers to Dunnottor. It is a short 2-hour flight from Bloemspruit to Dunnottor and the smartly dressed gents include the Commanding Officer, Col Van Heyningen and his wife. Clad in dress uniform with medals the group disembarks and quickly finds the location of the UT F/E's who are about to receive their wings. With pats on the back and pumping of arms, the group is congratulated on their achievements.

The parade is taken by the Chief of the Air Force, Lt Gen Mike Muller. The new pilots and flight engineers proudly accept their wings from the General, after which the Air Force Band leads the Squadron off the parade ground. Steve and the rest of the F/E's move over to the hangar to grab grub and refreshments. Naturally there is liquid refreshments as well, which Steve, George and a number of the other F/E's quickly consume as quickly as possible. Their time is limited as the DC3 will be taking off in less than an hour. Lt Henry Nichols, the Technical Officer of 87 HFS has joined the group and soon a plan is formed to annex a few of the parade ground marker flags for the squadron. On the way to the aircraft the flags are liberated by a very loud and mischievous group of misfits.

The DC3 taxis and takes off for Bloemspruit and soon enough the rowdy group of now inebriated F/E's are up to no good. The Commander of the DC3 has just leveled off at cruise flight level when the group all run to the front of the cabin, upsetting the C of G of the aircraft. They huddle together while the trim is readjusted once more. Once the aircraft levels out they all race to the back of the aircraft to repeat the process, all the time to huge fits of laughter. Next Johnny Beukes, who does parachuting as a sport, decides to tutor the drunken F/E's in the art of skydiving. They gather at the cargo door of the aircraft and then pretend to exit as a group, next they form up in a star formation in the cargo area. First connecting by hand and ankle then swapping to the other foot. This continues until the Commanding Officer demands that the motley group behave. Steve at this point has become sleepy and decides to lay his head down on the bench. Suddenly he is awoken by someone tugging a hat from underneath him. George is attempting to remove the Commanding Officer's wife's hat that Steve has inadvertently fallen asleep on. George takes a look at the flattened hat, punches the form back with his fist, places the hat on Mrs. van Heyningen's head and wipes his hand down her face while calmly saying.

"Looks like a cowboy's hat, and cowboys don't cry!"

Giggling George sits down with the Colonel scowling at him and Steve. Not long after the aircraft starts a decent for landing. The rowdy group has now settled down completely and is moping in the background. After the aircraft is shut down, all disembark and saunter off to their respective modes of transport. Steve and George are walking down the main drive to the security gate and then home to their respective Potlucks. They are walking in the middle of the road when a car honks a single warning for them to move over.

Steve motions without looking back for the car to pass. Once more the car honks and this time George motions for it to pass. A third time the horn honks, this time a little longer, and both George and Steve turn around to see Col Van Heyningen at the wheel. Jumping smartly out of the way and saluting the two quickly make way for the colonel to pass.

In the crew room the next morning Steve and George are summoned to FSgt Webb's office to explain their side of the story. The Colonel is expecting an apology. Steve and George rush off to the local SADF Store to buy a card and then to the local garden to picks flowers so that the lady they both know at the duty room can fashion an acceptable bouquet for them. Next, they report to AFB Bloemspruit HQ in wait for their punishment. Col Van Heyningen beckons them in. They march in, salute and remain at attention.

The Col gives them a once over and attempting not to laugh, starts chastising them for their behavior. Both Steve and George are looking very sheepish and embarrassed at the same time. They offer to buy the Colonel's wife a new hat and offer up the flowers as a consolation in the meantime. Col Van Heyningen bursts out laughing and punishes them with an extra duty each. With a hand wave he motions them to leave. Steve and George are relieved that they did not get more punishment.

As they enter the crew room back at the squadron the story has already reached everyone, and to howling fits of laughter Steve and George have to re-enact their apology and punishment to a very appreciative crowd.

Sound of Bullets

It's late in June 1981 and Steve arrives at AFB Ondangwa to meet Arthur Walker, the Gunship Flight Commander for three years at AFB Ondangwa. Arthur had obtained his pilot's wings in 1977 and flew for 7 Squadron, Rhodesian Air Force, before re-joining the South African Air Force in 1980. While flying Alouette III helicopters based at AFB Ondangwa in 1981 he was awarded the Honoris Crux Gold for risking his life during a night operation in Angola, by turning on the lights of his helicopter to draw enemy fire away from another helicopter.

The Honoris Crux Citation reads as follows: During January 1981, two Alouette's, with Lieutenant Walker as flight leader, carried out close air support operations resulting in the Alouette's coming under intense enemy artillery and anti-aircraft fire. He only withdrew when ordered to do so. Later Lieutenant Walker returned to the contact area to provide top cover for a Puma helicopter assigned to casualty evacuation. Again, he was subject to heavy enemy anti-aircraft fire. During the withdrawal the second helicopter developed difficulties and called for assistance. Yet again Captain Walker returned to provide top cover, drawing virtually all the anti-aircraft fire to his Alouette. His courageous act prevented the loss of an Alouette and crew. Lieutenant Walker's actions were not only an outstanding display of professionalism, devotion to duty and courage, but also constitute exceptional deeds of bravery under enemy fire and make him a worthy recipient of the Honoris Crux Gold.

Arthur and Steve hit it off immediately, both very professional and critical on equipment condition and serviceability. Arthur is called to Sector Command Post at Oshikati and Steve is assigned Commandant (Cmdt) Chris Hartzenberg, Officer Commanding 17 Sqn at AFB Swartkop, who is currently doing his tour of duty. Steve and Cmdt Chris get on well and are soon into a rhythm of how to operate efficiently and effectively together. At this point the Gunships are deployed to Angola daily but must return at night to the safety of AFB Ondangwa. This resulted in crews having to get airborne an hour before sunrise and then land late in the evening. Its early one morning at the HAG after Steve had just completed refueling from the stash of fuel drums flown in by the "Giants", when Cmdt Hartzenberg comes running out of the HAG Command Post.

"Steve, get ready we have a call out!"

Steve quickly prepares the aircraft while Cmdt Chris straps in and initiates the start-up sequence. Soon the two Gunships are enroute to the contact location. Koevoet had chased a group of SWAPO Special Forces back into Angola and are hot on their trail. Within 20 minutes the two Gunships are in range and Arthur Walker in the lead Gunship calls for smoke from the Koevoet Team.

Koevoet Smoke Signal

Almost immediately both Gunships make out the Yellow Smoke and space to orbit as per standard follow up operation. No sooner are Cmdt Chris and Steve in orbit when Steve spots the first Gook. Cmdt Chris sees him at the same time and in the excitement, banks the aircraft too steeply for Steve to pull off a shot.

"Roll out, roll out for Fucks sake!" Screams Steve.

Cmdt Chris rolls out but unfortunately loses speed, rendering the canon harmonization ineffective. Steve pulls off a shot and then adjusts aiming over the barrel, as the sight is now no longer of any use. The second shot takes the Gooks head off.

"Watch your speed, you are far too slow!" Says Steve.

The contact lasts another three minutes and any resistance is quenched. A huge plus factor is two captures who are standing in the center of the clearing with hands up. This is truly a successful operation as much intelligence will now be obtained with respect to what SWAPO is planning. After landing and debriefing with a grinning Koevoet team, the two Gunships return to the HAG for standby once more.

Debrief after Contact

It's a couple of days later, and the two Gunships are once again enroute to the HAG. It had been a quiet period after the contact with Koevoet. A Parachute Battalion has been deployed to the north and they have informed the HAG that they have just started a follow up and may be requiring Gunship Top Cover soon. Steve and Whitey Myburgh, Arthur's F/E, quickly prepare for a potential contact. As it's still early in the morning and Steve managed to sneak some groceries from the mess, he quickly builds them breakfast.

Breakfast with Eggs Sunny Side Up

No sooner had Steve and Whitey finished up when Arthur and Cmdt Chris come running up to the aircraft.

"Ok Chaps, we have a potential contact. Parabats have the Gooks visual and are going to engage, let's go!" says Arthur.

The two Gunships get airborne and hightail it to the coordinates. They are flying in loose battle formation across a long north south running Shona, when all of a sudden there are rounds flying all over. Both aircraft have been hit hard. Inside the Cabin Steve is spitting out Maltoprene filler from the Cabin Floor, while there is deathly silence from Cmdt Chris. Steve panics and reaches over to grab the Cyclic Control to fly the aircraft away to safety. As if being woken from a trance Cmdt Chris turns to Steve.

"I am ok Steve, just my finger hurts, but I don't see any blood."

Steve reaches down and checks Cmdt Chris's hand.

"You are right, looks like a bullet just glazed your glove, and you are one lucky man Sir!"

Steve carries on inspecting the cabin to check for further damage. Cmdt Chris contacts Arthur and they agree to land and check the aircraft for more damage. The Main Rotor Blades are making an odd whistling sound, indicating that one or more of them has been hit. Both aircraft retreat the way they came and find a clearing to land and check out the damage after informing the HAG of the situation and location.

With the aircraft shut down, Steve and Whitey immediately assess the damage to aircraft. Although there have been multiple hits, these are all superficial, with the exception of the holes in two of the Rotor Blades. These are not structural, but the Rotor Blades will have to be changed. The group gathers round and Steve and Whitey brief Arthur and Cmdt Chris on the status of the aircraft.

"It is going to be safer to fly the aircraft back to Ondangwa so that we can properly assess the aircraft with all panels removed. Right now, they are both safe to fly back, but we will have to change both aircrafts Main Rotor Blades for starters." Says Steve, with Whitey nodding in agreement.

With all in agreement, Arthur gets on the radio and informs the HAG of the situation, then they start-up and set course back to AFB Ondangwa. No sooner had they taxied in and shut down when the Base Ops Officer meets them for a debriefing with the Base Photographer in tow to record the event.

Angolan Contact

Steve, Whitey, Cmdt Chris and Arthur

The next two days Steve and Whitey are very busy in the Hangar changing Main Rotor Blades and patching up superficial holes in both aircraft. Fortunately, both of the aircraft do not have any critical damage with the exception of the Blades. During this downtime Steve and Whitey take the time to also wash the aircraft completely and process additional maintenance actions that would ensure they have good aircraft for the next few weeks ahead. There is something in the air and both Steve and Whitey want to be ready for the action when it happens.

It's a normal workday for the Flight Engineers and at supper time everyone clambers in the F/E Truck for a ride down to the Mess. Tonight, is Steak and Egg night, so nobody is late, to ensure access to the biggest and best steaks at the front of the queue.

With supper sorted its refreshment time at the pub next door. Steve and the rest of the F/E's saunter over to the long bar counter and order up. In the Chopper Corner sits Sarmajor Daantjie. "Oom Daantjie", as he is affectionately called is a bit of a drinker. What makes it entertaining is his speech impediment that improves drastically the drunker he gets. Oom Daantjie will normally plant himself down at pub opening time and stay there until pub closing time. He then gets into his short wheelbase Landrover and proceeds to navigate his way to his house on the base approximately a kilometer away. The F/E's have seen this procedure happen many nights and tonight Steve decides it's time to have some fun. Steve grabs the truck key and races up to the hangar to collect four small aircraft jacks. Upon his return, Steve and Whitey rig the jacks under the Landrover so as to just lift the wheels clear of the ground. Everyone returns to the pub and continue to order rounds. Eventually its closing time, and with that all the F/E's go into hiding behind the Landrover to watch the upcoming spectacle.

No sooner had everyone taken cover when a pretty wrecked Oom Daantjie comes staggering out of the pub. He leans up against the driver's door while trying to locate his keys. With these in hands, he battles his way into the driver's seat amongst a lot of groaning and sighing. Eventually safely located in the driver's seat, he inserts the key and starts the vehicle. Next the door shuts and vehicle started, with lights switched on. The clutch pedal depressed and reverse gear engaged he is ready to go. Slowly releasing the clutch and accelerating gently he turns the wheels to reverse out of the parking space. When he feels he is sufficiently out of the parking spot, he applies the brakes, depresses the clutch, and engages first gear. Turning the wheels in the direction he wants to go, he accelerates and releases the clutch. The next obstacle is the upcoming Stop sign. He judges this perfectly, stops, turn signal on, and turns right to go 200 meters down the round to his driveway. At his home, he signals left, gently brakes and turns into the driveway. He stops the Landrover and turns everything off. Struggling out of the driver's seat he goes to move forward and then realization hits him that he is still in the parking spot at the pub. By this time Steve and his buddies are screaming with laughter. Oom Daantjie wobbles over to them and drunkenly shouts!

"Fok julle, julle doose!" (Fuck you, you fannies!)

Early the next morning Steve is woken by the base intercom system calling all Chopper Crews to the Ops Room immediately. It's still dark out, and Steve struggles into his flight suite and Veldskoen. The briefing room is packed with Puma and Alouette crews. This was the start of the offensive against SWAPO and first on the map are the strategic towns just over the Angolan Border. This would also be the beginning of the Choppers being deployed out in the field with the troops for long periods during the operations. If crews are required to be changed the aircraft would be handed over in the field and the replacement crews flown in to complete the exchange.

Steve is once again flying with Arthur Walker and they are soon airborne with the rest of the Choppers taking off at three-minute intervals to prevent any incidents, as it's still dark and pre-dawn is just starting to light up the sky. Today the HAG would be moving to just south of the Angolan town of Ongiva, where SWAPO has created an open air garage to service and repair their vehicles. The Garage would be approached in typical attack formation with the escape path being blocked by stopper groups and frontal attacks from north, east and west. The Gunships are to provide Top Cover and attack if targets are visible.

The fleet of 6 Gunships and 8 Giants arrive at the HAG, refuel and prepare for the day's events. By midmorning the Flight Commanders are informed that the Garage has been taken with no shots fired. All aircraft get airborne to relocate to the Garage. At the Garage the Choppers space out and settle to land in the available open areas. With the aircraft settled, attention is now focused on setting up the HAG. There are ground troops sweeping the area amongst the fleet of Puma's and Alouette. Arthur lands the Gunship far forward, close the trees. After shut-down both Steve and Arthur decide to have a look around the Garage. With weapons hanging loosely around their shoulders, they investigate the equipment, tools and vehicles left behind.

They are all scrutinizing the layout of the garage, and the primitive environment that SWAPO had to repair their vehicles. Most had wondered far from the aircraft at this stage and the area seemed clear and safe, when all of a sudden, a Brown Job (Army) Major screams at the top of his voice.

"Kry daai Chopper's in die lug". (Get those Chopper's in the air)

By the shrill sound of his voice nobody hesitates but run for their respective aircraft. Aircraft are starting left and right, Arthur does not even do up his safety harness and starts the aircraft. Steve dives in and places the cannon's barrel in, after which he picks up the chock and jumps into the cabin. Arthur immediately takes off. All around Puma's and Alo's are taking off. In the consternation the one gunship takes off leaving his Flight Engineer looking up in surprise, still holding the wheel chock in his hand. Both Arthur and Steve burst into laughter at the amusing sight. The Flight Engineer's Pilot does a quick circuit and then sheepishly lands to pick up his engineer.

About 10 Minutes later the Pongo Major radios the aircraft to confirm that all is clear. All the Choppers once again land. Once all have shut down, the Major approaches Arthur and Steve, taking them over to a clump of bushes where his troops have secured a SWAPO Terrorist.

<u>SWAPO's Garage</u>

The Gook had been in the Tree in front of the Gunship with a sniper rifle in his hands, and when he sees Steve and Arthur, he indicates that these were the two he had in his sights. It is a rude awakening as to how close both of them had come to being taken out. The HAG is abandoned and all aircraft retreat to AFB Ondangwa that evening. Another week goes by quickly and Steve's replacement has arrived. Another Bush Tour concluded, Steve packs his kit and heads home.

Half of the year had just sped by and Steve did not even notice that it's almost mid-winter in Bloemfontein. He spends the evenings tidying up the yard and constructing temporary garages for both the vehicles. He then makes some improvements to the Potluck, so that Zella can be more comfortable.

There is not much flying at the Squadron, so Steve has a lot of down time to complete many of the overdue tasks that he needs to catch up on. All the while the big offensive into Angola is still constantly on his mind. Not even the midyear Squadron function sets his mind at ease. Zella has also become secretive and defensive. Steve writes it off to his pensive mood of anticipation.

A Sad Time

Once again Mike Webb approaches Steve and asks if he wants to do another Bush Tour. Steve says he just wants to clear it with Zella, but that it should not be a problem. Zella is not impressed but does not put up an argument. Steve feels it's his duty to fight for his country and ensure the "War Against Terror" does not cross over into the borders of South Africa.

By the middle of August 1981 Steve is once again on his way to AFB Ondangwa, this time to take part in the beginning of the largest offensive against SWAPO. There would be three offensives, namely the initiation Operation Carnation, followed by the Main Offensive Operation Protea and the cleanup Operation Daisy.

The offensive is to be launched primarily against SWAPO but any assisting forces supporting SWAPO would be prone to attack as well. To this end Angolan Towns and Cities identified as being supportive of SWAPO are prime targets. The first two of three of these are Ongiva, Xangongo and Mupa. Air Force Bases in the Operational area are abuzz with aircraft and personnel, covering everything from transport, bomber, fighter, ground attack, gunships, troop carriers, and UAV's.

F1 Mirage in front of Revetment

AFB Ondangwa looks like a little city with an international airport covered all over with aircraft, flight and ground crews plus a hoard of support staff. The Chopper Units would be deploying to the HAG's as soon as possible, leaving more room for transport, support and fighter aircraft. Steve's first Air Force Squadron namely 1 Squadron, is here in full force. Steve's chest swells with pride as he sees the Mirage F1's lining the revetments.

Steve is flying with Lt Abe Byleveld and completing Top Cover for all the aircraft arriving into AFB Ondangwa. Every evening the F/E's would race off to the Mess to get supper before there are only scraps left. At the same time, they barter with the Cooks for fresh meat, so that a late-night Braai can be initiated that evening. With fresh stocks, the group withdraws to the Air Crew encampment and proceeds to entertain themselves for the evening. Tonight, the Parabats are also having a gathering and are making a lot of noise just next to the Chopper crews. It's not long before the anticipated Blue Job, Brown Job fight ensues.

Armed with smoke grenades the Brown Jobs attack, but little do they know that the Blue Jobs have much more up their arsenal. The first pencil flare is released followed by a barrage of different coloured flares lighting up the sky while Parabats are diving for cover left and right. The battle ensues for another 5 minutes until the Military police sound their siren threatening to lock everyone up. The Blue Jobs invite the Parabats over for a truce drink, and the party continues.

The next morning Steve is up early to clean up the mess from the evening's horse play. Next, he heads off to the Hangar to prepare his aircraft for a 25-hour inspection. Steve has decided to complete the inspection a little earlier, in the anticipation of many hours being flown in the next few weeks.

AFB Ondangwa Alouette Hangar

Another day of Top Cover arrives, and Steve enjoys the opportunity to test the Canon. Abe Byleveld praises Steve's accuracy and the two discuss the upcoming operation while ensuring Top Cover for the arriving and departing aircraft. By midmorning the orders for the operation are going to be communicated. All crews are summoned to the Ops Room for a briefing. The prelude to Operation Protea is now underway.

Operations Protea and Carnation

The encounters with FAPLA in Operation Sceptic are the prelude to further conflicts during Operations Protea and Carnation in July and August 1981. As a result of the setbacks in 1980 SWAPO moves its bases further north in proximity to and even among the forces of FAPLA to discourage attacks by the South African forces. SWAPO's logistic system virtually becomes part of that of FAPLA. By mid-1981 the military situation on the northern border of SWA has become serious. The stockpiling of large quantities of ammunition and the increase in FAPLA and SWAPO forces in South Angola has become a real conventional threat to SWA. In July 1981 several skirmishes take place between the security forces and PLAN.

The General Officer Commanding of the SWA Territory Force announces on 6th July that 52 terrorists have been shot in contacts with the security forces in a period of four days. This sharp increase in skirmishes with SWAPO terrorists' results in the launching of Operation Carnation. Although 225 terrorists are shot during this operation, it does not prove to be a complete success.

The security forces do not operate further than 25 km north of the border while the larger terrorist bases are situated much further north. At this time FAPLA also adopts a more provocative attitude towards the security forces. Its air defense system becomes a real threat to the South African air support operations during Operation Protea.

Early in the evening of 23rd August the group of Gunship Engineers gathers in the pub. A great evening is had by all. Only one altercation takes place when Clifton Stacey puts out a cigarette on Steve's leg. Steve nearly loses it and threatens to take Clifton's head off. Fortunately, the situation is defused as Steve identifies that Clifton is drunk and seems very nervous about the impending attack the next few days. After a peace offering drink the motley group head for bed with the knowledge that tomorrow was going to be a very tough day.

Operation Protea's objectives are to destroy the SWAPO command and training center at Xangongo and its logistic bases at Xangongo and Ongiva. Xangongo is the headquarters of SWAPO's "northwestern front" from where it directs SWAPO units operating primarily in the Kaokoland and in western and central Ovamboland.

There are also other SWAPO bases, which are used as supply depots and training bases for SWAPO recruits, sited to the south and southeast of the town. Ongiva a town located less than fifty kilometers north of the Angola / South West Africa border is an important SWAPO logistical and personnel centre which supports operations in central and eastern Ovamboland and in the Kavangoland.

Both Xangongo and Ongiva are key bases in supporting SWAPO's war effort in South West Africa, because of their location close to its border. Their destruction would undermine SWAPO's ability to conduct operations in their "north western front" and also have a psychological impact by reinforcing the message to SWAPO that it no longer had the luxury of sanctuaries in southern Angola.

During Operation Protea several SWAPO bases and command posts in the vicinity of Xangongo and Ongiva are attacked and destroyed by three task forces. SADF units leave their bases and head towards the Angolan border.

The entire Gunship Fleet with the exception of Top Cover and Standby Aircraft will be deploying to the HAG in Angola, situated close to Xangongo. The Air Force launches a strike with various aircraft against air-defense targets in Angola at Cahama and Chibemba.

Ground troops advance along three separate routes to Xangongo. A mechanized force attacks the bases in the town where the headquarters of SWAPO's north western front has been established. At the same time other elements destroy SWAPO bases south and southwest of the town.

Xangongo is isolated and cut off from any possible intervention by FAPLA forces from Humbe and Peu-Peu in the North West and North East respectively. The combined force of SWAPO / FAPLA defenders are soon driven out by an attack on the tanks and infantry which are dug in and around the town.

After FAPLA and SWAPO have been driven from Xangongo, the main task force proceeds to the east and south driving the FAPLA force from Mongua. The attack on Ongiva takes place after a combined force of SWAPO / FAPLA, which had dug in, is defeated. Several Soviet officers are killed in this battle and a Russian warrant officer is captured. Thereafter, SWAPO facilities in and around Ongiva are destroyed and the operation is concluded on by the first week in September 1981.

Humbe

Battle Group 10 crosses into Angola at Ruacana just before midnight and heads northwards through dense bush to their forming point that is 12 km north-west of Humbe. They arrive at their form-up point on time. As Battle Group 10 follows the road south-east to Humbe, the Air Force begin to bomb the town of Xangongo.

The group's artillery begins firing artillery rounds at Humbe but is informed by their aerial spotter plane that the trenches close to the town seem abandoned with no enemy to the battle group's rear in the direction of Cahama.

The artillery fire ceases and their alternative target at Techiulo, that is closer, is then taken without incident as FAPLA soldiers flee on seeing the battle group arrive, leaving behind a group of Irish Catholic nuns at the mission station in the village.

By 12h30 the group heads back towards Humbe passing by the empty trenches and sighting no fleeing enemy from Xangongo, enter the empty town of Humbe. They soon leave the town and position themselves within 3 km of the bridge over the Cunene River and Xangongo.

The two combat teams of Ratel-20's and paratroopers are then sent closer to the river and begin to encounter contact with FAPLA troops fleeing Xangongo. By dusk the river plain is under the battle groups control and they laager there overnight though sporadic fire can be heard overnight from Xangongo. Apart from being woken and called to arms when a FAPLA column attempts a breakout from Xangongo via the bridge which is taken care of by the other battle groups.

The rest of the night is peaceful for Battle Group 10. At the end of August, after gathering up enemy equipment on the river plain, Battle Group 10 crosses the bridge over the Cunene River and by 09h00 they are in Xangongo. Their mission is to hold the town, protect the task force from FAPLA to the north-west while the other battle groups pursue their objectives in the south-east.

Xangongo

Battle Group 20, 30 and 40 cross the border at Ombalantu into Angola just before midnight at the end of August and head northwards through dense bush. By 09h15 the next morning, the battle groups find themselves too far east due to a navigation error and lost time.

The three battle groups would find their way to their forming-up point west of the town and wait for the air and artillery attack. The air attack on Xangongo begins at 11h50 when four Buccaneers from 24 Squadron attack installations and anti-aircraft sites with AS-30 missiles, while five Canberra bombers from 12 Squadron dropped bombs, followed by dive bombing 8 Mirage

F-1AZ's from 1 Squadron; 6 Mirage F-1CZ's from 3 Squadron; and 4 Mirage IIICZ's from 2 Squadron. The last wave of rocketing is carried out by eight Impala's. A twenty-minute artillery barrage of the town's defensive positions by G-2 guns and Valkiri multiple rocket launchers completes the bombardment.

Early the morning of 24th August 1981 Steve rises to prepare for the deployment. He is flying with Lt Andre Schoeman for the next few weeks. Steve packs his kit and heads to the aircraft to start the preparations. He checks that there are sufficient consumables to service the chopper, enough Rat (Ration) Packs to last for at least a week, and sufficient fresh water to last for at least the next two days.

Pre-Flight Inspection completed by flashlight, Steve heads to the Tech Control Office and signs up the Aircraft Log. He then prepares a Travel Log which he will take with him for the deployment. Next Steve heads over to the Ops Room and signs off next to the entry made by Andre. He finds Andre in the Briefing Room and informs him that the aircraft is ready. The Gunships will be flying is loose battle formation to the HAG, so group take off has been planned for a low fly past over the domestic area to say cheers to the sleeping crowd.

Battle Group 40 is tasked with taking the town of Xangongo, its defenses and the bridge over the Cunene. The plan is to attack from two places, the north-east with Combat Team 41 and the south-east with Combat Team 42. The teams begin to assault the layers of trenches and bunkers that make up the town's defenses. The fort and water tower, key targets in the town, are eventually reached and taken.

The bridge is reached by the combat teams by 17h30 and is immediately prepared with demolition charges by the engineers. It is later discovered that FAPLA and PLAN officers and their Soviet advisors have hurriedly fled the town while the FAPLA and SWAPO soldiers held their positions and fought furiously.

HAG Briefing

With arrival at the HAG just east of Xangongo, the aircraft are flying low and space for landing. The Giants would be arriving in a little while too with more equipment and troops for the impending operations. After refueling the aircraft Steve and the rest of the F/E's gather at the Briefing Area to get the latest Int on what is taking place. The phased Operations are now officially underway. The attack had been initiated with 122 mm rockets and 155 mm Howitzer rounds raining down on the target areas. The next few days are going to be hectic with advancing forces requiring Top Cover, Casevac (Casualty Evacuation) and Supplies. Steve prepares himself for a long haul. Everyone has to dig trenches to sleep in, as the imminent danger will still be a surprise Mortar attack at night. Early the next morning Steve awakes to the most amusing site. The pilots had dug their trenches off to one side, but every single one of them had erected stretchers to sleep on, which now stuck up above the trench they had dug. If any Mortar had fallen, they would have been defenseless, elevated as they are. Steve wakes the rest of the F/E's up and the comments are thrown across at the group of pilots.

"Looks like the ground mattress is a bit hard for the soft butt's" Laughs Steve.

Captain Laubscher, flying an observation aircraft, has fired smoke rockets to direct the Mirages' attack, but fails so he decides to attempt a direct hit with smoke rockets to accurately mark the target for the Mirages. He dive bombs the target firing one smoke rocket directly into the gun position but by this time the Mirages are out of ordnance and fuel. It is later found that his smoke rocket had hit the operator of the gun. Captain Danie Laubscher of 42 Squadron is awarded the Honoris Crux decoration for bravery. Two and a half hours later the ground attack has resumed, this time with limited enemy ZU-23-2 AA fire, attacking bunkers and trenches and eventually the airfield is captured. By 18h00, Battle Group 20 is in control of its objectives, having destroyed at least four tanks and capturing vehicles, guns and ammunition. Battle Group 20's rest overnight is disturbed by an enemy truck column that advances from the south into the groups positions and is then destroyed by Ratel 90's. By midday on 25th August, the battle group is in control of all positions south of the town but loses one soldier in the process. Later Battle Group 20 would attack a PLAN base to the south of Xangongo towards Cuamato, but it is found to be abandoned with the exception of equipment.

After gathering up enemy equipment on the river plain, Battle Group 10 crosses the bridge over the Cunene River and by 09h00 they are in Xangongo. Now based at Xangongo, Battle Group 10 is allocated to protect Task Force Alpha from a FAPLA counterattack from Cahama towards Xangongo. It is also tasked with protecting the bridge and ensuring readiness for demolition when required. The paratroopers attached to this battle group are sent to seek out PLAN positions further north of Xangongo, but all the bases are found to be abandoned. Meanwhile the pathfinder group which had been operating around Peu-Peu are attached to the battle group. Combat Team 3 is commanded by Major Joe Weyers and would position itself close to Chicusse about 18 km south-east from Cahama. If contact with FAPLA takes place, then the plan is to stop FAPLA's movement or fight a delaying action back to Xangongo. The combat team consists of three armoured car troops of Ratel and Eland 90's, platoon Ratel-60's, one Ratel-20 Mechanized infantry platoon, troop of 4 G-2 artillery pieces, engineer section, an unmanned aerial vehicle and 44 Parachute Brigade's pathfinder group. The combat team advances north-westwards and takes up positions across the Cahama / Xangongo highway with the pathfinders in the flanks to the south and guns in the rear.

Around 22h20, the artillery troop reports eight enemy vehicles heading for the combat team's rear from the southeast. The enemy artillery unit, consisting of a BTR-152, Armed Personnel Carrier, BM-21 Multiple Rocket Launchers and 23 mm AA guns, pass into the combat teams laager and are ambushed and destroyed with the SADF taking three wounded and capturing two BM-21's.

Two troops of Ratel-90's are withdrawn from Combat Team 3 the same day and attached to Combat Team 2 and sent towards Ongiva via Mongua as a reserve and join up with Battle Group 30 around 13h00.

Peu-Peu

At 11h05, anti-aircraft sites at Peu-Peu are attacked by four Air Force Impala's using rockets. By 11h45, attacks are continued by four Buccaneers who fire four AS-30's air-to-ground missiles. Battle Group 30 advances to a position north-east of Xangongo and discover the FAPLA troops, tanks and artillery at Peu-Peu are preparing to support their troops in Xangongo. The South African battle group attacks first and after a short fight forces FAPLA to flee the town destroying tanks, artillery and personnel carriers. Unable to mop-up in the town as night fall's and with reports of enemy to the west, the town is captured by the South Africans the next morning. FAPLA leaves behind up to 300 tons of ammunition, 120,000 liters of diesel and 90,000 liters of gas. Battle Group 30 then releases a combat team to back up Battle Group 20 who has thrown in their reserve in Xangongo. Battle Group 30 is back in Xangongo and joins Battle Group 20 for the advance to positions north of Ongiva.

Mongua

Combat Team Mamba is tasked with taking the village of Mongua east of Xangongo. This is a precursor to an attack on Ongiva by Battle Group's 20 and 30. FAPLA maintains a mechanized force including tanks around the village and whose size has been underestimated. The combat team attacks first with Valkiri rockets but soon encounter enemy trenches, 14.5mm anti-aircraft guns and 76mm artillery that holds up the infantry attack. Ratel 90's and Ratel 60 mortar teams are deployed to silence the guns.

Bosbok Telstar

Back at the HAG the MAOT (Mobile Air Operations Team) calls all for a briefing. The Mechanized attack was in position and would be advancing. There was a problem with the Telstar aircraft, a Bosbok, which carries two crew, the pilot and Army Command and Control Officer.

The aircraft was unserviceable at AFB Ondangwa and the Mechanized attack is advancing without full aerial command and control. The purpose of a Telstar is to direct the attack and also be an observation post for any potential threats so that a counterattack can be accurately launched. With no Telstar available the MAOT at the HAG decides to utilize the next best thing. Two Alouette Gunships to act as Telstar and Top Cover. The difference between the applications had never been put to practice, as the Bosbok operates, and is safe, at altitude, whereas the Alouette is slow and not very affective at altitude. The side firing cannon is harmonized for a maximum of 600 to 800 ft altitude with a forward airspeed of between 50 and 70 Kts.

Andre, Steve, Brut Roos and Clifton Stacey are dispatched early the morning for the Mechanized attack on Mupa. The flight out is uneventful and once over the advancing Ratel's they climb to 1,500 ft and start orbiting above and ahead of the advancing mechanized attack group. The two Gunships are spaced 180° apart and continue to orbit. The Commander of the advancing Ratel's radios that he is hearing 20mm cannon fire and wants to know if the Gunships have started shooting at any targets. Both Andre and Brut confirm no, and Andre requests from the Commander where the firing is coming from. There seems to be confusion as to where the cannon fire is. A tense couple of minutes ensue but still no confirmation on where the firing is. The Ratel Commander keeps asking if the Gunships are firing. At this stage there is stress in both Gunships, as confusion has set in on the advancing group and they cannot ascertain as to where the Cannon fire is. Andre radios Brut.

"Brut, waar is julle?" (Brut, where are you?)

No response.

"Steve can you see Brut?"

Steve looks out the side of the open Cannon door and looks back.

"Andre, they are burning and going down, turn left, turn left, and drop altitude quickly!"

The whole Alouette is one ball of flame and is angled in a dive to the ground. Andre autorotates the Gunship quickly to the ground and reports the incident to the MAOT at the HAG. The MAOT orders them to return to the HAG. One last look and they both see the aircraft impact the ground in a huge ball of flame. A huge black and blue cloud of smoke rises up, indicating the location of the impact. Andre and Steve head back to the HAG at low altitude both shocked at what they had just witnessed. There had obviously been an AA stationed in the town and was taking shots at both aircraft the whole time. It was just sad that nobody had identified where the firing had been coming from. If this had been done, both aircraft could have dropped to low altitude and flushed the AA out and easily eliminating it.

The infantry is then released to attack and clear the trenches. The Ratel 20's and 90's soon overrun the village destroying several T-34 tanks and forcing FAPLA to flee towards Ongiva. The Air Force loses two men when their Alouette III helicopter is shot down by 14.5mm anti-aircraft guns while providing fire support for the combat team. Combat Team Mamba would now wait until the following day to be joined by the two battle groups for the attack on Ongiva.

Later the afternoon Steve is asked to assist in identifying which body was that of the Flight Engineer. Andre and Steve fly out to the impact area and land. Steve walks over to the bodies and immediately identifies Clifton as the Flight Engineer, as he had died with the Cannon still in his hands and been burnt into a crouch position over the Cannon. Brut's body had been thrown clear through the plexi-glass but he had been hit with AA rounds and would have been dead before the aircraft hit the ground.

The Final Flight

Don't grieve for me; for now, I'm free, I'm following the path God laid for me.

I took His hand when I heard His call; I turned my back and left it all.

I could not stay another day, to laugh, to love, to work, to play.

Tasks left undone must stay that way; I've found that peace at the end of the day.

If my parting has left a void, then fill it with remembered joy.

A friendship shared, a laugh, a kiss, ahh, yes, these things too I will miss.

Be not burdened with times of sorrow, I wish you the sunshine of tomorrow.

My Life's been full; I savoured much, good friends, good times, and a loved one's touch.

Perhaps my time seemed all too brief; don't lengthen it now with undue grief.

Lift up your heart and share with me, God wanted me now,

He set me free.

The HAG is relocated to the town of Mongua with the Choppers landing in and around the outskirts of the town and camouflaged as best as possible. The chopper crews gather around a campfire to remember the fallen comrades and reminisce on the day's events. A very somber group of air crew gathers around the MAOT's Ratel to debrief on the incident.

As the daylight fades into night the fire is stoked. The Intelligence Officer makes his rounds to all the fire pits and warns of the possibility of night attacks by fighters. The Mig 29 is a very capable night fighter and the East German and Cuban pilots have been known to patrol the areas at night in search of the SADF. An hour later Org Kriel, one of the nervous Gunship F/E's screams from the darkness, "Maak dood daai fokken vuur". (Kill that fucking fire).

Just then, as if by premonition two fighters fly low over the town. By the time the sound of the jets is still audible the fire is extinguished, and crew's bomb shelled to any available cover. There are only a few embers left flickering in the night from the huge Bon Fire that was burning a few minutes before. The Int Officer comes out from his Command Ratel with a grin on his face. The fighters are two F1 Mirages conducting a sweep of the southern region on the lookout for Mig 21's in hope of a contact. Everyone has a very disturbed sleep that night.

After the contact the day and scare by the fighters, Steve and a bunch of the guys lay back quietly in the night. The adrenalin warping the bush as they re-live in whispers the contact, the noise, the machine gun and cannon fire, the urgent calls on the radios. Steve realizes that he has tapped into the warrior gene coursing through his bloodline.

A line of men queued behind him into history, each one fighting the conflicts of his day. Past Jesus and Genesis they ranged, the fathers of his father, extending to the forbears among the apes, fighting in tribes fighting for territory, fighting to survive.

Steve has no idea if there was an afterlife but if there is, those men are around tonight, lurking in the shadows. From the mists of their unwritten history he can sense them watching. Observing without judgement the pain that they have inflicted to dominate, for this is the way of our species, the way we persist.

Their blood runs through his veins, a continuity and inheritance spanning millennia. Steve is their most recent edition, an accumulation of their experience touching the origins of time. Steve feels the strength inside and knows he will always be.

Lying back on his sleeping bag, he glimpses his future in the Moon; spliced by branches, veined with roads to walk and mountains to climb. An easy prospect, well illuminated and inviting, compared to the battle they had fought. Steve has approached it with his warrior's gene, fearing nothing, and shaping it to his liking.

Author's note: Now in my 60's I realize I've done so. If anything, I get stronger as I get older.

Ongiva

Battle Group 20 and 30 depart Xangongo, leaving the town under control of Battle Group 10, and follow the road east to Mongua. There Combat Team Mamba, who have taken the town the day before, join them and would act as the two-battle group's reserve during the attack on Ongiva. They then head south-east to their assembly point north of Ongiva in preparation for the attack at 07h00 the next day. The Air Force completes pamphlet drops on the town with cargo aircraft, warning civilians and FAPLA to leave as the South African's fight was with PLAN. The PLAN 11th Brigade is instructed to stay and defend the town. The Air Force opens the attack early in the morning with the first rocket attack by two Mirage III's, against anti-aircraft positions north of the runway at Ongiva. One of these Mirages is struck by a SA-7 missile but makes it back to base in SWA with serious tail damage. The second rocket attack at 07h45 by four Mirage F-1AZ's on anti-aircraft positions close to the airport also draw anti-aircraft fire, SA-7's and 57 mm guns but without any hits. A third rocket attack at 07h48, by four Mirage III's destroying targets close to the town. The fourth rocket attack at 07h52, by four Mirage III's destroy targets close to the town drawing anti-aircraft fire and SA-7's with no hits. By 08h00 another attack, this time by five pairs of Canberra and Buccaneer bombers dropping bombs north of the town. Six Mirage F-1AZ's drop air burst bombs on the airfield at 08h10 and the last attack at 08h15 is on 11 Brigade headquarters by six Mirage F-1AZ's air burst bombs. After bombarding the targets with artillery fire, Battle Group 20 sets off for targets in and around the airfield. Battle Group 20 is divided into four combat teams. Combat Team 50 is the reserve, while Combat Team 10 hit targets south of the airfield, Combat Team 20 attacks targets south-east of the airfield and the last team 30 directly at the airfield and its installations. Combat Team 10 encounters a 23mm anti-aircraft gun as its target and clears them with artillery and infantry attacks. A counterattack by three Russian T-34 Tanks is beaten off by Ratel-90's with two tanks destroyed. FAPLA then flees their positions. Combat Team 20 takes the enemy positions by 15h30 but is slowed by 23mm anti-aircraft guns and RPG-7s, but mortars and infantry clear the positions. Combat Team 30 attacks the airfield from the south-east and east west along the runway. The team meet fierce fighting from FAPLA infantry and anti-aircraft guns and all movement forward by the SADF is held up for two hours despite artillery fire. Mortar fire is directed against a water tower which stop the guns receiving information on the South African positions, and the airfield is taken around 14h00 with FAPLA fleeing. With Battle Group 20's control of the airfield, it secures Battle Group 30's flank for its attack on the positions in and around the town of Ongiva.

Battle Group 30 begins its attack on the town defenses, but their advance is slowed by minefields and heavy resistance. Reports come in of the sighting of T-34 tanks from the east. The commander summons additional anti-tank armour and Battle Group 10 detaches Combat Team 2's Ratel-90 troops and are hastily sent to Ongiva arriving around 13h00. In the meantime, they attempt to slow the advance by attacking with 120 mm mortars. Combat Team 2 goes into action immediately, but dusk is falling, and they fire only to discourage the tanks advance. As night falls, all that can be seen is the flashes from the tanks. The Ratel's fire on the position and succeed in destroying two tanks and ending further enemy fire. Battle Group 30 then pulls back and laagers for the night readying them for an attack the next day. On the 28th August, Battle Group 30 resumes their attack on Ongiva only to find the FAPLA defenses, equipment and town abandoned. By 12h08, Ongiva is under South African control. By the next morning, a FAPLA convoy is discovered fleeing northwards from Ongiva towards Anchanca by a company from 32 Battalion who are attached to Battle Group 60. They call in an Air Force airstrike of Mirage's and Impala's that attack the convoy followed by an attack by Alouette Gunships.

Andre and Steve are part of the attack group and this is the first time Steve has had the opportunity to fire on vehicles, in particular Tanks. The vehicles are quickly set alight with the 20mm HE rounds, but the Tanks keep lumbering on. Steve reaches for a length of 50 Ball rounds and loads them into the Cannon. He then instructs Andre to come into a hover to the rear of the tank while he takes aim over the barrel and empties the rounds into the engine vents at the rear of the Tank. It has the desired effect. They succeeded in destroying tanks, trucks and armored personnel carriers. As the 32 Battalion company moves into to mop up, they discover the bodies of four Russians, two Soviet officers and two civilian women. One soviet soldier Warrant Officer Nikolai Feodorovich Pestretsov is captured when he remained behind with his wife's body. It is later discovered that thirteen Soviet military advisors had died that day.

Burning Russian Tank

Steve instructs Andre to fly low over the trenches surrounding the camp and readies to throw a White Phosphorous Grenade into the bunker to clear any enemy hiding inside. The grenade travels clear into the bunker opening and a few seconds later explosion confirms a direct hit. The troops are now clear to enter and check the bunker out. The Choppers fly many hours per day and soon the strategic attacks are well under way.

It is early morning when Steve and a group of the Chopper Guys borrow a Buffel Troop Carrier from the Brown Jobs. With everyone aboard they take the road down to Xangongo to see what they can raid for their living quarters at Ondangwa. It does not take very long to find the local Hotel, where there is a supply of Fridges that would be a welcome addition to keeping the Chopper stocks cold.

It does not take the group long to raid the best-looking Fridges and load them onto the Buffel. Fridges duly loaded, the group heads back to the HAG. At the last Stop Sign of the City a very familiar face of the Chief of the Army, General (Gen) Jannie Geldenhuys is observed on top of his Command Ratel. The ranking officer on the Buffel is a Captain and smartly salutes the General as they race by. Gen Jannie salutes back and shouts!

"More Kerels!" (Morning Boys).

The fridges will be dispatched with the first Giant back to Ondangwa that evening.

That night at the HAG in their Dugout Trenches the Pilots and Engineers are in a very somber mood and a toast to Brut and Clifton is made. SWAPO has struck and is going to pay. Andre and Brut had been very good friends and he is devastated at the loss of his pilots course buddy. The MAOT instructs Andre to return to AFB Ondangwa as his tour would soon be ending.

Combat Team 2 returns to Xangongo from Ongiva. Combat Team 2 replaces Combat Team 3 as the stopper group and the former returns to Xangongo for rest. Later the day Combat Team 2 is recalled too, as Battle Group 10 has received orders to return to SWA and preparations are required to return with the captured enemy equipment.

On the same day Combat Team Mamba disbands and their units rejoin Battle Group 10 and become the stopper group. Combat Team 3 escorts an artillery group to a position north-west of Mucope. The artillery group fires on Cahama but on their return to Xangongo, they discover an FAPLA battle group close to Mucope. After the combat team receives reinforcements from their battle group, they attack only to find the FAPLA forces have retreated to Cahama.

Xangongo and its bridge are handed over to UNITA and their SADF military intelligence liaison Commandant Mo Oelschig and head for Ongiva via Mongua collecting the remains of the Alouette that had been shot down the day before. After spending the night at Ongiva, the underground fuel tanks at the airfield are destroyed.

Battle Group 20 would begin to garrison the town of Ongiva. Battle Group 20 begins to prepare the captured equipment for its return to SWA while other elements of the battle group patrol the road from Ongiva through Namacunda to Santa Clara clearing it of mines as this would be the route the battle groups would leave Angola.

Battle Group 30 is detached from Task Force Alpha and is attached to Task Force Bravo, who is conducting operations against PLAN bases to the north-east of Ongiva and sent to the town of Anhanca.

Back at the HAG it's very early morning, and there is a chill in the air. Steve dons his captured Rice Camo Chinese Jacket and stirs the fire to brew some coffee. He opens a Rat Pack and adds some water from his Canvas Water Bag to the Breakfast Porridge. He takes a few mouthful's but does not have much appetite. Steve brews a large pot of coffee and wakes the rest of the crews up.

"Coffee's ready boys!" Offers Steve.

Andre and Steve prepare for departure and greet the rest of the Chopper Crews at the HAG. It's a wind still cool morning and the campfire smoke is kept low with the thin layer of mist hanging just above the trees. It's an eerie site as Andre and Steve lift through the mist and set heading back to AFB Ondangwa. The flight is just on an hour and both men are left to their own thoughts, only disturbed occasionally by the radio calls of ground troops wanting to check their Comm's (Communication) Strength.

Operation Protea is the biggest mechanized operation undertaken by the SADF since the Second World War. During this operation the security forces lose ten men against the more than 1,000 casualties of SWAPO and FAPLA. The approximately four thousand tons of equipment captured included several tanks and armoured cars, a large quantity of anti-aircraft guns and about 200 logistic vehicles.

The end of Operation Protea did not signal the end the South African activity against SWAPO in southern Angola as Operation Protea was quickly followed up by another attack, Operation Daisy.

Operation Daisy

Upon arrival at AFB Ondangwa, Steve is partnered up with a new pilot, Capt. Nealle Ellis "Nellis", an instructor from 87 HFS and also veteran of the Rhodesian conflict. Nellis and Steve know each other well and are soon chatting about the goings on, back at the squadron.

Nellis and Steve will be departing back into Angola this afternoon, as the second wave operation is about to begin. Steve takes the downtime to restock his aircraft with amo (Ammunition) and food. At lunch Steve catches a ride down to the Mess to enjoy a prepared meal. The last couple of days have been crazy, grabbing a snack between refueling sorties, or not eating all day and then stuffing whatever he could find in his Rat Pack into a stew meal late the evening.

It is midafternoon when Steve and Nellis, together with a second Gunship, get airborne for Angola. Their destination is a refuel at the captured Airfield of Ongiva, then off to Mupa at the second HAG established recently.

At home in the Bush

The flight is uneventful, and it is early evening when the two Gunships arrive at the second HAG. The HAG is a buzz with Brown Jobs, all busy preparing for the sundown defense perimeter. Steve busies himself in getting the aircraft camouflaged so that it is not visible to low flying enemy fighters or helicopters. Situated in the HAG is a batch of 122 mm Rocket Launchers. It's after 22:00 when Steve eventually slips into his sleeping bag laid into the trench he has dug in the very hard clay. What seems like a couple of minutes Steve and the rest of the Chopper crew are awakened in the middle of the night by the loudest discharge of 122 mm rockets from the Valkiri's. It was in fact 04h00 in the morning and sleep from then on is going to be impossible.

It is still a couple of hours before sunrise, so Steve lays back and tries unsuccessfully to ignore the whoosh and load bang as the rockets go supersonic after leaving the launch tubes.

In the distance 120 mm Mortar fire was also in progress, as well as the 155 mm G5 and G6 Howitzer's.

122 mm Valkiri Rocket Launchers

Today was going to be a long day for sure. At sunrise the Chopper Crews are summoned to the MAOT.

"Morning Gents, today we are supplying Top Cover for Willem Ratte and his 32 Battalion strike around Mupa".

Willem Ratte volunteered to join the Rhodesian Army in 1973 and was in the Rhodesian Light Infantry and later transferred to the elite Rhodesian Special Air Service. After six years in the Rhodesian Army and before the 1980 disbandment of the Rhodesian Special Air Service, Ratte left and joined the South African Defense Force. He was transferred to the elite 32 Battalion in 1979 with the rank of lieutenant. His command and reconnaissance skills earned him recognition as being simply the finest, most professional soldier ever trained by the South African Defense Force.

The tasking was for six Gunships to support the advance on a position south of the town of Mupa, where a large training camp had been identified by intelligence. It is mid-morning when Nellis, as the Gunship Flight Commander, radios for smoke. Willem responds immediately and requests that the Gunships orbit to the east and west of the present smoke. Nellis radios acknowledgement and the six Gunships break off in three groups as pre-planned. All over trenches are visible but there is no movement of SWAPO at all. There are however tracks into the town.

SWAPO Camp Trenches

Nellis dials in the HF (High Frequency) Radio and requests permission to enter the town from Sector Command at Oshikati. As this is becoming a political issue, authority first had to be obtained before advancing into any town in Angola. The response is that advance into the town is only authorized if the tracks lead into it and that there is visible activity of SWAPO. Willem and Nellis discuss the problem, which is quickly resolved by Willem confirming.

"Gunship, tracks lead straight into the town, we are proceeding toward Mupa".

Mupa has been badly bombarded and there is evidence of a hasty withdrawal. The advancing force is checking trenches and structures for SWAPO, Booby Traps and anything that can be of value for intelligence. Very soon the whole town has been swept and it is safe for the Gunships to land. All six aircraft land on the main road in the center of Mupa. Willem informs Nellis that he found two brand new Toyota Land Cruisers just on the outskirts of the Town, but without any keys could not start them.

"I can start them"! Says Steve.

Quickly a plan is formulated. Nellis and Steve together with a second Gunship for Top Cover will land near the vehicles where Steve will start them and show the assigned 32 Battalion driver how to operate them. Nellis lands close to the first vehicle and Steve jumps out with weapon slung over his shoulder and knife in hand. Once at the Land Cruiser, Steve pulls the wires at the steering column away to identify which is the ignition and starter wires. Next, he cuts three wires, joins the power supply to get the ignition lights on, and then touches the starter wire to the power wire to swing the engine to life. With the engine purring, Steve shows the driver how to kill the engine and then how to start it again. Also making sure that once the engine is stopped how to disconnect the ignition, thereby ensuring that the battery is not drained.

The black driver is grinning broadly, and all Steve sees are a huge set of white teeth grinning back at him. The driver jumps in and goes careening through the bush towards Mupa. With one down, there is one to go. Steve jumps back into the Gunship and Nellis heads off to the second vehicle. This one is a diesel engine Land Cruiser, but with the same process, Steve has no trouble in getting it started. All too soon both vehicles are on their way to Mupa. Nellis gets airborne once more, and radios the rest of the Gunships to set heading for the HAG.

The HAG is to be relocated closer to Xangongo and most of the vehicles have already departed, leaving the two Gunships with 1 platoon for defense. No fires are made in camp as intelligence had been obtained of a Battalion of FAPLA troops moving in the area. Nellis is off to one side while Steve has dug a trench to sleep in a dozen yards off.

It is a dark Moonless night and in the distance the sounds of vehicles moving in the bush can faintly be heard. The concern on everyone's mind is that they would be heading towards the HAG and by morning would be there. Eventually the sound stops indicating that the enemy have either stopped for the night or have veered off in a different direction. Steve settles in to catch some shut eye.

Steve is just dozing off when he hears light footsteps ahead of him. He strains to see in the darkness but cannot make out anything. Every minute or so the sound repeats, and Steve reaches out for his CZ75 9mm Pistol and slowly cocks it. Releasing the safety, he strains once more to see if he can make out any shadow but sees nothing.

Steve safeties the weapon but lays it on his chest and strains to focus on the sound. This continues until a purple smear is visible on the horizon as pre-dawn arrives. The sound disappears and Steve falls into an exhausted sleep until awoken by the Sun's rays.

Steve jumps up to investigate the footsteps he heard. Carefully checking for tracks Steve moves forward and to his surprise finds a field mouse hole with a bunch of fresh dirt piled up around it. The mouse had been building its nest and every time the dirt was thrown on the dry grass around the hole it sounded just like light footsteps on the ground. Steve giggles to himself at the silliness of the event.

The two Gunships depart back to the new HAG after breakfast. The next couple of days are filled with many hours of Top Cover follow up and occasional contacts, and then it's time to head back down south for Steve. He will be catching a ride back with the Giant that is coming in with fresh stocks from Ondangwa in the afternoon.

Steve packs his kit and then goes over the aircraft, cleaning and servicing to make sure that he is confident of handing over a safe machine to his replacement.

As an added bonus, he replaces the Poly Urethane Blade Tapes on all the Blades leading edges. The Tape prevents erosion of the stainless-steel leading-edge surface from sand and dirt during landing and take-off in the dessert and bush. In the distance the drone of the approaching Puma could be clearly heard. At 50 ft. and approximately 140 Kts, it is an awesome sight to watch approaching over the bush.

The Giant flies overhead and the undercarriage extends as the pilot banks in a tight circuit to space for landing. Coming into land, the nose lifts to slow the aircraft down and the engines spool up to provide power for landing. A huge dust storm is created and then she is down, and the shutdown procedure is completed.

Steve's replacement jumps out and comes ambling over. The two greet like long lost friends and Steve briefs him on the aircraft, operation and what to expect. Next Steve collects his kit and heads over to the Ops Tent to say cheers to all. The Puma crew is there as well and with goodbyes said, the group disperses to the aircraft for the flight back to Ondangwa.

Steve had not unpacked much kit on his arrival, so he won't have much to do in the morning except Clear Out and book in at Movement Control for his flight back south. So, with an early start at the Pub Steve has a heavy night drinking ahead of him.

The next day, and Steve is sitting in the Hammock seats of the SAFAIR C130 L100 that is taking them back to AFB Waterkloof. With a hangover and lots on his mind, he is not interested in any chit chat with anyone, so pushes his Bush Hat over his eyes and pretends to be asleep for the 3 and bit hours to the States.

SAFAIR C130 L100

It is already Mid-September 1981 and the year is quickly coming to a close. Squadron life brings Steve back to reality and he can relax once more. The squadron end of the year function allows the members and families to gather round and enjoy the joys of upcoming holidays. AFB Bloemspruit hosts a wonderful function and all members not on deployment enjoy a lovely evening. Steve and Zella drink and dance the night away until the wee hours of the morning. All the courses at 87 HFS have concluded and squadron life is very relaxed with very little daily flying. The downtime affords the opportunity to complete many of the squadron projects, of which one is the building and inhabiting an Avery for birds, tortoises and fish. Steve being an excellent welder brings his arc welder from home and soon he and Corrie van Wyk, a fellow F/E, are manufacturing the structure of the Avery. The rest of the F/E's are constructing the pond and nesting area. By week's end the Avery is complete and with great fanfare it is filled with wildlife and officially opened. This is going to be a lovely introduction to visitors of the squadron.

The weeks fly by and the next function to attend at the Warrant Officers Mess is that of New Year's Eve. AFB Bloemspruit always delivers, and a wonderful evening is prepared for those that attend. Steve, Zella, George, Suzette, Ben and Marina are seated at the same table. The three couples are having a great time and all too soon it's time to say goodbye to 1981 and welcome in 1982 with the boisterous singing of "Auld Lang Syne".

A new course of Pilots and Under Training Flight Engineers will soon be arriving to start their courses, so the squadron initiates the course preparation by ensuring aircraft availability by reviewing that no large maintenance actions will be required, course materials are updated and printed, and that AFB Bloemspruit Stores has sufficient stock to kit the new students with. All F/E's at 87 HFS have to complete a monthly technical quiz, thus ensuring that they are up to date on the standard and emergency procedures for the Alouette Helicopter. Straight after the quiz, FSgt Mike Webb then informs all that the Bush Tour Roster needs to be reviewed. Due to the upcoming courses all Instructors will not be able to share in the Bush Tours for the next six months. If there are any concerns, then it must be discussed now as the students will soon be arriving. Steve speaks up and says that he is available for any tour. The rest of the Base F/E's concur, and the meeting is adjourned.

In the first month of the New Year 5th January 1982 a Puma is shot down close to Ongiva in Angola. It is a sad moment and another reality check for Steve. Kenny Dalgleish was a fellow F/E who Steve had met in 1978 when he first joined 22 Squadron. The Chief of the Air Force, Gen Earp's son Mike was the Co-Pilot with John Robinson the Commander also lost in the shoot down. The Giant was returning across a Shona after dropping their troops further north. The random small arms fire had severed one of the main rotor servo hydraulic lines, causing the Puma to tumble forward into the ground, exploding in a ball of fire on impact. They never stood a chance. The second Giant in formation could only fly an orbit to confirm that no one survived before setting heading for Ondangwa.

The Super Fight

January and February are not very busy months for Steve and he does very little flying. Steve is headed back to Ondangwa at the beginning of March 1982. He arrives at Ondangwa and finds the new Gunship Flight Commander Capt. Nealle Ellis "Nellis" waiting for him at movement control.

"Steve", calls Nellis.

"Get your kit, we are leaving soon."

Steve looks up in surprise but hurries through to retrieve his kit and throws in the back of Neale's truck. Nellis, as he likes to be called, tells Steve that they are being deployed immediately and that he wants Steve to be his engineer. Honoured by the praise, Steve thanks Nellis and gets his Route Form ready for Clearing In. Nellis takes the Route Form and gives it to the Ops Clerk, requesting him to complete the process for Steve.

Steve packs minimum kit and races off to prepare the aircraft he has been allocated. He checks the aircraft, replenishes stocks and ammunition. Next, he checks that his rifle and pistol are clean and fully loaded with sufficient ammunition. Steve has manufactured his own survival jacket with a holster sown into it. He ensures that all the survival gear is in good order.

Steve is issued with an "R5" 5.5 mm Assault Rifle, which he has returned and now carries a captured Russian AKM-47 that he obtained from a previous Bush Tour Contact. Should they get shot down and need to run for it, the possibility of finding more 5.5 mm ammunition versus 7.62 mm ammunition on the run would be very unlikely. Many of the aircrew now have adopted a similar approach to weaponry. Steve had purchased a CZ75 9 mm pistol in favour of the 9 mm Star issued weapon, as it has a 16 shot magazine.

Steve meets Nellis, Angelo Maranta, and Eugene van der Merwe at the Ops Room and after a quick Int Briefing, signing of the Authorization Log, they move over to the Tech Control Office to sign up the aircraft log. They are on route to Marienfluss, Steve's first introduction to Angola a year before.

A Recce Team has been deployed in the mountains to the north of the Fluss in Angola. The intelligence gathered so far indicated that there was a huge buildup of SWAPO forces in the south western part of Angola with an inevitable infiltration plan to SWA.

Both Gunships get airborne for Ruacana where they are to refuel before setting heading to Marienfluss. It is déjà vu for Steve as they crest the saddle to drop down into the Fluss below. Although excited about the operation, Steve cannot help to be concerned with the memory of the last incident at Iona when he and Mike Hill had been hit with small arms fire.

In the distance they can make out the HAG Ops tent at the Rocky Outcrop next to the desert runway. Soon the Gunships space for landing with Nellis heading in first. After shutting down, the crews unpack and head towards the Ops Tent for Briefing.

Recce Team South Western Angola

Two Puma's had deployed a group of Recce's in the mountains to the north of Iona and they are currently searching for the location of the SWAPO training camp. The two Gunships will be on constant standby for them should they run into a contact. Steve and the rest of the HAG Team settle into a long wait while the Recce Teams follows up. It is late spring in the Marienfluss and every afternoon like clockwork a Thunderstorm passes through the area. This is welcome site in the desert, and Steve takes advantage of fresh water by turning the empty fuel drums upside down to catch all the rainwater in the base. This will serve as a basin for him to wash himself after the storm.

The Kunene River is approximately 5 minutes flight away, and therefore far too expensive to have a bath with a ferry flight by Puma. There are also huge Nile Crocodiles in the river, just waiting for some easy meat.

Kunene River

The storm subsides, and everyone follows Steve's lead in grabbing a quick bath for the day. Every half an hour or so, Steve wanders over to the Ops Tent to listen in on the radio for feedback from the Recce Team. Early evening everyone gathers round the fire pit to enjoy their Rat Pack meals and chat. Steve and Nellis are about to turn in with a very bright moon shining over the desert. The brightness of the moon makes visibility very clear. The next minute there is an urgent call on the radio, the Recce Team have a visual on a group of SWAPO moving north. Nellis wants to fly but Sector Headquarters won't allow it. The Gunships are not cleared to fly at night. Steve agrees with Nellis and wants to get airborne; the moon is bright enough for them to fly safely. Sector 10 emphatically refuses, grounding them till daybreak. The Recce Team is told to stand down and hide. Early next morning the Recce Team is on the move again and tracking the SWAPO group. The whole contingent at the HAG is huddled around the radio listening for updates. Steve and Eugene decide to prepare the aircraft as there could be a call out happening any minute. A Dakota from AFB Ondangwa has flown in fuel drums for the helicopters from Ruacana and stockpiled them in Marienfluss for the upcoming operation.

Steve is just about to remove the canopy cover, when he sees Nellis running with his kit. Angelo is short on his heels, it was happening. Steve and Eugene get the aircraft final preparations completed while Nellis and Angelo strap in for start-up. Within 5 minutes they are airborne and on route to the Recce Team. At this point the Recce Team, clad in SWAPO uniforms are having an argument with the Swapo Team, each group accusing the other of being FAPLA.

HAG Marienfluss

Just after take-off, Nellis makes radio contact with the Recce Sgt Jose' Dennison, who is very unhappy. The SWAPO patrol is approximately 18 strong and has begun to fire on their position with mortars. The next 20 minutes flying time are critical, and the gunships arrive overhead and can see signs of the battle. The veldt has started to burn, and it serves as a homing beacon to the contact area.

Jose' and his team are situated on a small kopje, some 100 meters high. The kopje is adjacent to a large rocky ridgeline, with steep cliffs overhanging the contact area. The top of the kopje is flat, where Jose' and his team have taken up defensive positions facing the enemy. It is not necessary for Jose' to indicate the enemy position, as the bush cover is relatively thin, and the enemy can easily be seen, sprawled out on their stomachs facing each other's position, rifles pointed at the nearest threat.

To Steve and Nellis they look like the little toy soldier's, completely inert and harmless. The SWAPO insurgents are halfway up the kopje, the nearest approximately 40 meters from Jose's position. They have spread out and are steadily advancing onto Jose's position, using well-disciplined fire and movement tactics.

In the meantime, 32 Battalion, Lt Kenneth Schwartz "Blackie" has been given orders to get one section in the Puma. Accompanying Blackie and the section is Sgt Wally Haldane, who did not want to miss the action. Blackie's reaction force is restricted to a single sweep line and no stopper groups because of its strength. However, if SWAPO could be duped, the sweep line could initially act as a stopper group, and once the main fight was over, could stand up and sweep through the contact area, mopping up any remaining resistance.

Nellis tells Steve to start firing at the rearmost SWAPO. Hoping that this would cause confusion as they would be caught in a crossfire between the fire from the choppers and own forces. Just as the first shot is fired, with the two Gunships over the target, SWAPO is caught completely off guard. Steve and Eugene pick targets and start firing. The one SWAPO has an RPG 7 Rocket Launcher and extra rockets strapped to his back. Steve hits him with a 20mm HE round and the rockets create a firework's display as they all ignite. With both Gunships attacking from the rear and the Recce Team shooting from their position has the desired effect, and the insurgents decide to make a break in the direction of more open ground and less cover. Before the break becomes an uncontrolled panic, the Puma drops Blackie in the expected breakout direction. Everything is going according to plan, and those enemies who have not been killed from the initial fire from the Gunship are running headlong, like sheep, into Blackie's group.

At this stage, both Gunships are low on fuel, and as the Puma has not returned with fuel, Nellis lands and conducts the controlling of the sweep line from the top of the cliffs overlooking the contact area. The enemy offer very little opposition during the contact, directing minimal fire at the helicopters and ground forces. It appears that the sudden appearance of the helicopters has taken them completely by surprise and knocked the fight out of them.

There are no casualties to South African forces, and the final score against SWAPO is fourteen dead and six captured.

The two Gunships start up and initiate the return flight to the Fluss. Nellis leading with Angelo following higher and further behind. As the two aircraft crest the huge mountain next to a valley that runs directly down to the Fluss, Nellis realizes that he is caught in a powerful downdraft as the airflow down the valley moving down towards the Fluss has increased drastically. Nellis increases collective pitch to no avail, the little Gunship is rapidly being pulled down the valley at a phenomenal rate.

Nellis radios Angelo, "Angelo I am in a down draft and in the shit, how are you faring?"

Angelo responds, "We are higher, and air is still here, are you ok?"

Nellis responds, "Fuck no, we are descending too fast!"

Just then at around 300ft from the base of the Fluss, the Alouette grabs air and stabilizes, allowing Nellis to gain control of the descent. Both Nellis and Steve breath a huge sigh of relief. The rest of the flight to the HAG is uneventful. They space for landing and after shut-down while the pilots debrief at Ops, Steve and Eugene refuel and refill the ammo pans. They don't cover the aircraft, as there may still be a follow up operation later in the day.

After the contact, the Recce Team, prisoners, and Blackie's section return to the tactical headquarters at Marienfluss with the Giants. The intelligence officer begins the interrogation of the prisoners. The prisoners are zipped tied and brought in one by one and questioned. The Int Officer is patient and questions them calmly for purpose, number of troops, location and force strength.

The captured soldiers are very forthcoming with information, as it is determined that they are underfed and have not been paid in many months. This makes the interrogation much easier, as they are watered and fed while they sing out a wealth of information. It is ascertained that they are SWAPO and not FAPLA. Their task is to build a transit camp and cache arms for a new infiltration route through the Kaokoveld into central SWA.

According to the prisoners, there are about 250 to 300 insurgents in the base. The prisoners confirm the presence of shoulder-launched anti-aircraft missiles, presumably SA7s, but they are not sure about anti-aircraft guns. They are armed with the normal small arms, such as RPGs, AKs, RPDs, PKMs, and RPKs. In addition, there are vast amounts of anti-tank mines and rifle grenades, but they did not mention anything about mortars.

Sector Headquarters' concern is that if the camp is not attacked within the next 24 hours, the remainder of the group would disappear into the bush. No planning is made to attack the base should it be located by Jose'.

At Sector Headquarters in Oshikati, the high brass is starting to plan. The only force available for an immediate attack is 32 Battalion's Alpha Company, who has just arrived from Buffalo, the SWA home of 32 Battalion, and Blackie Schwartz's Foxtrot Company platoon.

Lt Du Plessis "Duppie" is called and asked to get one platoon ready for the attack. Duppie calls JC and Piet, instructing them to prepare their platoon, Alpha 4, to troop immediately. It takes some time for Alpha 4 to get mortar pipes, ammunition, and rations, and change into camouflage clothes, and Captain Jan Hougaard decides to use the Golf Company platoon of Lt Fanus Nel "Nella" and Corporal Peter Burley, who has just landed and thus are ready to immediately return for the attack.

Peter is still sitting in the Puma that brought them from the bush when Jan Hougaard's order comes through for them to be trooped to Marienfluss tactical headquarters. 32 Battalion's mortar group of Lieutenant Buks, which is doing tactical headquarters protection for another operation, is withdrawn to give support for the attack.

Most of the night is spent listening to the interrogation of the prisoners and logistical planning for the extra aircraft and troops. There is a critical shortage of fuel and ammunition, and to truck in fuel from Windhoek could take anything up to a week. A fuel drop by air is requested.

This is subsequently carried out by C130 transport aircraft and completed by lunch time. The ammunition and the rest of the assault force are flown in by Dakotas and Pumas from Ondangwa and Ruacana. More equipment and aircraft fuel will be flown in later by C160 and C130 aircraft that will complete airborne Fuel Drops at Marienfluss.

C130 Fuel Drop

Two additional Alouette gunships from Ruacana are attached to the tactical headquarters. The pilots are Major Charlie Bent with Mike Bartlett and Lieutenant Andre Schoeman and Gary Golding. At midday, all the required forces are gathered for the attack. By now, Sector Headquarters has decided that the attack has to take place at 13:00 that afternoon. A plan for the assault is agreed upon.

Operation Super is now in full swing and the plan is as follows. The platoon from Foxtrot and Alpha would be the attack group with Jan Hougaard, Duppie and Wally as command group, and are to depart first to the target area. Thereafter, the two sections of Golf Company are to follow as cut off groups and the mortar fire group for indirect fire support. After a final briefing, the attack force takes off, only to return to the tactical headquarters, aborting the attack due to a territorial rainstorm over the enemy camp area.

In the meantime, a senior intelligence officer arrives at Marienfluss and manages to obtain a clearer idea of where the SWAPO camp is situated. He builds a sand model of the area and at last is able to pinpoint the enemy camp. It is fortunate that the attack had been aborted as the position indicated by the prisoners on the sand model is almost three kilometers away from the position initially determined. The delay in the attack also allows Piet to check on his platoons' preparations and to mentally prepare.

With the initial attack abandoned, Jan becomes concerned that the enemy could withdraw during the night. He deploys Nella and Peter's platoon, fully equipped with everything they needed, to ambush positions.

The plan is to initiate the attack at 08:00. The reason for this being that the enemy has a parade at that time every morning when orders for the day are issued. This suits the Gunships as the sun would be high enough to lighten the shadows, and observation of any enemy hiding underneath the bush cover would be easier. Nellis, Steve, Angelo and Eugene are to search for the camp, and once it is identified, deploy the assault force and mortars.

Four Pumas will transport the sweep line and the fifth is to deploy the mortar group. Once the forces are deployed, the two remaining gunships will supply top cover to Nella and Peter's ambush groups, which are already in position to monitor any forces trying to reinforce the SWAPO elements and to prevent any SWAPO forces from escaping while the battle raged.

A mini HAG will be established about eight kilometers away from the enemy base. The gunships will refuel and rearm at this position. If a Puma could not get into a landing zone in the contact area for an evacuation, the casualty would be transported by gunship to the mini HAG and the Puma would evacuate the casualty back to the tactical headquarters for further treatment.

Mini Hag

Before the men begin boarding the Pumas for takeoff on what would become a day long battle, Phil unexpectedly arrives at the tactical headquarters. Piet is glad to see him because they would need all the leaders, they could get to control the assault in the rugged terrain. Everybody only has webbing, and as much ammunition as possible, and with only one water bottle each. They have very little food as directly after the attack it is planned to return to Marienfluss. Jan Hougaard makes contact with Nella and informs him that the moment the choppers have offloaded the attack force they would uplift him and Peter and drop them on the eastern side of the target in two different ravines to act as stopper groups.

The Gunship's primary task is to locate the base. Only after it is located would Nellis determine where to drop the assault force and mortar crew and then call in the Pumas. The takeoff is uneventful, and the aircraft proceed to the target area. The visibility is good, and no rain clouds are present. As a child, Nellis tells Steve he had always thought that when battles were fought, the weather would be bad, low cloud with rain and thunder, as if the Gods were also sizing up for the battle. Here they are, on their way with clear blue sunny skies, to kill what possibly could run into hundreds of men.

Once over the river, Nellis and Steve get down to the serious business of navigation. The trick is to stay as low as possible so that the noise of the helicopters does not carry too far and give the enemy warning of the approach. Navigation in mountainous areas when flying at ultra-low level can be difficult because of the limited horizon, and the many ridges and gullies can cause confusion. The Alouette does not have any navigation aids, and therefore, all navigation is carried out by eyeball, and if the pilot does not concentrate at all times while flying, he could quite easily become uncertain of his position.

At the two-minute mark, Nellis calls the climb and confirms that the Pumas are in the holding area. Nellis climbs over the ridge overlooking the camp area and hopes that there will be complete surprise. The suspect target area is in a large bowl, surrounded by high mountains. They fly close to the side of the mountain, hoping to use echoes from the engine noise to confuse the enemy as to which direction they are approaching from and to use the aircraft camouflage to prevent visual detection. At this stage, Nellis is extremely apprehensive, as the anti-aircraft capability in the camp has still not been determined.

There is however nothing, only flat scrub. Nellis enters another orbit over the area. Even if the camp is deserted, they should still pick up the path pattern, and where is the parade ground? Nellis has the distinct feeling that they are there somewhere, and every now and then he has to check the altimeter as he is sub-consciously gaining height. All he can see is a large number of dew-soaked rocks, very dark brown in colour. Nellis sends Angelo to the north of the area to reconnaissance for any signs of the camp.

Just then, Steve shouts over the intercom that he can see tents below. Nellis has a look and can see nothing. Steve is adamant that he has tents visual and describes them as squares and dark brown in colour. The scene immediately changes, and the dark brown rocks became bivouacs, the path pattern emerges like a spider web on the ground, clothing hanging out to dry, the camp debris, carefully concealed, become apparent, and then, jackpot. Under every bush lay inert soldiers, under some bushes up to five. One small bush looks like a star fish. The enemy has tried to find cover under the bush, but has forgotten about their lower torsos, which stick out in an almost symmetrical star-shaped pattern. Nellis and Steve have never seen so many enemies on the ground before; they are all over the place. The camp is built around an old derelict kraal and covered an area of roughly one by one and a half kilometers. It is situated in a rocky area, with small trees and scrub. The ground cover, therefore, is not too thick from the air, and they can quite easily observe the enemy.

Bivouacs

The adrenalin is now pumping, Steve and Nellis both have the feeling of been punched in the lower gut. The first task is to get the troops on the ground as soon as possible, because once the insurgents on the ground start to break out of the area, the movement would become a flood. The secret is to keep them guessing as to whether they have been observed or not. Nellis instructs Angelo to widen his orbit, climb higher and try to act as nonchalant as possible. While waiting for the Pumas to come in, Nellis works out a plan of action and decides to drop the sweep line to the west of the camp and the stopper groups along the river lines to the south and south west of the camp. There is a conical hill quite close to the camp on which the mortar team can be deployed. An added advantage is that that the hill overlooks the camp and they will easily be able to observe the fall of the bombs and make their own corrections.

The enemy has still not made a concerted effort to reveal their positions and seem to be fairly relaxed, although some of them are starting to crawl slowly towards the edge of the camp. They have at this stage shown no sign of aggression and the South African's are trying to act in a non-threatening manner. Nellis and Steve feel very apprehensive flying lazy circles above the camp, while trying to act as though they are still unaware of the enemy's presence. They see the Pumas approaching and the insurgents seem to hear the noise of the thumping blades and they start moving more quickly towards the edges of the camp. Nellis orders Steve to open fire to slow down the movement, as experience has shown that once one person moves in a set direction, the rest follow like sheep, and it will be difficult to contain the large numbers present.

The first rounds from the gunships stops the run and the enemy dive for cover. A battle ensues in which the Gunships would play the leading role and account for most of the enemy kills. Nellis and Steve hear a large bang towards the rear of the aircraft and the accompanying tightening feeling in the stomach from the adrenalin flow.

Angelo shouts over the radio, "SAM launch, six o'clock!"

Nellis and Steve see the distinctive thick whitish-grey smoke trail of a SA7 twirling up into the sky. Nellis immediately puts on more bank to find the firing position. Steve takes aim and illuminates the SAM team. As they turn through 180 degrees, they see a second SA7 launch; this time it is directed at Angelo and Eugene.

Nellis shouts over the radio, "SAM launch nine o'clock."

However, they are so low that by the time Nellis called the launch, the missile is already travelling at Mach 1.5 and it passes just in front of the Gunships nose. By now they are coming under heavy automatic weapons fire. The sound of rounds accompanied by a curtain of tracer is like hundreds of typists pounding their typewriters in a typing pool. The SAM firing position is easy to find because of the smoke from the launch rising lazily into the air. As they come over the position, they see the missile operators trying to take cover beneath the bushes, and Steve quickly kills them with a few well aimed rounds. By now, both Gunships are on the receiving end of a large volume of hot lead. The RPG's are also starting to make life uncomfortable. Although considered fairly ineffective against aircraft, when they explode in the immediate vicinity of an aircraft, there is an extremely loud bang accompanied by a large puff of black smoke. This can be disturbing when one is trying to concentrate on the job of directing a battle. Steve sees another SA7 shoot past the nose of their aircraft, and once the firing position is identified, Steve once again kills the operators.

By now, the Pumas are close to the landing zone, which is less than two kilometers from the base, and Nellis moves them over to the position for Steve to mark the landing zone with smoke and give the Pumas top cover. With the breakout, some of the enemies are running in the direction of the landing zone. Polla Kruger, in the lead Puma, followed by three other Pumas, has to offload the assault force and command group at different positions because of the terrain, making it difficult for the assault force to get in an assault line.

Buks, with his mortar platoon, is dropped on the north eastern side on high ground, where they prepare their mortars. Blackie is to the far right, then Louis, then Phil, then Buks, and completely to the left, JC. Whilst landing and preparing to get in an extended line, the Gunships start to shoot at the base. Mortars fall, SA 7s firing in the direction of the gunships, and small arms fire is everywhere. With lots of shouting to the troops to get in extended line, the attack line is ready.

Louis changes the direction of the assault line and starts the attack. The terrain is very mountainous and rough, so they move very slowly forward. Within minutes, some of the gunships have fired all their ammo and two of them retreat for re-supply while Nellis and Angelo continued command and control.

The next task is to drop the mortar group. When the Puma flies over the base area, a SA7 is fired at it, but the task is accomplished without any serious problems. The Pumas, after their drops, return to Marienfluss to uplift fuel and ammunition to establish a mini HAG.

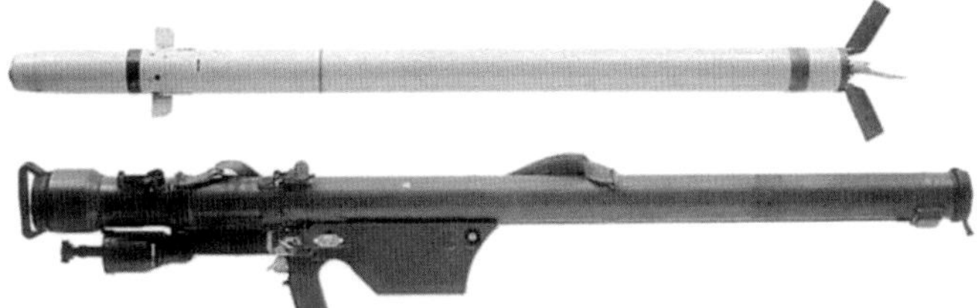

SAM 7 Rocket and Launcher

Duppie is dropped about two kilometers from the target by the Pumas. Two Pumas go in, dropping half the attack force. Duppie starts to form up in an extended line while the other two Pumas fly in and drop the remainder of the attack force. While forming up, they can hear and see that SWAPO on the ground is firing SAM's at the Gunships, which are circling their position. Mortars are also being fired. The terrain where the battle is taking place is very undulating, rough, and the attack force are having problems going over the crest, breaking the skyline and thereby creating good targets for the enemy forces. They advance over difficult terrain and try to keep in attack formation. Fortunately, from time to time there is high ground where the commanders could sit and observe the attack force make contact with enemy.

At this stage, the enemy realizes that they are contained and begin to direct heavy fire at the gunships as well as mortar fire onto the troops in the assault line. Although the mortar fire is not very effective, it is disconcerting for the gunships, as apart from all the other fire coming their way there are also mortar bombs passing through their orbit. Fortunately, Angelo quickly finds the mortar position and Eugene neutralizes it.

In the meantime, the two Pumas that had dropped the attack force, collected Nella and Peter and drop them in the two ravines. As the force moves into the base, some of the SWAPO's flee in the direction of the ravines, where Nella and Peter are waiting for them. From time to time, the attack force is forced to ground as Buks bombards them with mortars from the ridge. The advance moves very slowly due to the heavy rifle fire. The Gunships relieve each other for refueling, thus ensuring Top Cover for the Attack Force at all times. After a considerably long time advancing, the force starts finding dead enemy... lots of them. As they move past, they collect extra ammunition as their stocks are running low.

Once the troops start moving through the outskirts of the base, they come under heavy fire and their progress slows down. This is not a problem as they have contained the breakout and have the whole day to get through the objective. The slower the pace is, the less chance of casualties. At one stage, the fighting on the ground becomes so intense that the Gunships are killing isolated pockets of enemy approximately five meters from their own troops. The lethal radius of the 20 mm cannon shell is five meters, and the troops have to keep their heads very low during the firing.

At one point, Wally radio's "Gunship can you see our Day-Glo? Don't fire on us!"

Nellis, Steve, Angelo and Eugene's Gunships are short on fuel and are running out of ammunition. They are replaced by the returning Gunships, who are given the task of controlling the sweep line and giving close air support to the troops.

JC forms up and advances once again. Phil comes up behind him and starts moving into position to the right. He is about a step behind JC and two steps to the right, next to a shrub. The next moment, JC is knocked off his feet by a sledgehammer shock on his chest and side of the ribs. He falls backwards and looking to his right and sees Phil's head jerk back twice, first hole through the forehead and the second through the cheek and out the back of his head. As JC hits the ground, he cannot breathe. With his chest and ribs sore and right arm numb. Almeida is there in an instant checking him out. There is blood on him, but it was not his. Phil is still jerking on the ground, but there is nothing more that can be done for him. Half of the back of his head was gone. JC gets the line formed up again with Joaquim and Almeida, but it is very difficult to get the line up to advance. At this stage, there is no Gunships Top Cover, he advances into cover ahead of the line, and the rest would have no choice but to follow, and it worked! The terrain is now broken up into very deep and wide gullies. Soon after, they find themselves behind the SWAPO defensive line. The terrain becomes very difficult and the attack line breaks up several times. The whole area of the base is made up of deep gullies that make it impossible to keep formation. The Gunships return, but the area is too large to cover. By this time, JC has already given away all his loose ammo and started on the magazines in his chest webbing, when he discovers that there is a round that had gone straight through the first and halfway into the second magazine. On his AKM, he has a beautiful copper streak on the right-hand side. As the gunships are leaving, the message comes through that Phil is badly wounded and Angelo evacuates him. He carries out the evacuation under fire, landing meters behind the sweep line.

Duppie moves forward with the fire fight using mortars. It is difficult at this stage to supply accurate fire control orders to the mortars due to the nature of the terrain. It is also difficult to observe the enemy positions as they are hiding behind high ground and withdrawing just ahead of the advancing force. Several times, Duppie notes enemy slipping behind the advancing force, but are not a threat to the positions with both he and Wally keeping an eagle eye to the rear, and the of the Gunships doing a tremendous job in the air.

While Blackie's platoon is advancing, they come under heavy enemy fire, and Corporal Yobi João is killed. They get pinned down on the left flank; every time they move to advance, they draw heavy enemy fire. Louis calls Blackie over the radio to inform him of Corporal João's situation. Blackie moves over to Louis to assess what can be done, but Corporal João's is dead. On his way back to the formation, there is a SWAPO soldier who has pretended to be dead when the line moved past him. He is busy leopard crawling towards the machine gunner, Gomez, from behind, but Blackie is passing by and takes care of the problem. The group that pinned them down is dealt with by the Gunships. While Steve is shooting, Blackie radios that the Gunship is going to shoot one of them, they are shooting too close.

Nellis responds "Blackie, don't worry, there's a group in front of you which we've just sorted out."

Nellis and Angelo are relieved by the next two Gunships and break away for refueling and re-arming. While refueling, Steve grabs a quick snack. He is hungry and thirsty, the excitement, fear and adrenalin have consumed all his energy. Eugene does not look any better, but they put on a grin and get back to it. Upon returning, the Gunships arrive on the scene of the battle and relieve the next two Gunships. There are unfortunately not sufficient troops on the ground to prevent the enemy from escaping. The assault started at 08:00, and by 12:00 it is still in progress. The heat and thirst are beginning to have an effect on the men on both sides as the assault develops. For Duppie and Blackie, although they did not know it, the decision not to evacuate the body of João from the battlefield would later cause some problems when the troops confronted them about it.

Throughout the battle, an Impala ground strike aircraft is on standby for close air support should the need arise. Just after 12:00, Jan Hougaard and Nellis decide to call in a strike on a hot spot area that is very difficult to approach. Nellis requests the strike with napalm as air support. After flying low over the target Nellis tells Steve to mark the target area with smoke. They ease away to clear the area for the jets. After some minutes, there is no sign of the strike aircraft. Nellis enquires over the radio as to what their position is and when would they strike.

The answer comes back, "We have been orbiting the position you gave us but can find no signs of the battle or see your smoke. Are you sure that you are in the right valley?"

Nellis tries one more time to supply them with the grid position, but to no avail, the Jet Jocks have no clue where they are and are bumbling up and down a valley that only they will know about. The air strike is given up and the Gunships focus on trying to eliminate the threat. There are only a few rounds left and Steve warns Nellis that they won't be able to hold for much longer. Nellis takes another run over the target and Steve empties the last 20 mm rounds into the area.

At this stage, the stopper groups did not have much enemy to sort out as the Gunships kept the enemy's heads down. Between the Gunships and the ground force, the battle was being controlled and the enemy is taking a heavy toll.

Nella's group is picked up by the Giants and flown closer to the northwest. Peter is also air lifted and dropped on the edge of the base and told to expect SWAPO to retreat over the saddle in front of them. As they could not see the base or initial attack, they did form the stopper group preventing those retreating and have constant communication with all concerned.

Giants Trooping

Just before the Puma drops Nella, a group of approximately 30 enemies have managed to get to the position where the landing zone is to be. Angelo and Eugene, supplying top cover to the Puma, engage the enemy and become involved in a fairly heavy fire fight. After a few minutes, the Gunship neutralizes the position, but not before receiving light battle damage from small-arms fire. Nellis and Steve supply top cover to the Puma dropping off Nella's group in stopper position. While the Puma is on short finals for the landing zone, Steve picks up a group of enemies running along the gully in which the Puma is going to land. The gully sides are rocky and steep, and the enemy cannot climb out. It's like a duck shoot. All Steve did was to fire above their heads, and the ricocheting shrapnel did the rest. By the time the Puma takes off, a few of the enemy have progressed to within 50 meters of the landing zone, and Nella finds himself in a contact seconds after being dropped. He is in an exposed position and the Gunships have a few anxious moments before they are able to neutralize the survivors. Once again, Steve's accurate firing saved the day.

When the main attack is mostly completed, Nella and Peter are called by Nellis to clear an area to the west of the main attack zone. Nella unexpectedly runs into a group of SWAPO. He is shot and killed instantly. The confusion he caused by running straight into the enemy enables the rest of his group to take cover and start returning fire. The rest of his group not knowing whether he is dead or alive return fire on the enemy. Under heavy enemy fire, Sergeant Victor Dracula runs forwards, covered by Rifleman Bernardo's rifle fire, and extracts Nella's body, lying directly in the line of fire in front of the SWAPO positions. Nellis and Steve arrive overhead and begin firing at the enemy while guiding Peter towards Nella's position.

Peter was about 100 meters apart from Nella's group when he was shot. The platoon sergeant, Victor Dracula, is next to Nella, and grabs Nella's radio, shouting,

"Nella is dead! Nella is dead!"

Wally immediately responds to Dracula in Portuguese over the radio, calming him, and calls Peter, to support them as soon as possible.

Peter runs the stretch to Nella's position to help, but to no avail. He has been shot squarely between his eyes and must have been dead before he hit the ground. Nella's death was avenged by Kingutu, Peter's RPG carrier. Peter then loaded Nella onto one of Gunships for evacuation. Peter then moves the platoon over to join the main attack group about one kilometer away.

In the meantime, while the Gunships supply Top Cover, Major Jan Hougaard coordinates the Ground Forces closer to the contact area. The fighting has now subsided and to save fuel Nellis and Steve land close to Jan for a consolidation discussion. Both aircrew jump out of the Gunship after shut down and find the closest spot to relieve themselves. The next instant there is the almighty report of RPG-7 rockets across the treetops. Steve and Nellis race back to the Gunship but have to find cover as a firefight between SWAPO and the Ground Forces breaks out. The RPG-7's had been fired from across the donga. Blackie keeps looking over the ridge to see where the fire fight is coming from to be hurried back to his hiding place as more RPG-7's are sent his way. SWAPO is hell bent on getting a Chopper.

The moment there is a relief in the firefight, Nellis and Steve sprint to the Gunship. Nellis dives in and starts the aircraft while Steve grabs the chock and slams the barrel in place. Within a minute the Gunship is taking off straight up and backward away for the firefight zone. Nellis brings the aircraft to a safe orbit and they quickly identify where the firefight is coming from. With some well-placed rounds Steve quickly silences the attack, giving the Ground Forces time to move forward and mop up the operation.

By 14:30, the firing gradually dies down and the last shots are fired at 15:00. Most of the men have run out of ammunition and have to resupply themselves within the field from the dead SWAPO. By now, the men are mentally and physically exhausted after fighting for seven hours non-stop and could only hope that there would not be a counter-attack by SWAPO reinforcements coming from the north.

On the morning of 14th March, reinforcements comprising 24 men from Alpha Company commanded by Sgt Pikkie Meyer and another Foxtrot Company platoon are flown to the contact area, and together with Blackie's Foxtrot Company platoon they begin sweeping south of the base area while Peter's platoon continues with the clearing of the base. Another enemy is killed and one, who has been hiding in the captured base, is wounded.

When the top brass from headquarters in Windhoek and Oshikati arrive at the scene, Duppie is still in control of the clearing of the base. Only now it dawns on him how extensive the base really is, and he notices that a large number have escaped. Henk Coetzee comes in to blow up a large cache of ammunition found. While the clearing up continues, the captured documents are studied, and it is found that the strength of the base was 250 SWAPO in the base are from the mechanized base at Lubango and were busy establishing caches in the area to open a new front against the Kaokoland. The enemy in the base are from the July 1981 intake, with a group of 50 "old" cadres deployed more to the south in the direction of the Kunene River. One of the prisoners also mentioned that they are expecting another group of 200 SWAPO from Lubango to join them. The existence of a boat capable of carrying 18 men is also mentioned. This boat would possibly to be used to cross the Kunene River.

The SWAPO plans of establishing the Kaokoland front are disrupted. Supplementary Operations Order are issued to Jan Hougaard on 16th March, with the mission:

"You must clean the area south of Iona and execute an area operation to locate SWAPO as from 14 March for a period of three weeks", and tasks: "Locate the SWAPO base of 50 men south of Iona and destroy it. Locate the 18-man boat and report it to Sector 10 for further action."

Two days after the assault, the media is allowed to visit the contact area. Peter is still in the enemy base area. Alpha Company, with strength of 126, commanded by Duppie, is assigned the operation to locate the boat. Du Plessis also had Buk's 12-man mortar group, as well as air support consisting of two Gunship and two Puma helicopters, a Bosbok reconnaissance airplane, and a Dakota to be used for resupplies.

The company could not locate any more SWAPO or the boat in the next three weeks. Operation Super's main effort was in the past, and the helicopter crews could relax at the Alpha Company tactical headquarters waiting for any call from the patrols for assistance. None came.

The 32 Battalion and Air Force contingent at the HAG in Marienfluss spend the next day's relaxing and recuperating. Early morning and two Pumas get airborne to fly a Recce mission to the Skeleton Coast 40 minutes to the west. The Pumas are loaded with as many of the group as they can take.

It is a spectacular flight across the desert to the famous Skeleton Coast. The Skeleton Coast is the northern part of the Atlantic Ocean coast of SWA and south of Angola from the Kunene River south to the Swakop River, although the name is sometimes used to describe the entire Namib Desert coast.

The Bushmen of the SWA interior called the region "The Land God Made in Anger", while Portuguese sailors once referred to it as "The Gates of Hell".

On the coast the upwelling of the cold Benguela current gives rise to dense ocean fogs (called "cassimbo" by the Angolans) for much of the year. The winds blow from land to sea, rainfall rarely exceeds 10 millimeters annually and the climate is highly inhospitable. There is constant, heavy surf on the beaches.

In the days of human-powered boats it was possible to get ashore through the surf but impossible to launch from the shore. The only way out was by going through a marsh hundreds of miles long and only accessible via a hot and arid desert.

The war weary bunch enjoys a day of fun at the beach and decide to do some mortar fishing. A mortar is fired into the surf where the fish are jumping and then after the explosion the guys run into the freezing water and try to extract them. No fish are caught. The only thing that everyone does catch is a serious bout of sunburn in the nether region.

Skeleton Coast

This battle was the biggest and most successful for 32 Battalion up to this time. The Air Force, especially the Gunships, play a vital role in this success.

The Gunship crews killed most of the enemy, but never receive the credit. Without their support, 32 Battalion would never have achieved this major success.

Major Johan "Boela" Niemann and Lieutenant (Reverend) Manie Taute attend Nella's funeral in his hometown, Vryburg. Yobi is buried in the Kimbo cemetery at Buffalo Base.

Phil was cremated, and one morning a few weeks later Taute and his platoon have a ceremony on the banks of the Kuvango River. After a prayer, his ashes are thrown in the river near to the living quarters at the request of his family.

Ops Super Jan Hougaard with some Captured Ammunition

Nellis, Steve, Angelo and Eugene return to Ondangwa with the rest of the Choppers to resupply for their next deployment to Omega a 32 Battalion Base to the east.

Ops Super and some of the Air Force Contingent

Back; Monty, Sewes, Puma Co-Pilot, Polla, Eugene
Front; Nellis, Angelo, Steve

The conflict in South West Africa and Angola continues to escalate, and Steve spends the next year completing many tours in the operational area. His time at home seems like a blur and then it's on to the next fight.

Operation Meebos and the Fight Carries On

Operation Meebos occurs during July and August 1982 with the objective of attacking SWAPO's People's Liberation Army of Namibia (PLAN) bases and new regional headquarters in Southern Angola by the South African Defense Force (SADF) based in South West Africa. The plan involves the use of South African Air Force helicopters flown from mobile helicopter administrative areas (HAA) with a SADF Tactical Headquarters based deep in Angola and protected from possible People's Armed Forces for the Liberation of Angola (FAPLA) attacks by 61 Mechanized Battalion. These helicopters would fly 32 Battalion and paratroopers from the HAA areas to SWAPO targets identified by reconnaissance teams deep in the Angolan bush and by signal and human intelligence.

Planning for Operation Meebos begins when the SADF fears that PLAN and FAPLA would attempt to retake the Angolan towns of Xangongo and Ongiva. These towns had been captured by the SADF during Operation Protea and had been occupied ever since. Ongiva contains a SADF tactical and logistical headquarters with an airfield to support ground and airborne operations to conduct counter-insurgency operations in Southern Angola. The second part of the operation involved identifying the SWAPO bases and headquarters which appeared to be constantly on the move. The plan calls for 61 Mechanized Battalion to protect the Mobile Advance Airfields from possible FAPLA and SWAPO attacks while the Air Force helicopters are to transport 32 Battalion and 1 Parachute Battalion companies to attack SWAPO bases identified by reconnaissance teams.

A company of 61 Mechanized Battalion moves from Ongiva up to Xangongo where combat readiness training begins, practicing for the forthcoming operation. Air Force Mirages attack the FAPLA air defenses at Cahama, while SADF reconnaissance units discover a possible SWAPO headquarters near Mupa.

Steve leaves Bloemfontein at the beginning of August 1982 for AFB Ondangwa, and is once again partnered up with Nellis, and has been deployed to the captured airport of Ongiva in Southern Angola. There are six Gunships posted here for daily call out should contacts take place. The Giants still fly in and out of Angola from Ondangwa. It's a scorching hot day and the aircrew are all entertaining themselves with various tasks for the day. Based at Ongiva is a contingent of 32 Battalion under the command of Captain Gary Wright. Gary and Gunship Pilot Dick Paxton, an ex-Rhodesian have become good friends and subsequently terrorize everyone else with shenanigans.

Every evening at sunset a captured Anti-Aircraft weapon is fired from the roof of the Ongiva airport building. Unfortunately, there has been a problem with the weapon, and for the past few days could not be operated. Steve grabs some tools and saunters over to the 23mm AA Gun and tinkers a little here and there. He then climbs onto the firing seat, winds the wheel to align the cannon with a skyward pointing aim, and depresses the foot firing mechanism. With a loud report the huge weapon comes to life. With a long burst and yells of excitement the men gather round, and everyone has a go at letting off a couple of rounds into the twilight. It is an awesome sight with the 23mm rounds exploding at altitude with an amazing display of fireworks.

Early the next morning the Gunships and Giants are deployed to Mupa to initiate the attack on the SWAPO headquarters. It is attacked firstly by Alouette Gunships followed by an airdrop of ground troops by helicopter which kill around 18 PLAN soldiers. The attack is not as intense as has been experienced in the past, but the target area is cleared and the mop up operation is started. In the next few days, 61 Mechanized Battalions mortar and gun batteries are moved up to Xangongo.

61 Mechanized heading in the direction of Mongua hoping to confuse FAPLA and PLAN intelligence as to its final destination before disappearing off into the Angolan bush. Finally, after three days of pushing through the bush, 61 Mech meets up with two companies of 32 Battalion, 25 km east of Mupa. There they find what they hoped would be a suitable site for a Helicopter Administrative Area (HAA) position. On the same day, 32 Battalion reconnaissance units discover a PLAN base close to the Calonga River, 21 km on the western side of the Cuvelai / Techamutette road and about 31 km south-west of Techamutette. A plan is formulated for a parachute drop at first light, north of the target and a helicopter drop of 32 Battalion at three other points with protection provided by Alouette Gunships.

The day did not start well as the vicinity of the HAA is attacked by FAPLA artillery. The FAPLA unit expends its artillery shells in the attack and the HAA has to be moved. The tactical headquarters is moved up to the new HAA from Ongiva. At the same time the 32 Battalion reconnaissance units cannot find a suitable drop zone and also notice the base is being evacuated. The airdrop is cancelled, and the paratroopers called back to their base in SWA. The plan is modified, and the paratroopers are collected and join 32 Battalion for a delayed helicopter drop. By the time the SADF arrive at the target all that can be found are PLAN stragglers.

The HAA is now moved further north as a few days earlier aerial intelligence had discovered a base close by. The Tactical headquarters at the HAA begins planning another mission consisting of an air attack by Mirage's followed by a helicopter troop assault with air protection by Alouette Gunships.

The attack takes place around midday with an attack by Mirages followed by Alouette Gunships that are attacked by 14.5 mm AA guns and RPG-7s. 32 Battalion is the first wave of ground troops dropped in by Puma helicopters followed by a second wave of paratroopers. The battle ends after some fierce fighting. One soldier of 32 Battalion is killed and two are wounded. As for the PLAN soldiers, 144 died during the battle with weapons and ammunitions captured.

Distorted Images

On the 9th August 1982, close to the Techamutete and Cuvelai road, right next to the Mui dry riverbed, 61 Mech is preparing to attack together with 32 and Para Battalions with the Giants loading up the troops and head out to the attack area.

The camouflaged enemy's 14.5mm AA fires off long bursts at one of the Giants with direct hits and the Puma almost immediately erupts in flames and cartwheels nose first into the bush, exploding on impact. Twelve troops and three air crew are trapped inside the burning mangle. One troop is thrown clear, and the enemy drags him clear to the closest tree and shoots him at point blank range. All of the aircrew are from 31 Squadron AFB Hoedspruit. The Commander John Twaddle, Co-Pilot Chris Pietersen and F/E Coert Grobler have all taken the final flight.

61 Mech "Bundu Bashes" to the crash site and an hour later find the smoldering Puma wreck strewn around with bodies broken and burnt. The sight leaves everyone quiet in their own thoughts, while they rummage through the wreck to see if anyone has survived.

With great sorrow, bodies are placed in Body Bags, and with sobering heart wrenching truth the zippers are closed. Ratel 90 approaches and the Officer deplanes to review the sight. As he makes his way through the branch of a tree he steps on a mine. The deafening explosion leaves him mutilated, groaning and bleeding. Troops rush in to assist but his strength fades quickly. 16 young dead, dreams lost in this God forsaken bush.

The Troops withdraw and dig in for the night, each with their own thoughts and smell of the sight they just encountered. The deathly silence a sign that everyone is playing the scene over in their mind with vivid images of the carnage they had come across. Red tears flow over dirty soldiers' cheeks with the reality of the loss, and their next of kin has no idea as to what has transpired.

Early morning, and the area is swept for mines and made safe. A SAMIL truck is brought in to load up the remains of the broken and mangled Puma. The scene is unrealistic and unimaginable, the images keep flashing in each troops head as they all struggle to cope with reality of the event. Families pride and dreams destroyed these are the images of a war that has no end. Many will never have rest from that which they have seen.

Signal intelligence concerning FAPLA proposing to move a twenty-two-vehicle logistics convoy from Techamutette to Cuvelai is received. This is to resupply the 11th Brigade with artillery shells it has expended during the attack on the HAA. A plan is quickly prepared for an airdrop by helicopter of a 61 Mech ambush platoon along the road. The ambush begins around 05h30 the morning, stopping the convoy and destroying some of the vehicles. Alouette Gunships follow up, and by 08h00 the ambush is over with twenty vehicles destroyed and two captured. Steve destroys the vehicles with the 20mm HE rounds. It is an impressive site to see the rounds hit, explode and then the flames start as the flammable materials light up. The rest of 61 Mechanized Battalion reaches the ambush platoon later that day.

A week later a PLAN base is discovered north of the Mui River about 15 km to the west of the Cuvelai / Techamutette road by members of the 32 Battalion reconnaissance units. 32 Battalion and 1 Parachute troops are airlifted by Puma's accompanied by Alouette Gunships around midday to the base. During a second airdrop, the helicopters are ambushed enroute to the base by hidden PLAN anti-aircraft teams, resulting in one Puma helicopter being shot down killing the three airmen and twelve paratroopers.

Alouette Gunships attack the crash site dispersing the PLAN soldiers around the downed helicopter and 61 Mechanized elements move up to site to retrieve the bodies and the helicopter. The helicopter wreck itself is removed the following day. In total, 106 PLAN soldiers are killed at the base that was attacked. Another PLAN base is discovered on the next day by the 32 Battalion reconnaissance units about 30 km north of Cuvelai. Again, it is attacked by Mirages and Alouette gunships. Around 11h00 the infantry companies of 32 Battalion and 1 Parachute Battalion are air-dropped into the contact area guided by the Gunships and attack the base. The attack kills 116 PLAN soldiers with no loss by the SADF forces.

"Bushmen" 31 Battalion Omega

Two of the Gunships are instructed to withdraw to Omega Base in the Caprivi Strip, where they will be on standby to support a follow up operation in South Eastern Angola. Steve and Nellis together with another Gunship Crew pack up and head south toward Omega. Omega Base serves as HQ for 31 Battalion, also known as the "Bushmen" Battalion. The Battalion consists primarily of Bushmen soldiers from the Mbarakwengo and the Vasquela tribes in SWA. These soldiers have exceptional natural tracking and bushcraft abilities and are organized into a specialized counterinsurgency unit. There has been intelligence received that some Special Force SWAPO troops have infiltrated the area, and the Bushman are the right group to track them down.

31 Battalion Bushman

It has been a very busy tour for Steve, and he is relieved to be packing up and heading back to Bloemfontein. This was also to be his last tour for 87 HFS, as he and Zella have decided to relocate to Cape Town. Before this tour Steve had applied for a position back to 22 Squadron at AFB Ysterplaat in Cape Town. He is very hopeful that this will be approved. Exhausted after the heavy action, Steve settles into the 3-hour flight back to the States.

Back at the Squadron Steve is elated to be told that his transfer request has been approved. Steve and Zella begin planning for their departure to Cape Town. Unfortunately, there is no military accommodation available, so Steve has to come up with an alternative plan. On the last tour he befriended Pierre Louw from 22 Squadron, and the two hit it off. Pierre invited Steve and Zella to stay at his apartment until they can find suitable accommodation. With this offer the planned move is prepared for execution.

1982 quickly draws to a close and end of year functions are in full swing. At AFB Bloemspruit this year the Warrant Officers Mess is having an end of the year bash for the base. Steve and Zella together with many of the other married couples are partying the night away. Amid much drinking and dancing, the RSM Des Fountain has brought with him the whistle of happiness. He gives the whistle to Steve and instructs him to place the index finger over the hole and then to blow hard on the whistle to rotate the wheel in the front. With lungs sucked to the max, Steve exhales and is rewarded with a face full of Baby Powder. Howling with laughter Steve grabs Zella and smears his covered face all over her. The evening becomes a joyous occasion and the men have an opportunity to relax and bring sanity back to their lives amidst all the action that has been transpiring the past three years. With the boisterous singing of Auld Lang Syne, the evening is brought to an end. The New Year will bring about more threats and changes.

Unfortunately, the terrorist campaign against the SADF has increased dramatically and Steve prepares for another trip to AFB Ondangwa. It is early February 1983 when Steve departs Bloemfontein for his next tour.

Operation Phoenix

Operation Phoenix is an operation in 1983 by the South African Defense Force and South West African Territorial Force in response to a major incursion by PLAN fighters from Angola into the white farming areas of northern South West Africa. SWAPO's military wing PLAN has created a specialized infiltration unit called Volcano.

Members of this unit have spent the second half of 1982 receiving training from East German, Cuban and Russian instructors and are regarded as the best PLAN soldiers. By January 1983, 1000 to 1700 members of Volcano begin the journey south to the Angolan / South West Africa border. They are then formed into fourteen companies of 50 to 70 soldiers.

Their mission is for thirteen of these companies, to cross the border and engage the SWATF and SADF forces while the last company is to head southwards to the white farming areas of northern South West Africa. By February 1983, the thirteen companies head into Kaokoland, Ovamboland and Kavango.

The Fourteenth Company head for the white farmers in Kamanjab, Outjo, Tsumeb and Otjiwarongo. The South African Forces operation begins by mid-February when the incursions come to their attention.

Iondi 32 Battalion

The first night at Iondi the chopper crews end up playing cards with the Commanding Officer and his team while drinking the night away. Eventually in the wee hours of the morning everyone slinks off to bed to catch some shut eye. Arthur Walker requested an early wake-up call the next morning.

The sun is already baking in the sky when the next instant an explosion goes off next to the tent where the aircrew is still fast asleep. In a split second everyone has reached for their weapons and hit the floor. Flat on their stomachs, Steve and the rest of the Air Force Contingent, leopard crawl to the tent opening. Steve peers out and standing outside next to the weapon check pit is Friedrich von Solms, with his hands on his hips and a huge grin on his face, who had just fired an 81 mm Mortar on full charge at 06:00 sharp. The pit was about 10 meters away from the bunker. Werner Scott had arranged with Friedrich do a silent set-up and the first noise was the bomb departing.

To the 32 Battalion Troops amusement, the Air Force Crew looks a bit the worse for wear. Grumpily everyone heads off for Brunch. After Brunch the Gunships get airborne where Arthur hovers over the Ops Room, nearly taking the roof off, which is a standard army tent pulled over the bare rafters, before setting heading back to Ondangwa.

Steve and the rest of the Gunship Crews are kept busy daily on callouts for attacks on follow-up operations. Many hours are flown by the crews and fatigue is starting to show. The Gunship Crews are called to the Operations room and briefed that they all need to report to the Field Hospital at the Base for a quick check-up. They are also informed that if they have flown 100 hours in four weeks, that they will be grounded due to fatigue. Steve has exceeded the 100-hour limit but only has a week to go before heading back. His check-up at the Hospital gives him the all clear and he heads out on another call-out for the day. Very soon the week is over, and Steve is heading back home. He can now concentrate on the impending move to Cape Town.

By the beginning of March, the PLAN soldiers in the main force, who are kept busy by the SADF / SWATF forces, have taken 155 casualties but have succeed in laying mines and attacking and kidnapping civilians. The small PLAN force, being chased by the South African's, are now 50 km from the white farming areas. By early March, the smaller force has reached the farmlands and has attacked a homestead. But by early April, SADF / SWATF soldiers have caught up to the group and no PLAN fighters from the Fourteenth unit are alive and have failed to achieve their objectives. The operation winds down with mopping up operations and ends by mid-April. In the two-month operation 27 members of the SADF and SWATF lose their lives with PLAN's Volcano unit loss of 309 fighters.

Chapter 8 - MARITIME ROUND TWO

The Move to Cape Town

Steve is an avid restorer of motorcycles and cars, a hobby he has come to enjoy. He recently bought an MGA Roadster that is roadworthy but requires a rebuild. Zella has managed to start packing and is glad that Steve has returned to help finalize everything before the removal company arrives.

Steve has arranged that he can store all their furniture in Pierre's garage until they can find a place. Steve's father, Frank, has been having trouble with his car, so Steve and Zella decide to lend their Alfa Romeo Giulietta to Steve's parents, while they take the MGA and the XS1100 Yamaha motorcycle to Cape Town.

It's mid-March when the removal company arrives to load all Steve and Zella's belongings for the long trek. Steve feels excitement building for the up-coming trip. As the MGA's engine is burning oil, he instructs Zella to keep the speed at 50 to 60 MPH. He will bring up the rear on the Yamaha.

They leave early the morning, planning to complete the trip in one day. It is a good 10 hours to Cape Town and Steve wants to make sure that they have enough time in hand to make the trip. The long road starts off well and both soon set into a rhythm. Every 200 km Steve refuels the thirsty 1100cc Yamaha. He also checks the oil level of the MGA and then they set off again.

The road seems never ending, and through the Karoo Steve tells Zella to keep going as he will stop off for a fuel top up, while she makes up time. After the refuel Steve steps up the pace to catch up with Zella. After 30 minutes he has still not caught up with her and is concerned that she is going to fast with an engine that is using oil. Eventually Steve is cruising at 160 KPH when in the distance he spots the green MGA with a plume of blue smoke emitting from the exhaust.

Steve is angry as Zella had decided to floor it causing the MGA to burn more oil. He catches up with Zella and indicates to her to stop. A heated discussion takes place with both of them sulking back to their respective rides and settling in once more on the road to Cape Town.

The trip is pretty uneventful going forward with both Steve and Zella settling into a rhythm of pulling over when either one needed a rest, refreshment or washroom break. It's early summer in the Cape Province, with hot and long daylight hours. At 33-degree Latitude, Cape Town has daylight of around 14 hours in mid-summer. It is early evening as Steve and Zella come over the top of the Du Toit's Kloof Pass, enter the long tunnel and exit with the beautiful view of Paarl, Stellenbosch in the foreground, and Table Mountain on the horizon with Cape Town lined along the mountain and coastline.

View from Du Toits Kloof

They are heading to Pierre's apartment close to Sea Point in Cape Town. Within an hour they both take the last turn into the apartment parking lot. Pierre is there to greet them and soon everyone is settled in for a chat. Pierre is a single father and has his daughter living with him.

Table Mountain from Milnerton

"Motto Ut Mare Liberum Sit" - That the Seas may be Free

While Zella settles in for the arrival of their belongings, Steve leaves for the Squadron with Pierre early Monday morning. Steve clears in at the Duty Room of AFB Ysterplaat and 22 Squadron, once again back where he left off a few years back. Zella has been referred to a Dentist in Rondebosch for potential employment. As Steve is still classed as a qualified Rescue Swimmer, he is placed on the standby list for call out at the Squadron. Being a Maritime Squadron, 22 has the duty of responding to all ASR (Air Sea Rescue) call outs for people that have got into difficulty at sea or in the mountains. He completes standby for one week as a Rescue Swimmer, one week off and then one week as a Flight Engineer. Steve settles into Coastal Squadron life and very soon is back flying as Flight Engineer on the Westland Wasp and the Alouette III.

Living with Pierre and his daughter is a bit trying for Steve and Zella, so he approaches the Duty Room at the Base to get guidance on how to purchase his own home with Government assistance. Very soon Steve and Zella are given authority to start looking for a home. They find a place in Sanddrift Milnerton and decide to put in an offer. To both their surprise the offer is accepted, and they are now the proud owners of a Mortgage. Within a month Steve and Zella move into their new home and can at last unpack their belongings and furniture. Zella is enjoying Cape Town and the new practice that she is working at. She has also approached Stellenbosch University to enquire about studying for Oral Hygienist.

It is midmorning when Steve is summoned to the Tech Control Office for a phone call.

"Sgt Coetzee" Steve answers.

"Hello Sgt Coetzee, this Lt. Prinsloo from Air Force Head Quarters, may I ask you a few questions on security please"? Requests the lovely voice of a lady.

She then proceeds to question about events in his Air Force career and then informs him that he has Secret Security Clearance. Steve is puzzled by the phone call and as he walks out of the office down the passage, Major Charlie Bent summons him into the OC's Office. Charlie is the acting OC while Cmdt. Theron is readying for transfer in from Pretoria. Charlie accepts Steve's salute and then indicates for him to sit down.

"Steve, I would like to congratulate you on being awarded the Honoris Crux Decoration" says Charlie.

Steve looks at Charlie with a dumb expression on his face. He cannot process what he has just heard.

"I beg your pardon Sir" says Steve with disbelief on his face.

"I have just received a phone call from Air Force Head Quarters informing me of the event" says Charlie.

They chat a little longer and Steve walks away in disbelief as to what he has just been informed. Steve cannot process where, why or what he could have done to deserve receiving the decoration. After all he was trained to do a job and that is what he has strived to accomplish to the best of his abilities. Steve is lost in his own thoughts for the rest of the day and is reluctant to share the news with anyone. Even at home he cannot bring himself to tell Zella what has transpired.

The next day at the Squadron Steve receives a signal informing him officially of the decoration and where the parade would take place. The Honoris Crux (Cross of Honour), post-nominal letters HC, is a military decoration for bravery which was instituted by the Republic of South Africa on 1st July 1975. The decoration is awarded to members of the South African Defense Force for bravery in dangerous circumstances. This decoration is presented at a large military parade by either the State President or delegated Minister. The parade for 1983 Honoris Crux awards will be conducted at the city of Port Elizabeth on the Eastern Cape Coast.

Unlike a few years back, 22 Squadron now also participates in the escalated Border Conflict and therefore supplies crews for a tour every month. Just after Steve's 26th birthday he packs up and is on his way for the first time to the Caprivi Strip in SWA. AFB Rundu is located at the beginning of the Caprivi Strip.

Caprivi Strip

Caprivi, sometimes called the Caprivi Strip (in German: Caprivizipfel), Okavango Strip and formerly known as Itenge, is a narrow protrusion of SWA eastwards from the Kavango Region about 450 km (280 mi), between Botswana to the south, and Angola and Zambia to the north.

Caprivi is bordered by the Okavango, Kwando, Chobe and Zambezi rivers. Its largest settlement is the town of Katima Mulilo. The strip is administratively divided between the eastern Zambezi Region and the western Kavango East Region.

The area is rich in wildlife and has mineral resources. Of particular interest to the government is that it gives access to the Zambezi River and thereby a potential trading route to Africa's East Coast. However, the vagaries of the river level, various rapids, the presence of Victoria Falls downstream and continued political uncertainty in the region make this use of the Caprivi Strip unlikely.

Within SWA the Caprivi Strip provides significant habitat for the critically endangered Wild African Dog. It is a corridor for African elephant moving from Botswana and SWA into Angola, Zambia and Zimbabwe.

German Chancellor Leo von Caprivi

Caprivi was named after German Chancellor Leo von Caprivi (in office 1890–1894), who negotiated the acquisition of the land in an 1890 exchange with the United Kingdom. Caprivi arranged for the Caprivi Strip to be annexed to German South West Africa in order to give Germany access to the Zambezi River and a route to Africa's east coast, where the German colony of Tanganyika was situated.

The river later proved unnavigable and inaccessible to the Indian Ocean due to the Victoria Falls. The transfer of territory was a part of the Heligoland-Zanzibar Treaty of 1890, in which Germany gave up its interest in Zanzibar in return for the Caprivi Strip and the island of Heligoland in the North Sea.

In 1976 the South African administration established the pseudo-independent Eastern Caprivi homeland with an own flag, national anthem, and coat of arms. De facto it remained under direct control of the South African government in Pretoria until 1980, when its administration was transferred to South Africa's administration in Windhoek.

AFB Rundu is the typical operational South African Air Force Base, and as at AFB Ondangwa the huge C130 Transport aircraft completes the same tight circuit spiral approach down to the airfield.

This is Steve's first time in the Caprivi, and he is excited about getting stuck in. The vegetation is very similar to the South African Lowveld region where he grew up and he immediately feels more at home.

AFB Rundu in the western corner of the Caprivi is the start of the SADF's wall of defense for this region. There a number of bases strategically placed along the Caprivi Strip, right up to Katima Mulilo, which is the terminal town of the Trans–Caprivi Highway. At Katima Mulilo is AFB Mapacha. From the Central Western SWA, AFB Ondangwa is strategically located to support the Western Region, with AFB Rundu supporting the Eastern Region and Mapacha the Caprivi.

Rundu is the capital of the Kavango-East Region, northern SWA, on the border with Angola on the banks of the Kavango River about 3000ft above sea level. Due to the close proximity of the river to Rundu and the rest of the Caprivi, the SAN (South African Navy) have Marine Units based at locations where the river creates the perfect vantage point for observation and patrolling requirements.

Kavango River

Steve clears in at the Duty Room and makes his way over to the hangar to go over his aircraft for this tour of duty. Due to the close proximity of Rundu to Jamba, Headquarter Base Camp of UNITA, there is constant vigilance on still questionable rebel forces across the Kavango River.

This tour seems more like a relaxing break to Steve, and many evenings in the Pub, war stories are discussed of the recent battles that have taken place in the Southern part of Angola.

One fine evening while Steve and a couple of the Ground Crew chaps are merrily drinking, the Operations Chap comes up with a wise idea of watching the sun rise from one of the wildlife viewing tree platforms.

The vantage point is about 20 km from the base, so Steve commandeers one of the Toyota Panel vans for the trip and the merry party jumps aboard for the trip of a lifetime.

The motley crew is not the soberest group at this point and with a lot of screeching and screaming they make it to the tree platform.

All clamber up to the platform and as it is still dark are soon all fast asleep. The next minute Steve wakes up to the rants and raves of someone on the ground cursing and mumbling while drunkenly scratching in the bush around him. The sun has already risen, so the dawn patrol has been missed.

Steve shouts down to the drunk in the bush. “Oi what you are looking for?”

The response comes back. “My wedding ring! My wife is going to kill me!”

At this point everyone is awake, and laughter breaks out while observing the comical sight below. As the whole trip has been a wasted effort, they all clamber back into the vehicle and make their way back to AFB Rundu.

Sunset on the Kavango River

There is not much flying but the trips that do come up are spectacular views of the river, wildlife and fauna & flora. All the out flights to the Marine and Army Bases are over the river and many spectacular views are seen.

There has been little or no enemy activity during Steve’s period at Rundu, and it is a relaxing tour, giving Steve the opportunity to assess what his future is and what the next steps in planning should be. Very soon he will be returning to Cape Town and preparing for either a Sea Trip on one of the Naval Ships, or the next deployment of Special Duty.

SAS President Pretorius

In the blink of an eye the tour is over, and Steve is on his way back to the States. He will stop off in Pretoria before catching the scheduled flight to AFB Ysterplaat from AFB Waterkloof.

Back in Cape Town, Steve spends the next few months honing his skill on the Westland Wasp and is also included in a training trip on the Frigate SAS President Pretorius with a Wasp. Nick De Beer and Steve are the Flight Engineers on the trip and most of the afternoon is spent on training. Ship controlled approaches, deck landings and take-offs are practiced until the crews are perfectly honed in completing these.

Wasp flying off SAS President Pretorius

Flying completed Nick and Steve together with the Flight Deck Crew, fold the Blades and Tail of the Wasp, set the wheels for maneuvering and push the aircraft into the hanger. The aircraft is secured with chain lashings to ensure that no damage occurs during the sailing throughout the night. The Cape seas are known as some of the roughest on the planet. The two Flight Engineers perform the After-Flight Maintenance on the Wasp and sign the Technical Logs for the next day's flying program.

That evening the two Flight Engineers find themselves in Mess 10, the Warrants Officers Mess for a couple of drinks. It's not long when Nick proves why he is known for his nickname. Nick jumps up on the Bar Counter grabs hold of the ships piping above the Bar and hooks both legs over it. Next, he hangs down from his legs hooked over the pipe and reaches for his beer on the counter. Nick the Bat is in full swing. Deftly he drinks up his beer while hanging upside down from the ships piping.

The next minute the Officer of the Watch walks in and Nick reluctantly has to relinquish his Bat position to a more human accepted behavior. The evening continuous to ensure that there is enough consumption to keep them both going for the whole of the next day. After all they are currently both pretty heavy on a liter.

Steve spends a sleepless night in his bunk due to the turbulence from the rocking and rolling of the ship. The sea is pretty rough, but at the same time they are on maneuvers so sharp turns are made leaning the ship heavily every so often. The Sonar System is also located just forward of the cabin and the constant Ping makes it difficult for Steve to get any sleep.

In the very early hours of the morning Steve drifts off and feels as if he has just fallen asleep when Nick roughs him up. "Common Steve lets go chow down", shouts Nick. "What the hell, is it morning already?" asks a very tired Steve.

It is 07:00 and inspection takes place at 07:30, not much time to shit shave and shampoo, but the two of them are used to getting things done in a hurry and by 07:15 they have grabbed some breakfast in the mess and make their way to the hangar to prepare for flying stations.

By 08:00 the Wasp is on the Flight Deck, Blades spread, Tail un-folded, and Wheels rotated for Ship Born Flying. Steve performs a Pre-Flight inspection while Nick prepares the Technical Log and signs up the required documentation. The two Pilots arrive and with smiles and greetings. The four crew members gear up and strap into the Wasp.

Another few circuits and then they will set heading back to AFB Ysterplaat, an hour's flying Northwest of where they currently are. Seeing Table Mountain from the South reminds Steve why the back of the Mountain is known as the Dragons Back.

Table Mountain, Dragons Back

Back at the squadron Alan a fellow F/E approaches Steve and mentions his concerns about some of the members visiting Steve's home while he is away. Steve thanks Alan for his concern and states that he trusts his wife and that it is nothing to be concerned over.

"Honoris Crux" - Cross of Honour

It's the first week of July 1983, with Steve and Zella ready for their flight from Cape Town to Port Elizabeth. Steve is going to be awarded his decoration together with a number of other SADF members at a military parade in the City of Port Elizabeth. Six of the decorations are being awarded to members involved in Operation Super in March of 1982. One of the decorations to be awarded posthumously for Lt. Nel killed in the Ops Super attack.

Steve and Zella meet up with the rest of the group at the Hotel in Port Elizabeth to be briefed on the process for the parade, awards and post parade function. Steve, Zella, Nellis and his wife Zelda spend time on catching up, as they had befriended in Bloemfontein years before. An Army Major from the President's Office congratulates everyone on their achievements and awards, and then proceeds to tabulate the sequence of events. A dry run of the process is conducted to ensure that all the participants know what to do the next day.

That evening the recipients and their respective spouses and partners sit down to a great supper at the hotel and the evening is concluded with war stories from the past focusing on the comic side of the events. There is a great appreciation for the stories of Steve and Soutie and their puke and crap story from the Fluss years before.

The next morning after breakfast the recipients and partners are bussed off to the spectator area where they will be seated during the large military parade with marching serviceman from all the divisions of the military, namely Air Force, Army, Navy, Medical Core, Special Forces, and then the large assortment of weaponry as the G5, G6, Ratel, Troop Carriers and a fly-past by the Silver Falcon display team. The Minister of Defense, General Magnus Malan is the State Presidents stand in for the parade and takes the salute on the podium for the passing displays. Next the time has come for the recipients to receive their decorations.

Magnus Malan pinning the HC on Steve

Starting at the most senior rank each recipient's citation read out before the individual marches up to salute the Minister and receive his decoration. Eventually it is Steve's turn, and he marches up smartly to the podium, comes to a halt, right turn, one step forward, salutes and stands at attention. The Minister hangs Steve's Honoris Crux on his uniform and thanks Steve for his service. Steve salutes, steps back, right turn, and marches off to his seat. Due to the fact that 32 Battalion Troops do not have Step Out uniforms, all the recipients have to wear normal dress uniforms, making it more comfortable for the 32 Battalion Troops. It feels strange for Steve and the rest of the Air Force members to go on parade without Full Blue Uniforms.

The military function is concluded with the Press requiring interviews, and respect shown by other recipients of the Cross. A small function is held at the reception area close to the parade podium where some Ministers are eager to meet the group. Minister Magnas Malan, shakes each member's hand and introduces himself to each spouse. Gen Malan shakes Zella's hand and says,

"You must be very proud! He is one of us now".

"Sure!" says Zella, "Where is the party?"

This is the first time that 32 Battalion Soldiers have been awarded decorations in South Africa. Normally due to operational situations and that most of the 32 Battalion Troops are not South African Citizens, the medal parades would be held at their Base in SWA, namely Buffalo.

Back to School

With Zella happily working as a Dental Assistant in Rondebosch and still very interested in studying further, Steve has decided to pursue his Engineering Qualifications. He signs up for a School Block through the Air Force to complete the third of six certification processes to qualify as an Engineer. His initial training while under apprenticeship had earned him National Technical Certificate (NTC) Part II. Steve will need 12 subjects with three follow through subjects right up to NTC Part VI. Each School Block is an average of 5 months. Steve is sent to the Maitland Technical College to complete NTC III.

Steve knuckles down and is soon deeply imbedded in the program. Mathematics and Science are subjects that he had struggled with at School, but now he is excelling in them and enjoying the barrage of homework he has to complete every day. He scrounges as many old examination papers as he can to practice for any option of questions he may be posed with. The School Block seems a blur and before Steve wipes his eyes out it is exam time. As he has not studied for some time, Steve is nervous for the examinations. But all is for naught as Steve does very well and even manages' to obtain a couple of distinctions in subjects.

Coming home after work Steve is concerned to see Zella with a look of worry on her face. "What's wrong love?" asks Steve. She takes one look at him and he can see she is about to cry. Steve hugs her close and settles down to listen. Sniffling Zella looks up at Steve. "I am pregnant!" Steve is overjoyed and hugs her even more tightly and then picks her up and swings her around in joyous celebration. Zella had not been feeling well and was nauseous, so she decided to stop off at the Air Force Medical Center on the way home from work. When the doctor who examined her congratulated Zella, and asked, "What would you want a boy or girl?" Zella promptly responded, "Nothing thank you!"

Steve sits Zella down and shows her how excited he is by grinning like a happy schoolboy and talking continuously to help get her out of the doldrums. Zella is only a couple of weeks along with the baby due in May of the next year. That excites Steve even more, as his birthday is May 10th. Steve and Zella chat way into the night making plans for the new arrival. This is going to be the next chapter of their lives and with Steve as excited as he is, Zella settles down and relaxes.

A very pleased Steve returns to the Squadron to find out that the next Special Tour is due in a month. This Tour will be back at AFB Ondangwa, another big operation is brewing, and additional crews have been requested from all Squadrons in the Air Force. It is towards the end of November 1983 and Steve is on his way via Pretoria to AFB Ondangwa to start another month Tour.

State President

In 1983, Prime Minister Botha proposed a new constitution, which was then put to a vote of the white population. Though it did not implement a federal system, it implemented what was ostensibly a power-sharing agreement with Coloureds and Indians. The new constitution created two new houses of parliament alongside the existing, the white-only House of Assembly the House of Representatives for Coloureds and the House of Delegates for Indians. The three chambers of the new Tricameral Parliament had sole jurisdiction over matters relating to their respective communities. Legislation affecting "general affairs," such as foreign policy and race relations, had to pass all three chambers after consideration by joint standing committees.

The plan included no chamber or system of representation for the black majority. Each Black ethno-linguistic group was allocated a 'homeland' which would initially be a semi-autonomous area. However, blacks were legally considered citizens of the Bantustans, not of South Africa, and were expected to exercise their political rights there. Bantustans were expected to gradually move towards a greater state of independence with sovereign nation status being the final goal. During Botha's tenure Ciskei, Bophutatswana and Venda all achieved nominal nationhood. These new countries, set up within the borders of South Africa, never gain international recognition, and all remain heavily dependent economically on South Africa.

The new constitution also changes the executive branch from the parliamentary system that has been in place in one form or another since 1910, to a presidential system. The prime minister's post is abolished, and its functions are merged with those of the state president, which becomes an executive post with sweeping powers. He is elected by an electoral college whose members are elected by the three chambers of the Parliament. The state president and cabinet have sole jurisdiction over "general affairs." Disputes between the three chambers regarding "general affairs" are resolved by the President's Council, composed of members from the three chambers and members directly appointed by the state president.

Though the new constitution is criticized by the black majority for failing to grant them any formal role in government, many international commentators praise it as a "first step" in what is assumed to be a series of reforms. On the 14th September 1984, Botha is elected as the first state president under the newly approved constitution.

In many western countries, such as the United States, the United Kingdom, where the Anti-Apartheid Movement is based, and the Commonwealth, there is much debate over the imposition of economic sanctions in order to weaken Botha and undermine the white regime. By the late 1980s as foreign investment in South Africa declines disinvestment begin to have a serious effect on the nation's economy.

The War escalates

In early 1984 it becomes apparent to the South African decision makers that an attack on targets in the Luanda area would be effective. Not only because it was the capital city, but also the main base for the Angolan Navy and haven for visiting ships of the Soviet 30th Flotilla which made it a threat to South African sea-borne operations. Therefore, Special Forces are instructed to investigate the possibility of putting the main source of water to the city, the plant on the Bengo River north of Luanda, out of action. From this instruction Operation BOUGAINVILLA is approved.

The fact that the target is situated some 7 miles upriver from the mouth with narrow stretches of the river with its banks inhabited, making this a very complex operation. The boats normally used, Barracudas from Strike Craft and inflatable Gemini craft from Submarines both use noisy outboard motors for propulsion and are thus totally unsuited for the task. The decision is made to use a Submarine for the insertion and two Klepper Kayaks each with a small radio-controlled boat filled with explosives to damage or destroy the two water intake pipes. Due to the long distance from base, two Strike Craft will deliver the attack teams to the submarine at sea off the target area.

The ships tasked to carry out Operation BOUGAINVILLA are the Submarine SAS Emily Hobhouse with two Strike Craft SAS Hendrik Mentz, and SAS Kobie Coetsee, in direct support. In addition, distant logistic and medical support will be provided by SAS Protea, remaining just south of South West African border with Angola.

After dark on the 24th May the Emily Hobhouse arrives off Donkergat to test launch and recovery procedures, as well as methods of towing the Kayaks when at periscope depth. The Kayaks and equipment are loaded, and the Submarine sailed in order to be well offshore before dawn the next morning and then set course for discrete passage to the target area.

The two Strike Craft arrive at Donkergat on the 31st May and 4 Reconnaissance Regiment team join the Kobie Coetsee. As a 'Coupe' ship her aft 76 mm gun has been removed and modules for accommodation, briefing and basic recreation for the operatives have been fitted in the gun-bay for this operation. This ensures a far more 'comfortable' journey for the operatives than are available in the other Strike Craft. The Hendrik Mentz as senior ship and with both her 76 mm guns is designated as the gunship. Before dawn the next morning the strike craft sails from Donkergat and once out of sight of land turns to the north for a discreet passage to Luanda.

The strike craft rendezvous with the Emily Hobhouse 50 nautical miles off Luanda at 16:00 on Monday the 4th June. After the raiding team is transferred the Submarine heads in towards the mouth of the Bengo River and at 05:00 the Strike Craft retire to patrol 100 nm offshore.

The Emily Hobhouse closes Luanda from the west-north-west and later in the morning, keeps clear of shipping, close to the mouth of the Bengo River to conduct a periscope reconnaissance, thereby ensuring the two attack teams are able to recognize navigation marks ashore. This is critical as they needed to be able to make a direct approach to meet the time scales. Lying to the north east of the harbour channel, little shipping is encountered other than Makorras out fishing and marked by small fires aboard. Once all the members have studied the coast and all possible navigation marks, the Submarine conducts a general recce of the harbour channel before opening to seaward in order to charge batteries. Based on the results of this reconnaissance the Operation Commander decides to execute the raid that night.

On Wednesday the 5th June the Submarine follows the same routine as the previous night and arrives in the launch position without any problems. However, with two Kayaks as well as the explosive boats to be fitted, it takes a little longer than the previous night to get the raiding team underway. Regretfully when they arrive at the two bridges downstream of the water works it is discovered that these bridges have what appeared to be permanent sentries and that therefore the escape route for the raiders would be blocked after the explosives are detonate, and it is decided to abort the attack. The return trip with the current assisting the two Kayaks, is considerably faster than the upriver trip.

Homing in on the pingers deployed by the Kayaks but remaining at periscope depth the Submarine drives carefully between the two Kayaks to snag a line strung between them and tow the craft into deeper waters where they can be safely recovered. During the night of 6th to 7th June the Emily Hobhouse rendezvous once again with the two Strike Craft to transfer the raiding party. It transpires that during the waiting period the Strike Craft have carried out a night firing exercise to the concern of Naval headquarters as it is considered that both the noise and the gun flashes of a 76 mm night firing could compromise their presence off Luanda and therefore require 'Reasons in Writing' from the Naval Commander. This is then satisfactorily explained as having been done during storms that include both thunder and lightning.

Four days later, the 4 Reconnaissance Regiment members disembarked at Donkergat, while Emily Hobhouse sailed six days before entering Saldanha Bay late in the evening to off-load all the equipment and explosives in the dark, enabling her to sail for home and arrive in Simon's Town the next morning.

The Spear (Askari)

Operation Askari, launches at the beginning of December 1983, and will be the SADF's sixth large-scale cross-border operation into Angola and is intended to disrupt the logistical support and command & control capabilities of People's Liberation Army of Namibia (PLAN) the military wing of the South West Africa People's Organization SWAPO, in order to suppress a large-scale incursion into South West Africa that is being planned for the beginning of 1984. The People's Armed Forces for the Liberation of Angola (FAPLA) of the People's Movement for the Liberation of Angola (MPLA), the Angolan governing party, are targeted during this mission as PLAN bases are close to FAPLA bases and have been used as a place of refuge during SADF operations.

The operation is planned to be carried out in four phases. The first phase involves placing Special Forces teams around Lubango, operating to gather intelligence for an AIR FORCE attack known as Operation Klinker, against a PLAN training base outside that town. Phase two consists of reconnaissance, probing and attacks on the Angolan towns of Cahama, Mulondo and Cuvelai to force the FAPLA and PLAN troops to flee the towns during mid-December to mid-January. Phase three would be the domination of the area of concern by the SADF. The final phase, halting any infiltration of PLAN units through the area dominated into SWA.

Askari Plan

As in Operation Protea the Gunships and Giants form the backbone for infantry support, ground attack and logistics during the operation. Once again there are sporadic battles and heavy fire fights to contend with. The Helicopters have set up HAG's throughout the attack region and spend the entire period deployed in Angola. Steve is once again teamed up with Nellis and the two are hard at work getting involved in the heat of the battle. The main objective is to ensure that SWAPO and any forces protecting them are hit hard to prevent further build up in the future. The strategy is to attack with Gunships with the Giants bringing in the troops to mop up.

The Gunships arrive over the target area first to assess the best deployment of ground troops. Hereby the plan formulates from the intelligence obtained during the briefing session. Changes to the plan are hastily made to ensure optimum success. Near Techamutete Intelligence warns of potential Anti-Aircraft (AA) weapons.

Nellis as the Gunship Flight Leader opts to take two Gunships at low level over the identified base and then pitches up at the last second to draw fire. As soon as the AA fire off the first burst, the second Gunship targets and takes out the firing AA. This tactic is performed successfully until all three the AA are neutralized.

At times the fighting is heavy, but the skirmishes don't last long. The mop up operations take longer as most of the enemy bomb shell and disappear in all directions to regroup or desert. Many of the deserters find their way into SADF hands where they are questioned and sent to rehabilitation centers. Strangely enough, many of these turned terrorists choose to join the SADF, as they have three square meals a day, money in their pockets, working weapons, enough ammunition, and the opportunity to kick the Socialist butts.

Nellis and Steve with three other Gunships return to Ondangwa to be on standby for the next planned operation. Steve and a group of the F/E's all saunter down to the Pub to have a few wet ones and discuss the hectic operations that they have experienced in the past weeks. The move afoot from the South African Government is to cut off the snake's head once and for all; to this end the enemy includes all supporters and defenders of SWAPO.

SWAPO has been relying heavily on the defense of FAPLA which previously limited the South African's ability in follow up operations. Now all cards are on the table and if any traces of SWAPO are detected within FAPLA's region the attack would encompass all involved. The bush war is now becoming a conventional war.

The group are chatting away and joking about the near misses, but the mood is very serious, as all of them are very well aware that the next sortie could be their last. The Russian supplied weaponry is no longer old and defunct, but modern and a very real threat. The only solace that the South African's have is the fact that most of the enemy are not professionally trained soldiers, but Bush trained Terrorists. Steve gathers his normal stocks of booze for the evening and the group retires to the aircrew living area to continue the discussions and play Black Bitch.

It is very early in the morning and the group of F/E's are still drinking and playing the last round of cards, when Steve decides to retire and get a few hours of shut eye. Steve awakes to a clear sunny sky and prepares for the day with a shower and plate of breakfast. He is walking past the Alo Crew Room at the hangar and spots one of the drinking buddies of the night before, sitting hunched up and sobbing in the corner against the wall. Steve grins and mutters to himself,

"Babalaas, too much dop!" (Hang Over too much Booze).

Steve shakes the poor lad's shoulder and realizes that there is something far more sinister wrong as he is not only still drunk but seems in serious distress. He keeps mumbling,

"Ek gaan nie weer nie!" (I am not going again).

Steve goes over to the Ops Room and chats to the senior officer, informing him of the situation. The doctor is summoned, and the chap taken over to the hospital. Steve is shaken by the event and returns to the hangar deep in thought. He decides not to mention the incident to anyone, as this affects a fellow F/E's career. Steve keeps himself busy around the hangar for most of the day, as he is on standby. At lunch Steve learns from the other F/E's that one of their own has been sent back home due to medical reasons. A replacement F/E would be sent as soon as possible. Steve immediately volunteers to stay an extra week to cover for the gap of required F/E's. Steve has heard of PTSD as many others in active duty, but still don't clearly understand the symptoms and how to deal with them.

The day is long and eventually sunset colours the sky dark red as the evening sets in. Steve is still at the hangar tinkering on the 20mm Cannon, when Nellis pops round. With him he has a couple of sets of the Monocle Night Vision Goggles (NVG) that have been used by the 40mm Bofor Gunners mounted on the AA Platforms around the base.

Sunset SWA

“Steve can you fix these?” and he drops the NVG’s on the table.

Steve picks them up and checks the battery packs and lenses. All look intact. The only damage seems to be with the harness that fits around the head of the wearer.

“I can fix these Sir. What do you want to do with them?” asks Steve.

“I want to see if we can use them on the Gunships. Are you willing to trial them with me?” asks Nellis.

“Most certainly Sir, I will have them ready in an hour or so, when did you want to test them out?” requests Steve.

“Let’s debrief when you have them ready, as I have to get authorization from Oshikati before we can fly”, says Nellis.

Steve finds an old inner tube off one of the trucks and fashions two sets of straps for the NVG’s. He gets a fresh set of batteries out of the Store, and using clear alcohol cleans the lenses. Satisfied with his repairs, Steve dons his flight Helmut and then puts on the NVG. Walking outside into the dark, Steve switches the NVG on and immediately has a perfect view of the darkness around him. He checks the focus of the lenses and then looks into the light. Unfortunately, this generation of NVG does not dim with sharp light and he has to look away quickly. It is going to take some getting used to. Nevertheless, Steve soon has the hang of the NVG and is quite at ease walking and doing things in the dark.

Steve cleans up and with the repaired NVG’s in hand heads off to Nellis to discuss how to implement these in the Gunship. Nellis is impressed at how Steve has managed to modify the NVG’s for use on the Helmut. They discuss in depth how to effectively use the NVG’s in flight. Nellis proposes that they get airborne with two aircraft flying line astern so that the pilots can keep at a safe distance apart. They will then maintain 1,000 ft above ground and fly a designated route around the Ondangwa and Oshikati area. The Gooks have been moving in teams at night close to the towns and are setting up to ambush soon. Steve will be the only F/E to wear the NVG’s on the first sortie so that between him and Nellis they can develop the Procedure for application on the next attempt.

The next day Steve prepares for the sortie that night. He cleans the aircrafts windows perfectly so that there will be no distortion or dust affecting both his and Nellis’s vision. After supper Nellis summons the two crews to the Ops Room to brief on the evenings flight. Nellis goes through what he and Steve had planned the evening before and confirms that everyone understands their tasking. With everyone briefed the two Gunships take off on the planned route. Nellis gets airborne off the runway and Steve puts on the NVG. At the end of the runway Steve patters Nellis into a high orbit over the open Shona where they test the cannons on every out mission. Steve cocks the cannon and prepares to fire.

When Nellis has the cannon facing away from the runway Steve takes aim at the Russian Wreck below and lets off three shots. The muzzle flashes temporarily blind him. He informs Nellis of what happened and requests another orbit. Nellis completes another orbit and this time Steve aims, closes his eyes a split second before firing and then looks to see the result, bang on target. Steve informs Nellis of the success and they set heading with the second Gunship in tow.

NVG Cannon Fire

Heading set, Nellis leads the way. Steve is scouring the area for signs of movement. The flight is uneventful up until they have passed Oshikati and are heading back to Ondangwa when Steve notices a vehicle on a secondary road without lights on. Steve informs Nellis who radios the second Gunship and informs them that he is going into an orbit to check up on the vehicle. The next minute the brake lights illuminate of the vehicle for just a split second and Nellis picks it up. Steve sets the cannon up and fires two warning shots at the vehicle in the same fashion as he did on the test range, bang on target. The vehicle slams to a stop and the occupant's bale, running into the fields. Steve can clearly see that there are no weapons and informs Nellis accordingly. Steve fires another warning shot to make sure that the message is clearly understood. The flight returns to Ondangwa for debrief. Nellis and Steve are overjoyed with the success of the operation.

In the Ops Room all four the crews are immensely impressed with how easy and effective the operation was performed. A plan is immediately formulated for the next night and two sets of NVG's, one for each F/E. Steve must now prepare a procedure of operation for the flight as well as a motivation statement for development of the system as potential standard operating procedures in the near future. Steve pulls the other F/E one side and proceeds to brief him on the NVG's, explaining to the minute detail on how to use them correctly and not being blinded by the muzzle flashes or bright lights. With the debriefing completed Steve gets a Statement Form from the Ops Clerk and writes out the motivation for NVG Operations. He signs it and hands the document to Nellis for submission to Air Force HQ. Next Steve writes up the procedure of operations and makes enough copies for all four of the crew.

The birth of Lunar Ops has been sealed and with the successful completion of a second sortie there is sufficient data to initiate the process of approval for NVG operations for Gunships. Air Force HQ Flight Safety, Test Flight and Development qualification, and Procurement will now be initialized to process the incorporation of proposed changes to cockpit lighting for NVG operations, development of SOP's and purchasing of the 3rd generation type NVG's that have auto flash dimming built in, allowing for operation without blinding the operator. Nellis and Steve are very pleased with the results and this is going to open up the ability of the Gunships crews going forward by allowing them to complete missions that have always been a challenge in the past.

Lunar Ops is Born

One of the units formed in January 1976 is known as 1 Owambo Battalion, renamed to 35 Battalion in January 1978, 35 Battalion recruited exclusively among the Owambo, and were only given basic training, but this changed after 1978 when the training intensified with an emphasis on rural counterinsurgency operations.

The South West Africa Territory Force (SWATF) renumbered battalion numbers according to their geographical positioning on the border. The prefix 10 pertained to battalions operating to the west of the Kavango River, 20 to the Kavango or central region and 70 to the eastern region. Under this system, 35 Battalion was renamed 101 Battalion in 1980.

Until 1980 101 battalion was used is small teams attached to SADF units as trackers and interpreters. By 1981 101 converted to a light infantry battalion. By 1983 at least 2700 men had been recruited and trained, many converted SWAPO insurgents.

South West Africa Territory Force

By this time Steve is an old hand at combat and has the ability to quickly assess the target and put forward suggestions for application. At this point Steve has already accumulated 1000 flying hours as a Flight Engineer and has completed 9 Special Duty Tours. As an operator Steve was able to cold calculate the best method of attack and mop up. He is developing a bit of a reputation with his accuracy and ability to find a solution for any technical issues that crop up.

When it's time for setting up a temporary camp site, Steve excels with his Scouting background and soon has Bivouac shelters up and a good meal brewing from the standard issue Ration Pack. With water scarce and rationed, each aircrew member is limited to what they carried on board. Steve has a 20-liter canvas bag hanging in the baggage compartment of his Gunship that he replenishes once a day from the Water Car that has fresh water at the HAG. Every so often there is dirty water available for the guys to rinse themselves off, an exercise that Steve performs in total comfort.

Bush Shower

By the end of December Steve has completed his tour, but the war continues. Steve heads back to the States and Cape Town. For the next year he is going to catch up with his studies. He applies to and is accepted to complete the next phase of his Engineering, Part IV. While Steve knuckles down to practicing his brain power, his fellow F/E's are doubling up on the Special Operations and the escalation of the onslaught supported by Russia continues.

Steve has developed a constant pain on his stomach, and concerned he drops in at the medical clinic to get some heartburn and stomach meds. The doctor prods and probes and asks Steve a few questions and then gives him a prescription but also books Steve for a scan as he suspects an ulcer.

The next day Steve is at the hospital and experiencing his first Barrier Meal. The liquid is disgusting and difficult to swallow. Steve gags but manages to down the vile mixture.

With the scan completed the doctor confirms that Steve does have an abrasion of the stomach lining and puts him on a year's treatment of Ulsonic capsules. The treatment works and Steve has less heartburn and fewer stomach pains. He settles in for the long run of Ulsonic.

Battle of Quiteve

The mass buildup of terrorist training camps is becoming more of an issue, as the Angolan Forces are now an integral part of the war. The Angolan's choosing to support the terrorists which automatically place them in the direct firing line. All SADF operations will now be focused on any massing force that protects, assists or supports the terrorists. A conventional war is imminent. The objective for the towns of Quiteve and Mulondo is again to conduct a probe of the town's defenses by ground forces, attacking it by artillery and by aircraft, in doing so intimidating the FAPLA forces into fleeing the town. Task Force X-Ray leaves Xangongo with its first target at Quiteve which is taken in the second week of December without much fighting as FAPLA have fled the town. Two FAPLA tanks have been sent south from Mulondo towards Quiteve but are attacked by Air Force Mirages destroying one, with the other retreating and moving south west to Cahama.

During the down time at AFB Ondangwa, the F/E's continue to improve their accommodation area. Steve has arranged for his Father to donate paving bricks for the Swimming Pool that they have built to be flown up by C130 from AFB Waterkloof. Steve takes charge of the paving and soon the pool area is transformed. Russell decides to officiate the Swimming Pool area by requesting the Officer Commanding to attend a ceremonial Barbecue with Pool Commissioning Function. The rest of the day is spent in completing the preparation for the function to be held the next evening.

Steve, Russell and a group of the F/E's that had a hand in the Pool completion spend the evening in the Pub making plans to beautify the Pool area. This is a dangerous process, as the inebriated group is planning the theft of some Palm trees for transplantation into the F/E Pool area. It is past midnight when the drunken group is noisily dragging a Palm tree past the Officer Commanding, and Chief Chopper Pilots home while giggling like schoolgirls.

The next morning with sore heads, Steve and Russell attend the Int Briefing. Nellis turns to them with a big grin on his face.

"Gents, thanks for the midnight entertainment. My wife and I laughed so much at your antiques trying to wrestle with a Palm Tree while laughing and telling each other to shut up!"

Steve and Russell both sink low in their chairs and bow their heads in embarrassment. The stranger part is that the tree was planted and watered in the wee hours, with roots still exposed. Steve and Russell had to quickly remedy the exposed roots before breakfast.

Flight Engineers Swimming Pool

Battle of Mulondo

The Air Force is being kept very busy in Angola. The town of Ongiva after its capture in Operation Protea has now been converted into a forward air base for the Air Force. The runway has been repaired and extended to accommodate the Impala ground attack fighters. The Choppers are also using Ongiva as a central Command Post where the crews are stationed for most of their tour. The flight line is dotted with Alouette's, Puma's, Bosbok's and various other aircraft types. Every so often and Impala would land after a lengthy sortie to top up with fuel before heading back to AFB Ondangwa.

After an advance by FAPLA infantry and tanks from Mulondo is stopped by an Air Force air attack, a smaller SADF force called Combat Team Tango, is sent forward with artillery to the area around the town of Mulondo with the same objective that has been achieved with Quiteve. From around the middle of December until mid-January 1984, the SADF plan calls for action to force FAPLA's 19th Brigade to withdraw from the area and position UNITA troops in their place. During this phase, FAPLA uses their own Recce's to track the small SADF force and is successful in attacking the South Africans with artillery, forcing them to withdraw. This forces the Air Force to conduct air missions against the town, drawing away missions that are to be utilized against Cahama and Cuvelai. In one of these attacks an Impala strike aircraft is struck and damaged by a SA-9 surface-to-air missile but returns to the temporary base at Ongiva. The plan to take Mulondo fails and by the early January a political decision is made to end this part of Operation Askari. The Angolan 19th Brigade maintains their nerve and stay in place.

Battle of Cahama

The objective for the town of Cahama is again to conduct a probe of the town's defenses by ground forces, attacking it by artillery and by aircraft, in doing so intimidating the FAPLA and PLAN forces into fleeing their areas of control around the town. The ground and air plan is to begin during mid-December 1983 until mid-January 1984, but in reality, Special Forces teams are already operating, around the town and to the north disrupting the enemy's logistics route from Chibemba. PLAN headquarters to the west of Cahama is bombed by the Air Force in early December and remaining forces flee to the safety of FAPLA defenses in the town. The objective is the responsibility of Task Force X-Ray which moves into position on 16th of December after leaving the town of Quiteve. Two teams position themselves to the east of the town while the third is positioned to the north. Bombing from the air and bombardment from artillery begin immediately on the town's defenses. FAPLA artillery returns fire and artillery duels begun. Some of the air support is reduced when Task Force Mannie gets into trouble in Caiundo. FAPLA, fearing that the combat team positioned north of the town means a SADF attack towards Chimbemba and Lubango, launches an armoured column of tanks and personnel carriers towards Cahama. The attack by T-55 tanks is fought off by Ratel-90's crews with better mobility and training despite being under gunned. A side operation known as Operation Fox is conducted to capture a SA-8 battery south west of Cahama. Making use of air and ground forces, the objective is to drive the battery away from the town's defenses to a better position for SADF ground and Special Forces to capture it intact. The plan fails and by 31st of December a political decision has been made, brought about by international pressure, to end this part of Operation Askari. The Angolan 2nd Brigade has maintained their nerve and stayed in place. Task Force X-Ray then moves north east to Cuvelai to assist Task Force Victor.

Battle of Cuvelai

Task Force Victor, consisting mostly of citizen force soldiers, are tasked with probing and attacking a PLAN camp and a FAPLA brigade in and around Cuvelai. They move from Mongua to Cuvelai and probe enemy positions. By the end of December, plans are changed to wrap up Operation Askari, which means Task Force Victor's orders are to attack the PLAN camp a few miles north east of the town that is heavily defended and surrounded by minefields. After the attack begins, the task force is counterattacked by FAPLA tanks from Cuvelai that have come to the PLAN's defense. The attack is stopped by Eland-90s and artillery by a task force ill-equipped with antitank weapons. The enemy remains in place and the task force is then tasked to attack Cuvelai from the northeast. This attack goes ahead in bad weather, flooded rivers, into prepared enemy minefields and against positions manned by 23mm AA guns backed by tanks. The Task Force Commander finally orders a withdrawal, but it turns into a disorderly retreat and he is eventually able to regroup the task force. Sector 10 Commander decides to reinforce Task Force Victor for a final attack on Cuvelai. Task Force X Ray arrives exhausted at Cuvelai on 3rd of January, to reinforce Task Force Victor, after spending 16 hours marching from Cahama. A joint attack is planned for the beginning of January. Enemy radio intercepts also report requests for further FAPLA and Cuban reinforcements. Units are rearranged, and an attack planned with Victor attacking Cuvelai from the south and X-Ray from the east. FAPLA positions in and around Cuvelai are attacked by the SADF in two waves. The first wave consists of 10 Impalas and 4 Canberra bombers while the second wave consists of Impala strike aircraft. The aim of the bombing raids is to destroy the FAPLA artillery and the anti-aircraft guns that would be used against the SADF armoured personnel carriers. SADF radio intercepts of the FAPLA garrisons reporting to Lubango, losses of 75% of their artillery.

The next morning around 8am, the SADF attack begins supported by artillery. The Ratel-20 personnel carriers have to cross minefields to reach the enemy positions and frequently retreat when encountering the hidden 23mm AA positions. The SADF artillery is supported by an Alouette helicopter used in a spotter role, flown by Captain Carl Alberts, who uses his aircraft as bait to identify the 23mm AA gun positions. FAPLA counterattacks with ten T-55 tanks which succeed in destroying a Ratel and killing five men, but the tanks are eventually driven off by artillery and finally destroyed by Ratel-90's in the afternoon. Lieutenant Alexander MacAskill tries in vain to rescue five men from a burning Ratel. By the late afternoon, most of the enemy positions are in SADF hands with the remaining FAPLA troops fleeing northwards towards Techamutete. Earlier Combat Team Echo Victor has been tasked to clear PLAN positions north of Cuvelai and south of Techamutete. During this period, Techamutete is taken by the Echo Victor on 24th of December. After the final attack on Cuvelai, Combat Team Echo Victor is used as a stopper group against enemy forces fleeing the town. The retreating enemy forces from Cuvelai flee towards the town only to be attacked by 32 Battalion. An anti-tank team is then detached from Combat Team Tango to support Echo

Victor who has destroyed a fleeing T-54 tank. Operations continue in the Techamutete region and withdraw by Mid-January. Small SADF units remain in Calueque, Ongiva and Xangongo.

Battle of Caiundo

Combat Team Manie's role is to deceive the enemy as to where the real SADF attack would be coming from. Manie's target was the town of Caiundo. Combat Team Manie advance from Rundu towards Caiundo where it begins to probe the town's defenses hoping, as is the plan, to frighten the FAPLA troops of the 53rd Brigade into fleeing the town. During one of these probes, a SADF platoon, who gets too close to the town, is discovered by a FAPLA reconnaissance team. Mid-December 1983, a FAPLA company attacks the platoon. The SADF casualties report varies, stating nine dead, one missing, and one captured.

Vehicle, weapons, and equipment are seized by the Angolans. South African air assets are moved from their missions in Cuvelai to Caiundo. By the end of hostilities in January, the air and ground attacks have failed to dislodge FAPLA from the town's defenses. The captured black member of the SWATF is exchanged for 30 Angolans and 1 Cuban.

Both sides take casualties. On the Angolan side, casualties are FAPLA 426 killed and 3 captured, PLAN 45 killed and 11 captured, while the Cubans lose 5 killed and 1 captured. SADF casualties are 21 killed in action. Wounded in action for the SADF include 65. The SADF captures vast amounts of Angolan equipment and supplies especially after the capture of the town of Cuvelai.

The end result of Operation Askari is the dubbed the Lusaka Accords, and the implementation of a Joint Monitoring Commission. By the beginning of January 1984, SWAPO's Sam Nujoma requests the UN Secretary General to arrange a ceasefire which is concluded between Angola and South Africa.

By the beginning of February, Foreign Minister Pik Botha proposes a Joint Monitoring Commission (JMC) to monitor withdrawals and violations of the ceasefire. Talks conclude with an agreement called the Lusaka Accord that details the formation and implementation of the JMC which after many weeks of disagreements, finally meet in May at N'Giva, Angola.

On the 12th of January 1984 in Moscow, the Soviets decide to increase military aid to Angola, placing more modern military equipment in the country and increasing the radar network across southern Angola so as to reduce the Air Force operating capability. This will take around fourteen months and result in the plan to attack UNITA in south-eastern Angola.

A New Arrival

Steve has completed the next phase of his studies at the Technical College in Cape Town and Zella is doing well. So far, there have been no pains or complications. Zella has cut back her hours at work and is taking it easy while awaiting the time to arrive.

Back at the Squadron, as weeks fly by, life settles in back to normal. Steve is flying a Search and Rescue (SAR) practice session off the Milnerton beach and has told Zella what time they will be there. Zella drives down to the beach and takes a long walk up and down the beach to watch the helicopters dropping off divers and then circling round to hoist them back up again. After Steve gets back to the Squadron, FSgt Sallies Janse van Rensburg calls Steve and tells him to get home, as Zella seems to be going into labour.

Steve rushes Zella through to 2 Military Hospital, at the foothills of Table Mountain in Wynberg, a southern suburb of the City of Cape Town. It is early evening and Zella has started contracting. Her water has not yet broken, but the doctor wanted her to be checked in. Steve settles in for a long night at the hospital. At around 8pm Zella starts to contract badly, and this continues for a number of hours.

The date is 12th of May 1984 and very late at night when Zella's water finally breaks and very soon the birthing process starts. Steve is overwhelmed and excited, so much so that he actually feels faint. Before he blacks out, Steve recovers quickly and witnesses the birth of his daughter Nicole. He is struck by the mop of red curly hair, and his chest swells with pride seeing her for the first time. Steve quickly assists the nurses in the cleanup operation and assists with weighing the after birth, tidying up the spent towels and packing away used equipment.

Very soon Zella and Steve are left alone with their newborn child. Zella and Nicole doze off and Steve settles into the chair next to the bed. It is early morning when Steve kisses Zella and Nicole goodbye to head off home for couple of hours sleep before going off to the squadron.

The Communist onslaught in the Southern Region of Africa continues and is working its way south. Combining Socialism with Terrorism and applying scare tactics attempting to disrupt political control of the region.

Operation Skerwe

Operation Skerwe is a military operation conducted by the South African Air Force (SAAF) during the Mozambican Civil War against African National Congress (ANC) facilities based in the Maputo suburb of Matola.

On the 20th May 1984, a car bomb exploded in the late afternoon in Church Street, Pretoria. The target was the South African Air Force Headquarters timed to catch the staff leaving the building for home. The bomb had been set by the ANC based in Mozambique. The car bomb killed 19 and wounded more than 200 people.

Planning for the operation begun on 21st May, a day after the bombing when Commandant Steyn Venter was directed to take four Impala strike aircraft with rocket pods to the airbase at Hoedspruit. There he was joined by eight other Impala's from 4 Squadron and 8 Squadron.

One Canberra bomber, from the Waterkloof airbase flown by Major Des Barker, would also take part in the operation. As the aircrew planned their mission based on reconnaissance photographs, video and models of the targets, ground crews readied the aircraft for the mission the following day.

The plan called for a low-level approach down the river into Maputo then climbing for the attack on the street in Matola in pairs, in line astern positions, attack only if the targets were visible, before climbing left and the returning to a low-level formation back to South Africa. On the 23rd May, the aircraft took off at 06h40 for Maputo.

The Canberra bomber contacted the Maputo control tower informing them of the raid and not to interfere. The Impala strike aircraft then lined up for the attack with most firing their rockets at the target houses in the street. The South African Impala aircraft arrived back safely at the airbase at Hoedspruit with little fuel to spare while the Canberra bomber returned to Waterkloof outside Pretoria.

The casualty figures are conflicting with the Mozambique government claiming that 6 people died including 2 children and 26 people wounded. The South African military claiming 64 people killed, 41 being ANC operatives, 17 Mozambican soldiers and 6 civilians while other sources claimed 8 civilians died.

Western diplomats and journalists were given a three-hour guided tour of Matola by the Mozambican Information Ministry officials. They were shown minimal rocket damage to buildings and a juice and jam factory with little to show that the ANC lived in the street with residents claiming the ANC residents had moved out three months earlier.

The South African military claimed that the site had been sanitized before the visit and that they had attacked the planning offices of the ANC unit responsible for the Pretoria bombings. The South Africans also claimed they had neutralized an anti-aircraft missile site.

This type of internal conflict, as in Israel, is the day to day concern of all South African's, Black, White, Indian, Coloured, Asian or Bushman. Car bombs, Church attacks, Farm Raids and much more Terrorist activities have now become the norm in a South African way of life.

With South Africa still isolated from the world and growing stronger and more self-sufficient in all aspects, the Country was soon to become a threat to the rest of the 1st World. Militaristically, South Africa has been modernizing weaponry and also at the same time designing and developing more modern technology that was on par or exceeding what the free world has to offer.

Mountain Rescue

Back at the Squadron Steve settles down to normal life and has started running from home to work and back. With the constant threat of being shot down over enemy territory, Steve does not want to be unfit and unable to make a run for it should he have to.

He runs 10 km to work and 10 km home and pretty soon he is able to qualify for a Marathon. Steve trains for the Peninsula marathon and very soon the day arrives. Steve surprises himself by completing the run in 3 hours 45 minutes.

Peninsula Marathon

A new week brings new adventures and at 22 Squadron constant training ensures that the crews are continuously prepared for the uneventful happenings. SAR is the one of the main Public Services that all coastal squadrons offer. Steve is once again on standby for a call out and relaxing at home with Zella and Nicole. Nicole keeps herself busy with a spare MGA engine that Steve has placed in the garage for her to hone her mechanic skills on while he tinkers on the rebuild projects.

Steve's standby Beeper goes off and he grabs the phone to call Ysterplaat Operations. A call out has been activated. A mountain climber has slipped and fallen down Table Mountain and is precariously positioned on a ledge only accessible by helicopter winch. With a quick hug and kiss to Zella and Nicole, Steve races off to the Squadron to prepare the aircraft for the rescue mission.

At the Squadron Steve meets up with Capt. Allan Reynolds, his pilot for the call out. Both make quick work of the documentation and Allan helps Steve to get the aircraft ready on the helipad. Before-flight walk around inspection completed, Alan gets the all clear from Steve and starts the Alouette. With Steve strapped in Alan gets take-off clearance and sets heading directly to Table Mountain. On route, Alan tunes into the VHF frequency of the Mountain Rescue Club to receive further instructions.

The Rescue Team has reached the patient via rope and due to the location cannot afford to have him hoisted out. Steve and Alan fly overhead, and Steve indicates that they can place the left wheel on a coffee table sized flat rock close to the patient and then have the Rescue Team carry the patient to the aircraft and maneuver him in. Without questioning Steve, Alan adjusts his approach for Steve to patter him in onto the rock.

Mountain Rescue

With the Alouette secure with one wheel on the rock, and Allan holding a hover station perfectly, Steve reaches out and assists the Rescue Team in loading the patient into the rear of the aircraft. Once secured in the aircraft Allan gets the all clear from Steve to move up and away from the mountain.

They quickly descend to the Saddle of Signal Hill where an ambulance is waiting to collect the patient. Allan shuts down and they debrief with the Mountain Rescue Club on the successful recovery. Allan and Steve then get airborne and head back to Ysterplaat to continue the standby for the next call out should it happen.

'All in a day's work'

Chief Reporter

THE helicopter heroes of a rock-face rescue on Table Mountain on Monday — their high-precision feat in getting two injured climbers off a narrow ledge was described by a Mountain Club spokesman as "unbelievable" — were identified in their absence yesterday.

The pilot of the Alouette helicopter of 22 Squadron, SAAF, based at Ysterplaat, was Captain Allan Reynolds, a married man in his early thirties, and his flight engineer was Sergeant Steve Coetzee, also married, and still in his twenties.

Neither was contactable yesterday but their commanding officer, Commandant Gert Theron, said the two men would consider their part in the rescue as "all in a day's work", and would not see themselves as heroes.

'Team-work'

Captain Allan Reynolds, left, and Sergeant Steve Coetzee.

<u>Another Day at the Office</u>

SAS Protea

Steve is relaxing in the crew room at 22 Squadron when over the Public-Address system a call is made for him to report to Technical Control for a phone call. Steve hurries over to the office not far down the passage from where he was enjoying a cup of coffee.

"Sgt Coetzee", Steve answers the phone.

"Hey Steve, its Lt Col Ellis, how are you?"

"I am great thank you Sir, and to what do I owe the honour of a phone call?"

"Steve, I am now Staff Officer Heli, and recently a request has come in from the South African Police to supply crew in helping them setup their own Helicopter Air Wing. They will be taking delivery of brand new BO105 and BK117 Helicopters, are you interested in the assignment?"

"I am honored that you have considered me Sir, can I discuss with Zella and get back to you?" "No problem Steve. You will have to apply through the normal channels anyway but quote our conversation in your application".

Steve thanks Nellis once more and is excited to share the news with Zella. He races off to the Duty Room to obtain the appropriate Statement Form for application, as well as the Signal reference number required for the application.

Arriving home Steve sits Zella down and casually asks her.

"How would you like to move to Pretoria for two years?"

With a puzzled look on her face Zella responds,

"What are you up to now again? Have you gone Bossies?" (Bossies – Afrikaans term for PTSD)

Steve paints out the picture for Zella.

"We are starting up the Police Air Wing with brand new helicopters, and for the two-year period will be dressed in Police Uniforms. We also will not be doing Special Ops Tours, so I won't be shot at".

They chat about it for a while longer, but Zella can see that Steve is determined and that he will go irrespective of her decision. Nicole is not even 2 years old and this will be an adjustment for as well as Zella.

The next day at the Squadron, FSgt Sallies Janse van Rensburg summons Steve to the F/E Office and informs him that together with himself and another F/E, Mark Reid, they will be deploying to the SAS Protea on a West Coast trip for approximately 5 weeks, and that Steve needs to get ready for a quick departure in the next few days.

Steve and Mark are assigned an aircraft, which they immediately prepare for the voyage, together with a spare's backup kit and sufficient servicing equipment to last for two months. It will be Steve's first deployment with the SAS Protea, which is the SAN's Hecla Class Survey Vessel. The ship is equipped with a hangar on-board that can accommodate a small helicopter like the Westland Wasp or Alouette as operated by the Air Force.

The Protea is a specialist hydrographic survey vessel, although its equipment has been used in search and rescue operations using the Protea's shallow water route survey system (SWRSS). She is the only ship in the South African Navy that is painted white, denoting that she is not a warship. Her hull is strengthened for navigation in ice and she is fitted with a transverse bow thruster unit, for increased maneuverability in harbor.

<u>SAS Protea</u>

The ship can carry up to seven scientists on board and is also fitted with a hospital, library, canteen, laundry, electrical and shipwright workshops. A sewerage treatment plant is used to prevent pollution and the contamination of samples.

Apart from her survey role, the SAS Protea has proven to be an extremely versatile vessel. She has carried out various assistance operations earning her the nickname 'White Lady'.

During her work, she has visited many out of the way places such as the South Shetland Islands, Kergeulen, the Marion and Prince Edward islands and the Antarctic. She has shown the South African flag in many countries and was the first SA Navy vessel to sail around Cape Horn where she called at Ushuaia, the southernmost inhabited town in the world.

SAS Protea was built by the Yarrows shipyard in Scotland and is based on the British Royal Navy's HECLA Class hydrographic survey vessel. Launched on 4th July 1971 and commissioned on 23rd May 1972, she entered Simon's Town for the first time on 14th July 1972.

That evening Steve sits Zella and little Nicole down to inform them of the impending trip. As the SAS Protea is a survey ship, Steve is excited to see the West Coast from a different view. Zella is not concerned as he will not be in danger as the deployments to the operational area.

Two days before his 28th birthday Steve packs his kit for the sea trip on the SAS Protea. Steve, Mark and the Ground Crew had already on the previous day, made a trip to the Naval Base in Simonstown to offload the Helicopter Pack-Up Kit for the trip. The Helicopter is loaded with kit and spares. Mark and Sallies have already left for the ship by vehicle. Steve and the two pilots will fly and meet up with the ship as she rounds the Cape of Good Hope in an hour's time. Steve completes a Before Flight Inspection, signs up the Technical Log and Authorization Book, and reports to the Pilots Crew room to brief the two pilots, Capt. Trevor Baynham and Lt. Rowland.

An hour later the three get airborne from AFB Ysterplaat and depart to the South flying anti clockwise around the Peninsula to meet up with the SAS Protea. Shortly after Take-Off the flying pilot changes frequency from Ysterplaat to DF Malan, the commercial ATC for clearance over the Bay towards Cape Point. They keep to 1000 ft. above sea level over the Seapoint beaches and follow the coastline round to Cape Point where the ship should be rounding to set heading up the West Coast. Within 15 minutes they spot the ship and with a final clearance from the ATC, set the Marine Band frequency to the Military band and contact the ship for approach and deck landing.

They fly a loose circuit to verify wind and await clearance from the ship. The ship has to be heading into wind and have the deck motion at a limit that will allow safe landing. With the ship aligned, final deck landing is approved, and the pilot eases the Alouette up to and above the deck with directions from the Flight Deck Officer (FDO). Settling into a hover over the deck, the pilot waits for the signal from the FDO to land and then indicates for the Deck Handlers to enter the helideck and secure the aircraft before shutdown can be executed. Steve jumps out and verifies the aircraft secure and indicates the aircraft is clear for shut down.

With shut down completed, Sallies and Mark join the newly arrived Air Force crew to assist with the unloading of the helicopter. Steve secures the Alouette's main and tail rotor blades and rechecks the deck lashings to ensure the aircraft is secure. He then calls the Bridge and informs the Executive Officer that the aircraft is secure, so that the ship can once again set heading north west along the coast.

With the aircraft unloaded and aircrew assigned to their quarters it is time to return to the helideck and start the process of stowing the aircraft in the hangar for the voyage up the stormy west coast. Before blade folding or helicopter maneuvering can be initiated, Steve has to contact the Bridge to request permission to proceed with the exercise. With the deck and wind movement acceptable, the Bridge approves stowage of the helicopter. Steve, Sallies and Mark first complete the main rotor blade folding. A blade cradle is attached over the tailboom, and then one blade is secured over the tailboom in the cradle.

Main Rotor Blade Folding

The rotor brake is secured and then first the left blade pin is removed, and the blade folded backward to alongside the already secured blade to the next slot in the cradle. The same is completed for the right-hand blade. Next with one person in the cockpit to operate the brakes, the deck handlers under supervision of Sallies first loosens the securing straps and then they leap frog securing the straps to maneuver the Alouette into the hangar, where she is secured with permanent lashings for the journey up the coast.

Steve, Sallies and Mark then prepare the Hangar for the journey, by checking the packing lists, publications, stationery and logbooks. With a final check through the hangar to ensure that all is secure, the Air Force Technical Team moves off to their respective quarters to prepare for supper. The atmosphere onboard the SAS Protea is a little more relaxed than the other Naval Vessels and the crew much more approachable.

Many of the crew are from all race groups and have formed a well-knit organization. The Air Force Crew is welcomed into the naval fraternity as the mission starts. As the ship makes its way up the west coast of Africa, they will be sailing along one of the world's most dangerous coastlines. After supper the ships whistle sounds, and an announcement is made for the Air Force Crew to attend a trip brief in the Navigation Room.

Steve, Sallies and Mark join the two pilots in the Navigation Room to be briefed by the Captain. The tasking is for survey work along the coastline North of Lüderitz in SWA right up to the Kunene, the border of SWA and Angola. The helicopter will be utilized to fly survey equipment teams to the coast while the ship completes the survey from the sea. When the survey is completed, the aircraft will return with the survey team to the next coordinates and continue until complete. The Captain ends off with a possibility of an additional tasking, pending requirement over the next two weeks, but that he will brief them accordingly, as the helicopter will be required.

That evening the three F/E's are in the Warrant Officers Pub when Sallies issues an order requiring Mark and Steve to report to the Hangar on the double. Normally a hangar watch is set for the aircrew to share during the trip, whereby one person makes occasional trips to the hangar to check all is secure and safe. This was something new to Mark and Steve. Nevertheless, the two slightly inebriated F/E's make the swaying way up to the hangar to see what the fuss is about.

Once in the hangar, Sallies brings out a bottle of hooligan juice for the three of them to enjoy. The rest of the evening is spent joking and drinking until the wee hours of the morning before they all sneak to their bunks for a couple of hours kip before inspection rounds.

Steve wakes up to a very dry mouth and throbbing head. He slowly gets himself ready for a day of punishment, praying that he won't be the F/E for the day. Both he and Mark are looking far the worse for wear but manage to tidy themselves up for inspection.

Breakfast is forced down as Steve knows if he does not eat he will be very ill for the rest of the day. Fortunately, the weather is not the best, and with grey rainy skies, there is no hope of flying. Steve and Mark find a hole to hide in the hangar and settle in to sleep off their hangovers.

The next few days are spent reviewing onboard operating procedures and keeping abreast of the survey requirements. Early morning and the ships whistle sounds to inform the entire crew that the ship has reached Seamount Vema.

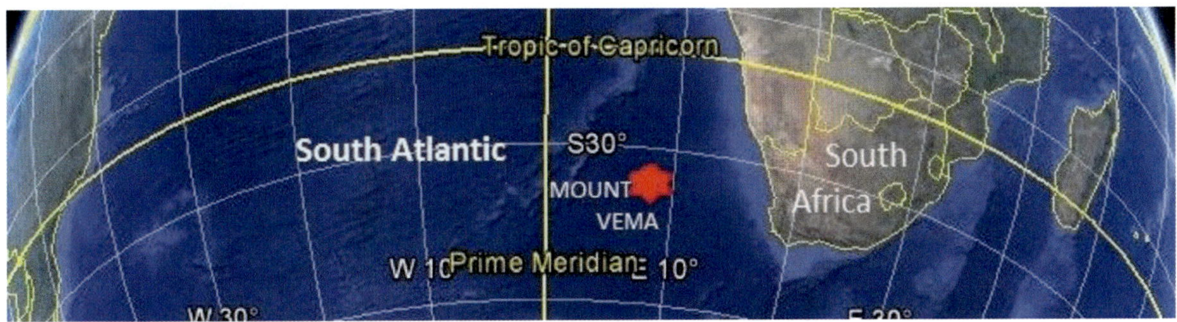

Seamount Vema

When you look at the world map, you soon realize that volcanically formed Vema Seamount, a mere 1000 kilometers from Cape Town, is not an island in the strict sense. However, it is a rock uniquely classified as an island. This is because this unique underwater mountain is among the very few seamounts in the world that meets most of the characteristics of an oceanic island. Furthermore, a study published in 1966 by the University of Cape Town recorded the probability that Vema Seamount was once an island at the surface of the sea.

Despite the fact that Vema Seamount was once an island with its top at the surface of the sea, eroded by millions of years of wave action, the best answer to that question today is that seamounts are defined by oceanographers as independent features that rise to at least 1,000 meters above the seafloor, and are considered to be within the deep sea. For that reason, Vema Seamount is unique. It rises 5000 meters from the seafloor and parts of its peak are only 4 to 10 meters below sea level. Therefore, Vema Seamount is more than just a seamount, and its existence is no different from that of an Oceanic Island. Being a dormant volcano, the water temperature on top of Vema is warm resulting in a multitude of sea life flourishing.

The ship's crews bring out hand lines and bait and soon everyone is pulling in all sorts of fish including Yellow Tail, Rock Cob, Concha and many more. "Nine Oh Clockers", a Navy snack tradition was going to be very good tonight for sure. Steve and Mark manage to bring in some fish as well, including the biggest Yellow Tail for the day. Steve gives the fish to the ships cook to prepare. The ships catering staff do an excellent job of preparing all sorts of starters and main courses from the days catch. The off-duty crews then break away to the respective Messes for liquid sustenance in anticipation of the Nine Oh Clock snacks. The catering crew does not disappoint, and the Yellow Tail has been prepared to perfection. Everyone bites in and soon there not a morsel of food left on the platters. A good day and night are had by all. The visit to Vema had been a surprise to all with the exception of the ship's officers and navigation crew. It was a well enjoyed surprise, one that very few people in the world will ever, if ever experience.

The ship turns north to continue up the west coast of Africa and on route to Lüderitz for the first stop and initiation of the survey work. The next three days are relaxing, and the mood is good. The Air Force Crew enjoys the off time and the F/E's take turns in Hangar watch and maintenance checks on the helicopter.

Lüderitz

Waking up the next day the ship's crew is met with a wonderful sight of Lüderitz dotting the horizon. Lüderitz is a harbor town in the ǁKaras Region of southern SWA, lying on one of the least hospitable coasts in Africa. It is a port developed around Robert Harbor and Shark Island. The town is known for its colonial architecture, including some Art Nouveau work, and for wildlife including seals, penguins, flamingos and ostriches. It is also home to a museum and lies at the end of the railway line to Keetmanshoop.

The bay on which Lüderitz is situated was first known to Europeans when Bartolomeu Dias encountered it in 1487. He named the bay Angra Pequena (Portuguese for Small Bay) and erected a padrão (stone cross) on the southern peninsula. In the 18th century Dutch adventurers and scientists explored the area in search of minerals but did not have much success.

Further exploration expeditions followed in the early 19th century during which the vast wildlife in the ocean was discovered. Profitable enterprises were set up, including whaling, seal hunting, fishing and guano-harvesting. Lüderitz thus began its life as a trading post.

The town was founded in 1883 when Heinrich Vogelsang purchased Angra Pequena and some of the surrounding land on behalf of Adolf Lüderitz, a Hanseat from Bremen in Germany, from the local Nama chief Josef Frederiks II in Bethanie. When Adolf Lüderitz did not return from an expedition to the Orange River in 1886, Angra Pequena was named Lüderitzbucht in his honor. In 1905, German authorities established a concentration camp on Shark Island.

The camp, access to which was very restricted, operated between 1905 and 1907 during the Herero Wars. Between 1,000 and 3,000 Africans from the Herero and Nama tribes died here as a result of the tragic conditions of forced labour. Their labour was used for expansion of the city, railway, port and farms of white settlers.

In 1909, after the discovery of diamonds nearby, Lüderitz enjoyed a sudden surge of prosperity due to the development of a diamond rush to the area. In 1912 Lüderitz already had 1,100 inhabitants, not counting the indigenous population. Although situated in harsh environment between desert and Ocean, trade in the harbor town surged, and the adjacent diamond mining settlement of Kolmanskop was built.

After the German World War I capitulation, South Africa took over the administration of German South West Africa in 1915. Many Germans were deported from Lüderitz, contributing to its shrinking in population numbers.

From 1920 onwards, diamond mining was only conducted further south of town in places like Pomona and Elizabeth Bay. This development consequently led to the loss of Lüderitz's importance as trade place. Only small fishing enterprises, minimal dock activity and a few carpet weavers remained.

Kolmanskop "Ghost Town"

Hand's to flying stations is piped and the Air Force Crew prepares the helicopter for flight, by reverse process of stowage. Once the blades have been spread, the before flight is completed, documents, and authorization book signed, do the crew gather for a briefing. The tasking is to fly the Supply Officer to Lüderitz for replenishment of some wet rations. Mark is the F/E for the day and the flight is concluded within the hour and the helicopter is once again refueled and stowed, while the ship sets sail to the survey sight further north.

For the next few weeks daily flights are conducted taking the survey teams to the shore and then waiting until the ship has completed the survey and then returning to the ship for the evening. The west coast of Africa has the cold Benguela Current, a northward flowing ocean current that forms the eastern portion of the South Atlantic Ocean gyre. The current extends from roughly Cape Point in the south, to the position of the Angola-Benguela front in the north, at around 16°S. The current is driven by the prevailing south easterly trade winds. With the very cold ocean waters cooling the air and forming adiabatic warming of the air as it moves over the coast results in a thick band of fog all along the western coast. This fog can last from an hour or two to a couple of days.

It is Steve's turn to fly a survey sortie, and once they have landed high up on the beach, Steve assists the survey crew in setting up for the next survey. The survey has only been underway for a couple of hours when a heavy fog quickly sets in. The pilot Capt. Trevor Baynham turns to Steve and they quickly decide that it is best to try and return to the ship. The nighttime temperatures on the Skeleton Coast of the Namib Dessert are very cold. Not the place to spend the night in a very small helicopter. Trevor radios the ship only to be informed that the visibility around the ship is pea soup. They are ordered to stand by and call in every 15 minutes. On the next call the Captain of the ship asks if he holds station in a clear patch, would the crew be able to find the ship. Steve does a quick calculation and with the fuel on board they will have more than enough time to search for the ship, return to shore, and fly again the next day. Within 10 minutes the survey crew is strapped in and the aircraft is airborne. They fly in the general direction of the ship, which is tracking their flight path on Radar, but cannot see anything. The second pilot Lt. Rowland, using the ships radar, is trying to guide them in, but the fog is too thick. With that the Captain of the ship has a brain wave and requests the Chief Engineer to throttle up all four diesel engines to max RPM for a few seconds. Like magic a huge plume of black diesel smoke billows up in front of the helicopter a quarter mile away. Like a magnet Trevor homes in on the ship and slaps the aircraft on the deck before the Fog locks them out again.

That evening there is a lot of joking about how the survey crew should have been left in the cold. Survival stories continue deep into the night until Steve goes on deck and sees the beautiful night sky above them. The Milky Way looks like a splash of white across the sky with closer planets seemingly just out of reach to touch. Steve is deep in thought as he takes in the beauty of the view above him. He has been privileged to have the opportunity to travel to places that very few people have or will have; doing what he loves most, namely flying. Steve retires to his bunk and falls into a restful sleep, unaware of what lurks in his future.

For the next few weeks the survey continues with no hiccups, and the ship has progressed past Walvis Bay and further up the Skeleton Coast towards Angola. It's a clear day and calm sea when the Captain of the Ship pipes the Air Force Crew for a briefing. The briefing is quite a surprise to the group. The survey work for the ship was a ruse to prevent the enemy from suspecting the true mission. The SAS Protea, with its Helicopter, is one of the extraction mechanisms for a Recce Team that have been sent into the Cabinda Province of Angola via Strike Craft for a reconnaissance mission. They will continue to sail up the African Coast to the northern region of Angola but stay out to sea just within range of the Alouette for extraction if required.

The next few days are quite anxious for the team, as they have no idea what the details of the extraction would be, how many Recce's there were, what the enemy has in terms of weaponry or what aircraft are available by the enemy that would pose a threat. By the 21st May 1985 the Ship is in position and crews are on the alert in case the call comes. In the very early hours, the next morning orders are issued for the crew to stand down and that the ship was setting sail back to South Africa. It takes another eleven days of sailing before the Air Force Team can get airborne and set heading for AFB Ysterplaat.

Back at the Squadron Steve and the rest of the crew find out what actually transpired during the raid. On the 13th May 1985 a South African Navy Strike Craft carrying a Recce team as well as a back-up team left Saldanha Bay and travelled to a spot some way off the Angolan coast near its border with Zaire. The mission was to confirm the existence of African National Congress (ANC) bases and South-West Africa People's Organization (SWAPO) bases near Cabinda. The area contained oil storage installations run by the Angolans and Gulf Oil, and because of this, several large military bases were also in the vicinity.

The Recces landed on the coast at night on the 20th May following an advance scouting party sent to gather intelligence on the beach where the party would land. Under ideal cloudy skies, the Recce team's trip had been slowed by the need to launch their boats further from shore than anticipated. The longer journey, as well as rough seas, threw off the precise timing of the mission. Near shore, Captain Wynand Du Toit noticed a small fishing vessel in the area of the landing zone and that the occupants were on shore around a fire. This forced the team to wait offshore until the boat left the area. They were now three hours behind schedule, and the danger of being detected grew.

Upon landing the boats were hidden and a rendezvous point set up. The men climbed a bluff and followed a route that skirted a small village and led to a road. They miscalculated the distance to the road and turned back, losing an hour of valuable time. Wynand decided to continue and reach the lying up position (LUP) in a densely wooded area within the two hours prior to dawn. South African Intelligence and aerial photographs showed an uninhabited area, but in fact it was surrounded by camouflaged People's Armed Forces for the Liberation of Angola (FAPLA) bases. The hide was finally reached as day broke. This proved to be far from ideal as a hiding place, as it was not part of the jungle, but an island of dense growth some distance from the jungle. The Recces hid in the undergrowth and spread into a defensive perimeter, one man at an observation post several yards to the north with a view of the course they had travelled.

As dawn broke, the features of a well-hidden FAPLA base became clear some 910 meters from the LUP. A few hours later, a small FAPLA patrol could be seen following the tracks they had left the night before. The team watched as the patrol withdrew, and then came back with a larger patrol which passed the hide. At 17:00 a three-man patrol followed the team's trail directly to the thicket where the Recces were hidden. They stopped short of entering the brush and returned to their base. Meanwhile, a second patrol approached the hide from the other direction and opened up heavy fire on the hidden position. As rocket propelled grenades (RPGs) struck their position, Wynand ordered the withdrawal of his troops. They had no choice but to double back on the trail that brought them to this position the previous night.

Two of the men were wounded as they exited the trees. FAPLA troops deployed 46 meters west of the site opened up with RPD machine guns, RPG and many AK-47s. The team turned north, pursued by FAPLA soldiers. Another group of Angolan soldiers advanced from the west, flanking the Recces so that they could only go east now. They could see a group of trees but needed to cross 40 37 meters of waist-high grass to get to this cover. Wynand took two men and made his way through the grass as the rest of the team hid in the thicket. The small team drew fire as over 30 troops moved onto the exposed position. One Recce, Corporal Rowland Liebenberg, was killed as his two comrades fought on. The fighting continued for a full 45 minutes. The two men started to run out of ammunition and were both wounded, Sergeant Louis van Breda later died and Wynand nearly so.

The contact was over and two South African soldiers were dead. While Wynand lay on his stomach, FAPLA soldiers approached and, thinking he was also dead, stripped his equipment, only then did they realize he was alive and shot him again through the neck. He remained awake with wounds in his neck, shoulder and arm as the FAPLA soldiers began to savagely beat him. The soldiers thought that he was a mercenary; though Wynand tried to explain that he was in fact a South African Army officer. After being severely roughed up, he was finally taken to Cabinda for medical treatment then to a Luanda hospital. The remaining six Recce soldiers carefully made their way north, where they regrouped and were eventually picked up to be returned safely to South Africa. Their escape was due in part to being ignored after the Angolans captured Wynand.

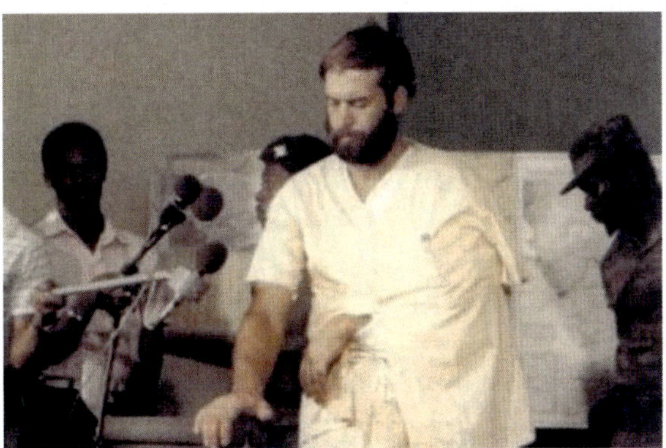

Wynand Du Toit captured

Steve is angry that they could not do anything to help but realizes with the limited intelligence available it would have been a suicide mission. In the meantime, Steve is summoned to the OC's office.

Steve salutes Cmdt. Theron smartly as he enters. "Sit Down Steve".

"Let me be the first to congratulate you on your transfer. You have been seconded to the South African Police (SAP) Force to establish their Air Wing".

"Thank you, Sir. When do I have to report?"

"It seems that you have until the end of the month of June, so use the authorization as approval to get your move quoted for and booked".

Steve thanks the OC, takes the Signal and hurries off to the Duty Room to start the process of obtaining moving quotes, travel allowances, and SAP accommodation in Pretoria. With all the required documentation processed, Steve heads home to inform the family and start the packing. As the secondment is only for a maximum of two years, Steve has offered his home to one of the apprentices at 22 Squadron for the period.

The next few weeks pass in a blur, and soon Steve, Zella and little Nicole are on the long road north to Pretoria. This will be their new home for the next year. They have been allocated an Apartment on Church Street in the Northern Suburb of Pretoria, not far from the newly established SAP Air Wing.

Chapter 9 - POLICING

It seems as if the weeks have flown past since June when Steve first submitted his application. With his transfer approved Steve gets the removal company in to quote for the move to Pretoria. The 1959 MGA Roadster is in pieces and will have to be transported with the Removal Company. Steve has decided that the Yamaha would also be trucked up and that Zella, Nicole and he would drive with the Alfa Giulietta. This will be Nicole's first long road trip, and therefore could potentially be a problem.

SAP Air Wing

With the contents of the house packed and on the way with the Removal Company, the family prepares for the long trek north. The trip is long, hot and tiring. For Nicole it is a bit much, as she has never been in a car for this length of time. With the summer heat she cries uncontrollably, until Steve decides they need to stop off at a town and seek medical help. The doctor has a look over Nicole and suggests fluids and frequent short stops. The rest of the trip is uneventful. Steve, Zella and Nicole spend the night at Zella's parents' home in Brakpan. Steve will go to SAP Headquarters the next day to report for duty.

Smartly dressed in his Air Force Blues, Steve reports to SAP Headquarters, where he meets his fellow F/E also assigned for the secondment, Hans Arnold. They are briefed by a Police Colonel and sent down to the Quarter Master to be issued with Police Uniforms. Steve is given his apartments keys and heads out to meet up with Zella and Nicole so that they can look over the new home. Their furniture arrives, and unpacking is started to establish some type of order. Their new life has just started. The Motorcycle was sent with the move, so now Steve has transport to and from the Air Wing. Zella has, through her connections managed to obtain a reference for work at a local Dentist and makes an appointment to go and see them.

Steve and Hans are sent to Lanseria where the Air Wing Helicopters are being assembled after arriving from Germany. They both report to Lanseria early the morning and are given a Technical course on the MBB BO-105 Helicopter.

The Messerschmitt-Bölkow-Blohm BO-105 is a light, twin-engine, multi-purpose helicopter developed by Bölkow of Ottobrunn, Germany. It holds the distinction of being the first light twin-engine helicopter in the world and is the first rotorcraft that could perform aerobatic maneuvers, such as inverted loops. The BO-105 features a revolutionary hingeless rotor system, at that time a pioneering innovation in helicopters when it was introduced into service in 1970.

Steve and Hans complete their training and immediately assist in the assembly and implementation of modifications to the new helicopters. The additional modifications give the helicopter the ability of improved performance in the South African climate. Once the assembly is completed, each aircraft is sent for spray painting in the SAP colours and then final decals. An acceptance flight is then conducted before dispatching the aircraft to the Air Wing in Pretoria. Steve enjoys the aircraft as the semi rigid rotorhead makes the helicopter incredibly maneuverable. With the twin-engine pack and responsive flight controls the BO-105 is the Ferrari of Helicopters.

MBB BO-105

Both the Engineers now start the process of establishing the Air Wing as an approved Air Operating Certificate (AOC) in accordance with the local Civil Aviation Authority. They have to ensure that there are sufficient tools, manuals and trained personnel available with the appropriate Policies, Procedures and Processes for the Air Wing to operate as an AOC.

With their military background and training it does not take them long to get the AOC ready for approval. During the time at Lanseria, Steve gets the opportunity to assist with the BO-105's bigger brother, the BK-117. The helicopter is very similar in design but a bigger version with more power.

Steve and Hans arrive back at the Air Wing to meet up with the rest of the Air Force seconded team of pilots. Lt Col Zack Zunckle is the Officer in Command with pilots, Maj Smiley van Zyl, Capt.'s Ricky Vergotinni and Duncan Gillespie.

There is tension in the air as the OC is not in favour of having F/E's onboard when they fly. "These aircraft are single pilot rated and do not require additional crew" says Zack.

Fortunately, not all the pilots share Zack's point of view. Smiley invites Steve to bring Zella and Nicole along for a training flight over the weekend. Nicole seems pretty excited and sits happily on Zella's lap as they take off for the flight. Steve looks back from the co-pilots seat and sees that Nicole has fallen asleep and will therefore have no recollection of the flight. Steve grins at Zella, who just shakes her head in acknowledgement. Smiley takes them on a long tour of the area and after an hour returns back to the Air Wing.

Monday morning Ricky asks Steve to prepare one of the aircraft for hoisting operations, as the Public Relations (PR) personnel want to take photos of the new helicopters at work. Steve gets to work and installs the electric powered hoist to the port side of the aircraft and tests it for function. Steve makes the entry in the Technical Log and then prepares the aircraft for flight. Ricky briefs Steve of the flight and the two walkout to the Bölkow. The PR crews are there with their cameras.

One of the crew is a very attractive young lady who asks if she can be hoisted from the aircraft. Ricky and Steve answer together as if one voice speaks, "Most certainly". Ricky then briefs the whole crew on what was to transpire during the shoot. Steve then briefs everyone to be hoisted on the Strop and hoisting positions. They are going to take off from the pad and fly a circuit to come into hover over the training tower, where the PR crews are to be assembled for the hoisting exercise of the Special Force Police Officers. The operation will be as realistic as possible with a pickup and assault drop off, followed by a precision hoist from the training tower. Next the PR lady will be hoisted into the aircraft and then a short flight around the area to land back at the pad.

With the briefing completed the PR crews disperse while Ricky and Steve prepare the aircraft for start-up and take off. Steve locks the rear sliding door in the open position in preparation for the flight and ties his restraining harness to the aircraft floor. Ricky lifts the Bölkow off the ground, dips the nose and picks up speed and then starts to bank out to the right. They fly a short circuit and line up with the training tower to complete the approach for a hoist of the SAP Assault team. Steve patters Ricky into position and then moves the Jib of the Hoist out to clear the landing Skids, before letting the hoist cable out.

With small corrections Steve talks Ricky into a position where the hoist strop is directly in front of the first team member. Steve informs Ricky of the hook up and confirms the team member is secured in the strop and starts hoisting him up. The cable is approximately 50 ft below the aircraft when Steve reels it in. The hoist travels quickly and when the Team Member is close to the aircraft Steve stops the hoist and reaches out to turn the Team Member around so that he can put his arm around the chest and pull the hoisted man back into the aircraft before releasing the tension on the hoist and removing the strop. The first hoist goes off smoothly and the PR Team has the opportunity to get what they need. The exercise is repeated with the remaining three members until everyone is onboard. Ricky then lands close to the training tower so that the SAP Team can disembark.

Now Ricky takes off again and flies a short circuit to line up with the training tower once more, this time to hoist the attractive young PR lady. The approach is perfect, and Steve already has the hoist cable out ready for the PR lady to hook into the Strop. She duly slips the strop around her chest and under her arms, and then indicates with a thumb up that she is ready for the hoist. Steve takes the strain on the cable and lifts her up. The hoist goes off well until she reaches the downwash height of the helicopter, when all of a sudden, her loose cotton top blows up over her, exposing what Steve thinks as the best pair of tits he has ever seen. As she has been instructed not to move her arms while hoisting, she was stuck with her top over her face and chest bare. When she is close enough, Steve reaches out and placing his arm around her chest, turns her and brings her into the aircraft. Only once the cable tension is released can she at last pull her top down, and with a red face grins up at Steve and Ricky. This was going to be one of those stories that will be told over and over.

Township Uprising

On the 3rd September 1985, the Parliament opens in Cape Town while protest demonstrations begin in the Transvaal, marking the start of the longest and most widespread period of black resistance to white rule. Stay Away, School Boycott and March, which lead to clashes with both police and township councilors and leave thirty people dead. The marchers also loot shops, set fire to houses and kill 4 councilors. By the end of the year almost 150 people have been killed in political violence, which increases to 600 by September 1985 as the revolt spreads across the country and the government declares a State of Emergency.

The demonstration on the 3rd September is not the first protest caused by local circumstances, flare ups increase across the country. Although the United Democratic Front (UDF) plays no direct role in these protests, the increased resistance and awareness brought about by them does affect the people. The UDF at this stage is still only thinking along the lines of affiliate-based campaigns and resistance against the state and does not plan to get involved in township militancy. The UDF is aware of the civic problems affecting people and mentions these in speeches in order to get support for national campaigns, but it feels such issues are the concern of local organizations. It is also more concerned with coloured and Indian issues surrounding the Tricameral Parliament and do not pay much attention to black townships at this time. Some activists are aware of the UDF's standpoint, and even discourage UDF involvement.

The UDF take little notice of township revolts of 1984, and only started to get involved as a result of police violence and state repression. The State however places a lot of the blame for the revolts on the UDF and begin to arrest and detain leaders of the UDF. At a meeting the main focus is however the form and direction of the UDF, not the revolts. The UDF feels sure that the revolts would not be able to continue without Grassroot Organization. The UDF feels it should rather focus on state repression and the school boycott, which are both national issues.

The lead in the revolts is therefore taken by Charterists. Many of the affiliates of the UDF do not support the distant position of the UDF and would rather it take a more confrontational position. The uprising spreads rapidly and is accompanied by looting and vandalism. Police presence in the areas causes further riots. By October about 30 organizations, many of them affiliates of the UDF, form the Transvaal Regional Stay Away Committee. The main strategy used in this period was Stay Away, and an important Stay Away is called for in the Transvaal in November. Although the UDF initially does not get involved in the call, the Transvaal UDF does endorse the call, in early November. The strike is very effective, with numbers of between 300,000 and 800,000 staying home, and unions being active in the organization. After the success of the Stay Away, the UDF feels it is time to reconsider its position. It realizes it has not reacted quickly enough, and that others have now taken the lead. It wants to rectify this situation but continues to follow rather than a lead the riots. The UDF, and the Federation of South African Trade Unions (FOSATU), do not support a second call for a strike as they both feel that it has already been shown that they have the power in their hands. The UDF rather supports a call for a "BLACK CHRISTMAS" to mourn those who have died in revolts and those in detention. The call is not for a consumer boycott as such, but rather for people to show self-sacrifice through not purchasing luxuries and not holding parties from 16th to 26th December.

In early 1985 the UDF is still very aware of the problems it is facing with regard to direction and strategy. It is becoming clear that the UDF is not as accountable to its affiliates as has been expected, and that it is starting to act more like a movement than like a front. Many also want the UDF to have more autonomy and to be able to make decisions on its own with the affiliates following it rather than it is following the affiliates. This leads to a streamlining of national and regional structures, and a move towards greater militancy as it decides to involve itself in existing political struggles, although organization remains important.

The UDF also begins to move closer to its black ties, although non-racialism is still of utmost importance. In this way the UDF starts playing a bigger role in the townships and uses funerals as an opportunity to address people. School boycotts are another form of protest that appear continually after the 1976 uprising. By the end of 1984 there are about 220 000 children absent from school in various parts of the country. Parents become concerned with the situation, and the Soweto Parent's Crisis Committee is formed to try and solve the problem. The UDF leadership, is against the continuation of the school boycott, and feels discussions should be started with the state on this issue. In this respect they face opposition from Congress of South African Students (COSAS), a key affiliate. Although many students return to school in 1985, there are still as many as 70,000 boycotting.

March sees the explosion of resistance in the Eastern Cape after the organization of a "BLACK WEEKEND" of consumer boycott and Stay Away. Once again, the UDF plays no role in the organization of the event. Violence escalates, with police killing about 20 people on their way to a funeral on 21st March. This results in more riots, the killing of a counselor and his family, and mass action around the funerals, which are attended by between 35,000 and 60,000 people. The UDF condemns the police violence and calls for a day of mourning, but also calls for non-violence on the side of the people, unless it is "DEFENSIVE VIOLENCE".

The government increases its attacks on the UDF, and arrests leaders in preparation for the Pietermaritzburg Treason Trial. The state stops the UDF and some affiliates from holding indoor meetings, while outdoor meetings are already prohibited. The UDF continue to attempt to connect the local struggle to the national struggle, and to focus on organization rather than on leading the people's riots. The first National General Council of the UDF since its formation is held in April, and discussion on strategy and form continues.

Purple Rain

With the riots playing havoc internally within South Africa, the SAP are deployed throughout the country to tend to the rioting, looting and murdering that is taking place in the Townships. It seems more like organized Tribal War than revolt against the Government. Many innocent parties that don't want to be involved are classified as traitors and either burnt by necklacing or beaten to death. It is during this turbulent period that Steve and Ricky are called to riots taking place near Soweto. Utilizing the BO-105 with a Fire Bucket attached to the Cargo Sling, filled up with Soluble Tear Gas and a mix of Water and Jenson Violet, they would bomb the rioting crowds. With Purple Rain falling down from the sky, the uncontrolled rioting crowd becomes more of run for cover crowd. The soluble Tear Gas burning, and Jenson Violet, effectively marking those taking part in the riots. For the next few weeks the SAP can follow up and make house arrests on all guilty parties that partook in the rioting.

To add injury to insult, Ricky puts on his Prince and the Revolution recording of Purple Rain over the Public-Address Speakers of the Helicopter, putting all fear of God into the rioting masses. With every drop that Ricky and Steve make the crowd disperses quicker, until eventually there are only stragglers left behind, making it easy pickings for the Police Constables on the ground to sort out and arrest. The adaption of a Fire Fighting Bucket to disperse a riot has been an effective additive to the SAP Air Wings ability in resolving issues. After a successful day of riot control, Ricky and Steve return to the SAP Air Wing in Pretoria. Steve completes the required maintenance on the aircraft after the days flying and signs up the Technical Logs accordingly. Both Ricky and Steve then report to the Briefing room to debrief on the day's events. During the briefing, Zack informs the team that they will be deploying to other parts for the country to complete a tour of duty for the same purpose, namely riot control and follow up action. Cape Town, Port Elizabeth and Bloemfontein are becoming problem areas as well. By now all six BO-105 and two BK-117 Helicopters are being operated in the SAP. Six of the BO-105's are based at the SAP Air Wing, with the two BK-117's stationed at Lanseria Airport. In the next few weeks the SAP negotiates Office and Hangar space at AFB Ysterplaat in Cape Town for the first deployment of the SAP Air Wing.

FLIR System

Smiley and Hans are deployed to Cape Town for the first tour and depart on the long flight down to Cape Town. They have installed a long-range fuel tank into the cargo compartment of the BO-105 which will improve the helicopters range. They will fly direct to Bloemfontein, refuel and continue via Touwsrivier for a second refuel and then Cape Town to AFB Ysterplaat. Steve is left to tend to the rest of the fleet at the SAP Air Wing. Smiley, Ricky and Duncan share the daily tasking. A local company arrives to display the latest technology in Policing. Steve assists in the mounting of the Forward Looking Infrared (FLIR) equipment.

The system is mounted on the nose of the BO-105 and connected to a remote control operated by the observer in the cockpit. A monitor displays the infrared image on the screen. Any heat source is displayed clearly on the screen. Vehicles that have been parked stay warm for a long time and clearly show a heat signature all around them. The image displayed on the monitor is very clear and allows the helicopter crew to home in on targets easily.

Early evening, Ricky and Steve together with the rest of the Air Wing Crew, brief on a test flight for the night to test the system in the field. After a quick supper Ricky and Steve prepare the aircraft for the flight. Steve will be monitoring from the back while the demo team member sits in the co-pilots seat to operate the system. Ricky takes off and heads towards Johannesburg. Within a few minutes the FLIR is tested and all systems are ready. The images are clear and if you look away from the monitor to see where the area is that you are viewing it is dark and black. The FLIR will definitely benefit Policing and follow up from the air. The test flight is a success, and now it will be up to the SAP Bean Counters to approve a budget for procurement. Steve is not very confident that this will not be a rush purchase.

The equipment is left as a loaner for the crew till the end of the week. The crews take full advantage of testing and using the system, and all conclude that it would be a positive tool in the Air Wings arsenal in the policing of crime.

Steve is going to re-leave Hans in Cape Town after the weekend, so he plans a weekend away for the family. One of the advantages of being in the Police Force is the availability of vehicles and fuel. Steve and Hans have learnt very quickly that if they needed transportation to go somewhere far without having to use their own vehicle and fuel, all they need do is request a vehicle for the period. Steve duly does this and on Friday afternoon picks up a Mazda sedan. The family packs up and heads out to Witbank, where Steve's parents live at Corobrik, a paving company near Duvha Power Station.

Steve's dad Frank and his mom Nellie, live on the Corobrik premises in one of the allocated houses. It is a huge four bedroomed home with all the requirements. A quiet weekend is spent catching up with the family. Since being back in the Transvaal, Steve and Zella have not spent much time visiting, so it means a lot to the grandparents to see little Nicole. Frank mocks Steve about his position in the SAP and keeps referring to him as Constable Coetzee. All too soon the weekend has come to an end and the family heads back to the city.

Early Monday morning Steve reports to AFB Waterkloof to catch the weekly Schedule flight down to Cape Town. It will be a three-hour flight with the C130 and to Steve's surprise, his very good friend George Avis is now a Flight Engineer under Training on the C130. Steve and George catch up and before they can wipe their eyes the trip is over and the big C130 is heading in to land at AFB Ysterplaat.

The Fairest Cape

Steve gets his gear and makes his way to the office that has been allocated to the SAP Air Wing at 22 Squadron. In the crew room is Hans and Smiley. They jump and greet Steve with smiles all round. Both Smiley and Hans will return today with Duncan flying in later this afternoon. For Steve it's an emotional adaption as he has come to love the Cape and it really feels good to be back. The last months in the Transvaal had reminded him of why he requested Cape Town as a transfer in the first place. The people are much friendlier in the Cape and there is much more to do, with everything available within an hour's drive. The Witwatersrand Metropolitan Area combining the Cities of Pretoria, Johannesburg, Germiston, Springs, Benoni, Brakpan and Boksburg have grown so large that it takes more than three hours to travel through.

Early the next morning Steve meets up with Duncan to brief on the days flying. They are deploying to Langa Police Station to support the follow up operations in the Langa Township where unrest has been brewing for some time.

They get airborne and head in the general direction of Langa. Duncan who has not flown in the Cape region looks to Steve to guide him to the area. Steve loses his bearings and they end up flying around in search of the Police Station. Just as Duncan is about to give up Steve spots Langa and points Duncan in the right direction. Duncan deftly maneuvers the BO-105 into an approach and lands on the Helipad.

They make their way to the Station and meet up with the Commandant. There have been sporadic bursts of unrest, rioting, looting and burning taking place in the last weeks. The task force has identified most of the ring leaders and is planning a raid to arrest them in the next few days. This morning with the assistance of the local Military Cape Coloured Core, they will be a force approach on a number of targets to make as many arrests as possible. The Chopper will be the Telstar in the sky and direct operations of the raids.

Briefings completed Duncan and Steve head out to the Chopper to await the signal for take-off. They don't have to wait long when the call for them to get airborne is requested. They start up and head out toward Langa. Duncan keeps the aircraft below a thousand feet and circles above the Casper's that have headed toward their respective targets. All too soon the troops deploy, and the raid is initiated. Steve spots a runner heading off in the opposite direction and brings it to Duncan's attention, who immediately radios the Task force leader of the respective Casper. Many arrests are made this day and the next day's forward. A multitude of arms, ammunition and explosives are found and removed. The eye in the sky operation is reaping huge rewards and the tide on the unrest is quickly turned.

During his downtime in Cape Town, Steve takes a day to check up on the family home. Arriving at the house, Steve is very disappointed to see that the yard in a state of disrepair, with the lawn growing wild, weeds in the garden and papers all over the driveway. Steve ambles over the road to his neighbor and loans a lawnmower shovel and rake to tidy up the yard and make the home look presentable once more. It is a very hot sun shining day and Steve spends shirtless hours in the burning sun to complete the clean-up. Very sun burnt and exhausted Steve heads back to the Air Force Base to recover, in preparation for the next day's flying.

This is the final week in Cape Town, and with the unrest under control there is not much flying. The crew keeps themselves busy by catching up on tasks required to keep the aircraft serviceable and police documentation updated. All too soon both Steve and Duncan are ready for replacement, this time they don't have to wait for the arrival of the crew as they have been summoned back to the Air Wing in Pretoria.

No sooner when Steve arrives back at the Air Wing, Ricky approaches Steve and asks him to prepare an aircraft for 30 hours of flying. They are deploying to Natal in search of cattle thieves in the Drakensburg Mountains near Pietermaritzburg. Steve calls Zella and informs her of the trip. Fortunately, being an old hand at this, Steve always keeps a night stop kit in his locker at work for these call-out events.

The Dragons Back

With the helicopter packed, long range fuel tank installed, fueled, and pre-flight completed, Ricky and Steve get airborne via the outskirts of Johannesburg for Natal. Ricky decides to do a shoot up over his home and at the appropriate time noses the BO-105 down towards the houses. The Chopper picks up speed as the dive down, and about 200 ft Ricky pulls the cyclic back to climb away. The aircraft continues downward in its nosedive. The cargo is too heavy in the rear pushing the center of gravity too far to the rear for the recovery. At the last minute and very low over the rooftops does the aircraft respond and gains altitude quickly. Ricky looks at Steve and they both break out into a nervous laugh.

"That was too close", Says Ricky.

"Confirm, the C of G is way too far back, I will repack the cargo at the refuel, we don't want to have those limitations in the mountains" Responds Steve.

The rest of the flight is uneventful, and Ricky lets Steve fly for most of the way. This opportunity was soon going to end, as Zack Zunckle has informed them that the Co-Pilot controls must be removed when the aircraft get back to the Air Wing.

Steve refuels the BO-105 at the Police Station in Pietermaritzburg, repacks the cargo and they are ready to set off to the Champagne Castle area of the Drakensburg Mountains where the Cattle thieves are operating. The thieves sneak across the border over the 14,000 ft. peaks of the Drakensburg via gorges, valleys and mountain passes, to steal cattle in Natal and then herd them back across the border to Lesotho. With the Chopper it is hoped that Ricky and Steve, together with a SAP Tracker will be able to pick up the trail and leap frog the spoor to catch up with the thieves. This is the same process that Ricky and Steve had used during the war in Angola to track Terrorists.

Ricky Steve, and the SAP Tracker, head out to the last known location of the thieves. The plan is to circle the area and then find the general direction of the spoor, and then fly overlapping circuits in the general direction until contact is made. It is a quick 45-minute flight to the area. Ricky makes comms with the ground force and confirms the direction of the spoor they are following, as well as the quantity of chopper fuel they have available. The team has 6 drums of Jet A1, more than enough for the afternoons flying with sufficient fuel to head back to Pietermaritzburg.

During the first circuit overhead, the tracker already has a clear picture on where the thieves are heading, and a quick plan is discussed to shorten the search area. By reviewing the terrain ahead and checking the map, there is only one way out of the area where the spoor is being followed. Ricky radios the ground troops and informs them to head in the direction of the twin butts on the horizon in a north westerly direction. The course is confirmed, and Ricky heads off to narrow gorge which will be the only way out of the area. Within 10 minutes they reach the area and climb to get a better view of the terrain, all the while keeping a good lookout for the thieves and cattle. With the gorge to his left, Steve spots a dust cloud and points it out to Ricky and the Tracker. With a yell all of them confirm that the thieves have been spotted.

Ricky heads back to the ground troops to pick up some reinforcements for the arrests to be made. Ricky makes an assault landing next to the ground troops and two constables quickly run forward to board the Chopper. No sooner are they onboard and Ricky lifts off in a cloud of dust. Ricky lands the aircraft ahead of the driven cattle and drops the two constables off. Next, he gets airborne and sets up a circuit above the stolen cattle, high enough not to spook them, but low enough to monitor what the thieves are planning. As this is the first encounter with a flying Police Car, the thieves have no idea what is happening. The reinforcements are closing in quickly with the Casper Troop carrier. At the last minute the thieves try to make a run for it and end up in the waiting trap set in the gorge. The arrests are quickly made, and the cattle corralled. Ricky radios the refueling truck and requests a location to land for refuel.

At the refuel excited chatter on how smooth the operation had gone is the order of the day. The praise for the Chopper is hearty and many cheers and thanks shared. Ricky and Steve are invited to share in the meal that is quickly thrown together, while they debrief over the successful operation. The sun's rays are shortening over the horizon when Ricky gets the Chopper airborne. They are heading back to Pietermaritzburg for the night before returning to the Air Wing the next day.

Back at the Air Wing the tension between the F/E's and Zack Zunckle is reaching a breaking point. Steve and Hans request a meeting with Lt. Col Nealle Ellis at Air Force Headquarters to discuss options. It has been just short of a year that the two had built the Technical side of the Air Wing where it is ready for Certification and Approval by the CAA. Nellis sympathizes with the F/E's and contacts the WO in charge of F/E's in the Air Force. The only available posting currently for Steve in the Cape region is at 25 Squadron. But he will be able to request a transfer to the Chopper Squadron as soon as posts become available. Steve takes the offer and heads home to inform the family.

25 Squadron operates the World War II DC3 cargo and troop-carrying aircraft, where the role of the F/E is more one of flying mechanic and load master. Steve makes peace with the time he will have to spend at 25 Squadron and prepares for the family's return to Cape Town. Zella on the other hand is furious, as she has been accepted to study for Oral Hygienist at Pretoria's University. Steve is appalled that she wants to stay and convinces her to reconsider.

Chapter 10 - IDLING

Combined Operations

It is 1986, and the U.S. conservatives convince President Ronald Reagan to meet with Savimbi at the White House. While the meeting itself is confidential, Reagan emerges from it with support and enthusiasm for Savimbi's efforts, stating that he could envision a Unita "victory that electrifies the world," suggesting that Reagan sees the outcome of the Angolan conflict as critical to his entire Reagan Doctrine foreign policy, consisting of support for anti-communist resistance movements in Central America, Southeast Asia, and elsewhere.

Back at Special Operations, the positive results of a reconnaissance operation meant that planning could proceed for an attack on the Namibe logistic infrastructure. The planning is for the Submarine SAS Johanna van der Merwe to carry out a final reconnaissance. The main raiding teams from 4 Reconnaissance Regiment would be carried by the two Strike Craft SAS Kobie Coetzee and SAS Hendrik Mentz as they were 'Coupe' ships so the aft 76mm gun could be removed to allow a modular accommodation unit to be installed in the magazine space which could up to 20 operators in relative comfort. They also carry the more modern and more reliable BLYTHE hydraulic stern ramps from which they will deploy both the Barracuda Mk 1 as well as the bigger and longer Barracuda Mk 2.

The support ship SAS Tafelberg will provide refueling and medical support south of the Cunene River mouth and also carry two Puma helicopters from 30 Squadron for medical evacuation if required, as well as a small Special Forces communications team to provide rear-link communications with the forces at Namibe.

To avoid the long debilitating journey in the Submarine the reconnaissance team will first join the P1561, at Donkergat and then transfer to the Johanna van der Merwe when she was off shore at Namibe. For this evolution the strike craft would have two of the older hydraulic ramps with a Barracuda Mk1 on each one. Once the reconnaissance team is transferred the P1561 will act as back up to the other two strike craft for the actual raid.

With all planning and preparation completed the submarine sails from Simon's Town at 11:00 on the 21st May in a thick fog to spend some time at Saldanha for final rehearsals and to load boats and stores. After successfully completing these tasks she sails from Saldanha at midnight on 22nd May and sets course to the north. She has a relatively uneventful passage to the target area, avoiding what little shipping there is, diving before first light to transit during the day at a depth of 70m and at 7 knots. Surfacing after dark she can then run on the surface whilst charging her batteries through the night.

On the morning of Friday, the 30th May, whilst the assault force is still packing their kit at Donkergat, the Johanna van der Merwe arrives off Namibe and commences monitoring shipping, fishing movements, radar and air activities off the port and its approaches. Just after 14:00, at periscope depth, she enters Namibe Bay to ascertain the number of vessels alongside the two quays or in the anchorage. Once she has completed a circuit of the Bay and in order not to take any further risk of detection, she exits the bay but remains off the port until 04:00 the following morning in case any vessels enter or leave the harbour. An important result of this reconnaissance is the confirmation that the two OSA Mk 2 missile boats are no longer present.

Meanwhile P1561 with the reconnaissance team sails from Donkergat on the evening of the 28th May and sets course to join Johanna van der Merwe rendezvousing with her some 70 miles off the coast on the 31st May. By 20:00, the Seaward and Tactical Reconnaissance Team as well as four days of victuals have been transferred and the Submarine heads back towards Namibe whilst P1561 heads south to rendezvous with SAS Tafelberg which has sailed from Simon's Town on the 29th May in order to replenish fuel and victuals. The other two Strike Craft with the raiding teams sails from Donkergat on the night of the 30th May.

In the dark Johanna van der Merwe closes the harbour on the surface to allow the teams to orientate themselves. At daybreak they dive and conduct a periscope reconnaissance of the harbour and missile sites in the forenoon. They then spend the remainder of the day monitoring traffic entering and leaving harbour. By 20:30 on the 1st June the two inflatable boats and the reconnaissance teams have been launched to carry out their task. The land reconnaissance team are successfully landed on the beach and the boat reconnaissance continued whilst the submarine keeps a listening watch at periscope depth. All goes well and by 04:30 both boats and teams are back on board the Submarine. On being debriefed it is decided that a second night of reconnaissance is not needed, as all the gaps in intelligence have now been filled and the main operation could go ahead. P1561 is informed and a rendezvous fifty miles offshore arranged for the evening and by 18:50 all the Special Force operators are on board the Strike Craft.

As intelligence reports have indicated that a Russian Tango class submarine has been attached to the 30th Flotilla and could possibly be in the area, the Submarine returns to Namibe by following a north easterly course and then approaches the port from the north. By 09:45 on Tuesday the 3rd June the Johanna van der Merwe is back in the bay at periscope depth to confirm that the targets are still there. It takes a little more than an hour to ascertain that there is one ship at the iron ore quay, three on the commercial quay and two at anchor. The situation in the port has not changed and D-day is confirmed for that night. The Submarine then reverts to her monitoring task.

In the meantime, the two Durban-based strike craft have encountered heavy weather and fallen behind their schedule but still expect to arrive in a designated waiting area 100 nautical miles west of Namibe in time, albeit a bit later than originally planned. Unfortunately that evening preparing to launch the Barracudas, first Kobie Coetzee reports a hydraulic fault on one of her ramps and although this is quickly rectified, one of the on board engines of a Barracuda won't start and by the cut off time of 21:30 the boats have still not been launched. As this was only the second of a total of ten days allocated for execution of the operation, the Operations Commander postpones the operation for 24 hours. As the Submarine also reports a high density of vehicle traffic that night it is indeed a wise decision.

On Wednesday morning the Submarine carries out a periscope reconnaissance from 11:30 to just after midday and reports that there is now an LPG tanker alongside at the iron ore quay with four vessels lying at the commercial quay even though one vessel has sailed in the morning. All ramps, boats and engines are thoroughly tested and found serviceable; the countdown commences at 13:00 and with the tactical headquarters for the operation now on the Kobie Coetzee the strike craft commence their approach. The Strike Craft are 'scattered' in a loose formation so as not to be identifiable as an obvious naval force if detected on radar as they approach, however, at the launch point, required to be more than five miles offshore. All boats are launched, and the diving attack teams embark on time. Regretfully one of the big targets, the LPG tanker at the iron ore jetty, sails at 22:00 just as the teams are approaching the harbour, and in fact pass the darkened Strike Craft all playing 'fishing boat' without noticing them. A lucky escape for both sides!

In despite the apparently calm sea a heavy swell results in big breakers on the fairly steep beach which means that the boats have to remain in fairly deep water, making it difficult for the heavily-laden and booted assault team members who have to be helped into the boats by divers and swimmers. After experiencing considerable difficulties in getting the boats loaded in chest deep water and clear of the landing beach, all the teams, tired but elated by their success, are underway for recovery by the strike craft before the cut off time of 03: 30. Unfortunately during the difficult recovery from the beach a number of items, including a night vision scope and diving items are lost in the shallow water and cannot be recovered in the dark. Although of limited monetary value the concern is that their discovery would confirm the attackers have come from seaward, an aspect that everyone has taken great pains to hide.

The boats are quickly recovered, and the Strike Craft clears the coast without delay. Shortly after 05:00 a number of radars, including Barlock are suddenly detected emanating from Namibe. This is an indication that something has woken the local community up. Although by now 25nm clear of the coast, those on the bridge can see the sky over Namibe being illuminated, confirming that the fuel depot is ablaze. Later that morning, a commercial radio station, Capital Radio broadcasting from the Transkei on 604 kHz announces that UNITA has claimed an attack on Namibe with much damage caused.

Meanwhile the Johanna van der Merwe, as she could not remain in the area dives observing an explosion from the area of the fuel tanks at 05:33 that morning, followed by flames which can be seen above the cliffs and at 06:15 she makes her way into the bay with extreme caution to observe the visible results of the attack. The fuel farm can then be seen clearly with fires burning fiercely but the LPG gas tank and one of the fuel tanks still appear intact amongst the flames. At the commercial quay she can see four vessels plus the tug. The first vessel, a small unidentified and undamaged Cuban ship lying at the southern end of the quay, seems to have avoided the attention of the SA Forces and is still with its lights on. The second vessel is a Cuban registered general cargo ship of about 6,000 tons, which has been severely damaged and is lying with a severe list to port and sinking at the berth. Behind her is a large Russian cargo vessel of some 15,000 tons listing about 30° to port and with no lights on and no movement visible aboard. The fourth vessel, another Russian cargo ship estimated at about 12,000 tons, is about 2m down by the stern and listing 15° to port, also with no lights or movement visible. Four small fishing boats are active in the bay and another five off the Giraul Plateau – the largest number observed by the Submarine during her period off the port.

Having completed her task, the submarine exits the bay just after 08:00 and once in deep water has a last look around and can see the fires still burning fiercely some 3 hours after the explosion. She then turns south and heads for home at best speed as her priority is to clear the area as soon as possible while remaining undetected.

Author's Note: Details of Operation DROSDY can be found in the book 'Iron Fist from the Sea'.

Table Cloth

Steve, Zella and Nicole arrive back in Cape Town to settle back into their home and life at the coast. Steve will be reporting to 25 Squadron after the furniture has been unloaded, house unpacked, and the family settled back into a normal life. The disruption of living in an apartment in a city that they barely knew has taken its toll on the little family. Zella will be returning to the Dental Practice in Rondebosch and Nicole re-enlisted at the Day Care in Bothasig. With life almost back to normal, Steve knuckles down to start his career in Fixed Wing aircraft as an F/E.

At the Squadron Steve is immediately put on the Technical Conversion course to get the DC3 Engines, Airframe, Instruments, Electrical, and Avionics Competencies. He is also allocated to large maintenance tasks like engine changes, under carriage checks and fuel tank replacement. Very soon Steve is confident enough to tackle any corrective maintenance task on the old bird.

The Douglas DC-3 is a fixed-wing propeller-driven aircraft. Its cruise speed 333 km/h and range 2,400 km revolutionized air transport in the 1930s and 1940s. Its lasting effect on the airline industry and World War II makes it one of the most significant transport aircraft ever made.

Cloth over Table Mountain

Together with its military derivative, the C-47 Skytrain, designated the Dakota in British Royal Air Force (RAF) service, and with Russian- and Japanese-built versions, over 16,000 were built. Following the Second World War, the airliner market was flooded with surplus C-47s and other ex-military transport aircraft, and Douglas' attempts to produce an upgraded DC-3 were a failure due to cost.

While the DC-3 was soon made redundant on main routes by more advanced types such as the Douglas DC-6 and Lockheed Constellation, the design continued to prove exceptionally adaptable and useful. Large numbers continue to see service in a wide variety of niche roles well into the 21st century.

"DC" stands for "Douglas Commercial". Production of DSTs ended in mid-1941 and civil DC-3 production ended in early 1943, although dozens of DSTs and DC-3s ordered by airlines that were produced between 1941 and 1943 were impressed into the US military while still on the production line. Military versions were produced until the end of the war in 1945. A larger, more powerful Super DC-3 was launched in 1949 to positive reviews. The civilian market, however, was flooded with second-hand C-47s, many of which were converted to passenger and cargo versions. Only five Super DC-3s were built, and three of them were delivered for commercial use. The prototype Super DC-3 served the U.S. Navy with the designation YC-129 alongside 100 R4Ds that had been upgraded to the Super DC-3 specification.

"ADIUVAMUS" – Help

The South African Air Force obtained all their DC3's after the Second World War and due to current embargoes have successfully managed to keep the aircraft in top condition. There are sufficient new parts still in long-term storage to support the aircraft for many years. At 1 Air Depot is a fully developed maintenance and repair capability for all components, including the engines.

25 Squadron DC3's over Cape Town

Steve passes his F/E check ride and is allocated trips on the Roster, which will take him all over the country. The DC3 or Dak and also known as "Kots Koets" (Puke Wagon) is utilized extensively for Rat Runs (Ration Supply) in the Operational area, Para Trooping, Personnel and Cargo Movement and a variety of other Special Operational tasks.

Steve is allocated an aircraft to prepare for a west coast trip in the next few days. He gets his checklist out and starts assembling all the items he will need for the trip which will last a couple of days. Major Jan Brandewyn van Zyl and Captain Herman Habig are the Pilot's for the trip. It is early morning when Steve completes the Pre-Flight Inspection and Ground Run of the aircraft, ensuring that all systems are serviceable and functional. The pilots arrive and after a short briefing the aircraft is prepared for the trip. They are parked at AFB Ysterplaat's Movement Control and will be taking on a number of PAX (Passengers). As if ordered, the movement's clerk leads out the PAX to the aircraft. Steve goes to the rear doors to ensure that the PAX move as far forward as possible, to keep the C of G forward. Once everyone is located, Steve joins the pilots upfront for the Pre-Start Checklist. With the checklist done, Jan instructs Steve to perform the Start Up.

They taxi out and obtain clearance from the Tower to line up for take-off. Herman is the flying pilot for this part of the leg. Pre-Take Off checks completed and Herman advances both throttles to 25 inches of boost. Jan is monitoring boost and taps Herman's hands when 25 inches is reached. Steve monitors RPM, Temps, and Pressures also ensuring that all the other systems remain in the green. The DC3 rumbles down the runway and the tail lifts off the ground. As the speed builds up the aircraft becomes more stable, and very soon Jan calls V1, committed speed for take-off. A short while later Jan confirms V2, take-off speed and Herman pulls the yoke back to lift the DC3 off the ground and into the air.

As the non-flying pilot Jan sets the radios and navigation systems for the flight and makes the required transmissions to the appropriate traffic controllers. Heading and climb power are set, while the aircraft continues to climb to 10,000 ft where they will level off and continue their flight up the west coast. The first port of call will be Alexander Bay.

Alexander Bay (Afrikaans - Alexanderbaai) is a town in the extreme north-west of South Africa, also known as the region of Little Namaqualand. It is located on the southern bank of the Orange River mouth. It was named for Sir James Alexander, who was the first person to map the area whilst on a Royal Geographical Society expedition into Namibia in 1836. It is mistakenly believed by many locals that it was he who first established commercial copper mining in the area. With diamonds being discovered along the West Coast in 1925, Alexander Bay was established to service the mining industry.

The town of Oranjemund lies on the northern bank of the river, which forms the international border with SWA. The two towns are linked by the Harry Oppenheimer Bridge, named for Harry Oppenheimer in 1951.

The town is served by an airport known as the Alexander Bay Airport. After diamonds were discovered along this coast in 1925 by Dr. Hans Merensky, Alexander Bay became known for its mining activities. The resulting diamond rush led to the Diamond Coast rebellion of 1928. Copper ore were shipped through the Richtersveld in barges down the Orange River for export from this bay. The town was a high security area and permits were needed when entered. It is no longer a high security area and no permits are needed.

Alexander Bay

Alexander Bay is the most northerly situated town along the west coastline of South Africa. The Orange River enters the Atlantic Ocean at Alexander Bay. The Orange River wetland forms the border between South Africa and SWA.

Fields of green and orange lichen grow on a hill near the turnoff to Alexander Bay town. It is 150 miles (240 km) north-west of Springbok, the administrative center of Namaqualand. Being near the southern end of the Namib Desert, it is officially also the driest town in South Africa with an average annual rainfall of less than 2 inches (50 mm). The cold Benguela Current in the Atlantic Ocean has a moderating influence on the coastal climate with only small variations in diurnal and seasonal temperatures.

Alexander Bay Airport is the destination for today, and at the top of climb, 10,000 ft. above mean sea level, Herman throttles the boost back and sets the propeller RPM for cruise. The flight will take them just under 3 hours to reach Alexander Bay. Steve settles in at the Navigators Table and updates the aircraft travel log. He checks the hydraulic fluid level and verifies all the systems are still in the green. Jan is updating the radio work and verifying position on the map. The view is spectacular at this altitude and the route they are following crisscrosses the coast line all the way to their destination. The three of them get along well and both Herman and Steve have beards so immediately a nicknaming convention is initiated. Due to Steve's height he is dubbed KBB "Klein Baard Bek" (Small Bearded Face) while Herman is called GBB "Groot Baard Bek" (Large Bearded Face).

As in Steve's last trip up the west coast on the Navy Ship SAS Protea, the cold ocean current and warm coastal air combine to form a large bank of fog all along the coast line. The concern for the Dak crew now is how long the fog was going to hang around. They will soon need to descend for an approach and landing. The jostling and jokes lighten the trip and very soon Jan is requesting approach and landing instructions from Alexander Bay Airport. Alex Bay confirms that the airfield is closed due to the weather conditions. Alex Bay ATC clears them down to 5,000 ft initially till overhead the field and then to enter an orbit around the airport, in anticipation that the fog will clear. At 5,000 ft Herman levels off, and they enter a wide orbit around Alex Bay. A strange site below shows the tail of a C130 sticking up out of the fog and the Control Tower windows and roof are also some of the few visible items indicating that they are indeed overhead the airfield. The C130 had taxied out to the runway threshold and was completing power checks when the fog quickly moved in, stranding them where they currently are. Inside the Dak cockpit, Steve and the other two are immediately aware of how hot it is and a quick glance at the outside air temperature (OAT) gauge confirms that it is 30 degrees Celsius at this altitude. The ATC has reported the OAT at 19 degrees. So there was an inversion due to the fog moving in under the warmer air.

Just as they thought that a diversion airfield may have to be selected the Alex Bay ATC informs them that the fog is starting to clear and that they would be able to continue an approach within 15 minutes. Right to the minute the fog starts to clear and the C130 lumbers down the runway for take-off. Next it is the Dak's turn to land. Herman completes a downwind leg and sets the aircraft up for a final approach to land.

The landing is completed and the DC3 taxis into the commercial parking area where the PAX are disembarked. Steve jumps up onto the aircraft wing and checks the engine oil for both engines while he awaits the refueling Bowser to top up the fuel tanks for the return trip to Ysterplaat. Within 40 minutes the crew is ready to receive their new PAX and begin the return trip. Steve starts the DC3 and soon they taxi out for take-off. The return flight is as uneventful as the flight up. Steve gets to know his pilots much better during the hours between landings. Jan was previously an instructor on the Impala at AFB Langebaan Weg, on the west coast about 200 km from Cape Town. He was also a member of the elite aerobatic flying team the Silver Falcons.

Closing in on Engineering

It is back to School for Steve, as he enters the final phases of the Engineering qualification. This time he is completing NTC V of the qualification process. Steve does well in all the subjects with the exception of Science, as the Teacher is more concerned about sharing stories than teaching the class. For the younger generation this is great as they don't have to knuckle down and study. For Steve this is frustrating, as he has limited time to study due to Air Force commitments and needs to get as much tutoring under the belt as possible. Steve approaches Mr. Louw, the teacher, to discuss the issue who nonchalantly states that Steve must get with the program. Steve loses it and states that he will report the teacher, to which Mr. Louw responds.

"Come with me to the Principal".

"No, I am taking you to the Principal", says Steve, and he marches off to the Principals office.

A very surprised Principal allows Steve to proceed with his complaint.

"Sir, I am here to learn and not listen to an old man brag about his life time escapades. The Air Force does not allow me to waste its money at a College that does not take education seriously. If this person is not spoken to or replaced I will not return to his class and also report this to my superiors".

With that Steve marches off and finds an empty class to go over the Science lesson himself and work through old examination papers.

The following week is slightly improved and then Mr. Louw is suddenly on vacation and is replaced by another teacher who enthusiastically conducts the Science lessons. The weeks forward Steve crams as much as he can into his study schedule to ensure that he obtains good marks. He cannot afford to rewrite any subjects and must do well. By the end of this term he will have accumulated 12 of the 16 required subjects.

At home in the evenings Steve spends as much time with Nicole as possible. She is growing up quickly and with a mop of curly red hair is the center of attention where ever the family goes. The bond with Nicole is tight and Steve is overwhelmed with emotion every time he has to leave them on a Special Operations Tour or extended duty. The time has come for exams and Steve dives into the past examinations, completing as many as possible in the short period before he starts to write his finals.

School Block completed Steve arrives back at 25 Squadron in time for his first Special Operations Tour on the Dak. This trip will take him to AFB Grootfontein for a two-week tour.

Grootfontein

At 25 Squadron Special Operations deployment, the crew teams up at the Squadron and are assigned an aircraft for the tour. Steve prepares the aircraft and ensures that the fly away pack up kit is complete with sufficient components, lubricants, parts and literature for the two-week deployment. He also verifies that the aircraft technical log is correct, accurate, and that no major component changes or maintenance actions will be required for the period they are on tour. At 16:30 Steve heads off to the NCO's Pub to have a few beers with the guys before heading home to pack for the trip in the morning.

It is the 25th April 1986 and Steve arrives extra early at the Squadron and with the assistance of the Ground Crew prepares the aircraft for the trip up to Grootfontein. They will be taking PAX and Cargo with them on this trip. Maj Jan Brandewyn Van Zyl and Capt. Mark Moses are the Pilots on this tour. It will be Steve's first trip with Mark, and Steve already has picked up a bit of tension in the air between Jan and Mark. The senior pilot did not seem to have much time for his co-pilot. The briefing, start-up and take-off are completed smoothly, and they are soon heading north towards SWA towards Grootfontein. The flight should take them approximately 6 hours.

Grootfontein (Afrikaans for Large Spring) is a city of 23,793 inhabitants in the Otjozondjupa Region of central South West Africa. It is one of the three towns in the Otavi Triangle, situated on the national road that leads from Otavi to the Caprivi Strip. Grootfontein receives an annual average rainfall of 557 millimeters.

The place was known to the Herero under the name Otjivanda. In 1885, 40 Boer families from the north-west of South Africa settled at Grootfontein. Part of the Dorsland trekkers, they were heading towards Angola. When that territory fell under Portuguese control, they turned back and established the Republic of Upingtonia at Grootfontein. Abandoned by 1887, it became the headquarters of the South West Africa Company in 1893.

In 1908 the Roman Catholic Church established a mission in Grootfontein as the basis of their eventually successful attempt to establish missions in Kavango.

Like all the towns in the Otavi Triangle, Grootfontein is very green in summer but drier in winter. In spring, Jacaranda and Flamboyant trees bloom. The town has an old German Schutztruppe fortress from the year 1896, which today houses a museum that expounds on the local history. The economic mainspring of the area was for many decades the Berg Aukas and Abenab mines to the north east of the town. These produced zinc and vanadium but have since closed. This is dolomite country and the carbonate deposits in the upper parts of the mine have yielded interesting fossils of Simian or Pongoid creatures that lived millions of years before modern humans evolved.

Twenty-four kilometers west of Grootfontein lies the huge Hoba meteorite. At over 60 tons, it is the largest known meteorite on Earth, as well as being the largest naturally occurring mass of iron known to exist on the planet's surface.

AFB Grootfontein has been established by the South African Government as the Forward Command Post for the Military in SWA. The Air Force Base has a long runway that easily accommodates large transport aircraft, bombers and fighters. Fully laden Mirage F1 and Buccaneer Bombers are launched from here for strategic attacks on SWAPO Bases in Angola.

During the long flight passengers come up to the front of the aircraft in hopes of looking into the cockpit area. Mark a lady's man tells Steve to bring the ladies up. Steve has welded together a stool for himself that he straps down between the pilots so that he can sit there during the flight instead of at the Navigators table. The stool is unfortunately not very lady like and when one is seated your legs naturally spread to allow a more comfortable position. The three-perverted aircrew therefore invite the ladies with the shortest dresses and skirts up front to judge the legs. Steve sits back in the Navigators table and passes comments forward to the pilots while they try and chat to the attractive passenger. What they don't know is that Steve has a cold mike switch and volume control to allow selectively what the lady can hear. At the opportune moment, when Mark has just asked the young lady where she is from? Steve would turn her volume down and comment how lovely her butt filled the seat. Both pilots would turn blood red and focus straight ahead. This carries on for quite some time until Jan catches a sniff in the wind.

"KBB, ek gaan jou bliksem" says Jan. (KBB I am going to smash you).

Steve bursts out laughing, and the rest of the trip is spent on teasing the pilots on being so vane. The time passes quickly and soon they are on a long final approach to AFB Grootfontein. Jan taxis the aircraft to Movements Control and completes the shut-down procedure. Steve exits the aircraft and allows the ground personnel to off-load while he completes an after-flight inspection, oils and refuels the aircraft in preparation for the next sortie in the morning. Jan has dispatched Mark to get a Truck for them so that they can take their night stop kit to the rooms and ready themselves for supper. The pilots are assigned officers' quarters while Steve is sent to the NCO quarters.

The Mess is a combined area and the three crew meet up for supper and a couple of drinks. Jan has been briefed on their first tasking the next day. They will be taking the same bunch of ladies with them on a tour of the operational area. Their first leg will take them to Mpacha, then Rundu, Ondangwa and back to Grootfontein. Jan and Steve keep the drinking down to a gallop while Mark ends up meeting some friends and disappears for the night.

Before sunrise the next morning, Steve is busy at the aircraft preparing it for the long flight of the day. He checks the engine oil levels, does a thorough inspection of the airframe and verifies that all the systems are functional. He completes a ground run to ensure that the magnetos are good, and the engines are operating smoothly. Just as Steve is about to shut down, Jan slips into the seat next to him and assists Steve in the shut-down procedure. Jan is not a happy camper this morning. Apparently, Mark did not return to his room last night and Jan is livid. He briefs Steve that if Mark arrives late for take-off that Steve must take over the co-pilots position for the trip and that Mark is going to be in big trouble. Steve is not concerned as he has enough piloting experience to be useful and knows the systems better than the pilots do.

At the last second Mark stumbles into the cockpit and receives a severe tongue lashing from Jan. Mark smiles sheepishly and takes his place in the co-pilots seat. The trip this day was going to be a very interesting one indeed. Jan ignored Mark for the rest of the trip with the exception of check list confirmation and instructions on what he needed for the flight. Tonight, they will be night stopping at Mpacha and the next night at Eenhana. The first landing of the day is Nkongo, where they are to drop off rations for the Army base. Jan is keeping the aircraft low and fast to evade any possibility of missile attacks. Small groups of terrorist's target runways and lay in wait for approaching aircraft to lock the SAM 7 heat seeking missiles onto. The aircrews of the South African Air Force are well aware of these tactics and have devised flight plans that shelter them from impending lock on by the infrared heat seeking missiles. You either approach high and spiral down with limited power setting, allowing less opportunity of lock on, or you approach low and fast to sneak in to the airfield and land before the enemy knows you are even there.

Army Base Ops Room

Jan deftly maneuvers the big aircraft into a short final approach and throttles back allowing the aircraft to sink onto the runway. After a short taxi to the holding area, the crew completes shutdown. Steve moves to the back to open the doors allowing the PAX to exit, and then guides the SAMIL Truck into position for the ration unload. Jan and Mark trudge off to the Ops Room, which is housed in a bunker built from galvanized Armco and layers of sandbags.

An hour later with PAX onboard and all briefed, Jan sets heading for the next base Nepara, only 30 minutes flying away. Jan keeps the Dak at low level just skimming over the tops of the tall Makalani Palm trees. Cattle and local population scatter beneath as the roar of the twin Pratt & Whitney Radials flashes over them. It is almost midday and the heat radiating from the earth together with the warm air creates a bumpy ride at this low altitude. It is not long before the first whiff of vomit filters up to the cockpit from some of the PAX that cannot hold out any longer and are ungraciously spewing into the Barf Bags.

The whoosh of the aircraft passing close by the tall Makalani Palms is calming during the bouncing cockpit and also quite an impressive site.

Makalani Palms

Once gain Jan completes a flawless landing and taxis the aircraft to the holding area. Steve repeats the offload process while Jan and Mark head off to the Ops Room to update Oshikati on the RAT Run Progress. The next landing will be Buffalo, the home of 32 Battalion. Once again, they complete the short 30-minute flight at low level, and this time picking up the mighty Zambesi river part way through the flight. It is a beautiful site flying so low and fast over this beautiful wetland area teaming with wildlife. Elephant, Hippo, Water Buffalo, and assortment of antelope cover the green plains along the river. The green belt of the Caprivi Strip is truly a sight to behold from the cockpit of any low flying aircraft. Once again, a repeat of the landing at Buffalo, and Steve reminisces the time he visited here when still on Gunships and fondly remembers the outing on the river with the large motorized barge the base used for floating Braai's on the river at sunset.

The next landing will be for the night stop at Mpacha. At Mpacha Steve refuels and replenishes the Oil of the Dak, and then performs the Post Flight Maintenance Inspection. He notices an oil leak from one of the rocker covers and decides to fix it. Fortunately, he has the required gasket in his flyaway kit and with the help of the local ground crew he removes the port engine cowling to replace the gasket. Within the hour Steve cleans up and enters the repair in the Technical Log, as well as the fuel and oil replenished.

The Dak Crew has a very entertaining evening at the Air Force Pub of Mpacha where Steve, Jan and Mark have met up with Chopper Crews that are stationed there for a month. Lots of war stories are shared, and then it's off to bed to catch forty winks before the continuation flight of the RAT Run. Mark seems to have learnt his lesson and is the very first one to go to bed that night.

First light the next morning Steve is surprised to see Mark join him in preparing the aircraft for the days flying. The SAMIL Truck fully loaded is already waiting to discharge their RAT's and Steve guides the loading of the DAK. He must ensure that the weight is evenly distributed so that the aircrafts C of G is at optimum, allowing for safe flight. Mark completes the Pre-Flight Inspection and turns both engine Props through a full rotation to clear the hydraulic lock that can form in Radial engines from oil draining into the lower cylinder heads over night.

By the time that Jan arrives with the trip authorization and maps, Mark and Steve have already run the aircraft and checked the systems. They now only have to await the arrival of the PAX for this leg of the trip. Included in this RAT Run is fresh meat for the next Bases they will be landing at. Jan does not have to convince Steve into ensuring that not all the meat ends up in the Brown Jobs camps, by hiding some of the Sirloin Steaks and Lamb Chops at the Navigators Table up front. By the time the PAX have boarded the reassignment of meat has been concluded. The route today will be Eenhana, Ruacana, Okongwati, Opuwa and Ondangwa for a night stop.

Early evening and the three tired Dak Crew members land at Ondangwa for the night. Steve puts the old girl to bed and then rescues the stolen meat from under the Navigators table. They will all be staying at the Fixed Wing quarters in the aircrew area.

Air Crew Area AFB Ondangwa

Steve grabs a ride down to the Pub with the Puma crews to get stocks and salads for the evening. It promises to be a fun evening for sure. Steve goes to the back door at the Pub and asks the Barman to help him out with some beers, a bottle of Brandy and Cokes. The money and goods exchange hands. Next Steve knocks on the Mess's back door and begs the Chef to give him a bowl of salad and to toss in some bread. Duly arranged, Steve jumps back into the Puma Garry and makes his way up to the aircrew area.

The hardwood fire has already been started and the flames licking up high into the night sky. Many of the gents around the fire are already on a station to happiness. Steve gets some utensils, spices, and cutlery from the kitchen and prepares the duly liberated steaks and chops for braai. Steve has also found a packet of Maize Meal and decides to make a serving of Pap and Sous. (Maize, Stiff Porridge and Sauce).

Within an hour Steve has the Pap and Sous ready and joins the already inebriated group to Braai the meat. Meat duly spiced, Steve places it on the grid above the hot coals and monitors it closely. The last thing he needs now is to burn the meat. The Beers are flowing freely, and the crescendo of voices is picking up considerably. Soon the food is ready, and the bunch of drunkards dig in for the feast of a life time.

Duly fed the serious drinking begins. Now Jan Brandewyn Van Zyl is true to his nickname and soon the Brandy and Coke is being generously distributed. Jokes are being shared and the laughter is unending. A couple of years previously, the legendary Soutie Sowden had started playing bag pipes with the local wild cats that come in to the Braai area for scraps. Steve decides it's time to continue the good work that Soutie started.

He grabs a cat which is trying to liberate the already liberated meat. Next, he swings the cat under his arm and without a shirt on, grabs the cat's tail, places it in his mouth and starts to blow. Gently squeezing the cat, a wonderful melody erupts, bringing the crowd to their knees in utter enjoyable laughter at the spectacle before them. The cat does a clawing action release and runs off into to the darkness like a deflating tire going pffft pffft all the way.

Steve wipes of the sweat from his chest and back when Mark turns to him and shouts.

"Shit Steve, you are full of blood man!"

Steve reaches back and realizes that the cat had clawed at his back to get free, and he was bleeding freely. Well it was time to visit the sweet nurses at the Ondangwa Hospital, and with Major Jan leading the charge, Steve is the Casevac on route to the Hospital across the road.

Steve and his drunken rescuers enter the hospital and are immediately chastised for their unruly behavior. Jan takes charge and soon Steve is receiving treatment, while Jan ensures that he is fed sufficient anesthetic in the Brandy and Coke division. The nurse shakes her head in disgust but cleans Steve up, and jabs him in the butt for safety. She then places band aids on the worst of the cuts and sends the drunks on their way.

Hospital at Ondangwa

The next morning it is a very hungover Dak crew that makes their way to the aircraft for the return flight to Grootfontein. They are to transport PAX only on the return trip. The trip is uneventful, and a grateful crew checks in at Grootfontein to spend their last night there before returning to Cape Town.

Steve's first Dak Special Operation tour has come to an end. He arrives back home in time for his and Nicole's birthdays. Steve is 29 and Nicole a beautiful 2 years old. The bond between them is growing stronger every day. Whenever Steve gets back from a tour Nicole would jump on his lap and put her arms around his neck and hug him and would not let go. Every now and again she would release here hold a little, lean back and look at Steve and then giggle and hug him tight again.

Fixed Wing Squadron Life

Back at the Squadron Steve is determined to get back on to Helicopters and takes a walk over to 30 Squadron to have a chat with WO Don Bacon, the F/E in charge of training at the Squadron. Don does not have good news and informs Steve that he has to have special qualifications to be able to join 30 Squadron due to the elite and challenging trips that they perform. Steve is not perturbed and goes looking for FSgt Russel Du Preez with whom he had shared a Tour at Ondangwa. Russel lets Steve know that he should apply for a transfer stating his desire to be on a Puma Squadron and validate it with his experience at 22 Squadron, the SAP and the training experience he has at 87 HFS.

Duly motivated Steve gets the applicable application forms and completes them. He then books an appointment with the 25 Squadron Technical Officer, to discuss the reasoning behind his request, in the hopes of a favourable acceptance and signed motivation so that he can submit the application. The CTO does not object and actually motivates that Steve will be an asset to any Squadron to which he is deployed. Jan Brandewyn Van Zyl had given the CTO feedback on the Operational Tour of Steve's professional and exemplar performance as an F/E. Steve is elated and embarrassed at the same time. He rushes to the duty room to get the application submitted for processing to Air Force Headquarters.

For the next two months Steve completes a number of trips which include east and west coast. He even gets time to spend an evening with Mike Freer, now stationed at 16 Squadron at AFB Port Elizabeth. Steve and Mike spend the evening catching up on old times discussing what each has been up to in the last 6 years since they last saw each other at Bloemfontein when Mike was completing his F/E Course.

Grootfontein Round Two

The winter in the Cape is still in full swing when it's time to head north once more for Steve. The rain is pelting down, and the southeaster is blowing up a storm, as Steve prepares his aircraft for his next Special Operations Tour to SWA. The schedule take-off is for 07:00 the next morning, and Steve has to ensure that the aircraft maintenance is up to date and he also reviews the Aircraft Log history to make sure that there have been no repetitive snags reported that he needs to be concerned about.

It takes Steve most of the day to check and repair minor issues on the aircraft until he is satisfied that he has done all that is required. He packs the fly-away kit and then gets the ground crew to assist him in placing the aircraft on the flight line. He secures the aircraft and then heads home for the evening.

Steve spends the evening entertained by Nicole and is enthralled as to how quickly she is growing up. Her beautiful red locks and splash of freckles on her light complexion face makes his chest swell in pride. Nicole fills a very big place in Steve's heart.

It is the 5th August 1986 early morning and the weather has not let up. Steve prepares and signs the aircraft documentation and then completes the Before Flight Inspection. Next, he calls on the ground crew and starts both engines to check the systems. With the run-up completed, Steve heads to movement control to check the cargo for the day's flight. He will have to complete the weight and balance sheet to confirm the aircrafts C of G. Steve's pilots for this trip are Maj Gawie Steenkamp and Capt. Herman Habig (GBB). Both are seasoned transport pilots and Steve has great respect for them.

The briefing is short and to the point, GBB will be doing the flying today with Gawie on the Navigation and Radios. This morning's take-off will be very marginal based on the weather conditions, and further up the coast it is not any better. Icing conditions are below 8,000 ft. so Steve double checks the De-Icing fluid for the Propellers and Windshields.

Their first stop is 200 km up the coast at AFB Langebaan Weg, where they are to pick up some spares for an Impala fighter based in SWA. The take-off is completed and as soon as the aircraft clears the airport fencing they are immediately in the cloud and in Instrument Flight Rules (IFR). Gawie is directing GBB via the Navigation instruments and completing the radio calls to obtain clearance to the north for AFB Langebaan Weg. GBB has the aircraft in a steady climb to the altitude they have been cleared by Cape Town International Control. Gawie sets the heading on the Navigation Instrument and confirms heading for GBB.

The next 30 minutes there is no visibility outside of the cockpit as the rain pelts down and the skies get even darker from the dense clouds. On approach to Langebaan Gawie requests an Instrument Landing Approach (ILS). The ATC sets them up on a long final approach and then proceeds to give 5 second interval corrections on heading and altitude. GBB follows the instructions to the last, and only at 200 ft do they eventually break cloud. The ATC continues to talk them down to touch down. GBB taxis in to Movement Control and they shut down for a well-deserved cup of hot coffee at the Ops Room.

Steve drinks up and returns to the aircraft to supervise the loading of the engine that they need to take with to SWA. By the time that Steve has loaded and checked the cargo, the weather has let up sufficiently to allow them to take-off. The crew obtains the required clearances and gets the show on the road. This leg of the journey they will have to fly at 10,000 ft meaning that they will pick up icing.

At 7,500 ft. ice starts to form on the windshield. Steve goes to the back and checks out the port and starboard passenger windows for icing on the wings. A thin layer has already started to form. Gawie opens the de-icing cock to start clearing the worst of the ice from the propellers. They continue to climb through the icing level until the windshield is completely iced up. At 9,600 ft. they break cloud cover into brilliant sunshine. Soon after there are loud thumps against the sides of the aircraft as chunks of ice start breaking off from the propellers. Very soon the windshield is clear enough to see out of and Gawie closes off the de-icing cock.

They start to relax after the tense IFR flight they have just come out of. Gawie looks out the port window and points to the aircraft shadow on the clouds surrounded by a perfect circular rainbow, known as the guardian angel to aviators. The rest of the flight is uneventful and the three take the time to chat and get to know each other better as a crew. Steve discusses his need to get back to Choppers with the two pilots, and to his surprise Gawie agrees with him.

"Steve, you are far to experienced to be a flying mechanic. I had always wondered why you came to Dak's in the first place?" says Gawie.

"Sir, it was a snap decision from Air Force HQ to get me back to the Cape, and it was agreed that I should apply for transfer to the first available posting on Choppers", responds Steve.

"Ah, that makes sense, well you are a good man Steve, and I wish you the best. I will chat to the OC of 30 Squadron when we return", says Gawie.

And so, the conversation moves on to all the contacts that Steve has taken part in, with both pilots pumping him for more details. Steve elaborates on the bad and good and all the jokes that were pulled on the various people during the tours. Gawie is laughing so loud that he did not even hear the ATC calling them to check position and ETA. With a nudge from GBB they quieten down and listen to the repeat call from ATC. Gawie responds accordingly and updates ATC on ETA.

The weather has now cleared up completely and they can see the earth below at 10,000 ft. Very soon they will change frequencies once more and then make their final heading corrections to Grootfontein. The landing, Taxi and unloading take a short time to perform and while Steve completes the Post Flight Inspections, the pilots take their kit to the living quarters and get the keys for the assigned rooms for all.

Steve joins them an hour later and they all cleanup for supper at the mess. Tonight, is a quiet night and Gawie knows a local bar where they can enjoy a couple of drinks before settling in for the night. The next day will be the long RAT run along the Caprivi Strip. This will once again present the Air Force Crew with an opportunity to liberate some meat along the way. The three discuss where they should plan the barbecue for and all agree that as they are not night stopping anywhere on the way, they would ask the ground crew chief Jorrie Jordaan to prepare for a Braai the next evening. Gawie asks Steve to take care of getting Jorrie squared away and he and GBB will take care of the liquid refreshments.

As aircrew it is always good practice to take care of the ground crew who work tireless hours in making sure that the aircraft are well maintained and safe. This small token of appreciation is an untold rule in the Air Force. The next day's flight is completed in record time, and the Dak is back in Grootfontein by 16:00. Jorrie is there to greet the crew and helps Steve to put the aircraft to bed for the night and completes the Post Flight Inspection. At the back of the Hangar is a Braai area that Jorrie had built over the years that he has been stationed here. The fire was already lit and pots on the side of the fire place indicated that the traditional Pap and Sous were ready, as well as a lovely Pot Bread.

Jorrie had also arranged for a bath tub of ice to cool the liquid refreshments in. Gawie and GBB make quick work of the Ops debrief and soon return with crates of beer for the tub of ice. All the ground crew has gathered round and Gawie has invited the ATC and Ops personnel to share in the spoils. Steve presents the liberated offerings to Jorrie who happily gets busy at the braai to prepare the final additive to the meals. The long-term personnel have their families here as well, so it is truly a gathering and fun evening ahead. The beer flows freely, and a hearty meal is enjoyed by all. Steve takes center stage with a stream of jokes that just keep on pouring out, one after the other. The appreciative gathering just keeps on pumping beer in his hands, so he can continue the charade of accents, facial expressions and mimics.

Eventually the fire burns down, the beer is finished, and people start moving off to bed, a truly great evening for everyone. Steve gets to bed very contented at a great day's flying and then celebration of good people he has had the honour of working with. The rest of Steve's tour is relaxed with many hours flown on short trips ferrying PAX, Cargo or both. Before the three can really settle in to the tour it is time to pack up and head back south. It has truly been an enjoyable two weeks and the three chat about it all the way back to Ysterplaat. Thankfully the weather is slightly improved on their return to the Cape and only traces of ice are visible on the wings.

On the descent the propellers throw off the melting ice with thuds against the airframe once more. This time they break cloud cover at 3,000 ft for a visual approach to Ysterplaat. A standard landing, taxi and shut down are completed.

The waiting ground crews help Steve to complete the refuel and Post Flight Maintenance before towing the aircraft to the 25 Squadron Flight Line. Steve gets his kit and heads home to the family.

The Apple of Dad's eye

Once again Nicole is overjoyed to see Steve and a repeat of grab dad around the neck, hug, grin hug again is completed for at least 30 minutes before Steve can sit down and catch up on the past two weeks. Zella has been enquiring to Stellenbosch University for the Oral Hygienist Course and has the opportunity to start studies in 1987, a few months' time.

The next morning Steve reports to the Squadron as normal and is called into the Technical Officer's Office. WO Du Toit asks Steve to sit down and smilingly shows him a signal from Air Force HQ. Steve's transfer to 30 Squadron has been approved and he has to move across today. He also has to pack and head to Pretoria for the conversion onto Puma Helicopters at 19 Squadron. Steve can barely contain himself from the excitement, his dream has come true. Steve thanks Oom Toit (Uncle Toit) and heads out to find a phone to call Zella. Zella does not sound very enthusiastic and Steve writes it off to her being concerned about the upcoming studies. Steve comforts Zella and confirms that he will be back before Christmas from Pretoria giving her freedom to start her studies.

Chapter 11 - CHOPPER POWER

It is the 22nd August 1986 when Steve arrives at AFB Waterkloof on the weekly Schedule C130 flight, where he is picked up by the 19 Squadron Duty Driver and taken to AFB Swartkop living quarters where a room has already been allocated to him. He unpacks his stuff and has a quick shower so that he can make it to the mess in time for a bite to eat. After supper Steve heads to the Warrant Officers Pub to meet up with rest of the students and 19 Squadron F/E's. He is greeted like a long-lost school friend and Ken van Straaten puts a fresh beer in his hand.

"Cheers Boet, and welcome, it's long overdue for you to be here with us"' says Ken.

Steve thanks Ken and the evening is off to a great start.

The next few weeks will be class room time where the students, pilots and F/E's will complete the technical training phase of Puma conversion. Steve enjoys the challenge of the Puma, a much more sophisticated aircraft than what he has had to work on in the recent past.

Puma - Cat of the Skies

The SA 330 Puma was originally developed by Sud Aviation to meet a requirement of the French Army for a medium-sized all-weather helicopter capable of carrying up to 20 soldiers as well as various cargo-carrying duties. The choice was made to develop a completely new design for the helicopter; work began in 1963 with backing from the French government. The first of two Puma prototypes flew on 15 April 1965. The first production SA 330 Puma flew in September 1968, with deliveries to the French Army starting in early 1969.

The SA 330 was a success on the export market, numerous countries purchased military variants of the Puma to serve in their armed forces; the type was also popularly received in the civil market, finding common usage by operators for transport duties to off-shore oil platforms. Throughout most of the 1970s, the SA 330 Puma was the best-selling transport helicopter being produced in Europe.

The SA 330 Puma is a twin-engine helicopter intended for personnel transport and logistic support duties. As a troop carrier, up to 16 soldiers can be seated on foldable seats; in a casualty evacuation configuration, the cabin can hold six litters and four additional personnel; the Puma can also perform cargo transport duties, using alternatively an external sling or the internal cabin, with a maximum weight of 2500 kg. Civilian Pumas feature a variety of passenger cabin layouts, including those intended for VIP services. In a search and rescue capacity, a hoist is commonly installed, often mounted on the starboard fuselage.

Pair of roof-mounted Turbomeca Turmo turboshaft engines power the Puma's four-blade main rotor. The helicopter's rotors are driven at a speed of roughly 265 rpm via a five-reduction stage transmission. The design of the transmission featured several unique and uncommon innovations for the time, such as single-part manufacturing of the rotor shaft and the anti-vibration measures integrated into the main gearbox and main rotor blades. The Puma also featured an automatic blade inspection system, which guarded against and alerted crews to fatigue cracking in the rotor blades. There are two hydraulic systems on board, these operate entirely independent of one another, one system powers only the aircraft's flight controls while the other serves the autopilot, undercarriage, rotor brake, and the flight controls.

In flight, the Puma was designed to be capable of high speeds, exhibit great maneuverability, and have good hot-and-high performance; the engines have an intentionally high level of reserve power to enable a Puma to effectively fly at maximum weight with only one functioning engine and proceed with its mission if circumstances require. The cockpit has conventional dual controls for a pilot and copilot, a third seat is provided in the cockpit for a reserve crew member or commander. The Puma features a SFIM-Newmark Type 127 electro-hydraulic autopilot; the autopilot is capable of roll and pitch stabilization; the load hook operator can also enter corrective adjustments of the helicopter's position from his station through the autopilot.

The Puma is readily air-transportable by tactical airlift aircraft such as the Transall C-160 and the Lockheed C-130 Hercules; the main rotor, landing gear, and tailboom are all detachable to lower space requirements. Ease of maintenance was one of the objectives pursued in the Puma's design; many of the components and systems that would require routine inspection were positioned to be visible from ground level, use of life-limited components was minimized, and key areas of the mechanical systems were designed to be readily accessed. The Puma is also capable of operating at nighttime, in inhospitable flying conditions, or in a wide range of climates from Arctic to desert environments.

From 1972 onwards, Pumas operated by the South African Air Force were deployed on extended operations in neighboring South West Africa and Angola during the Border War. During the first deployment to the Eastern Caprivi, one Puma crew member became the first member of the Air Force to be awarded the Honoris Crux. The Puma was involved in normal trooping; rapid deployment during "follow up" operations; acting as radio relays; evacuation of casualties; rescuing downed aircrew; insertion of Special Forces; and large scale cross border operations such as Savannah, Uric, Protea, Super, and Modular.

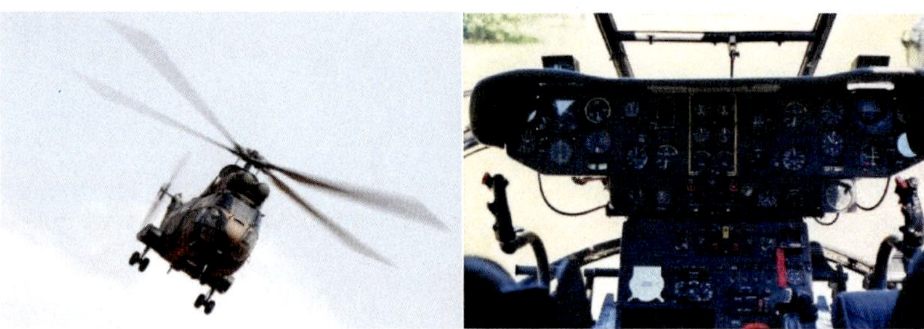

SAAF Puma

The majority of South African Puma purchases, including spare parts, were made in advance of an anticipated United Nations embargo that was applied in 1977. South Africa subsequently upgraded many of its Pumas. In December 1979, South Africa's government acknowledged the presence of its military forces operating in Zimbabwe; Pumas were routinely used in support of the South African Army's ground forces. In June 1980, 20 Pumas accompanied a force of 8,000 troops during a South African invasion of Angola in pursuit of nationalist SWAPO fighters. In 1982, the government confirmed that 15 servicemen had been killed when a South African Puma was downed by SWAPO forces; it was one of the worst losses suffered in a single incident in the conflict.

"Fama Ex Factus" - Fame Through Deeds

The Puma conversion course is in full swing and Steve knuckles down to ensure he learns all he can about this beautiful machine. He passes with flying colours and the next phase is set to start. They will be accompanied by a qualified Puma Engineer on their first few sorties until each student has been evaluated and graded. Only once the students pass the check flight, emergency procedures quiz and final technical exam are they entitled to fly as a solo F/E. The various phases of the conversion include general flying, instrument flying, confined area landing, hoisting, cargo sling, mountain flying, coastal flying and night flying. Most of the phases are completed at AFB Swartkop and the surrounding Rustenburg area.

On the course with Steve are Paddy More and a fellow newcomer to 30 Squadron Nic Henning. The three are as tight as the Three Musketeers, or as Steve refers to them the Three Mustard Queers. Steve enjoys the Puma immensely and can easily understand why his old friend Soutie Sowden from his Gunship days made the switch a couple of years ago. The Puma is fast, powerful and versatile. There is no lack of power when you need it and with the four-bladed main rotor she is smooth as silk. The F/E's workload in the Puma is an integral part of the cockpit and is therefore included into the checklists and vital actions. Pre-Start, Start-Up, Post Start, Fuel Management, Navigation and Vital Actions are all part of the F/E's tasking.

Peak to Peak

The weeks fly by quickly and soon the Squadron prepares for deployment to the Drakensburg for the Mountain Flying phase. With the jagged mountain peaks of the Drakensburg reaching up to 14,000 ft into the sky, this is the perfect platform for the next phase of training. Although Steve has been to the Drakensburg on many occasions with 87 HFS while at the training squadron in Bloemfontein, he has never had the opportunity to be part of this mighty machine in this constrained and dangerous environment. Here weather, wind and a multitude of other external factors add to make it the most difficult phase of flight training.

The forgiving Puma with its' power, autopilot and stable platform makes it the most versatile operating machine in the mountains. Steve enjoys every second he has onboard and loves the challenge he is faced with every time there is something new to train on.

Every day the crews brief before flying begins and every evening they debrief on the days sorties. Thus far they covered slope, pinnacle, and confined space landings in the lower altitudes of the Klein Berg (Small Mountains). This will be repeated at altitude in the Groot Berg (Big Mountains).

This adds in an additional risk as power at altitude and aerodynamic lift as well as overall performance all decrease with altitude. Add in wind and you have up and down drafts to wreak havoc with everything that they have just learnt. It is a full day flying for Steve and the pilot instructor that Steve is flying with is an exceptional pilot.

Dave Owen has an incredible ability to read the aircraft and instruct the student co-pilot on what to do and how to complete the exercise safely and efficiently. All through the flight Dave confers with Steve to ensure that he is fully up to speed with what the correct process is and where to identify if there is an error creeping in that could endanger the aircraft and crew. This type of cockpit management is precisely why the Air Force have such experienced and professional pilots.

Puma Mountain Cat

The team identifies a high pinnacle to land on and then circling it to establish up and down drafts drop a smoke grenade on the LZ (Landing Zone) to confirm wind direction. They then approach along the updraft side of the pinnacle and creep over to land on top, where Steve is now positioned on his stomach on the cargo floor to patter the flying pilot onto the LZ.

Coastal Prowling

With the mountain flying phase completed the aircraft deploy to Jozini up the northern Natal Coast. Jozini is a small town on the main route to Mozambique, and it is close to the Jozini or Pongolapoort Dam. Lake Jozini, as the dam is called, is a very popular Tiger fishing destination.

Because of its remote location, Jozini is the perfect place for a flight of noisy helicopters to complete the coastal flight training phase. The location is beautiful, pristine and offers many adventures for the outdoors man.

Once again, the flying program is crammed with various exercises for the crew to complete to further qualify and improve their proficiency on the Puma. The coast is a short 15-minute flight away from Jozini and then its drop down to 50 ft. above the ground and pull the power to watch the awesome Puma stretch her legs.

Northern Natal

With the thick coastal air, the engines provide maximum power and the rotor blades bite with the most effective lift hurtling the Puma through the air. With a power setting on the collective of 14.5 degrees pitch the aircraft quickly accelerates to just below VNE (Velocity Never Exceeded) and if you don't watch it she can easily exceed VNE of 165 Kts.

The awesome speed of the Puma at low level is truly a feeling that Steve gets thrilled by and cannot get enough of. The big Chopper is as agile as the small Alouette and can be thrown around or brought to a quick stop as easily.

With a couple of coastal sorties completed the final low-level phase is over the large Jozini Lake, which is the cherry on the cake for all the crews. The lake is a popular venue for fisherman and the lake and shore line are dappled with camp sites and boats on the water. To the joy of the spectators they are blessed with an aerial display of sleek fast-moving Choppers.

With the Coastal Flying phase nearing completion, it is time to relax and savour the moments that have transpired over the intense two weeks. Flying is completed early in the afternoon, and after completion Post Flight Inspections and Covering the Aircraft for the night, Steve accompanies the crews to the camp Pub for a bite to eat at the Braai and some Brown Gold liquid refreshments. It has been a very warm day and Steve together with Nic, Paddy and a couple of stragglers go for a last dip in the local swimming pool. Steve hops in with Beer in hand followed by the rest of the gang. The water is only 3 ft deep, so they lay back to cool off. Paddy in the meantime has gone for a pressure relief in the change room. As he comes out he sees everyone in the pool, and before Steve can shout out a warning Paddy launches a dive into the water. Paddy comes up spluttering and Steve jumps up to check him out. If he had hit his head, he could have a possible neck injury.

"Fuck who pulled the plug?" screams Paddy, as he gets up holding his forehead.

Steve giggling like a school girl is checking Paddy for physical signs of injury. His ligaments seem to be moving fine but there is a stream of blood running down the side of his face just above his right eye. Steve sees a cut where he had impacted the pool at the bottom.

"You need stitches Boet," says Steve.

Steve grabs his towel and gives it to Paddy to hold against his eye and guides him toward the Chopper Campsite. A Medic has been brought with on the trip as per operations standards. The group of guys sound like gaggling geese as they make their way to the Medics tents. Far too many brown bottles have already been consumed. At the Medic they discover that he is drunker than they are. Steve steps up and looks the lot over.

"Oi, I will stitch you up. Sit down let's clean it up," instructs Steve.

With that Steve pours some Whisky over Paddy's forehead and grabs a handful of swabs to dry it off. Next he tears open the needle and suture and squeezes the wound together and proceeds to stich the cut up. Paddy complains about the pain and Steve gives him a swig of Whisky.

"Here drink, Cowboys don't cry!" says Steve.

Stitches complete, Steve stands back to admire his job. Perfect stiches he thinks until he looks closer and sees that there are three more stiches past the cut. To cover up his over eager stiches, Steve slaps a Band Aid over the whole thing.

"There you go, good as new, now come buy me a beer", says Steve.

They saunter out of the Medics Tent and amble over to the Pub Tent to sing the evening away with all the choppers songs they can remember and those they are yet to invent.

Conquer the Night Skies

The crews arrive back at AFB Swartkop and prepare the aircraft for the final phase of the program in the coming weeks. They will have the weekend off and then it is back to classes and long hours of night flying, to hone their skills for operational flying they will soon be required to perform. Over the past few months Steve has been taking weekends off to his parents in Witbank. Slowly he has been assembling the MGA that he left with them after being transferred back to Cape Town from the SAP Air Wing.

Steve has had the car resprayed at a local panel shop while he rebuilt the Motor, Gearbox and Sub-Frame. With the spray job completed Steve is now in the final stages of assembly. The upholstery has been completed by his contacts at 2 Air Depot, and all the Chrome work done at 1 Air Depot. With the engine and gearbox re-installed, it is time to fire up the MGA for the first time since the rebuild. The car is Post Office red and looks stunning. Steve fuels up the tank, checks the oil levels and makes sure the radiator cap is secure. He primes the SU Carburetors and then gets in to swing the engine. The MGA roars to life on the first swing and purrs away like a very content kitten. Steve is overjoyed at the result. A few more weeks of work and he will be able to drive the car back to Cape Town after his Puma Conversion Course has come to an end.

<u>MGA Roadster</u>

It is Monday morning and Steve and the rest of the students are in class for the last phase of the Puma Conversion. Tonight, they start off with local area night flying to confirm the night flying procedures and the next evening they start a series of night navigation exercises which will be wrapped up by the end of the week. The final week will be final examinations and interviews, all in preparation of deploying operationally proficient Puma Crews into the Air Force.

As if planned there is a Chopper Reunion taking place at AFB Swartkop the coming weekend, which promises to be an almighty bash. All ex and present Chopper Crews will gather to celebrate 20 Years of Bush Chopper Operations in SWA. Crews from all over South Africa, serving and retired members will be attending. This is a fitting end of course for Steve as he proudly faces the next chapter in his Helicopter career.

Chopper Reunion Paintings

The first sortie of the night has them taking off at 15-minute intervals and joining the circuit at AFB Swartkop to practice what they have been given in the Classroom Instructions. The night flying procedures places an extra percentage of workload on the crews, as they have to work in unison to complete Vital Actions, Radio Calls, Aircraft Attitude, Altitude, Speed and Power settings. It is a busy office indeed and Steve is in his element for the whole sortie.

The next day Steve gets involved in the long night navigation planning exercise with his two pilots. The flight will take them as far as Louis Trichardt to the north and via a set route back to AFB Swartkop. They calculate fuel requirements, Waypoints for checking in accuracy, headings and time to go distances.

Ferry Fuel Tank

After sunset Steve has prepared the aircraft and secured three ferry tanks in the cabin of the Puma. With an additional 2,400 Lbs. of fuel there will be sufficient for the long navigation exercise they are going to complete tonight.

They are heading up to Nelspruit, Hoedspruit, Louis Trichardt via a set number of waypoints and return to AFB Swartkop. The flight will be approximately 4.5 hours.

At twilight Steve completes the Pre-Flight Inspection and readies the aircraft for the Long Night Navigation exercise. Additional equipment carried onboard for such extended flights is Toolkit, Aldis Lamp and Flashlight for any Corrective Maintenance actions should they arise. Steve methodically checks all the exterior and interior lighting, including the instrument panel, radios and navigational equipment lighting. He also packs in some illumination sticks, known as "Glow Sticks". A glow stick is a self-contained, short-term light-source consisting of a translucent plastic tube containing isolated substances that, when combined, make light through chemiluminescence, so it does not require an external energy source. The light cannot be turned off and can only be used once. These are used in Search and Rescue operations but are also handy source of soft light in the cockpit in case there is a lighting problem.

Shortly after twilight the two pilots join Steve and they complete the pre-start check list. While awaiting take-off clearance the crew briefs on the navigation ahead, heading distance, time, altitude, and reporting points. The co-pilot has prepared an information block for every leg of the navigation on the map. With clearance the flying pilot lifts off under ATC control and follows the heading set for clearance out of the AFB Swartkop airspace. Under controlled airspace the crew has to maintain altitude and direction as instructed by the ATC. Once cleared of the Air Traffic Controlled airspace they are clear to fly at the predetermined altitude as per the navigation flight plan that has been prepared. Steve assists the co-pilot in verifying all the waypoints for the flight are as planned and they set heading for the first waypoint. As they leave the city lights behind them, the beauty of the night sky surrounds them. The Commander is flying and between Steve and the co-pilot heading, speed and altitude are continuously monitored and verbally confirmed.

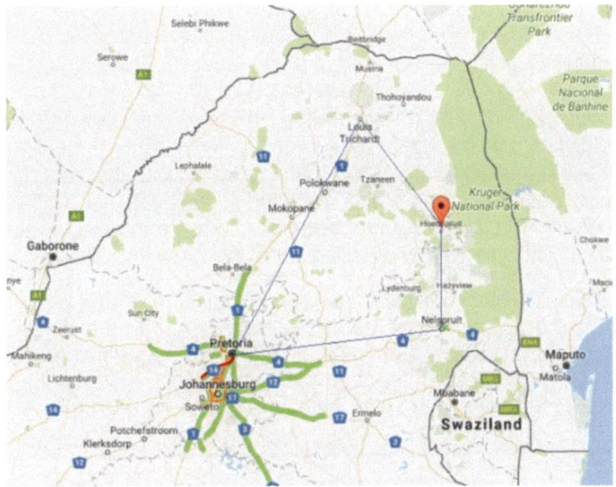

Puma Night Navigation

Steve in the meantime is also ensuring that the engines are performing correctly and verifies all other systems are nominal and functional. Soon he will be transferring fuel from the left-hand fuel system to the right hand to balance out the fuel quantities of the aircraft. The Puma has five main tanks, two on the left, two on the right, and a fifth tank between them. The left-hand system is fed by the two left tanks and the central tank. The right-hand system only by the two right hand tanks. To balance out the fuel usage Steve transfers fuel from the left-hand system to the right-hand system until both systems are the same. Once the fuel levels in both tanks reach below 1,000 lbs. each, Steve will open the additional Ferry Tanks in the cabin, releasing the extra 2,400 lbs.

The flight proceeds as per plan and all too soon they have Nelspruit in sight. Steve cannot help but to think back to many years before he had stood in the school yard and heard the approaching blade slapping Alouette which started the vision of wanting to fly in Helicopters. He smiles to himself and his chest swells with self-satisfaction on what he has achieved.

They are now heading north towards Louis Trichardt and are dead on track. Steve sets the VHF Radio frequency of the next traffic control zone for the co-pilot, who then makes the appropriate reporting call. Steve also dials in the HF Radio so that they can report back to Swartkop on their position and progress. They are once again heading into the dark night sky with occasional town and village lights visible in the distance. At Hoedspruit Steve enters another frequency change to the military VHF frequency of AFB Hoedspruit, where the co-pilot informs the ATC of position and route passing to the north. Steve keeps a close vigil on the instruments, making sure that everything is functioning normal.

They have now completed half of the navigation and are dead on track. At Louis Trichardt there is a waypoint that must be identified by the crew which then confirms an accurate navigation has been accomplished. Nobody has been briefed as to what to look out for. This to ensure that those who get lost don't radio their buddies for help. As the crew nears the coordinates at Louis Trichardt, they work together as a team. The co-pilot calls heading, while Steve confirms and then the Commander calls for speed and attitude which Steve verbally responds. They have slowed down to a 100 Kts to ensure that the waypoint is approached accurately. As they approach a valley between two hills there seems to be some type of light on the ground. The Commander slows down further and maintains heading and altitude. Steve moves to the cabin and opens the sliding door to get a clear look as they approach the waypoint. Then directly ahead of them is a military vehicle that suddenly puts his lights on and flashes his hazards. Bang on target they fly overhead, and Steve notes the letters on the roof of the vehicle, 19 Sqn. They have successfully accomplished this part of the navigation. They complete a lazy teardrop circuit of the area and then set heading directly back to AFB Swartkop. They climb to 5,000 ft agl and the Commander increases power to cruise. The big Puma stretches her legs and is soon cruising at 130 Kts.

The remainder of the flight is text book and much less stressful. With Pretoria's lights on the horizon the crew settles in to the standard protocol of approach path to AFB Swartkop. The landing is completed and after shutdown the ground crew quickly assist Steve in getting the aircraft into the hangar for an after-flight inspection. Then its briefing room, coffee and off to bed. This weekend would be the Chopper Reunion, and crews from all over will be arriving to participate in the celebrations.

Steve and Nic decide to start the reunion with a bang and head off to their favourite Hamburger Restaurant to stock up on the world-famous Garlic Burger. When the Burgers Bun is lifted, a white layer of Garlic hiding a big juicy Beef Pattie below is an indication of how much they are going to stink. With a few beers to help the mix they quickly polish off the Burgers and order two more to go. It is going to be a long hard night of celebration and they don't want to run out of energy. The two Garlic Buddies arrive back at the Warrant Officers Mess just in time to attend the start of the celebrations. There are many familiar faces and soon the war stories are being spread far and wide in the gathering. Steve and Nic are complimented on their most amazing Garlic Stink that they have brought along and rewarded with many beers for their efforts. There is a huge Spit Braai in process but with the size of the Ox on the spit it does not seem as if there is going to be food very soon. Steve and Nic munch into their spare stocks of Garlic Burgers and are set to go.

The evening turns into night, which quickly turns into very, very early morning. Steve wanders gingerly over to the Spit Braai and finds that the Ox has been nibbled away by hungry helicopter drunks and that there are very few pieces of meat left. In a couple of hours, the mess was going to serve the entire audience a champagne breakfast, so Steve decides to catch a couple of hours of shut eye. He meanders down to his room only to find a crowd of drunks sleeping all over. Steve runs in and dives on top of George Avis who is sound asleep in Steve's bed. After a couple of minutes of confusion and joking around, the group decides that it's time to continue sleeping. Steve spoons with George while two other idiots occupy the other bed with four more on the carpet.

The drunken group are awakened by some wise arse banging on a frying pan up and down the passage yelling on the top of his voice.

"Kos is op the tafel". (Food is on the table).

The heavily hung-over bunch splash water on their faces and make their way to the mess for the champagne breakfast. The cooks had outdone themselves and put forward and amazing breakfast. Champagne is served together with choice of eggs and boerewors. Fresh fruit, coffee, orange juice and champagne are readily available. A great breakfast for sure. While he is still sober enough Steve decides it's time to head to his parents and points the Alfa Giulietta in the direction of Witbank. Steve arrives at his parents' home and heads straight to bed to catch up on lost sleep. Steve is roused from his slumber by his Dad.

"Good Lord you stink man, open the windows" says Frank.

Steve just grins and looks at his watch, he had been sleeping most of the day. He slowly gets up and has a shower. His mom opens the door and windows wide to clear the garlic and beer stench that had been brewing in the room. Steve manages to recuperate for the rest of the weekend and leaves after supper on the Sunday evening. He will be back on the Friday to swap cars.

The students have now successfully completed their conversion to the Puma SA 330 Helicopter. All that is left is the final briefing from the Officer Commanding 19 Squadron and then clearing out for the return to their individual Squadrons. Steve will be driving the MGA back to Cape Town. It is going to be a long hard trip, as the MGA does not yet have its soft top fitted, leaving Steve exposed to the burning sun and wind for the trip down. With his fair complexion this is going to another grueling journey.

Apartheid government

In superficial ways, Botha's application of the apartheid system is less repressive than that of his predecessors. He legalizes interracial marriage and miscegenation, both completely banned since the late 1940s. The constitutional prohibition on multiracial political parties is lifted. He also relaxes the Group Areas Act, which barred non-whites from living in certain areas. In 1988, a new law created "Open Group Areas" or racially mixed neighbourhoods. But these neighbourhoods must receive a Government permit, must have the support of the local whites immediately concerned, and must be an upper-class neighbourhood in a major city in order to be awarded a permit. In 1983, the above constitutional reforms granted limits political rights to "Coloureds" and "Indians". Botha also becomes the first South African government leader to authorize contacts with Nelson Mandela, the imprisoned leader of the African National Congress (ANC).

However, in the face of rising discontent and violence, Botha refuses to cede political power to blacks and imposes greater security measures against anti-apartheid activists. Botha also refuses to negotiate with the ANC. In 1985, Botha delivers the Rubicon speech which is a policy address in which he refuses to give in to demands by the black population, including the release of Mandela. Botha's defiance of international opinion further isolated South Africa, leading to economic sanctions and a rapid decline in the value of the rand. The following year, when the US introduces the Comprehensive Anti-Apartheid Act, Botha declares a nationwide state of emergency. He is famously quoted during this time as saying, "This uprising will bring out the beast in us".

As economic and diplomatic actions against South Africa increase, civil unrest spreads amongst the black population, supported by the ANC and neighbouring black-majority governments. On 16th May 1986, Botha publicly warns neighbouring states against engaging in "unsolicited interference" in South Africa's affairs. Four days later, Botha orders air strikes against selected targets in Lusaka, Harare, and Gaborone, including the offices of exiled ANC activists. Botha charges that these raids are just a "first installment" and shows that "South Africa has the capacity and the will to break the ANC."

Long way home

Steve leaves his parents' home in Witbank in the early hours of the morning. The MGA is running well, and he keeps the engine revolutions low as he has just overhauled the engine and does not want to damage the new pistons and rings. By midday Steve has made good progress, but the sun has taken its toll and he is badly sunburnt. He decides to pull over for a rest and then fashions some protection for himself through the Karoo's dangerous desert sun.

Just after Three Sisters with the sun sinking fast there is a loud bang and a cloud of steam from under the hood of the MGA. Steve pulls over and shuts down to investigate. He pops the hood to see that the newly chromed radiator fan had broken a blade and it was imbedded in the radiator. He is stranded, despondent and angry all at the same time. He had specifically requested the plating shop to heat treat the fan blades which obviously had not been done. He is now stranded in the middle of nowhere. He cannot leave the car and has no idea how he will find a radiator at this time on a Saturday evening.

Steve flags a car down and begs the chap to tow him to the nearest garage. The two quickly fashion a tow rope and soon Steve is under tow to Touwsriver. All is going well until they arrive at Touwsriver where there is nothing open. Steve bargains with the chap to tow him to Cape Town. This will be very dangerous, as the MGA's vacuum braking system was now non-functional with the engine not running, and there are some very steep and treacherous mountain passes ahead. Steve informs the angel of mercy that he will coast down the passes and then take the tow up the other side. At this point the MGA's battery had been providing power to the headlights and they were starting to dim. The first pass went off without a hitch, but the Du Toitskloof pass is another animal completely with very steep and sharp turns. Steve is going to have to be wide awake. With limited visibility Steve tackles the decent, and very soon realizes that the MGA's brakes are not coping, overheating and the lights are getting even dimmer.

The car builds up speed on the steep decline and soon the tires are screeching as Steve navigates the corners. Steve holds on for dear life and navigates the pass like a professional hill climb racing driver. With a heavy sign of relief Steve feels the MGA slowing down as he nears the end of the treacherous mountain pass. He takes up the tow once more and an hour later at 1 AM in the morning Steve is towed into his driveway in Milnerton. Steve wakes Zella up and asks her for all the money she has in the house and gives it to the Good Samaritan and thanks him for the kind assist.

Chapter 12 - CATS EYES

"Summa Agilitas" - The Highest Agility / Unequaled Versatility

It is the 15th December 1986 and Steve arrives back at 30 Squadron with one goal, to qualify on the Puma SA 330 J Model's as soon as possible. The two J Model Puma's had been specially built for Antarctic conditions with additional hydraulic, deicing and anti-icing systems, more powerful alternators and additional Sponsoon Fuel Tanks.

The aircraft are owned by the Department of Environmental Affairs but operated and maintained by the South African Air Force. 30 Squadron has been assigned this accountability.

Since the acceptance of the two aircraft from France in 1980, 30 Squadron has developed into one of the world's most elite operators of the Puma in the most hostile conditions on earth. Steve is about to join this elite team of aviators in the next chapter of his life.

Steve and Nic join the next J Model conversion course and he is soon buried in the technical manuals of the aircraft, learning as much as he can about this beautiful beast. The aircraft are painted in the South African Flag colours Orange, White and Blue, which blend in beautifully with the lines of the Puma.

Puma SA 330 J

It is good to be back home with Zella and Nicole, and Steve wastes no time in catching up with the latest news. Steve has taken some time off to spend with the family. Steve also takes the time to repair the MGA and once fixed takes Nicole and Zella up the West Coast for a long drive. The Sports Car is running like a clock and with the lovely summer sunshine the family has a great outing.

Steve stops off at Melkbos Strand for a picnic. He builds a fire on the beach and gets the Chinese Stir-Fry Flat Iron that he made ready to cook up some fried eggs, tomatoes and bacon. He also places a Billy Can full of water in the fire to boil up water for coffee.

Melkbos Strand

Zella has prepared some sandwiches for them and gets a blanket spread on the sand dune to lay out the paper plates and eating utensils. With the meal cooked up and coffee served the family tucks in. Meal completed, Steve takes Nicole's hand and the two of them wander down the beach. The West Coast water is extremely cold and Nicole's screams in delight as she runs through the surf as the waves break and roll onto the beach.

Special Operations Puma

Steve packs his bags as his first Puma Bush Tour is about to begin. On the 22nd December 1986 he will fly out from AFB Ysterplaat to South West Africa for a short 13-day tour. He arrives to a hot dry Ondangwa and completes the clearing in process. Next, it's off to the Puma hangar to accept and inspect his aircraft for the tour. Steve is assigned Puma 180 for this trip and the aircraft has been well maintained so the inspection is quick and easy. Steve spends the rest of the day tinkering on the aircraft and catching up with the ground crew. As this is his first official Puma Operational Tour Steve feels excitement building up, as the Puma flying has been exhilarating already and now to experience it defending his country is going to top the list.

The evening is spent at the Ondangwa Tree Pub with the rest of the F/E's and a few of the pilots. A good night is enjoyed, but Steve takes his leave early to be refreshed for the potential call out the next day. As the enemy is non-religious there is no celebrating Christmas or New Year and the potential attacks are always more pronounced during these periods. Steve settles in under his mosquito net, on top of his sleeping bag, as it is a hot and wind still night. His thoughts drift to Zella and Nicole and he wonders what they are doing at this moment. Nicole will be three years old at her next birthday, and she is growing up quickly. Strong willed and determined she has definitely inherited Dad's personality. With a smile on his face Steve drifts into a light sleep.

It's the Christmas Eve and just after lunch when Steve has the opportunity to fly operationally in SWA in a Puma, when they are called out to a possible follow up operation. Two Puma's are tasked to a Trooping support of Gunships that have been called to a potential contact. The Parabats form up close to the aircraft while Steve and Capt. Mark Dutton complete the pre-flight walk around of the aircraft. Steve then quickly secures the access ladder of the Puma in the storage location at the rear of the aircraft, while Mark briefs the troops. With everyone embarked the Puma Flight Crew completes the pre-start and start up procedures.

The Co-Pilot obtains taxi clearance and Mark checks the brakes and then taxi's out to the taxi way. On the taxi way the ATC clears the Puma's for take-off. Mark pushes the cyclic stick slightly forward while pulling up on the collective pitch, adding power to the rotors. The big Puma stretches her legs and quickly picks up speed down the runway. With a small movement backward of the cyclic, the Puma is airborne and racing to the end of the runway. The Puma's form up in a loose battle formation and set heading to the coordinates they have been briefed.

The Gunships are already on station and orbiting around a Cuca Shop with trackers following up on spoor that has been detected heading in the general direction. Mark calls the Gunship on the VHF frequency and requests instructions on where to drop the troops for follow up. The trackers have radioed the Gunships and informed them that the Gooks must be in the Cuca Shop, as there are only tracks leading in but none coming out of the area. They have completed a quick 360 degree sweep of the area and have not picked up any sign of the Gooks leaving.

The Gunship Flight Leader then calls for the Giants to drop the troops north and west of the Cuca Shop. They are then to form sweep lines east and south and then move forward. With the trackers visual on the Cuca Shop and the Parabats moving in as stopper groups, it is anticipated that the escaping Gooks will get caught in the crossfire as they try to run for it. It is estimated that there are 10 Gooks in the group, all from the SWAPO Special Forces, trained in central Africa. Their tasking is to infiltrate SWA and set up ambushes at the Air Force Bases to bring down aircraft. The two Giants space for landing at the respective areas indicated by the Gunships. Mark brings the large aircraft into a quick stop as Steve completes the final vital actions. With the undercarriage down and locked, Mark flares the Giant and completes an assault landing in the SWA sand. This type of landing prevents too much sand blowing up into the rotors and engines. Steve indicates to the Parabats to deplane with horizontal thumbs indicating exit. In a few seconds the aircraft is empty, and Steve gives the all clear for take-off. Mark does not hesitate and quickly takes a hand full of collective pitch. The blades pitch increases quickly, and the engines spool up with the mighty Puma biting quickly into the air. Cyclic slightly forward with more collective and they speed through 60 Kts allowing Steve to retract the undercarriage. The two Giants will hold orbit outside of the potential contact area until called.

Cuca Shop "Local Shebeen"

The landing and take-off are the most dangerous zones for the Puma's in the Operational Area, as many pot shots have been taken at them during the vulnerable position at low speed. It does not take long for the sweeping troops to detect that the Gooks had practiced anti-tracking and were in fact already out of the crossfire opportunity. The Gunship Flight Leader calls the Giants back to pick up and reposition the Parabats in the general direction ahead of the escaping Gooks. With the troops relocated and the Giants safely back in orbit, the spoor is quickly picked up. The call on the radio from the Troops is excited and out of breath;

"Gunship, Gunship, the fuckers are flat footing it in the direction you are now flying, can you see them"?

With that the Gunship suddenly banks left, and the telltale sign of the 20mm cannon being fired can clearly be seen. Steve immediately knows how the Alouette F/E feels as he methodically picks out targets and fires at them. The second gunship joins in the fire fight. The troops on the ground are short on the heels, and with each troop wearing a day-glow patch on their bush hats, they can clearly be distinguished from the Gooks, so the Gunships will not inadvertently fire on them. Within 15 minutes the contact is over and the mop up operation begins. The four helicopters remain airborne until the troops on the ground confirm that the area is secure, only then do they space for landing and each chopper picks an open area to land in close proximity of each other. Steve's first Puma Tour is a bang and he could not be more pleased. The aircrew gathers around the contact area and reviews the carnage created. There is much babbling amongst the troops until the local Army Forces arrive to complete the mop up. The Giant's get airborne with their respective troops and head back to AFB Ondangwa, followed by the slower Gunships.

Steve spends the rest of the day cleaning all the dirt and sand from the Puma, and then heads to the Aircrew Quarters to have a quick dip in the pool, shower and heads down to the Pub for a cold beer. After supper the crowd of chopper crews assembles in the pub to pound liquid sustenance and Dutch courage away for the evening.

The next two days Steve is on Stand-By and spends his time at the Puma hangar assisting the Ground Crew with maintenance on other Puma's. Christmas comes and goes and so does Boxing Day without incident. It is the 27th December 1986 and Steve will be flying with Capt. Mike McGee this morning into Angola to complete a supply drop for troops deployed at the HAG. Steve has completed the Pre-Flight and signed all the documentation. A SAMIL Truck approaches the two Puma's to load up the supplies. These supply trucks are South African Manufactured, and Landmine resistant vehicles used extensively in the operational area.

<u>SAMIL Truck</u>

Once airborne and heading set, the crew gets chatting. Steve went to Primary School with Owen McGee and wondered if he was related to Mike the commander of the Giant today. To Steve's surprise Mike informs him that Owen is his cousin and that they are pretty close. The rest of the trip Steve and Mike share stories and experiences they both had with Owen. The supply drop at the HAG is uneventful and the two-and-a-half-hour flight is completed without incident. The rest of the afternoon Steve lounges around the hangar on standby in case there is a Casevac call.

Still on Stand-By on the 29th December 1986 at 10:00 the morning Steve gets the call for a trooping sortie to Angola. They will be flying direct to the HAG for refuel and troop uplift and then into a potential contact for deployment. Steve is once again flying with Capt. Mark Dutton as the commander. This time the Co-Pilot does the flying out to the HAG while Steve and Mark catch up on each other's careers. The landing at the HAG is completed and Steve quickly rolls drums closer to refuel the thirsty Giant. He tops up the internal fuel tanks and saunters off to the HAG Command Post to listen in on the briefing. A potential SWAPO camp has been identified and the tasking is for four Giants to relocate troops in an advance and stopper group at strategic points of the target. The four Gunships will deploy first, and the Giants will meet then over target. Once the troops are deployed the Giants are to return to the HAG and load up fuel for all aircraft and create a Mini HAG in close proximity of the proposed target.

The deployment and Mini HAG establishment are completed like clockwork. The potential camp however has been abandoned. The troops mop up and sift through the camp, very weary of Booby Traps to establish how long ago the withdrawal had taken place. By indication the camp had been hurriedly abandoned the previous night. The spoor clearly indicating a withdrawal in a north easterly direction. At the Mini HAG a new plan is formed, and a Telstar aircraft requested to establish if there is any movement afoot in the direction indicated by the spoor.

Fortunately, a Telstar Bosbok is available at AFB Ondangwa and deploys immediately to the area. Within the hour there is confirmation of the SWAPO movement and the Telstar relays current location, size and direction of movement. The Army Commanders quickly develop an attack plan at the Mini HAG and by early afternoon the authorization has been received. The Mini HAG is abuzz with Gunships, Giants and Troops as the attack is initiated. The Gunships arrive over the target area and are immediately engaged in a firefight with the retreating SWAPO. The Gunship Commander calls for Giants to urgently drop their troops at the designated areas. The Terrs have bomb shelled and are discarding uniforms, dropping weapons and mixing in with local population making it very difficult to complete the attack. The attack is called off and the aircraft collect the troops for withdrawal to the HAG. The Gunships pack up for the night while the Giants return to AFB Ondangwa. During the return flight Steve notices that Puma 180 has developed an auto-pilot problem and Steve makes note to enter a defect into the Technical Log on their return to base. Back at AFB Ondangwa Steve quickly completes his after-flight inspection and then delves into his note on auto-pilot problems to identify the snag with Puma 180.

The end of the year is closing in quickly. Steve has completed some maintenance on the auto-pilot system and requires a test flight to verify that the snag has been rectified. He contacts Mike to arrange the test flight with Ops. The test flight is a short circuit in the area of the Ondangwa airfield and is successfully concluded with the auto-pilot now fully functional once more.

It is the 31st December 1986 and Steve is on Casevac Standby. The crews not on standby are already celebrating the end of the old year. Early evening arrives and Casevac callout is broadcast over the Public-Address System. Steve gathers his kit and heads for the Ops Room to get briefed. There he meets up with his Commander Major Dave Owen. Dave is also a decorated pilot and received the Honoris Crux while he was on Gunships as well a number of years ago. The local Medics are ready and within ten minutes the Puma is airborne and heading set to the coordinates of the Casevac. An hour a half later they are back at AFB Ondangwa with the ambulance ready to whisk the injured soldier off to the hospital on the base. The rest of the old year is a sober one for Steve, as he is the Casevac Standby. The rest of the crews are much the worse for wear as much celebration has been concluded. There will be sore heads tomorrow for sure.

New Year's Day is extraordinarily quiet and there has been no action. Steve is no longer on Casevac Standby and can enjoy a few cold one's after supper. The next day Steve is once again activated for a resupply drop in Angola, this time at a HAG just over the SWA Border. The out flight is uneventful, and once landed Steve shuts down the powerful Turmo Engines. The troops are rewarded with a box of goodies put together for them from the base and there is excitement to see what has been supplied. Fresh rations are the most cherished, as these chaps have been living off Rat Packs for weeks now.

The next day Steve is assigned to complete a Cuca Shop sortie. Two Gunships and Two Giants are deployed with Parabats to a selected Cuca Shop at sunset to conduct a search for Terrs. A number of Cuca Shops are checked out to ensure that no SWAPO are present. At the same time the troops are building up good relations with the local population by showing their willingness to defend and support them. The sortie is concluded two hours later. Steve and his F/E Mates spend the rest of the evening in the hangar servicing aircraft, then braaiing and drinking until the early hours.

In less than a week Steve will return to Cape Town and continue his education on the Puma J Model. He has his sights set on deploying to Antarctica with the SA Agulhas.

The Learning Continues

1987 at 30 Squadron starts off with a bang and Steve is actively assigned many new maritime operations that assist him in honing his skills as a Flight Engineer on the Puma. In a few short weeks he completes emergency procedures, instrument flying, cargo slinging and hoisting operations, gunnery, firefighting and dingy drops. The flying is most enjoyable, and Steve loves the crew management requirements that give him much more responsibilities. Zella in the meantime has started her studies as an Oral Hygienist at Stellenbosch University. She will need to complete two full years of study before being able to qualify. Her years as a nursing student at the University of the Witwatersrand have afforded her some credits. Nicole is still at the Crèche in Bothasig and has made many friends. One very amusing event that takes place is one evening when Zella fetches Nicole while Steve is deployed. Zella sits Steve down after supper to enlighten him into Nicole's escapades. Zella had just picked Nicole up when she turned to Zella and said;

"Mommy Pietie said Fuck"

"Nicole, I don't want to hear such language from your mouth"!

"But Mommy, I didn't say Fuck, Pietie said Fuck".

Zella reports that this banter continued until she threatened to spank Nicole. At this point Steve was laughing uncontrollably, as he knew how stubborn Nicole could get, and just visualizing the discussion in the car between mother and daughter is too much for Steve to bear.

Steve has been selected to complete the Puma J Model conversion and must attend the Technical phase first. The standard assortment of lectures takes place, but this time the pilots are also on course with the F/E's. Steve passes the technical phase with high marks. The additional systems in the Puma J are amazing and Steve enjoys learning all about them.

The next couple of months Steve continues to hone his skills in maritime operations as he volunteers for deck landing, ship-controlled approach, formation flying and more cargo slinging and hosting. The big helicopter is a joy to fly in and maintain. When Steve arrived at the squadron Russell had asked him if he was interested in reviving a hangar queen. A hangar queen is an aircraft that has become a supply of parts for other aircraft and then is at a point where it is no longer an aircraft but just a shell in the corner. Steve jumps at the opportunity and together with Piet, they make a list of spares required to bring the old girl back to life. Most of the major components have been robbed for other aircraft so the list is quite extensive. Main Gearbox, Head, Blades, Engines, Gyro's, Auto-Pilot etc. to name a few of the items required. Steve and Piet validate part numbers required from the Illustrated Parts catalogue and then complete the Stores request forms for ordering of the parts. In the meantime, any parts that are available in stock are drawn from Stores to initiate the resuscitation process. One big task is the replacement of all the internal rubber fuel tanks. The tanks are available, so Steve and Piet set to work and within a day the task is completed. On the 30th March 1987 the Squadron is informed of another loss amongst the aircrew fraternity, Danny Lan a F/E was killed by small arms fire in his Gunship while on a follow up operation near Oshivello.

It is the end of April 1987 and Nicole's 3rd birthday is soon coming up. Steve will be 28 years old as well. Unfortunately, war does not have patience or wait for anyone. Steve is about to board the Flossie to head back to SWA and AFB Ondangwa for his next tour of duty. He will miss Nicole's birthday but decides to spoil her before he flies out. Steve takes Nicole and Zella to dinner for the evening and then a sunset drive along the west coast near Blaauberg Strand. The family has a great time, but it is a teary departure as Zella drops Steve off at the Movements Control at AFB Ysterplaat.

Blaauberg Strand

Operations Once More

Steve arrives at AFB Ondangwa on the 1st May 1987. This will be a full tour with many Cuca Shop sorties and Casevac's. Steve knows the drill now and is accustomed to sorties being changed at short notice. Early trooping deployments at first light and late night Casevac's become the norm. Ken van Straaten, Steve's friend from 19 Squadron is also doing a tour. Ken remembers that it was Steve who initiated the NVG flying a couple of years back. Currently Ken was part of a team that developed NVG Cockpits for the Puma. An Ultra Violet Lighted Instrument Panel had been constructed to supply soft lighting on the Instrument Panel. Infrared covers are attached over the landing and navigation lights and Lumi Sticks kept in the cockpit for emergency should there be a failure. All this then afforded two of the three crew, to wear NVG's in the cockpit without interference. Ken shows Steve the modifications and briefs him on the jerry-rigged installation direct onto the secondary electrical buzz bar.

Steve is intrigued but even more surprised when Cmdt John Church, Commanding Officer of 19 Squadron, requests him to attend a briefing at the Ops Room. To Steve's amazement he has been selected to accompany the deep penetration sortie to drop off Recce Units behind enemy lines. Steve will be flying with Capt. Steve Gallinetti and Capt. Herbs as Co-Pilot. Four Giants deploy to Marian Fluss, each with four ferry tanks fitted. On this trip the Giants are armed with 7.62mm Machine Guns in the doors. At the Fluss the Recce Teams have setup camp and are already preparing for the drop. The rest of the day is spent in preparing the aircraft for the sortie. Cmdt Church has instructed that all aircrafts Main Rotor Blade tapes are to be removed. The reason is that should any of the tapes develop a hole the whistling sound it makes will be a dead giveaway as the noise is quite loud.

It is already dark when the order for startup is given. Radio transmissions will be limited and only used for landing or an emergency. Steve spent the afternoon with his pilots to brief on how to patter their requirements during the flight. The co-pilot will navigate, the commander will fly and therefore both will be looking outside all the time. The F/E must patter altitude, attitude and air speed. A minimum altitude will be adjusted by the commander as the terrain demands. The F/E must also complete all internal vital actions, navigation waypoint updates and engineer tasks as required.

Steve can feel the excitement building as they lift off in the pitch-dark night. With the infrared covers on the external lighting the other Puma's are invisible to the naked eye. Only NVG's will be able to see them. Steve sets up his routine and as they set off ensures all vital actions are completed with verbal confirmation to the pilots. Next, he confirms minimum altitude warning. Steve Gallinetti confirms 100 ft. As they track through the Zebra Mountains only the pilots can see what the terrain looks like. All that Steve sees is the Radio Altimeter and aircraft Attitude Indicator as they meander through the valleys and climb over the saddles into the next valley. It is at one of these crossings that Steve starts to get excited as he notes the Radio Alt drops quickly below 100 then 60 then 50 and then 30 ft. All the while he is pattering and requests;

"Are you visual, minimum exceeded"?

Steve Gallinetti grins back at him and tells him to take a look through the NVG's. They had just climbed up a valley and over a saddle into a huge open area and were now cruising happily over an open expanse of flat topography. The flight continues all the while Steve is pattering and updating way points in the Doppler. After what seems like hours, Steve starts the fuel transfer to balance out the left and right tanks. He will need the space in both tanks to dump the additional 3,200 Lbs. of Ferry tank fuel. They set into a routine, every now and again the Co-pilot goes off NVG's and Steve must drop his NVG's so that there are always two sets of eyes outside. They crest another mountain range and it is a magnificent sight to see the Puma's in a lose battle formation flying stretched out to the right and behind each other. As they are the last Puma in the formation it is truly a sight to behold. The dark shapes look enormous through the NVG's with exhaust fumes deflecting back and downward on each side of the aircraft.

The Recce's in the back of the Puma are quietly preparing for the tasking and are checking and rechecking their equipment. It is time to open up two Ferry Tanks, so Steve makes his way back and opens the two rear tanks which will drain into the left and right main tanks respectively. By the time they reach the target the tanks will have drained and there will be enough fuel left to fly all the way back to AFB Ondangwa via any current route they select. The route up and back has been carefully planned so that they do not fly in a straight line at any point. There are a select number of waypoints set in the Doppler that they will follow, ensuring that there is no possibility of them being detected. Should they be detected on the outward leg, they will not be returning that same way, so the navigation must be accurate. All four aircrafts Co-Pilots are following a map and the Doppler Navigation system.

Without warning the VHF Crackles to life and Cmdt Church barks out;

"Space for landing".

The three remaining aircraft click the transmit button twice after each other to confirm. Steve performs the vital actions and waits for Steve Gallinetti to request Finals. As planned, only two aircraft will land at a time. The other two will orbit and provide top cover. Giants three and four are spaced and ready to land. Steve Gallinetti calls for finals and Steve confirms;

"Three Greens, Park Break Off, Nose Wheel Locked. Finals Complete".

Steve then moves to the back and opens the right hand sliding door, drops his NVG's into place and patters Steve Gallinetti in to the landing zone. The second aircraft is off to the right and about 100 meters ahead. Steve indicates to the Recce's that it is safe to deplane. The Recce's vanish into the darkness and both aircraft lift simultaneously. Once back in orbit the lead Puma and number two go in for a landing. Steve remains in the door on the machine gun should there be a need. A few minutes later both the aircraft on the ground lift off and the lead sets heading to the assigned waypoint. The return flight seems much longer to Steve, and he is thirsty from the continuous pattering. The two liters of water he brought with him have been consumed a while back already. It is past midnight when the four aircraft make it back to the Fluss. The teams are exhausted, and as soon as the aircraft have been secured, they are retiring to the Ops Tent for debrief and beer. The group quickly disperses, and everyone gets some well-earned sleep.

The sun is already high in the sky when Steve throws back his mosquito net. He rubs his eyes and struggles out of bed. Outside he can hear the radio in the Ops Tent. He puts on his Vellie's and saunters over to the Ops Tent to see what's happening. At the Ops Tent Cmdt Church is already up and has a steaming cup of coffee in his hand.

"Morning Steve, grab a cup of coffee off the fire, its fresh". Says Cmdt Church.

Steve thanks him and pours a mug of black gold to start his day.

"What's news Sir? Were we successful"? Asks Steve.

"The Recce's report that everything is going according to plan and that they will be moving to the extraction point in two days".

This is good news indeed as the operation has been in the planning phase for a number of weeks and everytime has been postponed due to enemy movement. This time however everything is working as planned. Once the Recce's complete their mission the supply route to western Angola will be seriously disrupted, placing a huge burden on the convoys. The railroad west was currently the only logistic supply route for the enemy. During summer the rainfall in this region of Angola is so heavy that the roads become completely impassable, and without the railroad it will almost impossible to supply the huge force that FAPLA is building to attack UNITA with.

Steve is looking through his logbook to update his flight hours when all of a sudden, he realizes that he has forgotten his birthday. He grins to himself and shakes his head.

"What are you grinning at Steve"? Asks Cmdt Church.

"I forgot my birthday 7 days ago Sir"!

They both burst out laughing. Cmdt Church asks about Steve's family and he informs the Cmdt of Nicole's birthday 2 days after his own. Cmdt Church then instructs Steve to dial up the HF Radio on 8975 and request a phone patch home.

"Mention my name Steve and they should give you a couple of minutes with Nicole".

After having a bite to eat from a Rat Pack, Steve makes his way down to the Puma to dial up the HF Radio for a phone patch home. He selects 8975 on the HF Radio and tunes the set.

"ZRB, ZRB this is Puma 188 over".

"Puma 188, this is ZRB, go ahead".

"ZRB may I request a phone patch to my daughter for a belated birthday"?

"Puma 188, ZRB, what is the phone number"?

Steve supplies the Radio Op with the phone number. The phone patch works with a dual system, the transmission from the aircraft is sent on 8975 and then once completed the return signal from the phone call is connected to a return frequency. When each party has completed talking, they must end the conversation off with "Over", so that they talk over each other.

Zella answers the call and Steve can hear how the Radio Op is briefing her. Next the Radio Op informs Steve to proceed.

"Hi honey, how are you"? Asks Steve.

"Wow this is a surprise, where are you"?

"I am still in SWA, how is Nicole"?

"She is fine and is listening in, all excitedly, she wants to say hello"!

"Hi my baby, how are you, I am calling to find out if you had a lovely birthday"?

"Daddy when you coming home? I love you daddy".

Steve feels his throat tighten and his eyes moisten.

"I will be home soon Nicole. Take care of Mommy. I love you".

Steve and Zella chat for a little longer and then they hang up. Steve calls ZRB back and thanks the Radio Op for his kindness.

The camp demobilizes and returns to AFB Ondangwa. Steve, Ken and the rest of the F/E's get to work to clean and maintain the aircraft. The Main Rotor Blade Tapes must be replaced, and this is a long tedious job. Steve manages to get his aircraft completed just in time to hand over to his replacement. Another tour has come to an end and he is on his way back to the States. This has been an amazing experience, one that he will remember for a long time.

J Power

Back in Cape Town Steve wastes no time to catch up with his family and spoils Nicole to a day out. The family travels to Spiers, a local wine farm near Stellenbosch where they have a collection of animals including cheetah. Nicole is thrilled to see the animals and Zella enjoys the wine tasting. After an exhausting day Nicole is fast asleep in the back of the car as they head back home to Sanddrift.

Back at the Squadron Steve focuses on the last courses and emergency procedures for the Puma J. It is the beginning of June 1987 and Zella is progressing well in her studies. Nicole at three years old is cute as a button and the center of attention at any gathering.

The month flies by with Steve completing another VIP trip with Cmdt Theron, this time with the Minister of Defense, Gen Magnus Malan. The Gen recognizes Steve and greets him by hand. Gen Malan had placed the Honoris Crux on Steve's Chest in 1982. The trip is to the coloured area of Langa on the Cape Flats.

Langa is a township and suburb of Cape Town, South Africa. It was established in 1927 in terms of the 1923 Urban Areas Act. Similar to Nyanga, Langa is one of the many areas in South Africa that were designated for Black Africans before the apartheid era. It is the oldest of such suburbs in Cape Town and is the location of much resistance to apartheid.

As the Puma settles to land there is a huge crowd of people gathered to see the spectacle of a helicopter landing in close proximity. Gen Malan is to meet with local leadership to discuss agreements. As soon as the VIP's are ushered away the aircrew is left to fend off the hordes keen in touching and feeling the Puma. After an hour the crowd has amassed to a huge throng and the excitement is building. Fortunately for the aircrew the meeting has adjourned and the VIP's return. Cmdt Theron stands on the Pilots access step and warns the crowd to stand back to no avail. The crew decides to start up anyway, as the high frequency sound of the turbines will be deafening enough to force the crowd back. The startup does not have the desired effect, but once the take-off vital actions have been completed and Cmdt Theron takes power on the collective, the force five hurricane force wind from the rotor wash has the desired effect. The crowd quickly moves back as the Puma climbs into the air. They return to AFB Ysterplaat was a repeat discussion on how comical it was to see the crowd disperse.

Steve continues his Puma J training and, on the 3rd July 1987, is the F/E onboard ZS-HJA, the civilian registered Puma J owned by the Department of Environmental Affairs (DEA) and operated by the Air Force's 30 Squadron. The crew is practicing Ship Controlled Approaches, where the aircraft is directed by the ships radar and validated from the aircraft on the aircrafts radar. Steve has spent many hours training on the radar operation and it is now paying off. Steve manages to get the radar set correctly for each approach and ensure that the flight path and distance out from the ship are accurate.

The next day with ZS-HJA the sortie is Cargo Slinging, and Steve enjoys it immensely. The additional systems and checklist make the Puma J a very interesting aircraft to operate. The Cargo Sling has a strain gauge incorporated that supplies the pilot with a load read out, thus allowing him to validate load weight when he takes the load. The DEA has opted to utilize their own aircraft for forming the base construction of a radio tower to be erected on "Ou Kaapse Weg" Silvermine Nature Reserve. The mountain overlooks the Cape Flats and will provide coverage for a variety of communications. Steve fits the Cargo Sling to the aircraft and prepares for the days flying. Major Trevor Jew is the Commander with Major Paul Shemer as the Co-Pilot. The three get airborne and head straight for the Silvermine area to meet up with the Public Works Department (PWD) Team that will be completing the foundation of the tower. Paul is flying and lands in a confined area close to the PWD Team. Steve hops out after shutting down and inspects the concrete bucket that they will be cargo slinging. It is a simple construction as used on construction sites when suspended from a crane. The hookup is safe, and Steve is satisfied. The PWD Team has done many cargo sling operations with the Puma's before and therefore Steve gives them a short safety brief to confirm the process.

The concrete mixer trucks are lining up at the base of the mountain where the Puma has landed. Once the Puma is airborne they are going to hover over the bucket and the PWD Team will attach the cargo sling cable hanging below the aircraft to the bucket. They will then move over with the bucket attached to the first truck and fill up with concrete. With the current fuel weight of 5,000 Lbs. the aircraft can stay airborne for up to five hours. The bucket weight of concrete is 1,000 Lbs. placing the total all up weight of the aircraft over the allowable limit of 16,300 Lbs. Steve briefs the loading crews to limit the bucket fill to three quarters for the first hour of flight, there after a full bucket can be lifted every time until they run out of fuel. For the next five hours the upload and dumping of concrete is performed like clockwork, giving both pilots and Steve plenty of practice for the work ahead when they will complete their first Antarctic trip.

By late afternoon the foundation is complete. Steve patters Paul into position to gently lower the bucket and once settled, Steve jettisons the cargo sling strop. Paul maneuvers the aircraft back to the confined area landing zone with Steve pattering the way for him and then lands. Steve unplugs his helmet and runs over to collect the strop. A quick flight back to AFB Ysterplaat and debrief with both pilots on the sortie. Steve is very pleased at the days flying. The ground crew assists Steve in getting the aircraft fueled and towed back to the hangar so that the required maintenance can be completed.

Tower at Silvermine

The next day Steve is assigned the same task with ZS-HJA and the same pilots. The tasking is to complete the foundation pour for the tower stays that need to be installed. Once again Trevor lands the Puma in the confined area landing zone and Steve shuts down. The crew then debriefs with the PWD Team. Steve informs the Team that as the aircraft only has internal fuel today that the bucket can be completely full for every lift. Safety briefing completed the aircrew retreat to the Puma and start up for the day's cargo slinging sortie. Two hours later the pour is completed and the Puma heads to AFB Ysterplaat. A job well done by all and for the years to come Steve will fondly remember the hand he had in constructing this very visible tower on Silvermine.

Steve gets home and spends time with Nicole. Zella has become reserved and seems to be disinterested in what Steve shares about the squadron with her. He shrugs it off to her studies and retreats to the garage to tinker on his hobbies. Nicole follows and immediately starts placing all sorts of tools and parts in the engine block that Steve has placed in the corner of the workshop for her. The two bond and Nicole keeps Steve entertained until supper time when they both wash up and sit down to eat. The rest of the evening Steve finds it very uneasy to talk to Zella and rather opts for channel hopping on the television.

Steve has been expanding on the house by adding to the back of the house and thereby creating additional kitchen, main bedroom, bathroom and shower. The work has been exhausting but rewarding. He is in the final stages of completing the project and must now just paint and complete some carpentry. Steve plans to have the extensions completed before he leaves on the next Special Operations Tour. He has also enclosed the porch and broken through into the living room, thereby creating a dining room off the living room. This weekend the task is to book the carpet company for laying of new carpets while Steve completes tiling and painting.

Night Skies

Steve arrives back in SWA at AFB Ondangwa to start his next tour of duty. This tour Steve spends many hours flying Casevac's at night, as the enemy are now getting bold and are patrolling Southern Angola with Mig Fighters during the day. The Puma's having to be cautious with any cross-border operations they fly. The aircrews remain vigilant and are always scanning the horizon for telltale signs of aircraft movement. Daily Int Briefings are a source of valuable information into enemy aircraft movements and Steve pays attention to all that is shared. The standard Cuca Shop sorties are still in effect and although not very effective they still ensure that the reaction time and practice prepare the fire fight force for the inevitable.

Steve flies twenty hours at night during the tour and is becoming very competent on the Puma. He assists the ground crew with a few engine and gearbox changes during the day and then relaxes in the afternoons at the pool in preparation for the night time Casevac. Soutie is also on a Puma tour with Steve and it is not long before the two start getting up to mischief.

Both Steve and Soutie fly a night sortie and return just before midnight. The ground crews are all tucked away in bed, so the two F/E's assist each other in getting both aircraft into the hangar. Steve and Soutie need to complete 50-hour maintenance inspections on the Puma's which requires the removal of some panels and clearance checks of the engines. Just to the right of the hangar is a 120mm mortar pit for airfield defense. Both Steve and Soutie are on the aircraft engine platforms when the next instant there is an almighty explosion. The F/E's bale off the aircraft and land squarely on the concrete floor two meters below.

"Fuck" screams Soutie, "What was hell was that"?

Just then another explosion and realization suddenly dawn on them. The idiot Parabats knew they were in the hangar and decided to throw some mortars as is authorized from time to time. The airfield defense units of mortars, Bofor's 40mm cannons and Missiles have a weekly night time firing sortie to keep the potential threats at bay. Steve and Soutie shake themselves off and have a cup of coffee. While drinking their coffee, Soutie concocts a plan of revenge. The next day they will be off flying for the day, so can put their plan into action without consequence. They complete the servicing's, sign up the technical logs and head for bed. Tomorrow was going to be a very interesting day for sure.

The scheduled weekly airfield defense firing is planned for tonight, so Soutie and Steve set their plan in motion by starting their day off on Rat Packs with dried fruit, prunes, chocolates and beans. Later in the afternoon they add in Brandy and Coke to the mix. Steve remembers that he had biltong and scrounges in his kit to find the remaining sticks. This is consumed with delight and washed down with more Brandy and Coke. By early evening the two inebriated F/E's have pretty loose stomach's, and each has a go at the fire bucket that they have liberated.

Pretty soon the bucket has sufficient ammunition and now they just need to wait for the opportune moment to enact the plan. With the bucket hidden the jolly twosome make their way to the Mess and then Pub to collect more stocks for the evening's entertainment. They return to the hangar and with the lights out attempt to be as quiet as possible. By the witching hour they sneak over to the mortar pit with the Fire Bucket in tow. As quietly as they can they descend into the mortar pit. Soutie reaches up and removes the tubes cover while Steve hands him the bucket. Carefully the contents are emptied into the tube. Soutie replaces the cover and trying to be as quiet as possible they retreat to the hangar. This time the lights are switched on and the hangar radio tuned in to the local station. More alcohol is consumed, and the crescendo of the two's joking and war stories blares away into the SWA night.

It is an hour before the witching hour when they observe movement around the mortar pit. Both sneak to the side of the hangar in enclosed the coffee area to hide and watch. The young Lt. is keeping his orders in a low voice, as they want to repeat the surprise of the previous evening. The order is given, and a mortar placed in the tube.

"Vuur" orders the Lt.

The next second the almighty bang and the mortar whooshes off in the distance to explode in the Shona. Another mortar is immediately launched and as the team readies the third the young Lt. puts his hand up and says;

"Wat de fok, ek ruik kak"! (What the fuck, I smell shit).

By this time the tears are rolling down Soutie and Steve's cheeks as they try uncontrollably to contain their laughter. A flashlight is brought to bear in the pit and it is layered in crap. The disgusted mortar team exits the pit to clean themselves up. This was going to one of those stories that Soutie and Steve can take to their graves with them.

The remainder of Steve's tour is a repeat of the first few weeks and very soon it is time to head back. The tenseness of flying under the stressful conditions is starting to affect the crews.

Night Skies Continue

It is mid-August 1987 when Steve returns to 30 Squadron. There is much emphasis placed on Night Flying and Steve enjoys these sorties immensely as Cape Town is a beautiful coast line to fly at night. Included in the honing of the Puma crew's skills is Instrument Flying (IF). The flying pilot is given a pair of UV Glasses to wear while the inside of the cockpit glass has amber IF screen fitted. With UV Glasses and Amber Screen, the pilot can no longer see outside of the cockpit and must rely entirely on his instruments and instructions from the ATC. In this instance the non-flying pilot acts as the ATC and is given the flying pilot instructions on what attitude, direction and altitude to fly at. As the F/E Steve assists the flying pilot with navigational, radio frequency and standard updates as per checklist.

Commandant (Cmdt) Theron, formerly Steve's Commanding Officer at 22 Squadron, is now the Commanding Officer at 30 Squadron. Steve has been assigned to a VIP trip with Cmdt Gert Theron and Maj Gary Hamilton. Steve hurries to the hangar to prepare Puma 173 for VIP Configuration. He has to fit a carpet, seats, and ensure that the aircraft is spotless for the trip. At 10:00 on the 2nd September 1987, Steve is introduced to the State President, his wife and their entourage by Cmdt Theron. Gary and Steve withdraw while Cmdt Theron briefs the VIP's and prepare the pre-flight and pre-start check lists. With Cmdt Theron strapped in they waste no time in getting the aircraft started and clearance obtained for the predefined flight.

Western Cape Flowers

The flight will be to the West Coast National Park to view the beautiful flowers and then after a short stop continue to the Cederberg where the State President has been invited to have dinner with the Niewout's on their farm. At the first stop Steve shuts down the Puma while Cmdt Theron jumps out to assist the State President. After a short walk around, they are once again airborne enroute to the Cederberg. Steve is unaware of the location of the farm and is pleasantly surprised when they arrive, that it is the farm of the wife of his friend Piet Brits. The Niewout's have been farming here since 1716 and their heritage is cemented in the region. A very pleasant afternoon is spent on the farm and the Air Force Crew is invited to join the spread for dinner.

Maltese Cross in the Cederberg Mountains

Steve, Zella and Nicole had spent a weekend with Piet and Mary-Anne at the farm the previous year and the family immediately recognizes him. With dinner completed Steve wanders down to the Puma to prepare for startup. Cmdt Theron busies himself with the VIP's while Gary and Steve complete the checklist. With Cmdt Theron strapped in Steve initiates start on number one engine. Immediately the Jet Pipe Temperature (JPT) climbs above the limits. Steve shuts the engine down and starts number two. Next Steve vents number one to clear any residual fuel and brings the temperature down before selecting ignition once more. Again, the JPT climbs quickly to above limits. Steve informs Cmdt Theron that he will have to shut down to investigate.

Cederberg Western Cape

With engine shut down, Cmdt Theron briefs the VIP's and requests that they retire to the farm house while the aircraft is repaired. Steve has already opened the engine cowlings and is inspecting the starting device, which supplies the initial startup fuel for the engine. It has a barometric pressure sensor that adjusts for fuel supply at altitude. The Cederberg is at 5,600 ft above mean sea level, making the air thinner than at Ysterplaat which is at 100 ft above mean sea level. The barometric pressure switch is stuck resulting in too much fuel being injected during start up. Steve taps the starting device and with Gary they retry the start with the same result. Steve shuts down and consults his F/E Notes. He gets a watch maker screw driver from his tool kit and adjusts the starting device completely inward and outward and then takes it back to the original setting. Next, he turns the setting to lean off the fuel for startup just to be on the safe side. By now Cmdt Theron is panicking, as the State President must be back at AFB Ysterplaat to take a flight back to Pretoria for an important function this evening.

Steve and Gary jump back in to attempt another start up. Steve has briefed Cmdt Theron that if the engine starts he would not shut it down in case the same problem arises once more. Steve cranks the engine up and selects ignition, the JPT climbs slowly and seems not wanting to complete the cycle. Steve helps the cycle along by reigniting the cycle. The JPT continues to climb and the engine RPM builds up to ground idle. Elated Steve reaches up and opens the throttle to bring engine up to flight idle. Steve now starts number two and the Puma is ready to go. Cmdt Theron in the meantime has ushered the VIP's back to the aircraft and ensures that all are safely strapped in the cabin. It is with great relief that Cmdt Theron, Gary and Steve lift off from the Niewout's and set heading straight back to AFB Ysterplaat.

Chapter 13 - HELDERBERG DISASTER

South African Airways Flight 295 was a Boeing 747-200B Combi, named The Helderberg that was delivered to the airline in 1980. The aircraft took off on 27 November 1987 from Taipei Chiang Kai Shek International Airport, on a flight to Johannesburg via Mauritius. Dawie Uys served as the captain of the flight.

The Boeing 747-200B Combi is a variant of the aircraft that permits the mixing of passengers and airfreight on the main deck according to load factors on any given route and Class B cargo compartment regulations. Flight 295 had 140 passengers and six pallets of cargo on the main deck. The master waybills stated that 47,000 kilograms of baggage and cargo were loaded on the plane. A Taiwanese customs official performed a surprise inspection of some of the cargo; he did not find any cargo that could be characterized as suspicious.

The flight crew consisted of 49-year-old Captain Dawie Uys with 13,843 flight hours, 36-year-old First Officer David Attwell with 7,362 flight hours, 37-year-old Relief First Officer Geoffrey Birchall with 8,749 flight hours, 45-year-old Flight Engineer Giuseppe "Joe" Bellagarda with 7,804 flight hours, and 34-year-old Relief Flight Engineer Alan Daniel with 1,595 flight hours.

Thirty-four minutes after departure, the flight contacted Hong Kong air traffic control to obtain clearance from waypoint ELATO (22°19′N 117°30′E) to ISBAN. A position report was made over ELATO at 15:03:25, followed by waypoints SUNEK at 15:53:52, ADMARK at 16:09:54 and SUKAR (12°22′N 110°54′E) at 16:34:47. The aircraft made a routine report to the South African Airways base at Jan Smuts (ZUR) at 15:55:18.

At some point during the flight, a fire developed in the cargo section on the main deck. The fire was probably not extinguished before impact. The 'smoke evacuation' checklist calls for the aircraft to be depressurized, and for two of the cabin doors to be opened. No evidence exists that the checklist was followed, or the doors opened. A crew member might have gone into the cargo hold to try to fight the fire. A charred fire extinguisher was later recovered from the wreckage on which investigators found molten metal.

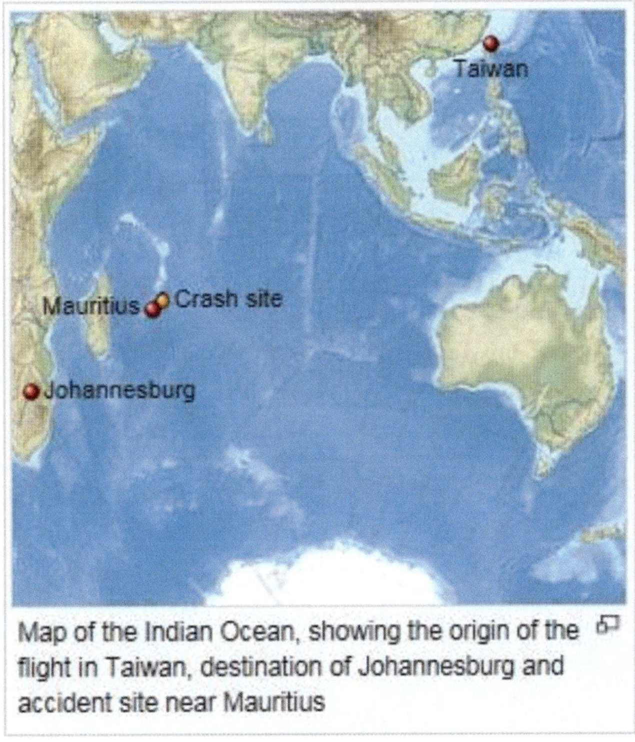

Map of the Indian Ocean, showing the origin of the flight in Taiwan, destination of Johannesburg and accident site near Mauritius

SAA Helderberg

The following communication was recorded with Mauritius air traffic control, located at Plaisance Airport Mauritius

Transcript of communication with Mauritius air traffic control			
Time	**Speaker**	**Dialog**	**Comment from official enquiry**
23:48:51	295	Eh, Mauritius, Mauritius, Springbok Two Niner Five.	
23:49:00	ATC	Springbok Two Nine Five, eh, Mauritius, eh, good morning, eh, go ahead.	
23:49:07	295	Eh, good morning, we have, eh, a smoke, eh, eh, problem and we're doing emergency descent to level one five, eh, one four zero.	
23:49:18	ATC	Confirm you wish to descend to flight level one four zero.	
23:49 20	295	Ja, we have already commenced, an, due to (a) smoke problem in the aeroplane.	
23:49:25	ATC	Eh, roger, you are clear to descend immediately to flight level one four zero.	
23:49:30	295	Roger, we will appreciate if you can alert the fire, ehp, ehp eh, eh	
23:49:40	ATC	Do you wish to eh, do you request a full emergency?	
23:49:48	295	*Okay Joe, kan jy...vir ons*	Okay Joe can you...for us
23:49:51	ATC	Springbok Two Nine Five, Plaisance.	
23:49:54	295	Sorry, go ahead?	
23:49:56	ATC	Do you, eh, request a full emergency please, a full emergency?	
23:50:00	295	Affirmative, that's Charlie Charlie.	
23:50:02	ATC	Roger, I declare a full emergency, roger.	
23:50:04	295	Thank you.	
23:50:40	ATC	Springbok Two Nine Five, Plaisance.	
23:50:44	295	Eh, go ahead.	
23:50:46	ATC	Request your actual position please and your DME distance?	
23:50:51	295	Eh, we haven't got the DME yet.	
23:50:55	ATC	Eh, roger and your actual position please.	
23:51:00	295	Eh, say again.	
23:51:02	ATC	Your actual position.	
23:51:08	295	Now we've lost a lot of electrics, we haven't got anything on the, on the aircraft now.	
23:51:12	ATC	Eh, roger, I declare a full emergency immediately.	
23:51:15	295	Affirmative.	
23:51:18	ATC	Roger.	
23:52:19	ATC	Eh, Springbok Two Nine Five, do you have an Echo Tango Alfa Plaisance please?	
23:52:30	ATC	Springbok Two Nine Five, Plaisance.	
23:52:32	295	Ja, Plaisance?	
23:52:33	ATC	Do you have an Echo Tango Alfa Plaisance please?	
23:52:36	295	Ja, eh, zero zero, eh eh eh three zero.	
23:52:40	ATC	Roger, zero zero three zero, thank you.	
23:52:50	295	Hey Joe, shut down the oxygen left.	Inadvertent transmission from the aircraft
23:52:52	ATC	Sorry, say again please?	
00:01:34	295	Eh, Plaisance, Springbok 295, we've opened the door(s) to see if we (can?)...we should be OK	
00:01:36	295	Look there (?)	Exclamation by someone else, and is said over the last part of the previous sentence

00:01:45	295	*Donner se deur t...*	Close the bloody door (Direct translation: Bloody door c...)
00:01:57	295	Joe, switch up quickly, then close the hole on your side.	
00:02:10	295	Pressure(?) twelve thousand	
00:02:14	295	*...Genoeg is...Anders kan ons vlug verongeluk*	..Is enough... ..otherwise our flight could come to grief (a more direct translation would be: otherwise our flight might have an accident)
00:02:25	295	Carrier wave only	
00:02:38	295	Eh Plaisance, Springbok Two Nine Five, do (did) you copy?	
00:02:41	ATC	Eh negative, Two Nine Five, say again please, say again.	
00:02:43	295	We're now sixty five miles.	
00:02:45	ATC	Confirm sixty five miles.	Incorrectly understood by air traffic control to mean that the aircraft was 65 miles from the airport; in fact it was 65 miles from waypoint Xagal, and 145 miles from the airport.
00:02:47	295	Ja, affirmative Charlie Charlie.	
00:02:50	ATC	Eh, Roger, Springbok eh Two Nine Five, eh re you're recleared flight level five zero. Recleared flight level five zero.	
00:02:58	295	Roger, five zero.	
00:03:00	ATC	And, Springbok Two Nine Five copy actual weather Plaisance Copy actual weather Plaisance. The wind one one zero degrees zero five knots. The visibility above one zero kilometres. And we have a precipitation in sight to the north. Clouds, five oktas one six zero zero, one okta five thousand feet. Temperature is twenty two, two two. And the QNH one zero one eight hectopascals, one zero one eight over.	
00:03:28	295	Roger, one zero one eight.	
00:03:31	ATC	Affirmative, eh and both runways available if you wish.	
00:03:43	ATC	And two nine five, I request pilot's intention.	
00:03:46	295	Eh, we'd like to track in eh, on eh one three.	
00:03:51	ATC	Confirm runway one three.	
00:03:54	295	Charlie Charlie	
00:03:56	ATC	Affirmative and you're cleared, eh direct to Foxtrot Foxtrot. You report approaching five zero	Clearance granted to the Flic-en-Flac non-directional navigation beacon.
00:04:02	295	Kay.	Last transmission from the aircraft
00:08:00	ATC	Two Nine Five, Plaisance.	
00:08:11	ATC	Springbok Two Nine Five, Plaisance.	
00:08:35	ATC	Springbok Two Nine Five Plaisance *(No answer)*	

After communication of flight 295 was lost for 36 minutes, at 00:44 (04:44 local time), Air Traffic Control at Mauritius formally declared an emergency.

South African Airways Flight 295 is located in the Indian Ocean near Mauritius. When the Helderberg last informed Mauritian air traffic control of its position, its report was incorrectly understood to be relative to the airport rather than its next waypoint, which caused the subsequent search to be concentrated too close to Mauritius. The United States Navy sent P-3 Orion aircraft from Diego Garcia, which was used to conduct immediate search and rescue operations in conjunction with the French Navy. By the time the first surface debris was located 12 hours after impact, it had drifted considerably from the impact location. Oil slicks and eight bodies showing signs of extreme trauma appeared in the water. All 140 passengers and 19 crew on the manifest were killed.

The South African Navy sent the SAS Tafelberg and the SAS Jim Fouche to assist in the recovery of debris and remains. The ocean tugs John Ross and Wolraad Woltemade also attended the scene, along with the Department of Environment Affairs vessels RS Africana and RS Sonne (The RS Sonne was not owned or operated by the Department of Environment Affairs but may have been chartered by them).

Searching for the Helderberg

Steve is still considered a junior engineer at 30 Squadron, when a call comes in that the SAS Tafelberg is deploying immediately to Mauritius to assist in the search for the SAA Helderberg. Russell calls Steve to the office and informs him that he feels Steve is experienced enough to be included in the trip. Steve together with Russell and Willie Beaurain and six pilots will be leaving the next day to join up with the ship which is already under steam up the east coast. Steve wastes no time in getting the assigned aircraft prepared for the trip. Puma 145 and 147 are the selected aircraft for the trip as they have both recently had Colour Radar systems installed. Steve ensures that the Technical Log is clear, packs sufficient fly away kit and ensures that the aircraft is clean. He installs ferry tanks and then hurries home to pack for the deployment.

It is mid-morning on the 2nd December 1987 when both Puma's get airborne from AFB Ysterplaat enroute to the SAS Tafelberg. Steve is teamed up with Paul Shemer as the Commander and Alan Reynold as the Co-Pilot. Paul had complete chopper conversion in 1980 when Steve rejoined the Air Force and Alan was at 22 Squadron with Steve in the mid 1980's. The two Puma's fly in loose formation along the east coast to join up with ship. Russell Du Preez is the F/E on the other aircraft and with him is Willie.

Stowing Puma on SAS Tafelberg

The flight to the ship is uneventful and once on board the aircraft are stowed and secured for the trip up the coast. The SAS Tafelberg will be calling in at Durban to top up with supplies. The Air Force contingent will also be able to get more appropriate clothing from the SA Navy Stores in Durban for the Tropical tour they are going to set out for. On this trip Warrant Officer Jackie Jacquet an ex F/E is going along as ground crew chief, accompanied by Vossie the Electrician. At Durban the Air Force crew gets a ride in with the Navy to the Stores and is issued with shorts, T-shirts and sandals. Once the ship is stocked they set heading toward Mauritius. It will be a full two days sailing before they reach the island on the opposite side of Madagascar.

SAS Tafelberg steams out toward the suspected crash site to hold station midway between Mauritius and the searching ship contingent. This to afford the two Puma's less flying time to the search area and allow for more hold time over the area. Steve together with Major's Louter Van Wyk and Trevor Jew, get airborne from the ship with the second Puma in tow. They are flying out supplies and equipment to the search group. The total flying time to the area two hours with fifteen minutes hold and a two-hour return.

Puma start-up SAS Tafelberg

The flight is long and intense, as there is nothing but Open Ocean all the way to Australia thousands of kilometers ahead. Should one of the aircraft develop a problem then ditching would be the only solution and the other Puma would be the rescue. Steve keeps a very close watch on the engines, gearboxes and instrument systems. He activates the radar to assist them with distance to the ships ahead.

They reach the search area and Steve winches down the supplies to the MV John Ross. They hold station while Louter communicates to the ship to clarify future drops. The two Puma's then set heading back to the SAS Tafelberg. Two hours later the relieved six crew members land on board the ship and shut down. For the next week the sortie is repeated daily. Willie has developed high blood pressure and therefore is unfit to fly, so Russell and Steve are the only fit F/E's left and complete the sorties.

On the 18th December 1987, Steve and Russell are once again the F/E's flying out to the search area. This time however it is decided that the two aircraft will not carry extra fuel as the equipment they are carrying is too heavy and will place the aircraft above MAUW. To counter the limited flight time the SAS Tafelberg is already steaming to Brenden Islands, which are islands that are so small that in heavy seas they are washed over. The flight out to the search area is uneventful, and the hoist is successfully completed. Now the challenge is the accuracy of Paul Shemer's flying and Alan Reynold's navigation to find a needle in a haystack in the middle of the Indian Ocean. Just before bingo fuel Steve spots the islands on the radar and Paul confirms he sees them on the horizon. A safe landing is executed by both aircraft and they shut down to await the SAS Tafelberg. The plan is to get airborne at sunset and head off to the ship with the remaining fuel they have. The crews do not want to take a chance on leaving too early and running out of fuel searching for the ship.

The rest of the day the guys walk around the small island. There is a barrier reef surrounding the whole island and there is the most amazing sea life all along the reef. The hours drag by until it is time to prepare for the return flight to the ship. Russell is already on pre-startup checks while Steve and Paul complete a walk around to check their aircraft. Russell indicates for Steve to come over to his aircraft. They have a starting snag. Steve runs over, and Russell explains to Steve that number one won't turn. As the Puma has an electronic starting cycle it is possible to by-pass the system with bridging clips, known as "Gippo Clips". Steve has fashioned his own an always carried them in his flight suite. He gives them to Russell who opens the 5 Alfa panel and bridges out the starting cycle. Russell reaches down and selects start, still nothing. The two of them confer and agree that the Starting Device is the culprit. This is the same component that gave Steve a hard time on his VIP Sortie a few months back.

Steve calls over to Paul and tells him to complete the exterior inspection and that he would join them as soon as Russell has his aircraft started. Russell has opened the number one engine cowling and Steve bridges out the Starting device with piece of stainless steel locking wire. Russell passes him a piece of string to tie to the bridge and then runs the string down to the cabin below. They lock the cowlings and Russell selects start. The pleasant whine of the starter is heard, and the engine starts normally. With a quick tug on the string the bridge is pulled from the Staring Device. Steve waits until Russell has both engines running and then races over to his aircraft.

Both pilots are already strapped in and have completed the pre-start check list. Steve asks Paul if he has completed the external inspection to which Paul confirms he has. It is already getting dark so Steve checks if he is clear to start. He switches on the booster pumps and then selects vent on number one. Nothing happens; he has the same problem as Russell. Steve will first attempt the "Gippo Clip" start. He removes the 5 Alpha cover and bridges out the start cycle. Fortunately, this method works on Steve's aircraft, and the Puma is soon alive and ready to fly.

Both aircraft get airborne and set heading for the SAS Tafelberg. With low fuel and flying at night it is a very tense time for both crews. Steve is monitoring the fuel levels closely and scanning the radar to detect the ship. Just as the first fuel low level warning light illuminates they spot the ship in the distance. A very relieved group of aviator's space for landing and in turn take up their spots onboard the SAS Tafelberg. With both aircraft safely on deck they initiate shut down.

Steve moves the rear of the Puma to extract the access ladder so that he can open the engine and gearbox cowlings. The ladder is not there. Steve feels a chill run down his spine, the pilots did not remove the ladder from the aircraft on their walk around and it flew off during the flight. Steve questions Paul on if he had removed the ladder to which Paul responded;

"But I thought you had"?

"Sir, I was at Russell's aircraft helping him, and asked you to complete the external pre-flight which includes ladder stowage".

"Oh shit, it must have dropped off in flight, is there any damage to the aircraft"?

"No Sir, the aircraft is fine, but this could have been a very serious incident if the ladder had contacted the tail rotor".

Steve reports the incident to Russell and Jackie, who write up a report based on the statement by Steve and Paul. Everyone is very relieved that there had been no damage or serious incident. For the remainder of the trip the crews would have to share the access ladder.

The Captain of the SAS Tafelberg decides that there is rest, and recuperation required for the ship. He steers the ship to the Brenden Islands and early the next morning he is easing the ship in between the small group of islands. At a safe depth below the ship, he calls for the anchors to be let loose. The rest of the day all hands not on duty are free to use the Delta Boats and have fun snorkeling on the reef. The Air Force Contingent makes full use of the opportunity and between Russel and Steve they collect enough Cochas and Coral to start a small gift shop. Amid sunburn and dehydration, much fun is had by all. Steve, Vossie and Russell are snorkeling at the edge of the reef and Steve sees a black tipped shark swimming close by. He calls over to Vossie to show him. With a yell, Vossie beelines it to the beach. Steve and Russell pack out laughing at the spectacle.

The ship sets sail back to Mauritius. Cmdt Rod Penhall is the Search and Rescue coordinator for the Air Force and has joined the crew onboard. He summons all to the bridge for a briefing. The SAS Tafelberg has been ordered to Madagascar where she will be accepting a civilian helicopter from Court Helicopters in Cape Town. The Sikorsky S61 helicopter is larger than the Puma and can carry more.

The S61 has been contracted to support the ships while the Puma's will be utilized to search for wreckage on the nearby islands that has been washing up in the recent few days. To this end the Air Force Contingent is to deploy to Mauritius and will operate from Plaisance Air Port out of Port Louis. They will also be housed in one of the hotels on the island for the duration.

A very excited bunch races off to their cabins to pack and prepare for their departure. Steve's aircraft has developed a fuel leak, so he ensures that he has sufficient parts to affect the repairs required. Both Steve and Russell must also ensure that they have sufficient support spares to keep the aircraft serviceable for the next few weeks. This is all loaded into the aircraft.

Mauritius Holiday Venue

It is the 22nd December 1987 and the two Puma's with all crew onboard get airborne from the SAS Tafelberg and set heading for Mauritius. They are heading to Port Louis, where the International Airport Plaisance is located. The crews will meet up with the command structure at Plaisance to establish the search operation. The Puma's will be utilized mostly in a support role by flying out supplies and personnel to the ships in the search area. They will also be on standby should any search and rescue be required. A very amusing radio call between Paul and Plaisance Tower keeps the flight light hearted.

“Plaisance we are two Puma Helicopters from the South African Ship Tafelberg, airborne and enroute to Plaisance, 20 miles out, clearance.”

“Eh, last call to Plaisance please say again”?

“Plaisance we are two Puma Helicopters airborne off the South African ship enroute to Plaisance at 18 miles out this time”!

“Eh, South African aircraft where are you coming from”?

“Plaisance we are two helicopters inbound at 15 miles and will be landing at Plaisance in 10 minutes, we are switching to Tower Frequency this time, good day”!

“Plaisance Tower, this is Puma Helicopters airborne off the South African Ship Tafelberg, currently at 2000ft agl and 13 miles out, request your joining and landing instructions”?

“Eh last call to Plaisance say again your intentions”?

“Plaisance Tower, Puma Helicopters request active runway, we are 5 miles out and are preparing to land at Plaisance”!

“Eh helicopter the active runway is 13, wind is calm, call 2 miles”!

“Plaisance Tower copy 13, 2 miles next, and we will land on the taxi way, Puma Helicopters”!

From that moment on it was clear that for any flights the Pumas would tell Plaisance what they intend to do instead of asking.

Both aircraft are instructed to taxi to a maintenance hangar at the airport from where they will be operating for the next few weeks. The rest of the day Steve spends time repairing the fuel leak to the aircraft until the pilots return from the search briefing. Everyone gathers their kit and the SAA Bus ferries them off to their hotel on the opposite side of the Island.

The hotel staff are very accommodating, and the Air Force Contingent is made to feel right at home. The next morning at breakfast, Steve orders an Omelet and after 20 minutes motions to the East Indian waiter to come over.

“Where is my breakfast”? Asks Steve.

“Oh Sir, it will only be two minutes”.

And off he saunters smiling and chatting. Another 15 minutes go by and Steve beckons him over once more;

“How long does it take to make an Omelet”?

“Oh Sir, it will only be two minutes”.

Eventually the breakfast arrives and is cold. As they are scheduled for an early take-off, Steve chows down and the group beelines it to the waiting SAA Bus. From this moment on all orders are jokingly referred to as “Two Minutes”.

The Court helicopter is stranded on Madagascar due to customs issues, so the Puma’s will continue their sorties to the search area from Plaisance Airport. The ferry tanks are reinstalled, and the aircraft filled to the brim. Both aircraft get airborne for the search area, this time to the MV Wolraad Woltemade to drop off a US Naval Officer as well as some supplies. On the return route all is well until Steve is alerted to a fuel low level warning light on the right-hand system. As he has already drained the ferry tanks into the main fuel tanks this does not make sense. The left-hand fuel system has more fuel, but Steve has balanced out the fuel by transferring it from left to right. The Fuel Booster Pumps are connected to an intricate piping and venturi system that ensures the engines are always supplied with fuel. If one of the Venturi Pumps is blocked by debris, then the Booster Pump will drain the main feeder tank quicker than the Venturi Pumps can supply, and thus the fuel low level warning light will illuminate. As they have nowhere to land Steve informs the pilots that he cannot transfer fuel at this time and that they should be prepared for fuel starvation and engine cut. A Puma can fly safely with one engine, but this far out to sea it is quite a daunting task. Paul decides to climb while both engines are functional so that if the engine fails they will have sufficient power to slowly glide down to Mauritius on one engine. The second Puma stays close in case something goes wrong.

Mauritius is still 75 miles on the radar and the fuel low level light is now steady red. Steve had started the stop watch at the first flicker, which would give them 15 minutes of flight time under normal conditions. 15 Minutes has come and gone, and the engine is still operating. At 20 miles it is obvious that Plaisance Airport is out of reach for them, so Paul requests Louter in the second Puma to break away to the SAS Tafelberg and pick up two drums of fuel. Paul keeps the Puma at altitude until they cross the coast line then Steve looks for a safe place for them to land. Once shut down Steve immediately accesses the

Venturi Pump via a drain hole at the bottom of the fuel tank. A ball of fluff and dirt are caught up in the center of the pump. Steve cleans out the Venturi and gets drenched with Jet A1 fuel. He secures the Pump and closes the panels. The second Puma arrives with two drums of fuel and Steve wastes no time in refueling. Back in the cockpit and checklist completed the crew is delighted to see that the fuel low level light is extinguished. The cleaning of the Venturi Pump and extra fuel has resolved the issue. A safe and happy crew returns to Plaisance Airport. For safety Steve decides to remove and clean all the Venturi pumps before refueling the aircraft for the next day's flying.

Mauritius Party Time

And then there is the "Day" when the Air Force conquers the hotels on Mauritius. Russell Du Preez, Jackie Jacquet, Steve and Vossie De Vos are having some downtime and they do what all Air Force guys do, they entertain. The team have just been relocated from the one hotel to another across the pond / bay / lagoon / open stretch of water. As they still have friends at the other hotel, it's decided after many "frosties" to make the trek across the pond / bay / lagoon / open stretch of water, with a water taxi. Russell does the bartering and soon has the "Captain Water Taxi Driver" take the team across the pond / bay / lagoon / open stretch of water to the previous abode of residence. There they meet up with some of their drinking buddies and a delightful day is spent by singing all the chopper songs they can muster and all the war stories they can dream up.

Eventually the sensible but wonderfully inebriated Jackie convinces all that it's time to depart back to the new residence. With a huge fanfare they depart, with Russell in search of the "Captain Water Taxi driver". The "Captain Taxi Driver" is not very impressed with his PAX, and it takes all Russell's negotiating skills to get him to agree to take the team for a reduced fare. With voices blaring "We are choppers, we are choppers we're a long way from home!" the Water Taxi starts making its way across the pond / bay / lagoon / open stretch of water. Midway across the pond / bay / lagoon / open stretch of water, Jackie gestures to the Creole Captain of the ship that he needs a bathroom break. The Captain just shakes his head and indicates that no pissing is allowed. Steve looks at Jackie, and a twinkle appears, and then the light goes on. "Man overboard", and there they are, swimming in ever decreasing circles leaving a large stain in the pond / bay / lagoon / open stretch of water. No sooner has the team baled when Russell and Vossie join in. The Captain is pissed at the pissing but has no choice as he is not going to get paid without any PAX onboard. So, he duly stops and waits for the giggling school girls to finish their escapades, and then helps them back on board, all the while loudly voicing his discontent in Creole. The team obviously thinks he is thanking them for not messing in his boat.

Needless to say, when dropped off at the other side of the pond / bay / lagoon / open stretch of water, there is a huge argument over what the payment would be. Russell is left to resolve the issue while Jackie, Vossie and Steve go in search of the next tin soldiers to fight with. It will be the last time they are able to utilize this mode of transport, as the rumour mill has spread very quickly about the chopper crew that are a bit of a hand full during transportation.

1987 Christmas and Russell decides that he must create an entertaining event for all the children at the hotel. No sooner said than done, and all Lumi Sticks are confiscated for use at the Christmas Party. At this point the Air Force contingent is pretty tanked up and with Russell in the lead the Lumi Sticks are activated, cut and splashed on the happy crowd. With cheers more Lumi Sticks are destroyed until the whole party is covered in the Luminescent contents of the Lumi Sticks. Great fun is had by all.

The crews have now been away from home for a month. It is still uncertain as to when they will return to South Africa. The search for the SAA Helderberg is still ongoing and the debris field is washing up parts of the aircraft on many of the Islands in the surrounding area. The flights out to the search area start waning off and it looks like they will soon be heading home. On the 29th December 1987 the Puma Crews are ordered back to the SAS Tafelberg to set sail to South Africa. New Year's Eve is celebrated onboard in full Naval tradition and a great evening is enjoyed by all.

It takes the SAS Tafelberg 3 days to get back to Cape Town and it is a pleasant afternoon on the 3rd January 1988 when the two Puma's take leave of the ship and head back to AFB Ysterplaat. It is really good to catch up with the family once more; Steve is missing too many birthdays, Christmases and New Year celebrations. Nicole seems to be growing up quicker everytime he is away on a trip.

It will be months until the SAA Helderberg's wreckage can be recovered from 4,000m below the surface of the ocean, the aircraft's fuselage and cabin interior would then be partly reassembled in one of SAA's hangars at Jan Smuts Airport where it will be examined and finally opened for viewing to the airline's staff and selected members of the public.

Mirage Down

On the 20th February 1988 Major Edward Richard Every from 1 Squadron is Reported Missing during an Operational sortie over Southern Angola after his Mirage F1AZ, 245 is shot down by a Soviet SA-13 Gopher Surface-to-Air Missile near Cuatir. The aircraft is seen to crash in flames and disintegrate on impact with the ground. Although he has no known grave, a Tribute Memorial Grave Headstone is erected in the Military Plot of the Voortrekkerhoogte New Military Cemetery in his memory. He was 31 years old.

A Special Forces team covering the area where the Mirage wreckage is located reports a large number of FAPLA and Cuban Air Force intelligence personnel picking through the wreckage and calls in an artillery barrage onto the wreckage. The 32 Battalion MRL Rocket-Launcher Troop hit the spot with a half-ripple of 127mm High Explosive Fragmentation Rockets. The Special Forces Team later observe two FAPLA Ural trucks collecting the bodies of more than 143 Cuban and FAPLA personnel that are killed by this rocket barrage.

Chapter 14 – FIRE AND ICE

The Western Cape is a winter rain fall area and therefore has very dry summers. 30 Squadron with the Puma helicopters is therefore strategically placed to deal with the inevitable fires that are the result of hot dry and windy conditions. The Puma with its cargo sling, can carry over 2,000 liters of water in a bucket for dowsing the flames. During these hot and dry summer months the Puma's work many hours fighting fires throughout the Western Cape. Steve has just settled back into routine after his trip on the SAS Tafelberg and is on Standby for the fires that are currently raging in the Silvermine area. It is four thirty in the afternoon and the Air Force Base is closing for the day, when the call comes in. Four aircraft are dispatched to Simonstown to fight the fire that is threatening Simonstown. There is still another five hours of daylight left so the crews ready the aircraft and depart en masse for Simonstown.

Steve is flying with Maj. Gawie Venter and Capt. Neil Reid. They are scooping water from the reservoir on top of Simonstown and dumping it along the fire line that is heading towards the town. With the Fire Fighters on the ground and the Alouette Fire Command and Directing the operation, the threat is soon under control. It is almost nightfall when an exhausted group of aviators make their way happily back to AFB Ysterplaat after successfully assisting to quench the serious threat of Simonstown. The summer is dry, hot and windy and Steve knows that this will not be the last firefighting call out.

The year has just begun, and Steve knows it is going to be a busy one. January comes and goes amid a flurry of training, VIP, Emergencies, Hoisting, Repelling and IF flights. Steve's Puma hours are quickly building up as he becomes more competent on the aircraft and its systems. It is the beginning of February and Steve takes two weeks off to spend with Zella and Nicole. It is good bonding time with Nicole. Zella is back at University and is doing well at her studies. Steve takes Nicole to Crèche in the mornings and picks her up in the early afternoons. It is one of those days when the Toyota E20 Taxis are once again abusively swerving in an out of traffic and cutting in front of cars. Steve's stress levels are at peak and as one of these irresponsive black drivers comes past with a heavily overloaded van, Steve leans out and shouts at the driver;

"You Bloody Black Bastard, look where you are going"!

Nicole looks at Dad with a beaming grin, and you know what is coming. Steve immediately regrets what he has done, but the damage has been delivered and he knows he will soon feel its wrath.

It is early evening and the family has been invited to a braai at Piet's, so they set off with the required stocks of beer, meat and salad. Steve is driving with Nicole standing between him and Zella. A Taxi passes normally on the right when sweet innocent Nicole makes Steve pay for his indiscretion this afternoon. She balls her fist and at the top of her voice shouts;

"You Bloody Black Bastard"!

Steve turns his face away with a sheepish grin. Zella chastises Nicole while looking sternly at Steve.

"This is your doing".

The story is repeated at the braai and Steve becomes the one to poke fun at all night. Nicole wakes the next day with a fever and Steve takes her to the Medical Clinic at AFB Ysterplaat. Nicole is diagnosed with measles and Steve takes her home to nurse her for the next few days. It is not too long before Nicole breaks out in the telltale spots and Steve immediately applies Calamine lotion to help with the itching. Nicole recovers well and can soon return to the Crèche.

Flood in the Desert

The north eastern part of South Africa is receiving an enormous amount of rain, and as the Highveld Plateau drains easterly and westerly there is flash flooding that can take place on the long flowing westerly rivers. It is the 25th February 1988 when 30 Squadron is activated to assist in flood rescues on the northern borders, Upington is under flood warning and the neighbouring farms are all being affected.

Upington is a town founded in 1884 and located in the Northern Cape province of South Africa, on the banks of the Orange River. The town was originally called Olyfenhoudtsdrif ('Olive wood drift'), due to the abundance of olive wood trees in the area, but later renamed after Sir Thomas Upington, Attorney-General and then Prime Minister of the Cape. It originated as a mission station established in 1875 and run by Reverend Christiaan Schröder. The mission station now houses the town museum, known as the Kalahari Orange Museum. The museum is also the home of a donkey statue, which recognizes the enormous contribution that this animal made to the development of the region during the pioneering days of the 19th century.

The elevation of Upington is 2742 feet. It is the closest large centre to the Augrabies Falls, arguably the greatest of South African waterfalls, and the Kgalagadi Transfrontier Park. The landscape is very arid, but the soil is fertile and crops such as fruit are grown in irrigated fields. The area is best known for its export-quality grapes, raisins and wines, which are cultivated on the rich flood plains of the Orange River.

Upington

Maj. Gawie Venter, Lt. Schalk Fourie, Lt. Snyman, Steve, and a ground crew member depart with full ferry tanks to Upington. The flight will take around 3 hours. They have been activated to assist with rescue and flood relief assistance in the Upington region. The flight is uneventful and upon arrival at Upington the Air Force Contingent quickly settles into the Motel they have been assigned. Steve and the Ground Crewman quickly unload the aircraft and prepare for the upcoming tasking.

Upington Floods

The rest of the day the Puma flies constantly to resupply farmers and townships that have been cut-off by the flooding Orange River. The river already has risen to above all of the low-level bridges and is now threatening the structured bridges in the city. This is a strange situation as there is not a cloud in the sky but the whole area is a flood plain. The Puma flies for the rest of the day providing vital supplies to cut-off communities. Early evening Steve and the Lt. Snyman together with the Ground Crewman complete the refuel, servicing and securing of the aircraft for the night. They then all saunter off to the Motel Pub for supper and nourishment. Steve and Lt. Snyman consume more than the required amount of red wine and retire to a restful sleep.

For the next three days the Puma is kept busy re-supplying many of the communities with supplies and assisting in planning for the cleanup operation that will be required. Steve has a headache and writes it off to the nighttime drinking escapades. On the third day Steve is busy refueling the aircraft and once again he is burning up. He opens his flight suite to cool off and his whole chest and stomach are covered in telltale dots, he has been infected with the Measles that Nicole had the previous week. Fortunately for Steve another Puma is en-route to Upington to replace them. Steve is feeling the after effects of the illness and is not a happy camper. The return flight to AFB Ysterplaat is long and painful.

Steve is booked off by the doctor for a few days to recover from the after effects of Measles. The days seem very long to Steve and the headache and body pain are truly irritating. Eventually the aches subside, and he is on the road to recovery. Steve is soon well enough to return to the squadron and continue the daily flight program. February melts into March 1988 and very soon April and May roll round. Steve's birthday arrives and at 29 he is fit and still running daily. Nicole will be 4 this year and Zella is holding a party for her the coming Saturday and then a braai in the evening for Steve. The standard entourage of bring and braai friends arrive, and once Nicole and her friends have enjoyed an afternoon of presents, cake and goodies, the adults dive into a hearty celebration of booze, boerewors, pap and sous.

On the 16th May 1988 Steve is packed and ready to catch the Flossie once more to SWA and AFB Ondangwa.

VIP in Angola

Back in SWA at AFB Ondangwa the mornings are cool as they head into winter. The days are still hot but without the humidity. Steve spends many nights flying Casevac sorties as the conflict in Southern Angola is on the rise once more. Late the evening at 21:00 Steve is in the hangar tinkering on the aircraft when another Casevac sortie is called. Steve races off to the Ops Room and meets up with his pilots for the sortie. There had been a contact just south of Mupa and the fire fight was still sporadic.

A number of troops had injuries and required extraction. They get airborne for the Casevac and take 45 minutes to reach the area. A signal flare marks the LZ, and Steve moves to the back to open the door so that he can patter the flying pilot into the LZ. There is still gunfire in the area and the night sky is marked with tracer rounds.

Steve indicates for the medics in the cabin to speed the extraction of the wounded. It is not very long when the Puma's cabin is full of bodies, and Steve screams to the pilots;

"How many Casevac's are we supposed to pick up? There are more than 6 we were told".

Steve closes the cabin door and the pilot, Mike McGee, takes power to get airborne. Steve is still in the rear and can hear the engines struggling to provide enough power. The rotor RPM is dropping when Steve screams;

"Watch the Rotor RPM reduce power or else we will run out of revs".

Immediately the Mike reduces the collective a bit and the rotor RPM stabilizes but remains low, indicating that the aircraft is very heavy. They limp forward and just scrape over the trees as they slowly gain forward speed. The aircraft is struggling to maintain altitude and Mike has to nurse the power very carefully until what seems like an eternity to reach 60 Kts.

Steve in the meantime has placed covers on the cabin windows and drops the curtain between the cockpit and cabin. He switches on the cabin lighting so that the medics can work on the injured.

Steve sneaks back to check up and counts 13 Casevac's with a doctor and two medics, making the Puma over MAUW and therefore very heavy. Because the cabin is so heavily loaded the C of G is far back and the aircraft can only maintain 110 Kts. Forward speed. It takes them an hour to get back to AFB Ondangwa. The injured are quickly collected by the ambulances and taken to the local hospital.

At the Ops Room the crew debriefs and amid raised voices from the crew the Int Officer is chastised for the inaccurate number of Casevac's. This could have turned sour very quickly. The Puma has flown into a fire fight situation where there were more injured than expected and no back up plan.

The request is put forward that for cross border operations Puma's must fly in pairs allowing for backup at all times.

Steve rests up the next day and is informed that he needs to prepare for a trip to AFB Rundu for a VIP sortie. Capt. Steele Upton is his Commander on the upcoming sortie. Steve sets to work to clean and install seats into the Puma for the upcoming flight. Early the morning two Puma's get airborne to AFB Rundu. The flight initially follows the border road running along Angola and SWA known as "Oom Willie se pad", (Uncle Willie's road).

Oom Willie se pad

The Puma's are flying in a loose battle formation and soon pick up the Cubango River and follow this to the town of Rundu. Once over Rundu they are cleared to land at AFB Rundu and after landing, taxi into the movement control area to shut down. Steve indicates for the refueling bowser to come closer and completes the refuel of the aircraft. He updates the travel log with fuel replenished and completes the sortie log. He joins the pilots at the Ops Room and there finds out that the VIP sortie would be the State President, PW Botha and Ministers of his cabinet, including Ministers Pik Botha, Dawie De Villiers, Magnus Malan and Barend Du Plessis. In the second Puma would be the State President's son and staff.

The VIP sortie is to Jamba in the South East of Angola, the HQ of UNITA and home of Dr. Jonas Savimbi. The two Puma's get airborne with their VIP's and head off across the border towards Jamba. The flight is a short 30 minutes from Rundu and once the aircraft land they are surrounded by UNITA.

State President PW Botha & Jonas Savimbi Jamba

UNITA has prepared a tour for the VIP's to display their self-sufficiency and origination. The aircrews of both Puma's are included in a guided tour of Jamba. Uniform making Kimbo's, Classes for teaching and parade grounds for drill training. The whole town is very well organized for a Rebel Force completely isolated in the Angolan Bush.

The tour is topped off with a parade in honour of the South African State President with a march past by well drilled troops, captured weapons and singing students. The parade is topped with a vocal speech by Jonas Savimbi himself in Portuguese. The final sentence of the speech directly aimed at PW Botha,

"Vida longo Presidente Pieter Botha", (Long live President Pieter Botha).

The crowd roars in response and slowly disperses. The rest of the day the VIP's are whisked away for talks and agreements on how South Africa would support UNITA in their struggle against the Communists. The aircrew are taken to their respective Kimbo's and told to report for drinks and supper at the main entertainment area close to Jonas Savimbi's abode.

UNITA VIP Visit

Unita General, General Geldenhuys, Minister Pik Botha, Jonas Savimbi, Minister Dawie De Villiers, President Botha, Minister Barend Du Plessis, Minister Magnus Malan, Unita General.

The sun sets red on the South Angolan horizon and the Air Force team meets outside the main table set for the VIP's. In front of the VIP table is a bed of burning coals to keep the chill of the cool evening off the VIP Guests. Across the fire is a large wooded table loaded with every type of drink imaginable. The Air Force Team does not need much encouragement to dive in and soon the drinks are flowing freely. The VIP's arrive and are seated at the table. President Botha and Jonas Savimbi in the center next to each other followed on either side, in pecking order the rest of the South African and UNITA delegation.

Food is served to the VIP's first, followed by visiting guests. A hearty meal is thoroughly enjoyed with the Air Force Team retiring once again to the Drinks Table. The evening turns to night and Angolan night sky is lit up by billions of stars forming the Milky Way Galaxy. The jokes and laughter at the Drinks Table are becoming louder and playful. Minister Pik Botha gets up from the VIP Table and comes walking straight through the bed of coals to the Drinks Table. With smoldering Velskoen, he walks over grinning and muttering.

"Ek vat nie kak van vonke nie!" (I don't take shit from sparks).

"Waar is die Brandewyn?" (Where is the Brandy)?

The spectacle results in a roar of laughter and appreciation for Pik's ability to join the crowd and have fun. He is clearly bored with the talks between the leaders and has decided to join the Air Force Team. The rest of the evening is enjoyed with his company and many servings of Brandy and Coke. The jokes and laughter recede into the night until everyone has eventually dispersed to bed to catch a few hours of sleep.

Steve is at his aircraft early to complete the pre-flight inspection and ensure that the Puma is clean for the VIP's. Oom Pik, as he has been affectionately dubbed arrives and seeks Steve out.

"Steve can you do one of those PAX Briefings that you Air Force guys are so famous for?"

"Most certainly Oom Pik, but the Commander normally does it!"

"I have already briefed him, just sit in your seat, turn around and then do it, ok?"

"Reg so Oom Pik". (Righty ho) Says Steve.

With all onboard and the pilots both strapped in, Steve turns around in his seat to face the PAX.

"Good morning Mr. President and Gentleman, just a few minutes of your time please. There will be no dancing, crapping or pissing on the seats. This is my cat and I will skin it as I see fit. Are there any questions?"

With that Steve turns forward once more and a roar of laughter from the back ensures Steve he still has a job. The pilots are grinning from ear to ear as they proceed through the checklist and Steve starts the engines to get the show on the road. The two Puma's get airborne from Jamba and form up in close formation for a fly past in honour of the meetings that have been concluded. Steel is flying the lead Puma with Steve and Tony while the second Puma forms up to the right and slightly higher. Lining up over the greeting area where Jonas is waving the two Puma's come racing over at 50 ft. agl and 130 Kts. Immediately after the fly past both Puma's climb to 1,000 ft. agl and then break left and right to bank round and complete a line astern fly past as a final gesture of farewell. The return flight to AFB Rundu is made all along the river so that the VIP's can enjoy the view. Once over the airfield the aircraft space for landing and Steve completes the vital actions. With the aircraft shut down at Movement Control the VIP's disembark and thank the Air Force Team for the flight. Oom Pik taps Steve on the shoulder and gives him a thumb's up and a huge grin as he follows President Botha to the waiting Falcon 900 Business Jet for their return flight to South Africa.

With the Puma's refueled they both get airborne for a return flight to AFB Ondangwa. Steve is getting to the end of another tour and must prepare his aircraft for the replacement F/E that will be arriving in a few days. Back at AFB Ondangwa Steve removes the seating and reconfigures the Puma back into a trooping aircraft. He starts cleaning the aircraft for the handover in two days. He must still fly one more sortie in the morning but wants to ensure that the aircraft is mechanically sound and serviceable.

Steve's mind wanders back through his experiences in the Border War years. Much has happened, and he feels a terrible urge to complete as many items on his bucket list that he can. He cannot shake the feeling of living on borrowed time. There have been too many close calls and he cannot help but wonder what the future holds.

Steve has lost too many comrades of late and the war is escalating with no end in sight. He needs to look forward but is struggling to shake the past and the eerie feeling that seems to overcome him. Nicole fills much of his happiness, but with Zella there is a feeling of unsureness. He does not seem to be able to communicate with her anymore and feels like a stranger. She still smokes when he is away, and he can smell it every time he returns. He wants to sit down and discuss these emotions with her, but every time so far, she has rebuffed him. He is in deep thought while working on the aircraft and does not notice that the sun has gone down and that he must hurry to make it to the mess for supper. He downs tools and rushes off to the showers and off to the Mess.

After a quick supper, Steve heads off to the pub and sits quietly at the far end of the counter, his thoughts still disturbed and uneasy. Before he realizes it, he is quite drunk, and wobbling finds his way out of the pub and along the open expanse of white sand to the air crew quarters. It is not an easy journey and he stops frequently and bursts out laughing at his own drunken stupidity.

Steve wakes early the morning with a banging headache. He slowly makes his way to the showers and stands there a long time. As he is returning to the States today, he dresses in his Brown Nutria uniform and forgoes breakfast with a strong cup of coffee at the hangar. He completes clearing out and reports to movement control to await the departure of the Flossie.

Puma NVG

It is 16th June 1988 when Steve gets back to Cape Town. It is really good to be home again, but the uneasy feeling keeps creeping over him like a shadow and he does not know how to broach a conversation with Zella, instead he makes a fuss over Nicole to settle his nerves. Steve arrives back at the squadron to be called to Cmdt Theron's office.

"Steve, you have selected to represent 30 Squadron for the official Puma NVG training which will take place from the 27th June 1988 for three weeks at 19 Squadron."

"Thank you Sir I am honoured to be considered and will keep 30 Squadrons name high."

Excitement overrules the feeling of doom and gloom, and Steve prepares for the trip to 19 Squadron. The two weeks fly by and once again Zella drops Steve off at movement control to board a flight to AFB Waterkloof for his NVG training. Major's Des Wellerblaber and Gary Hamilton are the selected pilots that will be on course with him. They are both good pilots and gentlemen. Steve has spent time with both of them at 87 HFS and in previous operational tours. The flight up is uneventful and by early evening the trio is imbedded at AFB Swartkop, the pilots at the Officer's Mess and Steve at the WO's Mess.

At the WO's Pub Steve once again meets up with Ken, and after a big bear hug the two get down to serious drinking and reminiscing. The syllabus for the upcoming NVG course is going to be very full and the students will not have much free time, according to Ken. But the course is interesting and requires accuracy and team work. Cockpit management is the main focus on getting it right the first time. Steve is excited and share Ken's enthusiasm, as this is what they are both very good at.

Steve joins Ken the next day to go over the Panel and NVG infrared cover installations required to dim out the white light on the Puma. This will allow the NVG wearer to safely utilize the NVG's inside and outside of the aircraft. The Panel is fitted in place of the Instrument Glare panel and contains a set of Ultra Violet Lighting that will illuminate the Instrument Panel. Internally the radio and navigation panel lighting must have covers installed over the illuminating, and warning lights.

Puma Engine Panel Warning Lights

Externally the navigation and landing lights are fitted with infrared covers as well. With the natural eye it is very difficult to see when the lights are on, the only confirmation is the heat given off when you touch the lenses. Steve learns from Ken how to connect up the UV Panel to the aircrafts Primary Buzz Bar. Once completed Steve and Ken verify that every installation is secure, completed and functional before signing of the aircraft's technical log book.

The students are gathered in the 19 Squadron Lecture Room where the lectures on NVG flying begin. All the aspects of cockpit management, flight conditions, sorties to be flown, and emergency procedures are presented. During the flight training phase each student will have a qualified NVG Commander and Flight Engineer onboard until a competency flight is completed.

Additional tasks to be completed are sorties that will include Hoisting, Cargo Slinging, Confined Area Landings, Slope Landings and low-level Formation Flying. All these sorties will be conducted at night under starlight sky, with little or no moon, thus giving all students the total effect of NVG Operations. The course completion will be an NVG navigation exercise to AFB Hoedspruit where the sorties are to be tested for each crew.

On the 30th June 1988 Steve is F/E onboard with Major "Rassie" Ras, who completed Helicopter Conversion when Steve was a UT F/E. Des Wellerblaber is the Co-Pilot and student. The sortie is in preparation for the NVG training to take place. They get airborne and Des is flying from the Commander's seat.

They form up in close formation with the lead aircraft and spend the next hour completing formation turns, climbing, descending, slow down and acceleration. All the while Steve is practicing the F/E role for NVG flying and patters attitude, altitude, airspeed and navigational position. All the while he also completes the Take-Off, Down Wind, and Final Vital Actions. The sortie is completed successfully and will be followed the next day by emergency procedures. This is required to ensure that the crews can handle any situation that arises.

The next few days the students spend most of the days preparing for the first flight. The moon is still rising too early and is too bright. For effective NVG training there must be mostly a starlit night. By the 4th July 1988 the sky is ready to be assaulted by a gaggle of angry Puma's. With Ferry Tanks installed Steve, Rassie and Des once again get airborne.

Take off is at 22:30 the night, with only stars lighting up the night sky. All three have NVG's attached to their helmets, both pilots have goggles down while Steve has his folded up and is completing all the internal checks and patters the flying pilot as per briefed altitude, attitude and airspeed. Generation 4 NVG's are the most modern sets, and only require starlight for effective operation. The sight through the NVG requires getting used to, but the visibility is clear and detailed.

The take-off is normal and Rassie lets Des complete the form up to the lead aircraft for a number of circuit flights.

Pilot with NVG's down

Next the formation completes a flight out of the AFB Swartkop controlled area and then doubles back to complete an approach and landing on the Taxiway. On short finals Rassie tells Des to slow down and position behind and above the lead aircraft. The two aircraft will then land line astern on the taxiway and perform a formation take-off.

Landing Approach with NVG's

The training continuous well into the wee hours of the next morning and eventually after five hours the sortie is completed. A very exhausted crew completes shutdown and debrief. Steve together with the ground crew make quick work of getting the aircraft refueled towed into the hangar and serviced. The aircraft must be in a readiness state at all times. Steve gets to bed and falls into a deep sleep. They are only required to report at 18:00 the next evening for the next sortie, so Steve makes the most of the relaxation to recuperate for the next flight.

At 17:00 the next evening, Steve reports to the squadron to be informed that the looming thunder storms will disrupt the training and that they should stand down for the evening. Steve takes the time to verify that the aircraft is still serviceable and completes a thorough inspection of the systems.

The next sorties will be a repeat of the previous night's exercise and then also include hoisting. Steve checks that the hoist installation is correctly mounted, and that the controller is functional. He then heads off to the WO's pub to meet up with the rest of the gang. Steve and Ken end up having too much to drink and are in deep trouble with Ken's wife, who has come looking for him at the pub. Steve sneaks away to his room to avoid the impending attack. Ken is in a heap of trouble tonight for sure. A hung-over Steve awakes to a late breakfast at the mess and a slow day for recovery. Fortunately, he will be taking off very late tonight so he has enough time to recuperate. At 18:00 Steve is back at the squadron feeling 100% better than he did in the morning. He checks the flight schedule to see which aircraft has been allocated for the sortie and wanders over to Technical Control to review the aircrafts technical log. There are no due items for maintenance and the aircraft has been signed up as serviceable for the next flight. Steve checks with Rassie what fuel quantity is required for the sortie and then gets a single ferry tank to install. Steve gets the NVG Panel and light covers required, and then completes the installation and testing before signing off the technical log.

The first sortie is scheduled for midnight take-off, so Steve relaxes in the crew room with a cup of coffee. Soon the crew room is filled up by the night flying ground crew and the other F/E's that will also be completing sorties this evening. The hours seem to crawl as they await take-off deadline, and Steve is left to his own thoughts. His mind is still dwelling on the uneasy feeling that has been plaguing him of late. He starts questioning himself on what the cause is, and if it is related to his marriage. He shrugs off the darkness and gets ready to start the flight.

Steve is once again flying with Rassie and this time the Co-Pilot is Maj Gary Hamilton, his fellow 30 Squadron team member. It was decided that the squadron crews will be kept together to ensure their compatibility and bonding for the stressful exercises that they need to complete. The two Pumas get airborne just after midnight and this time on final approach Steve is tasked to hoist one of the ground crew from the ground while they hover at 100 ft. agl. Steve selects the hoist controller to on, and hands over the cockpit management to Rassie while Gary flies the final approach. Steve moves to the cabin and drops his NVG's into position, opens the right hand sliding door of the Puma and with the hoist grip in his right hand reaches up with the left to grab the hoist hook and proceeds to lower it down from the aircraft. Steve patters the hoist cable extension and position of the aircraft to overhead the target is for the ground crew member that they will be bringing onboard. With the aircraft in position Steve lowers the cable the last 10 ft. to the ground and waits for the hoist strop to be secured onto the crewman. With thumbs up signal from the crewman Steve takes the load with hoist and reels it back into the aircraft. Steve keeps Gary informed by pattering aircraft position over the ground, hoist progress and stability until the crewman is level with cabin of the aircraft.

F/E NVG Hoisting

Steve reaches out and places his arm around the crewman's chest and with a gentle tug swings him backward into the cabin while releasing the hoist cable enough to safely lower him into the cabin floor. Steve helps the crewman out of the strop, unhooks it from the cable and then completes the hoist by reeling the cable up to the hoist motor. Steve closes the cabin door, lifts up his NVG's and moves back to the F/E seat in the cockpit. Once in position Steve informs Gary that he is once again in the cockpit and back on pattering and cockpit management. Rassie confirms he is once again on NVG's. The sortie is completed in reverse order with the crewman being lowered to the ground from the aircraft this time. A couple more hoists are completed and then Rassie informs them that he is satisfied and that they can form up with the other Puma, this time as the lead aircraft and practice NVG formation flight. By the time they land and shutdown it has been 2 hours and 45 minutes. This time the sortie seemed very quick as they have been busy all the time.

The next sortie is repeated but this time with Des in the driver's seat. Rassie is still the Commander and Steve the F/E. By now Steve is well versed with NVG hoisting and the sortie is completed 15 minutes shorter than the previous. At the debrief Rassie informs the 30 Squadron Team that they are good to go and that the final NVG flight at AFB Hoedspruit will be the wrap up of the training.

The next day Steve is off and takes the day to relax. Comic's, one of the 19 Squadron F/E's has invited Steve and a few of the other F/E's over to his house for a Braai in the evening, so Steve wanders down to the local SADFI to get stocks for the evening. Comic's picks Steve up early evening for the Braai from AFB Swartkop Domestic area. It does not take long before the beers are cracked and flowing freely. It has been a while since Steve has been able to relax in a setting where there is no pressure to be ready at the drop of a hat for operation or Casevac call out. Pretty soon the fire is lit, and the drinking continues until the coals are just the right glow for adding the impending Wors, Chops and Steaks. Being hungry Steve volunteers to be master braaier and is soon turning the meat to ensure an even braai is completed. Comic's wife has prepared the necessary sandwiches for braaiing as well. Steve grabs an Egg Lifter and proceeds to grill the cheese and tomato sandwiches. When they are perfectly toasty brown, Steve lifts the sandwiches and meat off the fire and yells out,

"Kos is op die tafel naaiers!" (Food is on the table screwer's).

Steve enjoys his meal and soon has consumed a sufficient delicacy to satisfy his hunger. The evening soldiers on until the wee hours when the night stillness is broken by drunken Chopper Song wailing. Comic's insists that the drunks retire to the house and he hands out everyone a sleeping bag for the rest of the evening.

For the next few days the weather has been typical of the Transvaal Highveld, with thunder storms brewing late afternoon and then continuing late into the night. This places a hold on the NVG training and it is only the next Monday, 11th Jul 1988 that Steve gets to fly again. This time he volunteers to complete an IF sortie, just to keep busy, as it seems as if the night time storms will still be a problem for the next few days. Steve has an enjoyable IF sortie and manages to rack up another 2 hours in his logbook. On the morning of the 14th July 1988 the NVG Crews depart for AFB Hoedspruit. Tonight, will be their final NVG sortie under training. Steve is assigned Puma 151 for the navigation exercise to AFB Hoedspruit with Cmdt Ströh as the Commander. Gary is the Co-Pilot and Des is PAX. It is a 1 hour 45-minute flight to AFB Hoedspruit from AFB Swartkop and the crews have time to relax and enjoy the flight. Six Puma's are on their way for the NVG training and will pair up into twos for the NVG Night Nav and Cargo Sling.

Upon arrival at 31 Squadron AFB Hoedspruit, Steve meets up with his old drinking buddy from 87 HFS, Johnny Beukes. Johnny is now an F/E on Puma's at 31 Squadron. The two catch up on the years past. The squadron has arranged meals and accommodation for the visiting crews at the local messes for officers and non-commissioned officers. Johnny takes the group of visiting F/E's to the mess to get rooms assigned and then they all have a meal. After lunch the group heads back to the squadron in preparation for the NVG flights in a couple of hours.

Steve installs a ferry tank and Cargo Sling for the exercise tonight. Once he has checked the sling for operation, he has the ferry tank refueled, completes a pre-flight inspection and then signs up the aircrafts technical log. He wanders off to the Ops Room to prepare for the NVG Flight briefing that will take place in the next while. Tonight Steve will fly two sorties, one with each of the 30 Squadron pilots, Gary and Des. They both have to be tested individually to certify that they can command an NVG flight.

NVG Navigation Exercise

Tonight, is a dark moon clear night and the aircraft can take off by 18:00 already. The first half of the sortie is a navigation exercise, followed by a confined area landing and then completed with a cargo sling pick up circuit and drop off. Gary and Steve are the first airborne with Cmdt Ströh as the Commander. Gary and Steve have worked on the night navigation together and Steve will update the Doppler Waypoints for Gary as they progress along the route. Steve has one Ferry Tank onboard and has it refueled as back up in case the flight is extended. The navigation exercise will be for one and half hours to set waypoints in the local area. Cmdt Ströh has given Gary control of the aircraft and takes the maps from him. Steve verifies the first Waypoint in the Doppler and Gary sets heading.

The navigation works out like clockwork and Steve even has the opportunity to navigate one leg. At the final Waypoint Steve notices a cargo net rigged with crates on the ground and realizes that this is the final test. Steve moves to the back of the aircraft and opens the Cargo Hatch to access the view below the aircraft. For improved visibility he also slides open both cabin doors in case he loses sight of the slung load. On final approach Steve takes up the control of the aircraft by pattering Gary into position over the load. Steve then brings Gary down until the crewman on the ground can clip the sling through the cargo hook. The crew checks the security with a pull and then indicates the load is clear to go. Steve gives the crewman time to clear the load and then patters Gary straight up to take the strain of the load. Once Steve is certain that the aircraft is correctly positioned over the load, he clears Gary to lift the load. Gary lifts the load by adding some collective pitch. The Puma's engines respond, and the rotors bite the air lifting the aircraft and load clear into the night sky. Steve clears Gary into forward flight and keeps a pattering watch on the load while Gary flies a full circuit to once again drop the load in the reversal procedure of pickup. On short finals Steve picks up the control of the aircraft and patters Gary into position to lower the load. Once the load is safely on the ground Steve calls for Gary to drop the hook. Gary depresses the cargo release and the sling falls away. Steve clears Gary to forward flight, closes the hatch and cabin doors and resumes his position in the F/E's seat.

The return flight to AFB Hoedspruit is a breeze and once shut down, Gary and Steve are congratulated for completing the NVG qualification. Steve now qualified, has the time of his life picking on Des who has yet to complete his exercise. Once again Cmdt Ströh is the instructor and Des the student. The flight is completed in the same successful manner that qualified Gary. It is close to midnight when the newly qualified NVG Operators are called to the 31 Squadron Crew room and drinks are offered around to the successful crews. It is after two in the morning when a singing bunch of Chopper crews are shuttled to their respective messes for shut eye.

The next morning after a hearty breakfast, Steve joins his pilots at the 31 Squadron crew room. The Officer Commanding 31 Squadron has organized a tour of the base and surrounding area for the visiting crews.

Hoedspruit Surrounding Area

The group is kept busy most of the day and Steve enjoys the Bushveld layout of the AFB. From the air you have look closely or else you mistake the AFB for a Game Farm. The fighters and helicopters are housed in mortar proof, revetments, strategically distributed around the base, that have been camouflaged on the roofs with natural fauna and flora.

Mirage F1 in Camouflaged Revetment Hangar

The squadron buildings are constructed in such a way as to look like a farmstead. By 15:00 it is time to return to AFB Swartkop and then get to AFB Waterkloof to catch the last flight out to Cape Town. Gary, Des and Steve get airborne and start the return flight, only to realize that they may just miss the flight to Cape Town. Steve pulls out the Manual and verifies the maximum power that Gary can pull on the Collective Pitch. Steve reviews the manual and informs Gary to add more power for maximum continuous power setting. The Puma stretches her legs and with an increased ground speed the team may just make it back to AFB Swartkop in time.

The threesome do make it back in time, and as Gary has the planning brain, he has the duty driver on standby to whisk them off to AFB Waterkloof for the return flight to Cape Town.

On the 1st August 1988 Steve is back at the Squadron where he concentrates on getting proficient with the Puma J as well as shipborne operations. Steve is tasked to prepare for a sea trip with the MV Agulhas to Marion Island in a month's time. Steve assists Willie Beaurain, the senior F/E for the trip in getting the ship pack-up kit for the aircraft readied, checked and loaded onto the ship.

Marion Island

Marion Island lies at 46°52'34" South 37°51'32" East in the Southern Indian Ocean, and is 19 km long by 12 km wide, and together with Prince Edward Island they have a combined area of 316 square km and politically form part of South Africa's Western Cape Province.

The islands are volcanic in origin, with Marion having many hillocks, secondary craters, and small lakes. Prince Edward Island has spectacular cliffs up to 490m high on its south western side.

Marion Island was first discovered in 1663 by the Dutch ship Maerseveen. The discovery was accidental, and no landing was made. More than one hundred years later, in 1772 Frenchman Marion du Fresne, who was looking for Antarctica, came across the island group.

Signs of early occupation

Thinking it was part of Antarctica, he spent 5 days trying to make a landing before discovering it was only two small islands. They left never to return.

Remains of Huts

Four years later, Captain Cook also saw the islands, but could not make a landing due to bad weather. The first recorded landing on the island was in much later in 1803 by a group of sealers, but they did find signs of earlier occupation.

In late 1947 and early 1948 South Africa took possession of both Marion and Prince Edward islands. Under the command of Lieutenant-Commander John Fairburn the two islands were annexed, and the South African flag raised.

The first expedition to the island was a meteorological team, led by Allan B. Crawford. Meteorologists have occupied the island ever since, joined in later years by scientists conducting research on the environment and ecology.

One of the first documented records of biological observations on Marion Island were those made by Richard Harris, who observed and collected seabirds during a British sealing expedition in 1830.

There are two major chapters in the history of Marion Island, sealing activities and the introduction and subsequent eradication of cats. Both had major impacts on the current state of the island and its wildlife.

During the 19th century elephant seal oil was the primary natural resource collected on the island. This was done by boiling the seal blubber in large tri pots either on the beach or on board the ships. Harvesting of fur seal and penguin skins for gloves also occurred on the island. Some remnants of these days still scatter the beaches. Remains of huts can still be seen but most sites are protected, and the artifacts stay undisturbed in their wet, cold graves.

The earliest documented evidence of sealing relates to the landing of a gang of sealers from the Catharine, Henry Fanning as captain, in December 1803. Sealers of different nationalities including American, French and British exploited the Islands. The second half of the 19th century saw a rise in the number of Norwegian sealers as well as sealers based in Cape Town. The first Cape Town based sea elephant oil industry on the Prince Edward Islands was established in 1833. Large-scale sealing occurred until November 1930 when seal numbers had dropped too low to be commercially exploitable. The ship SS Kildalkey made the final sealing expedition to the Island and took about 1,450 seals on this last trip. Today sealers still roam the Island, not carrying clubs and guns but tagging equipment and scales. Harvesting of seals has been replaced by research of these wonderful creatures.

Five domestic cats, including a castrated, orange striped male tabby and a black and white female together with three kittens were introduced during 1949 on Marion Island. These felines were brought to the island to help eradicate a mouse problem in the base. As cats do they soon multiplied, and the first feral cat was seen in 1951. By 1975 the population had increased to more than 2,000 cats feeding on thousands of burrowing Petrels, a much easier prey than the mice they were supposed to hunt. In 1975 alone, the cats ate just under half a million birds and species such as the Common Diving Petrel, the Soft Plumage Petrel and the Grey Petrel became extinct on Marion Island. With other remaining bird species also at risk it was decided to initiate the Marion Island Cat Eradication Program.

In 1977 the entire cat population was estimated around 3,405 individuals. A few animals were infected with the highly specific disease feline panleucopenia. By 1982 there were an estimated 615 cats remaining. During the spring of 1986 a secondary control measure in the form of nocturnal hunting was initiated on full scale. For three summers, eight two-man teams using battery-operated spotlights and 12-bore shotguns killed approximately 803 cats in total. The progressive decrease in hunting success and the sighting rate of cats suggested that hunting alone was no longer sufficient in reducing the numbers.

There are a number of Ship Wrecks around the islands. The best-known shipwreck around the Prince Edward Islands is the Solglimt at Ships Cove. The survivors constructed a small village against the cliff, housing 70 men. The wreckage lies in approximately 8 meters of water. Most of the wreck is covered by the sandy bottom with only four visible structures remaining underwater. The largest section resembles that of the engine room boiler, from where the displayed artifacts in the bar of Marion Base were salvaged.

Marion is the higher of the two islands, and State President Peak, its highest point at 1,230m, is permanently covered in snow and ice. It is surrounded by many secondary craters, betraying its volcanic origin. There is little vegetation, except for lichen, in the island's center. Elsewhere the vegetation is mainly mosses and ferns, and the terrain is very boggy. This is due to the abundant snow and rain. There are no trees, due to the persistent, strong westerly winds commonly termed the Roaring Forties.

Biological and environmental research is a major function of the Marion Island base with, weather data collection being the other. Close to 1,000 scientific papers and dozens of post-graduate theses have been produced from research on Marion, and the long-term biological monitoring programs provide exceptional research potential into the rate and impacts of climate change due to global warming. The research on Marion Island focuses mainly on the following themes:

- Weather and Climate studies; the interactions between marine and terrestrial systems;
- Life histories of seals, seabirds and killer whales;
- Structure and functioning of terrestrial ecosystems; and,
- Structure and functioning of near shore ecosystems.

The overwintering teams remain until the new relief team arrives. They spend about thirteen months on the island and consist of the following personnel:

- Senior meteorologist
- Meteorologist assistants
- Medical orderly
- Radio technician
- Diesel mechanic
- Various field assistants and biologists

On the 23rd August 1988 Steve is PAX on board Puma J, ZS-HIZ with Maj Boats Olivier as the Commander and Capt. Gert Uys as the Co-Pilot and Willie as the F/E. Their tasking is to join up with MV SA Agulhas which has left Cape Town harbour enroute to Marion Island.

MV SA Agulhas leaving Cape Town harbour

SA Agulhas is a South African ice-strengthened polar research vessel. She was built by Mitsubishi Heavy Industries in Shimonoseki, Japan, in 1978. The SA Agulhas is used to service the three South African National Antarctic Program research bases, Gough Island, Marion Island in the Southern Ocean and SANAE in Antarctica, as well as various research voyages. This annual trip by the Agulhas is to swap the over wintering teams and conduct any defined scientific research around the islands.

ZS-HIZ Deck Landing

The ship also has onboard a Public Works Department (PWD) Team and related equipment for repair, upgrade and maintenance of the base on Marion. It is a short flight out to the ship and very soon HIZ is on short finals for a deck landing on the Agulhas. The rest of the Air Force Team is already onboard and assist the aircrew to unload the aircraft. After greeting all onboard Steve and Willie get the Air Force Team to ready the aircraft for stowage in the hangar. First permission is obtained from the Bridge to proceed with the stowage, and then the Main Rotor Blades are folded.

Puma Blade Folding

The next step is to maneuver the helicopter into the hangar and secure it with chain lashings to the deck for the voyage down to Marion. The voyage will last approximately 3 to 4 days weather depending. The southern oceans are well known for stormy seas, and as the Agulhas is an Ice Breaker, she has a flat-bottomed hull, that does not take kindly to rough seas.

The Roaring Forties are strong westerly winds found in the Southern Hemisphere, generally between the latitudes of 40 and 50 degrees. The strong west-to-east air currents are caused by the combination of air being displaced from the Equator towards the South Pole, the Earth's rotation, and the scarcity of landmasses to serve as windbreaks.

The Roaring Forties were a major aid to ships sailing the Brouwer Route from Europe to the East Indies or Australasia during the Age of Sail, and in modern usage are favoured by yachtsmen on round-the-world voyages and competitions. The boundaries of the Roaring Forties are not consistent and shift north or south depending on the season. Similar but stronger conditions occurring in more southerly latitudes are referred to as the Furious Fifties and Shrieking or Screaming Sixties.

With the aircraft secured the Air Force Team gather in the hangar office for a briefing. "Boats" is in command of the whole Air Force Team with WO Jackie Jacquet in charge of the Ground Crew Team. There are three pilots and two flight engineers on this trip. Maj Manus Steyn is the other pilot and with Gert they will be completing their Puma J Command on this trip in preparation for the next trip down to Antarctica.

Steve on the other hand is being shown the ropes by Willie and between them they will share the flying for the trip. Life onboard the Agulhas is much more relaxed than the Navy ships, as there are many civilian personnel onboard from all levels of society namely Ships Officers and Crew, Public Works Department Teams, Scientists and the Air Force. Captain Bill Leith the Agulhas's Master calls all hands to the Ships Mess for a shakedown briefing.

Capt. Bill is a no-nonsense skipper with a huge responsibility, and his briefing is detailed and disciplined. Steve is feeling queasy already from the ships motion, so Willie takes upon himself to remedy the situation. A stiff Brandy and Coke never hurt anyone.

By the third drink Steve starts to feel much better and by supper time he is starving and joins the merry band in the mess for a good chow down. Not long after supper, in the ships lounge, the bar opens. The drinks are served on an IOU basis. So, the "more you drink", "the more you owe" the ship.

The Air Force Team typically ends up roaring until last rounds are called, and then slip away to the cabin to haul out hidden stocks to continue the party. This is the quickest that Steve has ever got his sea legs. The days end is repeated until Capt. Billy announces the arrival at Marion Island. For the first three days the Air Force Team will remain onboard to operate the Puma for offloading and scientific research support.

It is the 29th August 1988 when Steve is given the opportunity to fly as F/E off the ship. The sortie is with Boats and Manus, to take a group of Biologists to Prince Edward Island. Before the aircraft can land on the island, Steve and the Air Force Team must thoroughly wash the aircraft's undercarriage. The reason being, that no foreign bacteria must be introduced to the island which will disrupt the natural fauna and flora. It is a short 15-minute flight to Prince Edward Island and soon Manus lands at the designated site chosen by the Biologists. Steve shuts HIZ down and the Biologists gather their equipment to collect samples. Prince Edward Island has amazing steep cliffs with no beaches but the whole island is marshy and wet. The Puma's undercarriage is buried in the marshy growth. All too soon it is time to start up and return to the Agulhas.

Agulhas off Marion Island & Prince Edward Island

Once onboard and secured, the aircraft must once again be washed down, as the next sortie is to Marion Island. The Air Force Team is ushered into the Briefing Room where Boats informs them to pack kit for a week, as they are deploying to the Island while the ship conducts scientific research around both islands. Within an hour the aircraft is readied, and the entire

Air Force Team is onboard ready for takeoff to Marion. An aircraft hangar has been built on the island where HIZ will be secured for the non-flying periods, as the weather patterns on Marion change within 30 minutes, with hurricane force winds, snow, rain, ice or a combination of all. The hangar mimics that of the hangar onboard the ship, but for storage of one aircraft only. The helicopters blades also must be folded before being moved into the hangar.

ZS-HIZ in the Hangar

The Air Force Team and some scientists board HIZ and set heading for the base on Marion. This is Steve's first time on Marion and together with a group of other Greenhorns; they will be suitably initiated tonight.

With aircraft and kit stowed Steve, Robbie and Vossie venture out on the tundra for a hike to investigate the local fauna and flora. Suitably dressed the trio sets out in the marshy fields toward Seal Bay, where they hope to see the remnants of the seal hunting expeditions.

The walk is long and difficult, as the marshy landscape is difficult to navigate. Every so often one of them gets stuck and the others must assist to pull the stuck leg out of the mush. Occasionally a Gum Boot is left stuck in the tundra and must be forcibly retrieved.

The threesome, although exhausted are having the time of their life. Enroute to the bay they see fauna and flora that they have only heard or read about. They scale down the steep embankment down to the beach to where the last remnants of sealing are still evident.

Robbie, Vossie and Steve

Steve rounds the bend and is awestruck at the view ahead of him. The Volcanically formed island's coastline is steep and rugged but beautiful, and in front of him is a spectacular view of the small bay with two Butt Rocks reaching upward from the roaring surf.

The three of them are still staring in awe at the sight ahead of them without noticing that they have intruded on the local fauna's environment. A large Fur Seal is laying a couple of meters away and reacts vocally to the trio, who jump back in surprise as they observe the irate Seal barking at them.

Giggling like school girls after the fright they received Steve, Robbie and Vossie continue along the beach and are surprised by an even more impressive view. The reason the Fur Seal is so irate, is due to the pups hiding around the corner, tucked away in a cave with the remains of a Sealing Cabin.

Fur Seal, Sealing Pot and Penguins

Keeping the Fur Seal Pups company, are a school of penguins comically looking up at the humans while waddling around as if looking for attention. In front of the Penguins is an old Seal Oil Tri-Pot, evidence of the Islands history. Steve spends a long time searching around and investigating the area to see if he can scour up any additional evidence of the Sealers in the bay. Eventually it is time to head back. The sun sets quickly this far south, and the trio does not want to get caught outside in the darkness. The temperature also drops rapidly with sunset placing more urgency on their withdrawal back to the base.

They clamber back up the steep embankment and start the long trek back to the Base. They set heading back over the hill and with concern see that the weather is rapidly changing. First it seems to be only mist but very quickly turns to light rain. The temperature also rapidly drops, further urging the trio on. As they crest the hill which will bring the Base into view, the sight in front of them is once again breathtaking, and Steve takes a moment to capture it. Ahead of them they can see the base in the distance with the Agulhas just off the coast holding station. Where they currently stand they are in a light misty rain, but basking in sunlight is the base, which creates a picturesque view from where they are standing.

View of the Base and Agulhas

The exhausted but elated trio makes it back to the Base before sunset and in time for supper. The Bases cook has outdone himself and has set out a lovely spread for the visiting Air Force Team and Scientists. Steve is hungry after his walk and quickly wolves down his chow.

Willie is already at the bar and at this point a little the worse for wear. Boats, Manus and Gert join the rest of the Air Force Team at the counter and a round of drinks is addressed quickly. The drinks continue to flow freely until the Team Leader calls the rabble to order. Jackie, Vossie and Robbie are suitably seated as the Old Team members at the Base are soon to start the initiation ceremony for the new team taking over as well as first time visitors.

The guilty party is ordered forward to be initiated into trespassing the realm of Marion and must therefore partake in the required hooligan juice that has been painstakingly prepared and left to develop an aura of immense stench for the last week. There are a large group for the initiation ceremony consisting of, four from the Air Force Team, the New Marion Team, a few Scientists and PWD Team members.

A small speech is conducted by the Marion Team Leader and then all are supplied with a black bag to use for protection against what was to come. One by one the recruits are led to the kitchen and outside on the cat walk. Steve is one of the front runners but has no idea what awaits him through the closed door. All he hears is screeching, laughing and what sounds like puke.

Steve is still joking with some of the recruits when a Team Member grabs him and unceremoniously shoves him through the door. Outside on the catwalk is a large black waste bin filled with the vilest smelling brownish black liquid, causing Steve to involuntary start convulsing. For someone with a strong stomach Steve is surprised at the affect the concoction has on him. The Team Leader grabs Steve by the back of the neck and unceremoniously dumps his head into the bin, while demanding that he drink.

Steve comes up for air while he convulses and attempts not to puke. Next second, he is handed a mug full of the crap he just hauled his head out of and told drink. Steve knows he is going to puke, so without hesitation he chugs away and turns to the rail to empty the vile mixture from his body. With slaps on the back, Steve is escorted around the corner and sprayed down with cold water. The affect is immediate sobering and recovery of senses. He lifts the bag over his head and dumps it in the bin provided. At last he can grin and heads on back to the pub to clear the taste of crap from his mouth. Steve has endured many initiations but without a doubt this is the vilest tasting mixture he has ever had to endure.

Back inside the crowd roars every time an initiated member arrives, and a fresh drink is forced in his hand to help in cleansing the remnants of the bin from their mouths. Steve happily grabs his and gulps it down.

Marion Team Leader

Back at the pub Willie is a bit worse for wear and picks a fight with the new pilots. Boats intervenes and calms Willie down, bringing a very dangerous situation under control. Willie is sent to bed to lick his wounds, while Jackie and Steve continue to drink the night away with the rest of the Air Force Team.

At breakfast Boats calls Steve over and informs him that the team must meet in the Base meeting room in 30 minutes for a briefing. Steve hurries off to gather the rest of the team, after which they all gather in the meeting room. The sortie today is to deploy cat hunters and a few scientists around the island. The cat hunters will be flown to the temporary huts that have been constructed around the island for them. Some of these huts will still be replaced during this trip, a job that the Air Force will gladly do. Boats conducts the briefing and Willie indicates that Steve will be assigned the flying for the day.

ZS-HIZ outside the Hangar

Steve and the rest of the ground crew depart for the hangar to push the aircraft out and prepare it for the days flying. With the blades spread and secured, pre-flight completed, and documents signed the crew awaits their PAX for take-off. Jackie is standing at the hangar entrance, staring at ZS-HIZ and the picturesque sight behind it when Steve gets a brain fart. He runs to the back of the hangar and picks up a 2x4x8 length of plank and quietly approaches Jackie from behind.

Steve places the plank vertically on the ground and then jumps up against the length forcing it down to the deck with speed. With an almighty bang the plank makes contact. In front of him Jackie has reacted to the bang by jumping straight up while twisting his short fat body around and pumping his legs into a run, while violently shouting,

"Fok jou Steve Coetzee, ek gaan jou bliksem!" (Fuck you Steve Coetzee, I am going to smack you).

The whole Air Force Contingent is laughing helplessly at the spectacle while Jackie chases after Steve. Steve is laughing uncontrollably but stays out of Jackie's reach. Eventually the giggling subsides, and Steve catches his breath. He looks over at Jackie who is heaving heavily, and grinning.

"Man, Jackie but you can jump and run at the same time that was freaking awesome!"

Jackie turns to Steve and grins widely and says,

"Every dog has its day Steve, yours is coming".

With that the team settles down to release the blade tie-downs and remove the pre-flight covers from the aircraft. The PAX arrives, and Boats completes the briefing. Boats and Gert will be sharing the flying today, each one flying a leg. Steve starts the Puma and they complete the check list.

Take-off checks completed, Boats lifts HIZ off the pad and sets heading around the island for the first drop off. It is a spectacular view flying around the island, and within 10 minutes Boats identifies the first landing spot. He gently eases the big helicopter into a soft landing and then Steve indicates to the first team to disembark. Steve looks around and is amazed at the LZ they have landed. He jumps up and says,

"This will be an awesome photo, I'll be back!"

With that he grabs his camera and jumps out of the aircraft to capture HIZ sitting on the saddle.

<u>ZS-HIZ dropping off Cat Hunters</u>

The next week the crews fly many hours completing Cargo Sling sorties to rig up new huts and remove old ones from all around the island. The last batch of Cargo Sling work is the removal of an old hydro plant and all the accompanying piping back to the ship. All garbage is boxed and shipped back to South Africa for proper disposal. Eventually the trip to Marion is wrapped up and with goodbye's the last flight back to the SA Agulhas is completed and with the aircraft secured in the hangar the ship sets heading for Cape Town. No sooner has the ship started to rock and roll when the Air Force contingent is at their post in the Pub pounding away at the required nourishments. All that remains on the trip back is to wash and service the aircraft and ensure that the aircraft logs and spares lists are updated. The next day the weather is clear and the sea calm, so Steve and the ground crew decide to wash-down the aircraft and pack the hangar in order.

The trip back to Cape Town is a wind down for the Air Force Team and many evenings are spent in the pub. The scientists would filter in now and then but kept mostly to themselves. Steve has enjoyed the non-military type operation but even more so the aircraft. The J Model is a beautiful beast and Steve cannot get enough of the systems incorporated into the aircraft. He spends hours going over the technical data, operating and maintenance manuals to ensure he is well versed on all the systems. All to soon the Air Force Team is ordered to the hangar to prepare the aircraft for departure.

They are within reach of Cape Town and the Table Mountain is visible in the distance. The aircraft is loaded and then positioned on the flight deck, blades spread and pre-flight completed. A quick farewell to new friends and then all clamber onboard HIZ for departure to AFB Ysterplaat.

ZS-HIZ Ready for departure

Squadron duties

Nicole is growing up quickly and Steve cannot get enough of how she picks up little nuances, sayings and behaviors. Steve is a very proud father. With the escalation of conflict in Angola and rising tensions within South Africa, the constant reminder of war and its effects are always part of Steve's life.

He finds it difficult to communicate with Zella and is becoming short tempered. Many nights are sleepless and at times he gets searing headaches. Steve writes it off as being overworked as he is constantly upgrading the home, working on his car rebuild projects and volunteering for any additional flying that comes up.

Amongst daily flying duties involving an Air Show display at Hermanus, Radar Prototype testing, and aircraft test flights, Steve is kept busy until being deployed to Riemvasmaak for a weapons camp in the Northern Cape. On the 16th October 1988, Steve prepares for departure with Capt. Ken Hobson as Commander and Lt. Schalk Fourie as Co-Pilot, for Riemvasmaak.

Their tasking is to prepare the Range with targets for the Mirage F1's that will be starting a weapons camp in a few days. On this trip Steve has an apprentice ground crew, Paul, along for the ride to complete the cargo sling hook up for the loads they will be slinging.

Riemvasmaak is located near the Orange River, close to the SWA border, in the Northern Cape province of South Africa.

The name means 'tighten the strap' or 'tied with straps'. It was originally settled in the early 1930s by people of Xhosa, Damara, Herero, Nama, and Coloured origin, but in the early 1970s the community was sent back to their ethnic homelands.

The Damara group was sent to Khorixas in South-West Africa and became known as Riemvasmakers. Being in the Northern Cape region, the climate is "desert." There is virtually no rainfall during the year. In Riemvasmaak, the average annual temperature ranges between 30°C and 10°C with an average of 20.5°C. In a year, the average rainfall is 145 mm.

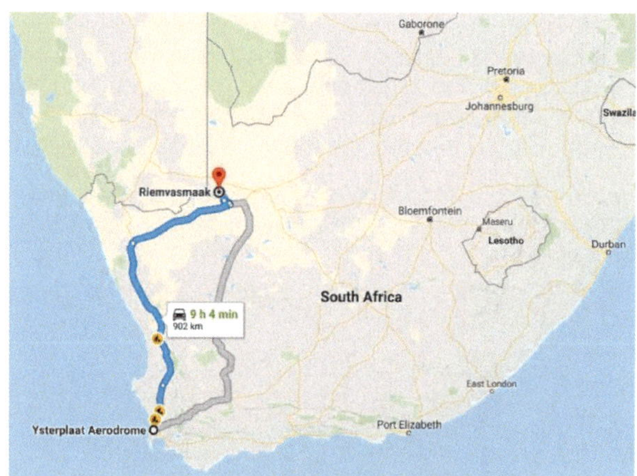

Riemvasmaak Weapons Range

The flight time will be approximately 3 hours 45 minutes, so Steve has installed and fueled up two internal ferry tanks. Also onboard Steve has a cargo sling and set of cargo strops, as they will be placing dummy fiber-glass Tanks and Armoured enemy vehicles on the range for the fighters to attack.

The flight is uneventful and the three crew chat freely about their respective experiences in the Air Force. Steve is reserved and quiet for most of the flight, only participating when asked to comment. Eventually the Range at Riemvasmaak comes into view with the camp buildings spread out near the foothills of the rock ridge. Ken takes over from Schalk and deftly puts the Puma down gently on the Helipad close to the Range Headquarters. Steve completes shut down and then exits the aircraft to begin the After-Flight Inspection. Ken and Schalk walk over to the Range Ops Room to find the accommodation for the Puma Crew.

Steve starts off towards the aircraft to install covers for the night. As he gets closer he is surprised to see two birds hopping in and out of the Engine Intake MPAI filters. Steve opens the engine cowling and moves forward to the MPAI filters to see what the birds had been doing. To his surprise they had been nesting, but most of all the materials they had been using were not twigs and grass but small pebbles.

Riemvasmaak Sunset

Steve decides to leave the nest in place and will remove everything on the Pre-Flight inspection in the morning. With Blade Tip covers installed and the aircraft secured with the sun setting, Steve saunters over to the accommodation block to join the pilots. Steve shares his bird nesting with the rest of the team and the evening around the camp fire continues after a braai with Wors and salads with two huge slices of toasted bread, cheese and tomato.

The first round of beers signals supper time and aircrew joins the Pongo's for an evening bush meal at the Camp Kitchen. In the morning the Puma is tasked to place the dummy tanks and artillery pieces at strategic places on the range. The group sits around the camp fire for a few hours sipping on hot coffee, as the evening dessert air has a chill to it. They all soon retire to their respective bunks.

It is early morning as Steve heads down to the camp kitchen to help himself to some bacon and eggs and a warm cup of coffee. The early morning air is still chilly and Steve elects to don his flying jacket over his flight suite. No sooner when he starts digging in to breakfast he sees Paul already at the aircraft removing covers and preparing the Puma for the days flying. Steve is suitably impressed and makes a mental note to add this to the apprentice's task book. Breakfast finished, Steve joins Paul at the aircraft.

"Can't you sleep Boet?" asks Steve.

"I slept well Flight!" says Paul, as they both open the Puma's engine cowlings.

Between the two of them the Pre-Flight Inspection and Cargo Hook installation is completed in double time. Importantly remembering to remove all the stones from the engine intake filters from the birds nesting habits. Steve then completes the Technical Log entries and asks Paul to roll some 44 gallon drums of Jet A1 closer so that they can refuel the aircraft. Paul complies and soon has six drums standing upright next to the starboard side of the Puma.

Steve has removed the refueling hoses and connects them to the internal electrical fueling system. Steve signals to Paul to hold the fueling nozzle to the left hand fuel tanks and then flips the Master Battery switch on. Paul reaches in the to select the electrical pump switches and the twin pumps starting working. Each drum will take around three minutes to empty.

Steve jumps down and opens up all the remaining drums and like Paul did on the first drum, inspects the fuel for water by shining a flash light in on the small breather hole while peeking in through the larger refuel hole to look for telltale shining globules of water at the bottle of the drum.

Thirty minutes later the Puma is fueled up and ready to start the days sortie. Steve and Paul join the two pilots back at the camp kitchen for a final cup of coffee before the briefing on the day's flight operations. Today they will be distributing BTR-60's dummy armoured carriers around the range by cargo sling.

A quick briefing by Ken and confirmation on the locations for the dummy targets with the Range Officer, and the Puma takes off on the first sortie. Steve requests permission to shut down at the first lift to ensure that the attachment points to the Dummy Target are secure enough and that the weight will hang properly under the aircraft.

Ken identifies the first target on the map and within a few minutes they are preparing to land. After shut down, Steve together with Paul wander over to the Dummy Target to inspect it. Steve immediately identifies that the Dummy Target is very poorly assembled, too light, and has very weak securing points.

Steve decides to utilize the tie-down straps he has in the aircraft to secure the weight. Steve instructs Paul to hook up the load and give way immediately so that if something does go wrong he won't be in the way when Steve jettisons the load.

Back in the aircraft, Steve briefs the pilots on the lift and warns them of the danger. With the Puma's hurricane downwash, the weight may fly up into the belly of the aircraft or worse into the tail or main rotors. Steve must be very vigilant at the cargo sling hatch.

Ken lifts the Puma into the hover and Steve quickly patters him over the Dummy Target. The load seems to hold station. Paul runs up and deftly hooks the cargo sling strop to the load. Steve gives the instruction to take the strain and lift the load. There is a swing backward and forward but Steve clears Ken to forward flight.

As soon as the Puma clears the ground cushion the load starts swinging violently up towards the aircraft whereby Steve immediately jettisons its. The Dummy Target falls back to earth in a cloud of red dust. The load is far too light for the Puma to sling. Steve instructs Ken to land, as he has just thought of a plan when he sees a stack of sandbags lying close by.

With the aircraft shut down, Steve explains his plan. He is going to pack sandbags on top of the Dummy Target in recessed areas where they won't move. This will then give the added weight needed as well as stabilize the load during forward flight. Steve calculates they need 50 bags packed onto the Dummy Target.

Once completed the exercise is attempted again. This time the load is much more stable and Steve instructs Ken to keep the speed below 60 Kts, limiting the backward swing. The plan works and by lunch time they have successfully placed all of the targets. The Mirages will complete their sorties in the afternoon and the Puma will then once again place different targets around the range the next morning.

The Puma is at the Range for two purposes, namely place targets and primarily to be on standby should one of the aircraft completing firing exercises end up in trouble and a Casevac is required. Steve and the Pilots remain on standby at the Range Headquarters close to the radio. The day is hot and the sun bright. The air is filled with Mirage F1 fighters diving in to attack the Dummy Targets. They are flying out of Upington a mere 100 km away.

By late afternoon the live firing has concluded and Steve makes his way down to the Puma to cover up for the evening. The guys limit the beers for the evening and by 22:00 they all head off to bed in preparation for an early flight the next day. For the next four days the exercise is repeated and in the late afternoon on the 20th October 1988 they pack their kit and Ken sets heading for the 3 hour 30 minute flight to AFB Ysterplaat.

Bottom of the Earth

Steve arrives back home and is starting to feel the excitement build for the upcoming trip down to the South Pole. Nicole is as excited, and she is all over the gear that Steve has been issued by the Department of Environmental Affairs for the upcoming trip down to the ice.

Cold weather clothing and sleeping bags are all fun for Nicole as she tries on everything while parading around the house. She has Steve and Zella in hysterics with her antics while she parades around with minus fifty-degree warm clothing ten sizes too big for her. With a happy face, giggling and falling Nicole tries on every piece of Steve's Antarctic Gear.

For the next few weeks Steve actively prepares for the trip while still conducting Squadron Flying operations which include NVG Flights, Instrument Flying, Aircraft Tests as well as Calibrating the Torque Meters for the J Model Puma's. In preparation for the trip Steve and the rest of the aircrew brush up on Ship Radar Controlled approaches while validating that all the systems are fully serviceable.

It is a hot day in Cape Town on the 1st December 1988 when Steve has Zella and Nicole drop him off at the Squadron. Steve, Cmdt Theron (Oom Gertjie) and Manus Steyn will fly ZS-HIZ from Ysterplaat to the SA Agulhas which is still tied up in Table Bay Harbour. Zella and Nicole will join Steve at the ship before they set sail for the South Pole.

Steve has already loaded the J Model Puma, ZS-HIZ with the fly away kit and all the crew's baggage. The aircraft spares kits have already been uploaded to the ship, including spare engines, rotor blades, gearboxes and a multitude of spare parts that will sustain them for the almost four-month deployment.

Zella and Nicole depart for the docks while Steve prepares the aircraft for the short flight to the ship. At 09:00 Steve cranks number one engine to get the show on the road. Ten minutes late with all Vital Actions and Pre-Take Checks completed, Oom Gertjie obtains take off clearance from Ysterplaat Tower. With clearance verified, Oom Gertjie takes a hand full of collective and HIZ stretches her legs and gets airborne.

A very short 10-minute flight later, Manus calls up the SA Agulhas requesting landing clearance. Master Bill Leith answers the request with wind direction, speed and clearance to land. Oom Gertjie completes a text book approach onto the left side of the Agulhas, next to the flight deck.

JD Van Zyl is the Flight Deck Officer and with Marshalling Paddles in hand guides the Puma over the deck and clears them to land. Once on the Deck, JD indicates to the ground crew to secure the aircraft to the deck before signaling that it is now safe to cut engines. Steve reaches up and throttles back both engines and sets the stop watch for the one-minute cool down run before he shuts the aircraft down.

Steve secures the aircraft and then opens the cowlings to complete the blade folding so that aircraft can be stowed in the hangar. Koos De Wet with Maj Gary Hamilton and Maj Alan Reynolds will be arriving soon with the second J Model Puma, ZS-HJA.

Steve and the ground crew make quick work of folding the aircrafts blades and then maneuvering it into the hangar.

With the hangar doors secured and deck cleared, the Agulhas is ready to receive the second aircraft. ZS-HJA lands and after shut-down the crews once again fold blades and stow the aircraft. Both aircraft are secured with chain deck lashings for the rough trip through the Cape of Storms. With the hangar secure the crews quickly disembark to have a last farewell with friends and families before the ship sets sail down South.

Quay Four at the V&A Waterfront

Steve finds Zella and Nicole and they head off for a quick bite to eat at Quay Four at the V&A Waterfront. Nicole is bubbly and excited to see all the ships in the harbour, but Zella is reserved and thin lipped. Steve tries to keep the mood jovial by cracking jokes and playing with Nicole.

Steve must be back on board in an hour, so the family quickly eats their meals and Zella drives them back to the dockside where the Agulhas is moored. A quick hug and kiss to his two ladies, and Steve waves a goodbye as he boards the ship. He rushes up to the flight deck to gather with the rest of the Agulhas compliment to wave goodbye to the small crowd that has gathered at the dock side. With moorings released the Agulhas slowly backs away from the dock and heads out of the harbour.

MV SA Agulhas leaving Cape Town Harbour

The South African Weather Service operates remote weather stations on Gough Island, Marion Island and at the SANAE base in Antarctica. Personnel at these stations make regular surface observations of the weather each day and feed these into the global weather observation network. Upper air soundings are also made every 12 hours at Gough and Marion Islands. These meteorological readings are very valuable as they come from regions of the world where weather observations are virtually non-existent. Observations from Gough Island, in particular, are extremely important for the Western Cape as most of the frontal systems approach the country from the West. The Marion Island station has been operating since 1948, Gough Island since 1955 and SANAE since 1960. Teams spend a year at each station and are deployed by the ship SA Agulhas, along with supplies to last the whole year.

The sea is calm, and the ship makes good speed as she heads down south. Steve and the rest of the Air Force contingent have headed to the cabins to medicate themselves against the dreaded sea sickness that will soon overcome them. The medicine in this case also improves their moods, looks, and bravery, as alcohol normally does. It does not take long for the jokes and pranks to start up. Steve although a little queasy has stabilized sufficiently so as not to need to empty his stomach, and by supper time even manages a hearty meal.

The ship sails steadily south and during the night the sea picks up substantially causing the flat-bottomed ice breaker to bob around a lot. The effects on her passengers is evident as many green faces are running backward and forwards to get to the toilets. Steve however has found his sea legs and completes his first duty of hangar watch. The aircraft and stowed spare components security must constantly be monitored to ensure that no lashings have worked loose or broken during the rough seas. Each member of the Air Force team will have a turn during the long trip down south.

Every evening after supper, the Pub in the ships lounge is opened and drinks are served on an "I Owe You" basis. The IOY's are consolidated and will be paid once the ship docks back in Cape Town. The pub remains open until 21:00 every night after which the Air Force Teams break up into smaller groups and head off to the selected drinking cabin to continue the party. As always with alcohol come's hunger and the need to replenish this shortfall must be quietly uplifted from the ships mess illegally. Steve, Koos, Gert, JD, Chris and Keith sneak down to the mess and into the kitchen. Once inside they uplift salami, cheese, French loaf and crackers. With drinks in one hand and food in the other they form a single line and as silently as drunks can be, sneak up to the first corner. Koos peeps around the corner and whispers back "safe" and giggling the rest pass on the message in turn. Steve at the back of the line, pretends there is someone behind him and imitates the message backward to nobody. This process is repeated at every passage corner they arrive at. Just as they are about to enter the last alley, Steve once again turns to whisper "safe" while giggling and looks straight into the face of the Master.

"Good evening Captain", says Steve.

"What are you doing Mr. Coetzee?" asks Captain Billy.

"Just walking," giggles Steve with salami under the one arm and a drink in the other hand.

Captain Leith just shakes his head and walks past, tomorrow he will resolve the issue with punishment as currently the stupid grin on Steve's face meant he would get nothing from him.

The next morning Captain Billy announces the entire ships compliment to gather in the mess for a briefing. An hour-long lecture is concluded on the ships rules, safety and pest control requirements. The last statement directly relating to the previous night's escapades by the Air Force.

No food or drink is allowed in the cabins, as research vessel the Agulhas is accountable by law to ensure that she does not introduce foreign items to any of the members of the Antarctic Treaty signed in Washington on 1 December 1959 by the twelve countries. In passing Captain Billy nods at Steve.

"See you on the Bridge for your first Ice Watch".

"Yes Sir", responds Steve.

Steve's punishment has begun.

<u>Ice Watch</u>

The ice watch is a necessary precaution and extra set of eyes on the ship's bridge to keep a look out for icebergs. Icebergs break away from the Antarctic ice shelf and drift north with the ice flows during the summer seasons. These icebergs range in size from small islands of floating ice to huge chunks of ice as they breakdown during their journey northward.

Steve's task on "Ice Watch" is to assist the crew in identifying Icebergs and ensuring that the ship is not being threatened in any way. The opportunity also offers Steve the ability to learn more about the Ship's systems and operation. Steve finds the punishment a blessing as he familiarizes himself with every bit of equipment on the Bridge.

As this is the first time that Steve will be crossing the Antarctic Circle he will be initiated with a crowd of new comers.

In the meantime, the ship has made good time down south, as the evidence of the icepack looms on the horizon.

First Pack Ice and Iceberg

In the next few days the ship will be forcing its way further south and breaking ice as it progresses. Captain Billy will not be resting during this time as the moment the ship stops then the ice flow northward will drift the ship back to where they started. Continuous ice watch is required so that Captain Billy can choose the route of least resistance by forcing the ship through already developed cracks in the ice flow.

Further south they plunge with the ice pack getting thicker and the temperature dropping steadily. Very soon they near the Antarctic Circle, where King Neptune rules supreme. The night before the line crossing ceremony the Kings henchman wander throughout the ship handing out subpoenas and charges to novices and roughing them up in preparation for the next day's event.

The ship sails steadily south through the thickening pack ice while the crew prepare for King Neptune's court arrival. All novices are summoned to the Helideck where they are unceremoniously gathered to await their fate. The crowd is becoming rowdy and joking when all of a sudden, the hangar doors open with the announcement of the arrival of the King and his Court.

Breaking Ice

With the King is his Guardian Bears who take no time in putting order to the crowd. The charges are read out aloud by the Messenger of King Neptune's Court. Each and every novice has a jumped-up charge against them, ranging from being ugly to stealing helicopters and boats.

Steve has been charged with illegally removing food from the ships mess and then refusing to share it with the Captain. With all the charges distributed King Neptune's Court prepares the guilty for their punishment!

The first part of initiation is the dunking of heads into cold seawater that had just been lifted into a large bucket. This is followed by dragging the accused across the deck to a large cooking pot filled with all sorts of goo and mess.

Before the head is forcibly dunked in, some rather smelly eggs are broken on the accused's head, adding to the mess already created and covered with flour. Should the accused retaliate in anyway, they are immediately hung up by strop from the ships aft crane.

The initiation continues until all inductees have been suitably introduced to the "Crossing the line" ceremony. The passageway to the showers has suitably been blocked so that the goo could set in the chill Antarctic air.

At the same time, should any accused have managed to slip by and get to their cabin, the water to the showers has been turned off. Every recruits goose has been suitably cooked.

Crossing the line

That evening the party continues in the ship's lounge where the drinks flow free and a great time is had by all. Steve and Koos are ruling the jokes as the alcohol flows and they are soon surrounded by an appreciative drunken crowd. Amid much yelling, laughter and back slapping the party eventually dies down in the wee hours of the morning. This far south the sun stays aloft for 24 hours, and Steve must constantly remind himself that it is actually still night time and not allow his internal clock to turn over. The rowdy bunches make their separate ways to the cabins and are soon tucked away for a few hours kip.

It has been 7 days of sailing and mostly all have got their sea legs. There are still a few of the scientists that are looking a bit green around the gills but are managing to move around the ship. As the ship is now fully locked into the ice pack there is no longer any pitching and rolling motion, only the sound of the ice scraping and breaking as the ships forces its way forward. Occasionally Captain Billy stops, reverses, picks up speed and rushes the ice pack to force the hull onto the ice and thereby breaking a crack open so that the ship can continue to move forward. This is sometimes repeated for a while when they encounter thick ice. Eventually the Captain takes a rest and the ship is brought to rest in the pack ice. Captain Billy will grab a few hours' sleep to recuperate before once again attacking the drifting pack ice.

It is 06:00 on the 14th December 1988 and Steve has just finished breakfast when there is an announcement to prepare the Helo for flying. Steve is the F/E on duty and makes his way quickly to the hangar to prepare the aircraft. Captain Billy in the meantime is using the huge crane, mounted just forward of the bridge to loosen the Agulhas from the pack ice. The ship had frozen in during the Captain's rest. By swinging the crane port and starboard of the ship, the heavy crane causes the ship to roll and thereby releasing the grip that the ice pack has on her. Just as the ship breaks free, Steve calls up to the bridge to request permission to move the Helo from the hangar and spread the blades for flying. Captain Billy authorizes the move and secures the crane. Steve and the ground crew maneuver the Puma out of the hanger and lash it in place to the helideck. Next, they spread the blades and Steve completes a pre-flight inspection before going to the flight office to sign up the technical logs and authorization book.

Oom Gert and Gert Uys are the pilots for the mission and are already in the flight office. Oom Gert calls the team over to brief them on the sortie that they are going to fly. The ship had drifted further north in the icepack than the Captain had expected, and he now wanted the Helo to fly an "ice recce" to find a shorter route through the pack ice. The ship had to reach the clear water where the icepack had moved away from Antarctica, normally an average of 60 miles of free Sailing Ocean that is void of ice. Once they reach this, the ship would set heading straight to South African North Antarctic Expedition (SANAE) Base. With everyone briefed the aircrew take their positions while the ground-crew man the lashings. Gert Uys reads the check list while Steve and Oom Gert complete the checks. This will be the first time that the entire checklist, which includes de-ice and anti-ice systems, is completed. These checks can only be performed in sub-zero conditions. Steve initiates start and gets both engines online for a full system check to ensure that all are working as required. Oom Gert gets take off clearance and indicates to Gert Uys that he must fly the sortie. Gert Uys shows the Flight Deck Officer (FDO) to release the lashings and awaits the FDO's signal to take off. The FDO waves the release lashings signal to the ground crew and then crosses the Marshalling Baton's in front of him in preparation to clear the Helo for take-off. Next, he indicates which direction Gert Uys must fly away and then with both arms outstretched he indicates for them to get airborne into the hover. Once stabilized the FDO clears them to port. Gert Uys moves the aircraft port into the hover and then takes power and dips the nose down to gain forward speed past the ship.

At 60 Kts Steve calls after take-off VA's and Gert sets heading to gain altitude and setup a search pattern so that they can indicate to Captain Billy the best route through the ice. As the Puma is now fitted with Undercarriage Ski's, Steve will not be lifting the undercarriage selector up, but has inserted the lock pin in place should anyone mistakenly do so. Within a couple of minutes flight, they spot a huge open piece of icepack to the starboard of the ship. Gert banks the aircraft back towards the ship so that they can find any open cracks that will allow the ship quick access to the open water. A couple of smaller cracks are identified and Oom Gert is chatting to Captain Billy on the radio, briefing him on what he sees. The Captain is satisfied and has already turned the ship in the direction that Oom Gert has proposed. Captain Billy then asks if they could fly a direct route south to establish how much more pack ice there was between the ship and open water. Gert banks due south and sets the Helo to cruise power. The sight over the pack ice is amazing and the three are in awe at the beauty unfolding in front of them. Steve calculates bingo fuel and confirms with Gert that they have to turn back in two hours to have enough fuel for the return plus a 40-minute reserve in case they could not find the ship. Oom Gert asks Gert to gain altitude so that they can easily spot the end of the pack ice. The Puma grabs at the cold air and quickly climbs to 5,000 ft. Gert is about to increase altitude again when they all spot the end of the pack ice in the distance.

The three quickly scan the horizon to ensure that it is not just a mirage reflection creating a false view of open water and they agree to continue in the southerly direction until they can confirm clear passage. It is a short 20-minute flight when they clearly see the clear passage between the pack ice and the Antarctic Continent. They are satisfied, and Steve verifies on the Radar what they see is fact. The ships beacon is on and Steve can see at their current altitude that the Helo's Radar is picking up the signal. By reviewing the ship's current location and the pack ice on the Radar Steve establishes that the ship is less than 30 miles from clear passage. Oom Gertjie confirms and instructs Gert to return to the ship. Oom Gertjie is briefing the Captain on the good news while they fly a zig zag pattern back to the ship, looking for cracks and a passable route for the ship to the open water.

Leading the Ship

With the Helo back on deck, Steve wastes no time in securing the Helo and blades. With the Helo secured the Air Force contingent head to the ships library for a briefing on operations for the next week. Upon arrival at the "Bukta" (Norwegian for Shore) where the Ice Shelf of Antarctica has formed a natural Bay, is the offload and upload storage area for the SANAE Base. The Helo's will be utilized to offload the ship by means of Cargo Sling. The priority items will be perishables and urgently required stock for the SANAE Base.

By 15:00 the same day Captain Billy calls hands to flying stations once more. The aircraft is being tasked to ferry the Public Works Department team with their equipment to the SANAE Base. The base is located another 50 miles inland from the ice shelf. Steve is flying with Gary and Alan and the 30-minute round trip flight is completed on schedule. The view is spectacular, and Steve feels the excitement building and looking forward to spending time on the most southern continent. The Main Base is an ARMCO Construction first assembled in 1979 above the ice on the Fimbul Ice Shelf near the Blåskimen Island. Built on the moving ice shelf, the station inevitably got buried, and will eventually break off as part of icebergs drifting away. Now in 1988 the Base is totally covered by ice and the entrance hatch takes you down some 50ft to where the corridors lead off to the various sections. Directly in front of the Chopper the Teams have constructed a distance signpost indicating to direction and distance to some notable cities in the world. The old SANAE Team greets the Chopper excitedly but also with sadness, as their stay on the Antarctic Continent is about to end in the next few months.

SANAE Main Base

In preparation the Old SANAE Team members have been preparing for the ships arrival and have built a ramp down to the bay ice with the D9 Caterpillar Dozer.

Ramp from Ice Shelf

The next morning Koos and Gert will be the F/E's for the day with Steve heading up the Cargo Sling hookup on the front deck of the Agulhas. For the next three days the Puma's will be flying Cargo Sling Sorties to offload the Ship.

Cargo Sling

With the ship secured against the bay ice, offloading for the base repair and upgrade stores and stocks will be loaded directly onto the sleds and towed by D9 up the ramp to the Bukta storage area before being moved off to the SANAE Base another 50 miles inland.

The Bukta storage depot is the location close to the ice shelf where all equipment is stored for after offloading from the ship, or transported form the SANAE Base to be returned to the ship.

At the Bukta is also storage of Helicopter fuel, Jet A1 that must be prepared for use.

During the long cold winter, the drums get covered by snow and ice and need to be removed by Cat. Poles are located at each corner of the storage location for easy identification after the long winter.

Bukta Storage

On the front Heli deck Steve is arranging and hooking up the loads for both Choppers as they fly sorties to off load the ship. Captain Billy constantly checks with the aircraft on fuel status and informs Steve on the next weight to prepare for cargo slinging. By adding weight to the cargo sling loads as the fuel burns off is the most efficient way of utilizing a very expensive method of ship off loading. Between sorties the ships main cargo crane gets into operation of unloading directly onto the bay ice, while the smaller crane prepares the next loads for the Choppers. Steve enjoys the high-pressure workload and volunteers to complete day two as well. On the 16th December 1988 it is Steve turn to fly and with HIZ completes Cargo Sling sorties with Gary in command. By 14:30 the afternoon they are tasked to complete a run to Grunehogna where the Sarie Marais Field Base is located. The Field Base is 120 Nm from SANAE located on land. SANAE is located on the Glacier and Ice Shelf overhang of the Antarctic Continent. The actual land is near two mountain peaks, Boreas and Passat approximately 80 Nm from SANAE. The sortie is in preparation of deploying the Scientific Research Teams from there in the next few days.

Location of Grunehogna

Over the next three days, Steve is allocated to ZS-HIZ and will be flying with Alan, Gary, and Manus to complete sorties between the Agulhas and Grunehogna, transporting PWD Teams, Supplies and Geo Survey Teams. In between the long flights to Grunehogna are also short runs to SANAE as well completing much the same.

By the 18th December 1988, ZS-HIZ and her crew are located at the E-Base, close to SANAE Main Base. ZS-HJA has departed to Grunehogna to be a support for the Geo Survey and Science Teams that will deploy to the field for the remainder of the summer.

E-Base at SANAE

The Air Force contingent settle in to life at SANAE, E-Base and make new friends as they use the down time to mingle at the Main Base's Pub in the evenings. Steve sets up the Skivvy Roster for E-Base and ensures that there are always two people assigned daily for keep the snow smelter full and general clean up and assistance in the kitchen and dining room area.

The Air Force crew have brought along a cook who takes care of the Brunch and Dinner for all at E-Base. On the 25th December 1988, the Air Force Cook has prepared an amazing Christmas Dinner for the whole crew at SANAE and E-Base. A great night is spent and then a rude awakening, as this is the first trip that Steve has done to the Antarctic, he once again has to partake in an initiation.

The first group will be the new SANAE Team followed by the rest of the first timers. The rites are read, and each recipient is blessed with a "Spanish Arsehole". The mug is in the shape of a woman's breast and the hole to suck to liquid out of is the nipple. The mug is filled with Tequila and a generous helping of Tabasco Sauce, thus the name "Spanish Arsehole".

After clearing the drink, one requires copious amounts of beer to stop the fire in your mouth and throat. A great evening is held and with drunken gaits Steve and his comrades waddle back to E-Base. The distance happens to be twice as long and try as they may they cannot maintain a straight route to E-Base which looms beckoningly in the distance.

They eventually stumble up the stairs to E-Base when suddenly Steve strips naked and dares everyone to do the Eskimo dash to the Met Lab and back. The distance there and back is close to 800 meters, so the race is on. A giggling bunch of drunkards makes the trip and freezing get back to E-Base for some more de-icing fluid to warm up. This time "Old Brown" Sherry is on the menu. For the next two days they all recover, before ZS-HIZ with her crew on the 27th December 1988, take off for Grunehogna where they will swap places with ZS-HJA who will return to SANAE, E-Base.

That evening a storm sets in and continues to blow for a week. With the aircraft secured to the ice with chains and blade securing poles, the crew must still complete visual inspection every couple of hours to ensure that there has been no damage. Due to the sub-zero temperatures and distance to the aircraft, a rope has been erected between the Bases Stairs to the Helicopters step.

Only by holding on to the rope can the inspection be conducted safely, as with the low visibility it is crucial to know where you are at. Previous teams from SANAE and other Bases on the Antarctic Continent have had team members lose their way and die of hyperthermia. Once you are lost in the storm you will end up walking around for hours trying to find your way and get completely disoriented, only to be overcome by hyperthermia. Not a pleasant way to die. The Air Force works the buddy system, and nobody goes out alone in a storm.

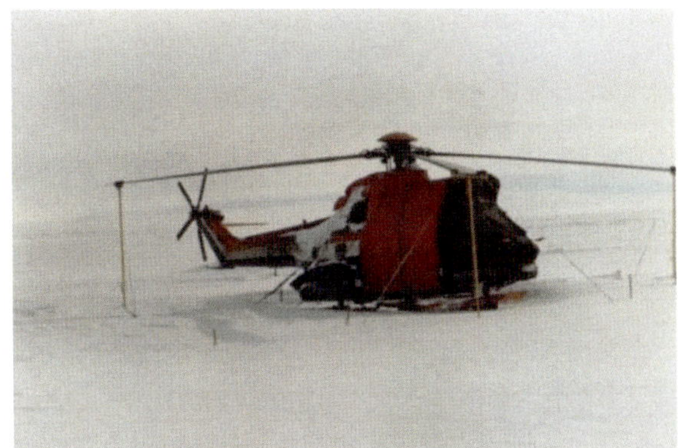

Secured J-Model Puma

During the blow, the Air Force decide that it's party time and set to have an evening of drinking and singing. Every type of alcohol is, tried, tested, and qualified to emptiness. Booming voices to Queen, Samantha Carlyle, Abba, Pink Floyd, Black Sabbath, Deep Purple and any band that ends up coming out of the Boom Box is enacted with an empty Brandy bottle as a microphone and the kitchen table as the dance floor. By early morning the next day, there are many corpses gathered around the kitchen table in various states of Compos Mentos. Steve is at the kitchen sink and sees that the urn could do with some snow. He wanders down the catwalk to the stairs and grabs a shovel to fill the bucket with fresh snow. Struggling back to the kitchen he dumps the snow into the Earn and switches it on and prepares a pot of coffee for the party boys. With the coffee brewed and mugs distributed, Steve cleans up the final dishes in the sink. He turns to the group of derelicts and says;

"Guys, I see the Cat Train on the horizon and they are about three hours away. So, I am going to get some shut-eye till 08:00, and then will come and make breakfast for the Cat Train guys".

CAT Train Leaving E-Base

The whole kitchen breaks out in a roar of laughter with every person in the room holding their gut in deep throated full blown gafuffle. Steve turns to the door and stomps out. Halfway down the catwalk to his sleeping container, he turns around and angrily returns to the kitchen. He swings the door open and shouts;

"Fuck you all!!"

Suddenly it dawns on him that what was actually coming out of his mouth sounded like;

"Foooo hhhuuuul wallllllll"

Shaking his head Steve turns and resumes his way to his bed. In the container are four sets of double Pine Bunks. Each Bunk has a pillow and mattress upon which the standard issue minus 50 degree sleeping bags are laid out. These are down filled sleeping bags and the quickest way to warm up is to sleep naked. Steve struggles out of his clothes, including the long johns and cuddles up in the sleeping bag. He is on the lower level with Spikkels the Fire Fighter above him. Steve has pulled the zipper right up and placed his head in the hoody portion. Heaving a sigh of drunken relief, he suddenly realizes that his bladder has the final say. He struggles out of the sleeping bag once more and with flip flops on, steps out naked onto the catwalk to relieve himself in the makeshift urinal that they had made out of a piece of Gutter and Downpipe. The flow starts off fine when suddenly he feels a twitch in his toes, as the cold starts to take effect. The twitch turns into a shudder and travels up his legs to his shoulders, and by the time the shudder reaches the top of his head, his whole body has starts to shake uncontrollably. Thankfully the stream of urine has stopped, and he hurriedly retreats to get back into the sleeping bag. Frozen, but back in the bag, he tries to relax and the next minute his teeth start chattering loudly. Steve bites down on his teeth to stop the chattering which automatically starts the shuddering. This continues until Spikkels shouts down at him;

"Fuck Steve stop shaking the bed, I can't sleep".

Needless to say, this was going to be one of those stories for the camp fire for many years to come.

A couple of hours later TV Terblanche the Radio Operator walks in the room with a mug for Steve. The telltale sign if it is clear flying weather is if the mug is filled with steaming black coffee. Should the weather still be un-flyable, the mug will be filled with Broffie. Broffie, a half filled black coffee and topped up with Brandy. Today was a Broffie day.

Steve rises with difficulty and sips the Broffie until the buzz gets him up to speed. He completes ablutions and after some resemblance of organization makes his way to the kitchen to start the breakfast for the Cat Team.

There are still a number of corpses in the kitchen that he unceremoniously dumps a cup of cold water on to get them out. Breakfast made, and Cat Train Team duly fed, he retires to the Radio Room to complete the daily radio schedule with the teams deployed in the field. This daily scheduled call is ensuring that the teams do not have any problems and are in good health. As soon as the weather breaks, ZS-HIZ will fly out to all teams and resupply their stocks and boost the guy's morale. They are working in teams of two and rely on each other a hundred percent to survive in the unhospitable continent of Antarctica.

Field Team Camp

The end of 1988 is looming quickly, and the weather clears up for the flying program to start up once again. Steve, Gary and Alan complete several sorties to the resupply the field teams.

The Old Year comes to an end and with hearty singing of Auld Lang Syne the New Year is welcomed in. It is late evening on New Year's Day when one of the field teams requires resupply. Steve and the crew quickly ready the Puma and at 21:00 Alan, Steve and Gary lift wheels for a one and a half hour round trip to complete the resupply.

By 2nd January 1989, ZS-HIZ is dispatched back to SANAE while ZS-HJA remains at Grunehogna. Gert and Steve are the F/E's at Grunehogna while Koos returned to SANAE with Oom Gert Theron and Gert Uys, Baas Gert and Gert!

The week passes quickly when Gary, Alan and Steve complete another resupply to the field teams. At this point Steve and Gert Stemmet share the sorties. By the 13th January 1989 a field team required relocation so Steve readies ZS-HJA for the sortie and ensures he has the Ski-Doo ramps loaded so that they can upload it in the field. The sortie is completed and upon return Steve retires to the radio room to take over the duties for the day.

Gary, Alan and Gert prepare for a field team deployment and load up the Puma. The aircraft is very heavy and therefore they need to ensure that the take-off is text book. Steve clears them for take-off on the radio and notes the time of take-off. The next instant TV Terblanche comes running into the radio room shouting.

"The chopper has gone down!"

Steve attempts to raise Gary on the radio but gets no response. Panicking Steve repeats his question to Gary.

"HIZ, Grunehogna! Are you chaps ok?"

Eventually Gary responds.

"Steve, we have an issue, but we are ok."

Steve dons his cold weather gear and rushes out to see what has happened. ZS-HJA is laying nose down in the ice with the tailboom wrapped around to the one side.

Decommissioned ZS-HJA

Steve checks the crew for injury and once satisfied tells them to get inside. Steve and Chris then assess the damage. The nose undercarriage extension jack has snapped folding the wheel back into the under carriage up position. The aircraft is resting on the ice on the nose floatation gear. The tailboom snapped with the impact and is hanging form the tail rotor control cables. Steve and Chris take notes and photos of the incident for the accident investigation that will take place. Steve and the crew secure the aircraft by digging dead men for the blade securing poles as well as the vertical support for the aircraft. The cargo is unloaded and secured at the storage depot. Next the aircraft covers are installed, battery removed, and aircraft strapped securely to the ice.

Gary has radioed SANAE and briefed Oom Gert of the incident. Steve debriefs the crew and starts the technical investigation. On take-off Alan was flying with Gert on the panel and Gary managing the radios. Gert locked onto the Torque Meter read out for take-off and did not see the Rotor RPM drop away until it was too late. The heavy aircraft with the engines at maximum power and Alan demanding more just bled off the Rotor RPM resulting in loss of lift, resulting in the aircraft dropping fast and impacting the ice.

A very somber crew spends the evening going over the incident and the sad state of affairs. Fortunately, the SA Agulhas has recently returned to Cape Town and was readying a return to SANAE with supplies and to collect the teams. Oom Gert contacts Silver Mine via HF Radio and requests that the Squadron prepare a Military L Model Puma to accompany the SA Agulhas back to SANAE.

After Brunch the next day, Steve and Chris start a plan of disassembling the Puma. Steve also chats to the Diesel Mechanic from SANAE to form a plan of modifying one of the sleds to load the Puma onto. Steve gives him the dimensions of the undercarriage and proposes that a channel be welded for securing the main and nose wheels in place. Steve has found a length of galvanized pipe that he can modify to replace the broken undercarriage jack. Chris is busy with the tailboom and has already cut the tail rotor cables off with a bolt cropper. Steve is clearing a hole under the nose of the aircraft so that the nose gear can be fully extended. He will need to ensure that the galvanized pipe locks the nose gear at full extension.

The work is slow and tiring, as the ice is hard. By late afternoon Steve has managed to fully extend the nose gear and starts to measure the length of the pipe required. With dimensions verified Steve retires to the generator room where there are tools available for him to form a temporary nose gear lock. Steve flattens the ends to simulate the attachment points of the nose gear jack. Next, he drills a hole to the exact size of the jack attachments on either side. An hour later the temporary nose gear lock is installed. The aircraft can now be safely loaded onto a sled with all three the landing gear down. After securing the aircraft for the night and exhausted Steve and Chris retire to the kitchen for some grub and liquid sustenance.

The sled modified by the Diesel Mechanic is also completed and the team have started the 72-hour trip from SANAE to Grunehogna. There is still a mountain of work to do on ZS-HJA in preparation for loading onto the sled. The aircraft will be too heavy to cargo sling, so the crew will have to remove as much of the heavy components as they can.

Early morning and the weather is holding. Steve and Chris gather the rest of the ground crew and install the mobile crane to the downed Puma. The task for today is to remove the Rotor Blades, Main Rotor Head, Engines, and prepare the aircraft for cargo slinging. With the mobile crane installed the first task is removing the blades. The de-icing looms and static bonds are carefully removed and with the blade sling attached to the mobile crane, each blade is carefully removed and lowered to the ice in the blade stands. The cold air slows the task down and under normal conditions an engine removal would take an hour, which includes the installation of the mobile crane; this engine removal is taking much longer. The aircraft is also leaning to one side making it difficult to swing the Engines and Main Rotor Head out of location. After much patience and heavy breathing both Engines are in the engine containers next to the aircraft. All that remains now is to secure the removed components, install the Main Gearbox Cover and cover the aircraft.

The cat train arrives two days later and Steve rushes out to greet the team. Rod the Diesel Mechanic shakes Steve's hand and leads him to the modified sled. Rod has done an amazing job of welding channels to the sled that will lock the undercarriage in pace. He has also welded lock rings in pace for the securing of the aircraft to the sled. Rod and Steve verify the measurements and are both pleased to see that the aircraft will fit perfectly onto the modified sled. Rod is staring at Steve with a glimmer of recognition. He looks Steve in the eye and asks.

"Did you go to Lowveld High?"

"Yes, I did!" says Steve. "Why?"

Rod replies, "I was two grades below you at school and payed rugby with you".

Grinning, the two old school mates shake hands and set out to start an evening of celebrations.

The SA Agulhas has taken a Military Puma onboard and is on route back to SANAE. It will take the ship approximately a week to make the journey. With the return of the ship there is going to a flurry of activity to ready the loading of ZS-HJA onto the sled, towing it back to the Bukta, and finally cargo slinging her onto the ship. The month of January is flashing past with all the activities that have taken place and before Steve knows it Puma 147 in her camouflage paint scheme is on final approach to land at Grunehogna. Due to the lack of de-icing and anti-icing systems on the military Puma she will be used only in clear weather. ZS-HIZ, has been lightened by removing all internal storage kit and just enough fuel on-board to sling ZS-HJA onto the sled. Steve has secured four lengths of rope to ZS-HJA on the aircrafts tie down rings to assist with guiding it down onto the sled. Oom Gert and Koos as the F/E are the only crew onboard ZS-HIZ. Steve is on top of ZS-HJA ready to hook up to the cargo sling. Oom Gert gets airborne with Koos flat on his stomach in the cargo compartment, pattering him in to hook up ZS-HJA. A long strop has been selected to give the flying pilot a better view of the load on pickup. Steve waits until the strop is within reach and in line with the lifting ring on the Main Gearbox Cover. He quickly connects the strop to the lifting ring and gets quickly off the aircraft. Once clear of the aircraft, Steve grabs the front rope and signals to Koos to lift.

Oom Gert starts taking power and slowly lifts ZS-HJA out its hole. The aircraft is hanging level and secure. Oom Gert starts moving over to the sled with the four anchors keeping the aircraft straight. The huge downwash from the rotors wants to spin the load and the guides must hold on for dear life. Oom Gert has lifted ZS-HJA to approximately 15 feet off the ground and is gently moving her over the sled. In position Steve indicates to lower the aircraft. As Oom Gert reduces power the load starts to move off to the right, and he immediately redresses back into the hover. Another attempt and the same thing occurs. Steve grabs his handheld radio and informs Oom Gert that he will just have to force it down, and even if it is slightly off the crew should be able to maneuver the aircraft correctly into position. With that Oom Gert aims and with Koos indicating that he is good, ZS-HJA drops perfectly into place on the sled. Steve indicates to Koos to drop the sling. With the sling released Oom Gert takes power and flies a short circuit before landing back at the designated landing spot.

With beaming smiles and lots of shouting the excited crews gather to see how perfectly ZS-HJA is poised on top of the sled. Chris and Steve start securing the aircraft to the sled with Tie-Down Straps and Chains. The removed components are loaded onto a low sled and secured. ZS-HJA's cover is re-installed.

Chris and Has Das are going to be riding back inside ZS-HJA to the Bukta. They will have to keep an ongoing watch on the aircraft for the 72-hour trip. With everything secured the entire Grunehogna crew retires to the kitchen for solid and liquid sustenance. The next day will be very busy as the Air Force contingent will be returning to SANAE. The Military Puma had already returned to the ship for overnight on-boarding in the hangar.

Back at SANAE Steve is assigned to Puma 147 to start the Cargo Sling loading of the ship. With Gary at the controls Steve and Gert as crew the 3-hour cargo sling operation begins. Steve patters Gary into position indicates to the ground crew to hook the load and then to Gary to lift the load. It is a short flight from the Bukta to the ship for the hook off on the forward cargo deck, and then return to the Bukta for the next hook up. It is high concentration work and the time flies. Pretty soon Steve indicates that the aircraft will need fuel, and Gary returns to the rear Heli-Deck of the ship to land.

The Cargo slinging continues for three more days with Steve flying in ZS-HIZ. ZS-HJA arrives at the Bukta on her temporary sled. Oom Gert and Koos once again lift the lady off the sled with ZS-HIZ and Cargo Sling her to the forward cargo hold of the ship. ZS-HJA will be secured in the cargo hold for the trip back to Cape Town.

By the 29th January 1989 the ship is loaded, and aircraft are stowed for the trek back to South Africa. It takes the SA Agulhas seven days to complete the journey back to Cape Town and on the 6th February 1989, early morning before sunrise the ship is laid up between Robin Island and Milnerton.

The Air Force contingent can see the Air Force Base from the Heli-Deck and are anxious to get home. Captain Billy cannot release the aircraft until the customs officials have been activated to accept them. With the first aircraft placed on the Helideck with Blades spread and loaded, the crew sets about preparing the second aircraft.

Steve is FE on HIZ with Koos on Puma 147. Steve signs up the aircraft log and author book and is in time for the pilots who have just been given the go ahead for take-off. HIZ will lift off first followed by the Military Puma and then both will fly in formation to AFB Ysterplaat.

The take-off is uneventful, and the remaining ground crew make quick work on getting Puma 147 ready for flight. After take-off the two aircraft form up and complete a fly-past of the ship to greet the teams that they had shared this exciting time with at the bottom of the planet. Clearance for approach and landing at AFB Ysterplaat is completed and the aircraft space for landing on the helipads at the base.

The crew's families have been invited to welcome the team back and Steve is overjoyed to see Zella and Nicole waving at him as he shuts down the aircraft. Nicole once again grabs Steve around the neck and grinning hugs him tightly. Steve reaches out and hugs Zella affectionately, as this has been a long tour and he has missed them both.

The customs officials approach slowly allowing the crews time to greet their families, and then pounce on the aircraft to check if the crews have not brought any items that require customs clearance and taxation, like for example "booze". Satisfied that there is just aircraft parts and kit in the aircraft, they depart.

The ground crew immediately tow the aircraft into the hangar away from prying eyes. In the hangar Steve and Koos open the compartments in the aircraft and remove all the hidden booze, which is quickly packed into the waiting cars for transportation off the base.

The team will take the rest of the day off and be in the next day to complete servicing's and unpacking of the aircraft and shipborne spares. At home Steve can't wait to hop in the shower and get the sweat off his body, as it is late summer and very hot in Cape Town. He has still to get used to the heat after being in Antarctic for the last three months. Steve's hair and beard have grown considerably, and Zella captures the moment as Steve gets out the shower.

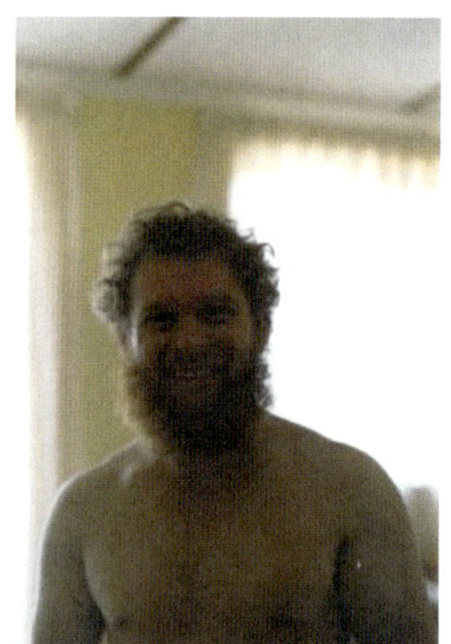

Three Month Growth

Chapter 15 – CONVENTIONAL WARFARE

The Republic of South Africa's ambitions to develop nuclear weapons began in just after the 2nd World War. South Africa reached an understanding with the United States after signing a 50-year collaboration under a US sanctioned programme, Atoms for Peace. The treaty concluded the South African acquisition of a single nuclear research reactor and an accompanying supply of Highly Enriched Uranium (HEU) fuel, located in Pelindaba on the outskirts of Pretoria.

The US delivered the 20MW research nuclear reactor, SAFARI-1, along with 90% HEU fuel to South Africa. South Africa decided to pursue plutonium capability and constructed its own reactor, SAFARI-2 at Pelindaba, that went critical using 606 kg of 2% enriched uranium fuel, and 5.4 tons of heavy water, both supplied by the US.

Pelindaba

The SAFARI-2 reactor was intended to be moderated by heavy water, fueled by natural uranium while the reactor's cooling system used molten sodium. The project was eventually abandoned by the South African government as the reactor was draining resources from the uranium enrichment program that had begun. South Africa began to focus on the success of its uranium enrichment programme which was seen by its scientists as easier compared to plutonium.

South Africa is able to mine uranium ore domestically and uses aerodynamic nozzle enrichment techniques to produce weapons-grade material. South Africa gained sufficient experience with nuclear technology to capitalize on the promotion of the US government's Peaceful Nuclear Explosions (PNE) program. The possibility of South Africa collaborating with France and Israel in the development of nuclear weapons is the subject of speculation during the Cold War.

Armscor builds the first operational weapon, code-named Hobo and later called Cabot. This device reportedly has a yield of 6 kilotons of TNT. It is eventually disassembled, and the warhead reused in a production model bomb. Armscor then builds a series of pre-production and production models under the code-name Hamerkop, after a bird. The Hamerkop series are smart television-guided glide bombs.

A-Bomb Casings

The South Africans select a test site in the Kalahari Desert at the Vastrap weapons range north of Upington. Two test shafts are completed. One shaft is 385 meters deep, the other, 216 meters. A gun-type device without a highly enriched uranium (HEU) core is produced. Atomic Energy Commission officials say that a "cold test" (a test without uranium 235) is planned.

An Armscor official at the time said that the test would have been a fully instrumented underground test, with a dummy core. Its major purpose is to test the logistical plans for an actual detonation.

Soviet intelligence detected test preparations and alerted the United States. US intelligence confirms the existence of the test site with an overflight of a Lockheed SR-71 spy plane. The Washington Post quotes a US official, "I'd say we were 99 percent certain that the construction was preparation for an atomic test."

The Soviet and Western governments are convinced that South Africa is preparing for a full-scale nuclear test. The Western nations press South Africa not to test. The French foreign minister warns of "grave consequences" for French-South African relations. Although he does not elaborate, his statement implies that France is willing to cancel its contract to provide South Africa with the Koeberg nuclear power reactors.

The sites are abandoned, and the holes sealed. One of the shafts is temporarily reopened in 1988 in preparation for another test, which does not take place. The move is intended to strengthen South Africa's bargaining position during negotiations to end the war with Angola and Cuba.

The warheads are originally configured to be delivered from one of several aircraft types in service with the South African Air Force, including the Canberra B12 and the Hawker Siddeley Buccaneer. Concerns about the vulnerability of the ageing aircraft to the Cuban anti-aircraft defense network in Angola subsequently lead the SADF to investigate missile-based delivery systems.

The missiles are to be based on the RSA-3 and RSA-4 launchers that have already been built and tested for the South African space programme. South Africa built six atom bombs, these missiles are incompatible with the available large South African nuclear warheads. The RSA series, being designed for a 340 kg payload, would suggest a warhead of some 200 kg.

Launch Vehicles

The RSA series is intended to display a credible delivery system combined with a separate nuclear test in a final diplomatic appeal to the world powers in an emergency even though they are never intended to be used in a weaponized system together.

Three rockets have already been launched into suborbital trajectories in support of development of the RSA-3 launched Greensat Orbital Management System, for commercial satellite applications of vehicle tracking and regional planning. Following the decision in 1989 to cancel the nuclear weapons program, the missile programs are allowed to continue.

Launch Control Room

In September 1979, a US Vela satellite detected a double flash over the Indian Ocean that was suspected, but never confirmed, to be a nuclear test, despite extensive air sampling by WC-135 aircraft of the United States Air Force. If the Vela Incident was a nuclear test, South Africa is one of the countries, possibly in collaboration with Israel, that is suspected of carrying it out. No official confirmation of its being a nuclear test has been made by South Africa.

In 1986, Jonas Savimbi visited Washington, where he met with American officials and was promised military hardware valued at about ten million dollars, including FIM-92 Stinger surface-to-air missiles and BGM-71 TOW anti-tank missiles. The US also pledged to continue its support for UNITA even if it lost the umbrella of protection conferred by the SADF presence in southern Angola.

At the US government's request, South Africa began lending UNITA more material assistance and aided the CIA in the acquisition of untraceable arms for the Angolan insurgents. The CIA was interested in acquiring Soviet and Eastern European arms for UNITA, as they could be easily passed off as weapons individual partisans had captured from FAPLA. South Africa possessed a vast stockpile of Soviet arms seized during Operations Sceptic, Protea, and Askari, and was persuaded to transfer some of it to UNITA.

While the Politicians never seriously considered the overthrow of the MPLA as a viable objective, they endorsed increasing aid to UNITA for many reasons, namely it would mend diplomatic relations with the US, UNITA could be molded into a proxy to harass PLAN and donating captured weapons to Savimbi was cost-effective and deniable.

After Operation Savannah had failed to prevent the ascension of the MPLA to power in Angola, the South African political leadership generally accepted that reversing that verdict by force was unrealistic. At the same time, the South African Politicians had recognized that a total military defeat of PLAN was elusive without the impossible corollary of a victory over the combined FAPLA-PLAN alliance in Angola. An offensive strategy which offered the chance to aggressively attack Angola by land, sea, and air and focus directly on the MPLA's centers of power was never discussed and became more remote as time went on. In its place, therefore, the other popular option was promulgated, which was to focus chiefly on fighting PLAN, the primary threat within the geographical limits of South West Africa and attempting to intimidate Angola in the form of punitive cross-border raids, thus assuming an essentially defensive posture.

The US and South African justification for arming UNITA lay partly in the increased supply by the Soviet Union of more sophisticated weapons to FAPLA, as well as the increased number of Cuban troops in Angola, which had rapidly swelled from 25,000 to 31,000 by the end of 1985. While the Lusaka Accords were still in force, the Cuban and Soviet military delegations had urged President dos Santos to take advantage of the ceasefire with the SADF to eliminate UNITA. A considerable increase in Soviet military assistance to Angola continued during this period, with the transfer of another billion dollars' worth of arms to FAPLA, including 200 new T-55 and T-62 tanks. Moscow also trained more Angolan pilots and delivered advanced fighter aircraft to Luanda, particularly the Mikoyan-Gurevich MiG-23s. Over a three-year period, Angola had become the second largest importer of arms on the African continent. FAPLA's arsenal expanded so exponentially that the SADF became convinced that the Soviet sponsored arms buildup was intended for deployment elsewhere. General Magnus Malan gave a speech in which he expressed alarm at the "flood" of Soviet military equipment and its sophisticated nature, claiming that it was much more than needed to cope with the SADF's limited expeditionary forces and UNITA. General Malan theorized that "the Russians want to develop a strong, stabilized base in Angola and then use the equipment and personnel positioned there wherever necessary in the subcontinent". South Africa gradually became locked in a conventional arms race with Angola; each side argued that it had to match the increased force available to the other.

Cheetah

To counter the appearance of advanced MiG-23 and Sukhoi fighters in Angola, for instance, South Africa began development on two sophisticated fighter aircraft of its own, the Atlas Cheetah and the Atlas Carver.

Project Carver

Both programs would consume in excess of 2 billion dollars.

Challenging the SADF

In mid-October 1987 FAPLA launched Operation Saluting October with the intention of severing UNITA's logistics lifelines to South West Africa and Zaire and forestall any future insurgent offensives. The impetus for Saluting October likely originated with the Soviet military mission, which pressed the idea of a major conventional thrust to destroy UNITA's southeastern front as early as 1983. FAPLA had received a new commander that year, Lieutenant General Petr Gusev, former deputy commander of the Carpathian Military District. Considering the war's length, its cost, the rising death toll, and looming cuts in the Soviet military expenditure which would limit future efforts to support FAPLA's war effort, Gusev wanted a decisive multi-divisional offensive to crush UNITA once and for all. Operation Saluting October was a two-pronged offensive aimed at retaking three major settlements from UNITA, Cangamba, Cassamba, and Mavinga.

The FAPLA command staff intended the attack on Cangamba and Cassamba as a feint, hoping to draw UNITA forces there and away from Mavinga. Once Mavinga was in government hands, FAPLA could expel the remaining insurgents from Moxico Province and pave the way for a final assault on Savimbi's headquarters at Jamba.

Approximately 14 Soviet advisers were to be attached on the battalion level, albeit with strict orders not to participate in the fighting and withdraw from the front as necessary to avoid contact with UNITA. They were accompanied by a small number of Cuban advisers and East German technical personnel serving in a variety of support roles.

Gusev and his staff appealed to Moscow for more aid to FAPLA, particularly strike aircraft, for another offensive; this request was granted. In what had become an annual practice, an estimated billion dollars' worth of arms was flown into Luanda by Soviet Antonov An-24 flights, as many as 12 per day for a six-month period. The equipment was offloaded in the capital and transferred to Angolan Ilyushin Il-76s, which in turn flew them directly to the front.

To FAPLA, the experience of planning and executing an operation of such massive proportions was relatively new, but the Soviet military mission was convinced that a decade of exhaustive training on its part had created an army capable of undertaking a complex multi-divisional offensive. The Angolan brigade commanders had repeatedly expressed reservations about splitting the force and fighting on two fronts, arguing that a single assault on Mavinga would be more linear and sufficient. FAPLA's Cuban advisers objected claiming South Africa might intervene on behalf of its erstwhile ally.

"Don't get into such wasting, costly, and finally pointless offensives," Castro had vented to Gusev's staff. "And count us out if you do."

General Arnaldo Ochoa, the senior Cuban military officer in Angola, also protested that the tactics FAPLA were being forced to adopt were more applicable to combat operations in central Europe than an offensive against an irregular fighting force on the broken African terrain.

Ronnie Kasrils, Umkhonto we Sizwe (MK) intelligence chief, warned the Soviet mission that if Saluting October proceeded an SADF counteroffensive was imminent. Gusev overruled the Cuban and MK concerns, and the operation commenced without contingency plans for a South African intervention.

Operation Modular

The preliminary phase of the new offensive begins in August 1987. Eight FAPLA brigades deployed to Tumpo, a region to the east of Cuito Cuanavale in early August, where on Soviet advice they temporarily paused for more supplies and reinforcements. On 14th August, having lost precious time, FAPLA resumes its efforts to advance; by then South Africa has launched Operation Modular to halt the offensive. The bloody campaign that follows entailed a series of engagements known collectively as the Battle of Cuito Cuanavale.

Because of FAPLA's delays, the SADF can assemble a blocking force strong enough to stop the FAPLA drive on Mavinga. By the end of August, South African expeditionary forces have built up to include 32 Battalion, elements of the 61 Mechanized Battalion Group, and the SWATF's 101 Battalion.

There are three major rivers and nine tributaries between Cuito Cuanavale and Mavinga. Although none of the rivers are especially large, all the prospective crossing points are adjacent to vast expanses of swamps and waterlogged flood plains. They stall the FAPLA advance and permit the SADF to create effective choke points which further hamper FAPLA's progress.

The South African general staff judge correctly that if these narrow entry points are seriously contested they have the potential to bottleneck entire brigades. They opt to launch a counteroffensive at the Lomba River, which is the last of the three rivers FAPLA must cross before reaching Mavinga.

The success of the South African counteroffensive is ensured by the rapid collapse of FAPLA's 47 Infantry Brigade, which is tasked with establishing a bridgehead on the Lomba's southern bank.

In conventional terms, the FAPLA troops possess more than enough strength and firepower to dislodge UNITA and the SADF from the Lomba River. Most however, are inadequately trained to counter the South African expeditionary force, which is composed of units selected for their experience in mobile bush warfare and are repeatedly outmaneuvered in the thick foliage cover.

The geographic separation of the brigades' positions, aggravated by the Lomba's swampy environment, hamper coordinated actions and allow the SADF to isolate and route each brigade piecemeal.

Between September and October 1987 FAPLA suffer almost 2,000 casualties during several failed river crossings. With much of its bridging equipment destroyed, FAPLA abandons the offensive and ordered its remaining brigades back to Cuito Cuanavale.

During Operation Modular, Cuban combat troops have remained well north of the Lomba River and decline to participate in the fighting, per Castro's instructions.

In Luanda, President dos Santos summons General Gusev and the senior Cuban general officer, Gustavo Fleitas Ramirez, for an urgent conference to discuss the worsening military situation and the failure of Operation Saluting October. Ramirez reminds dos Santos that Cuba has been opposed to the offensive from the beginning.

Gusev laments in his memoirs that, "I informed Chief of the Soviet General Staff, Akhromeyev about the result of the operation, but the most difficult task, in moral terms, is to inform the president of Angola, whom I had assured that the operation would succeed and that Savimbi would be crushed".

On 29th September 1987, President P.W. Botha adds a third objective to Operation Modular, namely the destruction of all FAPLA units east of Cuito Cuanavale. The reasons for this shift in objectives once FAPLA has abandoned its offensive are not apparent to everybody in the South African government.

Pik Botha and his senior colleagues in the foreign ministry caution against a major offensive north of the Lomba, citing potential diplomatic repercussions.

But confidence in the SADF has been buoyed by its effective defense of the Lomba, and members of the South African general staff successfully agitated for a renewed offensive towards Cuito Cuanavale. It is unclear whether they interpret their new objective as veiled permission to seize Cuito Cuanavale itself, although the option is discussed.

On 25th November 1987, United Nations Security Council Resolution 602 is passed, condemning Operation Modular as an illegal violation of Angolan sovereignty. The resolution expresses dismay at the continued presence of SADF troops in Angola and calls for their unconditional withdrawal.

South African foreign minister Pik Botha flatly dismisses the resolution out of hand, citing the unaddressed issue of Cuban linkage. He promises that the SADF would depart Angola once FAPLA's Cuban and Soviet advisers have likewise been withdrawn, or when their presence no longer threatens South African interests.

Operation Hooper and Packer

Per Pik Botha's new directive, the SADF commences Operation Hooper with the goal of encircling the retreating Angolan brigades and preparing for operations further east of the Cuito River. The decision to commence Hooper towards the end of the 1987 creates problems for the SADF, since many white conscripts involved in the Lomba River engagements are nearing the end of their national service, leading to a delay of several weeks while the existing troops are gradually withdrawn from Angola and replaced with a new intake.

The SADF has dispatched a second mechanized battalion, 4 South African Infantry, to Angola, as well as a squadron of Olifant Mk1A tanks and a battery of G5 and G6 howitzers. The failure of initial South African encirclement attempts necessitates a change in plans.

Between January and March 1988, the SADF and UNITA launch several bloody offensives just east of Cuito Cuanavale to destroy the shattered Angolan units that have succeeded in establishing a new defensive line there, an initiative which becomes known as Operation Packer.

They manage to drive FAPLA deeper into a shrinking perimeter between the Cuito, Tumpo, and Dala rivers known as the "Tumpo Triangle".

SADF Olifant Battle Tank

A complete brigade of tanks is advancing towards Cuito Cuanavale, where the Angolan troops in retreat from the South African attack are reassembling.

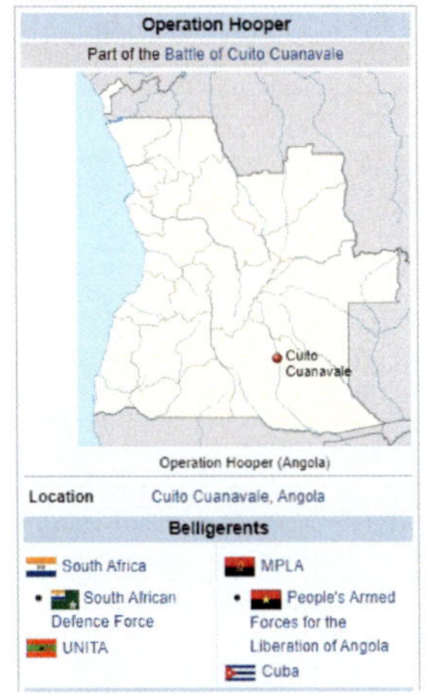

Cuito Cuanavale

Fidel Castro comments on the buildup of Cuban troops in Angola in late 1987 and early 1988. "We used helicopters to send in tank specialists, artillerymen, and experts in repairing military technology who could press into service the tremendous amount of Angolan technology and equipment that was there. Prior to that, we'd asked President José Eduardo dos Santos to turn over command of all the Angolan troops on the southern front to us."

The Cubans and Soviets concur with FAPLA's decision to withdraw to Cuito Cuanavale, with Castro pointing out that a strong defensive stand could plausibly be made there if the brigades manage to reach it. He also suggests that the only way to defeat the South African expeditionary forces in the long term is to outflank them and apply pressure to the South West African border. This would entail opening yet another military front, in southwestern Angola, well south of Cuito Cuanavale. On 15th November 1987, President dos Santos has written a letter to Castro requesting direct Cuban military assistance against the SADF. Castro agrees on the condition that he and General Arnaldo Ochoa receive command of all FAPLA forces on the front. The Soviet military mission is notably excluded from all future operational planning. Shortly afterwards, the Cuban government authorizes the deployment of an armoured brigade and several air defense units, about 3,000 personnel to Cuito Cuanavale. Castro suspects that the South Africans would not be content with eliminating FAPLA east of the town and that they intend to take control of Cuito Cuanavale's strategic airfield as well. His strategy is to strengthen the defense of that settlement while dispatching a few more brigades to Lobito, near the South West African border.

The FAPLA and Cuban defenders now ringed their defensive positions with minefields and interlocking fields of fire from dug-in tanks and field guns, into which they channel SADF assaults. On multiple occasions the combined UNITA and SADF forces launch unsuccessful offensives which become bogged down in minefields along narrow avenues of approach and are abandoned when the attackers came under heavy fire from the Cuban and FAPLA artillerymen west of the Cuito River. The defenders' artillery is sited just beyond the maximum range of the South African artillery and on high ground which give them a commanding view of the battlefield. This advantage, coupled with the proliferation of minefields, and heavily reinforced FAPLA-Cuban defensive positions render further attacks by the South African troops futile.

The bombardment of Operation Hooper starts on 2nd January 1988, with a mix of artillery and air strikes, and a UNITA infantry attack. Kentron, South African armaments development and manufacturing company has been involved in the development of guided weapons and missiles since the 1970s. The Raptor glide bomb is the first of these to go into service, with the H1 effectively being a technology testbed. It is used operationally in the final phase of South African involvement in Angola. Company officials are coy, but reports say the Raptor is used to successfully interdict the lone bridge crossing the Cuito Cuanavale River near the town with the same name.

H-2 Raptor Smart Bomb

24 Sqn Buccaneer Bomber

The Raptor is a modular system consisting of the glide bomb, the communications pod, pylons and control equipment. The bomb can glide to targets at ranges more than 60 kilometers but can be controlled at ranges of up to 250km, when the communications pod is fitted to a second aircraft. The weapon is integrated on the Buccaneer and the Mirage F1AZ, in which the pilot uses a small joystick control to steer the H2 to its target.

In later versions, navigation will be autonomous, by waypoint or by using GPS-assisted inertial navigation. The weapon is usually fitted with a passive TV seeker and can be upgraded to include an imaging infra-red or radar seeker. The weapon is accurate to within 3m CEP. In SAAF service it is either fitted with a fragmentation or penetration warhead.

The weapon is first used operationally against the bridge at Cuito Cuanavale during Operations Modular and Hooper. Buccaneer 414 drops the first H2 "Smart"-Bomb to be used operationally by the SAAF during an attack on the Cuito bridge in Southern Angola on 12th December 1987. Unfortunately, the H2 fails to destroy its target but a second attack on 3rd January 1988 proves more successful.

At approximately 05h45Z on 3rd January 1988, a formation of Buccaneers departs from Air Force Base Grootfontein armed with the glide 'smart-bomb' commonly referred to as "H-2 and HANTO", the first attempt of the day to destroy the Cuito Cuanavale Bridge is aborted.

The second attempt sees the aircraft take-off at 09h40Z while the Angolan Air Force launch a flight of MiG-23's to intercept, which never reach the Buccaneer formation, and Buccaneer successfully launch 'H2' and destroy the Bridge at 10h31Z.

32 Battalion and elements of other units harries the road convoys for weeks, destroying several hundred tanks and other vehicles, and inflicting an unknown number of casualties. On the 13th January 1988, the SADF attacks 21 Brigade, starting with air strikes and artillery bombardments. Over two days the FAPLA unit is driven out of their positions, and lose 7 tanks with 5 more captured, various other vehicles are destroyed and captured, and 150 men are killed or captured. UNITA loses 4 dead and 18 wounded, and the SADF has one man wounded and one armoured vehicle damaged. However, the SADF is again unable to exploit the momentum, due to a shortage or reserves and supplies. UNITA occupies the captured positions, and the SADF withdrew, but UNITA loses the positions later to a FAPLA counter-attack. A large Cuban and FAPLA column is on the way from Menongue for the relief of Cuito Cuanavale, but progress in the rainy season is slow due to the need to clear the UNITA minefields and guard against possible ambushes. They do not reach Cuito Cuanavale in time to take part in the first engagement.

The next attack is only on 14th February 1988, against the positions of 21 Brigade that UNITA has lost, and the neighbouring positions of the 59 Brigade. They are counter-attacked by Cuban tanks. Both 21 Brigade and 59 Brigade are forced to withdraw. FAPLA loses 500 men and a further 32 Cuban soldiers, along with 15 tanks and 11 armoured vehicles. The SADF loses 4 killed and 11 wounded, and some vehicles are damaged. FAPLA withdraw to the Tumpo river triangle, a smaller area east of the river and across from Cuito Cuanavale. The terrain is ideally suited to defense, and they lay extensive minefields.

In a skirmish on 19th February 1988 a FAPLA position is disrupted, and it results in the FAPLA 59 Brigade being withdrawn across the river. However, the SADF has two vehicles damaged in the minefield. In the following days the Cubans step up their air attacks against South African positions. On 25th February another assault on the bridgehead ran into a minefield and bogged down. In this engagement the FAPLA lose 172 men, plus 10 Cubans, and 6 tanks. In comparison the SADF loses 4 killed and 10 wounded, plus several vehicles damaged.

Due to the increased use of Angolan Fighter aircraft and Attack helicopters the South African Air Force is limited to flying support resupply and Casevac operations by helicopters at night. The Air Force helicopter crews are put under huge strain as they mount many hours flying from dusk to dawn. Lounging around the pool from midday and then spending the late afternoon preparing for the long night flights became the order of the day.

Due to the constant threat of enemy aircraft patrols, the routes flown into and out of Angola are constantly changed to ensure non-detection. Sorties start late at night, thus ensuring that enemy would be less vigilant and continue till early pre-dawn morning. The Chopper crews are then treated to an energizing breakfast of steak and eggs before showering and catching a few hours' sleep to repeat the process once again.

After the SADF completes the last attack of Operation Hooper on 1st March, FAPLA and Cuban forces begin aggressive patrols around 5th March into the minefields and land in front of their positions in the Tumpo triangle. This brings them into contact with UNITA forces patrolling the disputed land. On 9th March, Cuban MiG's bomb SADF supply lines around the Lomba River. This is the route the SADF use to move their supplies from Mavinga to their positions east of the Chambinga high ground. In preparation for the main attack on the 25 Brigade, UNITA forces attack and remove the FAPLA elements of 36 Brigade from the high ground north of the Tumpo triangle, between the Cuito and Cuanavale rivers. The positions on the high ground are taken over by 20th March, establishing forward observers for the SADF artillery. Members of 4 Recce infiltrate the west bank of Cuito with the aim of identifying targets for the SADF artillery batteries. The South African artillery engage many targets before the main battle and the Cuban artillery counter but are not as successful at hitting targets. On 18th March, two portable ferries to cross the Cuito River are destroyed by the SADF artillery. From 21st to the 22nd March, UNITA conducts numerous hit-and-run attacks on FAPLA/Cuban positions around Cuito Cuanavale to confuse and keep them occupied.

SADF electronic warfare operations intercept FAPLA communications on 22nd March which indicate that FAPLA wants to retake the Chambinga heights. These high grounds lay east in front of the Tumpo triangle and the SADF positions. SADF decides to go ahead with the operation planned for 23rd March. On the night of 22nd March, around 21h00, the SADF units begin to line up and prepare for the attack, which would begin the next morning. As they move forward during the night, the columns become temporarily lost and then must continue their advance with only one tank de-miner when the other overturns. Around 04h00 on 23rd March, SADF G-5 artillery begin to bombard the forward positions of the 25 Brigade. By 06h00 the SADF attack column is within 10 km of the FAPLA positions but has soon stopped as they are delayed by bad terrain. The attack resumes around 08h15. Not long after the attack column begin moving again, a tank hits a mine and the de-miner tank sent forward to clear the minefield is itself permanently disabled by a mine, unable to be moved. The column halts, and sappers are brought forward to clear a way through the minefield with their Plofadders (Automated rocket-fired explosive de-miner). These fail to work, and the mines must be manually detonated, further delaying the operation by three hours. Clearing of the minefields also attracts the attention of the Cuban artillery, which then fires on the SADF column. During this time, UNITA fights and loses a battle to recapture the high ground with elements of 38 Brigade.

The SADF's main column resumes moving around 12h30 towards 25 Brigade's positions, and just over an hour later hits another minefield. This once again disables three SADF tanks, attracting the Cuban artillery once more. One of the tanks is recovered while the other two remain stuck in the minefield. UNITA soldiers start taking casualties while being transported on the backs of the tanks and are exposed to artillery fire. The South African commander moves his forces back out of the minefield while attempting to retrieve the damaged tanks. By 14h30 a decision is made to withdraw completely due to the minefields and heavy artillery attacks from both sides of the river. A request is made for the SADF artillery to destroy the three damaged Olifant tanks which is rejected as it is believed that the tanks could be recovered. This however does not happen; one is retrieved by the Cubans and taken to the town of Cuito Cuanavale and the other two remain in the Angolan bush.

Operations Hooper and Packer are terminated after the SADF has killed almost 700 FAPLA troops and destroyed about half of the Angolan brigades' remaining tanks and armoured vehicles. Cuba has suffered 42 dead and the loss of 6 tanks. South African casualties are relatively light with 13 dead and several dozen severely wounded. Three SADF tanks are abandoned in a minefield, while most of the others are damaged beyond immediate repair or rendered unserviceable due to mechanical problems.

The Tumpo Triangle campaign exposes several flaws in the planning of the South African defense chiefs and general staff. They had estimated quite accurately that their forces would be able to inflict a crushing defeat on FAPLA in the flood plains and open terrain south of Cuito Cuanavale. But they had not anticipated so many Angolan units would survive and establish strong defensive lines in the Tumpo Triangle, or that the addition of Cuban troops there would stiffen the resistance considerably. Further South African miscalculations appear in the latter phases of the campaign. One is the assumption that the small and highly mobile but lightly armed SADF expeditionary force is suited to mounting frontal attacks on well-prepared defenders supported by dug in artillery west of Cuito. The use of battalions trained and organized for mobile warfare in this manner is in violation of the SADF's own mechanized doctrine. The defending Angolans had ample armour, anti-tank weapons, and the benefit of air cover. The Soviet Union's increased willingness to supply FAPLA with advanced fighter aircraft and even Soviet pilots on loan posed a serious threat to South African air operations over Cuito Cuanavale. As Soviet involvement grows, and the number of air battles increase, South Africa's air force begins encountering MiG-21 and MiG-23 fighters flown by well-trained Soviet pilots.

FAPLA Mig 21

Angolan pilots newly trained under Soviet supervision at Lubango are proving more capable of challenging South African fighters.

For the first time the SADF begin losing aircraft in numbers, indicating the contested extent of the Angolan skies.

FAPLA Mig 23

The SADF's declining air superiority force several operational changes. South African pilots exercise a standoff bombing capacity of twenty kilometers and time their raids, so they are out of range before FAPLA MiG's can be scrambled to intercept them. The necessity of avoiding prolonged aerial contact is partly dictated by fuel considerations.

Arthur Piercy downed by Mig 23

Mirage F1 AZ Landing AFB Ondangwa

Mirage F1's being prepped for battle

The SADF Mirage F1AZ and F1CZ fighters launch from distant bases in South West Africa, which means they have barely enough fuel for three minutes of combat once they reach Cuito Cuanavale. The impact on ground operations is more consequential.

FAPLA MiG's fly reconnaissance missions in search of the G5 and G6 howitzers, forcing the South African artillery crews to resort to increasingly elaborate camouflage and take the precaution of carrying out their bombardment after dark. Owing to the increase in losses and damage due to UNITA's US supplied Stinger missiles, however, MiG pilots must adopt contingencies of their own to reduce the vulnerability of their aircraft. Cuban and Angolan warplanes are forced to drop bombs from higher altitudes, greatly reducing their accuracy. FAPLA airfields are also monitored by South African forward artillery observers, who call in bombardments to destroy aircraft while they are exposed on the runway and preparing to take off.

Although the SADF and UNITA counteroffensive has been checked, FAPLA remains heavily strained and more dependent than before on its Cuban allies and Soviet materiel. This gives the Angolan President dos Santos an incentive to ease the military dilemma with negotiations and he reopens the possibility of reaching a new ceasefire and disengagement agreement with South Africa. As early as January 1987, Chester Crocker has responded to positive signals from Luanda, especially when President Denis Sassou Nguesso of the People's Republic of the Congo offers to mediate peace talks between the rival states. Yet preliminary discussions in Brazzaville throughout 1987 and 1988 remain stymied by the Angolan government's refusal to compromise on the timetable for a proposed Cuban withdrawal.

The Cuban government has not been consulted on the Brazzaville talks in advance and resents what it perceived as a discourtesy on the part of dos Santos. This factor has the effect of persuading Castro to make an authoritative bid to join the Angolan-US peace talks. He is determined that Cuba no longer be excluded from negotiations concerning its own military, and the results of any future settlement on the withdrawal process leave Cuba's image untarnished. Cuban S-125 "SA-3 Goa" missile systems are shipped to Angola in 1988 to provide air cover for Castro's offensive.

Cuban S-125 "SA-3 Goa" missile systems

While Operation Hooper is underway in late January 1988, Crocker relents to pressure and accepts Cuba as an equal partner in further peace talks. Castro agrees that he would not introduce extraneous issues to the agenda, such as Cuba US relations, and that discussion of a phased troop withdrawal would extend to all Cuban military personnel stationed in Angola, including combat troops, logistical staff, and advisers. With Cuba's entry into the Brazzaville talks, its desire to shift its military involvement in Angola from a passive, defensive role to an offensive one intensifies. Castro opts to escalate ground operations against the SADF, since he considers diplomatic progress impossible as long as South Africa still clings to the likelihood of a tactical victory. He retains a solely defensive posture at Cuito Cuanavale, keeping the SADF fixed in place, while carrying out his longstanding proposal to launch a flanking maneuver towards the South West African border.

It is a risky operation, beginning with a movement of Cuban troops in divisional strength west of the Cunene River, which has the potential to expand into an invasion of South West Africa. On 9th March, Castro sends the Cuban forces massed at Lobito, which have grown to about 40,000 men, southwards. He likens their movement to "a boxer who with his left hand blocks the blow and with his right strikes". "That way," Castro recounts, "while the South African troops are being bled slowly dry in Cuito Cuanavale, down in the southwest...40,000 Cuban soldiers...backed by about 600 tanks, hundreds of artillery pieces, 1,000 anti-aircraft weapons, and the daring MiG-23 units that take over the skies, advance towards the SWA border, ready to sweep away the South African forces".

As the Cuban brigade's advance, they accumulate thousands of PLAN insurgents, who depart their bases to join the offensive. The presence of so many Cuban troops effectively resuscitates PLAN's sagging fortunes, as it curtails new South African military initiatives against the insurgents not only in Angola but South West Africa as well. Firstly, the region being occupied by the Cubans just north of the border is the same territory the SADF has monitored and patrolled for almost a decade to prevent PLAN infiltration into Ovamboland. Secondly, all South African units near the border have ceased routine counter-insurgency operations while they are being mobilized to resist a potential Cuban invasion. Matters are complicated further when the Cubans form three joint battalions with PLAN fighters, each with its own artillery and armoured contingents. Due to the integration of the insurgents with Cuban personnel at the battalion level, South African patrols find it impossible to engage PLAN in Angola without risking a much larger confrontation involving aggressive and well-armed Cuban troops.

The limited SADF troops available near the border cannot halt the continued progress of the Cuban army or reduce the threat to South West Africa. There are simply too few men to hold the broad defensive positions along the Cutline against a conventional force in divisional strength. When South African officials warn against an invasion of South West Africa, Castro retorts that they are "in no position to demand anything". Havana also issues an ambiguous statement which reads, "we are not saying we will not go into SWA". The South African government responds by mobilizing 140,000 reservists, a figure almost unprecedented in SADF history and threatens severe repercussions on any Cuban unit which cross the border. Some facts of the battle:

- South African losses – 31 versus Cuban/MPLA losses – 4785
- SA Tanks lost – 3 versus Cuban/MPLA Tanks lost – 94
- SA Aircraft lost – 1 versus Cuban/MPLA Aircraft lost – 9

Points to remember about the battle are the failed Cuban/MPLA objectives. The objective was to capture Jamba. To achieve this, they had to cross the Lomba River, capture Mavinga and then Jamba. One SA Defense Brigade supported by UNITA prevented Cuban/MPLA forces form achieving their objective. The Cuban/MPLA forces did not cross the Lomba River, did not capture Mavinga and never came close to Jamba.

After the battle, Fidel Castro had General Arnaldo (Ochoa) Sanchez, one of the Cuban Commanders in the battle who had been called a "Hero of the revolution" by Castro, executed by a firing squad. Another Cuban General, del Pino Diaz, fled to the US after the war. Although the Cubans claimed they had achieved a glorious victory at Cuito Cuanavale, by the end of 1987 they were already suing for peace.

Furthermore, the Soviets, who were supplying the Cuban and MPLA forces with thousands of tons of weaponry worth over a billion dollars, were openly stating that the war in Angola could not have been won by the Cubans. Cuba during the negotiations, requested that they be allowed to withdraw from Angola in an honorable fashion, a strange request made by a supposedly victorious army. Cuba knew it was losing the war and did not want to leave in disgrace.

South Africa had no intentions of disgracing the Cubans and Soviets by revealing the true facts of the battle at the fragile negotiations. This would lead to the Cubans and Soviets sending more troops and supplies to regain their reputation. Humiliating the Cubans has no practical purpose. Furthermore, South Africa could not report the truth of the progress in the war for that would reveal their numerical weakness.

They have approximately 3000 lightly armed soldiers in Angola, yet the Cubans and Angolans are under the impression that there were 9000 soldiers due to the superior training and tactics of the SADF. For 48 hours without sleep during 2nd to 3rd October, the decisive day of the battle, the Recce's stand guard over the MPLA escape route across the Lomba River, neutralizing their armoured retreat.

While the MPLA T-55 tanks can fire while moving, the South African infantry fighting vehicles, Ratels could only fire when stationary, yet they are able to cause havoc amongst the MPLA vehicles attempting to use a single wooden road for retreat across a single bridge. Although the South Africans are outnumbered 4 to 1, they make the MPLA forces retreat towards the Lomba River on the 3rd October, the decisive day of the battle.

On the 3rd October, the enemy Air Force fly approximately 60 sorties attempting to bomb and strafe the South African positions, yet the enemy are widely inaccurate and do not have much effect.

The South African forces capture a SAM-8 Missile System intact, along with missiles, radar and logistics vehicles. This is the first example of the highly effective Soviet weapon to be captured by a western country. Several undamaged tanks are also captured.

The entire Cuito Cuanavale operation has been a Soviet invention. In 1987, over 1000 Soviet advisors have been assigned to Angola, the largest logistical operation to date, and approximately $1.5 Billion worth of supplies has been delivered. Vast amounts of Soviet equipment fall into South African and UNITA's hands, after MPLA's chaotic retreat. In both terms of arms and strategy, the Cuito Cuanavale Campaign is a stunning humiliation of the Soviets.

The loss of Cuito Cuanavale for MPLA means it would take at least two years to recover and regroup. During mid-November, the South African and UNITA forces have destroyed the airfield at Cuito Cuanavale and pinned down thousands of MPLA's best remaining units, still defending the towns perimeter.

The brave, courageous and valiant people of the South African forces who risked and lost their lives for the preservation of South Africa and the democratic freedom for which it stood. Their memory will live on forever, and their bravery will never be forgotten.

Destroyed MPLA T-55 Tank and SAAF Puma

1988 Tripartite Accord

Despite taking the necessary countermeasures on the battlefield, the South African government discerned it has reached the political limits of further escalation in Angola. The casualties sustained during the Cuito Cuanavale campaign have been sufficient to cause public alarm and provoke difficult questions about the tactical situation on the border and why South African soldiers are dying there. There is little reason to believe yet another bloody campaign would be successful in expelling the Soviets and Cuba from the region; on the contrary, as in the past, it could lead to an increase in the number of Soviet weapons and Cuban troops. The conflict has also evolved from a low-intensity struggle against lightly armed insurgents into protracted battles between armies backed by all the paraphernalia of modern conventional warfare, with the accompanying rise in human and material costs. This contributes to a sense of war weariness and increases the growing skepticism and sensitivity in civilian circles toward the SADF's Angolan operations.

The failure of the Soviet-supervised Operation Saluting October, along with the consequent destruction of hundreds of millions of dollars of FAPLA's Soviet-supplied arms, has the effect of moderating Moscow's stance on Angola. In a notable departure from its previous foreign policy stance, the Soviet Union disclose it too is weary of the Angolan and South West African conflicts and is prepared to assist in a peace process even one conducted based on Cuban linkage. Reformist premier Mikhail Gorbachev also wishes to reduce defense expenditures, including the enormous open-ended commitment of military aid to FAPLA, and is more open to a political settlement accordingly.

Chester Crocker, US diplomat. Crocker's influence and mediation are instrumental in talks which establish the Tripartite Accord. For South Africa and the Soviet Union, the two parties which had previously refrained from joining the US-mediated talks the point have now been reached where the costs of continuing the war exceeded its anticipated benefits. This necessitates a change in perceptions in both nations, which begin warming to the possibility of a negotiated peace. The Soviet government agrees to jointly sponsor with the US a series of renewed peace talks. For its part, South Africa makes its first bid to join the tripartite negotiations and agrees to send a delegation of diplomats, intelligence chiefs, and senior SADF officers.

The Soviet and US diplomats in attendance, including Crocker, make it clear to the South Africans that they want peace in Angola and a political settlement in South West Africa. They are also agreed on the need to bring pressure on their respective allies to bring about a solution. South Africa would be expected to comply with United Nations Security Council Resolution 435, in exchange for the complete withdrawal of Cuban troops from Angola. The Cuban and Angolan delegations have already assented to a complete Cuban withdrawal, and under US pressure produce an extremely precise timetable which extends this process over three to four years. South Africa finds this unacceptable but concedes that the withdrawal could be timed to certain benchmarks in the Namibian independence process.

Between May and September 1988, the parties meet for several rounds of talks in Cairo, New York, Geneva, and Brazzaville, but remain deadlocked on the nuances of the withdrawal timetable. The fact that there are two objectives Namibian independence and a Cuban withdrawal doubly aggravate the issue of timing and deadlines. In August, the Angolan, Cuban, and South African delegations sign the Geneva Protocol, which establishes the principles for a peace settlement in South

West Africa and commits the SADF to a withdrawal from that territory. As a direct result of the Geneva Protocol, PLAN declares a ceasefire effective from 10th August.

The 1988 US presidential elections lean new urgency to the negotiations, which have recently stalled after six consecutive rounds of talks in Brazzaville. Angola and Cuba have gambled heavily on a victory for Michael Dukakis and the Democratic Party during the US elections, hoping that this would spell the end of US aid to UNITA and a harder line on South Africa.

At the time of the Geneva Protocol, President dos Santos comments that, "If the Democrats had won the elections, there would be a readjustment in US policy, particularly on Southern Africa". The ascension of George H. W. Bush has the effect of persuading the Angolan and Cuban delegations to be more flexible. Crocker reiterates on several occasions that a new US administration means changes in personnel and basic policy review and presses them not to waste months of effort.

Three days after the US election results are released, the parties reconvene in Geneva and within the week have agreed to a phased Cuban withdrawal over the course of twenty-seven months. In exchange, South Africa pledges to begin bestowing independence on South West Africa by 1st November 1989. On 13th December, South Africa, Angola, and Cuba sign the Brazzaville Protocol, which affirms their commitment to these conditions and set up a Joint Military Monitoring Commission (JMMC) to supervise the disengagement in Angola. The JMMC is to include Soviet and US observers.

All hostilities between the belligerents, including PLAN, are to formally cease by 1st April 1989. On 22nd December, the Brazzaville Protocol is enshrined in the Tripartite Accord, which requires the SADF to withdraw from Angola and reduce its troop levels in South West Africa to a token force of 1,500 within twelve weeks.

Simultaneously, all Cuban brigades would be withdrawn from the border to an area north of the 15th parallel. At least 3,000 Cuban military personnel would depart Angola by April 1989, with another 25,000 leaving within the next six months. The remaining troops would depart at a date not later than 1st July 1991. An additional condition is that South Africa would cease all support for UNITA, and Angola likewise for PLAN and MK.

FAPLA and SAAF Crews for the JMMC

On 20th December, United Nations Security Council Resolution 626 is passed, creating the United Nations Angola Verification Mission (UNAVEM) to verify the redeployment northwards and subsequent withdrawal of the Cuban forces from Angola.

UNAVEM includes observers from Western as well as non-aligned and communist nations. In February 1989 the United Nations Transition Assistance Group (UNTAG) is formed to monitor the South West African peace process.

Pressures of Military Life

Zella has completed her studies and is offered a full-time position as Oral Hygienist in Cape Town. The last few years have been strange for Steve as Zella seems to have distanced herself from him and become confrontational. With Steve being away from home so often there has not been much chance to address concerns and each time the couple just moves on hoping that next time it will be better. Nicole on the other hand is prospering well and has made many friends at the Pre-School. Soon she will be old enough to start Primary School. Steve decides that he needs to address his career more earnestly than before. He wants to pursue Test Flying and therefore needs to complete his studies, apply for and completing Officer Forming and then a crash course on Aeronautical Engineering with Test Flight as the main subject line. Steve has been the Squadron Test Engineer for a few years now and loves the adventure and challenge of developing and testing modifications to the aircraft. With the Border War seemingly coming to an end there are going to be many changes within the country and Steve wants to ensure he can be part of the development process.

Zella has developed friendships with her colleagues and often goes out with them when Steve is home to look after Nicole. Steve does not mind as he has been operational for more than half Nicole's lifetime and enjoys the time with her. The distance between Steve and Zella is widening and he has no idea how to deal with it. He finds himself becoming cold and distant as he has been when operational. Without showing emotions of fear or excitement during his operational experiences, Steve managed to control his decision making. Burying the emotions become natural and normal to him. The less he shares the stronger he feels. So, this is just another process of closing off.

The family take a break and Steve books a hiking trip for them at Greyton a small town in the Overberg area of the Western Cape. Before Greyton was established in 1854, the verdant plains and forested ravines of the area were home to the Hassequas khoikhoi tribe who had their kraals near the Gobos river, which they named after their ancestral chief. Their many thousand heads of cattle and sheep were the reason why Ensign Schriver of the Castle of Good Hope was sent here in the late 1600s to barter with their head man, Captain Stoffel Koekson. So rich did Koekson become from this bartering that he eventually took his people to live in the Boschmanskloof, where he built them proper mud-brick houses, the foundations of which still lie under the old houses of Boschmanskloof today. Greyton owes much of its charm to the fact that its Cape Vernacular architectural heritage has remained largely intact. It is an extremely popular weekend and holiday destination for visitors who enjoy its combination of old-world charm and modern conveniences.

The Greyton McGregor Hiking Trail, also known as the Boesmanskloof Trail, is a 14km trail that winds through the Riviersonderend Mountains linking the towns of McGregor and Greyton. The hike is 2 days and staying overnight in McGregor. With accommodation booked they set off early in the morning on the first half of the trail. The day is hot and under clear skies Zella and Nicole soon showing symptoms of exhaustion from the strenuous hike. Fortunately, there is sufficient water on the trail and Steve stops long enough for the girls to recuperate.

<u>Greyton, Overberg</u>

The hike is spectacular, with steep gorges, large rock pools, waterfalls and beautiful Cape fynbos wildflowers. There is also plenty of birdlife and wild animals like Duiker, Grey Rhebuck, Klipspringer, Baboon, Dassie, Spotted Genet and Leopards. Early afternoon and they make it to McGregor to the cabin where they will spend the night. Steve prepares a quick meal while Zella tends to Nicole and herself. After supper the two are too exhausted to sit around the fire and are soon sound asleep.

Early the next morning Steve prepares a hearty breakfast for the return trip to Greyton along a different route. They will have to climb over the mountain ridge to access the trail leading down to Greyton. The day warms up quickly and soon the girls are falling behind. Steve takes Zella's Rucksack and straps it to his chest, balancing out the weight of his own Rucksack on his back. Next, he hoists Nicole up onto the back of his Rucksack with her feet hooked into the straps around his waist while she holds on to the side bags on the top. Satisfied that Nicole is secure with a belt around both, Steve continues up the mountain. At the top he rests the group before tackling the long steep route down. It's an exhausted trio that arrives back at Greyton early afternoon and all three make a beeline to the pool to recuperate.

Steve feels more relaxed and attempts to mend the fences with Zella, but she remains challenging as if rebelling against whatever is presented. Steve withdraws and keeps to himself as he looks back on the past nine years and realizes how much things have changes. Although satisfied and content with his position and work environment, something seems wrong and he cannot put his finger on what is bothering him. His temper flares constantly and he must watch how he reacts to conversations that don't support his beliefs. His love for Nicole however, remains the focus of his life, and he gazes down on her with pride. After the short holiday, Steve must prepare for his next tour of duty in a few months. This will be a big change, as the conflict in Angola has halted and now the SADF are assisting the UNTAG forces in the Security Council Resolution 435. All flying will be in support of preparing SWA for elections and the withdrawal of South African forces from the region.

Namibian independence

The initial terms of the Geneva Protocol and Security Council Resolution 435 provided the foundation from which a political settlement in South West Africa could proceed: holding of elections for a constitutional assembly, confinement of both PLAN and the SADF to their respective bases, the subsequent phased withdrawal of all but 1,500 SADF troops, demobilization of all paramilitary forces that belonged to neither the SADF nor to the police, and the return of refugees via designated entry points to participate in elections. Responsibility for implementing these terms rested with UNTAG, which would assist in the SADF withdrawal, monitor the borders, and supervise the demobilization of paramilitary units.

Since the early 1980s PLAN had consistently stated its intention to establish camps inside South West Africa during any future political transition, a notion rejected with equal consistency by the South African government. Compounding this fact was that PLAN insurgents also identified themselves as refugees without making any distinction between their civilian or military background, and the UN had explicitly invited refugees to return home. Indeed, PLAN did not possess many regular standing units and by the late 1980s many of its personnel followed cyclical patterns of fighting as insurgents before returning to refugee camps as civilians.

On 31st March 1989, Pik Botha complains to the JMMC that PLAN troops have advanced south of the 16th parallel and are massing less than eight kilometers from the border. He promptly intercepts UN Special Representative Martti Ahtisaari and UNTAG commander Dewan Prem Chand that evening and gives them the same information. On the morning of 1st April, the first PLAN cadres cross into Ovamboland, unhindered by UNTAG, which have failed to monitor their activity in Angola due to the delays in its deployment. Ahtisaari immediately contacts SWAPO, ordering it to rein in PLAN, to little avail. The South African foreign ministry also contacts the Secretary-General, who in turn relays the same message to SWAPO officials in New York.

At the end of the day, with no signs of the PLAN advance abating, Ahtisaari lifts all restrictions confining the SADF to its bases. Local police mobilize and fight off the invaders in a delaying action until regular SADF forces can deploy with six battalions. After the first two days the insurgents lose their offensive initiative, and the combined South African forces drive PLAN back across the border in a counteroffensive codenamed Operation Merlyn. Between 1st April – 9th April 273 PLAN insurgents are killed in the fighting. The SADF and police suffer 23 dead. On 8th April, the JMMC has issued the Mount Etjo Declaration, which reiterates that the Tripartite Accord is still in effect and that South Africa, Angola, and Cuba remains committed to peace. It also orders all PLAN insurgents remaining in Ovamboland to surrender at UNTAG-supervised assembly points.

Sam Nujoma denies any incursion has taken place on 1st April, claiming that he has only ordered PLAN insurgents already inside South West Africa to begin establishing base camps. He also points out that SWAPO has never been a signatory to the Tripartite Accord, and therefore the cessation of hostilities as dictated by its terms is non-binding. This draws some ire from Angola, which has given guarantees to the UN that PLAN would remain north of the 16th parallel. The SADF is re-confined to its bases on 26th April 1989, then released into Ovamboland again to verify that the insurgents have departed. By May 1989, all PLAN insurgents have been relocated north of the 16th parallel under JMMC supervision, effectively ending the South African Border War.

Rescue Recognition

Being a Maritime Squadrons 30 and 22 are constantly helping the civil organizations with disaster preparedness, rescues, flood and drought, and many more actions. For this the Air Force is recognized and often awarded the freedom of the city. The next city that invites the Air Force is George in the Eastern Cape. The city has opened one of the Campsites for Air Force and families to spend the weekend after the freedom of the city parade. Steve has prepared and flown as FE on Puma 145 for a fly-past on the day.

The two Pumas depart AFB Ysterplaat midmorning on the 2nd April 1989 enroute to George. The parade and fly-past are perfect, and the crowd applauds accordingly. After the fly-past Alan Reynolds lands close to the camp site and the crew enjoys some snacks with the parade members. The co-pilot is staying over so Alan and Steve will fly back to AFB Ysterplaat. Alan's daughter is accompanying them, so Steve offers up his seat and takes the co-pilot position.

Freedom of the City, George

The flight is uneventful until Alan's daughter starts looking very green around the gills. Without warning she barfs all over the radio panel in front of her. Alan is embarrassed as he will now have to clean up the aircraft after landing. The smell fortunately is not that bad, and the rest of the flight goes by smoothly. At base Steve gets the Clarktor to tow the aircraft and with the ground crew positions the aircraft at the wash bay. Alan gets a bucket with water and cleans up as best as he can. Steve completes his servicing on the Puma and helps the ground crew with stowing the aircraft in the hangar.

On the 4th April 1989 Steve accompanies Neil Wallace to Atlas Aircraft corporation to complete the test flight of the now repaired ZS-HJA, after the mishap in Antarctica. The test flight is completed with minor issues requiring attention. Once Steve has given the aircraft a full panel off inspection to confirm that all is in order, he accepts the aircraft and Neil prepares the navigation for the return flight to Cape Town. They will be leaving early in the morning and with the extra fuel the J-Model carries, they will only need to refuel once along the way. After take-off from Atlas they head along the route as planned and are handed over to Johannesburg Information. They are flying over the Witwatersrand area when suddenly the intercom system goes down. Manus, the co-pilot on the trip tries the radios but to no avail. Steve indicates to Neil that they should land so that he can check the system. Just then he remembers that the J-Model has communications circuit fuses in the cockpit, unlike the military Pumas that have these tucked away in the nose. Steve pulls the fuse and sees that it has blown. There are no spare fuses available, so he creates a quick fix. In his toolkit he always carries some copper locking wire. He wraps a single strand around the glass fuse and pops it back in position. Communications are re-established, and the flight continues uneventfully to AFB Ysterplaat. The flight takes seven hours to complete and an exhausted crew lands early evening at the base.

The next few weeks of squadron life are full of Test Flights, Training and VHF homing trials. In between all the Training and Test Flights, Steve manages to get a sortie of NVG training one evening to keep his skills honed should they be required.

Sinking Ship

Back at home the signs of spring are starting to appear. Zella and Nicole are both happy to sea Steve back again and the little family settles in to catch up on the last experience that he has just returned from. Steve has just turned 31 years of age a couple of weeks ago and has settled back into Squadron life and keeps building on his experience on the Puma, an aircraft he is enjoying immensely. Steve has just got back into the swing of military flying once more while sitting back at home the evening, relaxing and catching up with the family when he gets a call from the Ops Officer at AFB Ysterplaat.

As normal the Cape of Storms does not disappoint, and it is just after supper on the 31st May 1989 when a call out is activated for a night rescue of sailors from a ship that hit the rocks and is sinking. Steve grabs his gear and races to the squadron to prepare the aircraft for an NVG flight. Des Weller Blaber and Gary Hamilton are once again crewed with Steve as the NVG rescue team.

The weather is marginal and with heavy clouds, rain and wind the crew get airborne from Ysterplaat enroute to Cape Hangklip, where the rescue was to be attempted. At the Squadron Des informs Steve of the situation. A Taiwanese fishing trawler has run aground near Cape Hangklip and due to rough seas, they cannot get off the ship. The call out is to rescue the crew before the ship sinks.

Steve hurries to prepare the aircraft. He is using Puma 147 this evening and must therefore fit a sea tray, hoist, strops and rescue equipment into the aircraft. Additionally, he will have to install the NVG Panel and UV Lights, which enables safe operation of the Night Vision Goggles in the cockpit.

At 20:30 the evening Des lifts the Puma into the air. With clearance from AFB Ysterplaat they route directly past DF Malan International enroute to Cape Hangklip. The weather is not the best and as soon as DF Malan clears them to Cape Town Information, Des calls for NVG patter, as there are insufficient navigation aids to assist them in the flight. Steve gets on the panel and starts pattering, while Gary sets the navigation and follows the map.

Both pilots are on NVG's with Steve managing the cockpit. It is a quick forty-minute flight to the ship. Upon arrival the crew assesses the situation and contacts the local NSRI by VHF. The decision is made to proceed with hoisting the crew off and dropping them at the NSRI station, where they will be taken to the local hospital for medical attention.

Des elects to play the safe route and follows the coast line which provides more horizon than attempting to cut across the Cape Flats through the rain, wind and clouds. It is a tense flight to the stranded ship and as they arrive they can clearly see that the ship is doomed and is already listing badly from the damage incurred by the rocks. Gary makes comms with the ship and informs the Captain that they will be hoisting the crew aboard the aircraft.

Steve wastes no time in preparing the aircraft for hoisting. With Gary off NVG's and now monitoring the cockpit, Steve dons his NVG's, opens the right hand sliding door and has already selected the hoist switch. He leans out of the aircraft and patters Des over the ship to the most accessible spot for hoisting the crew off. Fortunately, the ship's Captain has the foresight to gather the entire crew at the foredeck where there are very little obstacles.

The ship is heaving and rolling heavily on the rocks, and Steve must time his reeling out of the hoist accurately while pattering Des in position. Steve has elected to use a double hoist, as they have enough power to lift two persons easily per hoist.

The NVG's Steve are wearing give him the ability to ensure that the hoist cable does not get entangled in the ships gear and antenna. In a short while the strops are on deck and the first two ships crew are secured and hoisted back up to the hovering Puma.

Steve grabs the center of the cable between the strops as the two crewmen reach the aircraft and swings them both into the aircraft while he unceremoniously releases the hoist to dump them in the cabin. Steve quickly unhooks them and then lets the hoist back out to pick up the next two crew.

In what seems like an hour Steve manages to hoist all the crew safely onboard while Des fights the weather to keep the aircraft steady and in position. The entire hoist has only taken 15 minutes. The Puma is heavy with all the rescued crew onboard and Des struggling to hold station. The last two ships crews are secure and Steve clears Des to forward flight, allowing the Puma to stabilize once more.

It is a short flight to the National Sea Rescue Institute (NSRI) Station where they land and shut down to offload their PAX. The Taiwanese crews are soaked and cold but thankful and happily praising the savior's that recued them. The Puma Crew grabs a cup of hot coffee and then head back to the aircraft for the return flight to AFB Ysterplaat.

It is early morning when they land back at base. Steve makes quick work of getting the aircraft refueled and back into the hangar. Des and Gary complete the paperwork while Steve finishes off the After-Flight Servicing and removes the NVG Panel.

With the aircraft ready for the next day, Steve helps the ground crew lock up and he sets heading for home. The family long-time asleep.

Combining Operations

For the month of June 1989 Steve is very active at the squadron and is flying most days. With the introduction of the NVG qualification at 30 Squadron, it has become essential that ship borne operations be adapted to include this type of flying which will give the maritime force an additional night time capability.

In preparation for this Steve is included in the Radar Controlled Approach sorties that are normally flown for ship borne operations. The purpose is to combine the NVG skill with the Ship Controlled Operations.

Vertical Replenishment at Sea (VERTREP's) include Cargo Sling and Hoisting work where the NVG operations will be key in giving the crew nighttime capabilities under low light conditions.

Utilizing the SAS Tafelberg Steve deploys in Puma 145 with Des and Gary to perform the additional skills onboard. The addition of NVG's gives the Puma the ability of not requiring any additional lighting for operations, meaning that the mother ship can be dark and remain undetected in enemy territory.

It does not take long before the crew masters operating with NVG's from the ship and after four days of deployment, they return to AFB Ysterplaat. The next generation of maritime capabilities initiated and giving the Navy an additional weapon in their arsenal.

Nicole is growing up quickly and has already developed a Taurus personality mirroring her father. Very defiant and determined she tackles anything and everything. Her first year at school Nicole tackles with vigor and soon has several friends.

Zella on the other hand seems happy with her friends and work colleagues and brushes off Steve's affections. They are now constantly bickering at each other and Steve is finding it very difficult to maintain and even keel. It is with a heavy heart but a mechanism of escape that Steve packs his kit for his next stint on the border.

It is the 10th July 1989 when Steve steps off the C130 Hercules at AFB Rundu. This will be his last tour of duty in SWA. He clears in at the duty room and then makes his way to the hangar to look over aircraft he will be flying for the tour. The first aircraft he will be using is Puma 185, a newer L Model.

The aircraft is clean and well maintained, so Steve verifies that the Technical Records are up to date and accurate. That night at the pub Steve meets up with the rest of the crews and recognizes Fanie Jordaan, the permanent pilot at Rundu, from AFB Bloemspruit when Fanie had completed Chopper conversion. They chat, and Steve discovers that Fanie will be joining him at 30 Squadron at the completion of his stint as Permanent Pilot at Rundu.

In the next few weeks the flying is much more relaxing as the tasking is in support of the UNTAG troops to ensure that the SWA election process is being affected correctly. As there are still SWAPO and PLAN soldiers that have not been briefed on the status of the operations, there are skirmishes resulting in casualties.

The odd trooping sortie is still carried out to counter terrorist activities. Mostly Casevac sorties are flown for sick local population and the odd injured soldier. The other sorties now involve registration of the population for the upcoming elections.

On the 27th July Steve in Puma 159 is flying with Major Carstens as the Commander for a VIP sortie. The diplomats are United Nations representatives monitoring the election registration process. It is a beautiful day and the scenic flights around the Caprivi Strip are a reminder of the beauty of Africa.

They follow the beautiful Okavango River to the election registration points

Caprivi Strip SWA

Back at base Steve completes the after-flight service, refuels the aircraft and covers it up for the night. The Pumas are always left on the flight line for potential Casevac call outs at night.

It is the 5th August and Steve is into his last week of tour when once again they are scrambled for a Casevac. The Casualty is a very thankful local population with a very bad case of malaria that would require hospitalization. The trip goes off smoothly and they are back at base before the pub closes for the evening. The doctor that was on the Casevac however requests that the aircrew report to the sickbay for a checkup as there have been reports of viruses being carried over from the local population. Steve first finishes up in the hangar and then jogs down to sickbay. The doctor is already waiting for him and instructs Steve to bare his butt for an injection. Steve shrugs and drops his flight suite for the stab. The doctor and medics are grinning and giggling but Steve laughs it off as it is obvious that they have started partying already. Steve makes a beeline to the pub and orders his first round. He is still busy finishing off his drink when he is overcome with stomach cramps. The penny drops, and he realizes that the doctor had caught him with an injection of laxative. Steve does not make it to the showers in time and must wash his flight suite and himself. The shitting takes a couple of hours to wear off, but Steve reports the incident to Ops, as he could have been on a Casevac callout and in his current condition that would be dangerous. The medical staff are duly punished for their thoughtless joke.

The next two days there are very short training and test flight sorties, giving Steve enough time to prepare his aircraft for handover to the next F/E. On the 8th August he clears out from AFB Rundu and boards the C130 Hercules back to the States. At AFB Waterkloof he will catch the last flight down to AFB Ysterplaat and get home the afternoon of the 9th August. Steve has now completed his last bush tour and is preparing the next chapter in his life. On the 28th August he starts his final studies to qualify for the Engineering Diploma. The next four months will be the accumulation of many years of studying. With this qualification he can start planning his next career as the war has ended and there is a political change on the horizon leaving doubt over a secured future.

Back at home Steve smells that Zella has once again been smoking while he has been on tour. He does not mention anything but is a bit alarmed when Nicole starts chatting about Mommy's new friends. Zella had mentioned a gay couple in the past but did not elaborate, just that they were friends with one of Zella's mates. Steve had met her mate whose children went to school with Nicole. Sharon and Jimmy had been over for a braai at their house a couple of times. Steve knuckles down and completes the final examination with all the subjects required to qualify as an Engineer. He has accumulated six subjects from National Technical Certificate (NTC) 4 through 6, with 3 subjects following through the qualification criteria. He has now obtained a total of 12 courses, the minimum to obtain and Engineering Diploma. Having completed NTC 6, all he needs to do now is apply for the Engineering Diploma to the National Administration House of Assembly.

Chapter 16 - POLITICAL CHANGES

Zella goes out occasionally with the dental group and is enjoying their company. Steve is concerned but while struggling with his own demons and keeping his temper in check he does not want to create a hornet's nest unless there was sufficient reason for it. Steve's brain is working overtime processing a million events, but his thoughts keep coming back to what's wrong with his marriage. He remembers back several years when one of his friends at 22 Squadron had dropped a hint that one of the F/E's from the squadron had been visiting Zella while he was on tour. At the time he brushed it off as he was certain that Zella would not allow such approaches. Now he was not so sure anymore. He decides to question Zella on the event to test the waters. Zella just brushes it off and says that all he wanted was a kiss. Steve is alarmed but is uncertain as how to proceed from here as his first instinct is to throw a tantrum. Steve calms down and retires to the garage where he is in the process of rebuilding a 1960 Rover 100 sedan.

Maritime Operations

For the next few months Steve focuses on the squadron flying and completes all available sorties that he can to keep him busy and his mind off his confused brain. He has this urge to be constantly operational and out there doing the impossible. He volunteers for every operation, sortie and stand-by. With emotions playing havoc on his stability there is a feeling of starting to lose control.

By December and Christmas drawing fast, Steve has calmed down sufficiently to manage daily life. As always family from up country utilize Cape Town as their favourite holiday resort where accommodation comes free at the Coetzee residence. This time its Zella's family with whom Steve has a strained relationship. Zella in the meantime has continued to act as if nothing is wrong.

It is a hot and dry December summer once again in the Cape Province and Steve volunteers for Fire Fighting standby. He is not disappointed as there are several fires roaring in the region and the squadron is activated almost daily to assist with fighting the fires. The one call-out is to Greyton where the family had hiked just recently.

Both Greyton and McGregor were on evacuation alert as the berg winds swept the fires quickly up and down the mountains. Steve is called out and with Puma 145 prepared they depart to the area. It is a 45-minute flight and as they top the mountain range to start descending a tremendous downdraft rips the Puma.

The negative G pulls the crew tight in their straps, and the Ground Crew with the fire bucket in the cabin are floating around as if there is no gravity. The next minute there is an almighty thump and whoosh as the downdraft kicks back and changes to positive G, with the opposite reaction. Pushed back in their seats the crew fights the forces while the cabin is a mess with falling crew and firefighting equipment.

Neil Reid, the commander is struggling to maintain altitude as the downdraft through the valley is pulling the Puma with it. A tense few minutes pass by with Steve diving into the cabin to check on the ground crew and firefighting equipment. All seem to be fine. As he rejoins the cockpit crew Neil is gaining control of the descent and manages to pull the Puma into a controlled flight path.

They land at Greyton on the rugby field where Steve immediately opens cowlings to check for buckling in the airframe due to the excessive "g" forces. He opens all the tailboom cowlings and checks all the rivets and Sheetmetal skin for any signs of stress, buckling, popped rivets and obvious damage. Fortunately, the Puma is a strong aircraft and took the bump in her stride.

Neil in the meantime, has contacted Silvermine on the HF to warn the next aircraft of the flight conditions and advises that a route from the coast would be safer. Steve assembles the fire bucket and tests the system to ensure the valve operates affectively.

Soon after the next aircraft arrives. The crews brief with the fire controller of the day and set out to start fighting the fire. The Pumas will utilize any open water to fill the fie buckets that is closest to the fire line that they must dowse. With the Fire Chief controlling the firefighting effort both aircraft get airborne and set heading to the are as directed. On route the both drop down to a lake closest to the fire and fill the buckets ready to be guided to the most threatening part of the blaze.

The Fire Chief must ensure that the fire is dowsed in an area where the fire fighters have immediate access so that the remaining embers can be tackled to prevent flareups after the Pumas drop their loads. Wind direction, fire direction and flight safety must be considered. The fire must be approached from the downwind side and drop to ensure that the wind will carry the drop over the flames.

Firefighting Puma

It is a hard and long day of firefighting, and fortunately the squadron has deployed a refueling bowser to Greyton the day before, so the choppers can refuel continuously and ensure that control of the fire can be maintained. By late afternoon the Fire Chief spots a fire jump across the ravine which has started up the opposite mountain and is racing up the cliffs. The fire will have to be tackled with the choppers alone, as the area is totally inaccessible to the fire fighters. With the winds and heavy load of the fie bucket it is a dangerous maneuver for the pilots. Once committed they will have no choice but to fly directly at the fire and cliff. Should the fire bucket mechanism fail there is very little room to maneuver the aircraft away from the cliff. Neil directs the heavy Puma to the fire and at the last moment calls to Steve to drop. Steve laying on his stomach and monitoring the drop through the cargo sling hatch opens the pneumatic valve and sees the spray of water hit the flames while Neil immediately adds power allowing the now lighter Puma to climb up and away from the cliff. Another 5 drops and the fire's quenched. The adrenalin of the day's work has had its effect on the crews, and it's an exhausted bunch that land back at Greyton to close for the night. After a quick meal at the hotel and a few beers the crews retire to their respective rooms to rest in preparation for the next day's fight.

Early morning Steve grabs a quick breakfast and makes his way down to the rugby field to get the Puma ready for the day's work. He has just completed the before flight and signed up the Travel Technical Log when the rest of the crew roll up. Everyone gathers round and Fire Chief briefs them on the day's activities. The fire remains mostly under control with a few flare ups that will threaten the towns if not addressed. Within 20 minutes the aircraft are airborne and attacking the fire once again. At the first refuel of the day, Steve grabs a bite to eat as they do not anticipate having much break during the rest of the day.

The fire is still raging in areas where the fire fighters cannot access and therefore the choppers need to focus continuous water bombing on these areas and positively ensure that there are no flare ups. By late afternoon the Fire Chief calls the choppers off and they land back at the rugby field. The fire completely contained. After a debrief with the Fire Chief and confirmation that the choppers have done their bit, they get airborne for AFB Ysterplaat. It is an exhausted group of aviators that arrive back at base early the evening. The Squadron Technical Officer has instructed the crews to go home and rest and report at mid-morning the next day.

Steve arrives home after 21:00 the evening and Nicole has already gone to sleep. He is still chatting to Zella about the fire when Nicole peeps around the corner and screeches her happiness as she runs and hugs him around the neck. Steve must give a complete rundown to them from the beginning without leaving out any piece of juicy news. The moment he does Nicole will remind him that he has not mentioned this! and what about this? and who did that? Eventually Steve pleads exhaustion and convinces Nicole to go back to bed.

December 1989 comes and without warning January 1990 rolls around, with Nicole attending Primary School for the first time. Dressed in her uniform she proudly walks up to the school entrance calmly informing Zella that she does not need to accompany her to the hall. Zella must then inform her that she must be accompanied so that the teacher can meet the parents.

"Oh ok, that's fine then," says Nicole. While she happily waves to her friends already at the entrance.

Resignation of Power

Steve is monitoring the latest political changes that are in process with the effects these will have on the country. The development of the country has progressed so far, even with 25 years of western embargos. Steve keeps mulling over what changes are going to do with the proposed moves in removal of "apartheid". The Black population are Tribal and don't work well together as a race. Unrest is easily provoked, and inter-tribal disputes remain common and dangerous. With the ending of the cold war and loss of communistic threat, South Africa was just another pawn for the West to move around the board. Trying times ahead are going to affect the country in many ways.

State President Botha's loss of influence can be directly attributed to decisions taken at the Ronald Reagan / Mikhail Gorbachev summit of the leaders of the US and the Soviet Union in Moscow during 29th May to 1st June 1988, that paved the way to resolving the problem of Namibia which, according to foreign minister Pik Botha, was destabilizing the region and "seriously complicating" the major issue which South Africa itself would shortly have to face. Soviet military aid would cease, and Cuban troops be withdrawn from Angola as soon as South Africa complied with UN Security Council Resolution 435 (UNSCR 435) by relinquishing control of Namibia and allowing UN-supervised elections there. The Tripartite Agreement, which gave effect to the Reagan/Gorbachev summit decisions, was signed at UN headquarters in New York on 22 December 1988 by representatives of Angola, Cuba and South Africa.

On 18 January 1989, Botha suffers a mild stroke which prevents him from attending a meeting with Namibian political leaders on 20th January 1989. Botha's place is taken by acting president, J. Christiaan Heunis. On 2nd February 1989, Botha resigns as leader of the National Party (NP) anticipating his nominee finance minister Barend du Plessis would succeed him. Instead, the NP's parliamentary caucus selects as leader education minister F. W. de Klerk, who moves quickly to consolidate his position within the party. In March 1989, the NP elect De Klerk as state president, but Botha refuses to resign, saying in a television address that the constitution entitled him to remain in office until March 1990 and that he is even considering running for another five-year term. Following a series of acrimonious meetings in Cape Town, and five days after UNSCR 435 is implemented in Namibia on 1st April 1989, Botha and De Klerk reach a compromise. Botha will retire after the parliamentary elections in September, allowing de Klerk to take over as president.

Botha resigns from the state presidency abruptly on 14th August 1989 complaining that he has not been consulted by De Klerk over his scheduled visit to see president Kenneth Kaunda of Zambia.

"The ANC is enjoying the protection of president Kaunda and is planning insurgency activities against South Africa from Lusaka", Botha declares on nationwide television. He states that he has asked the cabinet what reason he should give the public for abruptly leaving office. "They replied, I could use my health as an excuse. To this, I replied that I am not prepared to leave on a lie. It is evident to me that after all these years of my best efforts for the National Party and for the government of this country, as well as the security of our country, I am being ignored by ministers serving in my cabinet."

De Klerk is sworn in as acting state president on 14th August 1989 and the following month was nominated by the electoral college to succeed Botha in a five-year term as state president.

The new Political era

After De Klerk becomes acting president, the ANC leaders speaks out against him, believing that he would be no different from his predecessors, he still is widely regarded as a staunch supporter of apartheid.

The Arch Bishop Desmond Tutu shares this assessment, stating. "I don't think we've got to even begin to pretend that there is any reason for thinking that we are entering a new phase. It's just musical chairs".

Tutu and Allan Boesak have been planning a protest march in Cape Town, which the security chiefs want to prevent. De Klerk nevertheless turns down their proposal to ban it, agreeing to let the march proceed and stating that, "The door to a new South Africa is open, it is not necessary to batter it down".

The march takes place and is attended by approximately 30,000 people. Further protest marches follow in Grahamstown, Johannesburg, Pretoria, and Durban.

De Klerk later notes that his security forces could not have prevented the marchers from gathering. "The choice, therefore, was between breaking up an illegal march with all of the attendant risks of violence and negative publicity, or of allowing the march to continue, subject to conditions that could help to avoid violence and ensure good public order." This decision marks a clear departure from the approach of the Botha era.

As President, De Klerk authorizes the continuation of secret talks in Geneva between his National Intelligence Service and two exiled ANC leaders, Thabo Mbeki and Jacob Zuma. In October, he personally agrees to meet with Tutu, Boesak, and Frank Chikane in a private meeting in Pretoria. He also releases several elderly anti-apartheid activists then imprisoned, including Walter Sisulu. He orders the closure of the National Security Management System. In December he visits Mandela in prison, speaking with him for three hours about the idea of transitioning away from white-minority rule. The collapse of the Eastern Bloc and the dissolution of the Soviet Union meant that he no longer feared that Marxists would manipulate the ANC.

As he later relates, the collapse of "the Marxist economic system in Eastern Europe serves as a warning to those who insist on persisting with it in Africa. Those who seek to force this failure of a system on South Africa should engage in a total revision of their point of view. It should be clear to all that it is not the answer here either."

He further quotes: "History has placed a tremendous responsibility on the shoulders of this country's leadership, namely the responsibility of moving our country away from the current course of conflict and confrontation. The hope of millions of South Africans is fixed on us. The future of southern Africa depends on us. We dare not waver or fail."

Political events that change the country 1990

20th January – Thomas Mandlenkosi (Mshengu) Shabalala, an Inkatha Freedom Party National Council member, is shot dead outside his house in Lindelani's C Section, also known as eMadamini, near KwaMashu, Durban.

2nd February – State President F.W. de Klerk announces the beginning of the negotiated transition to end apartheid, the unbanning of the African National Congress, Pan Africanist Congress and Communist Party, the release of Nelson Mandela and other political prisoners, and the end of the state of emergency.

3rd February – Rainbow People's March, a small group of demonstrators, express support for the new South Africa by dancing down Adderley Street with a painting by artist Beezy Bailey.

11th February – Nelson Mandela is released from prison after serving 27 years.

4th March – Brigadier Oupa Gqozo of the Ciskei Defense Force leads a coup in Ciskei.

12th March – African National Congress president Oliver Tambo and vice-president Nelson Mandela meet for the first time in 28 years in Sweden.

21st March – Namibia gains independence with the United Nations supervising the withdrawal of South African forces and the first elections.

26th March – The Minister of Education, Piet Claase, announces that as of January 1991, the segregation of Whites and Blacks in state-run schools will end.

26th March – Eleven people are killed and more than 300 injured when police open fire on protesters in Sebokeng.

1st April – South African Transport Services become Transnet and the South African Rail Commuter Corporation, with Spoornet and Metrorail as respective railway operators.

16th April – Nelson Mandela thanks the world in the Wembley Stadium, London, for support during his imprisonment.

25th April – Dirk Coetzee, former South African Police Commander of the Vlakplaas counter-insurgency unit, testifies at the Harms commission.

28th April – Michael Lapsley, an Anglican priest and social activist, loses both his hands and an eye when a letter bomb explodes in his hands.

1st May – Jackie Matjili, Umkhonto we Sizwe member, is shot dead in Thokoza.

2nd to 4th May – The Groote Schuur Minute is signed after talks between the South African government and the African National Congress in Groote Schuur, Cape Town.

6th May – P.W. Botha resigns from the National Party in protest against State President F.W de Klerk's reform proposals.

4th June – Nelson Mandela starts a thirteen-nation international tour.

5th June – Colonel Gabriel Ramushwana, Chairman of the Venda Council for National Unity, announces the lifting of the state of emergency and the unconditional release of all political prisoners in Venda.

7th June – State President F.W. de Klerk lifts the state of emergency in South Africa that has been in place for ten years.

13th June – Sipho Phungulwa, one of a group of exiles who were held in African National Congress detention camps in Angola, is shot dead in Umtata while trying to seek an audience with the Transkei ANC leadership to expose the hardships they had endured in Angola. Ndibulele Ndzamela, Mfanelo Matshaya and Pumlani Kubukeli will be granted amnesty on 13 August 1998 in connection with this incident.

14th July – The Inkatha Freedom Party is formed when it is transformed from the Inkatha National Cultural Liberation Movement.

1st August – The African National Congress's armed wing, Umkhonto we Sizwe, suspends its armed actions after 29 years.

6th August – The Pretoria Minute is signed after talks between the South African government and the African National Congress in Pretoria.

12th August – Fighting breaks out between the Xhosa people and the Zulu people and more than 500 are killed by the end of August.

11th September – Seven political prisoners are released.

23rd to 25th September – State President F.W. de Klerk visits Washington on a state visit.

27th September – Fourteen political prisoners are released

October

15th October – The Reservation of Separate Amenities Act is repealed, ending racial segregation of public facilities.

19th October – The National Party opens its membership to all races.

4th November – South Africa announces that Harry Schwarz, a prominent anti-apartheid campaigner in Parliament, will be its next ambassador to the United States, the first serving politician from opposition ranks to be appointed to a senior ambassadorial post in South African history.

14th to 16th December – The African National Congress holds a national consultative conference in Johannesburg. George Bizos becomes a member of the African National Congress's Legal and Constitutional Committee.

Politics and a wave of Change

On 2nd February 1990, in an address to the country's parliament, President De Klerk introduces plans for sweeping reforms of the political system. A number of banned political parties, including the ANC and Communist Party of South Africa, would be legalized, although he emphasizes that this does not constitute an endorsement of their socialist economic policies nor of violent actions carried out by their members, and the Separate Amenities Act of 1953, which governs the segregation of public facilities, would be lifted and all of those who were imprisoned solely for belonging to a banned organization would be freed, including Nelson Mandela; the latter is released a week later. The vision set forth in de Klerk's address is for South Africa to become a Western-style liberal democracy; with a market-oriented economy which values private enterprise and restricts the government's role in economics.

De Klerk later relates, "that speech was mainly aimed at breaking our stalemate in Africa and the West. Internationally we were teetering on the edge of the abyss."

Throughout South Africa and across the world, there is astonishment at de Klerk's move. Foreign press coverage is largely positive, and de Klerk receives messages of support from other governments.

Tutu said that "It's incredible. Give him credit. Give him credit, I do."

Some black radicals regard it as a gimmick and that it would prove to be without substance. It is also received negatively by some on the white right-wing, including in the Conservative Party, who believe that de Klerk is betraying the white population. De Klerk believes that the sudden growth of the Conservatives and other white right-wing groups is a passing phase reflecting anxiety and insecurity. These white right-wing groups are aware that they would not get what they wanted through the forthcoming negotiations, and so increasingly try to derail the negotiations using revolutionary violence. The white-dominated liberal Democratic Party finds itself in limbo, as de Klerk embraces much of the platform it has espoused, leaving it without a clear purpose.

Further reforms follow, membership of the National Party is opened to non-whites. In June, parliament approves new legislation that repeals the Natives Land Act, 1913 and Native Trust and Land Act, 1936. The Population Registration Act, which established the racial classificatory guidelines for South Africa, is rescinded.

In legislative terms, he enables the gradual end of apartheid. De Klerk also opens the way for the negotiations of the government with the anti-apartheid-opposition about a new constitution for the country. Nevertheless, he is accused by Anthony Sampson of complicity in the violence among the ANC, the Inkatha Freedom Party and elements of the security forces.

Negotiations toward universal suffrage

De Klerk further states. "I believe the new political order will and must contain the following elements, a democratic constitution, universal suffrage, no domination, equality before an independent judiciary, the protection of minorities and individual rights, freedom of religion, a healthy economy based on proven economic principles and private initiative, and a dynamic programme for better education, health services, housing and social conditions for all... I am not talking of a rosy and tranquil future, but I believe the broad mainstream of South Africans will gradually build up South Africa into a society that will be worth living and working in."

His presidency is dominated by the negotiation process, mainly between his NP government and the ANC, which leads to the democratization of South Africa. Throughout the negotiations, de Klerk primarily attempts to prevent majority rule to preserve power for the white South African minority. His efforts, however, are thwarted when the Boipatong massacre causes a resurgence of international pressure against South Africa, leading to a weaker position at the negotiation tables for the National party.

Steve is getting concerned that all the efforts of the Settlers is coming to naught. While fighting his own demons he still must contend with why suddenly, the defenders of the country are now becoming ear marked as the destroyers. Like all the war hungry soldiers that have now been kept at bay, Steve struggles with his demons which he was able to feed on every contact, when the adrenalin flow kept him under control.

Professional soldiers and military hardware

In 1989, following the conclusion of South African Border Wars in Angola and Namibia, the apartheid regime in South Africa was beginning to dissolve. The South African Defense Force was looking at broad cuts in its personnel. The ANC leader Nelson Mandela demanded that then South African President Frederik Willem de Klerk dismantle some of the South African and South-West African Special Forces units such as 32 Battalion and Koevoet. One of these was the Civil Cooperation Bureau (CCB), a unit that carried out covert operations which included assassinations of government opponents and worked to bypass the United Nations apartheid sanctions by setting up overseas front companies.

Only Koevoet being part of the South West African Police (SWAPOL) was disbanded as part of independence negotiations for South-West Africa. Many members of the other units, or simply former national servicemen, are recruited by Executive Outcomes.

Eeben Barlow and Michael Mullen an Irishman from Dublin, formerly in charge of the Western European section of the CCB establish Executive Outcomes in 1989. Its aim is to provide specialized covert training to Special Forces members. Barlow is also awarded a contract by Debswana to train a selected group of security officers to infiltrate and penetrate the illegal diamond dealing syndicates in Botswana. When Debswana discovers Executive Outcomes is training the Angolan Armed Forces (FAA), it promptly cancels the contract.

The company also recruits many of its personnel from the units President F. W. De Klerk disbanded. At its peak, Executive Outcomes employs about 2,000 former soldiers. Barlow registers Executive Outcomes Ltd in the UK on the insistence of the South African Reserve Bank. Apart from founder Eeben Barlow (CEO), other senior Executive Outcomes personnel are Lafras Luitingh and Nic van der Bergh. Senior associates included Simon Mann and Tony Buckingham, who, along with

Barlow and Luitingh are the executive officers of Ibis Air, the aircraft procurement organization for Executive Outcomes which was essentially their private "air force". Pilot Crause Steyl is the South African-based director of Ibis Air.

Executive Outcomes is directly involved militarily in Angola and Sierra Leone. The company is notable in its ability to provide all aspects of a highly trained modern army to the less professional government forces of Sierra Leone and Angola. For instance, in Sierra Leone, Executive Outcomes fields not only professional fighting men, but armour and support aircraft such as one Mi-24 Hind and two Mi-8 Hip helicopters, the BMP-2 infantry fighting vehicle and T-72 main battle tank. It also possesses medevac capabilities to airlift the wounded out of combat zones via Boeing 727 D2-FLZ owned by Ibis Air. These are bought from sources in the worldwide arms trade within Africa as well as Eastern Europe.

The aircraft are owned and operated by a separate partner company called Ibis Air which also owns MiG-23 "Flogger" fighters and a small fleet of Pilatus PC-7 turbo-prop trainers converted for the recce and ground attack role (with the capability to fire SNEB air-to-ground rockets). Ibis Air also has the connections to operate MiG-27 "Flogger" strike aircraft and Su-25 "Frogfoot" close support aircraft for Executive Outcomes that are loaned out via the Angolan Air Force. Executive Outcomes has contracts with multinational corporations such as De Beers, Chevron, Rio Tinto Zinc and Texaco. The governments of Angola, Sierra Leone, and Indonesia are also clients.

Post war wind down

For the remainder of the hot and dry summer season there are many call outs for fire-fighting and Steve is kept busy almost every second weekend. The days melt into weeks which then melt into months and Steve is kept busy with general squadron flying, training, deployments, call outs, mountain flying and the occasional sea trip for a few days at a time. All the while he is training the local F/E's on the NVG's and preparing them for official NVG course training at 19 Squadron in Pretoria. Autumn arrives with the cooler evenings and soon accompanied by the winter rainfall. All to soon Steve and Nicole have their birthdays, Steve is 33 and Nicole a whopping 6 years old. Steve has also received his Engineering Diploma and immediately applies for Officers Course. He wants to get this done so that he can apply for the Test Flight Engineers Course.

Steve and Hennie Steyn have been selected as the F/E's to attend the helicopter competition that will be held at AFB Bloemfontein in August. There is less than 3 months to prepare so Steve and Hennie knuckle down to identify tooling, spares and ground support equipment that will be required to meet the competitions qualification criteria. A minimum fly away kit must accompany the choppers to the competition. Steve and Hennie decide to select the best two Pumas for the competition and select the best fly away kits. They will then clean, calibrate, paint and label all items accordingly. Next Steve decides that the aircraft need a paint touch up. He gets the required paint and mixtures from the paint shop and with his own equipment, he and Hennie paint both aircraft after hours. This is required as there are no extraction fans in the hangar and they do not want to cause any problems with squadron personnel. The aircraft touch ups are complete over three nights, and Steve has even stenciled the crew names on each aircraft as well.

The 20th August 1990 arrives all to soon when Steve and Hennie together with their pilots and two ground crew, are ready to depart for Bloemfontein. The fly away kits are loaded into the aircraft together with all the items, kit, and personal items they will need for the competition. Each Puma also has two ferry tanks fitted so that the flight can be completed with only one refueling stop. The aircraft get airborne and head out toward Touwsrivier where they will land for a fuel top up and then straight onto Bloemfontein. At Touwsrivier Steve and Hennie make quick work of refueling the aircraft. Pre-start checkups are completed and Steve cranks up the Pumas engine. After he starts number 2 engine, the second Puma radios that they have a starting problem. Steve jumps out of his seat and runs over to help Hennie with the snag. The problem is quickly rectified as Steve pulls out his "Gippo Clips" and bridges the T5 Relay of the Mobile Block, circumventing the electronic cycle. All to soon the sweet high-pitched sound of the engine firing is heard and Steve unclips his "Gippo Clips" and heads back to his own aircraft. Both aircraft take-off and set heading towards Bloemfontein.

The next four days are going to be strenuous with various competition items in ground support, flying exercises, and dress code being judged. The ground crew maintain the support equipment and must ensure that all activities are performed in accordance with Squadron Special Operating Procedures.

The competition starts in true military style with an opening parade and address by Senior Air Force Staff Officers. The competition is divided into various categories namely, precision hovering in Cargo Slinging and Hoisting. During these exercises the hoist and cargo sling loads must be maneuvered through obstacles and placed in a marked target area. These exercises require team work and coordination between F/E and Pilot.

While the flying exercises are being conducted the ground crew with support equipment are under constant scrutinization by the judges as well. All the SAAF helicopter squadrons are participating in the event with a huge diversification of aircraft including Westland Wasp, Aerospatiale Alouette, Puma, and Super Frelon. At the end of day one all participants report to the briefing area where the scores for the day are displayed. 30 Squadron is up there with a fighting chance in the flying category, so Steve and Hennie are pleased at the outcome.

The next day is initiated with a short navigation exercise. To test the skills of the crews, all navigational aids have been removed from the aircraft. Before each aircraft can depart a judge verifies that there are no navigation aids on board and clears them for the exercise. With so many aircraft, the exercise lasts until late in the afternoon. 30 Squadron has done acceptably but there is a concern over the accuracy on time flown versus planning flight time submitted for judging.

The final day of the competition is a long navigation exercise with the same rules as the day before. There are various routes, so the exercise is completed by midday. The scores tallied up and all crews are summoned to the briefing area. The Maritime squadrons have done well with 22 Squadron in the Wasps coming in first with the flying part of the competition. 30 Squadron wins the ground support side of the competition. Although disappoint in the flying side, Steve and Hennie are proud to be able to bring home the trophy for the hard work they put in preparing the ground support and aircraft.

Early morning 24th August both Pumas are packed and depart for Cape Town with their trophy on board. The four-hour flight back to AFB Ysterplaat is uneventful and they arrive late afternoon to a jubilant crowd of congratulators. Steve and Hennie unload the aircraft and complete the applicable servicing's before packing up and leaving for home.

Zella has been invited to one of her work associates home for a Braai on the Saturday evening. Steve accepts, and they pack in some meat and beer and make their way over to Bothasig for the evening. Steve has only met Sharon at Zella's work but does not know her husband Doug. The evening goes off well until Zella has had a bit too much to drink and starts a round of sarcasm. Steve gets up and helps with the dishes and cleaning up. Zella and Doug are having a deep conversation while Sharon and Steve continue cleaning up. They talk freely as if having known each other for a long time. There is a sexual tension between them that excites and scares Steve at the same time. They join the other two in the lounge and the conversation turns to car engines. Doug and Sharon are both from Rhodesia and therefore are used to having to fix things themselves. Doug is attempting to repair Sharon's car which has blown a cylinder head gasket. Steve offers his assistance which Doug quickly accepts, and they set a date for the repair to start.

Steve is busy completing a servicing on a Puma at the squadron when he gets called for a phone call. Steve picks up the phone and is surprised to hear Sharon's voice on the other end. They chat and then she says that she volunteered to call after speaking to Doug as they would appreciate Steve's help with the car and if they could impose on starting it the coming weekend. Steve responds that he will pop over this evening with Zella and Nicole to assess what tools he needs and format a plan of action. They chat a bit more and Steve hears a sadness in her voice. He does not push but says goodbye and walks away wondering. His own marriage is on very rocky grounds and his current mental state is in turmoil. He feels very confused, but deep down he has this insatiable desire to be loved and cared for.

Early evening after supper the family drives over to Bothasig so that Steve can assess the repair requirements for Sharon's car. Doug and Steve immediately go to the garage where Doug has already removed the cars bonnet and started loosening hoses. Steve looks and is satisfied that he can get the cylinder head off in an hour after which they will need assess the damage before buying spare parts. Doug agrees, and they return to the house to finish off some beers that Doug offers. Steve, Zella and Nicole leave for home. On the way Zella is extra friendly but with a hint of sarcasm in her tone. Steve laughs it off and responds by sharing his plan to repair the car.

Its Friday and Steve's settling into the last sortie for the day and then he can wrap up the after-flight servicing and relax for lunch with a layback afternoon. The intercom announces a call for FSgt Coetzee at Tech Control. Steve walks over and picks up the phone and is once again surprised to hear Sharon's voice. She starts off by thanking him for helping to fix her car. Steve can hear that something is not right and offers an ear. She hesitantly starts talking about her strained marriage. Steve looks at the clock on the wall and sees he has enough time, so he offers to meet with her for a cup of coffee. Sharon giggles and jokingly says are you asking me out on a date? They laugh, and she proposes a coffee shop in Green Point.

Steve quickly changes and races down to the car. He reaches the coffee shop 15 minutes later and sure enough Sharon is there to meet him. They greet and sit down, chatting about this and that until Steve says that she must spill the beans. Doug is and Anesthetist and has a bit of an attitude which causes conflict in their relationship. Sharon informs Steve that Michael, her eldest is not Doug's child, but only Candice her youngest was. Steve gets the message and his heart goes out to her. They chat for a long time and then Steve excuses himself as he needs to finish up at the Squadron. On the way back to the base Steve mulls over the meeting he just had and questions himself. Why was he doing this? What was he thinking? There is danger which gets his adrenalin going and the excitement in his gut wants to find out more.

Early Saturday morning Steve, Zella and Nicole take the short ride to Sharon's place. Steve and Doug immediately start working on the car. Steve gets the cylinder head off and with a quick look tells Doug that they will have to pull the motor. The pistons and rings are worn. Without a hoist or tri-pod Steve quickly forms an alternate plan. He noticed a pole lying next to the garage and secures the engine round the pole now laying cross wise over the front end of the car. With Doug on one side and Steve on the other they physically hoist the engine out. Steve makes quick work of stripping the engine down. Fortunately, the piston rings have not damaged the cylinders, so they can just clean up the pistons, replace the rings and reinstall. Steve recommends that they replace the big end and main bearings at the same time. The cylinder head is another issue. There has been repairs done on the head and it has also be skimmed. It looks as if too much has been taken off resulting in the head not seating properly causing the gasket to blow. Steve recommends a quick fix which should last for a couple of years. They will install a double gasket that will take up the spacing required. While Steve cleans up the parts he sends Doug to the Spares Shop to get the required parts. An hour later Doug is back with the parts and Steve makes quick work of assembling the engine. Together they hoist it back into the car and reinstall all the fittings. It is early evening when Doug turns the key and the Renault 5 fires up. Steve does some fine tuning on the ignition timing and carburetor. He stands back satisfied and Doug grinning from ear to ear. The families heard the car fire up and come running to the garage to see the successful repair completed. Doug throws Steve a beer which he cracks, and they raise one for success and quickly down them. Sharon insists that they stay for a Braai. Steve asks if they mind him using the shower, as he is covered in grease and oil from fingertip to elbow and sweaty all over. Sharon shows him where the shower is and offers him a towel. Steve thanks her and she winks at him with a broad smile. The evening is pleasant, and Steve has one too many. His emotions are in turmoil and the warning signals are ringing in his ears.

The CIA and Africa

With the war in Angola at an end Steve's concerns about South Africa's future are constantly in his thoughts. Was the west going to turn on South Africa the same as has been done in Rhodesia? During his involvement in Angola there were constant reminders that the US has a large involvement in the Angolan conflict. The Central Intelligence Agency is the US's front for conflict creation so that the politicians would have the ability to demand action against threats. Angola was an opportunity for the Russians to seize control which would not be in the best interests of the US. Instead of supporting South Africa, who were committed to fighting Communism, the US once again backed the rebel forces.

The following sequence of events create a foundation of concern for Steve. In Angola the US Central Intelligence Agency was having problems with transparency following piqued Congressional interest in the Executive Branch. One of these Senate investigations focused on the clandestine activities of the Central Intelligence Agency in Angola called, "Operation Feature". The US Central Intelligence Agency remained divided in its planning phase, and some had advocated against intervention. When President Nixon approved the plans for "Operation Feature", Nathaniel Davis, the Assistance Secretary of State for African Affairs, resigned. He advocated the Soviet Union would recognize American interventionism, in Angola and react negatively on the world's stage.

John Stockwell, the CIA's Station Chief in Angola, expounded on the processes the CIA failed to engage in regarding Angola. There was never a study run that evaluated the MPLA, FNLA, and UNITA, the three movements in the country, to decide which one was the better one. Prados, author of, The President's Secret Wars, expanded on this lack of consensus. He notes that before Davis's resignation, "Operation Feature", had begun and that Stockwell's planning activities were playing catch up with a decision process in which he was a reactive afterthought. "Operation Feature went forward on a very high priority. The operation was so urgent, in fact, that, the first planeload of weapons was on its way to the FNLA, via Zaire, before Langley even formed its task force to manage the program. Two more loads had been sent aboard Air Force C-141 transports, while a shipload of supplies was being assembled." Millions of dollars had been forwarded to rebel forces in the country under Presidential authorization with an initial investment of $6 million followed by an additional $8 million in July of 1975.

Opposing American interests and responding to the intervention of Americans in the region, the MPLA had received training and arms from Fidel Castro's Cuba. This aid continued into the conflict surrounding the Civil War. The MPLA was the largest group and was based on the capital, Luanda and was led by Agostinho Neto. The MPLA included members of the intelligentsia, academic community of the country and was decidedly Marxist. The American-supported FNLA operated father north of Luanda, closer to the border with Zaire. Roberto, the anti-communist leader of the FNLA, with socialist leanings, had links with neighboring Zaire and operated across borders during Angola's struggle for independence from Portugal. UNITA, led by Savimbi, was based in the south of the capital.

Russia had taken an additional interest in the outcome of the conflict due to Cuba's political role with the MPLA. On October 02, 1975, South Africa entered the conflict on the side of UNITA which had been supporting the FNLA. When South Africa became involved further assistance from Cuba was sought by the MPLA and the brinkmanship perpetuated political violence.

The US efforts failed to achieve the desired results and unable to secure immediate and additional funds in a tactical situation from the US Congress; the CIA began recruiting efforts for a mercenary force. The FNLA appeared to be the losing side and in doing so required additional training and manpower. The CIA secured approximately 300 men for the mission. The CIA's advisors were hard at work on the ground with FNLA troops. This mercenary force committed atrocities against the Civilian populations of Angola.

The CIA went to the Committee with requests for $30 million, $60 million, and $100 million to continue operations. Congress had been informed of Operation Feature, and not wanting to get the US embroiled in another Vietnam, proposed in opposition, an amendment to the Arms Control Act. Called the Clarke Amendment, it became law in 1976. This amendment explicitly prohibited the sale of arms for military or paramilitary operations in Angola. When the Clarke Amendment passed, and direct American arms stopped going to Angola, the war continued. The CIA Director, George H.W. Bush, who took over after Bill Colby in 1976, would not deny that arms were going to Angola. Allegedly the CIA through an intermediary in Israel continued to sell weapons to Angola. The war continued for decades, tens of thousands died, and more were displaced as refugees over the conflict.

If seen through a political lens of Communism versus Americanism, as was a common attitude the victory of Soviet-Cuban backing of the MPLA was a win for the pro-communist government who not only beat out the Portuguese imperialists, but the Anglophile-friendly, Fabian-socialist-backed interests of the FNLA. A unique phenomenon of this modern development in the post-civil-war Angola is the building of a ghost city called Nova Cidade de Kilamba by a Chinese Development Corporation.

<u>Nova Cidade de Kimamba – Uninhabited Chinese built City</u>

Kimamba is a residential development of 750 eight-story apartment buildings, a dozen schools, and more than 100 retail units and is mostly uninhabited.

The fact the Civil War in Angola lasts several decades created an environment of destabilization that was advocated as an American interest. The US domestic success or failure of "Operation Feature" are the sentiments of the Executive Branch and Legislative branches of government who were opposed regarding these operations. The anti-war sentiment of the Congress was successful in limiting the funds to conduct clandestine operations, but the subversion of the law by the US Central Intelligence Agency in exploiting political relationships with Israel may be viewed as an executive success.

For Angolans, the decades of war devastated their nation's capital amidst the hopes and promise of liberty from the rule of the crown and provided in that destruction a chance to rebuild. Their lives were sacrificed in the tens of thousands for the interests of the Soviets and Americans who were fighting a proxy conflict with Angolan pawns. Hundreds of thousands were made refugee in a country that was rich in natural resources and gave rise to the concept of 'blood' or 'conflict' diamonds. An entire generation remained captivated by political violence and at the end of it all, like their oppressors, the people's liberators through cronyism and favors, invited the multi-nationals, took money from big banks, mostly lead by the Americans, back into their backyard to draw upon their rich natural resources of oil and diamonds. Corruption became rampant in Angola with billions missing from the National Treasury. After fueling the colonial enterprise of slavery as a world leader of such decadent subservience at the behest of their Portuguese, Dutch and English traders for hundreds of years, the Angolans found themselves serving the corporation.

With these facts Steve has doubts that South Africa will be able to withstand what he sees as the reversion back to African Tribalism, as the continent is currently rife with conflict and rebel wars that remain a spin off from the misinterpretations from the west. Steve is convinced that the west incorrectly believes that one can enter a tribal region, preach religion, build schools and provide infrastructure. Tribal folk the world over are happy with their lot and do not need another God or modern amenities. They have lived the way they were raised for thousands of years. The west in all its ignorance fails to see this and Steve is more convinced that this will be the downfall of Africa. Mineral rich Africa with its huge agricultural infrastructure will always remain the political draw card. Steve is convinced that this be no different in his beloved South Africa of whom he is the fifth generation of those who settled here from Europe.

Frozen Continent

In a few short months Steve will be on his way down to Antarctica once again. On this trip Steve will be joining Russell and Bles as the F/E's. Russell du Preez is the squadron's Chief F/E and a true gentleman, respected by all. Steve is looking forward to working with him. Bles Bezuidenhout has been placed in charge of the aircraft covers and safety gear, while Steve and Russell complete the Pack-up Kits for the ship. The two Puma J Models are also being readied for the trip and Steve has taken upon himself to calibrate the aircrafts torque meters and verify both aircrafts serviceability status for the 3 months that they will be tasked.

The ground crew on this trip will be Herbie Malan Radio Technician, Ollie Kratschmar Instrument Technician, JD van Zyl and Jopie van Wyk Aircraft Maintenance Engineers. Steve instructs the ground crew to check the pack-up kits and ensure that the spares and tool lists are still accurate and ensure that the components and parts have the required certification and serviceability documentation. The spare engines, main gearbox, main rotor blades and additional large items together with the pack-up bins must be loaded on the ship in the harbour. Steve asks Piet Brits to arrange a truck large enough for the task and gets the ground crew to accompany him on the mission. Russell, Steve and Bles complete the aircraft preparation. This trip they will be flying Ice Thickness Surveys with doppler equipment installed into the cabin while they have the antenna flying below. The GPS and Doppler equipment will be installed once they are stationed at Grunehogna.

Before long Steve has been to the DEA Stores with the rest of the crew to collect his clothing and kit for the Antarctic Climate. The time is getting short, so Steve makes the best of the time with the family before he must depart. Nicole has mixed emotions, excited yet sad at the same time. She now understands that dad will be away a long time and she is not looking forward to it. Zella is friendly but detached and shrugs off the trip that Steve is excited about. Steve is also in contact with Nellis and Charlie Tait who are continuing the war as private soldiers with Executive Outcomes. Steve has some tough decisions to make but puts these to the back of his mind as he focuses on the upcoming trip to the South Pole.

It is the 29th November 1990 but unlike the previous trip Zella is too busy to join Steve at the dock before the ship sails, so he greets her when he leaves for the base the morning. A huge hug and kiss from Nicole and plenty tears rip at Steve's heart strings and with teary eyes he leaves for the base.

Steve and the ground crew tow the two J Model Pumas onto the flight line for the departure and joining of the SA Agulhas still in Cape Town harbour. Major Gawie Venter and Major Sloet Louw are Steve's pilots in ZS-HIZ. Russell with Maj Tony Johnson and Captain JC Kriegler are flying ZS-HJA. At the last-minute Steve loses his fear and half in anger at Zella calls Sharon and asks her to meet him at the SA Agulhas on the dock. He will give her a guided tour of the ship.

Both Pumas start up and fly together over the city with HJA going in for the first landing on the ship. Gawie flies a circuit over the city to give the crew time to fold HJA's blades and stow the aircraft in the hangar. With HJA out of the way, Gawie completes the landing and Steve shuts down the aircraft. The crew makes quick work of preparing the aircraft for stowage.

Steve takes up his position on the aircraft gearbox platform to pull the pins for the blade folding. In short time the aircraft's blades are folded and stowed in the hangar. Steve grabs his gear and takes it down to the cabin he will share with Bles and Russell.

Steve races to the dock side and sees Sharon waiting for him. He motions her to join him and he takes her on a grand tour. They board the ship and Steve shows her around. He escourts her to the hangar and shows her how the helicopters have been secured.

Sharon turns to him and they kiss passionately. Steve's heart is racing and a million visions flash through his brain. What has he done? Does he deserve this, which is more than what he is getting? What must he do? He accompanies Sharon to her car where they kiss once more, and she drives off.

Later the afternoon the SA Agulhas sets sail for the deep south towards the frozen continent. The next few days will be once again acclimatization to get their sea legs for the chopper crews.

Steve has been allocated as one of King Neptune's Bears and has also prepared all the jumped-up charges for the new recruits at the "Crossing of the Line" ceremony that will take place once they cross the Antarctic Circle.

Steve is in utter turmoil, and he attempts to bury what has happened in the last few weeks. He has a lot of thinking to do for the next four months. There won't be any contact with South Africa, so he will have to make up his own mind as to what must be done.

Tug of War

The ship has introduced several activities to prevent mischievousness during the voyage, of which the "Tug of War" is one. A rope is fed through two pulleys at the far end of the Heli-Deck with the two teams pulling against each other.

For the ships entertainment, Steve and a group of the Air Force contingent come up with an interesting dress code to keep the morale up.

Ladies of the Day

With inflated contraceptives the female appendices look real enough and to the entertainment and pleasure of the whole crew the Air Force takes a bow and loses the Tug of War.

Further south the ship ventures until meeting the pack ice and within a few days this becomes thicker so that the Captain must plot a clear route through to make headway. Due to the movement of pack ice away from the continent during summer, the ship cannot afford to stop as the retreating current will just carry it back further than the distance covered for the day's journey.

Pack Ice

The day of initiation arrives and with fanfare King Neptune's court arrive and gather the unsuspecting first timers for their initiation. The Kings Clerk of the Court orders the Bears to line the recruits up which he prepares for the arrival of King Neptune and his Queen. No quarter is given and to those who resist the Bears unceremoniously drag the victim closer to get dunked in ice water, lathered with egg and covered with flour. All the while the Clerk of the Court reads out each charge and sentences the guilty to be initiated. To aid in the demise of the new recruits the showers have been turned off to keep the spirit of the day alive and make the comfort level of those afflicted more unbearable. A great day is had and onward the ship sails south toward Antarctica.

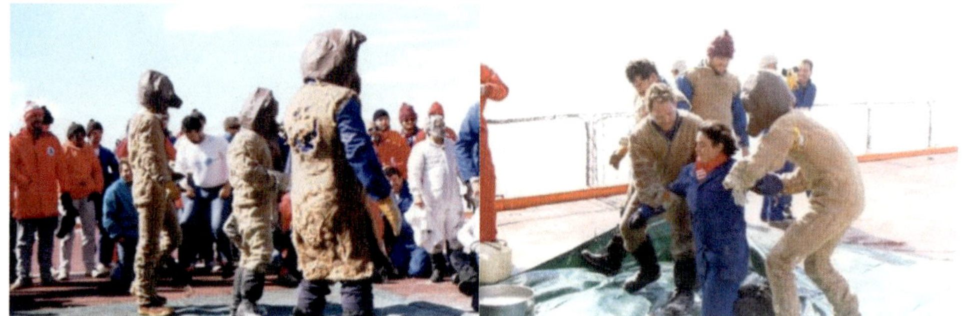

The Bears in action

By the 10th December the ship is struggling to maintain course and the Captain requests the Air Force to assist with flying an Ice Recce to establish if there is an open patch of sea that he can steer the ship to, enabling him to break through the pack ice and head along the open sea that now surrounds Antarctica. Steve with Gawie and Sloet get airborne in ZS-HIZ, setting heading along the course the ship is following in search of cracks and open water. Within a few minutes they notice a huge portion of ice that has large cracks heading in the direction of where the ship needs to go. Gawie radios the ship and informs them of the direction to steam.

They proceed further south and following the crack lines find an easy route through the pack ice that will eventually lead them to the open water. The sooner the ship can get to open water the sooner they can make the deadline to the Bukta at SANAE. Satisfied that they have given the Captain what he needs they return to the ship for landing. The ground crew assist Steve and quickly stow the helicopter in the hangar where Steve and JD finish the servicing and sign the Technical Logs. With a final check for security of the aircraft and spares in the hangar the crew retires to the pub for the daily celebratory drinks.

Three days later the ship arrives at the Bukta where the bay ice seems solid and the ramp built by the SANAE team is complete. The ship edges toward the bay ice while the local population observes. The inquisitive Emperor Penguins never disappoint and are always there to observe the strange visitors to their permanent home. The Emperor Penguin is the only living creature that lives permanently on the frozen continent. With the ship secured to the bay ice the unloading begins with gusto. The choppers will fly non-stop for the next hours to unload the New SANAE Team, Public Works Department (PWD) Crews, and fresh food for the Main Base at SANAE. The PWD Team will prepare the Emergency Base (E Base) for occupation while the New Team will start with the handover tasks from the Old Team.

Bay ice with the local population

For three days the ship offloads onto the Bay Ice and the heads along the Ice Shelf towards the German Base Neumeyer arriving there on the 14th December. Steve prepares ZS-HIZ for flight and with Tony in command and Christo Strobel as co-pilot of the flight they depart to Neumeyer to meet up with the Germans. The German base is built on much more stable ice and therefore they do not have the same Glacier movement as SANAE does.

The base entrance is controlled with a huge trap door, allowing them to park all their equipment under the base during storms. SANAE does not have this luxury and the vehicles are constantly having to be dug out after storms.

The German base is very well equipped and has all the modern amenities required to support a team for the year which includes, operating theatre, dentists chair, science laboratories, communications center and much more. The Germans welcome the South Africans with open arms.

The non-flying crews are already participating in the daily beer protocol and the grins with loud laughter is getting very prominent. The German Team take the crew on a tour of the base and describe the process of occupation, maintenance and support of the base.

The German supply vessel that sails from Germany every year, stops off at Cape Town to restock on fresh food before arriving at Neumeyer. As the Ice Shelf is very low at Neumeyer, the off and uploading is completed easily with the ship alongside. They do not have need for heavy equipment to complete the tasks. The bases lifespan is also much longer that SANAE as there is hardly any movement of the Ice Shelf.

Because the base is so close to the ocean, there are amazing views of wildlife during the year. On this visit the crew sees a colony of Emperor Penguins within a short distance. It is an impressive site to behold. The Penguins have just come out of a long cold and bitter winter.

Emperor Penguins

They are using the opportunity to gain their strength and fatten up during the short summer period by feeding close to the Ice Shelf. Steve watches in amazement how the Penguins nurture their young while each parent takes turns in fishing for sustenance to feed the young. The babies are hobbling about calling to their parents and looking for food. The next step in their survival will be to learn to fend for themselves.

German Base Neumeyer

The day comes to an end and the crew must return to the ship. A very rowdy bunch of passengers are in the back of the Puma and thankfully it is a short flight back to the ship for Steve, Tony and Christo.

The next few days are spent preparing for first flights to the Mountain Base Grunehogna. The base will have to brought up to scratch by having the PWD teams ensure that everything is still in working condition. The base will also be raised on its stilts as the accumulated snow below the base is dangerously close.

The Old SANAE Team has paid Grunehogna a visit during the early Spring and has therefore prepared a report on what need to be maintained.

On the 17th December Steve prepares ZS-HIZ for the flight to Grunehogna. The first flight out is with skeleton Science and PWD teams to ensure that the base is livable for the rest of the Geologists and Scientists that will arrive later. Steve with Gawie as the Commander and Thys Carstens as the Co-Pilot depart the ship on route to Grunehogna.

The flight to Grunehogna brings back fond memories to Steve from his last trip here a couple of years ago. As the Jutulstraumen Glacier flows off the Antarctic Continent it is some 5 kilometers thick in places with mountain peaks sticking out on either side of the valley created by the massive ice flow.

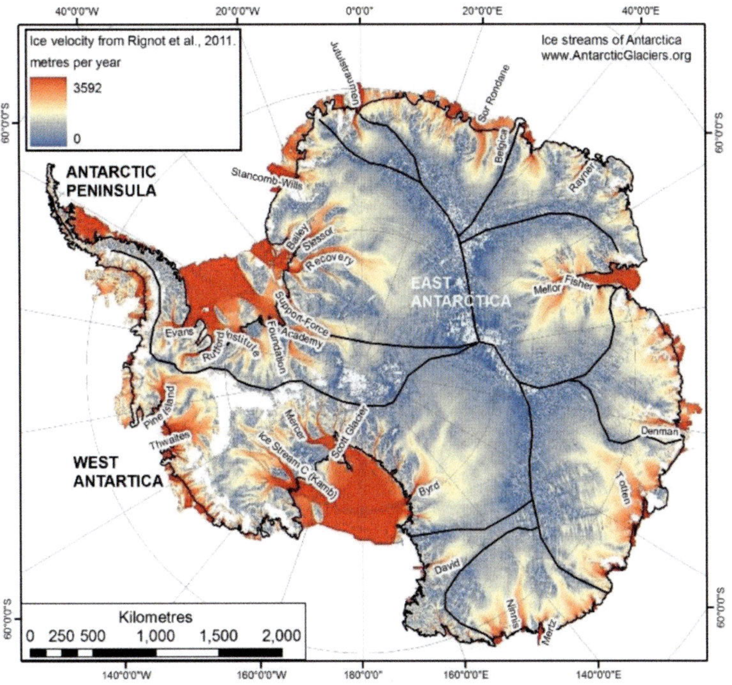

Ice Streams of Antarctica

The first site of land Boreos and Passat Nunataks are some 60 nautical miles from the Ice Shelf. These Nunataks, also called glacial islands, are exposed portions of ridges, mountains, or peaks not covered with ice or snow within, or at the edge of an ice field or glacier. Nunataks present readily identifiable landmark reference points in glaciers or ice caps and are often named. The term is derived from the Inuit word, nunataq.

With the two Nunataks to the right of their course and the inverted "A" against the mountains in the distance, they are on track for Grunehogna. The flight as always is awesome, and Steve assists the pilots in identifying the markers that they follow on their navigation between SANAE and Grunehogna. Even though the Tans Navigation Computer and GPS have been programmed for the flight, it is still essential that the crew familiarize themselves with the landmarks. The next land to pass is Vesleskarvet, a Nunatak on the west side of Ahlmann Ridge in Queen Maud Land, Antarctica. Its western side consists of a series of cliffs, approximately 250 m high, while the eastern side slopes more gradually down to the icefields. The accessibility of the relatively level wind-swept snow-free summit makes it ideal for the establishment of the new permanent base SANAE IV. It was mapped by Norwegian cartographers from surveys and air photos by the Norwegian-British-Swedish Antarctic Expedition in 1949 to 52 and air photos by the Norwegian expedition in 1958 to 59 and named Vesleskarvet, meaning "the little barren mountain."

Grunehogna can now be identified in the distance as they approach the final leg of their outbound journey, 120 nautical miles from SANAE. Gawie approaches Grunehogna and they elect to complete a slow flyover to ensure that the base is still intact. With the headwind identified Gawie spaces for landing and lands the aircraft within walking distance of the base.

After Shut-down, Steve secures the aircraft and double checks the fuel state for the return flight. He had topped up to internal fuel only and will need to add at least two more drums of fuel for the return flight. He makes his way over to the Generator shack and retrieves one of the Skidoos stored there for emergencies. Steve checks the Skidoo over and ensures that the engine is free. He tops up the fuel and then replaces the battery with a spare he brought with. After a couple of tries the Skidoo fires up and Steve rides out to the fuel dump to retrieve two drums of fuel.

The PWD and Science Teams have in the meantime made their way to the base to complete an inspection. If they cannot get the generator started, then the base will not be able to support the teams. Fortunately, there has been very little snow accumulation in the various buildings and in a very short time the telltale sign of the diesel generator smoke and rumble can be heard. Grunehogna is open for business.

Field Base Grunehogna

With the PWD and Science Teams comfortable the Chopper crew can retreat to the ship. Steve cranks the engines and with the checklist completed, including the deicing and anti-icing systems Thys takes a handful of collective and lifts the big chopper into the air, setting course back to the ship. They arrive back on the Agulhas 1.9 hours later. The ground crew assist Steve in stowing and servicing the aircraft for the next sortie.

The next morning, 18th December at 09:00 Steve has prepared ZS-HJA for a flight to SANAE Main Base, where the occupation of the E Base can now commence. Steve, Russell and Bles will swap flying duties on HJA for next few days while the flights to SANAE are completed. Steve has discovered that Bles had not completely inspected the aircraft covers and that one aircrafts nose cover had been left at AFB Ysterplaat. Steve switches to plan B mode and finds a tarp that will be big enough to do the job and then goes in search of a strong enough tape that he can join the main aircraft cover to the modified nose cover. If this cannot be achieved, then the aircraft will ingest snow in the first storm and not be flyable until they can defrost it. Steve's quick fix works, and the grey plastic tarp stays in place with the Duct Tape that he used to join the covers.

Aircraft cover quick fix

By the 22nd December the last flights to SANAE for the year are being concluded, all that remains now was to the get the Geomagnetic Equipment to Grunehogna where the Ice Thickness Surveys would be initiated. Together with Tony and JC, Steve completes the flight. ZS-HJA has relocated to Grunehogna with Russell, JD, Bles and Ollie to prepare for the survey. On the 24th December Steve prepares ZS-HIZ for a flight to join the rest of the Air Force at Grunehogna. It is decided that

Christmas would be spent together as a team. JC, Steve and Thys leave the ship at 16:15 the afternoon for the 1.9 flight to Grunehogna.

They arrive to a jubilant Air Force crew already in party mode. The party continues till late the evening until everyone is shooed off to bed by the Dominee (Pastor). He has accompanied the crew to conduct a sermon on Christmas day. After Brunch on Christmas day and the first celebrations completed Russell orders all the troops to form up for Church Parade. With the Dominee on the Catwalk the inebriated Air Force contingent form up to "Get on Parade" with Squadron Sarmajor Russell taking command.

"Get on Parade"

With the Dominee grinning from ear to ear from the spectacle in front of him, he conducts an amazing sermon. Sermon concluded Russell brings the bunch of misfits to attention and then dismisses them with the order, "to your duties dismiss". The group races back to the kitchen caboose to continue celebrations.

For the remaining days of 1990 Steve will be flying various sorties to the ship, SANAE and back to Neumeyer. By the last day of the year Steve once again prepares ZS-HIZ for a flight to Grunehogna where they will join the rest of the crew once more to bring in the new year.

The flight as always remains spectacular and Steve relishes in the site of this pristine continent that he has grown to love. The deathly whiteness dotted with darker rock formations lurks with many dangers but is blessed with unimaginable beauty. One mistake in the work that they are doing could easily result in a sudden death. Bearing this in mind safety remains of the utmost importance in everyone's mind.

Even the celebrations and inebriations are always treated with the utmost safety measures. The buddy system is preached over, and over, again. Nobody wanders away without a buddy and informing others of their intended trip. Each flight is carefully planned, and reporting points and times strictly adhered to. For those that have been here before it is easy to switch into safety mode, but for first timers a quick gentle reminder of the dangers brings them back to reality.

Strong winds are quite common in Antarctica and at Grunehogna the base is beside a small mountain range that interrupts the bulk of the North Antarctic ice sheet from the coast. Over the ice sheet there is commonly a high-pressure system that forces the air to flow to the low pressure closer to the coast.

The greater the difference between these pressures, the stronger the wind. Windscoops are a feature common to this part of Antarctica, especially when there are rocks or mountains that are elevated above the ice sheet.

The rocks, which could be considered small mountains, stick out from the ice sheet they are called Nunataks. When the wind from the ice sheet reaches these Nunataks, the wind pushes snow up the windward sides, where the wind is coming from. However, on the leeward side of the Nunatak, the wind is focused and scours the snow away from the blue ice. This means that on the leeward side of Nunataks, there is often very hard blue ice that is much lower than the snow on the windward side. Some Windscoops are subtle, but most are big.

A Braai in the Windscoop has been planned for the 31st December. Once Steve and the rest of the ZS-HIZ crew have covered the aircraft and stowed their kit in the caboose, they make their way down to the Windscoop to participate in the festivities.

Once in the Windscoop Steve remembers on his last rip how they used to slide down the sides at alarming speeds and skate over the Blue Ice to a stop.

Today is no different, with a gentle breeze there is a chill in the air, but the sun is bright, and the exposed rocks are creating a melt leaving a thin layer of water on the Blue Ice. This seems the perfect conditions for a long slide and challenge for Steve. He grabs the homemade wooden sled and from the top of the Windscoop picks up speed.

Sledding the Windscoop

Unfortunately for Steve he picks up so much speed that as he hits the Blue Ice the sled ejects him, and he continues along the Blue Ice on the film of water until he eventually comes to a stop.

By this time, to the amusement of all, he is soaked to the bone, and has to strip down to his underwear, draping his flight suite over the rocks near the Braai fire to dry. The party continues with Russell preparing an amazing Pot Bread as well.

Windscoop Braai

Copious amounts of alcohol are consumed to complete the wrap up of 1990 and it's a very worn-out group that eventually retreats to the kitchen and slowly the celebrations wind down and all go to bed.

On the 2nd January 1991 Bles and his crew board ZS-HIZ for SANAE where they will take up residence in E Base until crew change over. Russell and Steve will share sorties on ZS-HJA for the Geo Surveys that will be conducted over the next month. The aircraft is loaded up with the Geomagnetic Equipment and Global Position System accurate to 5 meters.

Each flight will be conducted with the aircrew, Pilot, Co-pilot, F/E and the Geomag Survey operators in the cabin. On the 3rd January Russell JC and Sloet conduct the first sortie.

With the aircraft refueled to max at 5000 pounds, they will have four hours of flight time. The survey will take them onto the Antarctic Plateau at 9800 ft where the air is extremely cold and thin.

The Geomag survey will follow a Line of Longitude to the plateau where they will then turn ninety degrees and fly a short Line of Latitude before returning on the next Line of Longitude. The average flight time is planned at 3.5 hours per sortie. There will 15-minute calls, initially on VHF and then when out of range on HF.

Steve will man the radio at Grunehogna for the first sortie. The current struggle they are having is with the Satellite availability, as the GPS requires a minimum of 5 satellites to ensure accuracy. The antenna that is flown below the aircraft is released after take-off.

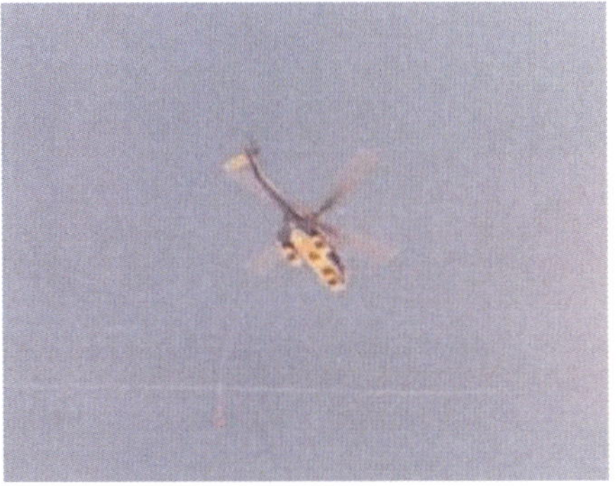

Geomag Survey Antenna

The first flight is concluded with no mishaps and the Geo team are happy with the results. The next day there are 1 or maybe 2 satellites available which do not make a flight viable, as the navigation accuracy must be within the parameters to ensure the correct measurements. The day goes by slowly and it is late in the evening when suddenly, the GPS spikes with full 5 satellites. Steve prepares the aircraft and with JC and Gawie they take-off on the next leg of the Geomag survey.

Antarctic Plateau

The flight is awesome and the Antarctic Plateau for the first viewing, barren bare and desolate. The strong winds are blowing snow drifts off the mountain tops and the Puma is flying crosswind to maintain the heading they need to fly. Steve and Gawie shares the Ops normal calls every 15 minutes as they continue onto the Plateau.

Early the next day Russell once again flies the first sortie with Steve manning the radio at Grunehogna. The sortie concluded, Steve takes over with Sloet as the commander and JC the Co-pilot. The barren Plateau has been the gathering place for many expeditions that have failed from the first time and up to present day when man has fried to conquer the frozen continent. Russell once again flies the next sortie and they are just heading out when the aircraft turns around with Sloet informing Grunehogna that they have lost an engine and are coming in for a single engine landing. This is going to be tough as the aircraft is full of fuel and heavy making a single engine landing impossible from the hover. Sloet does a very low and slow approach and at the last minute uses all the available power to land with some forward speed. The Puma slams downs but is secure and they can safely complete the shutdown. Steve has already requested that the next Cat Train brings the spare engine and mobile crane from the pack up at SANAE.

Engine Failure

Late the evening the Cat Train arrives with the spare engine. Russell and Steve have already prepared the aircraft for the engine change and have released fuel lines, electrical connections as well as loosened the engine mounts in preparation.

Cat Train

Early the next day the engine change is in process with the mobile crane assembly being the longest task to complete. The engine change itself takes very little time and within 30 minutes the new engine is secured, and all vital connections made. Russell get the Cat Driver to assist with reinstalling the MPAI Filters, instead of using the mobile crane which is tedious. With two guys standing on the Cat blade and Steve on the engine platform they muscle the filter in place and Steve engages the lock rails.

The last items to complete now are duplicate inspections, removal of the mobile crane and the technical log sign off.

Puma Engine Change

Sloet, JC and Russell complete a 30-minute test flight to ensure that the engine is performing within parameters. After shut-down the crew covers the aircraft for the night in preparation for the next day's sorties. As there are viable satellites available the Geomag Team wants to catch up on the survey which will entail round the clock flying to complete the delays already incurred.

This plateau was first sighted in 1903 during the Discovery Expedition to the Antarctic, which was led by Robert Falcon Scott. Ernest Shackleton became the first to cross parts of this plateau in 1909 during his Nimrod Expedition, which turned back in bad weather when it had reached a point just 97 nautical miles from the South Pole. Shackleton named this plateau the King Edward VII Plateau in honor of the King of the United Kingdom. In December 1911, while returning from the first journey to the South Pole, the Norwegian explorer Roald Amundsen decided to name this plateau the Haakon VII Plateau in honor of the newly elected King Haakon VII of Norway.

The Antarctic Plateau was first observed and photographed from the air in 1929 from a Ford Trimotor airplane carrying four men on the first flight to the South Pole and back to the seacoast. The chief pilot of this flight was Bernt Balchen, a native of Norway, and the navigator and chief organizer of this expedition was Richard E. Byrd of Virginia, an officer in the U.S. Navy. The other two members of its crew were the co-pilot and the photographer.

The high elevations of the Antarctic or Polar Plateau, combined with its high latitudes, and it's extremely long, sunless winters, mean that the temperatures here are the lowest in the world in most years, compare with central Siberia in the Northern Hemisphere. The nearly continuous frigid winds that blow across the Antarctic Plateau, especially in the long, dark wintertime, make the outdoor conditions there very inhospitable to life. Microbial abundance is low is mainly composed of bacterial groups in marine habitats. Based on research, polar microorganisms should not only be considered as deposited airborne particles, but as an active component of the snowpack ecology of the lofty, icy Antarctic Plateau. No penguins live on the Antarctic Plateau and no birds routinely fly over it either, except south polar skuas. There are no land animals on Antarctic or Polar Plateau, except for nematodes, springtails, mites, midges, human beings and their laboratory animals.

The Geomag Surveys continue with round the clock flying. On the 15th January Russell, Thys and JC are airborne and are almost at the furthest point of their leg on the Plateau. Steve gets the 15-minute Ops normal calls and steps out to grab a bite to eat. ZS-HJA reaches the end of the survey line and calls in that they are starting the cross leg before turning back on the return leg. Steve notes the time of call and waits for the start of the second leg call. Nothing is reported and 5 minutes later than expected Steve receives the call he does not want to hear. The aircraft has sheared an engine shaft and is stranded on the furthest leg on the Antarctic Plateau. Steve calls Christo who immediately activates ZS-HIZ from SANAE to scramble a rescue mission. The temperatures on the Plateau will not give the crew much time to survive and a long night there will be very tough. Current temperature is minus 20 with a 20 Kt wind increasing the chill factor to minus 33 degrees Celsius.

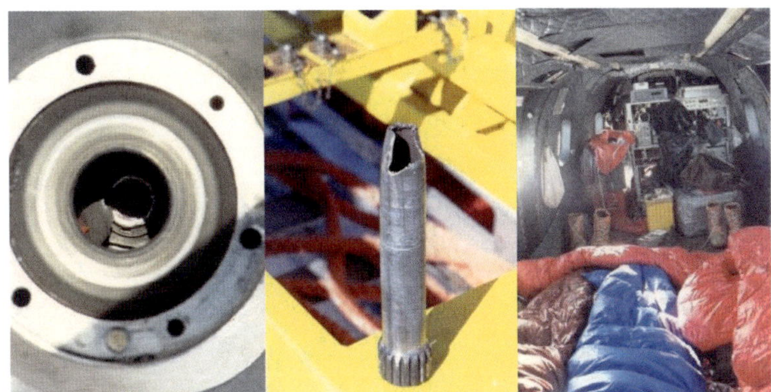

Stranded on the Plateau

The next radio call from SANAE is even worse news, the second Puma will not start, and they are trying everything they know. Christo contacts the Agulhas and Captain Bill informs him that the German Support Ship Polarstern was in the area with two BO105 helicopters onboard. Christo contacts the ship and discusses the rescue with the pilots of the BO105's. A plan of action is initiated and set into motion.

The Polarstern currently at Neumeyer will set sail for the Bukta near SANAE. Steve and Christo will make the voyage to SANAE with the Challenger and meet the BO105's there. Christo will accompany the BO105's to the rescue site to extract all the crew of ZS-HJA.

It takes the Challenger 5 hours nonstop to make the return trip to SANAE. As soon as they arrive Christo heads to the radio room to chat to the Polarstern while Steve makes a beeline for the other Puma to investigate the starting problem. Christo comes over to Steve and lets him know that the BO105's are on their way and if there are any changes in the situation of ZS-

HIZ to call him on HF. Steve wishes him luck and continues to diagnose the starting issue with Bles. 15 Minutes later the two aircraft land close to E Base and collect Christo for the return flight to Grunehogna.

Steve continues his fault diagnostics for the next couple of hours. He has been awake for more than 20 hours and the exhaustion is setting in. He has tried every bypass he knows and even tried some unaccepted practices to fire up the one engine but to no avail.

In the meantime, Christo with the two BO105's, have reached Grunehogna, refueled and were on their way to the recovery site of the downed Puma. One of the pilots monitoring the situation of the rescue progress informs Steve of more bad news. One of the BO105 helicopters has burnt the engines rear bearing and that they were abandoning the aircraft next to the Puma.

Rescue goes wrong

They are currently flying out the crew in three sorties with the one aircraft. With renewed energy Steve tackles the fault diagnostics. They had changed and engine on ZS-HJA a week before for a sheared engine shaft. Steve knows that this has nothing to do with the engine but solely with the gearbox alignment to the engine.

Steve opens the engine cover up and starts investigating potential sources of the non-startup. He narrows it down to no fuel mechanically as he has by passed all electronic process to no avail.

Steve decides to pull the Fuel Control Unit of the suspect engine. To his surprise and joy he finds that the fuel pump shaft has sheared at the shear point designated. This meant that the fuel pump may be suspect. He strips the Fuel Control Unit from the spare engine previously removed from ZS-HJA and compares the resistance to rotation between the two.

The resistance in turning the suspect Fuel Pump is less than that of the spare engine. When you change a Fuel Pump on the Turmo IVC engine you must conduct numerous calibration engine runs and test flights.

Steve decides to go for option B and just replaces the sheared Fuel Pump shaft. By this time the BO105 has recovered all crew to Grunehogna and will thereafter be returning to the ship.

Even though exhausted Steve gets an additional adrenalin rush and completes the re-installation of the Fuel Pump with the borrowed shaft. With the ground crew in the cockpit with him, as Bles has given up, Steve cranks the engine over and lets it build up sufficient speed before selecting ignition. The sweet sound of the engine firing is music to his ears.

With the BO105 and ZS-HJA stranded on the Plateau a decision is made to cancel any long navigation trips with only ZS-HIZ serviceable. The only flying Puma will remain at SANAE and be used for short trips to the ship or only for Casevac if required.

The Navy support vessel, SAS Drakensberg has been activated and will be bringing a military Puma to assist with the recovery operation of the two aircraft from the Plateau. The Agulhas will set sail to meet up with the Drakensberg at Bouvet Island.

SAS Drakensberg and SA Agulhas at Bouvet Island

On the 22nd January Steve, Bles, Tony, Christo, and Sloet depart for the ship with ZS-HIZ on route to Bouvet Island. Steve, Bles, Tony and Christo are the only drinkers of the contingent and end up partying the way by dancing on the counter, gaffuffling and getting up to mischief whenever they can to the Captains dismay. They meet up with the Drakensberg at Bouvet Island 7 days later. Steve, Tony, Sloet and Christo fly over with ZS-HIZ to the Drakensberg to meet up with Willie Beaurain, who has accompanied the military Puma down on the Drakensberg. With Willie is a SAP Crew and Pilot who will recover the BO105. They have brought a spare engine with them that they will assemble at Grunehogna before going out to the recovery site. Christo meets up with the Captain of the Drakensberg while Steve, Bles and Willie catch up on what the recovery plan would take.

Sloet, Christo, Willie together with the SAP Crew will return to the Agulhas with the military Puma. Steve and Tony take ZS-HIZ back to the Agulhas and with the limited ground crew stow the aircraft in preparation for the arrival of the military Puma 148. With Puma 148 on deck the crew makes quick work of stowing and securing it in the hangar, so the Captain can set heading back to SANAE.

The plan of action for the recovery is now set in motion. Both Puma 148 and ZS-HIZ will fly together to assure backup. The aircraft will depart the ship directly for Grunehogna where the crew for the recovery will be designated. An additional spare engine has been supplied from the Squadron. Steve, Bles, Ollie and Herbie will complete the engine change with Russell and Willie conducting F/E on the flying aircraft. As Puma 148 is the lighter of the two aircraft the spare engine and Hot Air Blower unit will be loaded into the cabin for transportation to the recovery site. ZS-HIZ will carry the tool kits and personnel. The plan of action is to use a parachute to cover the front of the aircraft with the Hot Air Blower directing warm air to keep the crew warm. Most of the work will have to be accomplished with bare hands. A tent will also be pitched with a Primus Burner for the backup crew to keep warm. As the air is very thin and will expend energy quickly, Steve has packed in two Turfor Winches to assist in locating the heavy engine and Hot Air Blower. The first flight will drop off the Mobile Crane which is required for the winching up and down of the engine.

It is the 6th February 1991 when the recovery operation is launched. Willie in ZS-HIZ arrives first at the recovery site. As is normal practice Willie reaches up and pulls both fuel flow levers back to idle to conserve fuel while the aircraft is being unloaded. At almost 10,000 ft with the temperature below minus 20 and the wind blowing hard, the conditions are not very favourable. The aircraft is unloaded and as Willie closes the cabin doors, number two engine flames out. Willie immediately spools up number one and warns the pilots to radio Puma 148 and inform them not to retard the fuel flow levers.

Steve and the rest of the crew leave the situation with Willie, as it is imperative that they pitch the tent and move the equipment closer to ZS-HJA which is still 200 meters away. They initially try to drag the Hot Air Blower but are soon too exhausted to continue. The cold and altitude taking it out of them. Steve rigs the Turfor's and starts cranking. It's a slower but much less exhaustive process. Herbie and Ollie pitch the tent and get the Primus going. Willie in the meantime has tried everything he can think of to start number one engine, but it refuses. They abandon the effort and resort to installing the aircraft covers. They will accompany Puma 148 back to Grunehogna after the last drop of equipment.

Recovery mission on the Antarctic Plateau

Steve and Bles have removed the cover from ZS-HJA and covered the front of the aircraft with the parachute. The next task is to start removing the engine. Steve works for 10 minutes and then with freezing hands goes to the tent to call Bless to take over. While they are completing this task, Herbie, Ollie, Sloet and Gawie are assembling the Mobile Crane. Puma 148 has returned to Grunehogna with the crew from ZS-HIZ and will await the radio call to collect the team. The SAP Crew at Grunehogna are making good time in getting the replacement engine ready to change the next day.

A task that under normal conditions would take an hour to complete is taking them more than four hours. Steve and Bles complete the before flight inspection of ZS-HJA and then set to work to get the aircraft started. Number two engine fires up but number one just completes initial light up and then flames out. They try this for the next hour and then Steve makes a command decision to fly the aircraft out on one engine. He instructs the crew to remove the equipment from the aircraft to lighten the load while he quickly briefs Gawie and Bles. Steve drains fuel leaving just enough for them to reach Grunehogna. Gawie and Bles will be alone in the aircraft. The tires are all deflated due to the cold and the aircraft is still heavy for this altitude. It is going to be very close to get airborne. While Gawie and Bles prepare Steve assists Sloet, Ollie and Herbie to move the Hot Air Blower over to ZS-HIZ. He wants to warm up the engines to see if he can start them.

All the while ZS-HJA has been sitting on the ice with number one engine running. Steve goes over to get a final brief from them and wishes them luck. Gawie takes power and ZS-HJA stretches out of her struts. She slowly starts taking to the air but there is insufficient power. Gawie reduces power and indicates for Steve to approach. He asks Steve to drain another 100 lbs of fuel. Steve crawls under the aircraft and opens the cock. Bles taps him when the gauges indicate 100 lbs are drained. Once again Gawie takes power. The aircraft slowly lifts in the air and Gawie nudges the nose forward to get speed. She drops down bounces once, twice and a third time. Steve is just about to give up hope when ZS-HJA shakes off the urge to want to land and shimmies up and onward. She is airborne to the jubilant screams of the crew on the ground. Once they have lifted off from the recovery site, Gawie selects a route that will get them off the Plateau the quickest and once they reach 4000 ft Bles manages to start the second engine. The flight back to Grunehogna is completed with no further issues.

With ZS-HJA on their way, there is no time to spare as the sun is low on the horizon and the temperature dropping quickly. Steve and Sloet complete the pre-flight inspection of ZS-HIZ. Sloet takes up the Command seat and Steve his F/E perch. Number one engine starts with difficulty but does spool up. Steve cranks number two engine and only gets initial light up and then flames out. Steve tries a trick taught to him by a friend who is a specialist on these engines. Leon a fellow F/E had spent many years in the Test Cell working for Atlas Aviation and had picked up many tricks in starting the Turmo IV C. Steve briefs Sloet to shut-off all electricals the moment he calls for it. Steve selects start once more, and the moment he selects ignition with the first indication of JPT rise he calls for electrics off. Sloet switches everything off and Steve quickly advances the Fuel Flow Lever. The JPT continues to rise when at 330 degrees suddenly stops. Steve's heart is about to drop when he notices that the engine was at Idle already. Without skipping a beat, he continues to advance the Fuel Flow Level causing the JPT to peak at almost 700 degrees. Sloet warns Steve but his concern is to ensure the engine makes it to full RPM. Just then the JPT drops back down to 350 degrees and the Ng reads Flight Idle. Steve lets off a yell and with a great big grin slaps the electrics back on. He briefs Sloet that he must stay in the cockpit and monitor while Steve helps to load the equipment into the aircraft.

Steve and the crew load the spare engine, mobile crane and remaining Geomag equipment removed from ZS-HJA. At 22:00 at night, everything loaded and the crew onboard, Sloet gets airborne for Grunehogna. Steve reaches up and turns the aircraft heaters to maximum as everyone is frozen to the bone. The flight back to Grunehogna is the happiest everyone has been since the incident. Sloet lands back at Grunehogna with the whole team applauding their arrival. Steve alights from the aircraft and is immediately tackled by a jubilant Bles to the snow. Bles hugs Steve and the two of them smile and laugh at the extreme relief of the very tense and dangerous recovery they had just experienced. Steve is exhausted and does not even take time to have a shower. He wolfs down a meal that the team has prepared for them and then attends a briefing for the next day's activities.

Willie requested not to be included in the next day's recovery plan as he was having a hard time with palpitations. Steve volunteers as he has BO105 experience and can assist the SAP crew in the aircraft recovery. Herbie and Ollie both volunteer as well. With the plan formed the exhausted group dive into their bunks and are soon all fast asleep.

The next day both J Models will be going to the ship to start the upload for the return trip to Cape Town. Puma 148 with Steve and crew aboard return to the recovery site to assist with the BO105. They drape a parachute over the aircraft and direct the Hot Air Blower in to warm the work area. Steve assists the SAP Crew to complete the engine change. With the engine change completed Steve leaves the SAP chaps to get the engine started while he warms up in the tent. The two days in these conditions are affecting the three and they are physically and mentally shutting down. The BO105 also only fires up one engine. The second wont light up at all. Steve suggests that they attempt a single engine take off like they completed with ZS-HJA. The BO105 cannot fly on a single engine and at this altitude won't even lift a skid. The two SAP gents work feverously at trying to start the engine, when at long last the telltale sign of blue smoke is emitted from the exhaust with the accompanying whine as she spools up.

With a few fine adjustments the thumbs up sign and Bees, the SAP pilot and his Crewman get airborne for Grunehogna. Steve gets on the HF and informs Grunehogna of the good news and then requests a 30-minute call for pickup. He will keep the tent up until the aircraft is on the horizon, as the cold is causing medical conditions with all. They huddle in the tent next to the Primus to keep warm. JC, Sloet and Willie are on the way to collect the recovery team with Puma 148. Steve is the first to hear the advancing aircraft and instructs the team to strike down the tent and pack up the equipment. JC takes a route further away from the recovery site and just as Steve gets on the VHF he sees them turn back towards the recovery site. Once the Puma lands, the team makes small work of loading everything including the Hot Air Blower. The problem however is that the Blower fits in lengthwise through the doors. With a section sticking out each side the cabin doors cannot be closed. The resulting cold air is not making it easy on the already frozen recovery team. The flight back to Grunehogna seems to take forever.

Puma 148 with Hot Air Blower

Upon arrival at Grunehogna Steve, Herbie and Ollie make a beeline for the Generator Shack to warm up next to the exhaust. The camp has already been mostly closed for the winter, so Steve and his crew must hurry to collect all their gear as they are heading straight back to the ship. At Grunehogna Willie and Bles change the flat wheels and complete a final inspection of the work performed in the field. Satisfied Christo, Sloet and Willie returned to the Agulhas. The ground crew assists Willie in stowing and securing the aircraft.

Steve gazes out over the tundra and is pleased to see the fruits of their efforts are parked out there. A very successful operation has been completed.

Recovery safe at Grunehogna

All three aircraft get airborne and set heading for the ship. The BO-105 will be stowed in the ships hold and will therefore land on the forward cargo hold. Puma 148 will land on the helideck and stowed in the hangar, while ZS-HIZ will land on the Helideck and be secured there for the remainder of the voyage. On the return voyage to South Africa the ship will be dropping weather buoys along the way. Once onboard Steve makes his way to the cabin, dumps his kit and passes out in his bunk. He sleeps through supper until the next morning when Russell gently wakes him.

"Steve, can you fly some Cargo Sling sorties with ZS-HIZ please?"

"Sure Boss, no sweat" says Steve.

Steve grabs a quick shower and makes the last call for breakfast before heading up to the hangar to prepare for the sorties of the day. He is surprised to see that the ship was already loaded and sailing towards Neumeyer. Steve with Tony as the Command Pilot and JC as co-pilot fly the first 2.5 hours of Cargo Slinging bringing in the last items from SANAE. The next sortie is a normal flight with passengers from SANAE and as the ship is now already under sail takes 2.1 hours to complete. The ship is now heading towards the South Sandwich Islands where the Puma will be used once more to locate weather Buoys on land.

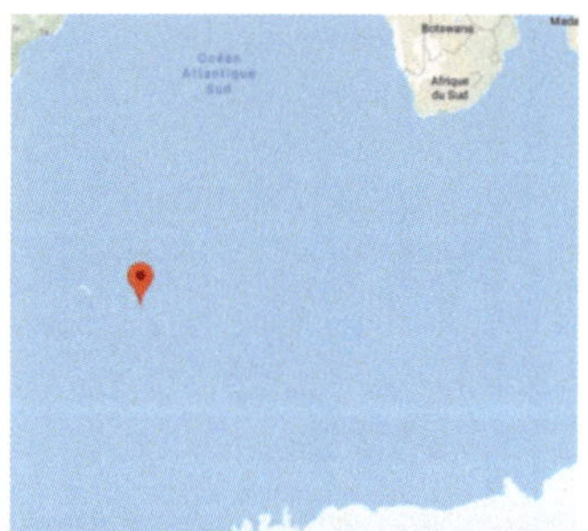

South Sandwich Islands

It takes the ship another three days to reach the South Sandwich Islands where the first weather Buoy is going to be erected at Southern Thule Islands. Southern Thule is a collection of the three southernmost islands in the South Sandwich Islands, Bellingshausen, Cook, and Thule (Morrell). The Southern Thule territory has been administered by the United Kingdom since 1908 and claimed by Argentina since 1938. The island group is barren, windswept, bitterly cold, and uninhabited. It has an extensive exclusive economic zone rich in marine living resources managed as part of the SGSSI fisheries. The Admiralty's

Antarctic Pilot says that Southern Thule is part of an old sunken volcano and is covered with ash and penguin guano. There are seals, petrels, and a bank of kelp just offshore, especially around a small inlet on Morrell called Ferguson Bay. The island group was first sighted in 1775 by the expedition of James Cook, who named it Southern Thule because it seemed to lie at very much the extreme end of the world. It was further explored in 1820 by Fabian Gottlieb von Bellingshausen who established that it consisted of three separate islands.

Early morning Steve must prepare a frozen ZS-HIZ for a 06:30 take-off with Sloet and JC. With the Military Puma and ZS-HJA occupying the hangar, ZS-HIZ has been secured on the heli-deck for the remainder of the voyage.

Frozen Puma

ZS-HIZ get airborne with a Meteorologist Team to head to the Thule Island. It is a short 15-minute flight to the coordinates that they need to assemble the Buoy. Sloet locates a safe landing zone and Steve completes the pre-landing vital actions. After Shut-down the Met Kassies make short work of erecting and initiating the Buoy. Once satisfied they scramble onboard while Steve completes the start-up. A short return flight to the ship and they stand down for the next drop off.

Southern Thule Islands

The ship is now sailing along the South Sandwich Islands towards Zavodovski Island, which is an uninhabited volcanic island in the Traversay Islands subgroup of the South Sandwich Islands. It lies 350 kilometers southeast of South Georgia Island. It is the northernmost of the South Sandwich Islands and the nearest to South Georgia. The island is home to around a million pairs of breeding chinstrap penguins, which is the largest besides Antarctica.

Zavodovski Island was discovered and named by Russian Antarctic explorer Fabian Gottlieb von Bellingshausen in 1819. Bellingshausen named it after Lieutenant Ivan Zavadovskiy, who was captain of his ship, the Imperial Russian Navy sloop-of-war Vostok. The American schooner Pacific under Captain James Brown landed at Zavodovski Island in 1830.

The island was surveyed in 1930 by Discovery Investigations personnel. It is approximately 5.6 kilometers across with a peak elevation of 1,808 ft above sea level. Mount Asphyxia, a stratovolcano also known as Mount Curry, dominates the western side of the island while the eastern half is a low-lying lava plain. It is an active volcano, with fresh lava reported in 1830 and numerous indications of activity since. Approximately 50% of the island is composed of tephra, a fragmental material produced by volcanic eruptions.

At 17:30 Thys, Sloet and Steve get airborne once again with the Met Kassies and a Weather Buoy to drop off on the Island. It is quite an awe-inspiring site to observe an active volcano out in the middle of the Atlantic Ocean. The weather is very marginal, and the wind is blowing in gusts. Thys must have his wits about him flying this sortie. The flight out takes them almost 30 minutes with the weather buffeting the Puma.

Zavodovski Island

Thys selects a landing area on the snow-covered slope of the Volcano and the Met Kassies hurry to complete setting up the Buoy. Thys has elected not to shut down due to the weather conditions. With the Buoy erected, tested and initiated the Met Kassies scramble onboard and Thys gets airborne for the return flight to the ship. The landing is quite hair razing as the flat-bottomed Ice Breaker is being tossed around like a rubber duck.

Thys must concentrate as each time he approaches the deck to land the pitching of the deck is countering his intentions, once that is corrected the ship rolls out of limits. It takes Thys a full two minutes to get the Puma back on the deck before the crew can secure her after shut-down.

With shut-down completed, Steve instructs the ground crew to ready the aircraft covers and chains to lash it securely to the deck. Part of the Hangar watch would now include a cold inspection of the flight deck to ensure that ZS-HIZ is still secure and undamaged.

Air Force and SAP Crews

The Captain now sets sail directly for Cape Town. On route to Cape Town the Air Force and SAP pose for a photo, a memory of a very trying event they had all shared in.

Nine days later the SA Agulhas can see Table Mountain on the horizon. The three aircraft will fly off approximately 50 miles from land. During the day the Air Force crew packs their bags and load up the helicopters. Take off is scheduled for late afternoon. Sad good byes are made as the Air Force prepares to leave. At 18:00 ZS-HIZ with Tony, Christo and Steve have part of the Ground Crew on board and they get airborne to fly a large orbit around the ship while the next aircraft is prepared. It takes the Crew less than 15 minutes to get Puma 148 readied and airborne followed by another 15 minutes with ZS-HJA. The three aircraft form up in a formation to give the ship a fly-past before setting heading to AFB Ysterplaat. It is a short 35 minutes to the base where the aircraft space for landing and then land on the taxiway before being directed to the flight line for shut down. As it is long after home time for the Squadron there are only a skeleton crew available to help refuel and tow the aircraft to the hangar. The families are there to greet the crews and Steve is overjoyed to see Zella and Nicole. Nicole races up to Steve and grabs him around the neck for a big hug and kiss.

With the aircraft unpacked and secured in the hangar Steve collects his kit and the family makes their way home to Sanddrift. Nicole very talkative asking Steve a million questions. Steve just grins and tries to answer as best as he can. Zella is very subdued but smiles and welcomes Steve back. He tells them about the experience and is very glad to be home. Steve has less than a month to prepare for the Officers Forming Course that he applied for last year. At home Zella gives Nicole a task leaving her alone with Steve. She turns to him and asks him what his intensions are with Sharon? Steve looks at her dumbstruck, but answers truthfully that he may be in love and that they should talk. Zella storms out and drives off in the car. Steve is a mess, he loves Nicole and does not want to disrupt her life. He is sure that he does not love Zella but cannot decide what the right thing is to do.

He calls Sharon and discovers why Zella had found out. She had filed for divorce from Doug and was moving out to her own place. Zella had put two and two together and without questioning her just knew that there was more than just friendship. The next few weeks before Steve leaves for the Air Force College in Pretoria to start his Officers Training are going to be monumental in the lives of a number of people. Towards the end of the trip he had made up his mind to work it out with Zella and approach a marriage counselor. By Zella's actions it did not seem that this would be possible. When Zella returns Steve can smell smoke and alcohol. He decides not to broach the subject and they keep to themselves. Steve tries unsuccessfully to stay away from Sharon, but the excitement and urge to see her is overpowering. They continue to meet and spend time with each other. There is no discussion of a future but just the present. In a week Steve will leave, and for three months will not have any contact with both Zella or Sharon.

In 1990, de Klerk gave orders to end South Africa's nuclear weapons programme; the process of nuclear disarmament was essentially completed in 1991. The following changes within the political arena for 1991 in South Africa are a prediction of what is to come;

9th January, Black children are admitted to schools previously reserved for whites only. In Sebokeng gunmen fire on mourners attending the funeral of a leader of the African National Congress, killing 13.

12th January, 45 mourners are killed during an attack on a funeral vigil for an African National Congress member.

13th January, 45 football fans die in the Orkney Stadium Disaster in the Oppenheimer Stadium in Orkney.

29th January, State President F.W. de Klerk, deputy-president of the African National Congress Nelson Mandela and Inkatha Freedom Party leader Mangosuthu Buthelezi meet for peace talks.

1st February, at the signing of a national peace accord State President F.W. de Klerk promises to end all apartheid legislation and to create a new multi-racial constitution.

25th February, Chief Mhlabunzima Maphumulo is shot dead by an alleged hit-squad outside his home in Pietermaritzburg.

11th March, a curfew is imposed on black townships after fighting between rival political gangs kills 49.

12th March, the government tables a white paper to end racial discrimination in land ownership and occupation.

24th March, twelve people, including a police officer and two children, are killed when police open fire on a crowd of African National Congress supporters attacking the police in Daveyton.

15th April, the European Economic Community lifts economic sanctions on South Africa.

30th April, a coup d'état is executed in Lesotho.

14th May, Winnie Madikizela-Mandela, dubbed the "Mugger of the Nation", is found guilty and sentenced to 6 years imprisonment for her involvement in the death of 14-year-old Stompie Moeketsi. The sentence will never be carried out.

28th June, the Population Registration Act in terms of which South Africans were classified into racial groups is repealed.

30th June, the laws enforcing geographical segregation, including the Group Areas Act, the Native Land Act, the Native Trust and Land Act and the Asiatic Land Tenure Act, are repealed.

2nd to 6th July, the 48th National Conference of the African National Congress takes place in Durban, the first to be held in South Africa since 1959.

9th July, the suspension of South Africa from the International Olympic Committee is lifted.

10th July, President Bush announces the United States is ending its 1986-enacted sanctions on South Africa.

4th August, the Greek-owned cruise ship Oceanos sinks off Coffee Bay and all 571 passengers on board are safely evacuated by SAAF helicopters.

9th August, right-wingers of the Afrikaner Weerstandsbeweging clash with the police in the Battle of Ventersdorp.

4th September, State President F.W. de Klerk announces a new constitution that will provide suffrage for black people.

2nd October, Minister of Foreign Affairs Pik Botha visits Beijing to strengthen South Africa's relations with China.

3rd October, Nadine Gordimer is awarded the 1991 Nobel Prize in Literature.

4th to 5th November, the African National Congress leads a general strike to demand a role in governing and an end to value-added tax.

8th December, Chris Hani becomes leader of the South African Communist Party.

Leadership Training

On the 22nd April 1991 Steve arrives at the Air Force College, wearing his full blues and white Candidate Officers strips. He joins the rest of the CO's on the parade ground and they are instructed to report to the Quarter Master for kit. A distant memory is sparked in Steve as he recalls a similar process many years before, when he joined the Air Force the first time. He finds himself surrounded by mostly young men fresh out of school. Most of these have applied to the Air Force for pilot's course and must first complete the basic officers forming course before they are sent to the Flight Training School. The recruits are issued with the kit they will need for the course and then hustled into buses. The pain and suffering is about to begin. They are given 15 minutes to don the Browns and Boots they are issued and must form up at a rough looking parade ground in the bush a number of kilometers away from the College.

The Physical Training Instructors (PTI) and Officer Instructors don't have any sympathy for the recruits and treat then one and all the same. There is no leeway for age, sex or colour. The dreaded "Gogga" was under way.

"Gogga" Starts

The physical abuse is double that which Steve had experienced in the past and he grits his teeth and bares through.

There are about 10 CO's the same age group as Steve, but the rest are all school leavers, and this is their first introduction to the military. The younger recruits have still to understand the military way of life whereby an order is not questionable but executable. Do it or die! The continuous exercising is taking its toll and slowly but surely the exhaustion starts taking effect and the mental challenge begins. "Om die bus" (Around the bus) is shouted by the Instructor.

<u>"Om die Bus"</u>

As the CO's get back and form up the mental abuse begins with the statement;

"If you are tired and want to give up then stay behind the bus. We won't question you or name you, just stay there and we will make sure you get home to a nice bath and warm bed."

And so, the pain continues. After each bout of PT, the CO's are offered the same option with;

"Om die Bus."

Morning becomes midday and soon the sun starts dipping the horizon. The "Gogga" only now getting momentum. At dusk the numbers start falling as more and more dropouts stay behind the bus. Suddenly it's a moonless night and still the PT and Mental challenges are stepped up. False hope is thrown at midnight when tents are brought out and the CO's given 15 minutes to raise them without any light. Even with light this is a challenge.

<u>"Hit the dirt"</u>

Everytime some progress is made; an order is screamed to hit the ground. All CO's then hold onto what they have and hit the dirt. Eventually the tents are pitched and the CO's ordered to unpack their sleeping bags, take off their boots and sleep. The CO's are just getting comfortable when the order to break up camp is given, and the process is started all over. June is winter in Pretoria and the cold night air does not help tired muscles, so muscle cramps and seizures start talking place. The CO's are ordered to run on the spot when Steve's calf muscle freezes up in a painful cramp. He falls and an Instructor is immediately at his side.

"Giving up old man?" shouts the Lt.

"No Lt.", answers Steve, "cramp!" and he immediately gets up but is unable to straighten his leg.

The medic is immediately on hand and confirms it is a cramp and gets Steve to lay down while he stretches the muscle out to relieve the cramp. Within a minute the cramp has subsided, and Steve is back on his feet to face the rest. The next exercise is very strange indeed. All the CO's are blindfolded, and they are ordered to form up in single file and lock their hands in front persons belt. With that the "Slang" (Snake) has been born. The front of the snake is led into a ravine and bush area and let go. The snake must move with their feet together at the same time and in the same direction. Not even 30 minutes into the Slang, a squeaky voice screams from the middle.

"Korporal! Korporal! my onderbroek skuur my!" (Corporal! Corporal! My underpants scour me.)

A giggle breaks out and the momentum picks until everyone is hollering. The Slang halts and falls over like a row of dominos. The Instructors are laughing so much that they cannot give the order to keep quiet. The recruits are ordered to form up back at the parade ground at double pace. The first break of dawn appearing on the horizon. The group has shrunk massively through the night and only 75 of the original 130 remain. Exhaustion has taken over completely and the movements are robotic with actions retarded and mental functionality very low. Still the PT continues but thankfully a quick break for some grub allows the weary bodies a few minutes of recovery. Then off they go again. At midmorning the mental tests begin, and the CO's are constantly questioned as to why they want to be officers, none of them have the endurance and tenacity to complete this. They now must write an essay in 15 minutes with an introduction, purpose, and factual statement, followed by a summary of why they want to be officers. Steve manages to get the basics but starts laughing when he sees the chap next to him is sleeping but the motions of writing are continuing. It was a comical sight to behold.

At midday the recruits are formed up once more. Steve wonders if this will ever end, when suddenly, they are ordered to take positions in the buses. The recruits make a Beeline for the buses and hop onboard. The Instructor boards the first bus and informs them that once at the college they will have 30 minutes to change into half blue uniforms and fall in on the parade ground. 24 Hours of Gogga have concluded and Steve has survived. He is amazed to see how many did not make it through the night but is too exhausted to dwell on it. He catches 40 winks on the short ride back to the College.

The next 46 days are going to be a constant process of leadership development under incredible physical and mental stress through ongoing tasks, exercise, inspections and route marches.

Route March

On the second day Steve is summoned to the Air Force College's Officer Commanding and informed that he will be the Course Leader. A big target has now been placed on his back. Being a FSgt and now only a CO meant that an Instructor Corporal is ordering him around as if he is a troop with no rights. Steve sucks it up and knows that at the end of this the same Cpl is going to have to salute him. He smiles inwardly while taking the abuse and responds respectfully, "Yes Cpl!"

Pole and Tire PT are daily occurrences followed by long lectures and tests. There are no passes or weekends off, just more lectures, PT and inspections. Slowly but surely Steve wins the younger group over and applying the reverse phycology approach gets them to fall in line and stops the whining. A few find out that Steve is an Honoris Crux recipient and soon there is a much greater respect for his leadership. They have reached the midway point of Officers Forming and the Instructors are less autocratic but still very disciplined. Steve sees the change and knows that they are now bringing the younger recruits into the military family. In a few short weeks they will start preparing for their pass out parade. The Technical recruits will all receive Officer's Rank while the CO's will now be treated as members ready for their new training.

The recruits are informed that their next of kin will be invited to the passing out parade and that they need to ensure the family contact details are correct. Each CO checks that the data he filed on the first day is still correct and legible. The College has sent out invites to all family members with transportation and accommodation arranged. Zella and Nicole will both be at the parade, but Zella has elected to stay with her parents in Brakpan.

S.A. LUGMAGKOLLEGE
OFFISIERVORMINGKURSUS
705 POD 07/9102
22 APRIL 1991 — 14 JUNIE 1991

VOORTREKKERHOOGTE

S.A. AIR FORCE COLLEGE
OFFICER FORMING COURSE
705 POD 07/9102
22 APRIL 1991 — 14 JUNE 1991

Officers Course

The passing out parade day arrives, and the CO's are marched smartly onto the parade ground. The Chief of the Air Force (CAF) and other high-ranking officers are in attendance. The Air Force Band leads the parade and the march past of the podium is conducted with spiff and span. The recruits pushing out their chests and Steve with his medals gently jingling as he marches and salutes the podium. The Flights of CO's form up in front of the podium and are individually congratulated by the CAF. As the CAF reaches Steve he shakes his hand and removes the CO bands under which are the rank of Full Lieutenant.

"Congratulations Steve!" says Lt Gen van Loggerenberg.

Steve grins from ear to ear with pride and the fact that CAF recognized him. The parade marches past and falls out at the edge of the parade ground where the tossing of hats ending this chapter is celebrated by all the recruits. Steve walks up to Zella and Nicole where Nicole grabs him for a big hug and kiss.

Zella smiles and says, "I would have loved to be an Officers Wife!"

Steve looks at her intently and she informs him that she is filing for divorce. Steve asks her if they can discuss this, as there must be a way to find resolution in the form of professional help. She shakes her head and says that she is not interested in listening to other people's stupid advice. Steve is shocked and asks her what must he do, he will still be in Pretoria for another three months at the School for Logistic Training? Zella just shrugs and tells him that they must leave now. Steve picks Nicole up and hugs her tight, then turns to hug Zella but she pulls away. He lets them go and returns to group of qualified recruits. Steve is sad, confused and uncertain what to do next.

The young CO's on their way to train as pilots are all clearing out of the Air Force College and heading to CFS Dunnottor to start their new lives. More of them will end up being scratched off the program as pilot training is a very disciplined process in the Air Force. The Technical Officers are given more appropriate accommodation at the Air Force College and will report to SLT early on 15th July 1991. Here they will receive training in Systems and Logistic Engineering, further developing them as leaders in the Air Force. There will be many lectures exams and finally they will pass the Logistic Technical Officers portion of their training development, after which they will be posted out to Units. Steve closes off to the outside world and gets his studies completed, as this is the only sanity he can see currently. He has applied for the Test Flight Course but is unsure if he will be accepted as his mental state is questionable. He is drinking far too much and has become withdrawn and distant. All this while Steve has not been in contact with Sharon, as he is unsure what she feels for him. He is undecided as to which direction he must go. He was raised to respect marriage and exhaust all avenues to make it work. Zella however is not even interested in talking about it with him. In a few short weeks he will be back in Cape Town and will have to make some hard decisions relating to his marriage. As Zella is not interested in joining him for the final formal dinner at SLT, he plucks up the courage and calls Sharon. She accepts excitedly and will be travelling up by bus with both children. Steve arranges accommodation with one of his friends in Voortrekker Hoogte for them.

The final day of the course arrives and Steve collects Sharon and the children at the Bus Terminal. She embraces him, and they set off to Steve's friends home. After the function Sharon and the children will drive with Steve back to Cape Town. The formal dinner goes off well and Steve finds out he will stay in the Cape Province but at Langebaanweg almost 200 kilometers up the west coast. The long drive back to Cape Town is very uncomfortable as Steve is withdrawn and only responds to questions when asked. Sharon reacts and lashes out at him, telling him to be a man. This angers Steve, but he controls himself and the air remains thick for the rest of the journey. Steve drops Sharon off at her apartment in Green Point and then makes his was to Sanddrift to face the music with Zella. Steve must report to AFB Ysterplaat on the Monday morning to permanently clear out there before officially transferring to AFB Langebaanweg.

As Steve pulls up the driveway his stomach pulls into a tight not, as he knows how stubborn Zella can be. He opens the door and Nicole screams in delight and races up to hug him. Steve drops all his belongings and moves to greet Zella. She brushes him off and asks him if he is going to visit his whore. At this point Steve loses control and asks Zella out about the past flirtations while he was away. She laughs at him and says he must try and prove it. This is doing nothing to calm Steve down and he is shaking as his temper flares. He screams at her that she never even wanted children and is therefore not worthy of being a mother or a wife. Zella lashes out at Steve and he grabs her arm holding it tightly. She cries out in pain and Steve lets her go. Nicole is crying uncontrollably which jerks Steve back to reality, so he turns on his heel and opens the fridge. There is beer, so he grabs a beer and drains the bottle. He goes out the back door and stands there contemplating what to do next. The more Steve tries to reason with Zella the more headstrong she becomes.

The next morning Steve is dressed in full Blue Uniform and reports to AFB Ysterplaat Duty room. It is strange to be an officer at the base where he had been a Non-Commissioned Officer (NCO) for so long. The guards and other NCO's salute him smartly as he passes them on his way. At the duty room the clerk informs him that he needs to report to Test Flight and Development Center (TFDC) Bredasdorp in two weeks for the Test Flight Selection Board. The transfer to AFB Langebaanweg will be postponed until after the Selection Board. Steve calls Sharon and she is happy to hear his voice. He apologizes for his mood and explains the situation with Zella to her.

"Why don't you come live with me? You can then work out what you really want." Says Sharon.

Steve accepts and goes home to collect his things and call Zella to inform her of where he will be. She shrugs him off and says,

"Do whatever you want to."

Steve leaves and goes to Green Point. He opens his books to start studying but cannot get any sense into what he is looking at. His mind is not into what he must get into his brain. Simple Math seems like a huge challenge, and aerodynamics suddenly impossible to grasp. He starts to panic but his mind stays confused and he cannot concentrate. Sharon is friendly and loving which helps Steve to relax. Late at night as they are nodding off to sleep the phone rings. Sharon answers and is immediately angry.

"It's your wife!" and throws the phone at Steve.

Steve asks Zella what she wants to which she replies,

"When are you going to see your daughter?"

Zella is playing the guilt trip on him and its working. Sharon is angry and lets Steve know exactly how she feels. She tells him to leave. Steve packs his stuff and makes his way back to Sanddrift. On the way he has a sudden urge to end it all and breaks into uncontrollable sobbing. He must pull over as his driving is becoming dangerous. The pain and emotions come out in deep groans and shudders and he looks up into the dark sky and screams, "Why, why, why?

Eventually Steve gets a grip on himself and drives the last distance to Sanddrift where he parks the car and lets himself into the house to fall asleep exhaustedly on the couch. He has two days before reporting to TFDC in Bredasdorp. He desperately attempts to get some of the studying to stick. The Test Flight Selection will take place over three days where the first day will comprise of introductions and briefing, the second examinations followed by personal interviews. Steve does not have a good feeling about the Selection Board.

The first day at TFDC Steve is wound up tighter than a coil spring. He recognizes most of the candidates there with him and knows that the Technical Officers will be giving it their all. The next morning Steve and the rest of the Candidates are ushered into a classroom and handed examinations to complete. Steve draws a blank and panic sets in. He reads the questions over and over to get some clarity and then tries his best to complete the answers.

The examinations last until lunch when the instructor collects them. Steve is very disgruntled and feels he has for the first time in his life failed miserably at a task. That night he joins the candidates for beers and they share border war stories. The Bush War has only just recently come to an end, but it feels like a lifetime ago. All of them are on edge and hoping to do well in the personal interviews the next day.

One by one the candidates are led into the Selection Board Room and remain there for approximately and hour. Eventually its Steve's turn. Steve marches in smartly and salutes the Commanding Officer Col Des Barker. Col Barker motions for the Steve to take a seat. In true military fashion the Selection Board has a number of members around a u-shaped table with the candidate facing them on a single chair. The focus of the room. Steve has been through a number of these before and has never been intimidated by them, but today he feels like his whole world is starting to crumble and collapse. First Maj Laurus Basson informs him that his score marks in the exam were not very good before firing off a quick batch of aerodynamic questions at Steve. Steve fumbles with the answers. Col Barker asks him if he is nervous, to which Steve replies that he has some stress he is working through. The Board pokes him for answers but Steve remains silent. The stress showing on his face. Col Barker calls a halt to the proceedings and follows Steve out.

"Steve are you having marital problems?" Asks Col Barker.

"Yes Sir, and I am afraid I am very poorly prepared for the most important test of my life!" Says Steve.

"Steve you are an excellent candidate, but your mental state will do you more harm than good on this course. You know the pressures we are going to be putting on the candidates. You have been on the support side of the courses a number of times now. There will be a next time for you." Says Col Barker.

Steve nods and shakes Col Barkers out stretched hand.

"I wish you success Steve, you deserve it." Says Col Barker.

With that Steve reports to the Duty Room at TFDC and collects his kit to travel back to Cape Town. The two and half hour trip back seems to last forever. Steve is not sure if Sharon is ready to settle down and he knows that Zella is on a mission to have fun. She has been going out often and leaving Nicole with friends. Steve has decided to accept that there is no going back. He will try one last time with Sharon before he leaves for Langebaanweg. Steve stops off at Sharon's apartment, but she refuses to let him in. Steve turns and walks away a very broken man. He drives through to Langebaanweg and settles in for the night at the Officers Mess. It is the 2nd September 1991 and the years has flown past. Steve reports for duty and is welcomed by the Officer Commanding AFB Langebaanweg. Steve has been appointed as the Base Logistics Officer.

As Base Logistics Officer one of Steve's tasks is to ensure that the Air Force emergency runways in the region are serviceable and stocked with fuel and equipment for fly away operations. To accomplish this Steve deploys with a Pickup Truck and Support Truck to the various runways for an inspection. The task will take a week to complete. Along the route they will make use of the local South African Police for sleeping quarters and meals.

The distances between each runway are great and the crew spends many hours driving but have the time to enjoy the beauty that surrounds them. One of these unique and amazing sites is the nests of the weaver birds. Steve is dumbstruck how many birds are in the closely weaved nests.

Sociable Weaver Birds and Their Nest

Steve gets back to AFB Langebaanweg and sees he has a message to call Cmdt Dempers at 2 Air Deport (2AD). Cmdt Fluffie Dempers was a Lt. at 87 HFS when Steve rejoined the Air Force in 1980, so Steve is very keen to see what he wants. Steve places the call and Fluffie answers.

"Steve, I need a Chief Technical Officer, when can you start?" Says Fluffie.

"Well Sir, I have just started working here but there is not much to do." Says Steve.

"I have already requested your transfer. I will see you on the 21st October at 2 AD." Instructs Fluffie.

Steve thanks him profusely and hangs up. He has less than a week to make arrangements. He calls Zella and tells her he needs a place to stay to which she responds, "That's fine, I have my own place and will be out by the weekend."

"Can we have a discussion before you leave?" Asks Steve.

"Sure, I will wait till you arrive." Says Zella.

Steve arrives back in Cape Town and true to her word Zella is there to chat with him. They sit down in the kitchen while Nicole entertains herself in the lounge. Steve tells Zella about the job offer at 2 AD, and that he starts there on Monday. He tells her that Sharon has moved on and has a boyfriend now living with her. Zella says that she was out most weekends while Steve was in Pretoria as well. Steve just nods and hangs his head. Next, he asks Zella if he can have Nicole as she seems very busy currently. To his surprise she readily agrees as the place she is moving to is on the other side of Cape Town and she won't be able to take Nicole to school. Steve is overjoyed but does not show any emotion in fear that she might change her mind. Steve gets up to chat with Nicole while Zella starts packing the rest of her stuff. Amazingly Nicole is excited to be staying with Steve and chats happily about what they need to do the weekend. Zella mentions that she would like to have Nicole over every second weekend to which Steve agrees.

Chapter 17 – A VERY DARK TIME

"Sustinemus" - We support

Air Depot based at AFB Ysterplaat.

Early on 21th October 1991 Steve drops Nicole off at School before heading back to AFB Ysterplaat where 2 AD is located. His mood is improving as it seems that his life is starting to change for the better. On reporting to 2 AD Steve is summoned by Fluffie for a briefing. Fluffie is currently the Officer Commanding 2 AD and is looking to build a strong team for the program that 2 AD has been assigned. 2 AD will be the Design Development, Production Line, Maintenance Repair and Overhaul facility for the Air Force modified C47 fleet. 2 AD will be the Air Forces first decentralized System House. To get Steve up to speed Fluffie wants him to establish the Chief Technical Officer process that will require the Design Development, Manufacturing Qualification, and Part Certification for all items designed, manufactured, repaired and modified at 2 AD. This is an enormous tasking and will take all of Steve ingenuity and dedication to effect the required changes. Steve is kept very busy but still finds time to visit the Squadron where he chats to Russell and asks him if he can fill in now and again as F/E. Russell is pleased to hear this as the Squadron are currently short staffed and could use a helping hand. Steve tells Russell to place him on the Standby Roster as well.

By the middle of the week Steve feels like he is in a madhouse with all the policies, processes and procedures that he must review and revise. Russell calls Steve and asks if he would like to do night flying. He assures Russell that he will be there, he must collect Nicole from school and then after supper she will go with him to the base where she can watch television in the squadrons officers lounge and finish her homework. Steve prepares the aircraft and checks up on Nicole before going out to the flight line for the first sortie. They fly for an hour and then take a break for one more sortie. Fanie Jordaan has been chatting to Nicole and as Steve comes in offers for her to fly with. Nicole's eyes widen and excitedly she runs with Steve to the aircraft. It is late the night when Steve and Nicole get home and she is already asleep in the car. Steve carries her through to the bedroom and takes hers shoes off and tucks her with her clothes. He is left to his own thoughts, he grabs a couple of beers and drinks them quickly. The feeling of dread just won't leave him. He shrugs and mumbles to himself, "Stop feeling sorry for yourself, face it like a man." But it's not just the rebuffing of the two woman that is plaguing him. He can't stop replaying events from the Bush War that have suddenly surfaced and are slowly driving him insane.

Without warning the end of the year arrives and although separated from Zella he keeps hearing of how she is messing with married men. Many years ago, she had told him of an episode when she was still a student that she had initiated an affair with a much older married man but did not get as far as a sexual encounter. She now seems to have tipped the scale and is sexually active with a number of married men. Steve is seeing her in a completely different light. The divorce hearing comes, and Steve accompanies her to the court. In 15 minutes it is done, and they are no longer married. Zella wants to celebrate but Steve feels like he is about to throw up. He goes home and waits for Nicole to come out of school, so he can collect her. They spend the afternoon at the beach where Nicole enjoys running in and out of the cold waves rolling up on the beach. Steve watches her with pride. She has recently started Gymnastics and was doing very well at it.

Single once more

At home the evening Steve gets a call from his father. He has retired and offers for them to come and stay with Steve, thereby helping with Nicole. Steve cannot think clearly and just accepts. Nicole is collected by Zella and Steve is alone at home. The darkness overwhelms him once more and he finds himself falling down a pit of despair with no way back. He calls Zella and tries to talk to her but breaks down miserably. Not wanting to embarrass himself he hangs up and reaches for something to drink. He is till sobbing to himself when there is a knock on the door. He refuses to answer it and the knock becomes insistent, still Steve ignores it. The next minute Russell is standing in the kitchen next to him.

"Steve, what is wrong?" Asks Russell.

"I don't know, I am losing it Russell!" Sobs Steve.

Russell stays with him for the remainder of the day and asks Steve to reach out for help. Steve responds that he does not know what's wrong so how to ask for help is a mystery. Russell takes matters into his own hands and knows how much Steve loves to fly. He reports Steve's condition to the medical clinic who immediately revoke his flying medical.

The next morning Steve gets into the office and gets a call from 2 Military Hospital. He must report for evaluation immediately. Steve goes to Fluffie to inform him that he needs to get to the hospital, and Fluffie nods. At 2 Mil Steve is directed to the Psychiatric Wing where he reports to the reception. The nurse checks the records and shows Steve to a consulting room. Steve has just sat down when the doctor comes in and introduces himself. He asks Steve out about his experiences, current situation and what his mental state is. After an hour of cross examination Steve is free to go but must come back for a minimum of 10 sessions. They also would like to speak to Nicole to establish if she is coping with the current family situation.

It will be a few months before Steve's parents arrive, so he attempts to control his rising depression and spends many hours away from the empty house when Nicole is with Zella. He is drinking far too much but at least he does not feel like the world is closing in on him anymore. He has completed the sessions at the hospital and they are happy with Nicole. She displays very little trauma of the events that are taking place. Steve is reissued with his flying medical and gives a copy to Russell for filing. Russell feels embarrassed at reporting Steve, but Steve thanks him. There was no way he would have coped alone. Russell is relieved as he and Steve are friends and he did not want this to be an issue between them.

Steve is doing very well at 2 AD and Fluffie is impressed at how quickly he has established the policies, processes and procedures to manage the CTI position. Steve is also the Chairman for the Configuration Control Board. It does not take long for headquarters to find out that 2 AD has a certification process that exceeds the commercial equivalent. Steve is invited to 1 AD to a work session where he is requested to showcase the process and assist the personnel there to do the same.

In the period that he was in Pretoria, Nicole had stayed with Zella as it is school holidays and she could go to work with her. Zella has also moved closer to Bothasig and has rented a house in Richwood. This meant she would be able to take Nicole to school. Steve is concerned that she would want to take Nicole back, but this was not the case at all. It seems that Zella was benefitting from her affairs and could now afford better accommodation, new car and furniture.

Life after marriage

A new year starts, and Nicole is back at home again. Steve is overjoyed to have her back and she chatters happily away about her holiday with the Grand Parents. The year starts off with many projects that Fluffie has allocated to Steve. Fluffie is desperate to get 2 AD on the map. The first project is modernizing the Plating Shop. Steve gathers as much information as possible. The most convincing item for his business case motivation is the R50,000 fine looming over 2 AD's head after heavy metals are discovered in the runoff water from the base by the City Council. Steve together with the Head of the Plating Shop create a full business case which includes layout, bath design, water treatment plants and recycling system. Steve finalizes the Business Case and presents it to Fluffie for approval and submission. Fluffie is impressed and submits the Business Case without requiring any amendments.

The next project Fluffie hands to Steve is the modernization of the Paint Shop. Currently one of the old 2nd World-War Hangars has been utilized as a Paint Shop. Steve sets up a meeting with the Head of the Paint Shop and starts formulating the conversion of the Hangar to a fully integrated Spray Booth. The requirements must be Health and Safety standards, requiring sufficient air movement to expel the whole Hangars volume of air in 3 minutes. The air must be filtered, cooled, humidified and vented pure enough to breath. Once again Steve gathers the required qualifying information to create a Business Case for presentation and approval. Before submitting this to Fluffie, Steve calls in a Commercial Contractor to verify accuracy of the calculations and alignment with regulations. Satisfied that he has covered all the requirements, Steve submits the Business Case for approval.

The two projects have taken up a lot of Steve's time but the opportunity to develop new facilities at 2 AD is very rewarding and exciting. While the summer months pass quickly Steve is still assisting the Squadron with standby and is occasionally called out to fly sorties. Steve has also established a new CTI Office and developed the Quality Management System for 2 AD.

Steve appoints four Quality Inspectors and arranges for each unit on the Depot to assign a Quality Representative for accountability within their respective departments. At this time the Manufacturing and Certification Program is in full implementation with all Units at the Depot following Procedures.

Steve has weekly Configuration Control Board meetings for the processing of Engineering Change Proposals. 2 AD is quickly becoming known as one of the foremost manufacturing shops in the Air Force and with Mig and Tig Welding, Plating, C&C Lathes, Grinding and many more capabilities. They currently manufacture parts and items for various programs including the C47-TP Maritime Patrol Aircraft, Rooivalk Attack Helicopter, Cheetah Fighter and many more.

Air Force Cross

Steve is rewarded when Fluffie summons him to the HQ Building and informs him that the Plating and Paint Shop Business Cases are approved and are a priority for initiating. Another interesting development is that Steve together with the Antarctic Recovery Teams have been awarded the Air Force Cross.

The decoration is awarded for exceptional ingenuity, resourcefulness and skill, and extraordinary leadership, dedication, sense of duty and personal example and courage in mortal danger, in non-combatant situations. The recovery of the crew and aircraft from the Antarctic Plateau in January of 1991.

Steve is surprised at the award but pleased that those that he relied on to support him during the very tough recovery have also been recognized for their efforts. On the 29th July 1994 at a medal parade on AFB Ysterplaat the proud recipients receive their decorations from the Chief of the Air Force.

Nege Lugmaglede vereer vir reddingspoging in Antarktika

Nege lede van die Lugmag het Lugmagkruise en Balkies tot Lugmagkruise ontvang op 'n medaljeparade op die Lugmagbasis Ysterplaat. Van die lede was 'n paar jaar gelede betrokke by die herwinning van 'n Lugmag helikopter en 'n Duitse helikopter in Antarktika. Te midde van stormsterk winde en temperature benede -20 grade C is die helikopters herstel en die gestrande bemanning na die Suid-Afrikaanse Nasionale Antarktiese Ekspedisie se basis teruggevlieg. Van links is maj. M. Louw (balkie), AO2 R. du Preez, vlugsers. D. Bezuidenhout (balkie), lt.kol. C. Stroebel, sers. A. Lewis (agter), lt. S. Coetzee, sers. O. Kratscmar, vlugsers. W. Beaurain en sers. H. Malan. **Foto: Peet du Toit.**

<u>Air Force Cross</u>

The C47-TP Program is now demanding more of Steve's time as the production timeline has been reduced requiring completion of the program a year ahead of schedule. The C47-TP project involves taking the old Piston Powered Dakota aircraft and completely refurbishing the airframe, adding in 46 inches to the length and then reengining the now new type aircraft with Turbo-Prop PT6 Engines. 4 AD and 2 AD are the Air Forces two production lines for 50 aircraft. 2 AD will additionally build the VIP and Maritime Patrol versions. Additionally, 2 AD will take over the System Management of the platform and sustain the through life support for all the Squadrons operating the C47-TP.

C47-TP

Steve attends monthly Project Meetings at 4 AD in Pretoria where is processes the Engineering Changes (ECP) and assesses the data for accuracy, applicability, quality, safety, budget and completeness. Each ECP must be fully processed for approval before being released for manufacturing and distribution.

Steve spends many evenings when Nicole is with Zella at the Air Force Base to keep himself occupied. The negative part is the constant drinking. He is not aware of the potential of alcoholism but finds solace in not having to be alone and moping. He vaguely remembers the chap who broke down at Ondangwa in SWA in the 1980's and how he had to be sent home. The memory fades and he signals for another round of drinks. It is past 10PM when he gets home and falls into bed.

Nicole is growing up quickly and is doing well at school he now freckled and open smiling face keeps Steve motivated to moving forward. Inwardly Steve has started despising woman and would not allow anyone to get close to him. His fear of making the wrong decision far outweighing his deep desire for someone to love and share his life with.

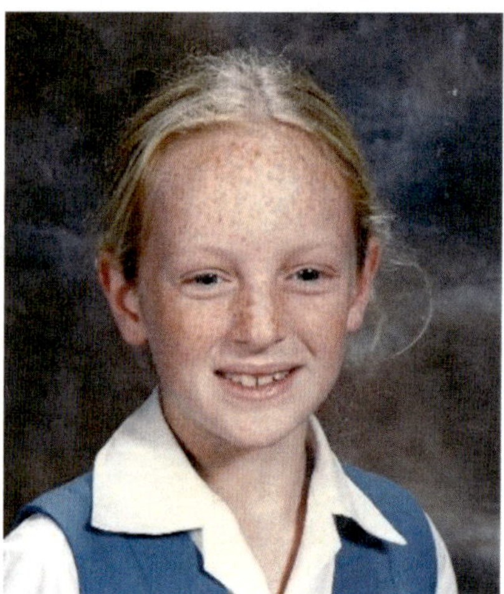

Nicole Growing Up

Frank and Nellie, Steve's parents with all their belongings are set to arrive in the next few weeks. Steve's father has become an alcoholic and is very difficult to get on with. Steve's mother on the other hand is a hypochondriac and is constantly ill with some or other ailment. Steve recalls when he first left home many years before, how he was glad to get out of the toxic environment.

Nevertheless, he puts it all behind him and makes them as comfortable as he can. It will be a relief to have someone at home when he must fly at the squadron for call outs or has to do a trip to Pretoria for the Projects he is managing. Steve has also decided to start looking for a home closer to Nicole's School and future High School. There are a number of homes available in Bothasig which is a stone's throw away from the Schools.

Frank and Nellie

Winter has come fast, and Steve is very busy at the Depot, implementing all the projects he has been assigned. Christo, now the Officer Commanding 30 Squadron approaches Steve and asks if he is willing to do one more trip to SANAE at the end of the year, as they are short of F/E's. Steve without hesitation accepts but asks Christo to make an official request to Fluffie. Christo happily obliges and Fluffie calls Steve in to discuss the trip.

"Steve as you will be away for almost 4 months you need to hand over your projects to accountable personnel. I do not want a fall back on all we have accomplished to now!" States Fluffie.

"I agree Sir, that is why I have handed over the tasks to my three most trusted Warrant Officers, namely Hennie, Alan, and Neville. They have proven their ability to manage the projects successfully that they were assigned. For the CCB I would like to nominate Capt. Chris Bothma, as he has been following what I do for the last year now." Says Steve.

"Perfect Steve, now go and get your head straightened and come back stronger." Requests Fluffie.

"I apologize, I did not know you were aware of my situation?" Says Steve.

"No apologies Steve, you have to sort out your life for your daughter, make sure you do." Says Fluffie.

Excited but also weary Steve sits and ponders over the upcoming trip to the South Pole once more. Hopefully Zella won't take advantage. Steve decides to confront her and settle any issues before.

As if arranged, Zella is at Steve's home when he arrives from work. He pulls her one side and clears the air with the upcoming trip. Zella's immediate reaction is that Steve is lucky that his parents are here as she has plans of her own for December. Steve breathes a huge sigh of relief. The next few months are frantic and amongst getting the aircraft ready, handing over projects, assigning workload and ensuring that there are no loose ends, Steve readies himself for the upcoming travels.

Nicole's cousins from Pretoria have come to visit with their Grand Parents and will also be company for Nicole over the December Holidays. Carla and Danni are Brenda's daughters. Brenda, Steve's sister requested them to visit so that they can catch up with the old folk. The three girls get on well and are continuously up to mischief in some way or other.

2 AD has the end of year formal function and Steve decides to ask the Paint Shops WO's daughter to accompany him. It is a strange situation for Steve at having to ask a woman out on a date again. He perseveres, and she accepts. The Officers Mess at Ysterplaat put a wonderful spread and Steve with his partner arrive timely for the start of the evenings proceedings.

Being a formal evening Steve is on his best behavior and after drinks in the pub after the formal, Steve excuses himself and takes the young lady home. Dating is definitely not easy, and Steve is very uncomfortable. He notices behaviors that send warning signals and cannot wait to leave after saying good night.

2 AD Mixed Formal

The longest trip

The 2nd December 1992 arrives without warning. It is Monday morning and Steve is packed and ready for the trip down south. Steve's parents will take him to the base and then find a parking space close to the SA Agulhas in the Cape Town Docks. The girls will accompany them to say goodbye to the ship. Steve arrives at the Squadron and prepares ZS-HIZ for the flight to the ship. Fanie Jordaan will be the Commander with Mark Fairley as the Co-pilot. With the aircraft loaded, fueled and documents signed, Steve walks into the officer's crew room and helps himself to a cup of coffee while waiting for the pilots. There are three officers in the cockpit of the Puma today, the Commander, Fanie Jordaan is a Major with the Co-pilot Mark Fairley a Lieutenant and lastly Steve Coetzee the F/E also a Lieutenant. They get airborne and leave for the ship. The ground crew is already onboard and are ready for their arrival. With the aircraft on deck and shut down, Steve opens the cowlings and rotates the Main Rotor to line up the marks for folding of the blades. The ground crew have located the blade folding poles and starting at the left rear Steve indicates he is ready to pull the blade securing pin. JD van Zyl has clamped the blade cuff on the blade and lifts the tip up to slacken the torsion on the blade pin. With a swift pull Steve removes the pin freeing the blade to be carried backward to be secured on the tailboom lugs. Within 15 minutes all the blades are folded, and the aircraft is being maneuvered into the hangar. The next aircraft is due to arrive in 20 minutes.

Steve debriefs the crew and then finds out from the ships purser that he has a separate cabin as he is now an officer. Steve rushes his kit downstairs to his cabin and then makes his way back to the hangar to assist with stowing ZS-HJA with the rest of the crew. Bles and Hennie and the fifth pilot Mac will be flying with JC and Kobus. The Air Force contingent gather in the library for a debrief. Mac checks that everyone has what they need and have been accolated accommodation. He then informs them of the latest time to be back onboard and they break off to meet up with family and friends for farewells before the ship will be escorted out of the harbour.

Steve makes his way to where his parents are waiting with the three girls and then goes in search of a place to enjoy a meal. Steve finds a restaurant close to the quay where there is a small water taxi operating around the harbour. He summons the operator and pays him to take the girls for a tour. Steve orders some beers for his father and himself and a glass of orange juice for his mother. They watch amusingly as the girls excitedly wave and point at every new unknown object they see. Steve feels a tug at his heart while watching Nicole, he hates to leave but he does not want to burden her with his dark emotions that still surface constantly. He will be better off focusing on the challenges ahead. The trip is destined to be the longest journey south by a South African team yet and will require him to be very vigilant. The girls get back with Nicole excitedly explaining what they saw and where they went. Smiling Steve hugs, her and then asks them what they want to eat.

As if in a chorus they have already decided that they want Hot Dogs. Steve places the order for all including the meals for the girls and more beer for his dad and himself. The hours fly by and then it's time to head back to the ship. Nicole is crying and won't let Steve go. Steve feels like a monster but tugs her arms from him, kisses her and moves away towards the gangplank. Onboard he makes his way to the helideck where he can see the girls with his parents. Nicole is wiping her tears but waves sadly at Steve. The ship is moving slowly away from the dock and Steve keeps staring at his daughter and thinking how blessed he was to have her. His heart swells with pride but he knows he must sort out his mind or else Nicole will suffer along with his downward spiral. For a fleeting moment he considers giving up Nicole to protect her and then immediately changes his mind, as Zella is not much of a mother and will do her more damage. He must work out what is messing him up and soon.

The ship clears the harbour and sets sail towards the south. Steve settles into his cabin and as he has been instrumental in implementing the aircraft into the Air Forces Computer Maintenance Management System he has brought along a laptop loaded with the program and their aircraft data for the trip. He will update the system daily and ensure that all maintenance activities are completed appropriately. Eventually he extracts himself from the cabin having spent a couple of hours preparing the logs and entries. The weather is changing and the ship rolling and pitching as she heads past the Cape Point and now sets heading on route to the ice. Two days later the crew has settled down and the drinking sessions are well under way. Mac finds Steve in his cabin and tells him that the ships engineer needs an urgent part for the ship. Would one of the aircraft be able to complete the flight as it would be messing up the ships schedule if they must turn around now. Steve confirms with Mac it's not an issue and that he will discuss with Bles and Hennie which aircraft to use.

By 07:00 the morning ZS-HIZ is airborne Fanie, Steve and Mark. They make good time back to Cape Town and land on the Dock to pick up the equipment for the Agulhas. Steve secures the equipment and rejoins the pilots in the cockpit for take-off and return flight. Steve sits back and realizes that as the Clerk of the Court for this trip he now has some jumped up charges for the two new recruits sitting in the cockpit with him. He jots down some notes in his pad and smiles to himself as the Puma speeds back towards the ship. The next few days Steve has a lot or preparation to do. His mother had kindly helped him fix all the costumes for Crossing the Line Ceremony, and all that remained now was to ensure that all new recruits had suitably jumped up charges. With clearance to land from the ship Steve completes the Downwind and Final Vital actions and Fanie brings the Puma into a steady hover on the port side next to the Helideck. The Flight Deck Officer (FDO) indicates him to move over to the Helideck and once in position indicates clearance to land. With the Puma safe on the deck, the FDO motions the deck crew in to secure the aircraft for shut-down. The FDO now signals aircraft secure and Steve initiates shut-down.

The ground crew are already preparing the aircraft for refuel and stowage. Steve first motions the ship's crew to collect the equipment that they had brought back before climbing up the ladder to open the cowlings and fold the blades. With the aircraft stowed and secured and final checks completed in the hangar the Air Force retires to their cabins for some drinks and then lunch. Captain Bill is ever so thankful and offers the Air Force a round of drinks. Big mistake, the Air Force runs the pub and are working on an IOU system that will be settled on the last night of the return voyage.

Captain Bill has just authorized a double of the best scotch for everyone, which they gleefully down and line up for another. The ships engineer is celebrating with them and states that he is sure that the Captain stated two rounds, and with that another round is quickly downed. The rest of the evening turns into a loud drunken, air guitaring piss up. Mark Fairley being the most prominent center stage performer. Hennie and Bles invite Steve to join them in their cabin, a deck below the officers. A bottle of Brandy and several Cokes are available. The three joke and drink the night away.

The next five days are going to be copy paste procedures of wake up, eat, drink, get up to mischief, check the hangar, eat, drink some more, back to cabin to finish left over drinks, sleep and then repeat. All the while Steve manages to complete the charge sheets for all the new recruits. The King and Queen have been selected and briefed. The Bears have been selected and briefed, the costumes final checks completed and assigned to the individuals. Steve is ready to present at the Line Ceremony.

All the while the ship is sailing steadily south and the greenhorns onboard are slowly starting to get their sea legs with less green faces at meals or in the bar. Eventually the ship is breaking ice and the sixty sixth parallel closes in. Captain Leith summons Steve and informs him the time that he will stop sailing the next day for the ceremony to take place. It is the night before the ceremony and Steve with his Bears in costume start their rounds to read out the charges to the newbies. Each cabin is entered, and the recruits name called for processing. The Bears then grab the newbie and rough them up a bit while Steve reads out the charge.

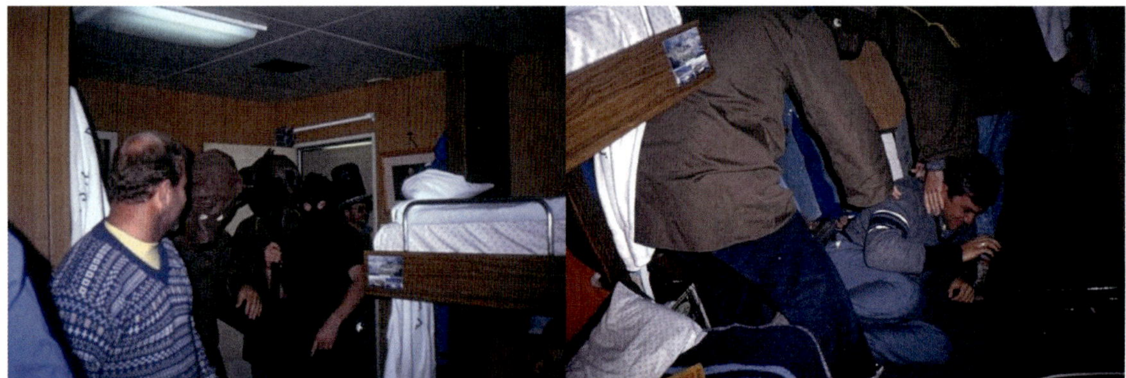

Reading the Charges

In the pilots cabin its Mark and Fanie's turn. Steve grins broadly as he ruffles them both while charging them with stealing a helicopter from the ship. Mark tries to spray Steve with a mouth full of water. Steve giggles and sits on his head.

"What's your name?" Shouts Steve.

"Fairley!" Shouts Mark.

"Fairly fucked!" Responds Steve, as they continue to the next cabin.

Early the morning Steve sets his plan in motion and ensures that all have their costumes ready and the ship's crew has prepared the dunking and flour pots for the occasion. With a final briefing, Steve requests the Officer of the Watch to pipe all to the helideck for the Crossing the Line Ceremony. The Bears are harassing all the newbies on the Helideck and ensuring that they are kept in a separate group like herded cattle for continuous abuse. With King Neptune's arrival with a fanfare blaring over the Public Address the hangar doors open to reveal King Neptune, his Queen and the Clerk of the Court. Steve with a Public-Address speaker is addressing the crowd and welcoming the king and queen to witness the ceremony. Steve insists on the crowd acknowledging royalty and for those who refuse the Bears are quick to correct the attitude.

Arrival of King Neptune and his Queen

Next Steve starts reading the charges while the Bears locate the culprit and bring them forward for initiation. First the cold sea water head dunk, followed by flour tub and then a pat on the head by King Neptune with the suitably prepared egg. Each recruit is processed and for those that misbehave the strop is connected to the overhead crane for a display of power. The guilty will remain there until pacified.

The ceremony concludes and with the withdrawal of the King Court a Braai is laid out on the Helideck for a scrumptious lunch. Unfortunately for the inductees there is no water for them to rinse off. This creates a comical spectacle as they try to get flour and egg off themselves so that they can at least enjoy their meal.

Eventually the Captain authorizes the water to be turned on and the thankful inductee's race to their cabins for a quick rinse off before the bar opens. Disrobed King Neptune once again becomes JC Kriegler and his Queen transforms into Hennie Steyn. Steve collects all the costumes and packs them away for the next years crew. He does a quick round in the hangar to ensure that everything is still in order.

During and after the ceremony there had been a large number of people in and around the aircraft and Steve needs to satisfy himself that there was nothing amiss, damaged or unsecure. Satisfied Steve makes his way down to his cabin to rest a bit before the bar opens.

Steve's mind dwells on the last year and what has transpired thus far. He is missing Nicole and is also fighting to control the darkness that keeps closing in around him. A great sadness starts sweeping over him. Steve jumps up, swears under his breath and makes his way to the bar via the ships rail.

Still further south they sail until eventually Captain Bill makes it through the pack ice to the clear water around the Antarctic continent.

It will be another day and a half before they reach the Bukta at SANAE. In the open water the ship can pick up speed without the threat of ice bergs, as these are all drifting away from the continent. The water is clear and smooth.

Looking over the side Steve makes out whales and seals swimming at great depths, but the visibility is so clear that the scene seems almost photographic. The sea is less salty and is of the purist oceans in the world.

Clear Water

The Southern Ocean

The Southern Ocean, geologically the youngest of the oceans, was formed when Antarctica and South America moved apart, opening the Drake Passage, roughly 30 million years ago. The separation of the continents allowed the formation of the Antarctic Circumpolar Current.

Water gets transported around the Southern Ocean fairly rapidly because of the Antarctic Circumpolar Current which circulates around Antarctica. Water in the Southern Ocean south of New Zealand, resembles the water in the Southern Ocean south of South America more closely than it resembles the water in the Pacific Ocean.

The Southern Ocean has typical depths of between 4,000 and 5,000 meters over most of its extent with only limited areas of shallow water. The Southern Ocean's greatest depth of 7,236 meters occurs at the southern end of the South Sandwich Trench.

The Antarctic continental shelf appears generally narrow and unusually deep, its edge lying at depths up to 800 meters.

The Southern Ocean contains large, and possibly giant, oil and gas fields on the continental margin. Placer deposits, accumulation of valuable minerals such as gold, formed by gravity separation during sedimentary processes are also expected to exist in the Southern Ocean. Manganese nodules are expected to exist in the Southern Ocean.

Iceberg near McMurdo Station

The icebergs that form each year around in the Southern Ocean hold enough fresh water to meet the needs of every person on Earth for several months.

For several decades there have been proposals, none yet to be feasible or successful, to tow Southern Ocean icebergs to more arid northern regions such as Australia, where they can be harvested.

Icebergs can occur at any time of year throughout the ocean. Some may have drafts up to several hundred meters; smaller icebergs, iceberg fragments and sea-ice, generally 0.5 to 1 meter thick also pose problems for ships. The deep continental shelf has a floor of glacial deposits varying widely over short distances.

Sailors know latitudes from 40 to 70 degrees south as the "Roaring Forties", "Furious Fifties" and "Shrieking Sixties" due to high winds and large waves that form as winds blow around the entire globe unimpeded by any land-mass. Icebergs, especially in May to October, make the area even more dangerous.

The remoteness of the region makes sources of search and rescue scarce. The Antarctic Circumpolar Current (ACC) is the strongest current system in the world oceans, linking the Atlantic, Indian and Pacific basins.

Antarctic Circumpolar Current and Antarctic Convergence

The Antarctic Circumpolar Current moves perpetually eastward, chasing and joining itself, and at 21,000 km in length, it comprises the world's longest ocean current, transporting 130 million cubic meters water per second, 100 times the flow of all the world's rivers.

Several processes operate along the coast of Antarctica to produce, in the Southern Ocean, types of water masses not produced elsewhere in the oceans of the Southern Hemisphere. One of these is the Antarctic Bottom Water, a very cold, highly saline, dense water that forms under sea ice.

Associated with the Circumpolar Current is the Antarctic Convergence encircling Antarctica, where cold northward-flowing Antarctic waters meet the relatively warmer waters of the Sub-Antarctic, Antarctic waters predominantly sink beneath Sub-Antarctic waters, while associated zones of mixing and upwelling create a zone very high in nutrients.

These nurture high levels of phytoplankton with associated copepods and Antarctic krill, and resultant food chains supporting fish, whales, seals, penguins, albatrosses and a wealth of other species.

The Antarctic Convergence is considered to be the best natural definition of the northern extent of the Southern Ocean.

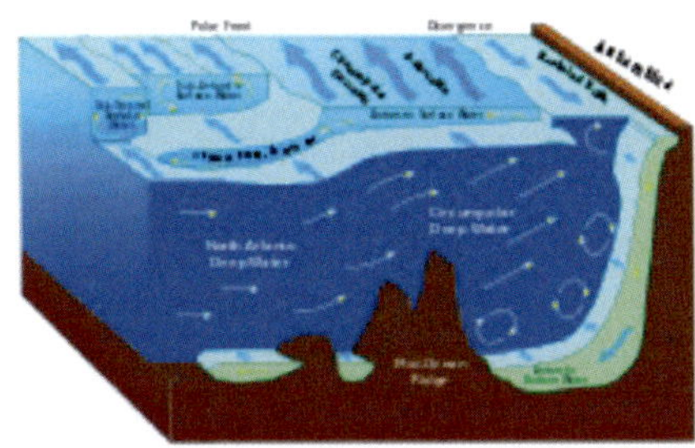

Upwelling in the Southern Ocean

Large-scale upwelling is found in the Southern Ocean. Strong westerly (eastward) winds blow around Antarctica, driving a significant flow of water northwards. Since there are no continents in a band of open latitudes between South America and the tip of the Antarctic Peninsula, some of this water is drawn up from great depths. In many numerical models and observational syntheses, the Southern Ocean upwelling represents the primary means by which deep dense water is brought to the surface.

The Ross Gyre and Weddell Gyre are two gyres that exist within the Southern Ocean. The gyres are located in the Ross Sea and Weddell Sea respectively, and both rotate clockwise. The gyres are formed by interactions between the Antarctic Circumpolar Current and the Antarctic Continental Shelf. Sea ice has been noted to persist in the central area of the Ross Gyre. Due to the Coriolis effect acting to the left in the Southern Hemisphere and the resulting Ekman transport away from the centers of the Weddell Gyre, these regions are very productive due to upwelling of cold, nutrient rich water. Sea temperatures vary from about minus 2 C to minus 10°C. Cyclonic storms travel eastward around the continent and frequently become intense because of the temperature contrast between ice and open ocean. The ocean-area from about latitude 40 south to the Antarctic Circle has the strongest average winds found anywhere on Earth. In winter the ocean freezes outward to 65 degrees south latitude in the Pacific sector and 55 degrees south latitude in the Atlantic sector, lowering surface temperatures well below 0 degrees Celsius.

Antarctic Animals

A variety of marine animals exist and rely, directly or indirectly, on the phytoplankton in the Southern Ocean. Antarctic sea life includes penguins, blue whales, orcas, colossal squids and fur seals. The Emperor Penguin is the only penguin that breeds during the winter in Antarctica, while the Adélie Penguin breeds farther south than any other penguin. The Rockhopper Penguin has distinctive feathers around the eyes, giving the appearance of elaborate eyelashes. King Penguins, Chinstrap Penguins, and Gentoo Penguins also breed in the Antarctic.

The Antarctic Fur Seal was very heavily hunted in the 18th and 19th centuries for its pelt by sealers from the United States and the United Kingdom. The Weddell Seal, a "true seal", is named after Sir James Weddell, commander of British sealing expeditions in the Weddell Sea. Antarctic Krill, which congregates in large schools, is the keystone species of the ecosystem of the Southern Ocean, and is an important food organism for Whales, Seals, Leopard Seals, Fur Seals, Squid, Icefish, Penguins, Albatrosses and many other birds.

Research is part of the global census of marine life and has disclosed some remarkable findings. More than 235 marine organisms live in both polar regions, having bridged the gap of 12,000 km. Large animals such as some cetaceans and birds make the round trip annually. The rocky shores of mainland Antarctica and its offshore islands provide nesting space for over 100 million birds every spring. These nesters include species of Albatrosses, Petrels, Skuas, Gulls and Terns. The insectivorous South Georgia pipit is endemic to South Georgia and some smaller surrounding islands. Freshwater Ducks inhabit South Georgia and the Kerguelen Islands.

The flightless penguins are all located in the Southern Hemisphere, with the greatest concentration located on and around Antarctica. Four of the 18 penguin species live and breed on the mainland and its close offshore islands. Another four species live on the Sub-Antarctic islands. Emperor Penguins have four overlapping layers of feathers, keeping them warm. They are the only Antarctic animal to breed during the winter. There are relatively few fish species in few families in the Southern Ocean. The most species-rich family are the Snailfish, followed by the Cod Icefish and Eelpout. Southern Ocean snailfish are generally found in deep waters, while the Icefish also occur in shallower waters.

Seven pinniped species inhabit Antarctica. The largest, the Elephant Seal, can reach up to 4,000 kilograms, while females of the smallest, the Antarctic Fur Seal, reach only 150 kilograms. These two species live north of the sea ice, and breed in harems on beaches. The other four species can live on the sea ice.

Crabeater Seals and Weddell Seals form breeding colonies, whereas Leopard Seals and Ross Seals live solitary lives. Although these species hunt underwater, they breed on land or ice and spend a great deal of time there, as they have no terrestrial predators.

The four species that inhabit sea ice are thought to make up 50% of the total biomass of the world's seals. Crabeater Seals have a population of around 15 million, making them one of the most numerous large animals on the planet.

The New Zealand Sea Lion, one of the rarest and most localized pinnipeds, breeds almost exclusively on the Sub-Antarctic Auckland Islands, although historically it had a wider range. Out of all permanent mammalian residents, the Weddell Seals live the furthest south.

There are 10 cetacean species found in the Southern Ocean; six Baleen Whales, and four Toothed Whales. The largest of these, the Blue Whale, grows to 24 meters long weighing 84 tons. Many of these species are migratory, and travel to tropical waters during the Antarctic winter.

Five species of Krill, small free-swimming crustaceans, have been found in the Southern Ocean. The Antarctic Krill is one of the most abundant animal species on earth, with a biomass of around 500 million tons. Each individual is 6 centimeters long and weighs over 1 gram.

The swarms that form can stretch for kilometers, with up to 30,000 individuals per 1 cubic meter, turning the water red. Swarms usually remain in deep water during the day, ascending during the night to feed on plankton. Many larger animals depend on krill for their own survival. During the winter when food is scarce, adult Antarctic Krill can revert to a smaller juvenile stage, using their own body as nutrition.

Many aquatic Molluscs are present in Antarctica. Moving around on the seafloor and in burrows filtering the water above. There are around 70 Cephalopod species in the Southern Ocean, the largest of which is the Colossal Squid, which at up to 14 meters is among the largest invertebrate in the world. Squid makes up most of the diet of some animals, such as Grey-Headed Albatrosses and Sperm Whales, and the Warty Squid is one of the Sub-Antarctic's most preyed upon species by vertebrates.

Increased solar ultraviolet radiation resulting from the Antarctic ozone hole has reduced marine primary productivity, phytoplankton by as much as 15%. Illegal, unreported, and unregulated fishing, especially the landing of an estimated five to six times more Patagonian Toothfish than the regulated fishery, likely affects the sustainability of the stock. Long-line fishing for Toothfish causes a high incidence of seabird mortality.

All international agreements regarding the world's oceans apply to the Southern Ocean. Many nations prohibit the exploration for and the exploitation of mineral resources south of the fluctuating Antarctic Convergence, which lies in the middle of the Antarctic Circumpolar Current and serves as the dividing line between the very cold polar surface waters to the south and the warmer waters to the north. The Antarctic Treaty covers the portion of the globe south of sixty degrees south, it prohibits new claims to Antarctica.

This year a full team of scientists will be conducting a multitude of scientific experiments including Earth Sciences and Physicists. Many researches will be attempted during the short summer in Antarctica including, botany, meteorology, biology and geology. A team of biologists onboard, led by Professor Martan Bester, will also be conducting a Whale and Seal count, where use of the helicopters will be made.

The Antarctic Pack Ice Seals (APIS) Program was developed and executed by members of the Scientific Committee on Antarctic Research Group of Specialists on Seals and their National programs to consider the functional significance of upper trophic level predators in the Antarctic pack ice zone and to investigate the seals' interactions with their biological and physical environments.

Recognizing the high cost and logistic difficulties in undertaking research in the pack ice on a circumpolar scale, scientists from the United States, Australia, Germany, South Africa, Norway, and the United Kingdom collaborated to implement a multi-disciplinary science program that would be far greater than the sum of its parts

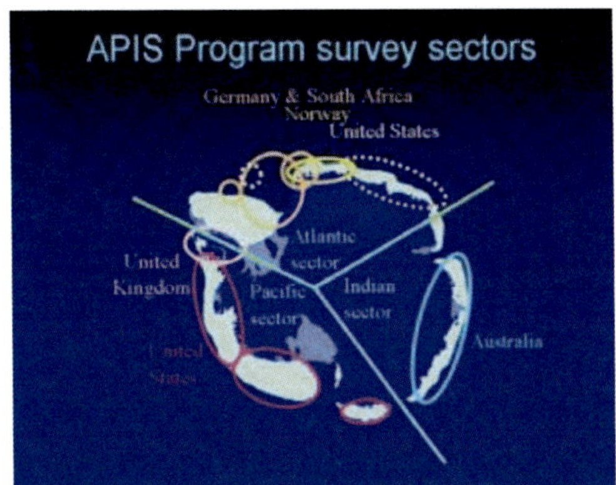

<u>Plan for National participation in the international Antarctic Pack Ice Seal (APIS) program</u>

The pack ice region surrounding Antarctica contains at least 50% of the world's population of seals, comprising about 80% of the world's total pinniped biomass. As a group, these seals are among the dominant top predators in Southern Ocean ecosystems, and the fluctuations in their abundance, growth patterns, life histories, and behavior provide a potential source of information about environmental variability integrated over a wide range of spatial and temporal scales. Variations in top predator distribution, abundance, behavior, and physiology can provide valuable insights into locations of oceanographic features and areas of high secondary production.

Seal Count

On the 16th December JC, Kobus and Steve get airborne with ZS-HIZ from the ship on route to SANAE Main Base. At SANAE they pick up the first batch of Scientists that will be deploying inland from Grunehogna. With the aircraft loaded and pre-flight completed, Steve starts up the Puma and Kobus gets them airborne. Their destination Grunehogna with the scientists. The flight time to Grunehogna will take 45 minutes. Steve has updated the Tans Computer with the navigation points and JC has updated the GPS that was recently installed before the trip. They will not be spending much time at Grunehogna, as the Captain wants to initiate the Seal count that must be conducted along the Ice Shelf and wants them back onboard before evening. The flight to Grunehogna as always, is spectacular and Steve loves identifying the prominent navigation points along the way. By ensuring that the new crew are fully aware of these is important in this unforgivingly beautiful environment. At Grunehogna the Scientists unload and ready themselves for their stay at Grunehogna while Steve refuels the aircraft for the return flight to the ship.

By late afternoon JC lands ZS-HIZ back on the deck of the SA Agulhas. Steve and the crew waste no time in getting the aircraft stowed so that Captain Billy can set sail for the Marine Biologists seal count. Steve gets out of his flight suite and dresses into more casual clothing for supper. Tonight, is steak night and the mess hall will be full, so he wants to be there early to get the best of the steaks. Steve, Hennie and Bles are almost at the front of the row and are already planning the evening in the bar later. The doors open and the crowd storm in. With the first seating filling up quickly the ships stewards start bringing out the food. The aroma of steak and chips is awesome, and Steve's mouth is watering in anticipation of the first bites. Steve begs fresh garlic from the steward, as this is how he loves to enjoy his steak. Hennie and Bles ditto the garlic. It was going to be a smelly evening for sure.

With supper taken care of the trio head up to the bar for after dinner refreshments. Tonight, Brandy and Coke are on the menu. It does not take long for the bar to fill up and the proverbial Ghetto Blaster for music. The evening is off to a good start and it does not take long for a few of the slightly inebriated party goers to break out into song. The evening soon develops into a full-blown party with Biologists, Air Force, Ships Officers and Scientists slamming drinks away and exercising their vocal cords on every song that blares out of the Ghetto Blaster. Bles has over consumed and is attempting to rest for a minute by lowering his butt toward the step between the bar and kitchen. Kobus has Steve's video camera and is giggling as he videos Bles rocking back and forth while aiming not to miss the step. Steve calls to Bles!

"Bles what the hell are you doing man, sit down the suspense is killing us."

Bles looks up trying to focus on where voice is coming from while indicating with a thumb up that he is in control. The bum swaying and aiming takes another minute while the amused crowd is roaring with laughter at the spectacle being captured on video. With Bles seated Kobus notices that Mac has become slightly exhausted and is resting his head on the bar counter and seems to be dosing off. JD sneaks up and starts loosening Mac's belt, so his pants drop down. Just as JD unbuckles the belt and start pulling it through, Mac jerks upright, grabs the belt and jerks it out of the loops himself while trying to stabilize himself. Kobus is attempting not to laugh while he videos the escapade but is unsuccessful with uncontrolled giggles and shaking shoulders while he captures the moment. In the meantime, Mac is attempting to rethread his belt on very unsteady feet. He manages the first two belt hooks and bending forward rests his head for a little nap before jerking upright to find the next hook and repeat the saga once more. It takes Mac fifteen minutes to complete the process after which he is exhausted and leaves for his cabin amidst howling laughter. Bles in the meantime has fallen backward off the step and with a backward drunken look tries to see who pushed him. By this time most of the party goers are beyond normal comprehension and Mark is air guitaring to almost every bit of music from the Ghetto Blaster followed by sharp whistle calls to accentuate his enjoyment of the music. Eventually the party quietens down, and the seats are accommodated to continue uncontrolled volume discussions. The Ghetto Blaster is turned down, but the voices remained raised. The Chief Engineer, Brian, is seated in one of the recliners with his head back and is fast asleep. This is an opportunity not to be missed and Steve races off to his cabin to fetch his electric razor. Steve quickly trims Brian's hairline from one temple to the next making him seem to have developed a massive receding hairline overnight. The whole episode is captured on video by Kobus. Brian wakes up and has no idea why everyone is laughing at him. With a backward wave he exits the pub for the night. Eventually it is closing time and armed with a fresh bottle of Brandy and some Cokes, Steve, Hennie and Bles retire to the F/E Cabin to continue the discussion. Steve enters Hennie and Bles's cabin where Donald has retained Steve's video camera and is capturing a very inebriated Bles trying to hold composure. Everytime Steve or Hennie ask Bles a question his head turns slowly while his eyes seem to lag and follow the direction of the voices he hears. Donald, Hennie and Steve are hollering at the spectacle. Eventually a fresh round of drinks is poured, and the chatter turns around woman. Bles insists that he has the prime story and starts the conversation off.

"Ek het va Helen Shuusman geshe!" Mumbles Bles.

"What are you saying Bles?" Questions Hennie.

"Helen Shuuusman, I did sheee her."

"Oh, you mean the politician Helen Suzman?" Says Hennie.

Nodding profusely Bles acknowledges, "Yeshh Helen Shuuusman."

Steve, Hennie and Donald burst out into a fresh round of uncontrollable laughter. Bles just having claimed that he has sex with the 75-year-old South African anti-apartheid activist and politician. Bles is still toppling around the cabin and trying to adjust the airflow.

"Open the Vans." Says Bles.

"Vans, what vans?" Asks Hennie.

"Fans, vans, daai goed." Mumbles Bles.

"Oh, you mean the Vents." Says Steve.

Steve opens the Vents for the overhead air-conditioning while he, Hennie and Donald are laughing uncontrollably at the drunken banter from Bles. The three settle down and continue drinking. Bles is becoming subdued and retires to the bathroom to ready himself for bed. Steve decides to return to his own cabin and drunkenly exists. A short while later there is a knock at Hennie's cabin door. Hennie opens the door and sees Steve swaying while holding a broken glass.

"I lost my drink!" Burbles Steve.

With tears running down his face while slapping his leg in laughter Hennie takes the broken glass from Steve who turns on his heel and heads up the corridor to find his own cabin.

At 11:30 on 17th December Kobus, Fanie and Steve get airborne with two Biologists to conduct a seal count. The start to sortie flying along the ice shelf while scanning all the floating pack ice for seals. In this region of Antarctica, the Crabeater and Weddell Seals are prominent, but there are also several of the ferocious lone wolf Leopard Seals that feed off the penguins as well. The flight along the ice shelf is beyond any describable beauty that Steve has seen.

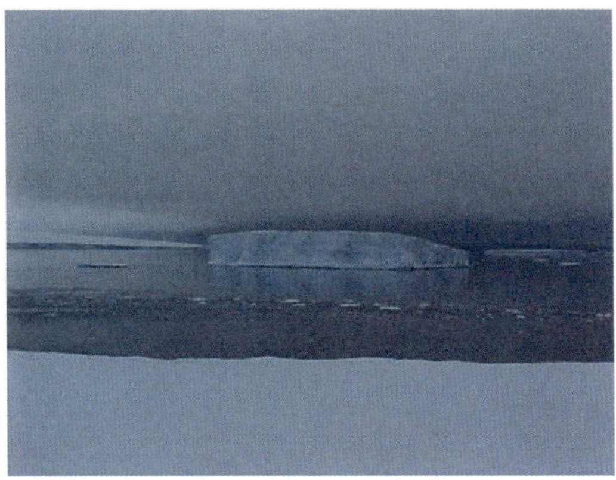

Iceberg and Pack Ice

Crabeater and Leopard Seals

The four-hour flight concludes very successfully with the seal count logged and happily all the species of the region noted. The next few days are scheduled to complete the same surveys and count as many species of wild life as possible. The Biologists will feed the information into an international database for the monitoring of the Antarctic species. At 12:00 18th December Fanie, Mark and Steve get airborne with ZS-HJA and two Biologists to complete the next survey. The same flight pattern is to be completed as the day before. They will keep a low cruise speed at just under 100 ft. above sea level and stick close to the Ice Shelf. They are not disappointed and are even rewarded with Humpback and Orca Whales this sortie.

Humpback and Orca Whales

Excited with the successful sortie Fanie lands the aircraft back onboard the ship. Steve prepares the aircraft for a long trip coming up and ensures that the survival kit is serviceable, maintenance completed and fueled. He signs up the Technical Log and retreats to his cabin to update the Maintenance Management System with the latest flight hours and Servicing data.

It is midday 20th December when JC, Kobus and Steve get airborne with ZS-HJA for a direct flight to Grunehogna. They are flying in Scientific Equipment and fresh supplies to the teams at Grunehogna. The flight to Grunehogna never seems to be the same, as the different lighting captures the most picturesque sights. On route they fly past Vesleskarvet which is the location of the new SANAE V base being constructed.

Vesles Karvet

At Grunehogna Steve once again refuels the aircraft and makes his way to the kitchen for a cup of coffee before they will head back to the ship once again. The teams are preparing their equipment for deployment that will only be initiated once one of the Puma's has relocated to Grunehogna after the survey is completed. With shopping lists from the team, the aircrew depart for the ship.

Back onboard the survey sortie for the next day is being briefed. Steve has noticed a hydraulic leak from the righthand hydraulic pump. Bles has already replaced the Alternator which is located beneath the Hydraulic pump on the previous sortie after losing current from the righthand system during the previous sortie. Steve notices that the pump seal is leaking and decides that he needs to replace it. He finds a hydraulic pump in the pack up kit and completes the Technical Log for the replacement action.

Steve installs the pump and signs off the snag. He summons the ground crew to the hangar for the required ground run of the aircraft to check for leaks. Steve contacts the bridge and informs the Captain of his intentions to check the aircraft. Captain Billy gives Steve permission and with the ground crews assistance he prepares the aircraft for ground run. With Bles in the co-pilot seat and Steve in the commander's seat they complete a start up and run the Puma for fifteen minutes.

Bles shuts down the aircraft and when all switches are off Steve opens the cowls to check the new hydraulic pump for leaks. The pump is dry, and Steve makes the aircraft serviceable in the Technical Log. The ground crew once again stow and secure the aircraft in the hangar.

The next day Sloet, Mark and Bles take off with ZS-HJA on the next seal survey. Steve and Hennie are still in the hangar when the Puma returns after only 30 minutes. After shutdown Bles informs them that the righthand hydraulic system was over pressurizing to maximum and that they could not continue the flight.

The ground crew once again stows and secures the aircraft while Steve and Hennie rummage through the pack up for another hydraulic pump. Unfortunately, there was only one spare pump that is now installed on ZS-HJA. Steve reviews the Illustrated Parts Catalogue, Maintenance and Repair Manuals to see if he can obtain information to repair the leaking pump or fix the over pressure on the new pump.

Steve concludes that the pressure relief valve located in the pump housing is factory set and cannot be removed. The pump shaft seal however is located on the other end of the pump housing. Steve decides to split the two pumps to make one serviceable pump. With the good seal casing and the good pressure relief casing he can build a serviceable unit. Steve mentions his plan to Hennie and Bles who vehemently oppose his plan.

"This is a maintenance action that only Atlas can perform!" Exclaims Hennie.

"Oh! and how do you propose we do that then Hennie, send it by FedEx?" Says Steve sarcastically.

"I am the senior Technical rank and will brief the Chief pilot of my intensions. I will then build a serviceable pump from the two we have and run the aircraft for an hour on the deck to check all the systems."

"We want nothing to do with this." Says Bles and Hennie as if speaking in once voice.

Steve shrugs and goes to brief Mac and Sloet on the situation. He informs them of the leaking pump being the reason for the Alternator failure. There are also no more Alternators in the pack up, so it would be useless to reinstall the leaking hydraulic pump and losing another Alternator.

Steve's plan is to split the two pumps and combine the serviceable parts for a non-leaking and non-over p Mac and Sloet agree with Steve and he proceeds to remove the pump from the aircraft. With the both the . leaking pumps in hand, Steve goes to the ships engine room workshop to create a clean workspace for the process. He not want to contaminate the pumps with dirt and grime from the hangar.

Steve first splits the leaking pump to assure himself of the process. He cleans all the parts and then lays them out in order of disassembly. Next, he strips down the over pressuring pump in the same way and repeats the cleaning and laying out process. Satisfied, Steve now starts the assembly of the two serviceable housings. He double checks the assembly and once satisfied completes all the required wire locking.

Steve calls for JD's assistance to witness the installation and counter signs the process. Next Steve obtains permission to conduct a ground run from the bridge. He then orders the ground crew to maneuver the aircraft onto the Helideck and contacts Sloet to join him for the ground run. With Sloet in the commander seat and Steve in the F/E's seat they obtain start up approval and initiate start.

Steve monitors the hydraulic gauges carefully and they are both normal in the green. With the engines at flight idle and the Rotor RPM stabilized, Steve informs Sloet that he is going to open the Cowl and check the hydraulic pump for leaks. Steve scrambles up the ladder and peaks in the cowl. There are no leaks from the pump.

Steve rejoins Sloet and they settle into monitoring the hydraulics for the next hour. Half an hour into the ground run Sloet says he is satisfied. Steve shakes his head and informs Sloet that this is about finding and proving a solution. The two senior F/E's have not met the grade and Steve is pissed. He is going to make an example.

Exactly 60 minutes on the clock, Steve reaches up and shuts down the aircraft. With the Rotors stopped he indicates to both Bles and Hennie that they must conduct a full inspection of the hydraulic repair carried out. Hennie's attitude has changed, and he humbly apologizes then completes a full check of the system.

Bles remains in the Technical Office and pretends to be too busy to check. Steve will have a word with him later. First Steve and Hennie satisfy themselves that the aircraft is once again serviceable and ready to fly the next Seal Survey.

Sloet has briefed the Biologists who have prepared themselves already. Steve volunteers for the next sortie as he is confident that the fix he completed is safe. JC, Kobus and Steve take-off at 13:30 and complete the 2.6-hour sortie with no further issues.

The aircraft is performing perfectly, and all systems are normal. On the post flight inspection Steve checks the hydraulic pump and is satisfied that the area is perfectly dry.

Steve calls Bles one side and has a quiet discussion with him. Steve reminds him that as the F/E he must exercise all options within his experience to find a safe and high-quality solution. He cannot deny that others may have solutions that he has not had exposure to before but needs to accept that as a team there is more experience. They shake hands and head for a meal and then the pub.

For the next week the seal surveys will continue with Hennie, Bles and Steve sharing the flying. In the meantime, the ship has made good speed towards the Bukta where the Norwegian base Troll offloads all their equipment. Troll is a Norwegian research station located at Jutulsessen, 235 kilometers from the coast in the eastern part of Princess Martha Coast in Queen Maud Land, Antarctica.

It is Norway's only all-year research station in Antarctica and is supplemented by the summer only station Tor. Troll is operated by the Norwegian Polar Institute and features facilities for the Norwegian Meteorological Institute and the Norwegian Institute for Air Research.

It is very close to Christmas and the Captain has authorized the kitchen staff to prepare a feast for Christmas Day. The Air Force will be onboard for both Christmas and New Year's. On Christmas day 25th December JC, Kobus and Steve get airborne for the last Seal Survey before the Christmas party on the ship.

A quick 2-hour sortie and a positive seal count result bagged, they land back onboard where the ground crew eagerly stow and secure the aircraft. Hennie meets Steve with a beer in hand and the two quickly wrap up the Technical Log and ensure the hangar is secured. They head to the bar to start the festivities.

The Team, from left to right back; Mark, Kobus, Fanie, JC, Bles, JD, Fireman 1.
From left to right front; Hennie, Steve, Fireman 2, Gerhard, Mac, Greg.
Not in photo, Sloet and Donald.

The celebrations continue till early morning when the Air Force Crew end up in one of the larger cabins where Fanie has managed to fill a garbage bag with Helium from the Met Lab. The bag is passed around while each member has a go at trying to say something in a helium infused voice without laughing. Very few succeed.

Kobus breaks out in laughter at the first word and the hysterical laughter that comes out sounds like a school girl being kissed for the first time. Fanie manages to give a Charles Fortune Cricket commentary rendition that is incredibly funny and in the boyish shrill voice has the expected results with a howl of laughter from the crowd. The evening winds down and the rowdy drunken participants make their ways back to their cabins to sleep off the over consumption.

It is 26th December, Boxing Day and Steve readies ZS-HIZ for another Seal Survey. With Kobus and Mark as the pilots the 2.1-hour sortie is completed with the Biologists extremely satisfied with the number of seals observed.

Helping the Norwegians

Contrary to most other research stations on the continent, Troll is constructed on the snow-free slope of solid rock breaking through the ice sheet at Jutulsessen, located 1,275 meters above mean sea level. The station opened as a summer-only station in 1990. It has an overwintering capacity of eight people and a summer capacity of 40. It is served by Troll Airfield, which is the base for the Dronning Maud Land Air Network.

It is the 27th December when the SA Agulhas receives a call for assistance. The Norwegian vessel, Polar Bjorn is currently stuck in pack ice and cannot break through to the Ice Shelf to offload their cargo.

In discussions with the SA Agulhas the Polar Bjorn is requesting assistance in offloading. Mac and Sloet call Steve to discuss what the limit is for Cargo Slinging.

The Puma J Model is rated at 2500 Kg from the hook and can easily lift the heaviest load from the Polar Bjorn. Kobus and JD will be dropped off on the Polar Bjorn on the first flight where after both aircraft will complete the offloading by cargo sling.

Steve and Hennie prepare both aircraft for Cargo Slinging. The ground crew prepare ZS-HIZ for first take-off. Fanie, Mark and Steve get airborne off the ship with Kobus and JD as Pax and land on the forward deck of the Polar Bjorn. They drop Kobus and JD off and pick up a Casevac from the Polar Bjorn to take back with them to SANAE where the doctor will treat him. He is suffering from pneumothorax or collapsed lung which occurs when there is a build-up of air in the space between the lungs and the rib cage. As a result, pressure on the lung is increased, therefore, it cannot expand as much as it usually can. He will be made comfortable onboard the ship for the travel back to SANAE.

Norwegian Station Troll

With Kobus taking charge on the Polar Bjorn bridge for the Cargo Sling work, he radios Fanie with the first load hook up. Steve confirms the maximum weight they can sling with the current fuel load. Both Puma's have internal fuel allowing more weight on the Cargo Sling.

As the fuel burns off so the weight on the sling can be increased. Towards the end of the sortie the heaviest items, the vehicles, will easily by lifted from the ship. Fanie brings ZS-HIZ in for the first hook up with Steve pattering him to where JD is ready with the first strop.

JD secures the strop and indicates load hooked and Steve clears Fanie to take the strain and lift the load. It is a quick flight to the ice shelf and then back to the Polar Bjorn to collect the next load. By the time ZS-HJA is airborne half the loads have been removed from the ship.

Between both aircraft the rest of the cargo and vehicles are slung from the Polar Bjorn. The pilots from the Norwegian crew are overjoyed at how quickly the two Puma's have managed to complete the task.

Cargo Sling from Polar Bjorn

Fanie flies ZS-HIZ back to the Agulhas and after landing, Steve shuts the Puma down. ZS-HJA has landed on the Polar Bjorn to pick up Kobus and JD before returning to the ship as well. Giving the ground crew sufficient time to stow and secure ZS-HIZ.

With both aircraft stowed and secured Captain Billy sets heading for the Bukta at SANAE. The Norwegian patient has settled in well, but the Captain wants the SANAE doctor to treat him as soon as possible. He summons Mac to the bridge to discuss flying the patient off earlier to ensure the treatment can be affected soonest.

ZS-HIZ will take off in the morning for SANAE to drop the patient off while ZS-HJA continues the Seal Surveys. The Norwegian Captain and pilots pay the Agulhas a quick visit with their EC130 Helicopter to thank the SA Agulhas for the assistance.

Polar Bjorn Crew

Early the next morning Hennie prepares ZS-HJA for a flight to SANAE to drop off the Norwegian patient. The doctor at SANAE wants the patient there immediately to start the treatment. He will remain at SANAE under the doctor's treatment until he recovers sufficiently to be returned to the Polar Bjorn. Soon after the departure of ZS-HJA, Steve and the ground crew prepare ZS-HIZ for another Seal Survey sortie. There are only a few surveys left to conduct, as the helicopters are now required for Geophysics and Public Works Department work. The construction of the new SANAE IV Base is underway and the preparation for the foundations of the elevated permanent base must be initiated.

The ground crew assist Steve in maneuvering the aircraft onto the helideck, where after Steve climbs up onto the transmission platform and locates the pins after the crew spreads the blades. Bles completes a duplicate inspection of the Blade Pin security as well as the reconnection of the De-Icing Looms for the Main Rotor Blades. Steve has initiated the Technical Log entries and completed the pre-flight inspection. Bles signs the duplicate inspections while Steve completes the Author Book and ensures that the survey team are ready for the flight. Steve keeps himself busy to prevent his mind from the dark place he finds himself in. On the trip so far, Steve has managed to control the Demons by forcing positive thoughts. Nicole features mostly and brings a warm feeling of protection in his heart.

ZS-HIZ flight preparation

Once again Kobus, Sloet and Steve complete the Seal Survey in a 2.7-hour sortie along the ice shelf. Martan is extremely satisfied with the count and his beaming smile at the end of the flight depicts his success.

A New Year

The Seal Surveys, as the Old Year, are coming to an end. This will be the first time that the Air Force crew will celebrate the New Year onboard the Agulhas. 31st December rolls in quickly and the Ships Catering Staff have prepared a feast in the celebration of the new year on the 1st January 1993. The yearend still however needs to be greeted and shortly after supper the festivities start. It is a decent group of Air Force that enter the bar to start the evening off. This for certain would not last.

Distinguished Gentleman from the Air Force

The party starts in earnest and very soon Mark has the Juke Box cranked up and is whistling loudly to his favourite hits. The rest of the party goers are in no better shape and the proverbial burble mode speech is in effect. Slurring, spluttering, laughing and shouting are the order of the evening. Kobus decides it's time to play a trick on Steve, who is an officer but not a pilot, so royal game for him. He sidles up to Steve and starts mumbling about personal family matters to entice Steve into a confrontation. The reverse happens and Steve storms out of the pub to the ships railing to curb his tears. He is forcing back emotions that seem to well up from deep within him and has no way of controlling what is happening.

Hennie in the meantime has updated Kobus on Steve's current marital issues. With shock on his face Kobus rushes out to apologize to Steve. Steve brushes him off with a nod of acceptance and disappears to the aft of the ship. Perhaps a walk on the helideck will help clear his demons. He stays on the helideck for a few minutes and realizes the danger of being with his own thoughts and moves back to the bar. Hennie already has a drink in hand for him which he quickly finishes. The celebrations continue and at midnight ships time the singing of Old Lang Syne commences. Drunken handshakes and hugs are distributed while the celebrations continue. South Africa is still an hour behind the ships current time. At 01:00 Hennie grabs a glass of champagne and with a loud retort exits to the helideck to bid South Africa a happy new year. Steve and a few of the Air Force Crew follow suite. The motley group raise their glasses and bid South Africa a happy new year. Hennie's voice chokes up and with tears in his eyes he turns to Steve and retorts, "Hoe Choke hy my nou!"

Steve bursts out laughing as Hennie had just re-enacted a video clip of a Coloured Woman sampling Hokes Wine laced with salt. Her response was exactly what Hennie had just done. The drunkards return to the bar to continue the celebrations to the wee hours of the morning. Captain Billy had decided not to limit the hours of operation for the celebrations. There were going to be some sullen hangovers in a few hours, but fortunately with the ship sailing back to the SANAE Bukta flying would only commence at midday on this new year.

Steve is the soberest of the F/E's and elects to offer his services for the Seal Survey on this first day of 1993. This 2.8-hour sortie is the second last survey for the season flown by Fanie with Kobus as co-pilot. The last sortie is on the 4th January with a flight conducted to the west along the ice shelf. Steve once again completes this 3-hour sortie together with JC and Mark.

The 7th January Fanie, Kobus and Steve depart with ZS-HJA to SANAE to begin the offload of the pack-up kit for the helicopters. The 1.5-hour sortie ensures that all pack-up and personal kits for the Air Force Crew staying at the SANAE Emergency Base are relocated from the ship. Both aircraft depart the ship for SANAE where they will be located for a few days before one aircraft is deployed to Grunehogna. The crews will swap after a week. At SANAE the Challenger Vehicles have now been fitted with GPS Navigation systems to assists the teams with accurately traversing the Glacier on route to Grunehogna. Fanie offers to train all the drivers on the programing and use of the GPS.

CAT Challenger

The New Base

It is early afternoon on the 8th January when Steve and Hennie prepare ZS-HIZ and ZS-HJA for a flight to the new SANAE IV construction site as Vesleskarvet. With Steve is Kobus as the flying pilot and Fanie as co-pilot. A PWD Team is flown to inspect the temporary living containers for condition and preparation of a small team that will start working there.

The construction of SANAE IV has been initiated in South Africa already and the respective modules slated for future trips to be transported by the SA Agulhas and South African Navy Supply Ships. The new base will be located in the Queen Maud Land region of Eastern or Greater Antarctica. SANAE IV is to be constructed on top of a distinctive flat-topped Nunatak, Vesleskarvet, on the fringe of the Ahlmann Range of mountains. The base will be approximately 80 kilometers from the edge of the continent and 160 kilometers from the edge of the ice shelf. Vesleskarvet is surrounded by the glacial ice sheet.

Vesleskarvet location of SANAE IV

The first three SANAE research stations were located on the Fimbul Ice Shelf near to the coast and were subject to the gradual snow burial and eventual crushing that occurs with all stations constructed in this fashion. With a vision of creating a more permanent station, SANAE IV will be completed using a design which is revolutionary with the structure raised on stilts allowing snow to blow through underneath and thus limits deposition. By constructing the base near the cliffs of Vesleskarvet, the concept is advanced further as snow that would collect downwind of the base and eventually advance to cover it is instead blown off the 250 m high cliffs into the wind-scoop beyond. By virtue of this feature, the station should far exceed the short useful life of its predecessors.

The station will have orange coloured roof for better visibility from the air. SANAE IV will consist of three linked modules, each double-story, 44 meters long and 14 meters wide. Two smaller nearby structures will contain the satellite dish to be used for communications and the diesel fuel bunkers. Joined end-on-end in a north-south orientation, the base modules will be complemented on the northern end by a large raised helicopter landing area with a lifting section allowing vehicles to be brought up into the hangar for maintenance.

The C-block, northern-most module, will contain the large hangar, generator room, workshop, water storage, sewage processing plant, equipment stores, offices of the mechanical and electrical engineers, flight operations office, gymnasium and sauna. The neutron monitors of the North-West University will also be housed in this area. The B-block, middle module, will contain the kitchen, dining area, two TV lounges, bar, games room, smoker's room, library, a laundry and accommodation units. While the A-block, southern module, will contain the radio room and communications hub, medical facility, darkroom, various research project offices, leader's office, two physics labs, wet lab, store-rooms, another laundry, and accommodation units. The modules are to be linked by single-story connections which also serve as entrances with stairways down to the surface 4m below the base. Each link will contain an entrance hall with two sets of doors, creating a rudimentary 'air-lock' to prevent excessive cooling when entering and exiting the base, as well as a change-room, ablution facility and electronic distribution boards.

The base generates power will utilize three diesel generators. Water is to be generated by manually shoveling snow into a snow smelter, which then melts the snow and ice and pumps water automatically into the holding tanks. Waste water and sewerage is to be treated within the base, with the only by-product being clean water which is then released back into the environment. All refuse will be sorted, crushed and sealed in empty fuel drums for return to South Africa.

The base will be well insulated by its 0.5-metre thick walls and triple-glazed windows, but the internal areas will have to be actively warmed. This will be accomplished by three means. Firstly, the heat generated by the diesel generators will be used to heat water for the taps and showers, which is then circulated through the base. Secondly, the same generator heat will be used to heat air which is distributed by the climate control system. Thirdly, small electric wall and fan heaters will be available in all indoor areas. Efforts are made to maintain the interior temperature at 18 °C although some areas, such as the hangar, do cool well below this in winter.

SANAE IV will have advanced communications capabilities using both satellite and radio systems. A permanent satellite connection to the SANAP headquarters in Cape Town will provide three telephone lines and one fax line, and near-broadband internet access. Team members in Antarctica will therefore enjoy fast internet access which allows them to correspond with colleagues and stay in contact with friends and family.

The base will be staffed and maintained year-round by a team of scientists and support personnel. Each overwintering team arrives during the summer expedition and take-over period aboard the research and logistics vessel SA Agulhas, stays at the base through the austral winter and returns to South Africa at the end of the next summer season, an expedition of approximately 16 months.

The summer expedition and re-supply team consists of 80 to 100 persons, and includes administrative staff, heavy vehicle operators, helicopter crew, maintenance staff, the new overwintering team and a large scientific contingent. During the brief summer, typically December / January to February / March, the base is resupplied with food, equipment and fuel, all waste products will be removed for transport back to South Africa, the new overwintering team will receive on-site training, and scientific investigations which cannot be undertaken in the winter months, such as extended field-work, must be completed.

The overwintering team remains at the base alone and isolated between the months of March and December. To be fully self-sufficient, the team typically consists of the following personnel:

- An electronic engineer who doubles as communications technician,
- A mechanical engineer responsible for the base systems,
- An electrical engineer who manages power generation and distribution,
- Two diesel mechanics responsible for maintenance of the diesel generators, heavy vehicles and skidoos,
- A meteorologist who performs both observations and forecasting,
- A cosmic ray physicist/engineer responsible for various research projects
- A high frequency radar physicist/engineer responsible for the auroral radar projects,
- A third scientist responsible for the International Polar Year projects and other installations, and
- A medical doctor

An expedition leader is selected from the overwintering team prior to the departure of the expedition, and a deputy elected to serve in his place should the need arise. The expedition leader is responsible for administrative tasks and reports to the South African National Antarctic Programme headquarters in South Africa.

SANAE IV's reason for existence is to provide a permanent year-round base for scientists undertaking research projects under the auspices of SANAP. Investigations carried-out year-round are predominantly in the physical sciences, while the summer months allow research in more diverse fields such as oceanography, biology, geology and geomorphology. Recent projects have also focused on sources of renewable energy such as solar and particularly wind power generation. Ongoing physical science research programs includes the Antarctic Magnetospheric and Ionospheric Ground-based Observation, Southern Hemisphere Auroral Radar Experiment and Super Dual Auroral Radar Network, Antarctic Research on Cosmic Rays very low frequency radio research and various International Polar Year projects.

Artist impression SANAE IV

Both aircraft land close to the temporary containers that will house the construction teams. While the PWD Team inspect the temporary living containers the Air Force contingent does a sweep of the area to see how far the base foundation has progressed. There is a high wind blowing loose snow around. The temperature is below zero so the aircrews dress appropriately. A number of the containers are packed with blown snow that has been forced through pin hole size gaps in the doors. The PWD Team manages to force the doors open and start removing all the accumulated snow inside the containers. Steve and Hennie use the video camera to capture the beauty from the top of the Vesleskarvet cliff which overlooks the valley to Boreas, Passat, Lorenson Piggen and Roberts Collen.

View from Vesleskarvet with Lorenson Piggen

Roberts Collen is one of the Nunataks that has the only sign of life in the region with the snow pectoral laying eggs and hatching them in the crevasses of the rocks during the summer period. In between these crevasses are also signs of vegetation that has adapted to surviving in this incredibly challenging environment.

The wind has picked up and the temperature dropped. By the time everyone is back at the choppers Steve discovers that there has been windblown snow buildup on the transmission and engine platforms. He checks the MPAI filters and engine intakes to make sure that there is no accumulation in them before closing up and completing the preflight inspection. Fanie reads the checklist while Kobus and Steve complete the checks. Steve starts the first engine and once at self-sustaining rpm he starts the second so that both can warm up before he advances the fuel flow levers. As he starts opening the throttle a fire warning light illuminates on number one engine. Steve retards the fuel flow and before jumping to conclusions gets out of his seat to visually confirm if there is actually a fire. The engine shows no sign of flames, so Steve is convinced that the cold windblown snow accumulation on the engine platform has caused a temporary malfunction of the fire detectors. Just then Hennie radios through from ZS-HJA that he has the same scenario and also on number one engine. Both Steve and Hennie concur that the snow buildup on the number one engine platform was causing the malfunction. Steve advances the fuel flow once more and this time the fire warning light flickers and remains extinguished. Both aircraft take-off and return to SANAE III.

SANAE first timers

The old SANAE Team has invited all occupants, visitors, new team members and the Air Force to a welcome to SANAE evening.

Main Base Bar

The old team has prepared a delicious round of bar snacks for everyone and it's not too long before the party is well under way. The old team leader however is keeping a watchful eye on the participants to ensure that there are no early party AWOL first timers.

Next without further adieu, he brings out his name list of first timers. In no particular order the names of the first-time visitors to SANAE III are read and ordered to come forward and form a line. Two drinks are offered up, first the Spanish Arsehole followed by a Beer Chugger.

The problem however is that both drinks are sucked from a mug shaped like a woman's breast with the nipple as the method of delivery. The Shot Boob Mug is filled with two tots of Tequila and two tots of Tabasco. Due to the size of the hole the poor victim has to suck hard on the nipple to get the mixture out.

Should any of it spill the immediate effect of the Tabasco infused Tequila starts a burn so bad that it turns the skin red. Thus, the term Spanish Arsehole is a very apt name for this shot.

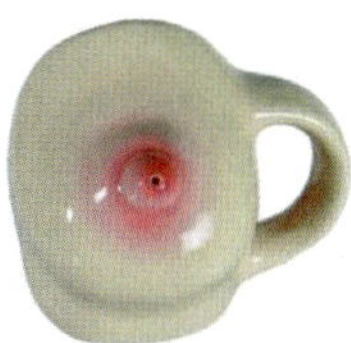

Boob Shot Glass for the "Spanish Arsehole"

Following the burn from the Spanish Arsehole the Larger Boob Beer Mug is offered to sooth the pain.

The problem however is that the hole is small, and the drinker must suck extra hard to get the beer out.

Beer Big Sipper

The Norwegian patient has recovered sufficiently to be included in the initiation after which he comments that it was the worst drink he has ever had in his life.

The comical scene is causing havoc as the participants battle to curb the burn and are sucking extra hard to get the beer out. Fanie does a good job and even complains that the Tabasco is blocking the hole and he cannot get it all out. Without missing a beat, the team leader fills his shot again for another attempt. This time Fanie makes sure to get it done right. Mark steps up and spills a mouth full of the Spanish Arsehole on his shirt front. The next minute he starts rubbing his chest. As he lifts his T Shirt the redness of the burn is immediately noticeable. This only encourages the crowd more and he is forced to have another because of the spill. Mark is a very unhappy camper. With all new comers initiated the party continues until late in the night. Eventually Steve, Hennie, Bles and the rest of the team make their drunken way up the 50 ft stairwell to the surface.

Main Base Entrance and Passages

Swaying badly the group aims for E-Base and 30 minutes later find themselves still the same distance away but in the wrong direction. They have ended up far to the left of E-Base amongst the equipment storage platforms.

E-Base

Steve takes the lead and giggling the drunken group follow. Steve keeps E-Base in his sights and keeps plodding along while the rest following at a slow pace. Eventually an exhausted and cold group of party goers are within reaching distance of E-Base.

Stumbling up the stairs Steve makes his way to bed and struggles himself out of his Antarctic clothing to fall back on the bunk into a deep sleep.

It is mid-morning on the 9th January when Steve stumbles into the kitchen to feed his hangover. Brunch is ready, and Steve helps himself to an extra-large helping. He will need it today as he has planned to complete a large servicing on ZS-HIZ. The rest of the Air Force crew is also looking very much the worse for wear. Very little chatter takes place and Steve grumbles a few orders informing the crew to be ready after breakfast for the servicing on the aircraft. Some resistance starts being mouthed but one look at Steve's face quickly quells the moans that were about to start. Steve dons his cold weather gear and heads down to the aircraft. Ollie and Herby accompany him down and they start removing the aircraft covers for access to the panels and platforms that need to be opened. Three hours later the hangovers have disappeared, and the servicing successfully completed. The aircraft is covered and secured.

At midday on the 12th January Steve together with Kobus and Mark are flying ZS-HJA to the Halgrens Nunatak where the Biologists are eager to check out the nesting areas of the Snow Pectorals. Landing on the top of Halgrens on a rocky outcrop gives the Biologists a quicker access to the nesting areas. The group spend a couple of hours clambering around the rocks oohing and aahing over amazing ability for life to exist in this hostile environment. They take-off and return to SANAE. For the next two weeks there are a number of flights to the field and back to resupply teams. Two trips are also completed to the Cat Train Challengers that are on route to SANAE IV.

On the 31st January Steve prepares ZS-HJA for a flight with Fanie and Mark to the Polar Bjorn. They return the recovered Norwegian crewman to the ship and assist with uploading the cargo for return to Norway. The Cargo Sling sortie is completed in record time.

The first month of 1993 has come and gone in a flash with Steve not having time to reflect on the ominous feelings deep down. There are still a number of flights to be conducted to Vesleskarvet for the PWD Team that are preparing the foundations for the new base.

The short Antarctic summer is quickly coming to an end and the sun is now reaching the horizon and staying there for a long time. Within a few weeks the South Pole will start experience darkness for a few short hours, which will quickly increase to total darkness.

On the 11th February Steve prepares ZS-HIZ for a flight to Grunehogna. Steve, Fanie, Kobus and Mark together with Gerhard and Greg depart at 14:00 to spend the next two weeks at Grunehogna. They arrive at the base 2.5 hours later and the crews quickly unload the aircraft while Steve, Gerhard and Greg set about to cover and secure the aircraft.

Over the next two weeks the Air Force contingent will be on standby for the PWD crews at Vesleskarvet as well as the Geologists and Scientists that have deployed in the field.

During the period Mark celebrates his birthday with Fanie and Kobus perfecting their culinary skills to bake a cake for him.

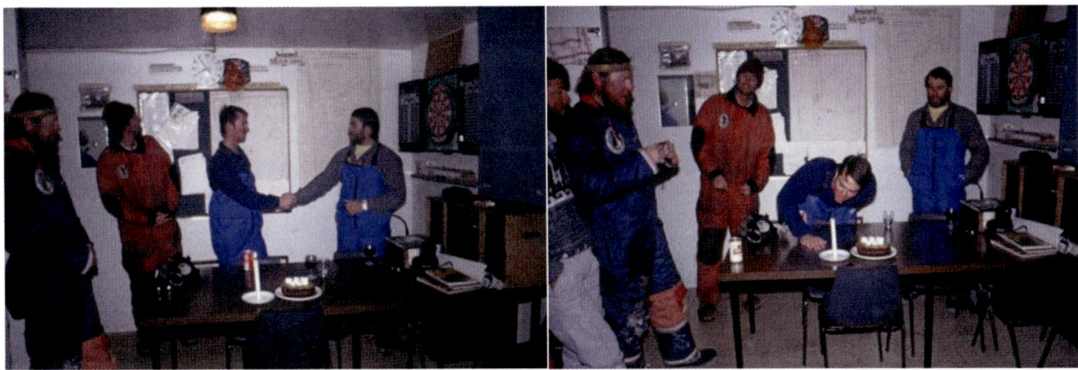

<u>The Birthday Boy, The Cake and The Candle</u>

The evening becomes a roaring party and soon the booze is flowing freely. It does not take long for the Juke Box to appear and at full volume is blasting from the kitchen table. Older numbers like "I can't dance" by Phil Collins results in a walking dance rendition that ends up on the tundra with Steve in the lead.

The results are predictable, somewhere, somehow there was going to be shoving and a human pile giggle in the snow.

I can't dance Rendition

Later the evening Steve and Fanie deliver a drunken performance of Queens "Bohemian Rhapsody". Both using empty Brandy bottles as microphones and singing as loud as they can pump their lungs to burst out, the two perform an amazingly comical enactment for a very appreciative audience.

Eventually the evening winds down with over consumption taking its toll on many. With heads buried on folded arms around the kitchen table and the music playing softly in the background the exhausted bodies requiring recuperation.

Bohemian Rhapsody

On the 25th February the crew packs up once more to return for the final stint at E-Base. At 18:30 Fanie lifts ZS-HIZ off to a spectacular flight back to SANAE.

The sun is low on the horizon and is dipping as they land at E-Base.

Sunset E-Base

With the setting of the sun for a few hours the temperature drops substantially. There is a frenzy of getting last minute tasks completed by all teams as the time at Antarctica is quickly drawing to a close. Equipment requiring repair or damaged are all packed up and taken to the Bukta via Cat Train. These will be loaded back onto the SA Agulhas for return to Cape Town.

Igloo Build

Steve and Donald decide to fill the time with the design and building of an Igloo at E-Base. In each aircrafts emergency kit is a snow saw that is specifically designed to cut blocks of compressed snow for the purpose of building Igloos. No sooner have Steve and Donald cleared an area to start the build when an audience of all knowing professionals have all the advice required to proceed. Steve shows them the middle finger and proceeds in the preparation work. This was going to be an Air Force special design.

Building the Igloo

They have cleared out a square area to begin the construction in the form of a pyramid. Mark and Fanie decide to join the construction and soon the shape starts to form.

Eventually the Igloo reaches the desired shape and the sealing block is prepared for location, thereby making the igloo secure as well as strengthening the walls. The first pyramid shaped Igloo is now in its final stages. All that remains is to clean up the interior and set the scene for a night as an Eskimo.

Settling in for the Night

With the required de-icing fluid and snacks the guys settle in for the night. After four hours the Igloo cools down substantially and soon the now drunken group are freezing. The Igloo, unlike the Eskimo's has not been designed to insulate against the cold. The entrance tunnel is short and allows cold air in. The source of heating to seal the Igloo on the inside is also insufficient. So, with drunken embarrassment the group withdraw to their warmer bunks for the rest of the night.

The next few days are a frenzy of packing and preparing the loading of the ship. The Air Force Crew will withdraw back to the ship to complete the loading work. As the sun is now setting completely at night and the temperature dropping steadily, the teams are experiencing a different view and feel for the frozen continent. It is late on the night before their withdrawal from E-Base when the teams are rewarded with the most incredible light display they have ever witnessed. The Aurora or Southern Lights are incredible. The sky changes colour as the display flashes from horizon to horizon. With deathly silence it is incredible to observe the night sky being painted.

Aurora Southern Lights

Loading the ship

It is the 9th March and the preparation for loading the ship is well under way. Steve, Fanie and Mark start Cargo Sling work to load the ship with ZS-HIZ. The hook up at the Bukta and drop off on the ship is a short 2-minute sortie and soon the Bukta is cleared from the piles that have been stored. Fanie lands back at E-Base where the Air Force contingent is readying for a return to the ship. The aircraft is loaded and prepared for its return to the SA Agulhas. In the meantime, Steve has prepared

ZS-HJA to complete the last of the Cargo Sling work. A number of Diesel Generators must still be uploaded. The PWD Teams have inserted lifting hooks into the engine blocks so that the ground crew will only need to attach the cargo sling strop at hookup for lifting. The loads are quickly processed until the last Generator is lifted and as Kobus proceeds through transition to forward flight, Steve sees the engine sway and break away on the one lifting hook. The shock of the engine swaying causes the Cargo Sling Pole to break away from the attachment point under the main gearbox of the Puma. Steve reaches out to catch the pole while he jettisons the load which falls away to the ice. Steve informs Kobus as to what has happened and requests that he land on the ship so that the aircraft can be inspected.

With ZS-HJA on deck Steve goes to the Technical Office to pull up the Manuals. The Cargo Sling attachment lugs under the Main Gearbox sump plate have broken clean off, but there was no damage to the Gearbox itself. Fortunately, there is no more Cargo Sling work required and the dropped Generator is recovered with the D6 Cat and loaded via the ships crane. ZS-HJA is stowed and secured for the rest of the journey.

Cargo Sling

With the ship loaded it is time to set sail for the South Sandwich Islands for the annual Weather Buoy dropping. The SA Agulhas will head out to the eastern tip of the South Sandwich Islands and then set sail for Gough Island where the ship is to make a stop for uploading cargo from the base. Steve in the meantime has conducted an investigation into why the load broke away during the cargo sling sortie. He locates the Generator in the hold and discovers that there was ice in the lifting hook locating screw thread, resulting in the hook not being completely secured. Once the load had been lifted it did not take long for the heavy Generator to break free from the one hook and jerk tight on the other. The resultant shock broke the Cargo Sling attachment lugs from the Main Gearbox sump plate. Steve types up his report with photos and schematics. He submits the report to Kobus who will process the enquiry at AFB Ysterplaat on their return.

Dropping Weather Buoys

The first weather buoy is prepared and released from the Heli-Deck with Steve and Hennie assisting the Met Kassies to complete the task. The weather buoy is prepared by the Met Kassies and checked onboard for signal strength and data capture before being suspended from the ships crane for deployment. Each buoy will be dropped at set intervals for transmission of weather data back to Cape Town via Satellite. The weather transmissions are available to all countries for utilization in the prediction of weather patterns.

Journey Home

With all the weather buoys deployed the SA Agulhas sets sail for Gough Island on her way back to Cape Town. At this time of year, it is the safest route to follow as the ship can sail directly into the heavy seas without the danger of hitting the waves from the side which would definitely not end well with a flat-bottomed ice breaker. The SA Agulhas is a Class three ice breaker with a flat-bottomed hull and therefore does not cut through the high seas as a conventional ship would. She is susceptible to the rise and fall of swells and therefore pitches and rolls in heavy seas. Sitting in the lounge having a midmorning coffee Steve looks out the porthole and sees only sky as the ship rolls heavily to the starboard. The next minute he only sees water as the ship now rolls over to port. At the same time the ship is riding up and over large waves resulting in movement around the ship to be very difficult with people hanging onto railings and support themselves on either side of passages. Meals are pretty entertaining as one chap found out. He had just collected his meal from the line and made his way gingerly to the table. The side rail of the table is up to prevent the plates from sliding off. He seats himself as the ship pitches and rolls heavily only to sweep his plate of food right over the side rail and deposits the broken plate and food all over the floor. He returns to the line for another helping.

Nine days later 18th March the ship arrives at Gough Island. Steve prepares ZS-HIZ for the flight to Gough and back.

Gough Island Base

Captain Billy has authorized the crews to visit Gough Island for the rest of the day while the cargo is being transferred to the ship.

Gough Island

JC, Fanie and Steve fly the guests to the Heli-Pad and Steve shuts down the aircraft. Steve then secures the Blades and the group move off to meet the Gough Team and take a tour of the base.

The time on the island goes quickly but Steve enjoys the sights and makes new friends with the current team members. It is early afternoon when they get airborne to return to the ship. The last leg back to Cape Town about to begin. It will take the ship another five days of tough sailing to Cape Town, so Steve uses this time to consolidate the Technical Logs for both aircraft and gets the crews to help him wash them. During the time at Antarctica the aircraft have not been washed and the black soot has coloured the sides of the aircraft and tailboom. Steve brings out the only detergent that works well "Handy Andy". A great time is had by all as a lot of horse play and alchohol are involved. With the aircraft spotless and the Technical Logs updated the party continues in the lounge bar area until the small hours of the morning.

It is the 23rd March and 50 miles from Cape Town when Captain Billy authorizes the Air Force to leave the ship. Steve is a passenger and with both aircraft packed, the Air Force is ready to depart. ZS-HIZ leaves first and orbits the ship while ZS-HJA is prepared and then takes off to join ZS-HIZ in a fly past of the ship before setting heading for AFB Ysterplaat. Steve sits silent gathering his own thoughts as he contemplates his return. What has transpired in his absence, was Nicole ok and did Zella keep her promise. What was in store for him going forward.

The aircraft land at the Squadron and Steve is delighted to see that his father had brought Nicole to greet him. With a shriek she runs up to Steve and hugs him tightly. Steve is overwhelmed with emotion and feels his eyes tearing up. He is speechless while Nicole babbles away continuously. Steve is thankful for this as he would not be able to talk without breaking down. Steve greats his mother and father while still holding onto Nicole. As with all his previous trips, Steve has kept all the chocolates that they are supplied for Nicole, which she is now questioning.

"Daddy did you bring me chocolates?" Questions Nicole.

"Of course my darling, let's go and get my stuff so I can get it out for you." Says Steve.

Steve collects his kit and Nicole immediately starts rummaging to find the treasure. With a shriek she finds the box of chocolates and starts opening one. Steve helps the ground crew to locate the aircraft in the hangar and then after greeting the team makes his way to the car for the trip home. He will return to the Squadron in the morning to complete the required servicing on the aircraft. ZS-HJA will also need an inspection and replacement of the Main Gearbox sump plate.

It is a warm clear day, so Steve prepares a Braai for the evening. Nicole has settled in with her grandparents and seems to be progressing well at school. Steve prepares the meat and builds a fire while his mother makes a salad. The family enjoys a meal outside next to fire and Steve is constantly peppered with questions from Nicole. He does his best to answer them. Eventually the excitement of his homecoming wears off and he can relax. Steve can see that his father is still drinking heavily and that his mother is very stressed out. He will have a heart to heart discussion with them. The first item on the agenda however is relocating closer to Nicole's school and Steve informs them of his plan to sell up and find a place in Bothasig that is closer to the school. Nicole is excited, but Steve's parents are dubious.

Back in the Saddle

Back at 2 Air Depot Steve quickly catches up on what has transpired in his absence. To his relief there are only a few items that require corrective actions which he can easily rectify. He reports to the Commanding Officer to get debriefed and to give a rundown of the trip down south. Fluffy is glad to have him back and issues a list of items that he needs to action in the next month. Steve thanks him for allowing him to do the trip and excuses himself to get on with the tasks at hand.

Being a single man is a huge adaption for Steve as all of a sudden, all the woman are giving him a come on. The problem however is that these are mostly married, divorced or problem ladies. Fluffy's secretary Anthea has made no bones about her intentions and is continuously inviting Steve out. She is divorced with two children and Steve shies away as he has other problems to contend with.

Steve contacts a real estate agent and within a few days she has the perfect house for him. The house is located at the top end of Bothasig not very far from the High School and close enough to the Primary School that Nicole is currently attending. The house is perfect with two bedrooms, garage, and all amenities including an apartment and swimming pool. Steve already has a plan of how to enclose a Braai area in front of the pool and create a covered walk through between the house and apartment. Steve signs the offer to purchase and now must receive an offer on his own home. The ink has hardly dried on the document when Steve gets a call at home that an offer has been submitted for the purchase of his home in Sanddrift. Things were falling into place at last and Steve is hopeful for the future.

The biggest challenge that Steve still faces is the constant sense of doom. Being back home again has brought this to the front again. Steve attends a function at 11 Air Depot that is located near the Cape Town International airport. He ends up drinking far too much and, on the way home, loses control of the car and smashes it into the guardrail destroying the vehicle.

The car still moves so Steve limps it home. The next morning Nicole sees the car and bursts into tears. Steve gets a lift to work and borrows a motor cycle from a friend until the insurance claim can be processed.

It will be at least a month before he will get an answer from the insurance. He settles in to deal with the issues at work and prioritizes the actions that Fluffy has issued him. One of the tasks is to upgrade the officers mess lounge and bar area. Steve is tasked to replace the curtaining and décor in the lounge. Steve obtains several contacts for the interior décor work and selects a reputable company to come in for a quotation. Alison an attractive middle-aged lady arrives, and Steve is impressed at what she has demonstrated can be accomplished within the budget provided. Once again Steve is getting the invitation to develop more than a friendship. He does not bother to question her on her marital status but plays ball and lets the situation progress. Eventually Alison asks him out for dinner to discuss the quotation. Steve knows this is not the truth but plays along any way. She would pick him up this evening for a bite to eat.

Alison picks Steve up and it is quickly evident to him that her intentions have nothing to do with the quotation. The evening passes like a whirlwind and Steve is still trying to make sense of it when he is being kissed and fondled. Still feels himself closing off with warning signals going off in all directions. What is it with woman he wonders! Alison is in a relationship, yet she is behaving just as Zella, and although it angers Steve he has stopped caring about what is right or wrong. He goes into it with no emotions just to move on to the next.

After getting home Steve shuts down completely, closing off all emotions that are trying to come to the surface. He no longer cared and has no intention of being caught in the middle of any relationship. He will just move around and keep his sanity by refusing to get any deeper into any relationship. The sale of the house comes through quickly and Steve approaches his friend Piet Brits to help him with the move. They plan accordingly and book the move for a weekend when the house will be available in two weeks.

The insurance has written the car off and pay Steve out the market value. Steve goes in search of a cheap car and ends up at a second-hand dealer in Parow. Steve walks in and spots the same vehicle that he had just written off, a Toyota Corolla. He is looking the car over when he hears a familiar voice behind him. He spins around and looks straight in the face of a fellow Lowveld High student with whom he played rugby. Kelvin Roberts immediately recognizes Steve and they spend an hour catching up on each other's lives since they parted so many years ago. Kelvin makes Steve a sweet deal on the Toyota and he leaves there a very happy customer.

He will collect the car next week after it has been thoroughly gone through and road worthy testing completed. Steve gets back to work and is just sitting down in his office when the phone rings. He answers and feels a cold shiver running down his spine. A familiar voice asks him how he is. Steve is in shock and must pluck up courage to respond.

"Hi Sharon and, how are you?" Stammers Steve.

"In a bit of a spot I am afraid and that's why I am reaching out to a friend." Responds Sharon.

The boyfriend she had replaced Steve with, bought a house which they moved into together. The relationship has turned sour and she wants someone to talk to. It has been more than two and half years since they last spoke. The warning bells are clanging loudly in Steve's head and he struggles to contain his emotions. Is this love that he is feeling that is causing him so much pain. Was it the wrong time for them before due the situation and now he has been given a second chance? Steve's hopes build up as he convinces himself that this must be right and the only explanation of why she would reach out to him. They arrange a meet and Steve excitedly jumps on the motorcycle to get there as quickly as possible.

Steve steps into the restaurant in Goodwood and immediately recognizes her. She jumps up and hugs him tightly thrusting her groin invitingly towards him. All common sense flies out the window and Steve's under her spell as she paints a picture of the past two and half years. They talk for hours and agree to meet soon again. Steve gets up to leave and his brain is in total turmoil. Were all the emotions he has been going through just because of the break up with Sharon and the divorce? He wants to believe this, but somehow, he knows that there are deeper issues that he must revisit to find answers on. Sharon may be able to help he hopes.

With the move coming up at the weekend Steve gets together with Piet at the NCO's Pub after work the next day and they plan the move requirements. Piet has a VW Combi and can loan a Pickup Truck. He has also arranged a car trailer to help with getting everything transported. They have far too many drinks and then head their separate ways to recover.

Its early Saturday morning and Piet arrives with his Combi and Trailer. While the help that Steve has arranged from the base loads up, Steve takes Piet to pick up the Truck. The move takes the whole day to complete as they cannot move furniture in until the previous owners have moved out. By dark the move is finished and so is everyone. Steve buys a bunch of Pizza's and Beer for everyone to enjoy. Steve is pleased as he and Nicole can now be on their own in the house and his parents have their own domain as well. The rest of the weekend is spent on cleaning up and unpacking everything. Steve has already started to formulate a plan on what to do for an enclosure in front of the pool.

At the back of his mind Steve is hoping that this time with Sharon will be different and he must control all his emotions and does not reach out to her. He wants her to start the first move as she has already done. Back at work there are many projects that keep him busy and therefore allow him no time to reflect on what may or may not happen. 2 Air Depot has been selected to assemble, install, test fly and deliver the new Pilatus Astra Trainers that have been procured from Switzerland. With the imminent political changes taking place in the country and the end of the border war, there is still much changes to be expected. Steve continues to fly at the Squadron at every opportunity he can.

It has been a couple of weeks and Steve is just starting to lose hope when a familiar voice calls out to him once more.

"Hi Steve, my car has broken down and is stuck in the middle of the road, do you know who I can contact to tow it away?" Asks Sharon.

"No problem, I will go and look at it, where is it stuck?" Requests Steve.

His mind is racing but he hangs up and gets Piet to help him to analyze her car. The front brake has seized when the car moves forward. By rocking the car back and forth he manages to release the brake and dives it home to fix. He calls Sharon and informs her that the car is at his house and that he will fix it the next day. As he can catch a lift with Piet she is welcome to use his car. She is delighted and agrees. Steve gets the address and drives over to pick her and the children up. Nicole is excited to see Michael and Candice again and they race off to the room to play on Steve's laptop. Steve explains the problem of the cars brakes to Sharon and confirms that he will have it repaired by tomorrow evening. Steve is in total turmoil and is scared to say too much or make any wrong move. He keeps the conversation light and after an hour of chit chat offers his keys to Sharon. She accepts and drives off.

After work the next day Steve quickly strips down the disc brakes of Sharon's Car and realizes that they had been incorrectly assembled. He cleans and services the brakes and reinstalls it correctly. He starts the car and takes it for a test drive. The problem has been corrected. He cleans up and calls Sharon to inform her of the good news. Sharon arrives and is very appreciative of the assistance. She sidles up to Steve and with a hug places a kiss on his cheek. Steve is elated but keeps his emotions in check. They chit chat some more and Sharon invites him and Nicole to supper. Her now ex-boyfriend has moved out and therefore Steve can freely visit. Steve accepts the invite and Sharon leaves.

Steve collects Nicole the next evening and they drive over to Goodwood to honour the dinner date with Sharon. After supper the children disappear to play outside. Sharon opens to Steve about what is happening. She is moving back to Howick in Natal. She wants to be near her mum and needs to get away from Cape Town. Steve feels the despair creeping in but maintains even keel. Sharon looks him in the eyes and with tears in hers she blurts out.

"We could be so good for each other, but our timing is terrible."

Steve just nods as he knows that once she has made up her mind that there would be no turning back. Steve gives her a hug and cradles her to stop the sobbing. His emotions are all over the map and he is hoping she will give him the opportunity to prove how he can be better at the relationship. Sharon has made up her mind but promises to keep contact. She gives Steve a deep kiss and holds him tight. Steve collects Nicole and drives home in total confusion, what just happened? Did Sharon dump him or put him in storage? What must he do keeps running around in his head!

Steve keeps his promise and with some of his staff from work he helps Sharon to load her belongings into containers for shipment to Natal. The loading takes most of the day, after which Steve runs the chaps back to 2 Air Depot so they can get their respective rides home. Exhausted Steve gets home and cracks a beer. Piet calls Steve and asks if he wants to join them for a Braai. As Nicole is with Zella for the weekend Steve accepts and jumps into the car. He stops at the local Bottle Store and gets a stock of beer and bottle of brandy to take with. At Piet's home Mary-Ann has already started the salads and accompanying side dishes. Piet is adding wood to fire for the appropriate amount of coals to Braai on. He already has a brandy and coke ready for Steve who accepts the drink gladly.

Piet and Steve have developed a deep friendship and Piet knows exactly what Steve is going through. He has met Sharon and understands well the confusion Steve has now. He also knows Zella and openly discusses that he is glad that Steve is divorced from her. The drinks flow freely and with the coals ready Steve assists Piet in getting the meat done to perfection. Mary-Ann brings out the rest of the food and they sit down to a hearty meal on the porch. After supper Mary-Ann withdraws to the house while Piet and Steve drink the night away. Piet is studying Information technology and has planned to leave the

Air force to start his own business. The discussion turns to politics and both the soldiers admit that the political arena is not looking good for the future. President De Klerk was systematically disassembling the powerful structure that had brought the country so far in such a short span of time. With 25 years of embargo South Africa was more powerful than any other country in Africa with a booming economy. The air of change however did not look very promising.

Sharon will be leaving in the morning so Steve heads home to sleep off his drunkenness. He would like to at least remember his last meeting with the woman he thought would be his love. The next morning Steve has a long shower and makes himself a hearty breakfast of bacon eggs and toast. After dressing he gets into the car and drives slowly to Sharon's place. He wants to believe that there is an opportunity, but the truth of the matter is that Sharon is on a different path. He knocks on the door with his whole being wanting to turn and run. Frozen he waits and then hears Sharon opening the door. She smiles and embraces him while kissing him openly. Steve responds accordingly and laughing they go inside. She offers him coffee which he accepts. In the kitchen Steve sits down while Sharon moves around the bare kitchen to scratch out coffee mugs for them. She seems excited about the upcoming trip. She has sold her car and is flying to Durban this afternoon. A friend from work will be dropping her at the airport. The children left yesterday, and she is just cleaning up before departing.

"Are you going to visit me?" Sharon asks as if teasing Steve.

"Only if you want me to!" Responds Steve.

"You are my special person whom I hold dear to my heart, of course I want you to visit!" Says Sharon.

Steve just smiles as he must be careful that he does not make a mistake again and mess it up. They talk for a few more hours with Steve keeping his distance as the sexual tension is very high and he is afraid that if he over steps the line he will lose her forever. The time comes to leave, and she embraces Steve tightly with much passion before releasing him. Steve makes his way to the car and cannot decide if he is happy, sad or confused. Everything was right but also so wrong.

The next month's slip by at a furious pace with Steve increasingly busy at work. Winter has come and gone, and Spring is around the corner. Steve gets a call from the Chief Technical Officer at AFB Durban. They are looking for a Squadron Technical Officer at 15 Squadron based in Durban. Steve says that he may be interested. He is instructed to go to the signals office as there will be a signal authorizing travel from Cape Town to Durban for him to meet with the Commanding Officer of 15 Squadron to discuss the position. Steve is excited yet scared as his motive for this move would to be near Sharon. There would be a host of problems that would accompany this as well, namely what about Nicole, his parents, his house. Steve puts it to the back of his mind and gets ready for the trip. He has Sharon's email and sends her a message informing her that he will be in Durban for a week and would she be willing to meet. He shuts down the computer as he does not expect any response.

The day arrives for the trip to Durban. Steve is dressed in full Blues for the interview and has packed a few things to tide him over for the week. He checks his email and is excited to see a response from Sharon. She will meet him in Durban. It has been six months since they last communicated. The flight to Durban is long and uncomfortable, reminding Steve of all his trips to SWA. At midday they land at Durban and he is met at the Movement Control by the base Ops Officer. Steve salutes smartly and introduces himself. The Ops Officer takes Steve to 15 Squadron and leads him to the Commanding Officer. Steve knocks on the door and hears a familiar voice.

"Come." Says Commandant Ray Barske.

Steve smiles broadly as he steps in. Ray was the Head Directing Staff of the Air Force College when Steve completed his officer forming, and the person who appointed him as the course leader. Steve had also flown with Ray in SWA and in Angola. Ray beams broadly as he recognizes Steve and grabs his hand while enthusiastically pumping it.

"Great to see you again Steve, so glad you could make it up here. I have already spoken to your boss Fluffy and he is not a happy camper but says that you are the best at what you do."

"Awesome to see you again as well Sir, and I am glad to have made the trip." Says Steve.

Ray does not mince his words and informs him of the opportunity and that he needs a good Technical Officer to run the show. Steve is confident that he can do the job and is not concerned about the challenge. He informs Ray that there are personal reasons that would be a challenge and elaborates about the divorce, Nicole and his parents. Ray nods his head and agrees with Steve that he would have to consider all the options before deciding, but he would not hold it against Steve if he did not take the post. After a long discussion Steve excuses himself with a promise to let Ray know his decision before he leaves.

They shake hands and Steve goes in search of crews that he knows. In the crew room the F/E's jump up and shake Steve's hand. The rumour of him potentially taking a post here is already hot off the press. Steve just smiles and states we will see.

The rest of the day Steve gathers as much information as he can with respect to accommodation, schooling, and security. At the end of the workday Steve is taken to the hotel by the Ops Officer. He books in, has a shower and settles in for a meal and some beers. Sharon had given him a number to call which he does. She answers immediately and sounds excited. They set up a time to meet the next evening. It is an hour's drive for her from Howick, so she will be at the Hotel in the early afternoon. Steve confirms that he will be waiting for her.

The next day Steve spends the morning visiting all the areas of the Squadron to familiarize himself with the operations. This was going to be a very difficult decision to make. If Sharon gives him an indication that there is an opportunity, then he has some very difficult choices to make. Steve makes his way back to the hotel by early afternoon and is just about to go up to his room when he sees Sharon walking through the entrance. He rushes up to her, but she just offers up her cheek. Confused he invites her to the lounge and asks is she would like something to drink. She would like coffee and he orders them two cups.

Steve looks deeply at her and asks.

"How have you been?"

"I am doing very well, it is so good to be near my mum again. They have helped me buy a house in Howick, and I have a new car as well. I have also met a wonderful guy and we are engaged."

Steve feels his world crumbling in with rushing sounds in his ears. He is not sure he heard correctly but remains quiet, so that she can confirm what he thought she had just said. She lifts her left hand and shows the ring. Steve feels like a knife has pierced his heart and his pulse is racing just to keep him alive. He breaks out into a cold sweat and realizes the big mistake he had almost made. He is now so glad that he never told the family about the possibility of a move to Durban. He cannot wait for this meeting to be over as he wants to get out of here as soon as possible. What seems like hours Steve answer questions monosyllabically while he tries desperately to maintain composure. Eventually the torture is over, and Sharon begs to be excused as she has a long drive home. She gets up hugs Steve and leaves. He just sits back in the couch and cannot believe what has just happened.

The next morning Steve reports to the Squadron and briefs Ray on his decision. Although disappointed Ray is very appreciative over Steve's openness and honesty and wishes him well. He picks up the phone and informs the duty room to arrange a return flight for Steve. Steve heads back to the hotel and mopes in the room. He goes to bed early not having any appetite or will to drink. He spends the whole night tossing and turning but cannot sleep. Early morning Steve packs his kit and checks out for the return flight to Cape Town.

This year was turning out to be a very dark one indeed. The walls constantly keep folding in on Steve. He hardly eats and reverts to long hours of silent staring trying to make sense of life. Nicole's school year is coming to an end and Zella has planned another trip for them over December. Steve does not want to spend the time alone, or with his parents and plans a soul-searching trip for himself.

Steve takes two weeks of vacation and decides to hike to Zimbabwe. He has no idea why or where he will go but feels the need to break away from anything that reminds him of his current mental state. Steve ends up in Rustenburg with his cousin and spends a few days with them. Both Cynthia and Gerhard are heavy drinkers and fight often. The situation does Steve no good and he hikes through to his aunt Bobby's home in Blairgowrie, a suburb of Johannesburg. After a few days of moping Steve stops off at a secondhand motorcycle shop and purchases a Suzuki GS 750. The bike needs work but will make the planned journey that Steve is formulating. He bids Bobby farewell and takes the road to the far north. As he travels further north he sees the changes in the country side and is saddened by the increase of Squatter Camps popping up randomly. A sure sign that the old South Africa was fading, and that border control was ineffective, allowing illegal aliens to cross into the country.

After a four-hour trip Steve reaches the border control post at Beit Bridge and presents his passport for processing. The Customs Official takes a long time to review his credentials and Steve feels a cold shiver up his spine. There had been rumors of Zimbabwe creating a Black List of South African Defense Members that had operated in the old Rhodesia before and that these lists were being used to capture and lock up people who then do not get the appropriate legal support. They end up jailed for months and sometimes years before settlements can be negotiated. Fortunately for Steve it does not seem as if has made the list. He passes through the border post and makes his way towards Harare, the capital. When Steve had been here last, this was Rhodesia and Salisbury was the capital. The sun has started to set, and the roads are inundated with pedestrians, cattle and animals, so Steve finds the first and best Motel to stop over for the night.

Early the next morning Steve is underway again. It will take him another 6 hours to reach Harare and he still has no idea what he is doing here. At midday Steve has reached Harare and the tingling at the back of his neck now a constant warning that he should turn around and get out of there. He finds a Café to purchase a quick meal, then refuels the bike and heads back south. He has this sudden drive willing to get back to Cape Town. He makes the border crossing before they close and is relieved when there is no interrogation, just a wave off and no interest in why he has only spent 2 days in the country.

Steve rides till late in the night until he is forced to stop as the Gas Stations are closed. He curls up next to the bike and catches a few hours of shut eye. In the cold morning air, he stirs and starts pacing around, a million thoughts flying through his brain. He plays the last years through his mind, recalls the narrow escapes, the loss of a marriage and the yearning to have someone to love and share life with. Steve feels the deep emotions building up inside him like a dark cloud again forcing a loud sob out of his hunched frame. He angrily gets up and kicks a branch laying on the ground, but it only delays the inevitable. Without warning the sobs turn into deep cries of pain and the tears run freely down his face, soaking his chest.

By the time the Gas Station opens Steve has gained his composure. He refuels the bike and sets heading for Cape Town. He will have to cover 2000 kilometers to get there. For the next 17 hours Steve heads steadily south, refusing to stop and catches a nap here and there, before hitting the road once more. Arriving home very late the night, Steve collapses on the couch and is fast asleep. He awakes late the morning and when he looks in the mirror is shocked at the skeleton face with big dark black ringed eyes starting back at him. It takes Steve the next four days to completely recover but he is starting to identify issues that spark the dark depths of despair within him.

The year of 1993 has been very trying for Steve and he finds it difficult to process days, weeks, months and even the past three years. The yearend arrives so quickly that he has not even realized the time passing. 2 Air Depot has a year's end function to celebrate the coming of the new year which Steve attends alone.

Steve has gone to the function on the now rebuilt Suzuki. He spent the time after arriving back from Zimbabwe in stripping the bike down and rebuilding it. The evening passes quickly and soon the singing of Auld Lang Syne resounds through the hall amid much cheering and drunken babbling. Steve realizes he has had a few too many and makes his way carefully to the bike. He rides slowly in the direction of Blaauberg Strand without having any intention of going there. At the beach he remembers parking the bike with the mist rolling in and then blacking out.

Steve awakes to pressure bearing down on him. Struggling to get sense of where he is Steve realizes that he fell over with the bike on top of him. Just as the despair of negativity starts creeping in, he sees a ray of sunshine reflecting of the mist and waves. The most beautiful rainbow with distinct clear colours accentuates the coming day and the beauty it brings. He continues staring and absorbing while slowly focusing on his past, present and future. He realizes that after life threatening operations, bad marriage and relationships he needs to focus on himself and determine what the source of his actual pain is. Struggling out from underneath the bike, Steve shakes himself off, picks the bike up and sits on it, contemplating where to go from here.

Post Traumatic Stress Disorder (PTSD) is something Steve has read about and has heard many discussions of but has never considered the cause or implications of those who have been affected. Glad that he is still alive Steve starts up and heads home slowly to research PTSD and see what his true issues are. At home Steve researches the World Wide Web for information. He quickly realizes that he has many symptoms related to PTSD and has been burying them so as not to expose those around him to the effects thereof.

As PTSD is a mental health condition characterized by either witnessing or experiencing a terrifying life event, with common symptoms that include nightmares, severe anxiety, flashbacks, and obsessive or uncontrollable thoughts, Steve starts to understand the dark emotions he has been fighting for so long. The events commonly associated with PTSD are military or combat exposure amongst others to which Steve has had multiple experiences. The treatment however is something that he does not grasp, as there are many veterans that are suffering the same issues that have no idea what is wrong with them. Steve starts to look back at his past to the first exposures and his reactions thereafter. South Africa operated mostly clandestine and the Operations were never publicly shared.

When returning home from a tour Steve had to keep silent of his experiences, resulting in burying his emotions as well. The result of this mental blockage of events that have transpired, caused an emotional change making Steve a capable operator. This then invested itself in what he now understands as the adrenalin drug from the action he had always been exposed to and why the need to continue wanting more exposure was a way for him to satisfy the urge. This scares him but at the same time he now thinks he knows how to counter the doomsday moods when they rise to the surface. He focuses on looking for something beautiful every day to draw his black mood swings away from focus. Steve spends the rest of the day contemplating his future and with renewed energy starts sketching out the plan to build an enclosed Braai.

Chapter 18 – A NEW LIFE

With a new year ahead, Steve looks forward to 1994 and better things to come. Nicole is very excited about the Braai area that Steve is planning, which encourages Steve to set the plan in motion. He orders the building materials required and starts the construction himself. Against the neighbours boundary wall he constructs a brick wall which will also be the load bearing support for the laminated beams to lay the roof over. During summer the sun sets late in the Cape Province giving Steve five hours to construct the Braai every evening. It does not take long until he can already see progress. The wall is up, and Steve's father helps to install the beams. This is quite the exercise as the old man cannot lift the heavy beam but supports it while Steve muscles it into place. Steve works till late every evening and by the weekend has the roof constructed. The next step is to have a Weather Vane type Extraction Flue installed. The Chimney will have a large extraction hood over a Braai Pit that Steve has built. With the Glass Sliding Doors installed the project is starting to look complete. There are no finances left to complete the floor with paving bricks so Steve focuses on covering the walkway between the apartment and the house.

It is the 21st January and Steve arrives home after a couple of beers with the guys at the Air Force Base. He parks the bike in front of the garage and goes in to chat to Nicole and his parents. He has just cracked a beer when his neighbour Sidney knocks on the door.

"Hey Steve, I have a chick that likes motorbikes. Don't you want to take her for a ride?"

"Sure, just finishing my beer will be over in a sec." Responds Steve.

Steve collects a spare Helmut and walks round to Sidney's house. In the porch area is Sidney, Michele and a lovely looking woman that Steve has not met.

"Steve this is Annie, my sister in law." Says Sidney.

"Nice to meet you, here is your Helmut, let's go." Says Steve

Annie's jaw drops open and she tries to resist but is being urged on by Sidney. She follows Steve out to the bike. Steve fires up the Suzuki and indicates for her to hop on. He takes the road up to the top end of Bothasig and then follows the route past Plattekloof to the N1 highway. He enters the highway and accelerates quickly down the hill to the next off ramp where he decelerates as quickly forcing Annie to slide up against him. Steve follows the route back home and parks the bike back outside the garage. Annie hops off grinning from ear to ear. Steve can see that she likes and enjoys riding on motorbikes.

"Did you enjoy that?" Asks Steve.

"Yes, thank you very much." Responds Annie.

They chit chat a little longer and then Annie rejoins the party next door as it is Sidney's birthday celebration. Steve likes the look of Annie, she is very attractive, neat but reserved. He must definitely find out more about her. This is something that he has not felt in a long time. It is a strange excitement urging him on to find out more about her. The previous flings have been for personal satisfaction without any emotional ties. Steve meets up with Sidney later in the evening and offers him a beer on his birthday. Sidney accepts and the two chat for a while.

"So, what do you think of Annie?" Asks Sidney.

"I like what I see. Is she married, divorced, or available?" Says Steve.

"She is married but her idiot husband has moved out. You should contact her and see what happens." Responds Sidney.

"I think I will. What is her number?" Requests Steve.

Sidney gets her number and scribbles it on a piece of paper for Steve. Steve folds it neatly and places it in his military identification holder. With the recent past experience still very fresh Steve is wary that he may open himself up to more hurt. He is going to take this very slowly to see where it goes before investing to deeply. He decides to contact Annie next week and set a date with her. The new year offers up many opportunities for flying at the Squadron for Steve, which he does at every possible moment. Mostly night flying or training sorties during the afternoons when he does not have meetings at 2 Air Depot. Fluffy is also delegating more tasks and projects to him which keep him busy. So far Steve has managed to keep up with working out the demons that plagued him in the past. The moment he starts feeling depression he focusses on anything that presents beauty. Today he looks out the office and stares at Lions Head part of Table Mountain and with the Clouds rolling over the mountain a most picturesque portrait unfolds in front of him. He looks down at his desk and reaches for his military ID pulling out the neatly folded phone number. Steve dials the number and the sweet voice of Annie answers quickly.

Long road back to Normality

"Hi Annie, this is Lt. Steve Coetzee, Sidney's neighbour, the chap that took you for a ride." He stammers.

"Hello Steve, good to hear from you." Says Annie.

Steve is nervous and cannot understand why. They chat a bit and then Steve asks her out for dinner. Annie accepts, and Steve is elated. He is looking forward to spending time with her to see where this will lead. Friday evening takes a longtime to arrive and Steve is nervous. He has been using woman as emotional detachments, but he is sure that Annie is different, there is just a calming feeling that he needs to nurture this relationship. This is going to be a very tough challenge as he has lost complete faith in relationships. Steve makes sure that his car is clean and takes extra-long in the shower. He dresses smart casual and awaits Zella to collect Nicole. Zella rolls up and thankfully does not stay long. Steve has made sure that Nicole has all her kit for the weekend and gives her a hug and kiss as she scampers out the door.

Steve takes the short drive up to Annie's place and knocks on the front door. David, Annie's son answers the door and smilingly greets Steve. Steve smiles back and asks if his mother is ready. He nods and runs to call Annie. Annie comes through and Steve catches his breath. Smartly dressed, with her long hair beautifully combed she looks gorgeous. Steve is momentarily at a loss of words as he takes in the beauty in front of him. He stammers a greeting to which she giggles a reply. They make their way to the car and Steve opens the door for her to get in.

The conversation flows freely as Steve drives down to Milnerton. He is taking her to a restaurant on Woodbridge Island in Milnerton. Steve finds out that Annie is in a bad relationship and her husband has moved out, leaving her and David to fend for themselves. He sympathizes with her and can relate to how she must be feeling. They arrive at the restaurant and Steve opens the door for her. The waitress leads them to a comfortable table where Steve lets Annie choose the seat she prefers. Steve finds out that Annie does not partake in alchohol and orders the same as her. They chat about everything that comes to mind and Steve is very relaxed as the evening progresses. He has not experienced such a relaxing evening with a woman for a very long time. All the woman of late were too demanding or only out for a good time. Although his emotions are still raw regarding the last episode he had in Durban, Steve is trying hard to bury them.

With dinner completed Steve asks Annie if she would like a drive to Signal Hill, as it is a beautiful windless evening. Annie agrees and Steve heads off to Cape Town. The drive is interesting as Annie questions Steve on what he does. Steve explains his position and his past as a F/E. Arriving at Signal Hill they take a short walk to look over Cape Town and then wander over to the opposite side to the Green Point view.

View from Signal Hill

The setting is incredibly romantic, and Steve has an urge to cuddle and protect this beautiful woman. He leans towards her and she turns to face him, and a natural lingering kiss takes place. Steve's emotions are in turmoil. He holds her comfortably while they chat until the sky deepens in colour and the stars shine brightly above. He does not want this to end. Eventually they walk to the car and Steve drives slowly back to Bothasig. Steve escourts her to the front door and they kiss once more. He turns and with a wave goes to the car.

Steve struggles to sleep as his mind keeps going over what he is feeling. He does not want to get involved unless he is confident that there is going to be a future. Yet the future scares him and he finds it easier to revert to the operator emotion within him. Those emotions that analyze, review, validate and then execute. He does not contact Annie for the next week, his heart still yearns for that which he cannot have. He knows he is acting out like a spoilt child and must get hold of his emotions and face them like the man he is supposed to be. At AFB Ysterplaat Steve throws himself into the projects he has been assigned and is soon buried in a mountain of work. Russell calls from the squadron and Steve accepts all the flying offered to him. He even offers his time to complete the Technical Training for new pilots that have arrived. All this time Annie has been constantly in his thoughts. It seems like a lifetime since they went out.

The squadron is having a tenpin bowling evening with families included. Steve takes the opportunity to invite Annie and David to accompany him and Nicole. Annie is delighted, and Steve looks forward to meeting up with her again. Steve and Nicole collect Annie and David and after quick introductions the children are chatting away in the rear of the car while Annie is telling Steve about what she has been up in the last while. The drive to the tenpin bowling alley seems to go by to quickly for Steve, as he has enjoyed chatting to Annie. They arrive at the venue and soon Steve is introducing Annie and David to the Air Force families.

The four of them have an amazing evening and it's a grinning foursome that get back to the car to start the journey home. Annie invites them in for something to drink and chat. Steve readily accepts. They are still talking away when Steve looks over and sees Nicole dozing. He winks at Annie and says that he should take her home. She smiles and prepares to leave. Steve gives Annie a kiss and she hugs him tightly. Steve promises to visit soon.

The dark demons are keeping away, and Steve is more positive about his future. He has been an officer for almost three years now and will soon be promoted. Steve has visited Annie on several occasions and spent evenings with her and David. David is a couple years older than Nicole and will soon be going to High School.

Steve probes Annie about her marriage and is sad to hear how she has been mentally and physically abused. He wants desperately to care for her but shies away as he is protecting himself from getting too deeply involved. He invites Annie and David to come to the house and enjoy the pool with them. He will Braai some meat after and then they can watch television. David is already off to fetch his swimming trunks, so Annie has no choice but to accept.

Steve has been gathering brick pavers where he can scrounge them to finish the Braai area off with. He has also created an indoor garden with all the plants that his parents have brought with them. The area is starting to look very cozy indeed.

Annie is suitably impressed and nods her appreciation of the design that Steve has developed and built. The children are already frolicking in the pool when the front door bell rings.

Piet and his family have decided its Braai time and have come loaded with meat and booze. Very soon the pool is full of bodies, including Piet and Mary-Ann's children Pieter and Heibre. The evening is pleasant and after a long exhausting evening Steve walks Annie and David back home.

Upon his return Mary-Ann communicates her approval of Annie to Steve immediately. Piet concurs, and the drinking gets way in earnest to Mary-Ann's disapproval.

The next week seems to pass very quickly and its early Friday evening when Annie rolls up with her Toyota Corolla fully loaded with brick pavers.

"Where the heck did you get those?" Asks Steve.

"From a building sight!" giggles Annie with Nicole laughing hysterically in the background.

"What have you lot been up to?" Demands Steve.

"Nicole and I stood watch while David and his friends loaded up bricks." Grins Annie.

Steve just smiles while shaking his head. They pack all the pavers in the Braai area where Steve will lay them in the next few days. The process is repeated until the whole area is completely paved. Annie is proving to be very resourceful.

The months seem to blend into one another for Steve as his relationship with Annie goes through a number of ups and downs. This mostly due to Steve's inability of wanting to commit.

Annie is struggling her own battles as she files for divorce and gets ready to sell the house so that she can setup away from where her husband could ruin her life once again.

Russell asks Steve if he could complete a quick three-week trip to Marion Island as the Squadron is short on F/E. Steve jumps at the opportunity and goes over to the Squadron to prepare the aircraft he has been assigned. As the J-Model ZS-HJA is receiving major maintenance currently, Steve will be using a military Puma L Model this trip.

On the 29th April they depart for the SA Agulhas with Puma ZS-HIZ and Military 147. They join the ship as she leaves Cape Town harbour and set sail for Marion Island.

8 Days sailing later the ship approaches Marion Island and Steve prepares ZS-HIZ for an offloading Cargo Sling sortie. A major storm had damaged the base crane, so all the offloading was planned to be completed by the helicopters. Steve in ZS-HIZ together with RF Botha and Sloet Louw get airborne off the ship for the first sortie of offloading.

The flying continues daily and once the offloading is completed the reversal is initiated. All the return cargo and rubbish are slung back to the ship for return to Cape Town. Steve's birthday comes up quickly and fortunately the 10th May is scrubbed for flying due to weather. The Air Force take a breather and celebrate Steve's 37th birthday.

Steve reflects back on the last few months after meeting Annie. He is drawn to her but has his guard up and keeps fighting the emotions welling up within. Initially he pines for his lost love but realizes that this is just an excuse he uses to manage the demons that still seem to plague him. Steve mulls over his lot and is having a tough time making up his mind in what direction he should go.

Annie, although awesome in many ways, also has many issues and this scares him, as he does not know how to react. Steve spends some quiet time on the Helideck longing for stability, the warmth of love by a woman and someone to share his life with. A very somber Steve saunters back into the bar and for the first time in a very long time does not join the drunken party.

With the turmoil in the political arena in South Africa, Steve has a further concern if the country would stay stable enough for him to offer Nicole and potentially Annie and David the future they deserve.

The newly elected National Assembly's first act is to formally elect Mandela as South Africa's first black chief executive. His inauguration takes place in Pretoria on 10th May 1994, televised to a billion viewers globally.

The event is attended by four thousand guests, including world leaders from a wide range of geographic and ideological backgrounds.

Inauguration of Nelson Mandela

Mandela heads a Government of National Unity dominated by the ANC which had no experience of governing by itself but containing representatives from the National Party and Inkatha. Under the Interim Constitution, Inkatha and the National Party are entitled to seats in the government by virtue of winning at least 20 seats. In keeping with earlier agreements, both de Klerk and Thabo Mbeki are given the position of Deputy President. Although Mbeki has not been his first choice for the job, Mandela grows to rely heavily on him throughout his presidency, allowing him to shape policy details. Moving into the presidential office at Tuynhuys in Cape Town, Mandela allows de Klerk to retain the presidential residence in the Groote Schuur estate, instead settling into the nearby Westbrooke manor, which he renames "Genadendal", meaning "Valley of

Mercy" in Afrikaans. Retaining his Houghton home, he also has a house built in his home village of Qunu, which he visits regularly, walking around the area, meeting with locals, and judging tribal disputes.

Aged 76, he faces various ailments, and although exhibiting continued energy, he is isolated and lonely. He often entertains celebrities, such as Michael Jackson, Whoopi Goldberg, and the Spice Girls, and befriends ultra-rich businessmen, like Harry Oppenheimer of Anglo-American. He also meets with Queen Elizabeth II on a state visit to South Africa, which earns him strong criticism from ANC anti-capitalists. Although dismantling press censorship, speaking out in favour of freedom of the press, and befriending many journalists, Mandela is critical of much of the country's media, noting that it is overwhelmingly owned and run by middle-class whites and believing that it focused too heavily on scaremongering about crime.

Steve shakes off the feeling of doom and focuses on the task at hand. There is still a large volume of cargo to be loaded and the helicopters will fly daily to get the task completed. It takes a further 7 days to complete loading up the ship before the Captain sets sail for Cape Town on the 18th May. The return trip this time of the year has all the favourable currents and the SA Agulhas makes excellent time back to South Africa. On the 22nd May both helicopters get airborne on route to AFB Ysterplaat, their trip completed. It's a Sunday so there are not many personnel at the Squadron. Steve's Father is there to collect him. Steve greets him and loads his kit into the car. He then assists in getting the aircraft refueled and stowed in the hangar at the squadron before leaving for home.

Back at 2 Air Depot Steve knuckles down to getting the Certification Program fully implemented for locally manufactured parts. The progress has been incredible from the defunct paper driven system to the first computer-based procedures. Steve is pleased with the outcome and the team he has put together to implement it. Already Air Force Headquarters are looking to standardize the process throughout the SAAF. Steve is kept busy with Engineering Change Proposals and conducts several Configuration Control Boards to process the proposed Modifications. The revised procedure making traceability and follow-up actions controlled and efficient. Fluffie is impressed and congratulates Steve on the successful implementation of the procedure. Fluffie also has another surprise for Steve and summons him to the 2 AD Headquarters. It is the 14th June 1994 and Steve has just been promoted to Captain. With promotion comes greater responsibility, and Fluffie elaborates changes he is planning. It has been a mere two years that Steve has been at 2 Air Depot and already he has managed to make constructive and progressive improvements to the manufacturing, repair and overhaul procedures.

Fish River Canyon

Russell approaches Steve and invites him to accompany a group of hikers to complete the 5-day Fish River Canyon hike. Steve accepts and together with Russell and Vossie they start planning. Steve digs up all his Air Force survival equipment, together with the 32 Battalion Rucksack and starts preparation for the journey to Namibia. The Fish River Canyon is in the south of Namibia and is the largest canyon in Africa. It features a gigantic ravine, in total about 160 km long, up to 27 km wide and in places almost 550 meters deep.

The Fish River is the longest interior river in Namibia. It cuts deep into the plateau which is today dry, stony and sparsely covered with hardy drought-resistant plants. The river flows intermittently, usually flooding in late summer and the rest of the year it becomes a chain of long narrow pools. At the lower end of the Fish River Canyon, the hot springs resort of Ai-Ais is situated. The Fish River canyon consists of an upper canyon, where river erosion was inhibited by hard gneiss bedrocks, and a lower canyon formed after erosion had finally worn through the gneisses. Both parts have been declared a national monument in 1962. Upstream, the river runs through horizontal dolomite strata; these metamorphic rocks formed part of the canyon. The Fish River Canyon Hiking Trail consists of hazards, steep descents, boulders, rocks, deep sand, slippery river crossings, baboons, snakes, scorpions and heat. The Fish River Canyon hiking trail is one of the more popular hiking trails in Southern Africa. The immense scale and rugged terrain has drawn many visitors from all over the world to experience what hiking or trail running the canyon can offer.

Steve, Russell and Vossie travel up in Steve's Toyota to the start of the trail, 13 Km from Hobas at the car park. They will overnight here at the campsite to be joined by the rest of the team the next day. The plan is to complete the 2-kilometer descent into the canyon on day 1 and then proceed along the 88 kilometers of the Fish River through to Ai-Ais the next five 5 days.

There are no amenities on the trail and hikers must carry all their needs with them. Upon arrival they pack their rucksacks and check the gear required for the hike. Steve has frozen vacuum-packed steaks that will last him for 4 days. He has also ensured that he has sufficient Brandy and Coke Syrup for enough refreshments for the 5 days. They complement the fresh meat with Rat Packs that Russell has managed to get from the Air Force Store. Each of them has a 2-liter bottle of beer for the first night and fresh Steaks and Wors to braai. They settle in for the night next to the fire and wake early the next morning for a relaxing bush breakfast. Steve surprises them with bacon and eggs with a fresh pot of coffee. At midmorning the rest of the team arrive, and they can descend into the Canyon.

Fish River Canyon from the Car Park

The weather is usually mild and typical temperatures vary between 5 °C and 30 °C with little humidity. Due to flooding and extremely hot summer temperatures reaching 48 °C in the day and 30 °C at night, permits are only issued between 1 May and 15 September.

The descent is steep, and chains are provided to assist hikers over the first 100 meters. Thereafter the unmarked path follows a gravel trail to the beach at the bottom. The descent down to Sulphur Springs takes them through the narrowest section of the canyon, layered with big boulders, rocks and deep sand making hiking slow and laborious resulting in an average hiking speed between 6 and 10 kilometers per day. With everyone safe in the Canyon they head down to a safe area to build camp for the night.

Fish River Canyon at the Start

Steve sets his sleeping place in the natural hollow of a boulder. He has brought a piece of parachute along to cover himself at night for protection from bugs and sand in case the wind comes up. Everyone pairs up with another member and supper preparation starts in earnest. Steve reaches into his stash of frozen vacuum-packed steaks and produces one that is big enough to share with Russell and Vossie.

The rest of the crew all have freeze dry rations and energy meals. The look on their faces as Steve prepares the steak over the fire is very amusing indeed. But not as funny as when he produces three plastic glasses and proceeds to pour Brandy and Coke from his stocks. The civilians amongst them just shake their heads with concern that the Air Force is nuts and with the weight that they are carrying, they will not make it to the end. Little do they know how many times Steve and Russell have completed similar hikes in the past and how many times they have had to help those proclaiming to be well prepared. Steve winks at Russell, this was not going to be any different. At the initial decent Steve hung back as he already saw that some of the ladies in the group were struggling. Steve has brought his medical kit with as he does on all hikes and keeps to the back of the pack to help stragglers. Tomorrow would be interesting for sure.

Steve the Fish River Buddha

The route from Sulphur Springs to Three Sisters is mostly on firmer ground with plenty river stones and frequent river crossings. The average hiking speed between 15 and 25 kilometers per day. The second day starts off well until the large boulders start posing challenges to those not accustomed to boulder hopping. This continues for the next two days and is starting to take its toll on those that experience this for the first time. Steve, Russell and Vossie bring up the rear and help the stragglers by lightening their loads and carrying the extra weight for them. Every evening the three of them sit down to braai steak finished with Brandy and Coke. A revised opinion from the rest of the hikers is formed of the rough and tough Air Force. A new view of admiration and appreciation flow forward as those who have been assisted spread the word.

Fish River Boulder Hopping

From Three Sisters to Ai-Ais the canyon widens out with some sections reachable by 4x4 vehicles. The average hiking speed increases between 25 and 35 kilometers per day. Exhaustion is starting to take its toll on the less fit members of the team but with grit and determination and moral support they push forward.

The canyon continuously opens with every kilometer they proceed down the river bed. The trail will end at Ai Ais where a resort with hotel rooms, chalets and camping grounds will allow them to relax and unwind from the grueling 5 days in the canyon. The Fish River has less pools and is looking more and more like a river. There are sections with deep areas of water that allow the tired and hot hikers to soak in the cool water and regain strength for the last stretch. Tomorrow is the last day before the exit the Canyon at Ai-Ais. The whole team is looking forward to fresh food and beer. Even the Air Force are sick of all the Brandy and Coke they have had to contend with.

Coming to the end of the Canyon

Although there are still plenty of rocks to clamber over, a trail can be found and followed, easing the pressure of jumping up or over the rocks. In the distance the trail becomes more pronounced and the hikers can pick up the speed. As if picking up the scent of beer and relaxation the hikers are now head down and flat footing it to the end.

Last stretch to Ai-Ais

Ai-Ais Hot Springs

Upon arrival at Ai-Ais even before checking in to their rooms, Steve and Russell order beer and down these in a few gulps. After checking into the rooms, they join the rest of the team in the hot pools and alternate between the hot and cold pools until their aching bodies have started to recuperate. Steve catches the courtesy bus back to the Hobas car park, to collect the Toyota. They will spend the night at Ai-Ais and return to Cape Town in the morning.

System Management

Steve's relationship with Annie is progressing but has many challenges. Steve cannot let go of the past and at the same time he is still plagued with his mental state and how to move forward. Annie has in the meantime managed to sell her house and has moved to a rental in Goodwood on the opposite side of the highway. The relationship between Steve and Annie has spurts of good and then bad toying with both their emotions. Annie has a lot of recovering to do and bravely faces the future with a positive attitude. Steve is not very helpful and either reacts in anger or clams up completely. The couple does continue to have a relationship and Annie accompanies Steve to numerous Air Force functions. The summer moves on quickly to Autumn and once again on the 2nd October at the 2 Air Depot management meeting Fluffie informs all that Steve has been promoted to head up the System House. Steve will now be accountable for the C47-TP fleet for full life cycle support. He will have a team of almost 30 people to cover all aspects of Systems House from Procurement, Supply, Engineering, Maintenance, Modification, System Performance, and Field Service Support. The challenge uplifts Steve's mood and spirit as he confidently directs the team to develop all the criteria for the platform.

Steve completes a number of courses that will assist him with managing his new position. Many of these courses are presented by International Instructors that have been brought in specifically to ensure the best training is provided. Steve completes System Engineering, Configuration Management, Workforce Activity Based Management, Safety Training, and many more. Well armed with experience and qualifications, Steve is poised to drive the programs forward for successful implementation. Aircraft acceptance by the various squadrons are conducted ensuring that technical, operator and maintainer training are effectively conducted, with contractual support commitments met to achieve operational availability objectives.

The production lines at 2 and 4 Air Depots are now delivering aircraft ahead of schedule and with few corrective actions. Fleet support is improving, and the aircraft are obtaining confident support by the operating squadrons. The power, efficiency and reliability of the converted aircraft have successfully presented a very modern capable platform that can improve on the long history of the legendary DC3.

C47-TP converted DC3

On the 9th November 1994 Russell approaches Steve to assist in an East Coast trooping trip near Port Elizabeth. Steve goes over to the squadron the same afternoon to get briefed and book his flight to East London with a Commando Pilot. The Commando Pilots own their aircraft and are assigned to the Air Force to fly small groups of personnel to various locations. This service is recorded as their respective national service call up periods. On the 10th November Steve flies up to East London with a twin-engine Beechcraft. He arrives by midday and is collected at the airport by the crew that he will be flying with for the next week. Both Maj Crafford and Captain Smuts are a bit dubious to having an officer as F/E with them. The F/E Steve is replacing gets onboard the Commando aircraft for a return flight to Cape Town. Steve senses tension of an officer of same rank being the F/E and puts it to rest by taking a first look at the aircraft they will be flying for the week. Puma 166 is seconded from 15 Squadron based out of Durban. Steve's first glance at the aircraft raises concerns. The aircraft is filthy, and the main rotor blades tapes are in tatters. He completes a before flight inspection and is not satisfied with the condition of the Puma. Steve signs up the travel log and the crew get airborne for Queenstown. Upon landing his first task is to wash the aircraft and then inspect it completely to satisfy himself that the aircraft is 100% serviceable. The previous F/E had not taken good care of the aircraft and Steve wants to ensure that the pilots clearly understand that he is here as the F/E and not on vacation. He spends the next four hours washing, inspecting, and replacing the main rotor blade tapes. Satisfied a very dirty Steve wanders up to the rooms where the crew has been accommodated. Willem is highly impressed at what Steve has done and thanks him for taking the time to sort out the aircraft. As reward Willem offers to pay for Steve's meal this evening.

At 08:30 on the 11th November the crew gets airborne for Burgersdorp to conduct trooping with the army. There have been reports of terrorist organization infiltrating into the region form the neighbouring states resulting in farm attacks and theft. The military has been mobilized to quench to infiltration and secure the safety of the local population. Back at Queenstown Steve completes the after-flight inspection and covers the aircraft for the night. The concerns the pilots had with respect to Steve being an officer now in the past as he has proven an invaluable part of the crew and they are functioning well together. By midafternoon they are airborne once more headed to Port Elizabeth to collect Major Crafford's replacement, a co-pilot from 15 Squadron. At 16:30 with the co-pilot collected they head back to Queenstown to secure for the night. There are now three Captains as crew for the aircraft, not a normal situation but strange anyway. The next few days are busy, and they conduct many trooping operations at roadside points to check cars, trucks and potential infiltrations. On the 13th November Willem gets a call from Port Elizabeth to collect a prisoner from an army base at McLear.

Maclear is a small town situated in the Eastern Cape province of South Africa, near the Mooi River a tributary of the Tsitsa River, 172 km north of East London and 80 km north-east of Elliot. It was founded in 1876 as a military camp, called Nqanqaru Drift and developed rapidly, reaching municipal status in 1916. McLear was named after Sir Thomas Maclear (1794-1879), a famous astronomer who laid the foundation for a trigonometrical survey of the Cape Colony. The town is some four thousand feet above sea level with a population of less than 10,000.

They get airborne at 14:30 and proceed direct toward McLear. As they make their way into the foothills of the Drakensberg the weather closes in and they are soon completely IFR. Willem takes control and with the co-pilot on navigation with Steve on instruments assisting Willem they progress through the storm until eventually they see a break in the clouds and dive down through a hole to pick up the route once again. The rest of the flight is conducted VFR and they arrive safely at the army base. Steve shuts down and they gather at the HQ for a briefing with the Officer Commanding. One of the integrated soldiers from uMkhonto we Sizwe had terrorized the camp the previous evening after over consumption of alchohol.

uMkhonto we Sizwe was the armed wing of the African National Congress (ANC), co-founded by Nelson Mandela. Its mission was to fight against the South African government. uMkhonto we Sizwe launched its first attacks against government installations on 16 December 1961. It was subsequently classified as a terrorist organization by the South African government and the United States and banned. For a time, it was headquartered in the affluent suburb of Rivonia, in Johannesburg. On 11 July 1963, 19 ANC and uMkhonto we Sizwe leaders, including Arthur Goldreich and Walter Sisulu, were arrested at Liliesleaf Farm, Rivonia. The farm was privately owned by Arthur Goldreich and bought with South African Communist Party and ANC funds, as individuals who were not white were unable to own a property in that area under the Group Areas Act. This was followed by the Rivonia Trial, in which ten leaders of the ANC were tried for 221 militant acts designed to "foment violent revolution". Wilton Mkwayi, chief of uMkhonto we Sizwe at the time, escaped during trial. uMkhonto we Sizwe was integrated into the South African National Defense Force in 1994.

The officer also a Captain was secured in the camps detention barracks and is suffering an immense hangover. He will be taken to Queenstown where he is to face a Board of Enquiry. He had secured a weapon and threatened lives of the troops. He had also discharged rounds resulting in damage to buildings and offices. He would be facing a dishonorable discharge. Steve wanders over to the detention barracks to collect the prisoner. Willem offers to help to which Steve replies with a grin.

"You don't want to witness this".

Steve collects the prisoner and grabbing him by the scruff of the neck forces him towards the aircraft. At the Puma Steve briefs the prisoner.

"Listen here and listen carefully, you will sit where I put you and not move. If you move I will crack your head. If you puke in my aircraft, I will throw you out, no matter how high we are. Do you understand me?" Says Steve with a very threatening growl.

"Yes boss!" Answers the prisoner.

The pilots join Steve at the aircraft and after the pre-flight inspection they prepare for start-up and take-off. The weather has cleared, and the flight back will be VFR. During the flight the prisoner starts mumbling and is starting to move forward. Steve looks back grins and excuses himself from the cockpit. He makes his way to the now slightly sober prisoner, who is mumbling threats. Steve checks his cuffs and throws him back to the area he was allocated. Next, he takes the aircraft blade cover and places it over the prisoner's head with a few solid smacks to convince him of the warnings he was given previously. He removes the blade cover and points to the door. With widening eyes, the prisoner immediately settles down.

For the next two days there are more trooping flights with positive outcomes, the infiltrations have subsided substantially, and the deployment can be completed. On the 16th November Steve readies the aircraft for flight to 15 Squadron AFB Durban. They get airborne early morning and set heading to East London for a fuel top up and then follow the coast line to Durban. At 15 Squadron Steve greets all the crews he remembers. The weekly Flossie is at movement control and Steve must hurry to make the flight down to Cape Town.

Steve arrives at AFB Ysterplaat as the base is closing for the day. He gathers his kit and heads out to the parking lot to collect his car for the ride home. He is looking forward to catching up with Annie tonight and calls her the moment he has dropped his kit in the bedroom and greeted Nicole. Steve and Nicole have a dip in the pool and he tells her he is going to visit Annie. Nicole has homework to do and cannot go with. Steve is excited to see Annie again and is elated to see she feels the same. They chat till late the evening until Steve begs tiredness from his trip and leaves for home. Christmas and New Year arrive quickly, and Steve asks Annie to attend the functions with him. They have a lot of fun and are beginning to enjoy their relationship.

The last months of summer pass quickly as Steve is extremely busy with project and program tasks which require him to attend progress presentations at Air Force Headquarters and various Subcontractors in Transvaal. Additional responsibilities require Steve as the Systems Manager to conduct a Staff Visit to all the Squadrons now operating the new aircraft type. It is already the first quarter of 1995 when Steve selects his team to accompany him on the staff visit. He obtains approval to task a Commando Pilot to ferry them around the country to the various squadrons. The trip takes them to Bloemfontein to 86 ADFS where the multi-engine training takes place. Steve meets with the officer commanding and pilots to obtain their collective input into the performance and operation of the converted C47-TP's. Steve's righthand man WO Theuns Scholtz and his team are doing the same with the Technical and Support group. After the debrief Steve consolidates the feedback from both meetings into a trip report. They will spend the night at AFB Bloemspruit and head off to 44 Squadron in Pretoria the next day. Steve meets up with the crew at the Warrant Officers mess for a few drinks and is pleased to see that the F/E from 87 HFS are there. They chat and drink till closing time after which Steve retires to the Officers mess for some shut eye. The rest of the Staff visit goes off smoothly and they return to AFB Ysterplaat late afternoon on the Friday.

Russell approaches Steve again as he needs an NVG qualified FE to conduct some ship-controlled approaches, cargo sling and hosting work from the SAS Tafelberg. Steve gets his night stop kit from his cupboard, calls Nicole and tells her he will be back the next day. He races over to the squadron and prepares Puma 145 for the flight to the ship later the evening. At sunset with the before-flight completed and briefing conducted, Steve accompanies Fanie and Kobus to the aircraft for the flight to the ship. The SAS Tafelberg is 20 miles off Cape Point and they soon pickup it up on the darkening horizon. Fanie lands on deck form instructions by the FDO and Steve shuts down the aircraft. The ships Executive Officer comes over.

"Fanie the Ensign will take your kit to the Ward Room. Flight the Warrant will get the Petty Officer to help you with your stuff." Says the XO.

"Thanks XO, Fanie I will catch up with you in the Ward Room, I am just fitting the Cargo Sling." Says Steve.

"Fuck Flight, you are a Captain!" Exclaims the exasperated XO.

The XO assumed that the F/E to be a Flight Sergeant and when the mistake registers, he cannot believe his eyes. The evenings flying is conducted successfully completing Cargo Slinging, Hoisting and Ship Controlled Approaches with a darkened ship. After the aircraft is stowed by Steve and the ground crew, he joins the pilots in the Ward Room for some refreshments and drinks. The XO sidles up to Steve and places a beer in his hand.

"Bliksim Steve you got me there. Cheers!" And the XO clinks Steve's glass before downing it.

The Air Force crew are up early the next morning to return to Ysterplaat. Back at the Squadron Russell tells Steve to leave the aircraft as it is going in for a major servicing. Steve thanks Russell and ambles over to his office to continue the day's work at 2 AD.

After a rocky start Steve and Annie's relationship has started to stabilize and they are spending more time in each other's company. Chatting on the phone to Annie, Steve invites her over. Annie arrives in her gown and slippers and by early morning she leaves to get showered and dressed to go to work. Both find this amusing but fun and the scenario repeats itself until early in May 1995 when Steve has once again to report to the Air Force College in Pretoria. He is attending a career qualifying course which will clear him through the promotions to full colonel. The Staff and Command Course prepares officers for leadership roles in all aspects which include running the units as businesses, force preparation for deployments and myriad of additional qualifications not dissimilar to the civilian Master of Business Administration (MBA).

Staff Course

Steve is accompanied by two more officers from AFB Ysterplaat, Gary Ramage and Deon Maartens. They depart AFB Ysterplaat on 31st April 1995 in Steve's car, arriving at the Air Force College in the early evening. The trio clear in and after being allocated individual Rondawels they wander over to the mess for grub and the pub for rubbing shoulders with rest of the course.

There is good bunch on the course and Steve feels comfortable with the workload he will have to tackle for the next few months. The course involves syndicates working to research material, develop planning, creation of presentation materials and the shared presentation to the Directing Staff and Members of the Course. The key role is team work, and for those with the experience in their previous capacities this is a method of blending all the knowledge into a single executable plan. In Steve's syndicate for the first phase he has Administrative, Supply, Logistic, Security and his own Operational expertise to combine efforts for the task at hand.

From the first day it is evident to Steve that the workload is going to be extreme. Already some of the course are nervous having never been exposed to this type of pressure. Steve knuckles down and tackles each task with the same vigor and dedication. He quickly ensures that the laptop he has is templated to automatically meet the Conventions of Service Writing requirements. He vividly remembers how strict the Directing Staff were when he completed the NCO development course a number years ago.

Gary and Deon are drawn to Steve for leadership and constantly request his assistance in tasks. Additional to the syndicate tasks are individual course submissions that must be completed and submitted daily. There is no exception, if the course is submitted a minute after the designated hour it is deemed a failure and will not even be marked. This results in each student spending the night working in syndicates until late in the evening and then till early hours of the morning on the personal tasks.

The pressure is unending, but Steve is having the time of his life and volunteers to manage the Pub for the course. The Pub with its content must be run as a business. This requires that the stock count when accepting the contents and keys to the Rondawel in which the pub resides places the accountability on the individual to manage the full business, namely stock replenishment, sales, profit margins, cleanliness, and rule enforcement.

Outside the Pub is a traffic light which had been installed by a previous course. The lights had long since stopped working, so Steve immediately contacts his friends from 1 Air Depot to send in an electrician to rectify the problem. In Steve's mind you cannot have a Pub that cannot signal open, last round and closed.

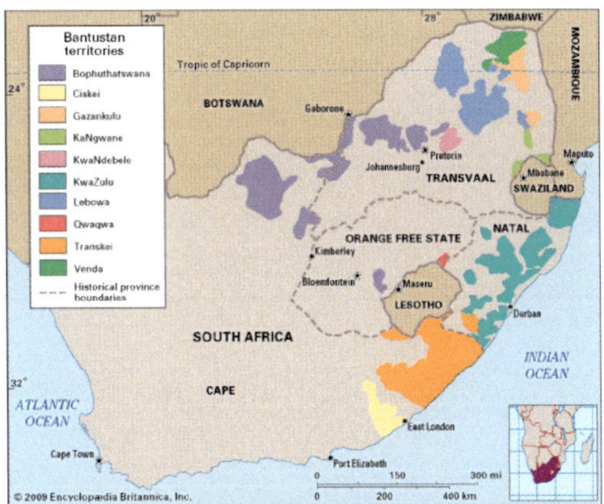

<u>Self-Rule Homelands</u>

The Rondawel becomes the go to place for study and preparation. Steve opens the Bar at 17:00 each evening and brings his study materials with him to complete progress during quiet times. JC Mothupi a Major in the Bophuthatswana Military steps into the Rondawel and ambles up to the counter.

JC is the Aide du Kamp to President Kgosi Lucas Manyane Mangope the President of the Bantustan homeland of Bophuthatswana.

With the ANC in power the current ruling Homelands are soon to be scrapped and once again incorporated into South Africa. The African "homelands" also known as Bantustans were established as part of the strategy of "separate development". The idea was to establish states to which black South Africans were provided full control over their own land to govern and defend accordingly.

Similar to the United States these Homelands would report to a central government for governing, budgeting, policy setting and laws. Unfortunately, these states are not recognized by the rest of the world. There are 10 homelands, each established for a specific "tribe" or ethic group. The notion of this ethnicity, these "tribes", was the previous government's simplification of complex linguistic and cultural groups. The ethnicity designated for each homeland currently:

Bophuthatswana – Tswana

Ciskei and Transkei – Xhosa

Gazankulu – Shangaan and Tsonga

KwaZulu – Zulu

Lebowa – Pedi and Northern Ndebele

Qwa Qwa – Basotho

Venda – Venda

"Hello Steeeve, can I pleez haf a beer?" Asks JC in his best English.

Steve reaches under the counter grabs a clean glass and wipes it with a clean dish cloth. While JC chats to a fellow course member Steve quickly laces the glass rim with chili. He pours the beer and offers it to JC.

"There you go old chap, enjoy." Says Steve.

JC takes a sip, smacks his lips together and takes a longer swig at the beer. Pretty soon the glass is almost empty. JC is not a drinker and having one beer is already an amazing feat. JC passes the glass back to Steve while wiping his mouth with the back of his arm. The chili obviously achieving the required results.

"Can I pleeez haf one more Steeeve?" Asks JC.

Steve complies and only puts a dab more chili to increase the heat as it were. By this time most of the course members have caught to what Steve has been up to and the laughter starts spreading. JC in the meantime has almost finished the second beer. Steve innocently looks at JC.

"What's wrong JC, are you thirsty tonight?" Questions Steve.

"Aaah, I do not know Steeeve, but my mouth she is burning, maybe I haf one more pleeez?" Requests a very perplexed JC.

Steve starts laughing and owns up what he has done to JC's beer and offers him a glass of milk to help calm the hot lips. JC just shakes his head and smiles at Steve.

"Ai ai Steeeve you are a clever one, well played my friend." Retorts JC.

Steve grabs his hand and they shake, a friendship solidified. JC and Steve are going to be a force to be reckoned with on this course. They have both seen and done things that only warriors would understand. They are friends for life. The course progresses, and students are getting in the daily workload that keep them up till late at night, but still have time to visit the Rondawel before the amber and then red light are switched on. It is on a cold wintery night that Steve has managed to complete his tasking for the next day and opens the Rondawel earlier than usual. He has hardly cracked a beer when some friendly faces peek in.

"You open yet?" Asks Deon.

"Yep, lets drink Boet." Responds Steve.

Steve has hardly opened a beer for Deon when the next two customers pop in with the same request. The evening progresses well with Steve teaching the non-chopper group the "Chopper Song". Very soon everyone is joining in and the party is under way. The party soon reaches a crescendo at which moment Steve decides it's time to start fun.

"Dead Ants!" Screams Steve.

Those familiar with the game fall to the ground on their backs with legs and arms in the air. Each one still holding his drinks.

"Did anyone spill a drink?" Asks Steve.

Deon giggling like a school girl on his back with arms and legs in the air indicates Gary.

"Your round Boet!" Laughs Steve.

Steve turns to the rest of the group and describes the rules. Upon the instruction "Dead Ants" everyone must fall on their back with arms and legs in the air while holding their drink aloft. Anyone who spills or is last down must buy a round for all.

JC comes into the Rondawel to see what the noise is about and at the most opportune moment.

"Dead Ants!" Screams Deon.

JC looks around in surprise as if he cannot believe what these stupid white men are doing. Steve jumps up and quickly inducts JC into the club. A couple of rounds later JC starts to excuse himself when Steve locks the door and throws the keys out of the window. Unbeknown to all the real keys are in Steve's pocket. JC loudly voices his dissatisfaction to which Steve offers him another beer, and the party continues. When a few of the heads start drooping onto the counter Steve miraculously opens the door and shoos them out so that he can close for the night.

While Steve is on course in Pretoria, the 1995 Rugby World Cup taking place in South Africa is the third Rugby World Cup. To unite the country President Nelson Mandela insists that South Africa hosts the first Rugby World Cup in which every match will be held in one country. The World Cup is the first major sporting event to take place in South Africa following the end of apartheid. It is also the first World Cup in which South Africa can compete as the International Rugby Football Board has only readmitted South Africa to international rugby in 1992, following negotiations to end apartheid. In the final, held at Ellis Park in Johannesburg on 24th June, South Africa defeats New Zealand 15 to12, with Joel Stransky scoring a drop goal in extra time to win the match. Following South Africa's victory, Nelson Mandela, the President of South Africa, wearing a Springbok rugby shirt and cap, presents the Webb Ellis Cup to the South African captain François Pienaar.

The Staff Course includes a Staff visit to AFB Ysterplaat where the students will prepare and conduct the Staff visit to obtain more in-depth knowledge of the Air Force Command and Control systems. Included will be a visit to Silvermine, the Southern Air Forces Underground Command Center. Silvermine also manages the international Search and Rescue (SAR) Control. They will be spending four days in Cape Town. Steve phones Annie and asks her if she would like to join him at a luncheon when they arrive at the Ysterplaat Officers Mess. Annie accepts and is excited to see Steve after him being away for such a long period.

On the 4th July 1995 the Staff Course meet at AFB Waterkloof Movement Control to catch the flight down to AFB Ysterplaat. This will be the courses Staff Visit for which they will be preparing individual and syndicate reports. The three-hour flight down to Cape Town seems to last an eternity for Steve, as he misses Annie and cannot wait to see her again. At AFB Ysterplaat the students get assigned rooms at the Officers Mess and are invited to the Rondawel behind the Officers Mess for a Braai. Steve can see the parking area from the Braai area and spot on time Annie arrives. Steve rushes to embrace and kiss her. She looks beautiful with her long dark hair falling down her back in gorgeous curls. Steve's breath is taken away and he feels a warm rush of emotion for this adorable woman. As he is in uniform he cannot hold her hand but walks close by her side to lead her back to the Braai area where the rest of the course are congregated.

"Look here comes Little Hitler and his woman!" Barks out one of the loudmouths, to which Annie responds with the most beautiful blush.

Annie is the only lady amongst the group and is initially out of place but soon sees Gary and Deon who she knows and can settle down to enjoy the afternoon. Steve stands proudly next to her while everyone tries very hard to get a word in with her. The evening ends off and Annie says goodbye to Steve. Steve has one more request and holding her tight gently asks he if she would honour him by attending the formal dinner at the end of the Staff Course in Pretoria with him. The Air Force will fly her to Pretoria and then she can travel back with him in his car. Annie is delighted and confirms that she will attend. Steve smiles and kisses her passionately before letting her leave.

The Staff Visit concludes on the 7th July when the course gather at AFB Ysterplaat Movement Control for the return flight to AFB Waterkloof. The Staff Course is now in the final stages and will be mostly report submission and presentations. A final video presentation will be judged by the entire Directing Staff to add the final marks for pass or fail. Fortunately, this course has had no failure or Return to Unit members. Even the Homeland officers had managed well. The course has gelled well and support each other in all aspects. Should one student struggle then there is immediately someone to assist and guide them to success.

Annie arrives on the 25th July and Steve is at AFB Waterkloof Movement Control to welcome her. He spots her smiling face as she exits the big C130 Hercules and walks proudly to the Arrivals Hall. She spots Steve and hurries over to hug and kiss him. Steve collects her luggage and they depart for the Air Force College. Annie excitedly tells Steve that she has met Gary and Deon's wives and they had an immediate connection. The formal dinner is scheduled for the Wednesday night so tonight was theirs. There is sufficient place in each Rondawel for the student's partners to join them for the duration. Steve shows Annie to the Rondawel so that she can freshen up while he wanders over to open the Pub. Annie soon joins him at the Pub with the rest of the motley crew. They move over to the mess for a lovely steak and egg supper to return to the pub for some more refreshments. As per normal the evening results in a drinking party but well behaved the gentleman treat their respective ladies well and are off to bed at a respectable hour. The next day will mostly be course wrap up and final interviews and showing the wives and girlfriends around the rich history of the Air Force College. On the 23rd April 1944 the Air Force College was established for the further development of the Air Forces Officers. After the official course photo, the group disperses to prepare for the evenings formal dinner.

JUNIOR BEVEL- EN STAFKURSUS 2/95
17 APRIL 1995 TOT 15 JUNIE 1995

VOORTREKKERHOOGTE

SA AIR FORCE COLLEGE
JUNIOR COMMAND AND STAFF COURSE 2/95
17 APRIL 1995 TO 15 JUNE 1995

Front row from L to R: Maj M Wimmers, Lt Col A Louw (DS), Lt Col PJ Merts (SDS), Col JL Somerville (OC), Lt Col IZ Lourens (DS), Lt Col MJ van Wyk (DS), Maj FW Conradie (DS), Maj AM Grundlingh.
Second row from L to R: Capt S Coetzee, Capt AR De Olim, Capt JD Gelderblom, Capt J Albertyn, Capt G Ramage, Maj JC Mothupi, Capt DT Delcarme.
Third row from L to R: Capt M Bergmann, Capt CJ Krüger, Capt HP van Heerden, Capt A Robinson, Capt AC Letcher, Capt DJ de Waal, Capt D Krüger, Capt D Maartens, Capt J Williams, Capt JB La Rouchelle.
Top row from L to R: Capt I Joubert, Capt HJ Potgieter, Capt HS Pretorius, Capt JJ Briedenhann, Capt LW Beer, Maj CJ van der Merwe, Capt JW Janse van Rensburg, Capt JA Vosloo, Capt A Kilian.

<u>Junior Staff and Command Course June 1995</u>

Steve and Annie relax in the Rondawel and by early evening Steve has polished his Mess Dress buttons, medals, wings and chain. He dresses and leaves Annie to finish off. Steve's breath is taken aback as Annie comes out of the Rondawel. She is impeccably dressed in a smart skirt, top and jacket and looks absolutely lovely. The couple joins Gary and his wife Janice, for a quick drink before ambling over to the Mess Hall for the formal dinner. The entrance hall has been decorated and laid out with the customary Sherry to start the evening off. As it is almost mid-winter the catering staff have lit a fire in the entrance hall firepit where Steve and Gary are chatting. The two ladies are at the Sherry table chatting away. After the last weeks drinking and steak suppers, both Steve and Gary have quite a gas build up. Steve releases a long burst followed by Gary and the two catch a whiff of their accomplishments and immediately back away from the fireplace. The ladies who have abled over to join them move closer to the fire and as they sniff the foul air the General and Senior Officers enter causing the ladies to be locked in. The smell at this stage is still waffling in the area. The General slows down looks at the red-faced ladies and moves on. By this time Steve and Gary are doubled up with laughter. Annie and Janice however are not impressed and let the two know very clearly how disappointed they are. The rest of the evening goes off smoothly and after delivering their respective speeches the senior staff members indicate to the Mess President to wrap up the evening. They all gather in the Pub for Port and the Smokers pick a cigar. It's a very proud Steve that accompanies Annie to the Rondawel. She is truly a wonderful woman and he has enjoyed having her with him.

The Next Chapter

South African politics is progressing slowly, and Steve is becoming concerned with respect to the future of his career in the Air Force and the stability of the country in the future. Zimbabwe, Mozambique and Namibia are not progressing but reverting to total tribalism where the most powerful chief creates a dictatorship and destroys all progress. Steve looks at the developments since the change of power and notes a few items that indicate that there are cracks. Thus far since 1995 the country has had some developments and issues namely;

- The President Nelson Mandela with Deputy President's F.W. de Klerk and Thabo Mbeki lead the country.
- 10th January 1995, General Johan van der Merwe, Police Commissioner of the South African Police Service, resigns and is succeeded by General George Fivaz.
- 25th January 1995, South Africa and India sign several agreements relating to political, trade, economic, cultural, scientific and technical co-operation.
- 27th March 1995, Winnie Mandela is dismissed as deputy minister of Arts, Culture, Science and Technology.
- 10th May, at Vaal Reefs gold mine in Orkney, there is a runaway locomotive that falls into a lift shaft onto an ascending cage and causing it to plunge 1,500 feet to the bottom of the 6,900 feet deep shaft, killing 104.
- 6th June 1995, the Constitutional Court abolishes capital punishment in the case of S v Makwanyane and Another.
- 19th July 1995, The Promotion of National Unity and Reconciliation Act, No. 34 is signed into law by president Nelson Mandela.
- August 1995, the serial killer Moses Sithole is arrested for the murders of 38 people.
- 29th November 1995, Desmond Tutu is appointed chairperson of the 17-member Truth and Reconciliation Commission (TRC) by president Nelson Mandela.

The TRC set up in terms of the Promotion of National Unity and Reconciliation Act, No. 34 of 1995, and is based in Cape Town. The hearings will start in 1996. The mandate of the commission is to bear witness to, record, and in some cases grant amnesty to the perpetrators of crimes relating to human rights violations, as well as offering reparation and rehabilitation to the victims. A register of reconciliation was also established so that ordinary South Africans who wished to express regret for past failures could also express their remorse. The TRC has several high-profile members, including Archbishop Desmond Tutu, chairman, Alex Boraine, deputy chairman, Sisi Khampepe, Wynand Malan, and Emma Mashinini. The work of the TRC was accomplished through three committees:

- The Human Rights Violations Committee investigated human rights abuses that occurred between 1960 and 1994.
- The Reparation and Rehabilitation Committee was charged with restoring victims' dignity and formulating proposals to assist with rehabilitation.
- The Amnesty Committee considered applications from individuals who applied for amnesty in accordance with the provisions of the Act.

The concern that Steve has is the fact that the TRC views the War against Terrorism as Human Rights Violation and wants to approach members of the previous SADF for potential questioning. This is an outrage to Steve as now the country's previous enemies, who were guilty of many atrocities through Church and Public Bombings, attacks, and kidnapping are now leading up a commission to place the blame against the defenders of the country.

President PW Botha refuses to testify at the new government's Truth and Reconciliation Commission, for exposing apartheid-era crimes, which is chaired by his cultural and political nemesis, Archbishop Desmond Tutu. The TRC finds that he had ordered the bombing of the South African Council of Churches headquarters in Johannesburg. He is fined and given a suspended jail sentence for his refusal to testify in relation to the human rights violations and violence sanctioned by the State Security Council (SSC) which he, as president until 1989, had directed. President PW Botha successfully appeals to the High Court against his conviction and sentence. The Court finds that the notice served on him to appear before the TRC is technically invalid.

Steve and Annie take the long road home and decide to stop over in Somerset East to visit and old friend of Steve's. They meet up with Dyke's and his family and enjoy relaxing for the two days before setting heading to Cape Town. With Steve's parents now living with him, there are a number of challenges that come with the advantages of having someone to look after Nicole and keep the house tidy. Steve's father "Frank" is drinking a bottle a day and is a confirmed alcoholic who is also suffering from depression. Steve mother "Nellie" is a hypochondriac and also suffers from extreme depression. Steve is at wits end trying to support them and make them understand how difficult is to be a single parent, follow a career and still try and court a woman. Steve has the impression that his parents insist on their blessing for the woman he dates. This infuriates him, and he is driven to staying away from home when Nicole is with Zella. With Annie living in Goodwood, Steve spends the lonely evenings visiting her instead. As if per blessing Annie must vacate the rental she is staying in as the owner has placed the condo up for sale. Steve pounces at the opportunity to invite Annie to come and live with him and Nicole. Annie agrees, and the move is quickly completed. Their life together may have many challenges, but Steve is feeling more apt to accepting her into his life. This is a step he was not even contemplating as he still has many dark moments but is excited about the future.

With Annie, and David now in boarding school at Riebeek-Kasteel near Malmesbury, living with Steve and Nicole the house has become alive with children popping in and out all the time. Annie is in her element and is constantly preparing large meals anticipating friends of David and Nicole dropping for a bite. Steve is busy with the System House Management programs and projects and is preparing for the upcoming responsibility of the new trainer aircraft procured.

The Pilatus Astra is a hybrid between the Pilatus PC7 and PC9 trainers with South African Avionics installed. This is to be accomplished at 2 Air Depot at AFB Ysterplaat. The aircraft will be received via ship at Cape Town harbour and then assembled at 2 Air Depot incorporating the South African installations before being test flown and accepted. Once the test flights are concluded one aircraft will be deployed to Test Flight and Development Center at Bredasdorp with the remainder being transferred to AFB Langebaanweg Flight Training School.

Pilatus Astra

A new family

With Annie and David part of the family Steve's life seems more stabilized as he focuses on the needs of being head of the house once more. David is a challenge as it is obvious that Annie had to raise him single handedly which has resulted in him taking advantage of her to some extent. What she has successfully accomplished is giving David the love and direction he needs as a teenager to form a strong character. What is lacking is the disciplining him on the straight and narrow. Between Nicole and David, they manage to manipulate Annie's support when they know that Steve will not approve. This situation adds a bit of tension between Annie and Steve, but they seem to cope with the challenges. Steve continues to discipline David, as he knows if not checked, will go off course and be more of a problem to himself and others.

What Annie brings to the family is something that Steve has let lapse for many years now. Before his separation and divorce Steve used to be a total disciplinarian with respect to tidiness, punctuality, clothing and behaviour. In the last few years Steve has become lazy on the keeping the house neat and tidy, leaving it to his parents to do. Annie sets the record straight and quickly gets the home ship shape. Steve's uniforms are once more beautifully ironed, and he always looks smart. There is always a cooked meal in the evenings and the family starts bonding. Steve feels himself withdrawing less and warms to Annie's care and love. They still argue a lot and have disagreements but seem to manage the ups and downs. The one issue that does create a huge amount of stress for Annie is the dislike that Nellie, Steve's mother has for Annie. Nellie believes her blue-eyed boy deserves better. Not to create waves Annie keeps the animosity to herself, not wanting to stir the pot. Steve feels the tension and forces Annie to own up. They have a long discussion and Steve requests Annie to see if there is an alternate solution that they can implement. Annie has done he homework and there is an Old Age Retirement complex in Goodwood that is very affordable which would suffice. Steve requests Annie to get more detail so that they can be prepared to present the option to his parents, as he knows there is going to a fallout.

The year 1995 is proving to be a much better year for Steve. His is getting control of the of the dark emotions and finds himself in a happier place. The state of the country still concerns him, and Nelson Mandela was requesting all Air Force Units to present a Business Case as to their existence right. Steve has a feeling of bad things ahead. Already major projects of the Air Force have been cancelled as the government is confident that the military modernization can now be procured from the west. Some of the programs that fall are very successfully designed and potentially world class for example, the Space and Missile Program, twin engine fighter Carver, the attack helicopter Rooivalk, Mirage F1 upgrade to name a few. Fortunately, the Rooivalk team has anticipated this move and have already taken the aircraft to the Paris Air Show where it obtains a stellar review. The government allows continuation of the program with a halt on 13 aircraft only. This to Steve are the warning bells he cannot ignore, and he starts formulating a plan. He does not share his idea with the family as there are still too many unknowns. He does upgrade his car to a BMW 318 which he purchases from Kelvin once again. With a grin on his face as he drives off he remembers the days he would pass similar cars on a hot day when they have the windows wound up and air cons running. With an audience Steve would blurt out.

"You capitalistic Bastard." Now he is one of them.

The year 1996 starts off with many questions and the C47-TP program is reaching the midpoint to completion. The fleet support Systems House at 2 Air Depot is established and functioning smoothly with great reviews by Air Force Headquarters. Steve works hard at given his staff all the tools they require to meet the challenges they face. More and more he is pleased at how quickly the team has grown and become incredibly proficient at what they do. With structure Policy, Process and Procedures in place Steve focusses on managing the open Subcontracted Projects which still have milestones to complete. One of these projects the full delivery of a publications package for the C47-TP currently under development and production by Log-Tek. Log-Tek is a Systems Engineering Company Headquartered in Midrand Johannesburg. Satellite offices are strategically located close to large military projects. One of these being the Codification of military hardware for the South African Navy. The office is in Diep River Cape Town.

Nicole has started High School at Bosmansdam in Bothasig and is doing well. David is still a challenge at Boarding School with Annie and Steve having to drive out to Riebeek-Kasteel occasionally to smooth the stormy waters. The trouble he is creating is not putting him on good standing with the Hostel Father. Annie fears he may be expelled. Steve has just celebrated his 39th year and will soon be expecting promotion to Major. He travels to Midrand to attend a project review meeting for which he is the chairman. At the meeting are representations from all companies that have a stake in publications, including Air Logistics Command. Steve flies up with South African Air Ways and is dressed in a civilian suite. He is collected at the airport by the duty driver from 4 Air Depot and they arrive at Log-Tek 30 minutes late. Without skipping a beat Steve hurries into the conference room with more than thirty high ranking officers, contractors and subcontractors. Steve takes his place and with an apology for his lateness he welcomes all to the project review meeting.

Several of the accountable leads did not provide updates to their progress. Steve indicates the urgency to timeline and accuracy of feedback reporting to maintain schedule and budget. He activates a number of actions to the responsible teams with defined feedback for completion requirements.

The progress meeting has lasted an hour and Steve keeps to the time allocated before wrapping up with a review of the minutes and open actions. He closes the meeting and turns to the CEO of Log-Tek seated next to him, Naested Moolman.

"My apologies for being so abrupt with your team as well, but we cannot afford any more delays." Says Steve.

"No offense taken Steve. Can I take you to lunch?" Asks Naested.

"I can eat." Responds Steve.

They walk out to Naested's car and he drives them to a rural restaurant between Midrand and Wonderboom Airport. They chit chat about the program and Steve's career when Naested cuts to the chase.

"Steve how would you like to work for me?" Asks Naested.

Steve is taken aback and cannot answer straight away.

"Well that depends on what is driving me to leave the Air Force!" Replies Steve.

"How about five times your current salary with a Petro and Maintenance Credit Card?" Asks Naested.

Steve is flabbergasted and tells Naested that it is an awesome offer and that he is humbled but will need to discuss with the family and his Officer Commanding. Naested has no problem and just needs Steve on his team. He is impressed at how Steve operates and controls the situation even if he is the most junior rank in the room. On their return to Log-Tek Steve catches up with some of the leads to discuss mitigating items and how best to present. The duty driver returns to collect Steve for his return flight to Cape Town.

The two-hour flight seems like eternity for Steve as he mulls over the offer that Naested has offered him. He loves the military but with the current political arena he must be ready to make a change. Already many of the senior military personnel are being made offers for early retirement. This experience and expertise will soon be lost and never be available to keep the point of the Air Force arrow sharp.

Annie is at the Airport to pick Steve up and he shares his surprise with her. Annie is excited as this will mean a change in their life style. Steve reminds her that he will have to make a huge adjustment in leaving the Air Force, as this is what he has become good at. There is still a lot to think about and Steve is worried. Already the brain drain from South Africa has reached a crescendo. The flow of people immigrating from South Africa had started shortly after Mandela assumed Presidency.

The personnel from programs that had been halted have been snatched up all over the world. The Space Program personnel were all now in the US working for NASA, the attack helicopter design team in France working for Eurocopter and many more special programs personnel have been relocated all over the world. Steve is starting to see the trend he observed in Angola, Rhodesia and Mozambique. This was not going to be any different. The process may take longer but the outcome is predicted. Steve makes up his mind to chat to Fluffie on Monday. He will have to make as much money as he can so that he will qualify to leave the country if required.

Alan Clark a F/E from 22 Squadron has recently completed an officer forming course and comes to chat to Steve about a possible post at 2 Air Depot. To Steve this must be sign that his decision is the right one. Steve takes Alan into his confidence and informs him of his intentions to leave the Air Force which will give him the opportunity to take over. Steve tells Alan that he will discuss this with Fluffie. Meanwhile George Mollison now also a Lieutenant is promoted to manage the Pilatus Astra program as Steve's righthand man. Steve is elated and decides to talk to Fluffie immediately. Steve makes an appointment with Fluffie's secretary and jots down the date and time in his diary.

Steve and Annie have an enjoyable weekend as he tries to mend the waves between them and his parents. The internal Braai is awesome, and the perfect winter gathering area to eat, drink and relax. Steve and Annie fall asleep in front of the fire on the couch to only awake as the cold sets in after the fire burns out. Steve shares his plan with Annie and the decision is made, he will resign from the Air Force.

Early Monday morning Fluffie summons Steve to his office. Steve is not surprised and accepts the fact the Fluffie and Naested have already spoken about the offer. Steve marches in and salutes smartly.

"Sit down Steve." Indicates Fluffie.

Steve seats himself and lays the cards on the table. He adds in his discussion with Alan and what his impressions of Alan are. Fluffie nods knowingly as Alan was on the same Squadron as Fluffie and he knows his capabilities well.

"You have set a high standard Steve and will be missed. But honestly I know here your heads at and I most probably will do the same." Responds Fluffie.

They chat for another hour with Steve clarifying how he will hand over to Alan. Steve still has 90 days of accumulated vacation to which Fluffie just waves a hand and tells him that he will be officially on vacation from the day he decides to and then after that his resignation will take effect.

Steve thanks him profusely and cannot believe that everything seems to be falling into place. It will take at least another month for Steve to hand over. Steve hurries back to his office and asks the office secretary to ring Log-Tek, Naested Moolman for him. A few minutes later his phone rings and he connects with Naested.

They exchange pleasantries after which Naested informs Steve that he has spoken to Fluffie already. Steve enquires about the salary and services plus location. Steve does not want to live in Pretoria or Johannesburg. Naested confirms the offer is being typed up and requests an email address. Verbally they agree on salary, cell phone, credit card and that Steve will be accommodated at the Diep River Office in Cape Town. Steve thanks Naested and hangs up. He is excited and immediately calls Annie to share the news.

He has a month to hand over his accountabilities and bring Alan up to speed. Steve is excited but in trepidation about the future. He has a good career and is on fast track promotion which could have in a senior leadership role in five years. Steve however has seen the degradation in politics and is more concerned over the future of the country.

Steve celebrates his 40th and Annie surprises him with a huge gathering and Braai. The evening is a roaring success, even when Steve and Hennie strip naked in front of everyone to enjoy a winters swim. The evening eventually returns to some form of normality and sober wives must drag inebriated husbands with tired children to their respective homes. Steve finds his way to bed grinning like a chechia cat. Annie just shakes her head at him and proceeds to clean up the kitchen.

The month flies past and although he has cleared out of the Air Force he is still officially on vacation until September 1996. In the meantime, Annie has secured an apartment for Frank and Nellie in Goodwood. Steve takes them through to have a look at the place and they seem pleased.

The clinic, shopping and support services are close at hand making their reliance on Steve less of an issue. Steve arranges with Piet once more to assist him in moving them in. With his parents settled, Steve focuses on the priorities for the next few months.

Deep Mine

Steve reports to Log-Tek, Diep River Office on the 3rd June 1996. Steve meets the team and is shown to his office by Gail who is the Engineering Secretary. Jonathan Morse is head of the office and reports direct to Naested. At Diep River are several military projects currently being managed for the Air Force and Navy. There are two floors of which the engineering and publications occupy the lower level with codification the upper level.

Steve is allocated all the projects for the Air Force, which are essentially those that he signed the contract for as System Manager while in the Air Force. Steve settles down quickly and calls a meeting with the teams he will be managing. Don Rothwell heads up the publications team while John Greyling is project managing a few engineering projects.

Steve settles in quickly with the Log-Tek team and travels monthly to Midrand for project progress meetings. He also now attends the C47-TP Program meetings as a contractor to provide schedule and progress reports. Steve quickly streamlines projects and ensures that timelines are maintained. Naested is wanting Steve to be involved with more than just the Air Force projects and requests that he accompany John on a Systems Engineering project for the Gold Mines.

Swartklip have developed a continuous mining program and require a full Integrated Logistic Support Plan to promote their project. Steve and John travel to Johannesburg and report to the Mine at Western Deep Level. Western Deep Level mine is the deepest Gold Mine in the world, descending to 3,9 Km below the surface. Steve and John will witness the continuous mining process and familiarize themselves with the Logistic Support Analysis required to further calculate system performance and reliability.

Gold Mine Shaft Cage Descent

They accompany the next shift down in the cage donned with safety gear and hardhats. This is both of their first time down a gold mine and therefore both have a feel of unease.

The cage falls at an alarming speed and the shafts leading off from the descending cage pass quickly by as the fall ever deeper into the dark. After what seems like an eternity the cage quickly slows down with a jolt and comes to a stop.

Journey at the bottom of the shaft

John and Steve exit with the rest of the miners and are taken by their guide to a transport coach that will deliver them to the location where the Swartklip Rocksplitter is in operation. The heat and claustrophobia are unbearable and both Steve and John are uncomfortable in this alien environment.

Steve's first impression of the Rocksplitter is one of amazement. Together with joint venture partners Swartklip is launching two new "continuous mining" products for the local and overseas markets. Hydrofracturing technology offers the mining industry a "non-explosive," highly efficient, fast and safe solution to breaking of hard rock.

Continuous Mining at the Rock Face

The crew briefs them on how they prepare and process the rock splitting. The process is simple, and the questions posed are primarily what stoppages for maintenance or breakages for repair occur at what frequency.

Steve is also interested to know what training is required to declare an operator proficient and how many operators are required per shift.

Miners installing Rock Props

Both Steve and John have prepared well with a list of questions that will give them the data they require to develop the Support Plan. They are sitting away from the Rock Splitter comparing notes and observing the layout of the mine. Steve is just eluding to the fact that they are almost 4 Km below the surface and the rock props seem like tooth picks holding back a mountain of rock when a siren goes off in the distance. Both John and Steve look up at each other and then at the miners to establish what the siren is for. Before Steve can ask the question, the earth shakes with a tremor and is followed by a deep grumbling thunderous boom. They are both totally out of their element when their guide turns around with a smile.

"Aaag don't worry man, that's just Piet popping a pillar!" Says their guide.

Further along the mine is a normal mining blasting operation that has just been processed. The area there will be vacated until the extraction systems remove the dust so that the safety crew can inspect the rockface before the rubble is removed.

The Rocksplitter will prevent this unnecessary downtime, as it continuously breaks rock without blasting. Eventually the two resurface and breath deep gulps of fresh air. This is an experience that they will remember for a lifetime. They have what is required to develop the full Integrated Logistic Support Plan for the Swartklip Rocksplitter.

Planning the Future

Frank's little VW 1600 is giving up, so Steve finds a Ford Cortina Station Wagon for him and buys it on the spot. Frank can now load up all his leather works tools and equipment to generate additional income for them by selling belts and paraphernalia on the side of the road. Frank is doing well with the sales and has several back orders. Steve is still concerned with the amount of drinking and sees depression taking over. This is confirmed when Nellie goes to visit her daughter Brenda in Transvaal while Steve is away on a Project that Frank take a turn for the worst. He hallucinates and calls Annie "Tony" as if she were his first born that had died at the age of two. Steve is the second born and never knew his sister as she had died 18 months prior to his birth. Upon Steve's return Annie quickly shares the experience with him and her concern that Frank is not doing well. Steve agrees and forces Frank to see the doctor who immediately recognizes severe depression and alcoholism. Franks is hospitalized but checks himself out a week later. This is a repetitive process and Steve is at wits end. Nellie wont force Frank and when Steve leaves he goes into a rant about how much he hates Steve. He throws down photographs of Steve and stomps on them.

Steve has been taking his BMW for servicing at the same place Don takes his car to. On this occasion the owner approaches Steve and indicates that he needs to come and see the cars he has for sale on the lot. Steve walks with him as spots a beautiful BMW 325. There was less than 50,000 Km on the odometer, so Steve was very interested. He takes the 325 for the evening and is very impressed at the power and comfort of the vehicle. As he now has a Petro and Maintenance card, paying for fuel and repairs was no longer an issue. Annie takes one look.

"I love it, it looks so sleek and the colour is perfect."

Steve returns the next morning and has made up his mind. He trades the 318 on the 325 and is the proud owner of another capitalist vehicle.

Sub-Saharan Africa comes from a low base and stability cannot be taken for granted. Despite improvement, there are still a significant number of armed conflicts and the risk of cross-border contamination is high as most countries have a conflict-torn neighbour. Moreover, there have still been spikes of violence, sometimes widespread, in recent years and even in more stable countries.

In post-electoral violence cost more than 1000 lives in Kenya and people died during strikes and conflicts between unions in South Africa, two of the few democratic countries on the continent. Grievances around political inclusiveness reignited an old conflict in Mozambique.

Democracy in Sub-Saharan Africa is scarce and flawed. Only 8 of the 44 countries included in the Democracy Index are classified as fairly democratic, while 22 are labelled as authoritarian. Progress is scant, being held back by poorly functioning governments. Resilience is also sparse, as countries with a high degree of fragility dominate the continent and the region has the highest average Fragility Index.

Sub-Saharan Africa is a resource-rich continent. While a blessing for USD revenues, resources can be a curse for economic development and peace, especially when governance is poor. Commodity price volatility can also trigger instability and a high proportion of food and fuel in the consumption basket is a bad spell, while an unequal society exacerbates the risks.

The risk of conflict increases the lower is the level of income, the lower is the rate of growth and the greater is the dependence on primary commodities, especially when institutions are weak. Therefore, the persistence of commodity dependence, poverty and weak institutions are a fragile base for building on the progress made on stability.

Steve notices a shift in the political arena where there is a common factor that underlies much of the weak institutional quality of Sub-Saharan Africa, namely corruption. This is because corruption acts as a tax on conducting transactions, which via various channels affects a country's institutions as well as its economy. Foreign Direct Investment (FDI) is an investment made by a firm or individual in one country into business interests located in another country.

Generally, FDI takes place when an investor establishes foreign business operations or acquires foreign business assets in a foreign company. However, FDIs are distinguished from portfolio investments in which an investor merely purchases equities of foreign-based companies.

Corruption reduces FDI, reduces the efficiency of governments since they maximize rents from bypassing red tape rather than welfare, reduces the tax-raising ability of governments because it fuels the size of the underground economy, increases inequality as tax systems, for example, are biased to benefit the wealthy and reduces confidence in public institutions and political processes, such as elections, which hinders democracy.

Despite these detrimental effects, corruption is still a major problem in Sub-Saharan Africa. A very large proportion of the countries in Sub-Saharan Africa scores poorly on the World Bank's measure Control of Corruption, which measures how well corruption is contained, thus the inverse of corruption.

Annie so much loves Steve's car that she drives it at any moment possible. Annie's Toyota Corolla has been over heating, so Steve suggests trading it for a BMW. Steve and Annie go shopping for a BMW for her.

The first BMW, a white 316 is a lovely vehicle, and Steve can see that Annie loves the car. She is undecided, and Steve takes her to a number of alternate dealers. While driving to the next dealer Annie looks at Steve and tells him that she really likes the first car. Without flinching Steve turns the car around and drives directly to the first dealer. She signs and becomes the proud owner of a white BMW 316.

Building Camaraderie

Steve maintains strong ties with the Air Force and ends up being elected to head up the Flight Engineers Association. The turnout for the meetings is overwhelming and Steve is energized to present a professional organization to the Air Force members, retired, civilian and serving.

Steve initiates monthly meetings and forms two branches, one in the southern part of the country and one in the northern part. He requests a motion to have two additional positions voted and accepted as deputy chairman for both branches. The monthly meetings grow in popularity and soon are drawing guests from other parts of the Air Force organization.

The Air Force Museum at Ysterplaat have recently established a replica Bush Pub on site and have offered the location as a venue for future gatherings. Russell and Steve pounce at the opportunity and set about planning a tree planting ceremony coupled with a time vault function.

Steve officially invites the Commanding Officers for Ysterplaat and neighbouring squadrons to attend the function.

Thanking the Officer Commanding Ysterplaat

The evening is once again a crowded event and is initiated by opening speeches from the hosting Officer Commanding and the Chairman of the Flight Engineer Association.

The Chairman welcomes all and dictates the events for the evening.

Opening Speech

Suitably initiated the meeting erupts to the joyful singing of the traditional "Chopper Song".

Chopper Song

Before there is time to consume the normal copious amount of alchohol, a tree is planted outside the Ysterplaat Air Force Museum.

Planting the Tree

The Flight Engineer Association continues to grow in popularity and Steve attends meetings in Pretoria and Cape Town respectively to ensure the membership remains strong and focused on the objective.

The focus on keeping the association alive spurs Steve on the encourage members to grow and plan their futures. In the current political situation, it seems as if most are playing a waiting game for the inevitable to happen, but not planning to react and create opportunities. The young people look up to those that have served on the Border for guidance and direction with the hope that there will answers available to help guide them forward. Steve focuses on building this opportunity and elects to have a team define a request to Air Force Headquarters for consideration of placing a F/E in the Rooivalk Attack helicopter as the Weapons Officer. The paper turns out to be comprehensive with many pros and minimal cons. Steve signs the document and submits it officially to Air Force Head Quarters.

Unfortunately, due to reduction in production of the Rooivalk and political pressure to scrap the program the F/E as Weapons Officer did not receive the appropriate prioritization and is shelved. Steve delivers a positive speech to the members ensuring them that the inputs and expertise provided has been very positively received.

Farewell to the work horses

The Department of Environmental Affairs (DEA) have previously tabled and obtained approval to have the Air Force supply two Oryx Helicopters to replace the aging Puma J Models. The Oryx M2's built by Denel Aviation will be upgraded to have Anti and De-Icing Systems and including additional avionics and navigation systems. With the delivery of the Oryx's the J Models are put up for sale. 22 Squadron and DEA arrange a farewell function to celebrate the service of the two aircraft at AFB Ysterplaat's Warrant Officers Mess. Steve uses Log-Tek's new digital camera to capture the evening.

Farewell function ZS-HIZ & ZS-HJA

J Model replacement Oryx M2

Steve and Annie are working on their relationship and are being drawn in various directions by the two teenagers. David being rebellious and Nicole not accepting Annie as the woman of the house. The situation has many challenges resulting in a number of conflicts, arguments and disagreements. Annie, however is determined to work hard at the relationship where Steve on the other hand is starting to clam up again. He flies off the handle for the smallest of issues and then refuses to talk to anyone. It seems as if he is withdrawing to escape matters he is afraid might destroy his sanity once again. Annie's bouncing spirit does bring Steve back again and they once again make up and move forward.

The year draws to a close and Steve has settled well into his Project Management position with Log-Tek. Naested is extremely pleased with program progress and urges Steve to focus on running the branch at Diep River. Steve is unwilling to follow the recommendation as he has started to look at immigration. He will soon have to sit down with the family and have a heart to heart discussion. He first wants to see what the new year holds in for them. Steve is concerned about his parents as Frank is not improving resulting in more pressure on Nellie. Steve spends as much time as he can, fixing items around the apartment only to be bombarded with complaints that they must climb the stairs to their place which is difficult for Frank. Steve just nods his head and carries on. The situation was not improving at all. Nellie is also in despair and no longer cares what Frank does.

End of an Era

The yearend functions give Steve and Annie time to reconcile and focus on their relationship. Frank is now chain smoking and is soon bed ridden. Nellie has given up and Steve fetches her for the day. Steve is concerned when he sees his father. His lips are blue, and complexion is very sallow. Nellie has a good day with the family and it is late afternoon when Steve takes her back.

The 10th January 1997 arrives, and Frank is now 71 years old. Steve and Annie pay him a visit and wish him for his birthday. His condition has not improved. They leave, and Steve's mind is a mess as he tries to make sense of what to do. On Monday the 13th January Steve gets a call at the office from Nellie.

"Steve your father has collapsed please come quickly?" Sobs Steve's mother.

Steve excuses himself from work but drives slowly to Goodwood. A sense of foreboding and deep sadness coming over him. He feels that his father has passed on and the emotions that rise are confusing. He arrives at the apartment and his mother is with one of the neighbours. Steve goes to comfort her and can see that it is too late. Frank died while trying to get up from the chair and the Ambulance Crew could not revive him. Steve gets Nellie to pack a few things and takes her home with him.

Steve invites Brenda his sister and father's sister Babs to stay with him and Annie for the funeral. The funeral is to be conducted at the Milnerton MOTH Club where Frank was a member. The funeral is attended by a number of MOTH Members and Air Force personnel that knew Frank. Steve attempts to deliver a speech but breaks down uncontrollably. The emotions he feels are incredibly strange to him. He respected his father and looked up to him most of his childhood. The last years however were very different and Steve has difficulty defining why he is broken. Is it perhaps because he could not mend the relationship or was it because Frank could not love his son. Steve vows never to shut out his children. Frank is cremated, and the ashes mounted at the memorial outside the MOTH Club.

Military Strength

One of Mandela's opening statements to Parliament was to realign and modernize the military. The SANDF took over the personnel and equipment from the SADF and integrated forces from the former Bantustan homelands forces, as well as personnel from the former guerrilla forces of some of the political parties involved in South Africa, such as the African National Congress's Umkhonto we Sizwe, the Pan Africanist Congress's Azanian People's Liberation Army and the Self-Protection Units of the Inkatha Freedom Party (IFP). The Azanian People's Organization' s AZANLA was invited but refused to be integrated and to this day remains the only guerrilla force not integrated into the current force. With the integration came the process of balance of power from white to black. Many of the white defense force members are now being offered early retirement packages, starting at the those at the age of 55 years and older. With the packages offered and the status of brain drain post 1994 from the country, many of the educated and experienced expertise are being lost. Nelson Mandela posed a statement claiming that there was peace after apartheid and therefore no longer a requirement for a military force but rather a system of Coast Guard and Policing force. With the threat still real in Africa Steve starts to see the reality of poor leadership taking effect. The shrinkage of the military is going to be the deciding factor of South Africa's peace keeping ability in Africa. Once known as the fifth most feared fighting force in the world the country was quickly becoming invisible as a strength in the region.

Steve has mentally made up his mind and now needs to investigate options. Steve browses the World Wide Web and discovers that there are a number of Immigration Services that have started up to capitalize on the outflux of people from the country. He discovers that there is a presentation taking place in Cape Town in a couple of days and decides to discuss the option with Annie. Steve explains the current situation of the political arena in South Africa together with his observations and fears for the future. Annie listens intently and does not oppose anything that he brings up. She agrees to accompany him to the presentation.

Chapter 19 – THE FINAL STRAW

A Canadian company "Soft Landings" are presenting immigration opportunities to Canada, Australia and New Zealand. The presenter gives an honest speech on the strict qualification criteria for application. Annie has her sights set on New Zealand and Steve feels that Canada would be a better option. New Zealand is 16 hours away from the west whereas Canada is surrounded with everything a first world country needs. On the way home Steve and Annie have made up their mind and agree to have a family discussion as soon as possible.

The next evening after supper Steve sits the family down and starts the discussion.

"Politically South Africa is in a very critical position. The current ANC Government, like Zimbabwe to the north will create a dictatorship and cripple the country in no less than 15 to 20 years. Reversed discrimination, corruption, crime and brain drain are already in motion. For the two of you, Nicole and David, to have any future we must find an alternate option. To that end Annie and I have attended an immigration seminar and have a proposal that the whole family must agree on before we finalize our plans. We would like to immigrate as a family to either Canada or New Zealand, depending on where we qualify." Says Steve.

Both David and Nicole surprise Steve when they excitedly agree that it is the best option and that they support the decision. Steve and Annie have a lot of work to do. Steve must have all his qualifications accredited and legally translated if not in English. Both Steve and Annie will have to obtain release for taking the children out of the country from their ex-spouses. The plan is set in motion and Steve completes the forms he collected from the presentation. The cost is huge but the benefits for the family bigger. Within a week Steve has completed the application, paid the fees and submitted all to the Immigration Company based in Midrand. The family settles down to the proposed 18 month waiting list.

Both George Mollison and Alan Clark have also started immigration processing to New Zealand. Steve remains headfast on Canada as his qualifications will be more readily accepted there. With the process initiated, Steve starts gathering data as requested by the Canadian Immigration Officials, which require him to dig deep and find information from Air Force Head Quarters, Technical Colleges and other Institutions where he has received accreditation.

Project Completion

The C47-TP Publications Project is winding down and the final deliverables are being processed. The Air Force are a happy customer and Steve is pleased with the product they delivered. Steve manages to pick up one additional project for the development and delivery of "Pilots Manuals" for the C47-TP. Fortunately, he had anticipated this and had ensured that Don Rothwell's team had captured relevant data during the development of the Technical Publications. All that had to be completed was inclusion of the data into the approved Test Flight reports from TFDC at Bredasdorp.

To celebrate the success of the project Steve obtains approval from 35 Squadron to take the Log-Tek Team in the newly commissioned VIP C47-TP for a flip around the Peninsula. With Champagne suitably cooled the celebrations are set and the team plus spouses meet at 35 Squadron for the scenic route.

Log-Tek Project Team

Steve has been incredibly busy since joining Log-Tek and with the decision to immigrate now in process he is mentally drained. Steve decides to revisit SWA, now Namibia, with the family to show them where he operated in the Air Force.

There is however, a deeper part of Steve that needs to go back, as if he is being urged to relive part of his past by visualization.

<u>Namibian trip</u>

Annie and the children are excited and Steve starts planning the trip. As winter fades and Spring moves into summer Steve has prepared the route to follow. This will be the first time that he sees the route from the ground as he has flown Namibia far and wide but never driven it.

The Journey North

It's early December 1997 when Steve services the BMW and his home-made trailer. The route is more than 9,000 Km and will take them more than 3 weeks to complete. Steve gets several Rat Packs from Russell at 22 Squadron to add to the grocery list of rations he is preparing. Steve and Annie do some last-minute shopping at Cape Union Mart to buy tents and camping equipment. All to soon the day arrives and early morning the family prepares for the long trek through Namibia. The trip North starts off well and Steve stops off at Clanwilliam for refuel and refreshments. The girls go off to the toilet while Steve and David refuel the car. Steve feels the need for pressure relief and lets off a humungous fart. David laughs so loud that he ends up farting as well. Steve looks down at David.

"That's not a fart man, here is a real fart!" And Steve propels a volume of gas from his rear end.

Suddenly Steve's expression changes as he realizes he has just shat in his pants. He walks off bow legged to the toilet where he strips down and washes himself off. The underpants cannot be saved so Steve dumps them in the trash and wearing shorts goes back to the car. David at this time has tears streaming down his face from laughter as he tries to explain the episode to the ladies. The trip so far is literally starting off with a bang. Further north they continue through Vredendal towards Springbok. Springbok is the largest town in the Namaqualand area in the Northern Cape province of South Africa. It was called Springbokfontein until 1911, when it was shortened to Springbok. Springbok is located on the national route which connects the Cape with Namibia, and at the western end connects it with Upington and Pretoria. It is the main town of the Nama Khoi Local Municipality, which also includes a number of surrounding towns such as Okiep and Nababeep.

The town lies at an elevation of 3,304 feet in a narrow valley between the high granite domes of the Klein Koperberge, Small Copper Mountains. This name gives away the reason for the early settlement which gradually turned into a major commercial and administrative centre for copper mining operations in the region. While the town initially developed rapidly, this slowed down when rich copper deposits were discovered in Okiep. As the main source of water, Springbok continued to develop as the commercial and administrative centre for different mines in the area. Even though mining activities have dwindled, the town remains an important administrative capital in the region and due to its location a favourite stopover for tourists on their way to Namibia. Today the main income is generated from tourism, mining activities, commerce and farming. The country side being dry is blessed with spring flowers.

Springbok the Flowering Desert

They will reach the border post at Vioolsdrift by late afternoon. A road bridge on the national road links South Africa with Namibia and the town is the South African border post. At the other end of the bridge is the small Namibian village of Noordoewer, meaning "north bank" in Afrikaans.

The area is profoundly arid, and the crossing is overlooked by steep and spectacular sandstone cliffs hundreds of meters in height. In general, the surrounding region is almost unpopulated. There are small pockets of fertile alluvial soil along the course of the river and these are used for growing crops, such as dates and melons, under irrigation.

There are two seasons, with a short winter season lasting from about May to July with almost no rain falls, and the weather is hot. The summer season lasts from August to April and is very hot with no rain whatsoever. Vioolsdrif is officially one of the hottest places in South Africa reaching a temperature of 47 C°.

Vioolsdrif Border Crossing

They arrive at the border crossing and after presenting their passports Steve drives to the campsite just across the Orange river to setup for the night. Steve is exhausted and catches forty winks before supper.

Steve snoozing

As he awakens Steve is reminded that he promised the family supper and immediately gets the Braai Skottel out to prepare Wors and the rest of the food that Annie had packed for the trip.

Supper is served

After supper the family takes a walk along the river to stretch legs and enjoy the scenery. Tomorrow is going to be a long day and Steve wants to make sure they are well rested for the next stretch up to Lüderitz.

The road to Lüderitz is through the Namib desert for 580 Km. Along the route they encounter the Namib Desert Horse, a rare feral horse found in the Namib. These are the only feral herd of horses residing in Africa, with a population ranging between 90 and 150.

Despite the harsh environment in which they live, the horses are generally in good condition. The most likely ancestors of the horses are a mix of riding horses and cavalry horses, many from German breeding programs, released from various farms and camps in the early 20th century, especially during World War I.

Whatever their origin, the horses eventually congregated in the Garub Plains, near Aus, the location of a man-made water source. In 1984, the first aerial survey of the population was made, and in 1986, their traditional grazing land was incorporated into the Namib-Naukluft Park. Driving along the dusty desert road they are fortunate to spot the horses in the distance.

Namib Desert Horse

The long straight desert road seems endless although the scenery is spectacular the children are soon bored and nod off to sleep. Steve updates Annie on the geography and history of this desolate place. The Namib is a coastal desert and the name Namib is of Khoekhoegowab origin meaning "vast place".

The Namib stretches for more than 2,000 kilometers along the Atlantic coasts of Angola, Namibia, and South Africa, extending southward from the Carunjamba River in Angola, through Namibia and to the Olifants River in Western Cape. The Namib's northernmost portion, which extends 450 kilometers from the Angola-Namibia border, is known as Moçâmedes Desert, while its southern portion approaches the neighboring Kalahari Desert.

From the Atlantic coast eastward, the Namib gradually ascends in elevation, reaching up to 200 kilometers inland to the foot of the Great Escarpment. Annual precipitation ranges from 2 millimeters in the most arid regions to 200 millimeters at the escarpment, making the Namib the only true desert in southern Africa.

Having endured arid or semi-arid conditions for roughly 55 to 80 million years, the Namib may be the oldest desert in the world and contains some of the world's driest regions.

The desert geology consists of sand seas near the coast, while gravel plains and scattered mountain outcrops occur further inland. The sand dunes, some of which are 300 meters high and span 32 kilometers long, are the second largest in the world. Temperatures along the coast are stable and generally range between 9 °C to 20 °C annually, while temperatures further inland are variable summer daytime temperatures can exceed 45 °C while nights can be freezing.

Fogs that originate offshore from the collision of the cold Benguela Current and warm air from the Hadley Cell create a fog belt that frequently envelops parts of the desert. Coastal regions can experience more than 180 days of thick fog a year. While this has proved a major hazard to ships, of which more than a thousand wrecks litter the Skeleton Coast, it is a vital source of moisture for desert life.

Namib Desert

The Namib is almost completely uninhabited by humans except for several small settlements and indigenous pastoral groups, including the Ovahimba and Obatjimba Herero in the north, and the Topnaar Nama in the central region. Owing to its antiquity, the Namib may be home to more endemic species than any other desert in the world. Most of the desert wildlife is arthropods and other small animals that live on little water, although larger animals inhabit the northern regions. Near the coast, the cold ocean water is rich in fishery resources and supports populations of brown fur seals and shorebirds, which serve as prey for the Skeleton Coast's lions. Further inland, the Namib-Naukluft National Park, the largest game park in Africa, supports populations of African Bush Elephants, Mountain Zebras, and other large mammals. Although the outer Namib is largely barren of vegetation, lichens and succulents are found in coastal areas, while grasses, shrubs, and ephemeral plants thrive near the escarpment. Several types of trees are also able to survive the extremely arid climate.

Thick morning fog rolls in from the ocean

Lüderitz and Kolmanskop

As the road winds down towards the coast the temperature drops, and the wind picks up. Lüderitz has a desert climate, with moderate temperatures throughout the year. The average annual precipitation is 17 millimeters. Windy and cold conditions can occur due to the cold South Atlantic current on the coast.

As they round the bend Lüderitz looms in front of them. The bay on which Lüderitz is situated was first known to Europeans when Bartolomeu Dias encountered it in 1487. He named the bay Angra Pequena Portuguese for Small Bay, and erected a padrão, stone cross, on the southern peninsula. Steve makes a quick detour to the cross. The wind is howling, and the air is much colder. In the 18th century Dutch adventurers and scientists explored the area in search of minerals but did not have much success. Further exploration expeditions followed in the early 19th century during which the vast wildlife in the ocean was discovered. Profitable enterprises were set up, including whaling, seal hunting, fishing and guano-harvesting. Lüderitz thus began its life as a trading post.

Bartolomeu Dias Cross

The town was founded in 1883 when Heinrich Vogelsang purchased Angra Pequena and some of the surrounding land on behalf of Adolf Lüderitz, a Hanseat from Bremen in Germany, from the local Nama chief Josef Frederiks II in Bethanie. When Adolf Lüderitz did not return from an expedition to the Orange River in 1886, Angra Pequena was named Lüderitzbucht in his honour. In 1905, German authorities established a concentration camp on Shark Island. The camp, access to which was very restricted, operated between 1905 and 1907 during the Herero Wars. Between 1,000 and 3,000 Africans from the Herero and Nama tribes died here as a result of the tragic conditions of forced labour. Their labour was used for expansion of the city, railway, port and on the farms of white settlers. Steve stops the car on a viewpoint just short of the town for the family to take in the view.

Town of Lüderitz

In 1909, after the discovery of diamonds nearby, Lüderitz enjoyed a sudden surge of prosperity due to the development of a diamond rush to the area. In 1912 Lüderitz already had 1,100 inhabitants, not counting the indigenous population. Although situated in harsh environment between desert and Ocean, trade in the harbour town surged, and the adjacent diamond mining settlement of Kolmanskop was built. Steve drives to the closest Motel and books a room for the night. With keys in hand Steve and Annie unlock the door to be surprised with a layer of desert sand inside the door. Annie quickly sweeps the sand up and places a damp cloth against the door sill to prevent further ingress. Lüderitz is spectacular and is rich in German history.

After the German World War I capitulation, South Africa took over the administration of German South West Africa in 1915. Many Germans were deported from Lüderitz, contributing to its shrinking in population numbers. From 1920 onwards, diamond mining was only conducted further south of town in places like Pomona and Elizabeth Bay. This development consequently led to the loss of Lüderitz' importance as a trading place. Only small fishing enterprises, minimal dock activity and a few carpet weavers remained.

Early the next morning Steve gets the family together as he is very keen to visit the ghost town close by. Just outside Lüderitz lies the ghost town of Kolmanskop. This previously bustling diamond town is now abandoned and fights a constant struggle against being buried under the shifting sand dunes of the Namib desert.

In April of 1908, Zacharias Lewala, a worker on the railway line between Lüderitz and Aus in what is now southern Namibia, picked up a shiny stone and showed it to his supervisor, August Stauch. Recognizing the find, Stauch got himself a prospecting license and then presented the stone for verification. State geologist Dr. Range confirmed it was a diamond, and within months the diamond rush was on around the site of Kolmanskop, 10 kilometers inland from the coastal town of Lüderitz.

The name Kolmanskuppe, Kolmanskoppe or Kolmanskop is believed to have originated from a transport driver named Johnny Kolman. He transported goods from Keetmanshoop to Luderitzbucht and it was his custom to outspan his oxen and make camp in the vicinity of a low-lying gneiss kopje (Kuppe) or hillock.

Ghost Town Kolmanskop

In September 1908, the Colonial Government declared a Sperrgebiet or 'forbidden zone' extending 360 km northward to latitude 26 Degrees South from the Orange River and 100 km inland from the coast, known today as Diamond Area No.1 in order to control the mining of the diamonds and in February 1909 a central diamond market was established. The Sperrgebiet was designed to give the government control over the region thought to contain diamonds and accounted for 20% of the worldwide diamond take. In 1909 almost 500,000 carats were produced there and yields almost tripled in 5 years. As the diamond mining progressed to Kolmanskop, a unique little settlement mushroomed in the desert sands. Improvised wooden buildings with corrugated iron cladding, prefabricated in Germany, gave way to solid and astonishingly impressive buildings that contrasted in a bizarre way with their desolate surroundings.

Among them, with an air of importance, were the double-storied homes of manager Hans Hőrlein and mining engineer Leonard Kolle. There was a police station using camels for their patrols, a post office, opened in February 1909, a general dealer's store, a bakery, butchery, lemonade and soda-water factory which used the same cooling facilities as the butchery. There was an ice making facility which provided each household daily with a free block of ice which was made in special upright, long and narrow forms. Each morning the ice vendor came down the streets, which were even then smothered with sand, to deliver the daily ration of ice blocks and cold drinks to each

There was a large workshop, a huge depot, a carpentry shop, offices and stables. There was a primary school with a playground complete with swings and merry-go-round. At the top of a sand-dune hill was a reservoir which served a dual purpose. It provided the mining plant with water for the washing and treatment operations and was also used as a swimming pool by the residents of Kolmanskop. Sea-water was pumped through a long pipeline from Elisabethbucht, some 28 kilometers away. A pipeline also served Charlottental. Occasionally there was a leak which was greatly enjoyed by the children, an unexpected shower in the desert.

Drinking water remained a problem. It had to be shipped from Cape Town to Luderitzbucht and then brought by rail to Kolmanskop. It was transported in barrels to the diamond fields. Initially these water barrels were conveyed in wagons, but their wheels got bogged down. The problem was solved with the barrels being pulled along the desert sands by two mules. Fresh water was also obtained from a spring at Garub, about 100 kilometers distant. It was transported in barrels in railway trucks, off -loaded at the depot and pumped into tanks. Prior to 1927 there was also a simple corrugated-iron recreation centre with a skittle alley.

In 1910 Stauch's Koloniale Bergbau Gesellschaft decided to erect a central power station at Luderitzbucht to supply electricity to the diamond fields. This ambitious undertaking was initiated by Stauch. A few years later the company floated the Luderitzbuchter Elektrizitats Gesellschaft, with a capital of two million marks, to run the power station. Housing, electricity and fuel were provided free by the company, which also maintained a well-built hospital. The hospital had one of the finest X-ray plants in Southern Africa.

In 1927 a magnificent new recreation centre was built where many functions and forms of entertainment were held. It had perfect acoustics, designed by an expert from Germany. Provision was made for gymnastics and film shows. There was also a large skittle alley a casino and a theatre.

Some 700 families lived in the town, including about 300 German adults, 40 children and 800 Ovambo contract workers. Wages were good and virtually everything was free, including company houses, milk deliveries and other fringe benefits. Large metal screens around the gardens and corners of the houses helped to keep the sand at bay and a sand-clearing squad cleared the streets every day. Many of the professionals in Kolmanskop had lavish homes. On the railway line between Kolmans and Pomona, sand was always a problem, causing long delays. The train was always accompanied by cleaners with shovels to clear the tracks.

South Africa gained control of SWA after World War I in 1920 and sold the diamond deposits to Consolidated Diamond Mines (CDM), which was transferred to De Beers, predecessor to Namdeb in 1929. In 1928, the discovery of Namibia's vast marine-terrace diamond reserves, just north of the mouth to the Orange River, slowed production in the north. The general exodus to Oranjemund began and many of the original prefabricated wooden houses were dismantled and reassembled again in Oranjemund. Kolmanskop remained the headquarters of the CDM until 1943 when it moved to Oranjemund. Mining operations ceased there in 1950.

Looking at Kolmans and the other towns, after the desert had taken over, it is difficult to believe that these places were once alive with people, and that some of them had beautiful indoor gardens. By 1956 the town of Kolmanskop was deserted and replaced by Oranjemund as SWA's diamond headquarters the beginning of the end started. Soon the metal screens collapsed, and the pretty gardens and tidy streets were buried under the sand. Doors and windows creaked on their hinges, cracked window panes stared sightlessly across the desert. A new ghost town had been born. Within 40 years the town was born, flourished and then died. One day Kolmanskop's sand-clearing squad failed to turn up, the ice-man stayed away, the school bell rang no more.

Sesriem

Leaving Lüderitz Steve navigates towards Swakopmund. The journey takes them back through the Namib desert to Sesriem 495 Km further north. At the entry to Sossusvlei is Sesriem Canyon, where centuries of erosion have incised a narrow gorge about 1 km in length. At the foot of the gorge, which plunges down to 30 to 40 m, are pools that become replenished after good rains. Sesriem derives its name from the time when earlier pioneers tied six lengths of rawhide thongs (riem) together to draw water from the pools. At Sesriem Canyon is scenic campsite that the family decides to call it for the night. Steve checks in at the office and secures a site for the evening. They set up camp and after an early supper relax at the bar. Steve and Annie retire early while the children are entertained by the young manager, who looks like he would be more comfortable sleeping out in the open next to a fire than managing a campsite.

Steve and Annie are relaxing on top of the sleeping bags as it is still very warm. In the distance Steve recognizes the grunting of a lion. He explains the sound to Annie.

"You are trying to scare me, there are no lions here." Responds Annie.

Steve reiterates that they are definitely in the bush and that the sound is a lion. But Annie won't believe him. They eventually drift off to sleep. After a quick breakfast Steve goes to the office to settle up and is surprised to receive a bill of R200 for alchohol. He questions the bill and the young lad informs him that the children had "Springbokkies". Steve is angry at both the manager and the children. David is 16 and Nicole 13 years old. How could this idiot feed them alchohol? The Springbokkie is Peppermint Liqueur laced with Baileys. Not a cheap drink at all. Steve chastises David and Nicole and they set off to Swakopmund.

Sesriem Campsite

Still travelling through the Namib desert, Steve heads north to Swakopmund. The desert road is dusty, desolate and long. There are many corrugations as the gravel road is a state of disrepair. Steve feels the rear of the car becoming loose and stops to take a look. He finds that the right rear wheel is totally deflated and destroyed. He swaps out the wheel for the spare. They still have over 300 Km to go and with the current state of the road he cannot guarantee that there won't be another blow out. Steve drives gingerly onward, gritting his teeth as the corrugations get worse in sections. All along the route he keeps an eye out for a service station and when they do reach one he finds out that a replacement would be same price for a set of new tires. Steve decides to continue and hopes for the best.

Swakopmund

Eventually the end is insight and Steve breaths a heavy sigh of relief. First order of business is to find have the tire replaced and then accommodation. Nestled on Namibia's Atlantic coast and surrounded by the sand dunes of the vast Namib Desert, the resort town of Swakopmund enchants visitors with its distinct German colonial architecture and pleasant climate. With scenic beaches, the town boasts the status of Namibia's adventure sports capital, where recreational opportunities abound.

There is everything from sandboarding and quad biking on the desert dunes, to surfing, golfing, and helicopter rides. The town's history starts with the landing of the Portuguese sailor Bartholomew Diaz on Namibian soil at Cape Cross in the year 1487 where he erected a stone cross. Much later, in 1793, two Dutch sailors were anchoring shortly at the mouth of the Swakop River. In 1862 the crew of a German gunboat hoisted the German flag at the mouth of the Swakop River to signal the territories occupancy. Another gunboat marked the possible landing site with poles in August 1892. With this sovereign act the occupation of this coastal area by the German Reich was demonstrated to the English who were occupying the harbour of Walvis Bay.

Geographically Swakopmund is situated amidst dunes and desert close to the mouth of the Swakop River. During the colonial period Swakopmund was an important harbour, although the conditions were not really favourable, as the coastal waters were far too shallow, a sheltered lagoon was missing, and the surf was much too strong. Additionally, the harbour of Lüderitz was too far away and the nearby Walvis Bay harbour was under British occupation. As the disembarkation of settlers and troops on surf boats was a life-threatening undertaking, an artificial harbour was built at very high costs. Initially a 325-meter-long, wooden jetty was built in 1902, which was replaced by an iron one in 1912. The complete supply of the colony was handled via Swakopmund. The remains of this Jetty can still be seen today.

To upgrade the means of transportation the first German South West African railway line between Swakopmund and Windhoek was opened on the 01 July 1902. The Namib Desert is over 100 kilometers wide; the track distance to Windhoek covered 382 km in which the railway had to climb to 1673 meters above sea level. This narrow-gauge railway runs today from Walvis Bay via Swakopmund to Windhoek.

Today Swakopmund serves mainly as a holiday resort and is thus of touristic importance. Due to its mild climatic condition especially during the high season December and January the town is an attraction to many tourists especially from the inland to such an extent that accommodation has to be pre-booked way in advance. Many South African and Namibian pensioners take up residence here. During colonial times Swakopmund was referred to as "Germany's most southern coastal resort", even though water temperatures, due to the cold Benguela current of the Atlantic hardly reached over 20 °C.

With the wheel repaired Steve drives northward up the coast to find accommodation for the night. At Long Beach they find room for the night with a restaurant close by. Steve decides to surprise the family the next day and goes in search of the plan he wants to put into action.

Quads in the Dunes

Without saying a word Steve drives to the Dune Quad Bike camp and pays for a guided tour of the Dunes. Annie and the children are excited and can't wait to go. After the required safety briefing, helmets and instructions, they follow the guide on a tour through the dunes.

They are rewarded with the fantastic beauty of the Namib Dunes and enjoy an exciting rush of racing up then down these huge moving mountains.

A very windblown group with big smiles eventually return the Quads. A perfect end to a perfect day. Steve treats them all to a meal at the local restaurant after which they take a walk on the beach to watch the sunset. Due to the high Mica content in the windblown desert the red sunsets of SWA are spectacular.

SWA Coastal Sunset

War Zone Post-Independence

The long trek continues as Steve has planned to start from the west and move along the top of SWA to the east in the hopes of stopping at places he operated from during the border war. The 700 Km trip to Ruacana would be a test for them for sure. They soon leave the Namib desert to the west as the road slowly creeps more inland and they are surrounded with semi desert bushveld.

They are now entering the OvaHimba a nomadic tribes people.

Himba mother and child

The OvaHimba are predominantly livestock farmers who breed fat-tailed sheep and goats but count their wealth in the number of their cattle. They also grow and farm rain-fed crops such as maize and millet. Livestock are the major source of milk and meat for the OvaHimba. Their main diet is sour milk and maize porridge and sometimes plain hard porridge only, due to milk and meat scarcity. Women and girls tend to perform more labor-intensive work than men and boys do, such as carrying water to the village, earthen plastering the mopane wood homes with a traditional mixture of red clay soil and cow manure binding agent, collecting firewood, attending to the calabash vines used for producing and ensuring a secure supply of soured milk, cooking and serving meals, as well as artisans making handicrafts, clothing and jewelry. The responsibility for milking the cows and goats also lies with the women and girls. Women and girls take care of the children, and one woman or girl will take care of another woman's children. The men's main tasks are tending to the livestock farming, herding where the men will often be away from the family home for extended periods, animal slaughtering, construction, and holding council with village tribal chiefs. Members of a single extended family typically dwell in a homestead, onganda, a small family-village, consisting of a circular hamlet of huts and work shelters that surround an okuruwo, sacred ancestral fire, and a kraal for the sacred livestock. Both the fire and the livestock are closely tied to their veneration of the dead, the sacred fire representing ancestral protection and the sacred livestock allowing "proper relations between human and ancestor".

Himba Herders

The route takes them past Kamanjab directly to Ruacana. The temperature once again is in the high 30's and thankfully the BMW's air conditioner is helping them keep cool. Fortunately, Steve remembers that there is accommodation available at Ruacana, so they will not have to camp out in the heat.

Ruacana

Ruacana is a town in Omusati Region, northern Namibia and the district capital of the Ruacana electoral constituency. It is located on the border with Angola on the river Kunene. The town is known for the picturesque Ruacana Falls nearby, and for the Ruacana Power Station. Ruacana was developed around a major underground hydroelectric plant linked to the nearby dam across the border in Angola at Calueque. The dam and pumping station were bombed in a Cuban airstrike in 1988, during the Angolan Civil War.

OvaZemba and OvaHimba people are native to the area. The name Ruacana originated from one of the first settlers in Ruacana called Ruhakana. The town was therefore named after Mr. Ruhakana although it is currently written as Ruacana. The place normally receives an annual average rainfall of 426 millimeters.

The 600 hectares farm Etunda is situated near Ruacana. It is run as a government supported irrigation scheme and has been established in 1993. Half of the farm is commercial irrigation land; the other half is allocated to 82 small-scale farmers. Etunda cultivates maize, wheat, watermelons, bananas, and other produce.

They arrive late afternoon at Ruacana and Steve immediately recognizes the houses that they accommodated during the border war when they were deployed here for special operations. These houses were now the rentals that they would spend the next few days at. Steve unpacks the necessities out of the trailer while Annie prepares a meal for them. The children have gone investigating and end up making friends with a family not far from them. Steve and Annie relax for the evening while the children join their new-found friends on an excursion of the town. They want to investigate the local swimming pool to see if they can have a dip.

Later the evening David and Nicole return excitement written all over their faces. The pool was closed so they jumped over the wall to have a swim, after which they went back to their new found friend's home and were subsequently invited for a tour of the Ruacana Hydroelectric Power Station the next day.

Entrance to the Ruacana Hydroelectric Power Station

They unwind after the travels of the previous day, but Steve knows the trip east is going to be tough. It is rain season and "Oom Willie se pad" will be treacherous. He aims to stop off at Oshikati, Sector 10 Headquarters and Ondangwa the Air Force Base during the border war. Steve packs the trailer early morning and they set out before the temperature becomes unbearable. The first stop along the route is Outapi, an old Army forward base. Most of the base has been ransacked and not worth stopping, so Steve continues to Oshikati. The communication towers that were extensively used as navigation points during the war clearly indicate the location of the town.

Communication Tower

They are now entering the land of the Ovambo. In Oshiwambo, the language of the Ovambo, the town's name means "that which is in between", although some believe that the name, Oshakati, was used to refer to the 275 m high broadcast tower, the tallest structure downtown and in Namibia. Oshakati is one of Namibia's largest cities. In February 1988, a bomb blast occurred in Oshakati at the First National Bank, killing 27 people and badly injuring nearly 30 others, most of them nurses and teachers. It is almost midday, so Steve stops off at the local Kentucky Fried Chicken for some take away meals. Amazingly the food is good and soon devoured by all.

Ondangwa

A short 35 Km down the road Steve turns into what used to be AFB Ondangwa. The bases water tower, a dead giveaway. This water is pumped directly from the Kunene river from Ruacana and was built by the SADF during the border war. The old Guard House in blue, still stands. Steve feels a shiver up his back as he turns into the entrance to Ondangwa.

Entrance to the Ondangwa Airport

Many tours spent here in the not too distant past bring back vivid memories to Steve, good and bad. A lot of ghosts exist here for him and uneasily he drives into the area.

The first stop is the hangars where many hours were spent at night maintaining the helicopters in preparation for war. The access road now in the advanced stages of over growth. Fort Rev, the old Recce Camp longtime removed and the veld already reclaiming evidence of past occupation.

Hangars and Control Tower

Most of the once proud Air Force Headquarter and Operations Briefing Buildings now form part of the Ondangwa Airport offices and are in disarray.

The Stores and Armoury already stripped of all the zinc cladding with just the metal frames still remaining on concrete slabs.

The once proud Lapa where a number of memorials were placed, and a beautiful garden maintained now derelict and destroyed.

The once famous Tree Pub and Restaurant just a memory. The many sad and happy times spent here will forever only be in the memories of those who had the privilege to be here.

Steve looks over the place and his heart sinks, remembering all the camaraderie and lifetime friendships formed in these walls.

With immense sadness Steve moves through the area remembering past voices as if they were calling out to him and beckoning him to remember.

Steve remembers sadly how the late Clifton Stacey and he had spent his last night in this very same pub. The emotions that are flowing over Steve are intense and frustrating as he knows they are his memories alone and will not be understood or shared with the family. It would be selfish of him to open up and share the times, as he knows he will most surely breakdown.

The touring members accommodation billets now in disarray. The zinc roofs removed, and the rooms now accommodate goat herds.

Wondering through the ruins of a once powerful, modern and bustling Air Force Base, Steve is overcome with emotions as he remembers the hard, fun, sad and fearful days that he and his fellow flight engineers had spent so many hours. The hard work, the fun and the many hours of high adrenalin reminding him of his journey through life and the current situation South Africa was in.

Remains of the Lapa

Remains of the Tree Pub

Remains of the Mess

Steve wanders over to the Aircrew Accommodation area remembering how with their own hands they had built swimming pools, gardens, braais and gardens. How they had decorated the entrances to the billets and created their own sanctuaries. Oh, how he remembers those days and how he longs for the times that people could stand together for a common cause and not be forced apart by idiocy or bad communication.

Steve remembers the times of hardship and the times of pain, the times of celebration and the times of happiness. Shaking his head, he wanders over the place he rested for so many years after very trying and dangerous days in the field.

Remains of Alo Den

Names in history

Remains of the Pool

<u>Remains of the Air Crew Pub Area</u>

<u>Remains of the Pool built by Steve and the Flight Engineers</u>

<u>Remains of the Ablution Block</u>

A very subdued Steve motions the family that it's time to leave. Steve drives slowly out of Ondangwa and heads east to Rundu. The road to Eenhana is mostly tarred but after that "Oom Willie se pad" is a wet mud mess.

Steve is anxious and is hoping that there will be no problems. The BMW is not suited for this type of bundu bashing and can very easily get stuck in the mud. During the rainy season Steve has witnessed the most effective military vehicles get bogged down quite badly on this very stretch of road. They make it to Eenhana in record time so Steve pulls over at the old Army Camp to recoup and show the family what a border protection camp looked like.

Remains of the Army Border Camp with kitchen and mess hall at Eenhana

To the left is what once was the Mess Hall with the Headquarters directly ahead under sandbags with a defense tower on top of it. Behind this is the Communications Tower with the Aapkas, lookout tower. Steve has spent many weeks here on deployment for follow up operations against SWAPO. Both Koevoet and 32 Battalion used to operate from here. Eenhana was strategically placed by the SADF to cover the area closest to the Angolan border had the highest potential of infiltration. Many a contact had been spearheaded from here. At one point the Air Force had a permanent Ops Officer and Communications Tech stationed here.

With Eenhana behind them Steve sets heading on the gravel road to Okongo, another Army Base that also covered the border for the same reasons. At Okongo is a giant Baobab tree that is hollow in the center. During the war years the Army Campers that were stationed here had built a chapel inside the hollow of the tree. Many Sunday Services were conducted from the pulpit.

Baobab Tree at Okongo

Leaving Okongo Steve starts to see the degradation of the road as the evidence of rain has already created large pools of mud along many stretches. Steve carefully navigates the safest parts of the road where he is sure the road is dryer. When unsure he stops to check the road out before plunging blindly into the unknown. The road is so desolate and isolated they will most probably be on their own for a number of days before someone passes by. In the next few miles there are a few trucks that have been bogged down and will need a dozer to extract them from the mud. They are axle deep all around and the drivers are camped out on the side of the road as they have no answer for extraction. Steve slowly makes his way through with the heavy six-foot trailer and at one point his heart loses a beat as the BMW slides precariously close to a deep pool of mud, but at the last minute gets enough grip and slides toward the dry area where Steve gains control once more. Eventually at 110 Km from Rundu Steve is back on the tarred road and can relax once more. They make quick time to Rundu and Steve stops at the first Motel so that they can bed down for the night as he is totally exhausted from the long trek.

Rundu

Rundu is the capital of the Kavango-East Region, northern SWA, on the border with Angola on the banks of the Kavango River about 3,300 feet above sea level. The place normally receives an annual average rainfall of 565 millimeters. Rundu has a hot semi-arid climate, with hot summers and relatively mild winters. Even though it has a hot semi-arid climate, the area experiences high diurnal temperature variation during the winter with average high temperatures at roughly 26 °C and average low temperatures at 6 °C.

At the Rundu Lodge Steve checks in for the night and the family settle down to catch up some well-deserved rest and recuperation. At check in the owner introduces the children to Koerie, the local pet Mongoose. Koerie takes to David and Nicole immediately and follows them to the room.

Currie the Mongoose

In the meantime, Steve has made his way to the swimming pool and is relaxing with beer in hand. Annie soaking up the sun as per normal.

Swimming after a long day

Suitably cooled down and refreshed they make their way to the restaurant and have a hearty well deserved meal. Steve enjoys a couple of beers before they make their way back to the room. It does not take long for the whole family to fall fast asleep. Sometime during the night Koerie crawls in with David and Nicole and spends the rest of the night sleeping with them.

From now on the tour will be mostly on tarred roads and Steve feels more relaxed about the route. The bad roads through the desert and the mud-soaked road on the border have taken their toll on him and the BMW. The car is in dire need of maintenance and tire replacement. After a good rest Steve gathers the family and they pack up for the next stretch to Katima Mulilo. It is a long stretch of road at more than 500 Km. Steve remembers the road teaming with wild life and often they saw Elephant, Giraffe, Kudu, Buffalo and many Impala.

Buffalo

Along the way Steve remembers that 32 Battalion had their main base, Buffalo, located next to the Okavango river. He checks the map and sees that it is still indicated as "Buffalo Park" with a gravel road leading up to it. He follows the road some 20 Km from the tarred road and memories start flooding back as he rounds the bend to see the entrance.

Entrance to Buffalo 32 Battalion

Although in disrepair the entrance still has that powerful pull of the camaraderie of the fighting Buffalos. Steve had many friendships here with the troops, black and white.

Politicians had visited this place of rest for warriors and families had created homes here. This was 32 Battalions Home Town "Buffalo".

The mighty Okavango river

The Okavango River is the fourth-longest river system in Southern Africa, running southeastward for 1,600 km. It begins in Angola, where it is known by the Portuguese name Rio Cubango.

Farther south, it forms part of the border between Angola and Namibia, and then flows into Botswana, draining into the Moremi Game Reserve. Before it enters Botswana, the river drops 4 m in a series of rapids known as Popa Falls, visible when the river is low, as during the dry season.

Discharging to an endorheic basin, the Okavango does not have an outlet to the sea. Instead, it empties into a swamp in the Kalahari Desert, known as the Okavango Delta or Okavango Alluvial Fan.

In the rainy season, an outflow to the Boteti River in turn seasonally discharges to the Makgadikgadi Pans, which features an expansive area of rainy-season wetland where tens of thousands of flamingos congregate each summer.

Part of the river's flow fills Lake Ngami. During colder periods in Earth's history, a part of the Kalahari was a massive lake, known as Lake Makgadikgadi. In this time, the Okavango would have been one of its largest tributaries.

Remains of the Ammunition Depot Buffalo

During the United Nations occupation of SWA 32 battalion had to be relocated to Pomfret in South Africa as SWAPO the leading political party at the time did not want them there.

The base was hastily emptied, and the occupants relocated. Since their departure the area has been left for nature to claw back.

Remains of the Headquarters Buffalo

Along the route Steve passes the old 32 Battalion Headquarters that has already lost its roof and contents. The local population have raided everything of value and taken this back to their kraals for use.

Remains of the Officers Mess Buffalo

The Officers Mess, a thatched roofed building was beautifully designed to blend in with the surroundings and reflected the rustic nature of the African influence.

Steve stops off at the graves and walks around looking for names that he can remember. A very real moment on which he reflects the war and how many sacrifices were made.

32 Battalion Fallen Warriors

A great sadness overwhelms him as he steps through the grave yard. The family having no idea of the emotions and memories that have been stirred in his mind. He shrugs off the dark cloud and makes his way to the area where they will erect their camp site.

Setting up camp on the banks of the Okavango

Steve and David erect the tents and set up the camp site while the ladies review their local art purchases. Steve collects ingredients for supper and ensures that he has the required utensils to complete what he is planning.

The girls checking their purchases out

Steve wants to share a border war HAG deployment meal with the family and settles down to prepare supper for the evening.

The campsite overlooks the awesome Okavango River with Angola on the other bank. Memories of events past keep Steve floating back.

View from the campsite Buffalo

The view from the campsite is spectacular, reminding Steve of the days he visited when there was a Lapa constructed for viewing the river from where one could sit back, relax and enjoy a few cold ones. There also used to be an old barge that 32 Battalion had annexed, repaired and used as a floating fishing, braai and sunset cruise vessel.

David and Nicole on the Kavango

Walking along the bank of the river they find a local who has some canoes. A quick barter and everyone jumps onboard for a quick tour up and down the river.

Cooling off in the Okavango

Just before supper a quick cool off in the river while being very alert for local flat dogs, crocodiles, that are abundant here. Steve starts the supper by browning some onions in a Billy can, followed by slice tomatoes, Canned Bully Beef, Canned Chili Con Carne, and lastly Vienne's in Tomato Sauce. He keeps stirring until the concoction has heated up appropriately and then calls for dinner is served.

"I am not eating that." Grimaces David.

"No problem, go hungry then." Responds Steve.

Steve takes a healthy helping and starts munching down. Annie and Nicole take a small helping and gingerly start eating. The next minute both Annie and Nicole grab a huge helping each and with a grin both compliment Steve on the amazing taste.

David is to hungry to ignore the food and after his first bite he too adds more on his plate. The meal is completely consumed with the children wiping out the Billy can with the remaining bread rolls. Steve just grins.

"So, you enjoy your first Air Force Bush Meal, did you?" He questions the family.

The evening camp out is amazing with the flowing sound of the river and animal night sounds they are completely alone in the wilderness. They all sleep soundly. Early morning Steve makes a scrambled egg and bacon breakfast before breaking camp for the journey to Mpacha.

Mpacha

Katima Mulilo is a town situated in the Caprivi strip and is the capital of the Zambezi Region, Namibia's far northeast extension into central Southern Africa. It is located on the national road on the banks of the Zambezi River in lush riverine vegetation with tropical birds and monkeys. The town receives an annual average rainfall of 654 millimeters. In 1971 the area around Katima Mulilo got involved in the South African Border War. As in World War II, it was a strategically important location, this time due to troop transports into and out of Zambia and Angola.

The settlement also was at the centre of the Caprivi conflict in the 1990s, an armed conflict between the Caprivi Liberation Army (CLA), a rebel group working for the secession of the Caprivi Strip, and the Namibian government. In the early hours of 2 August 1999, CLA launched an attack occupying the state-run radio station and attacking a police station, the Wanella border post, and an army base. A state of emergency was declared in the province, and the government arrested alleged CLA supporters.

Established and run as a garrison for a long time, Katima Mulilo still shows signs of its military role today. In the city centre was the South African Defense Force military base, almost every house had a bomb shelter. The town benefited from the military presence in terms of infrastructure and employment, and there are still a number of military bases surrounding the town.

At Katima Mulilo Steve finds the most appropriate accommodation for them and unhooks the trailer. He is taking the family to the Mpacha Airport, formerly AFB Mpacha to show them the layout and also see what is left. The town features an Export Processing Zone and the largest open market in Namibia.

There is an important international electricity interlink facility, the Caprivi Link Inter Connector; its inauguration has improved the power supply to the town. The town has been affected by corruption, financial mismanagement, and infighting between councilors ever since SWAPO took the majority on town council.

Water supply has been unstable because money is owed to the national water supplier. Katima Mulilo is the terminal town of the Trans Caprivi Highway, and the highway together with its extension to Zambia is called the Trans-Caprivi Corridor. The town is served by Katima Mulilo Airport, situated about 18 km to the southwest which is serviced by regular flights from the capital Windhoek.

Mpacha Airport

The tarred roads are in very good condition and it is a quick 20 Km ride from the town to the airport. The old security house with cattle grids still exists, but the booms have long since been removed. Steve drives through and keeps on the road to the old AFB Mpacha.

The previous domestic area security house and cattle grids are also still there. Thinking that these were still serviceable, Steve accelerates through them to discover that the grids have been removed.

There are two loud bangs as the wheel rims hit the trench that is over a foot in width and lined with angle iron. The next minute there is short bursts of hissing air escaping as the wheels rotate through the damaged part of the rims. Steve stops the BMW and on closure inspection realizes that he will have to bend the rims straight to prevent the air leakage.

Steve delves into the toolbox he packed and finds a claw hammer. Hitting with all his might he manages to straighten the damaged rims sufficiently to prevent further air escaping. He drives off slowly towards the base and realizes that there has been substantial suspension damage as well.

Steve will have to complete makeshift repairs back at the motel. He continues to AFB Mapacha and sees that the base is advanced disrepair.

Remains of AFB Mpacha

The hangars that housed the Air Force aircraft that were stationed there are still standing but are in various stages dismantle. The workshops next to the hangars have been stripped and anything of value removed.

Next Steve drives through the domestic area. At the one house where his friend, Jock van der Westhuizen, had stayed the place is empty and stripped.

Remembering the past as if it was yesterday, it was at this house when they were braaiing a number of years ago when one of the locals came in and started tending to the garden. Steve and Jock look on amusingly, as the base did not employ gardeners. Steve and Jock amble over to the local.

"Good day friend, and what are you doing?" Asks Jock.

"Hello, I am tending my garden and home." Replies the local.

"Oh, but I live here at the moment." Says Jock.

"Yes, you are, but soon Sam Nujoma will be in charge and he has told me I can choose my home, and this is the one I am taking." States the local.

"Ok then please carry on friend." Says Jock.

Steve grins as he remembers the story and shakes his head at the outcome while looking at the condition of the base post SWAPO.

Remains of AFB Mpacha living quarters

The only buildings that are well maintained at the base are the current airport offices and control tower. The taxiway, runway and supporting facilities have been maintained and the airport seems to have a fair amount of traffic.

Mpacha Airport

Steve turns the damaged BMW around and finds an alternate route off the base without further incident. At the motel he assesses the damage and realizes that he will have to find a heavier hammer and chisel to further straighten the wheel rims, as they are still allowing air to escape as the weight of the car rests on the damaged areas. The family spends the night at Katima Mulilo at a motel on the banks of the Zambezi river.

Motel on the Zambezi River

They are closely surrounded by four countries namely, Angola, Zambia, Zimbabwe and Botswana. Thus, the importance of this far eastern location of Katima Mulilo for Namibia. Steve informs the family that they will be making their way to Tsumeb where he will attempt to repair the suspension of the BMW, as there are no local garages equipped to complete the task. The front shock absorbers are damaged beyond repair and the wheel alignment is causing the car to pull badly to the left. A short distance from where they currently are, is the Chobe Flood Plains in Botswana. This is an opportunity to spend a few days and see abundant wild life. Steve points the BMW in the direction of the Chobe National Park a short 100 Km from Katima Mulilo. With limited speed due to vibration and lack of front suspension Steve takes it very slow. They arrive at the border crossing at midday with the temperatures in the high thirties. Steve is shirtless and strolls over to the Customs Shack to be scolded by the Customs Official.

"You are improperly dressed, go away!" Shouts the large black female customs official.

Steve can't believe his ears but turns away to retrieve his shirt for round two of the comedy strip. With the customs official taking her time to serve them, they wait a further half an hour before getting the passports stamped and are allowed to proceed into Botswana.

Chobe Lodge

The family spends the rest of the afternoon relaxing around Chobe Lodge and enjoy the sights. The lookout tower is an awesome vantage point to see animals from.

Annie, Nicole and David on the lookout

An amazing evening is spent at the lodge's luxuries accommodations, restaurant and location.

View of the river from the balcony

The next morning, they take a guided motor boat tour around the Chobe Reserve and are rewarded with many wildlife sightings, including Hippo, Giraffe, Elephant, Impala, Kudu, Fish Eagle and Crocodiles.

Hippo frolicking in the river

Chobe Wildlife

After a relaxing afternoon and evening Steve prepares the family for departure to Tsumeb where he needs to affect the repairs on the car.

The distance is a whopping 900 Km and will take them most of the day to complete. They depart shortly after an early breakfast and this time Steve ensures that he is appropriately attired for the border crossing which goes off without a hitch. The dirt road is winding and rough and Steve must navigate the twists and turns carefully. At a blind curve Steve slows down and is about to accelerate when two-armed militia jump out in front of the car. The children are fast asleep in the back. The first chap aiming his AK47 at Steve, orders them out of the car.

"The children are sleeping and have nothing on them, search us if you want to." Says Steve.

Steve indicates to Annie to exit the car, and behind his seat shows the children to keep their eyes closed. Steve has their passports ready and presents them. The militia accepts the passports and takes his time in verifying the content. Eventually satisfied he indicates to Steve and Annie.

"Ok you can go." The militia instructs them.

Shaken up Annie stares at Steve, who had anticipated that this might happen. SWAPO was still in the process of integrating all their freedom fighters and some of these are still enacting acts of terrorism. Fortunately for them these militia seemed to be looking for weapons only.

Eventually Steve turns onto the tarred road to Tsumeb, which is in good condition and he manages to keep up good speed that does not induce too much vibration. They stop briefly for lunch and continue the long road west. Eventually as the sun is edging closer to the horizon they approach Tsumeb and find the first hotel available to stay for the next two nights.

Tsumeb

Tsumeb is a city of 15,000 inhabitants and the largest town in Oshikoto region in northern Namibia. Tsumeb is the "gateway to the north" of Namibia. It is the closest town to the Etosha National Park. The town is the site of a deep mine, that in its heyday was known simply as "The Tsumeb Mine".

The town was founded in 1905 by the German colonial power. Tsumeb is notable for the huge mineralized pipe that led to its foundation. The origin of the pipe has been hotly debated. The pipe penetrates more or less vertically through the Precambrian Otavi dolomite for at least 1300 m. The pipe was mined in prehistoric times, but those ancient workers barely scratched the surface. Most of the ore was removed in the 20th century by cut-and-fill methods.

Many millions of tons of ore of spectacular grade were removed. A good percentage of the ore was so rich that it was sent straight to the smelter situated near the town without first having to be processed through the mineral enrichment plant.

Tsumeb, since its founding, has been primarily a mining town. The main shafts became flooded by ground water over a kilometer deep and the water was collected and pumped as far as the capital, Windhoek. The mine has since been opened up again by a group of local entrepreneurs. A fair amount of oxidized ore remains to be recovered in the old upper levels of the mine. It is highly unlikely, though, that the deepest levels will ever be reopened. The other notable feature of the town is the metal smelter, currently owned by Namibia Custom Smelters. The Annual Copper Festival is a well-known event on the local festival calendar.

Near to the town are two large sinkhole lakes, Lake Otjikoto and Lake Guinas. Guinas, at about 500 meters in diameter, is somewhat larger in area than Otjikoto. A pioneering documentary movie about scuba diving in these lakes was made by Graham Ferreira in the early 1970s.

The depths of the lakes are unknown, because towards the bottom both lakes disappear into lateral cave systems, so it is not possible to use a weight to sound them. Otjikoto, which has poor visibility, is at least 60 meters deep. The water in Guinas is completely clear and well over 100 meters deep.

Guinas has been in existence for so long that a unique species of fish, Tilapia guinasana, has evolved in its waters. When South Africa invaded German Southwest Africa, today's Namibia, in 1914, the retreating German forces eventually threw all of their weaponry and supplies into the deep waters of Otjikoto. Some of the material has been recovered for display in museums.

One of the largest and deepest underground lakes in the world lies a little to the east of Tsumeb, on a farm called Harasib. To reach the water in the cave one has either to abseil or to descend an ancient, hand-forged ladder that hangs free of the vertical dolomite walls of the cave for over 50 meters.

The largest meteorite in the world, called Hoba, lies in a field about forty minutes' drive to the southeast of Tsumeb, at Hoba West. It is a nickel-iron meteorite of about 60 tons.

The next day Steve finds a workshop that has two new shock absorbers that he can fit. He replaces the shocks and inspects the rest of the suspension. Fortunately, there is no further evidence of damage.

Steve has the wheel alignment corrected to prevent further damage to the tires and asks the workshop owner to balance the front wheels as best as he can. There will still be vibration due to the rim damage, but it should be acceptable for the journey back to Cape Town.

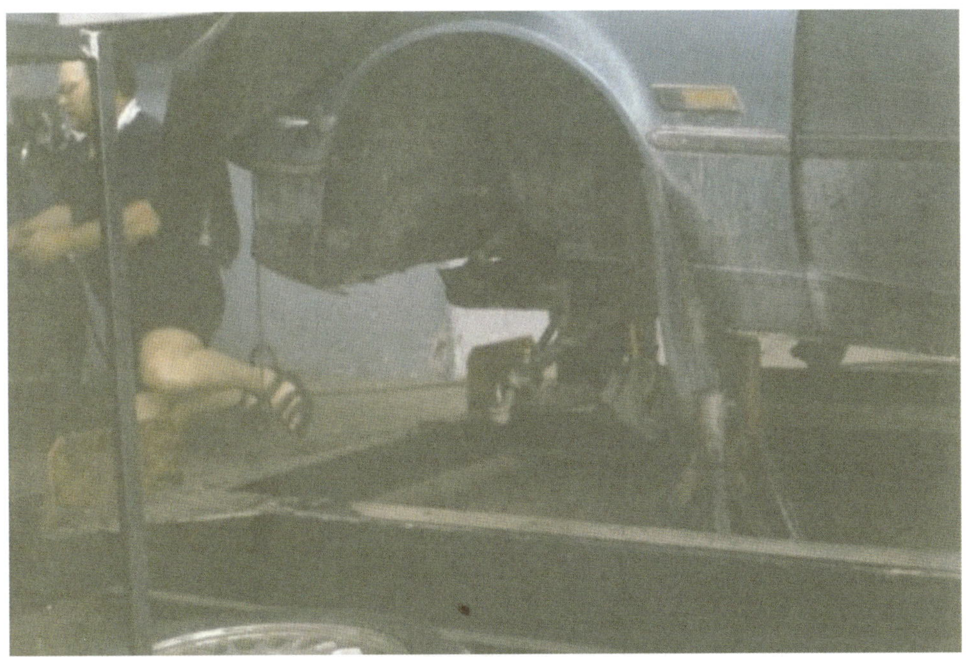

Damaged BMW Suspension Repair

Relieved that the car is in a somewhat safer condition that will not cause major problems, Steve returns to the hotel and collapses exhausted onto the bed. Annie wakes Steve early the next morning and they start preparing for the visit to Etosha National Park.

Etosha

The trip will take them less than two hours to complete. On arrival at Etosha Steve heads directly to the Namutoni Gate and books into the campsite for the next two days.

During the border war Steve had spent a week here completing the recovery of a helicopter that had crashed into the Etosha Pans.

It was a difficult recovery as the aircraft was badly damaged and had to be torn down to manageable pieces for the Alouette III helicopter to cargo sling.

Three people had died in the accident and one survivor had managed to walk out to find help.

Namutoni Etosha National Park

That evening Steve leads the family to the Namutoni Water Hole, where all the animals come to get their fill in the evenings. The water hole is full of wild life coming to get their fill in this dry arid climate before the sun sets. The water hole is fed from a drilled well that pumps the water into a hollow that naturally becomes a pond during the rainy season. There is an abundance of wildlife, Annie, Nicole and David have never seen them in their natural habitat before and are amazed at how close they are.

Steve explains why the natural tendency for animals is to grant the higher ranking first opportunity and then moving away for the next in line to get their fill. Steve has enquired about cats and the game ranger is certain that a pride of lions will visit the water hole tonight. In the meantime, all the other animals are getting their fill.

Various game at the Water Hole

Zebra, Impala, Springbok, Oryx and Elephant getting their fill for the day. They get there before the Lions will arrive so as not to become prey.

Various game at the Water Hole

At sunset the King of Beasts arrives, and the other animals quickly retreat. The lions lazily get their fill and then lay down to rest for a few hours before moving off to their sleeping place for the night.

After sunset they are blessed with the arrival of a heard of desert Elephants. The gentle giants taking their time to get their fill.

Various game at the Water Hole

The family retreats to the camp site to finish off supper. Annie has purchased some Wors and Steaks from the Namutoni Store and Steve has built a fire to braai them on.

The girls prepare tomato and onion sandwiches to accompany the meat. Steve shares some beers with David. The children excitedly discuss what they have seen today and are looking forward to the drive through the reserve the next day.

Eventually exhaustion takes over and they retreat to their respective tents. Steve is just dozing off when the pride of lions starts grunting in the distance. Wide eyed Annie looks at Steve.

"So those were lions we heard at Sesriem?" She questions.

"Now do you believe me?" Laughs Steve.

Just then Steve hears the tent zipper next door open and both children peak into the tent.

"What's that?" They both question in unison.

"It's the Lions." Confirms Annie, with her eyes just as wide as both children.

Steve burst out laughing and explains how the male lion holds his head close to the ground and utters a number of grunts to emphasize his pride and keep others at bay.

Early the next morning Steve rushes everyone into the car and they set off on a tour of the Etosha Pan and game reserve. They are rewarded with the great animal viewing.

Driving along the side of the Etosha Pan, Steve takes a turn off to get closer to the Pan itself. As they come around the first bend they spot a lioness with her kill that she has just brought down. Panting, with blood all over her mouth, the lioness just lays there catching her breath with her paws over the carcass of a Zebra.

Annie and Nicole are shocked but excited to see their first kill. Steve knows that the pride is close by and decides to move on. Two kilometers down the road the children both urge Steve to stop as they are close to the Pan now. The children want to collect some Etosha Pan sand for keep sake. With the children already collecting sand and Annie three quarters of the way down to the beach, Steve leans over the car's roof.

"Annie you do know that there is a lion........?" Steve says and cannot not even finish his sentence.

Annie lets out a yelp and comes racing back to the car faster than a bullet. Steve can't help but laugh at the spectacle. Annie is angry and calls to the children to get back to the car immediately. The laughing continues for quite some time until Annie informs them all to stop it or else.

The rest of the day is spectacular with wonderful animal sightings throughout the day. At midday with the sunroof open, Annie and Nicole decide to stand with their heads and chests outside of the car to catch the wind as Steve drives further in the reserve.

The girls are having the time of their life with hair blowing in the wind and singing to the music blaring from the car's stereo.

The next instant Annie is screaming that the is something in her hair and that Nicole must get it out. A Rhino Beetle had flown into and got caught up in Annie's long flowing hair. Trying to unhook itself the claws just caught more hair. Nicole giggling uncontrollably, manages to free the beetle, and both the ladies quickly return to inside the vehicle.

<u>Rhino Beetle</u>

Eventually they arrive back at camp and after supper settle in for an early evening. The route back to Cape Town, over 2000 Km, is going to be long and stressful. The BMW still has a vibration and the wheel alignment is not the best.

After breakfast Steve sets heading towards Windhoek via Grootfontein, a distance of 628 Km. They will spend the night in Windhoek before heading down to South Africa. The road is tarred and in good condition.

Steve does not have the same concerns as was in the Namib desert dirt roads with the possibility of burst tires. On the long straight stretch of road Steve lets David take the wheel. Two hours into David's drive there is a Police blockade across the road. It is too late to stop and change drivers and Steve urges David to act naturally.

The black policeman approaches the driver's side and asks David for his license. Steve reaches across and supplies his own license in hope to fool the cop. It does not work.

"How old are you?" Asks the cop.

"Sixteen." Answers David.

"You are too young to drive and do not have a license. Here is your fine and this must be paid now." Instructs the cop.

Steve reaches into his wallet and counts out the amount requested, takes over from David and drives off. The girls of course see this as payback and rile David and Steve for the next few hours to Grootfontein.

Windhoek

Steve stops off at Grootfontein for refreshments and then back on the road to Windhoek. They are travelling through the center of Namibia passing through places that Steve had flown to in his past life.

The route takes them through spectacular villages and towns like Kombat, Otavi, Okaputo, Otjiwarongo, Sukses and Okahandja. Most of these places have been heavily influenced by the German and Dutch Boer culture. These are evident in the architecture, farms and fashion of the people.

Early evening and Steve pulls up alongside the Hotel they will be staying for the night.

The name of the hotel brings everyone to laughter as they try to understand. Once at reception the penny drops and Steve puts two and two together. Hamburg a city in Germany is referenced, and the Hamburger Hof indicates that it is linked to the same hotel in Hamburg and Frankfurt. They settle in and then go in search of supper. The reception desk has indicated one of the oldest restaurants in Windhoek serves the best meals. The restaurant is a short walk away from the hotel and the family takes in the sites. At the restaurant the décor is old and rustic. The Oak flooring showing signs of many years of wear. The restaurant is filling up, so Annie selects a table with a view of the city.

Hamburger Hof Hotel Windhoek

Steve orders beer and soft drinks for Annie and the children. The meal arrives and is served to perfection. They are still enjoying their meal when a rowdy and obviously misbehaving little girl keeps running up and down between the tables, making an excruciating noise on the wooden floor. Steve is about to say something when there is an almighty crash and the little girl is sprawled face first on the floor. She gets such a scare that she jumps up and races to her mom and buries her head in shame.

"Oh my God." Says Annie.

"I was about to say something." Says Steve.

"No, no, I was just imagining her falling flat on her face and then it happened." Blurts Annie.

Steve and the children burst out laughing. Annie has the ability to see ghosts and feels strange powers. Maybe she is turning the tide now and dishing out payback where required. They finish off their meal with a lovely dessert and then proceed to walk around to see the sights of Windhoek.

Christ Church Windhoek

The Christ Church is a historic landmark and Lutheran church in Windhoek, Namibia, designed by architect Gottlieb Redecker. The church was built following the wars between the Germans and the Khoikhoi, Herero, and Owambo. The foundation stone was laid on 11 August 1907, while on 16 October 1910 the church was officially dedicated. It was originally known as the Church of Peace. Christ Church was constructed from quartz sandstone mined from the vicinity of Avis Dam. It has a mixture of neo-Romanesque, Art Nouveau and Gothic revival influences. Its spire is 24 m (79 ft) high. The colorful stained lead glass windows in the sanctuary were a gift from Emperor Wilhelm II.

The family are taking in the beauty of the church and its architecture when Steve notices that the beautifully manicured lawns were covered with black squatters laying, eating and drinking. Steve is shaking his head in disappointment when the next instant the grounds sprinkler system activates sending people running in all directions. Steve, David and Nicole burst out laughing while Annie shakes her head in disbelief.

"I did it again." Blurts Annie.

"What did you do again?" Asks Steve.

"I was just wishing that the sprinkler system would activate, not even knowing that there was one, and there you have it." Exclaims Annie.

Steve and the children put distance between themselves and Annie.

"You walk that side, we don't want evil things happening to us!" Giggle Steve, David and Nicole.

They discuss the happenings at supper and the church back at the hotel until late the night when Steve ushers them off to sleep. They still have many kilometers to travel.

Steve plans to make the trip down to Vioolsdrif a full day's travel so that they can camp out for the last time before setting heading for home. Early morning with bellies full they start the journey south. The stretch of road is desolate, hot and straight. They will be travelling via Keetmanshoop through Grunau to Vioolsdrif. The total distance of 800 Km will take them most of the day. Eventually at Grunau Steve passes the turnoff to Ai-Ais. Ais Ai-Ais Hot Springs is at the end of the Fish River Canyon hiking trail. Where the warm baths and spa after a grueling 5-day hike of the canyon ease the pain from very sore muscles. Steve fondly remembers his hike down the Fish River Canyon with Russel and Vossie.

Ai-Ais Hot Springs Fish River Canyon

Late the afternoon they stop at the Border Control to produce passports and leave Namibia. It has been a long exhausting but adventurous trip. The emotions that Steve experienced were not what he had expected, and he is pensive over how he feels about the remains of all that he had experienced. The trip did not satisfy what he had hoped. The one thing he had achieved was to share his experiences with Annie although he was not sure if she understood the depth of the experiences and the emotions that they had stirred.

Crossing the border once more

Steve sets up camp at the campsite on the South African side of the border and prepares a final meal for the family. The experiences they have gone through in the past four weeks will be memories for a life time. Although the children did not enjoy the long road between stops, the beauty of Namibia will forever be encased in their memories.

At sunrise Steve breaks up camp, packs up the trailer and car and heads south for the last 700 Km to Cape Town. The family have bonded, and Steve is comfortable that the decision to immigrate will work out. When required during difficult times they will be able to stand together.

The group are quiet in the car, each one buried in their own thoughts as the car plods on south. Steve keeps playing the political issues through his mind and his decision to leave his motherland behind. His roots started in the 1650's and his blood is African. Would all his experience and qualifications suffice, or will he be back to swinging wrenches once more. The unknown creates a disturbing feeling and he knows that he must maintain positive thoughts no matter what. There will be no future for the children in the new South Africa.

A New Car

Back at home Steve gets all the rims and tires of the BMW replaced. He also inspects the car and notices that there are signs of wear. Back at Diep River Steve pops in to the local BMW agent that sold him the BMW 325.

"Surprise me!" Says Steve.

"I have just what you need, come look at this!" Claims the salesman.

A beautiful BMW 320 new shape one-year old car beckons to Steve.

"Where do I sign?" Asks Steve.

Amazingly the paperwork and roadworthy are processed in record time and before Steve is about to leave he receives a phone call to collect his car. Steve loves the car and although 500cc less than the 325, the six cylinder 320 is not lazy at all and drives like dream. The car is full house with all the luxuries that he is sure Annie was going to enjoy. He calls her on the way home and tells her to wait outside for him as he has a surprise.

Annie is overjoyed with the lovely light blue colour that almost seems to be purple as the light catches it. Steve lets her drive it around the block and she is caught hook line and sinker. There is now a second love affair in the household, Annie with the BMW 320.

Chapter 20 - THE FALL OF POWER

> "In a multi-racial society where power must eventually be transferred into the hands of the numerically stronger Bantu, not only the White, but also the Coloured and Indian will go under. Over time even the Bantu masses will not benefit because on the strength of what has happened elsewhere in Africa, it must be taken into consideration that South Africa will develop into an autocracy or dictatorship. On account of their lack of ability to manage a complicated administration, the country will moreover administratively and economically be destroyed and for everyone - White and Coloured - end in chaos"
>
> Dr. H.F. Verwoerd.

In the echoes of political history Dr. H.F. Verwoerd's words ring true and the stage that has been set plays out the truth of Africa. Dr. Verwoerd was assassinated for developing and implementation of an African solution that would ensure the safety and progressive development of all peoples in South Africa.

South Africa now as a fully democratic country is already starting to show cracks. All that the previous government had built is being systematically disassembled. Steve is very concerned for Nicole and David's future. Africa as a continent was becoming war mongering gaggle of tribal led countries, that are very quickly becoming ungovernable. With the end of the SWA Angolan conflict many of the trained military South African operators are seeking alternatives to showcase their skills.

Eeben Barlow and Michael Mullen, an Irishman from Dublin, formerly in charge of the Western European section of the Civil Cooperation Bureau established Executive Outcomes take the opportunity to put a well-trained fighting force to work. Executive Outcome's aim is to provide specialized covert training to Special Forces members. Barlow is awarded a contract by Debswana to train a selected group of security officers to infiltrate and penetrate the illegal diamond dealing syndicates in Botswana. Debswana Diamond Company Ltd, or simply Debswana, is a mining company located in Botswana, and is the world's leading producer of diamonds by value. Debswana is a joint venture between the government of Botswana and the South African diamond company De Beers; each party owns 50% of the company.

Many of Barlow's Special Forces students later join him at Executive Outcomes after he starts recruiting men to assist with the training of the Angolan forces. The company also goes on to recruit many of its personnel from the units President F. W. De Klerk disbanded. At its peak, EO employs about 2,000 former soldiers. Barlow registers Executive Outcomes Ltd in the UK on the insistence of the South African Reserve Bank. Executive Outcomes assists Ranger Oil with an equipment recovery operation in the harbour town of Soyo. Ranger Oil Limited is an international exploration, development, and production company. The Company explores for crude oil and natural gas. Ranger operates in Canada, the United States, the Gulf of Mexico, the North Sea, Angola, Peru, Ecuador, Namibia, and the Cote D'Ivoire.

Dubbed by the South African media as an attempt to assassinate the rebel leader Dr. Jonas Savimbi, Executive Outcomes found itself under constant UNITA attacks where it loses three men. This action sees Executive Outcomes as being recognized by the Armed Forces of Angola (FAA) and a contract to train its forces is duly awarded. In a short space of time, UNITA is defeated on the battlefield and sues for peace. The Angolan government, under pressure from the UN and the US, are forced to terminate Executive Outcome's contract and they are replaced by the UN's peacekeeping force known as UNAVEM.

Executive Outcomes contains an insurrection of guerrillas known as the Revolutionary United Front (RUF) in Sierra Leone, regaining control of the diamond fields, and forces a negotiated peace. In both these instances they are credited with rescuing both governments against RUF and UNITA. In the case of Angola this leads to a cease fire and the Lusaka Protocol, which ends the Angolan civil war albeit only for a few years. In Sierra Leone, however, the government capitulates to international pressure to have Executive Outcomes withdraw in favour of an ineffective peacekeeping force, allowing the RUF to rebuild and sack the capital.

Steve monitors the political arena closely as the current scenario feels very similar to the demise of the Rhodesia. With the minority government displaced the country very quickly reverted to a dictatorship which is doomed to last a longtime. The economy and infrastructure have already collapsed. Ian Smith only once doubted the wisdom of his decision to declare Unilateral Declaration of Independence and lead Rhodesia into a 15-year civil war to protect white rule. That moment of doubt occurred in April 1980, during a meeting with Robert Mugabe, who the previous day had taken office as the first Prime Minister of Zimbabwe. Mugabe had summoned Smith to Government House and Smith was surprised to be greeted with a warm handshake and a broad smile; after all, the country's new Marxist leader had promised his people that, come liberation, he would have Smith publicly hanged in Harare's main square. At that meeting, Mugabe told Smith he was acutely aware that he had inherited from his old adversaries, the whites, a jewel of a country, and he praised its superb infrastructure, its efficient modern economy, and promised to keep it that way. Smith, completely disarmed, rushed home in a state of excitement, and over lunch, told his wife, Janet, that perhaps he had been wrong about a black government being incapable of running his beloved Rhodesia.

Ian Smith recorded the following to a press reporter from the Telegraph. "Here's this chap, and he was speaking like a sophisticated, balanced, sensible man. I thought! if he practices what he preaches, then it will be fine. And for five or six months it was fine..."

The simple, trusting banality of Ian Smith's words may, in fact, offer more clues to the catastrophe that has been Rhodesia/Zimbabwe over the past half-century than any number of political or academic tracts. The point is Mugabe was not the sophisticated, balanced, sensible man Smith had briefly hoped for. Even as he was shaking Smith's hand, he was plotting the destruction of another group of political enemies, the Matabele, and was soon to send Korean-trained troops into Matabeleland to conduct a campaign of torture and murder that has still to be fully exposed.

It is estimated that between 10,000 and 20,000 civilians were murdered and as many again disfigured and tortured in what the Matabeles call the gukuruhundi, the washing away after the storm. The sensible chap, in fact, turned out to be the type of African leader that "good old Smithy", as his supporters called him, had campaigned against throughout the Unilateral Declaration of Independence years. He has become the embodiment of corrupt, violent, amoral African dictatorship, just as Smith had warned his supporters.

At the time that Mugabe claimed to be defending "civilized standards", Rhodesians had already witnessed the flight of Belgian refugees from the Congo; Idi Amin had trashed Uganda, and Mobutu Sese Seko was about to introduce an even more brutal and dysfunctional regime in neighbouring Zaire; immediately to the north of Rhodesia, Kaunda's Zambia was in a mess, riddled with corruption and economically mismanaged, and Malawi was being similarly misruled by the eccentric despot Hastings Banda. So why, Smith argued, would Mugabe be any different? Why, indeed.

Smith is a simple man and it is his rather humourless, one-dimensional Rhodesian-ness that at once made him a hero among his own people and a figure of derision among his enemies. While being interviewed for an autobiography Smith spoke endlessly about how Rhodesians had been more British than the British, how Churchill, had he been alive, would almost certainly have emigrated from corrupt, liberal England to Rhodesia, and how this small community of decent, fair-minded whites had been betrayed by, well, just about everybody he could think of, the Tories, Labour, the Afrikaners, the OAU, the UN. Not surprisingly, Smith calls his ponderous autobiography "The Great Betrayal".

However ponderous, however humourless and unsophisticated he is, Smith had run a successful emerging African country and, although the whites were the main beneficiaries, there was increasing prosperity among the black population. Above all there was a sound, intelligently managed economy, free from the post-colonial blight of corruption. Today, Zimbabwe is a failed state with a non-functioning economy, a once-flourishing agricultural sector now moribund, and a population on the brink of starvation. According to a UN Development Programme index, life expectancy there today is one of the lowest in the world. So much for liberation.

Steve's main worries are that a convicted terrorist now leads the country, and that the cowardice of FW de Klerk had paved the way to make this happen. South Africa had withstood the western pressure by developing a powerful self-sufficient economy with an export market that has grown to include defense weaponry and systems. The South African military had been powerful enough to defend and logistically positioned to support a force from Cape to Cairo.

Spiral back to Tribalism

Summing up to what has happened to a once thriving country and its inevitable spiral to Tribalism. Within South Africa, terrorism and uprisings led by the African National Union grew in intensity in 1983 to 84. A state of emergency was declared in 1985, accompanied by renewed political and economic pressure from abroad. In 1986, Bishop Desmond Tutu, a leading black nationalist, addressed the United Nations and called for renewed sanctions. The Botha government announced an end to the pass laws and promised limited black participation in government. Fighting among black groups, Black on Black, in 1986 to 87 further increased domestic tension. These Black on Black attacks were mostly tribal related, these different groups vied for positions in the rebellion against stability. These attacks not unlike the Gang Wars seen in the United States.

In early 1989, in anticipation of elections to be held in September, various proposals were put forward for constitutional reform. Most called for expanded power sharing but still within the context of defined racial groups. In July 1989 President Botha had an unprecedented meeting with Nelson Mandela, amid strong suggestions that the white government was seeking an accommodation with the anti-apartheid leadership. Botha's successor, F.W. de Klerk, continued that policy.

A series of measures in 1989 to 90 resulted in the partial dismantling of apartheid, against the vehement opposition of the white right wing, but violence between supporters of the ANC and the Zulu Inkatha movement in Natal led to the declaration of a state of emergency in the province.

Mandela was released from prison in the spring of 1990 and received a rapturous welcome from South Africa's blacks, and later made a triumphant tour of Western Europe and North America. His glory was short-lived, however, as the struggle for supremacy again erupted in murder and violence between Mandela's ANC and Mangosuthu Buthelezi's Inkatha Freedom party throughout the latter part of 1990 and 1991.

At the same time, President de Klerk and Parliament continued to move the nation toward the ending of apartheid by repealing 60 years of segregation in hospitals, libraries, schools, and other public institutions. The government also released other political prisoners and completely repealed the legal foundations of apartheid: The Land Acts of 1913 and 1936, the Group Areas Act, and the Population Registration Act. The United States and other countries began lifting trade sanctions against South Africa in the summer of 1991.

In September 1991, de Klerk, Mandela, and Buthelezi, together with 20 smaller anti-apartheid groups, signed an accord to end factional violence. De Klerk proposed a new constitution that would provide universal suffrage and create a two-chamber parliament open to all races. The new constitution abolished the black homelands, consolidating them into one large, multiracial South Africa. In March 1992 a referendum of white voters overwhelmingly approved a government proposal to dismantle all forms of apartheid and to conduct talks with black leaders designed to end white-only rule.

The new constitution was approved on November 17, 1993, by all of the country's major political parties, except for Chief Mangosuthu Buthelezi's Zulu-based Inkatha Freedom party, which withheld its support until a week before the country's first-ever multiracial elections in April. More than 22 million voters cast ballots. An overwhelming majority chose the 75-year-old Mandela to lead a coalition government that included de Klerk's National party and Buthelezi's Inkatha Freedom party.

The 'Milk of Human Kindness' has left the room

The sad truth of South Africa...for 342 years Settlers built up the most powerful country in Africa, for which Tribalism has taken a few years to tear it down. Over the past years, the once-great land of milk and honey has changed dramatically; the milk has soured and most of the honey has been stolen. The reality is that the 'milk of human kindness' has been whipped into the sour cream of human anger and hatred through divisive, militant, nursery school, and populist politics along with a manipulated and invented history, and the subsequent results this brings.

There are people, on both sides of the political divide, who are consumed by hatred and determined to immerse the country into a cauldron of conflict. They hate success; they hate anyone who does not agree with them, they hate because they are ashamed at their own abilities; they hate because they have nothing better to do; they hate simply to hate, and they demonstrate it through their actions and words. They insist that their opinions are the only valid opinions and woe betide anyone who disagrees with those opinions; such people are regarded as 'the enemy'.

They exhibited some of this hatred in their xenophobic or rephrased Afriphobic, attacks against foreign nationals. They frequently exhibit their hatred towards women, children and other helpless citizens. They revel in their hatred. Some openly call for an armed struggle for 'freedom' despite the political changes following the 1994 elections, where everyone was given the opportunity to carve their own success. Even when the system of both employment and human protectionism acts to their benefit, they still blame and hate.

In reality they are the beneficiaries and victims of their own self-inflicted failures, yet they will continue to lay blame elsewhere for their misfortunes. Others call for the confiscation of all legal firearms to enable 'them' to continue their hate-fueled rampages against unarmed citizens.

Their hatred has no limits. The violence, deaths and chaos that has engulfed our country has surpassed the level most countries would consider to be a national crisis or a 'war'. Murders, violent crimes, infrastructure sabotage, gang wars, home invasions, cash-in-transit robberies, hijackings, and more, have become daily occurrences. These actions have resulted in several countries issuing travel warnings to their citizens who wish to visit South Africa.

The impact of this increasingly hateful and negative mindset effects every South African, regardless of ideology, race, ethnicity, or language. And the blame ought to be placed before the door of all political parties, along with their 'advisors' who have played to tune of negative and populist politics at the expense of the people, progress, and prosperity. It also adds to the distaste with which South Africa has come to be viewed, regionally, continentally, and internationally.

Of course, some journalists, social media armchair warriors and politicians add to the 'fog of hatred' without many of them realizing what they are actually doing. Others purposefully apply their poisoned keyboards in order to fuel further anger, concern and chaos. They promote hatred and discard progress. Their hatred for good order and stability is palpable.

The reality is that South Africa is in an unprecedented mess, driven by corruption and hatred. The dithering politicians across all political parties are apparently only interested in earning their salaries. Talking the talk without being able to walk the walk remains a waste of breath. Unless politicians actually take note and act on what is happening at ground level, instead of what is happening in their bank accounts and all citizens learn to work together to achieve success South Africa will never regain our status of the land of milk and honey. Instead, South Africa will be regarded as a nation driven by hatred for one another, and everyone else.

Immigration Progress

The decision made, Steve drives hard to get the immigration process back online. It is February 1998 and the local agent has not been proactive enough, so Steve makes an appointment to see them on one of the project meetings that he still attends in Midrand. Steve is disappointed to discover that little progress has been made. He collects all the documents and cancels the contract with the agency. Steve spends the next few weeks consolidating the application and submits it directly to Canada House in Pretoria. Within a month he receives confirmation that the process had been initiated and that he would be contacted if additional documents would be required.

At Log-Tek Steve is finalizing a lot of the projects and is involved in a few Naval projects as well. He is not very proactive in driving the projects as his mind is overwhelmed with getting the immigration process back on track. In a holding pattern he can only play the waiting game. He had thoroughly prepared the package with supporting documentation for each of the application paragraphs. Neatly attached as Appendices Steve is confident that he has provided more than enough data.

On his 42nd birthday Steve is approached by Pi-Log, sister company to Log-Tek to manage the implementation for the South African Air Forces Logistic Information System, SLIS. Naested had recommended Steve to Pi-Log and he will be seconded to Pi-Log for the program. With the amount of travel that he needs to do, Steve will need a low mileage car. He has a brainwave and contacts his friend at Diep River BMW who has the very car he needs. Steve collects the BMW 540I and takes it home for the evening. Annie is totally unimpressed and prefers the 320. Steve then rolls out the plan.

"Let's trade your 318 on the 540 so that I can have a low mileage car for the project I have just be allocated. Then you take over the 320." States Steve.

"That will work!" Beams Annie.

She has the prize and is completely satisfied. Steve returns the car to Diep River with a couple of items that need repair and starts the process of trading the 318 for the 540. By weeks end Steve has a low mileage BMW 540I and Annie is in dream world with her BMW 320I.

To Steve's amusement when he asks Annie to drop him off at the airport for his trips up north she insists they go with the BMW 540. Steve fills the tank before they leave, as he has the Log-Tek Petro Card. On his return Annie collects him with the BMW 540 with an empty tank.

"I thought you did not like the 540?" Questions Steve.

"Oh, the fuel is free." States Annie.

This was an argument that Steve was set to lose and hiding behind a smile he just nods.

Travelling Once More

Steve together with Johan Slabbert, Slabs, will form the Program Directorship for the implementation of SLIS. Steve would complete the initial audit, set up and then assist Slabs in completing the transition from Mainpack to SLIS. Mainpack is an old Mining software package that had been modified to suite the Air Force many years ago. SLIS on the other hand is a more comprehensive system that will take control of all facets, from Human Resources, Finance, Design, Production, Operations, Modification, Phase Out and Phase in of Platforms. In essence a complete business management package.

The project requires Steve to travel from squadron to squadron all over South African for the next 18 months. Before Steve can touch ground a year has passed and the SLIS implementation is on track. Steve has been driving to all the Air Force Bases in the country and is currently on his way from Pretoria down to 15 Squadron at Durban followed by 87 HFS in Bloemfontein.

Steve chats to Annie and asks her to join him in Durban after which they can have a break in the Drakensburg Mountains before driving to Bloemfontein, and then after completing the implementation at 87 HFS, back down to Cape Town. Annie agrees and contacts her ex-boss from Mondi Paper, Roger Jacobs in Durban, to request accommodation. Roger owns some vacation apartments and books this for them. Steve has also booked two nights at the Dragons Peak Hotel for them in the Drakensburg Mountains.

Steve reaches Durban by midday and proceeds directly to 15 Squadron to complete the initial audit. It will take the rest of the day to audit. The next day he briefs the squadron personnel on the process for phase in of SLIS. Each aircrafts records must be validated against the physical configuration of the aircraft. The aircraft technical logs must be a duplicate of the part and serial numbers installed on the aircraft. Mainpack will then be corrected to reflect the Technical Log.

Once this has been completed the SLIS software will be uploaded from a data dump extracted from Mainpack. A second verification from SLIS to the Technical Log will verify data accuracy and then only will normal operations continue. The program allows for aircraft on standby to be managed outside of the systems until the rest of the tail numbers are operational, and then only will these be updated accordingly.

The final task for the day, Steve conducts an audit of the IT platform to verify if the number of stations, WAN, LAN and current operating systems will meet the SLIS program requirements. Shortfalls are noted and reported to Slabs. Slabs will then activate the IT Team to install upgrades and prepare the platform for SLIS implementation. Steve completes his final report and checklist, says his good byes to the squadron and drives off to the commercial side of the airport to collect Annie.

It is good to see Annie again as Steve has been away for two weeks already. They hug and kiss and Annie chats away happily, updating Steve on the latest news. Steve heads south down the beautiful eastern coastline to Amanzimtoti where the vacation apartments are located. As they drive down Steve points out markers where as a young boy his family used to holiday in the past.

This coastline is also where in his F/E days they conducted many coastal flying sorties. It takes them 30 minutes to reach Amanzimtoti where Steve quickly locates the apartments. They quickly unpack, and Steve takes a quick shower, while Annie contacts Roger to make arrangements for the evening.

Roger and his wife Jean collect Annie and Steve at the apartment and drive them to one of their favourite Indian Restaurants in the city. The evening goes off amusingly as both Steve and Roger put away the drinks. Roger is East Indian but speaks English like a Colonial with perfect pronunciation. The more inebriated he gets the more perfectly he pronounces words. Steve on the other hand, a European South African with an English accent starts talking with an Indian accent. The ladies are entertained through the whole meal. After a wonderful evening Roger drops them off at the apartment.

Drakensburg Paradise

The next morning Steve and Annie pack and depart for the Drakensburg. The drive will take them through the most beautiful part of Natal to the foothills of the mighty Drakensburg. Along the way they pass through the valley of a thousand hills. Steve takes a slow scenic drive and enjoys the scenery with Annie.

Valley of a Thousand Hills

They stop off for some lunch close to Estcourt before entering the Drakensburg range proper. They will travel through the Kleinberg first but can already see the peaks of the Grootberg behind. The scenery is spectacular as they drive through the mountains towards the Dragons Peak Resort. Steve checks in and they are Allocated a Rondawel close to the lake. The room has a King Size bed and is covered like the old colonial beds with bed posts and drapes. It is late winter and the Drakensburg is covered in snow.

Snow covered Drakensburg

There is a huge fire place already lit to warm up the room. Annie loves the place and is babbling ten to the dozen about the resort. Steve grins and hugs her tight. They cuddle next to the crackling fire and chat away happily about the trip to Bloemfontein and there after home to Cape Town. Steve tells Annie that the trip to Bloemfontein is going to be as scenic as the road they have just driven up from Durban until they are on the escarpment. Then it is back to the undulating farmlands of the Orange Free State. They take a walk along the river and around the lake. The tranquility and beauty is captivating and they take it all in. Steve feels the tension edging out of his muscles and a calmness comes over him. He is content and has the most beautiful woman by his side. There are still dark corners in his mind that Steve struggles with, but this break from reality is giving him the opportunity to catch up with Annie. They have a lovely supper at the restaurant and then take a walk around the resort before getting back to the Rondawel. Steve stokes the fire and they chat until late before cuddling up in the huge bed.

Dragons Peak Mountain Resort

Steve plans to leave late morning for AFB Bloemspruit as it is only 450 Km to Bloemfontein. After a relaxing breakfast Steve and Annie take a leisurely drive away from Dragons Peak resort, having spent a lovely time there. The long drive affords Steve the opportunity to share his concerns about the politics of South Africa with Annie. He explains how he witnessed the spiral of Rhodesia and Mozambique to the fiasco that they have become today. Annie listens intently and responds positively that she supports Steve and trusts his judgement. If he thinks it is their best option, she will be at his side and see it through. The five-hour drive seems very short as Steve answers Annie's questions. All to soon Steve spots Signal Hill at Bloemfontein and within an hour they are turning off the highway towards AFB Bloemspruit. Steve has arranged accommodation in the Officers Mess for them for the next two days.

They spend a lovely evening at the Officers Mess enjoying the meal and then a few drinks in the Bar. Steve rekindles old friendships and buys a round of drinks. After a good night's sleep Annie accompanies Steve to 87 HFS where he completes the same process as he had done at 15 Squadron in Durban. As 87 HFS is a disciplined Flight Training Center, it does not take Steve long to complete the tasks required. All records are up to date, well maintained and the IT Platform has recently been upgraded. The next morning Steve concludes his visit with a debriefing and possible schedule for SLIS implementation.

It is midmorning when Steve and Annie point the big BMW homeward. This is a road that Steve has travelled many times and the 1100 Km trip will take them close to 11 hours. Steve settles in for the long drive. Annie is the perfect travel partner and keeps vigilance over Steve as well as a good look out on the road. They continue the discussion over South Africa and the immigration process. Steve has not had any feedback from Canada yet and is concerned that there may be issues. Steve tells Annie that if Canada does not work that they must investigate New Zealand or Australia, as he does not think Europe would be a good option. Already the UK and France have immigration problems with African refugees. Steve is making good time and with the speed cruise set at 150 KPH they are predicted to shorten the trip substantially. It is past nine at night when Steve stops at home in Bothasig. An exhausted Annie and Steve greet the children, quickly unpack, shower and crawl straight into bed.

Immigration Progress

Early the next morning Annie is already making breakfast when Steve joins her after a shower. He needs to go into the office for the day to finalize the reports and set some conference calls. Annie points to some official looking document on the kitchen countertop.

"Those look official from Canada and must have arrived while we were away." Says Annie.

Steve's heart skips a beat as he picks up the correspondence and quickly opens it. It is a confirmation letter from immigration Canada of their application requesting Steve and Annie to attend an interview session at Canada House in Pretoria. Steve's face breaks into a smile and he lifts Annie up by the waist and hugs her tight. He shows her the letter and they both breath a huge sigh of relief. The appointment at Canada House coincides with the Yearend function for Pi-Log. Pi-Log have made accommodation available for Steve and Annie for the weekend of the function. Steve contacts Pi-Log Midrand and requests to provide an additional two days prior to the function so that he can attend to project meetings at the same time. This will afford him the opportunity to complete the Canada Immigration Interview as well.

Genadendal Hike

Russell approaches Steve and asks whether he would like to do another Fish River Canyon hike. Steve chats to Annie and she is very keen to join. As Annie has no long hikes recorded, she will have to complete a qualifying hike locally first. Russell arranges with John the hike organizer, for Steve and Annie to complete a two-day qualifying hike at Genadendal. Genadendal has a rich spiritual history and was the first mission station in southern Africa. It was founded by Georg Schmidt, a German missionary of the Moravian Church, who settled on 23 April 1738 in Baviaanskloof in the Riviersonderend Valley and began to evangelize among the Khoi people.

Genadendal Hiking Trail

Steve and Annie meet up with John and his friend John at the start of the trail. John and Steve brief on how they will process. John will leave Steve to take care of Annie. The sky is laden with dark clouds, but it is warm. The first couple of hours are a gentle climb and the trail is clear and easy to follow. The gentle slopes suddenly become a steep gradient and soon Annie is lagging. The gradient is now so steep that they have to be careful not to stand up too straight or they would lose their balance. Steve lets Annie rest frequently and encourages her up the steep slope.

At last they summit, and Annie bounces back and leads the hikers along the trail. With invigorated energy Annie is hot footing it when all of a sudden, her toe kicks a root across the trail, and she trips heading face down in the dirt. Her backpack launches forward to rest on her head, pinning her down. Steve rushes forward to help her and sees that Annie is shaking. Steve is concerned until he realizes she is laughing. He helps her up and they break out in uncontrollable laughter at the amusing accident. Annie dusts herself and quickly heads down the trail.

The group comes into a ravine with a stream flowing through a refreshing pool. Steve strips butt naked and dives in while the rest of them do the civilized thing. Suitably refreshed they get back on the trail for the short distance to the overnight huts. John is impressed as Annie leads them to the overnight hut on one of the local farms.

The overnight hut is on a farmer's land and his wife has wisely stocked up on beer which she offers at a reasonable price to Steve. Steve buys six beers and sets about making a fire in the firepit for supper. He has brought chops and wors along for them. After the beers are consumed Steve and Annie retire for the night. John is impressed with Annie's performance and confirms that she will easily be able to handle the Fish River Canyon. John asks Steve if they can head out alone as he must get back to Cape Town the next day, while Steve and Annie can take a leisurely hike back.

Steve rises early and prepares a quick breakfast for them. He wants to be on the trail early as the weather looks threatening, and he does not want to get caught in a storm up on the mountain. The return trail follows a different route and is not clearly marked. John has already left while Steve and Annie set a pace according to Annie's comfort. Steve lets her lead until she can no longer make out the trail. Steve takes over and leads them on. The gradient sharply increases.

"Not far now, there over the next boulder is the summit." Says Steve.

Annie just nods and red in the face keeps struggling upward. They reach the boulder that Steve pointed out and stretching up is another 100 meters of climb.

"Fuck! You lied to me." Exclaims Annie, as her spirit is broken at still having to climb further.

Eventually an exhausted, red faced, and very tired Annie reaches the summit with Steve encouraging her on. A misty rain has set in as they reach the summit. Steve can see Annie is cold and tired and tells her that he is going ahead to make something warm to eat and drink. Steve accelerates and 15 minutes later comes around bend to a natural cove that forms a shelter from the rain and wind. He sets up a quick camp and starts the burner with a pot of water. Next, he gets some Esbits to warm the canned food he has opened, with some crackers. With the water nearly at boil Steve adds teabags and sugar just as Annie rounds the bend. Annie sobs when she sees the tea and food.

"I thought you had left me, it's so cold and wet." Cries Annie.

"Here love, sit down and sip the tea while I finish lunch." Comforts Steve.

They enjoy the warm tea and food and Annie wants to get going again. Steve insists that she relax as the descent down to Genadendal is steep, tricky and the trail is not clear. Steve packs up and pours another cup of tea for them. With Annie refreshed they continue along the now almost obscure trail. The mist and low clouds are now so thick that they can hardly make out the route at all. Steve creates his own contour path and winds slowly down the steep mountain side. The rain is starting to pick up and the trail is becoming slippery. Just as Steve is about to find shelter there is a break in the weather. Steve identifies that they are close to the parking lot where he has parked the car. Fifteen minutes later they make it to the car. Steve calls John on his cell to inform them that they are safe. John was concerned when the weather picked up so quickly but is very relieved that they are safe. Annie is now qualified to join them on the Fish River Canyon hike.

Immigration Canada

Steve and Annie once again take the long road to Pretoria and check into the accommodation that Pi-Log has arranged for them in Lyttleton. Early the next morning they arrive at Canada House for the interview. The interviewer informs Steve that he does not qualify on points due to his age but that his qualifications and experience are impressive. The interview questions focus mainly around Steve and Annie's relationship with a quick overview of Steve's work history. After a few more questions an hour has passed. The chap gets up and shakes both Annie and Steve's hand and informs them that they qualify for immigration to Canada. The next step will be police clearances and medicals for all of them. They are informed that this will be processed in the next few months.

A very relieved and happy Steve leaves with Annie. They celebrate with a luncheon at a top-notch restaurant. In the evening Annie dresses for the function. She takes Steve's breath away and he feels blessed to have such beauty accompany him to the function. The Pi-Log function is a formal event with many speeches and presentations. Eventually dinner is served followed by an open bar and dancing. Steve and Annie enjoy the evening and it is close to midnight when they arrive back at the Guest House. They spend the next two days enjoying Pretoria before taking the long trip back to Cape Town. Steve is relieved and carefree. They chat about the future and how to settle down in Canada. Neither of them has ever been to North America before and therefore have no idea what is awaiting them. Steve's main concern now is finances and with the limited pension he received from the Air Force, sale of the house and contents, there will not be much money available. He will have to come up with a savings plan to start building a nest egg before they leave.

Days seem to blur into weeks and Steve is getting concerned that Immigration Canada have misplaced their application. He calls but cannot be directed to anyone who can assist. As he arrives home from Diep River the evening Annie is smilingly waiting for him. The documents arrived, and they need to book their medicals with the doctor as provided in the correspondence. Included in the package are the police clearance requests for them which Steve processes immediately.

Steve checks in with Russell to see when the Fish River Canyon hike is planned for. Russell informs him that the hike is off due to flooding in the Canyon. Annie is disappointed when Steve informs her of the situation. This would have been their last opportunity to complete this hike before leaving the country.

1999 draws to a close and the SLIS program is being finalized. Steve is unsure whether to return to Log-Tek or wait and see what Pi-Log offers him. Dirk Barnard who he had reported to at Pi-Log wants him to stay, as there are many programs, he needs help with. By this time the Medicals for Steve and Annie are complete, and Police Clearance processed. Steve receives a notification from Immigration Canada that the process is progressing. Steve chats to Annie to make sure that her and David's Passports are up to date and valid. Steve does the same with his and Nicole's passports.

Mozambique Floods

Mozambique is divided into two topographical regions, to the north of the Zambezi river, a narrow coastline and bordering plateau slope upward into hills and a series of rugged highlands punctuated by scattered mountains. South of the Zambezi River, the lowlands and flood plains, are much wider with scattered hills and mountains along its borders with South Africa, Swaziland and Zambia. Monte Binga, peaking at 7,988 ft, is the highest point of Mozambique; the Indian Ocean is the lowest. The country is drained by several significant rivers, with the Zambezi being the largest and most important. The Zambezi is in fact the fourth-longest river in Africa, and the largest flowing into the Indian Ocean from Africa. Lake Malawi, Nyasa, is the country's major lake. The Cahora Bassa is Africa's fourth-largest artificial lake. A small slice of Malawi's Lake Chiuta sits in Mozambique. In October and November 1999, heavy rainfall affects Mozambique, followed by a period of heavy rainfall in January 2000. The heavy rainfall continues through February not limited to only Mozambique but most of the south eastern coastline. Other countries also affected, include Eastern South Africa, Swaziland and Botswana. Mozambique is hit the worst and in the first few days, the capital city is under water. The rainfall does not cease causing rivers that run down into the valleys to break their banks and flood the low flood plains. On the 11th February, the Limpopo River overflows, flooding villages for miles around.

Mozambique Floods

The Limpopo Valley suffers massive losses and damages, and disease spreads through the people who were affected. Dysentery is rife. Over the space of three days, the country has experienced seventy-five per cent the year's rainfall. The Incomati, Umbeluzi, and Limpopo rivers exceed their banks, inundating portions of the capital Maputo. At Chókwè, the Limpopo River reaches a level twice its normal level. Some areas receive a year's worth of rainfall in two weeks. The resultant floods were considered the worst to affect the nations since 1951.

Steve gets home the evening to watch the devastation in Mozambique on the news but is surprised by an official package from Immigration Canada. They have received their Residency Documents for Canada. Steve chats to Annie and they start planning when to leave South Africa. Several items require urgently to be arranged including selling the house, cars, and arranging shipment of the items that they need to take with.

Steve is still planning when he receives a call from Slade Thomas. Slade has leased the two Puma J Models from a farmer who bought the aircraft. Slade has secured a contract to support the rescue work in Mozambique and has offered Steve US Dollars to fly for him.

Steve accepts immediately and applies for his Mozambique Visa. This was going to give them tax free funds for settling in Canada. Steve opens a Canadian Bank account and provides the details to Slade's company NAC Helicopters. Steve shares the positive news with Annie, but it has a huge negative as well.

Annie will now have to conduct all the immigration processing on her own as Steve will be out of the country. Steve supplies Annie with all account details, travel reward miles and anything else she requires including Power of Attorney to sell everything. Steve packs and heads out to Maputo Mozambique.

The weather continues to batter the country. The coastal town of Beira is hit by an enormous cyclone causing further damage, especially from flash flooding. Farms and arable land are completely submerged in the towns of Xai-Xai and Chokwe. People are forced out of their homes and must climb onto roofs and into trees in the hope that they can be rescued. Over five hundred thousand people are saved this way as the waters continued to rise. The South African government sends helicopters. One woman gives birth in a tree but is luckily saved by the air force. The rainfall continues for five weeks.

People waiting for rescue on rooftops

Farmland and crops which villages rely on for survival are submerged. Many families are stranded with no food or clean water, and hundreds die from starvation, with over forty health stations destroyed. Irrigation systems all over the country are ruined. Over one hundred thousand farming families have lost their livelihoods, with nearly fifteen hundred square kilometers of land destroyed. Twenty thousand cattle are either swept away by the flood waters or die from disease shortly after.

The Mozambique government uses boats to evacuate residents in flood zones, setting up 121 camps for evacuees. However, the country has limited capacity for widespread rescues due to insufficient helicopters. South Africa sends a fleet of twelve planes and helicopters to operate search and rescue missions, as well as airdropping supplies. They are assisted by two helicopters from Malawi, six from the United Kingdom, and ten from Germany.

Flooded Rivers breaking Banks

By the 7th March, a fleet of 29 helicopters has rescued 14,204 people. Residual floodwaters contribute to outbreaks of malaria and cholera, with malaria infections at four times the usual rate killing a number or people. Areas in southern Mozambique also lose access to clean water, furthering dehydration and illnesses. In addition, the United Nations Mine Action Service expresses concern that the floods shifted the locations of landmines left over from the nation's civil war. Later, the remnants of Cyclone Gloria halt relief work due to heavy rainfall. Residents begin returning home in early March after floodwaters recede.

As Steve steps off the aircraft at Maputo he is struck by the way that Mozambique has degraded. Under Portuguese Colonial Rule, Mozambique was a thriving well developed and flourishing country. A modern airport and capital Lourenco Marques, now Maputo, was considered the paradise in the sun.

Walking towards the terminal buildings Steve just sees derelict and unmaintained buildings. The customs office is a hole in the wall with collapsible tables and plastic chairs. The officials rude and uncooperative and arrogant. Steve quietly informs the customs official that he is here to assist in the rescue operations with the helicopters. The response is indifferent and no care attitude.

Steve steps through and needs to relieve himself. He makes his way to the toilet and almost hurls as the stench from the urinal and toilet bowls overwhelms him. White bowls and urinals now darkened black from lack of cleaning for many years already. He decides to move through to the arrivals hall and rather hold his need for the hotel toilets.

J.C. Linde is there to collect Steve and they greet like long lost friends. JC was a pilot in the Air Force with whom Steve had many good times in the past. JC is heading up the operation for Slade in Maputo. They make their way to the hotel through very poorly maintained streets. Many of the buildings that had been started during the Portuguese era, stood as they were left, incomplete and slowly being reclaimed by nature. Fortunately, tourism is still a big attraction to Mozambique and most of the top hotels are in good condition with excellent service.

Early the next morning the team heads down to Maputo airport on the commercial side. Steve is elated to see the two J Models still in their original paint scheme parked on the apron. Each aircraft will fly with two qualified crew and a student co-pilot.

Steve thoroughly checks the aircraft log before going out to ZS-HIZ and performing a through before flight inspection. It is still raining, but most of the rescue work has been completed. The bigger task at hand now is to feed those that have been cut off from the flood waters.

The World Food Program has contracted NAC Helicopters to transport food and implements to the most remote communities first. Both aircraft get airborne and fly for nine hours the day, stopping only to refuel and reload with fresh cargo. Exhausted the crews get back to the hotel well after sunset. Steve calls Annie and briefs her about the work that he needs to do.

"Would you like to join me for a week?" Asks Steve.

"That would be lovely." Answers Annie.

They chat a little more and Steve reminds her that she will have to get a visa. They agree that she will come for a week in March 2000.

The flying is non-stop, but Steve is having the time of his life. Eventually there are no more student pilots and they operate with only two crew. In one day they move ten tons of cargo to a very remote village near Goba to the south of Maputo.

The villagers are excited and happy to see them and quickly help Steve to unload the cargo. Three trips later and all the cargo is supplied, enough to feed them for the next six months as well as seed to start fresh crops including implements to plant them. A good day's work completed, and the crews get back to Maputo after sunset.

The same process is repeated to the east, north and far north of Mozambique. Towns like Chokwe, Arruma, Chicumbane, Chongoene and Manjacaze are still cut off and require resupply. The two Puma's together with Air Force Oryx's, Court Helicopters S61's and Titan Helicopters Mil 8's are working long hours to keep the supplies flowing.

Steve chats to JC and poses an idea of rather cargo slinging the supplies from a central supply station which will be must faster than the current internal loading. Steve contacts Eugene from the Air Force group and requests them to loan him 10 cargo nets and strops for the plan he wants to enact.

Eugene delivers and two days later Steve has the means to speed up the supply. Steve decides to hand over the F/E duties to Org Kriel while he manages the first day's cargo slinging from the ground. Armed with a group of cargo packers, VHF Radio, water and determination, Steve sets to work. With each aircraft starting at 1-ton lift until the fuel load lightens, Steve keeps adding with every new sling until the loads are 2-tons.

Every three hours the aircraft would land for fuel and the process is repeated. Eventually after sunset Steve is picked up and they head back to Maputo. The two aircraft alone have managed to move 100 Tons of supplies and equipment for the day. The supplies can now be trucked to the cut off towns.

Early the next morning they deploy to Xai-Xai 200 Km to the north of Maputo. The town is totally cut off and is running out of supplies. The rich people are so desperate to get out of the town that they are offering cash to have their vehicles and personal effects cargo slung over the flooded water so that they can escape. Steve shakes his head and walks away. They are here for humanitarian reasons and not to satisfy the whims of the rich.

Steve is flying with Steve Whiteing the next day as they return to Goba to the south of Maputo. They have a team from the World Food Program onboard to follow up with the village to see if they are needing any more assistance. They land and Steve shuts down the Puma.

The villagers come rushing over and are disappointed to see that there is no cargo for them. When questioned about the 10-tons of food and equipment that was flown in a few weeks back, they respond that the Chief has confiscated everything and is demanding payment from them before he will supply. If Steve had any doubts about immigrating, then those thoughts are completely out of the window after witnessing this fiasco.

Tribalism rules no matter where or when. Life is cheap, and power is everything. Steve walks away disgusted and rather spends the time checking the aircraft for snags and cleans the engine and transmission platforms.

Xai-Xai submerged

Beautiful Annie

Annie will be arriving tomorrow so Steve focuses on having her with him. They have lots to catch up on. Has the house been sold, what about packing the contents for shipment and when will the cars be sold? Steve finishes up early and wanders over to the arrivals area. As aircrew he can approach the flight line and he impatiently awaits the SAA Flight from Johannesburg with Annie onboard. Just after 17:00 the Airbus A340 taxis in and shuts down. The access steps are pushed to the door and the passengers start exiting the aircraft. What seems like an eternity Steve spots Annie at the head of the stairs. His heart swells with pride, she is beautifully dressed and looks radiant as she comes down the stairs towards him. She recognizes him standing at the entrance to the arrivals hall and a smile lights up her face. They hug and kiss and Steve is elated to see her again.

He accompanies her to the Customs desk and the official recognizes Steve. With a wave he indicates Annie to approach, skipping the lineup. He stamps the passport without even glancing at it and with a beaming smile welcomes her to Maputo. Steve has ordered at taxi as the team is at a restaurant to the north of Maputo where JC is sponsoring supper for everyone. The taxi ride takes an hour over some of the roughest roads that Annie has ever experienced.

"Wow this place is really poor and unkept." States Annie.

"This is the precursor to what will soon happen in South Africa love!" Retorts Steve.

They join the group and JC's wife Sharon makes a fuss of Annie. It is good to have another woman in their midst. Later at the hotel Annie updates Steve on the progress at home. She has an offer in for the house and has sold the cars. Kelvin Roberts, Steve's school mate, has bought both BMW's and sold a Toyota cheaply to Annie. When the leave the country, he will buy it back from her at the same price. The packers will be coming to pack the house contents for shipment in May. The children are becoming a problem, as David is so in love with Bianca and does not want to leave South Africa. His negativity is affecting Nicole who is starting to mutter the same nonsense. They are both saying that the process took so long and that the country is still fine. Steve just nods and comforts Annie. He will deal with the children on his return.

Early the next morning Annie accompanies Steve for the day. They are flying back to Xai-Xai and the surrounding area to resupply some of the villages that the trucks could not reach. With Annie seated in the co-pilots position Steve and Anton go about operating the Puma and soon they are on their way. Annie is having the time of her life. As per normal when the Puma lands close to the first village hundreds of little black faces come running towards the aircraft. When the blades stop the crowd moves forward to have a look what is inside. Annie is overwhelmed by this activity and refuses to get out of the aircraft. Steve laughs and gets to work unloading the cargo. By midday Annie has still not moved from the co-pilots seat and Steve can see she is uncomfortable.

"What's wrong darling?" Asks Steve.

"I need to pee!" Says Annie.

"Well go in the bush, or we can quickly land in an open area and you can squat over the cargo hole in the cabin." Says Steve.

"No thank you, I can hold it in." Grimaces Annie.

On the last sortie of the day with the temperature in the high thirties, Anton grabs a hand full of collective and puts the Puma in an accelerated climb to get to cooler air.

“Let's go and chase some clouds!” Exclaims Anton.

Annie is having the time of her life and the view is spectacular. At just below 10,000 ft Anton levels off and heads towards Maputo. The look on Annie's face lets Steve know that she is uneasy at the altitude. The view from the co-pilots seat gives her an amazing vantage point and looking between her feet she sees the ground far below. Back at Maputo Steve quickly services the aircraft while Annie makes her way to the toilet. She has barely left when she returns.

“I am not putting my bum on that seat thank you!” says Annie.

Steve knows exactly what she is talking about. There are six of them that need a ride back to the Hotel and one rental car. Everyone squeezes in with Annie sitting on Steve's lap. The return route to the hotel is along a road that is full of potholes. In the evening the potholes are filled with loose gravel which is then removed by the locals at night to sell the next day. The road is rough and bouncy, making it very tough on Annie. She has now managed to keep her pee in since lunch time. They arrive at the hotel after dark and Annie makes a beeline to the hotel lobby toilets. By the time she returns Steve has ordered her a Vodka Passionfruit and Seven-Up with an umbrella to top it. The relief on her face is hysterical and Steve bursts out laughing.

The week goes by far too quickly and it is time for Annie to return home. It has been lovely having her with him and even nicer to experience the flying as well. They embrace and kiss and Steve promises to see her soon. Annie departs and with a final wave she disappears into the aircraft. There are still several contracts in place for the aircraft and Steve wants to capitalize on the tax-free money he is earning. The nest egg is building up in the Canadian Bank account.

Engine Loss

The Puma's deploy to Beira and are Cargo Slinging from an airfield inland located closer to the villages that require supplies. The first flights of the day off without any issues. Steve and Steve Whiteing are flying ZS-HIZ and are at Max All Up weight with a full Cargo Net. They have just gone through 1000 ft when Steve hears an Engine wind down. He jumps up and screams at Steve Whiteing that he has jettisoned the load as they have lost an engine. Steve checks the instruments are realizes the number two engine is at idle and making an awful sound. He shuts the engine down and Steve Whiteing brings the aircraft in on one engine then lands at the dispersal area of the runway.

After shutting down Steve cranks number two engine and even before ignition he identifies that the combustion chamber must have separated. This will require an engine change. Steve contacts JC on the HF Radio and informs him on the situation. There are no spare engines available in Maputo and Steve will have to secure the aircraft until they can get an engine shipped from South Africa. JC gets one of the Air Force Cessna Caravan aircraft to collect the Steve's and ferry them back to Maputo.

Slade has managed to get a spare engine shipped to Nelspruit on the border between Mozambique and South Africa. Both Steve's, JC and Sharon fly to Nelspruit in ZS-HJA to collect the engine. Upon arrival at Nelspruit an air show is in preparation and the organizers ask JC if they would like to participate with the Puma J Model. This will be the first time that these aircraft have been seen here. While JC enters the airshow and briefs the commentators, Steve loads the spare engine and secures it in the cabin. JC and Steve Whiteing return, and they prepare for the air show. Steve Whiteing performs a low fly-past and then into the hover for the crowd followed by a corkscrew climb and nose bunt fly away. They land, and Steve refuels for the return flight to Maputo.

Early the next morning Steve and the ground crew prepare for the engine change on ZS-HIZ. As the area is so muddy there is no way that they can get a crane into the area. The mob pack up kit mobile crane is still in Cape Town, so Steve comes up with plan B. Steve Whiteing is an amazingly steady pilot and can hover the aircraft perfectly. Steve and the ground crew loosen number two engine on ZS-HIZ and shift the engine forward. Steve secures the main rotor blades so that the forward-facing blade will not interfere. With Steve in the cabin operating the Cargo Sling they attach the strop and move over ZS-HIZ. Bubbles the ground crew chief secures the strop to the engine lifting sling and gives Steve a thumb up. He clears the area and Steve patters Steve Whiteing up, lifting the engine off. The engine is lowered to the ground on some old car tires and then the replacement engine hooked up. Steve patters Steve Whiteing into position and they lower the engine onto the platform. They have just performed the first engine change by cargo sling.

It takes another 30 minutes to secure and inspect the engine. Unfortunately, the fuel line has been damaged and requires replacement. It takes another two days to get one from South Africa and then Steve quickly gets the fuel line installed. He starts number two to check the settings and completes the required acceleration and slam checks. Without shutting down he beckons Steve Whiteing to take over the commander's seat for a short test flight. They complete a single engine power check and then a max stop check. The engine performs normally and after landing Steve refuels, packs the kit and they return to Maputo with the serviceable ZS-HIZ.

The crews have been operating nonstop for four months now and most of the contracts are in wind down phase. One last sortie is to fly Richard Attenborough film director and producer over the flood area. Richard has two Academy Awards for Gandhi in 1983, receiving awards for Best Picture and Best Director. He is also known for his work on Gandhi, Brighton Rock, The Great Escape, 10 Rillington Place, The Sand Pebbles, Doctor Doolittle, Miracle on 34th Street and Jurassic Park.

Richard Attenborough

JC has made friends with many of the local politicians and reputable businesses. He manages to secure a weekend rest and recuperation for the team at Inhaca Island, just off the coast of Maputo.

Inhaca Island

They land and secure the Puma on the beach, out of the reach of high water. The resort is amazing, and all the buildings are built from resources on the island.

There are no vehicles, but the restaurant, pub and resort are well stocked. The weekend is destined to be a serious unwind from the 9-hour flight days of the past four months.

Beach Resort Inhaca Island

All to soon their time is up and its back to work, the two days at Inhaca has refreshed them for the last stretch. Steve has just turned 43 and celebrates his birthday with the team at the hotel. In a few weeks he will return to Cape Town to finalize the immigration process. There are a few signatures and approvals remaining to close off his commitments in South Africa. JC wants to start collecting some ex Air Force Puma's as he has work in Africa for them. Steve makes some enquiries with his contacts and secures two aircraft for JC. He will have to take JC to the current owner and negotiate a deal.

Steve returns to Cape Town and is very impressed at what Annie has achieved without him. The house deal was completed, cars sold, and contents are in the process of being packed for shipment to Vancouver. Steve has one more trip to Johannesburg to meet up with JC for the potential procurement of the Puma's. The meeting goes off smoothly and JC secures a potential purchase. Steve thanks JC for the past five months and wishes him well before returning to Cape Town. By the time Steve gets home the packers have completed and the removal company arrive to transport everything to the shipping container.

Annie's aunt has arranged a farewell function for the family at her home in Kraaifontein. Annie has also used all Steve's British Airways airmiles and secured tickets for them from Cape Town to Vancouver flying out 25th June 2000 the day before Annie's birthday.

Steve gathers the family to have an open discussion on the move and reasons why. The mood is pensive, and Steve has to keep control of his temper. He starts off with a little history lesson of what his life was like as a teenager growing up in South Africa. As in the first chapter Steve reiterates the strong patriotism and pride of the country that had been nourished and cultured, how after independence in 1961 the country had quickly developed to become a world economic power followed by a military growth that made South Africa a force to be reckoned with.

Chapter 21 - TRIBAL AFRICA CONTINUES TO SPIRAL

Steve continues to create a visualization as he recollects the developing political reversal to tribalism. The spiral downward started in 1990, with de Klerk ordering to end South Africa's nuclear weapons program; the process of nuclear disarmament was essentially completed in 1991. The existence of the program was not officially acknowledged before 1993. The following events further solidify the decision to immigrate to Canada;

In 1992, de Klerk held a whites-only referendum on ending apartheid, with the result being an overwhelming "yes" vote to continue negotiations to end apartheid. Nelson Mandela was distrustful of the role played by de Klerk in the negotiations, particularly as he believed that de Klerk was knowledgeable about 'third force' attempts to foment violence in the country and destabilize the negotiations.

In 1993, de Klerk and Mandela were jointly awarded the Nobel Peace Prize for their work in ending apartheid. The awarding of the prize to de Klerk was controversial, especially in the light of de Klerk's reported admission that he ordered a massacre of supposed Azanian People's Liberation Army fighters, including teenagers, shortly before going to Oslo in 1993.

In 1994, de Klerk became deputy president in the government of national unity under Nelson Mandela, a post he kept until 1996. De Klerk's working relationship with Mandela was often strained, with the former finding it difficult adjusting to the fact that he was no longer president. De Klerk also felt that Mandela deliberately humiliated him, while Mandela found de Klerk to be needlessly provocative in cabinet. One dispute occurred after Mandela gave a Johannesburg speech criticizing the National Party. Angered, de Klerk avoided Mandela until the latter requested, they meet; when they ran into each other, they publicly argued in the street. Mandela later expressed regret for their disagreement but did not apologize for his original comments. De Klerk was also having problems from within his own party, some of whose members claimed that he was neglecting the party while in the government. Many in the National Party, including many members of its executive committee were unhappy with the other parties agreed upon new constitution. de Klerk withdrew the National Party from the coalition government. De Klerk declared that he would lead the National Party in vigorous opposition to Mandela's government to ensure "a proper multi-party democracy, without which there may be a danger of South Africa lapsing into the African pattern of one-party states".

In 1996, the chair of the TRC, Desmond Tutu, was frustrated that de Klerk did not take responsibility for the actions of the state security services. In de Klerk's view, his greatest defeat in the negotiations with Mandela had been his inability to secure a blanket amnesty for all those working for the government or state during the apartheid period. De Klerk was unhappy with the formation of the Truth and Reconciliation Commission. He had hoped that the TRC would be made up of an equal number of individuals from both the old and new governments, as there had been in the Chilean human rights commission. Instead, the TRC was designed to broadly reflect the wider diversity of South African society and contained only two members who had explicitly supported apartheid, one a member of a right-wing group that had opposed de Klerk's National Party. De Klerk was upset that Alex Boraine had been selected as its deputy chair, later saying of Boraine: "beneath an urbane and deceptively affable exterior beat the heart of a zealot and an inquisitor." De Klerk appeared before the TRC hearing to testify for Vlakplaas commanders who were accused of having committed human rights abuses during the apartheid era. He acknowledged that security forces had resorted to "unconventional strategies" in dealing with anti-apartheid revolutionaries, but that "within my knowledge and experience, they never included the authorization of assassination, murder, torture, rape, assault or the like".

In May 1996 South Africa completed the transition to democracy when it approved a permanent constitution to replace the transitional one implemented three years earlier. It created a strong central government, an independent judiciary, and a bill of rights with one of the broadest guarantees of liberty in the world. In addition to freedom of speech, movement, and political activity, the South African Bill of Rights protects rights to adequate food, housing, water, education, and health care. The day after the new constitution was approved, de Klerk and his colleagues in the National party quit their cabinet posts, saying that the government was strong enough to handle "robust opposition." Effectively destroying what had the previous regime had spent Billions of Dollars developing to afford blacks to have their own states.

In 1997 there were reminders that troubles remain with riots in Johannesburg suburbs by coloureds against discrimination in favour of blacks and, a mass rally, which turned violent in Johannesburg by still-unsatisfied Zulus. Bitter feelings between the Inkatha Freedom Party and Mandela's ANC surfaced again when the Truth and Reconciliation Committee reported testimony linking Inkatha leaders to assassination squads during the apartheid era. de Klerk resigned the leadership of the National Party and retired from politics.

On 2nd June 1999, South Africa held its second post-apartheid elections: the ANC won a gigantic victory, taking 266 seats in the 400-seat Assembly. An "alliance" with the one member of the Indian Minority Front gave ANC the 2/3 majority that permits it to amend the Constitution. Thabo Mbeki, who replaced Nelson Mandela as party chief in December, was elected unopposed to be his successor as South Africa's president as well. As inflation heats up strikes grow more frequent.

More recently we saw the brutal black on black murders with the necklace method. We saw blacks storming into white churches with AK 47's and hand grenades, opening fire on the unarmed congregation such as at the St James Church massacre. We have seen everything from brutal Muti murders to the evil torture preceding the brutal killings of White farmers and their family members in Rhodesia, Namibia and in South Africa, most of the time nothing stolen. More than 3000 White farmers and family members murdered to date since the ANC took over in 1994.

Black on Black Terror

It is necessary to reiterate that this violent nature of blacks are not directed at whites only, so the black behaviour apologetics who claim that this behaviour is retribution for wrongs committed by whites against blacks, have no leg to stand on, because most often than not this black violent nature is directed at their own kind as we have seen with Shaka's defecane, Muti murders and necklacing.

No, this brutality, this murderous, stealing and other asocial behaviour of Blacks could never and can never be reconciled with the behaviour of the deeply religious and pious Boers of South Africa. This violent behaviour of blacks was one of the rationales for Apartheid. The other was cultural differences. For now, it is important to realize that whites in South Africa never wanted to rule blacks. Whites wanted to separate from blacks and stay as far away from blacks as possible.

White South Africans are often accused that their "sense of superiority", their "white privilege" is the reason why the multicultural New South Africa and the Rainbow Nation is a failure. It is apparently the unwillingness of the white man to share property and wealth that is the cause of all the misery. How short sighted and selfish.

The white man has progressed with civilization and developed in all areas where the black man has remained mostly barbaric and 400 years behind in civilization development. What they have learnt well is to demand hand outs and lace their own pockets while still practicing tribalism in a more modern form.

Having spoken his heart out Steve hopes that the family fully understands the decision that he an Annie have made for them. It is not going to be easy, but life will be different with different challenges but most of all the children are guaranteed a future to mold as they want to.

Sunday the 25th June 2000 arrives, and family and friends have congregated to see the family off. Tears flow, and last calls are made for boarding when Steve forcibly gets them to move through to the departure area. This chapter in their history as a family closed and a brand new one just opening. The future of the children now afforded an opportunity to develop fairly without reversed discrimination and persecution. The great unknown for all of them ahead as none of them have ever set foot off African Soil to other civilizations. Everything they know has been via media, film or television. With mixed and varied emotions, the long trek away from Africa commences with many adventures about to start. There will still be many roadblocks, trials and tribulations ahead, but with determination, love and caring they will persevere. Many of the so-called friends and family have labeled them as cowards, running away from the country of their heritage. A bitter pill to swallow but with grit and determination Steve must lead the family forward and make a success to ensure a future.

Stop White South African Genocide

Now many years later with the family well settled and having achieved what they had set out to do Steve finds himself constantly having to defend the how and why. The statistics as defined below clarify many of the decisions that Steve and Annie had to make for this to be successful. After reading it and comparing the information to what we experience today, one wonders which state a crime against humanity is actually.

The Lies about Apartheid

In 1988, a German book published how benevolent the White giant of Africa actually was. Here are some of the facts;

In apartheid 1972, South African Blacks owned 360,000 vehicles. More than all the black African states together.

The monthly income of Blacks per capita in 1988 was R352 per month in South Africa, Malawi and Mozambique were less than R20 per month.

In apartheid 1988 Black people could undergo a complicated heart valve surgery for just more than $1 while Black Americans had to pay $15,000. In a Pretoria hospital between 2,000 and 3,000 of these surgeries were done per year.

In apartheid 1970, Black workers earned R1,751 million, or 25.5% of the total wage fees in South Africa and increased to R17,238 million in 1984 a 1,000% growth and 32.3% of total wages in South Africa.

In the apartheid 1986/1987 financial year, Whites paid tax of R9,000 million and Blacks R171 million, while Indians paid R257 million and Coloreds paid R315 million.

Between 1962 and 1972 the United Nations paid $298 million to underdeveloped countries compared to an apartheid South Africa that spent $558 million on the development of its Black areas.

The budget amount for Black education in apartheid increased every year from 1970 to almost 30% more than any other Government Department.

From 1955 to 1984 the number of Black scholars increased from 35,000 to 1,096,000. In 1988 71% of the adult Black population could read and write versus 47% in Kenya, 38% in Egypt and 34% in Nigeria. On average during the year 15 new classrooms per working day were built for Black scholars.

In apartheid 1985 there were 42,000 Black students enrolled at South African universities. There were 5 Black universities and 28 higher education institutions funded by the Government.

Soweto with its population of 1.2 million, had 5 modern stadiums versus Pretoria with its 600,000 Whites who had three. Soweto had 365 schools versus Pretoria 229.

In apartheid Soweto in 1978, there were 115 football fields, three rugby fields, 4 athletic tracks, 11 cricket fields, two golf courses, 47 tennis courts, 7 swimming pools, 5 bowling halls, 81 basketball fields, 39 children playgrounds and countless community halls, cinemas and clubhouses.

In Soweto in 1978, there were 300 churches, 365 schools, 2 Technikons, 8 clinics, 63 kindergartens, 11 post offices and its own fruit and vegetable market.

The White Government built a huge hospital Baragwanath 3,000 beds in Soweto. One of the largest and most modern hospitals in the world. Its 23 operating theaters were equipped with the best equipment money can buy. Here Blacks were treated at a nominal cost of R2 for an unlimited period. In 1982, no fewer than 898 heart surgeries were done here. Next to the Baragwanath Hospital is the St. John-eye clinic, famous for the treatment of glaucoma, previous fix retinas, traumatic eye injuries and rare tropical diseases.

There were over 2,300 registered firms, 1,000 taxi operators and 50,000 car owners in Soweto.

Dr. Kenneth Walker, a Canadian physician, visited Soweto and made the following observations; He saw several houses worth more than R100 000 with various BMW's at the door. Only 2% of homes were shacks with neat buildings with lawns. If he had to choose between the decaying apartments in New York, Detroit or Chicago than he would rather stay in Soweto. He'd rather be very ill in Soweto as in some Canadian cities. He says the city has more schools, churches, cars, taxis, and sports fields than any other independent African state.

In 1978, the apartheid South African Government built a highly modern hospital MEDUNSA on the border of the independent state of Bophuthatswana at a cost of R70 million on 35 hectares. In this "city" they had living and sleeping facilities for male and female students. Black doctors, dentists, veterinarians and para-medical staff were trained. It was the only specialized university of its kind in Africa and one of the few in the world financed by White taxpayers exclusively to benefit Blacks. Almost all students who mainly came from the national homeland's costs were taken care of by the Government.

The practical training took place in the nearby Garankuwa Hospital farm where the whole range of human ailments were covered. Garankuwa had the facilities for kidney transplants, isotopes units with specialized laboratories where 200 doctors were trained practically every year.

The apartheid South Africa provided training for the airline personnel of Swaziland, Botswana, Zimbabwe, Zaire and the Comores.

In 1979, when the train traffic to the Malawian capital Lilongwe was interrupted by rebels, the apartheid South Africa sent transport aircraft with fuel drums to keep their economy going.

In 1986, 80,000 Black businessmen from Africa visited Cape Town to finalize business deals.

The apartheid South Africa provided the grain needs of its neighboring countries and wider. In 1980, Zambia received 250 000 tons of maize, Mozambique 150,000 tons maize and 50 000 tons of wheat, Kenya 128,000 tons maize and Zimbabwe 100 000 tons. Other countries that also received South African grain were Angola, Ivory Coast, Malawi, Mauritius, Tanzania and Zaire.

At least 12 countries of Africa, according to the "Argus African News Service" were so dependent on apartheid South Africa grain that a total ban on imports and exports would have destroyed them economically.

About half of Lesotho's male population worked in apartheid South Africa, about 146,000 in 1983, and earned R280,6 million which was about half of Lesotho's treasury.

In the 1982/83 financial year the apartheid South Africa budgeted R434 million for assistance to the independent neighboring states.

The apartheid South Africa produced more electrical energy than Italy, as much crude steel as France, more wheat than Canada, more wool than the United States, more wine than Greece and more fish than Great Britain.

Apartheid South African trains ran on more rail lines than in West Germany, carried more passengers than Switzerland, had better punctuality record than Austria and exported car parts to 100 countries.

Apartheid South African mines bore down to the depth of 3,480 meters and holds the record for the deepest vertical shaft at 2,498m deep into the hardest rock in the world.

In apartheid South Africa had 1.4 police officers for every 1,000 people whilst the world had the following: United Kingdom 2.2, New York 4.3, and Moscow 10 per 1000. In South Africa there were 16,292 White Policemen versus 19,177 Non-White.

In 1979-1980 there were no deaths in apartheid South African prisons. In the previous 10 years 37 died versus 274 in the same period in Wales and England.

In 1974, the average monthly income of black workers in apartheid South Africa were $127 versus the $140 in the US, the richest country in the world.

In 1983, 127 political prisoners were confined in apartheid South Africa and 11 whose movements were limited. A further 32 were under house arrest.

Now, if we look at the recent history of South Africa, we will discover that power was not won by struggle as the ANC and the rest of black South Africa claims. Political analysts and experts such as the late Dr. F van Zyl Slabbert, are unanimous in this. The apartheid government could easily have hung on to power for at least another 15 years. The hand-over was done voluntarily through a majority "Yes" vote to a referendum by white South Africans in 1992. And with power, quite a number of other things were wrapped up in the parcel. 25 years later we need to assess what was done with that and with this assessment comes the question:

Tell us: WHY must WE give even more?

Tell us: Why must WE respect what black majority government did with what was given to them?

Tell us: Why YOU deserve even more trust, even more opportunities?

Tell us: Why do YOU believe that WE don't have the right to say: "Enough now. We're going to walk away and take care of our own future. We now demand self-determination."

Tell us why: YOU were given power and you corrupted government with it.

YOU were entrusted with education, transport and health!!!!

Today WE sit with School graduates who pass with 30%!!!

WE have patients bleeding to death on hospital floors while nurses have a tea break!!!

WE have a public roads system which was the best in Africa, now hardly suitable for any vehicle and we have trains constantly set alight.

YOU were entrusted with a heritage. National heritage sites such as Augusta Manor House, Bloemfontein Town Hall and numerous statues were burned and destroyed.

Places and streets were renamed after people who had no link with them at all. Our language was removed as a language of tuition in higher education centers founded through the existence of that language in the first place!

YOU were entrusted to make our sports teams internationally competitive. Through YOUR quota systems YOU turned us into the laughing stock of the world.

YOU were handed a civil aviation company which was one of the oldest and most reliable in the world. YOU bankrupted that.

YOU were handed Denel, the Post Office, Eskom, SARS, Transnet, Iscor...all functional and profitable. YOU bankrupted them, sold them off to Indians and Chinese, looted them and ran them ALL straight into the ground.

Everything YOU received was destroyed, corrupted, bankrupted and compromised.

The only ones YOU tried to set up in 25 years became a failure such as VBS Bank.

And now YOU claim that white arrogance is the reason why there is a lack of respect for black majority government.

We don't disrespect your government because it is black, WE disrespect it because it is dysfunctional, corrupt and incompetent!!!!!

So, tell us again: Why do WE need to keep giving you more and more opportunities when WE have seen what YOU did with what we have already given you?

Daydreaming of times gone

During sunrise one morning I was drinking a cup of coffee and gazing at nothing in particular out of the window. For some reason I started thinking about a time when I was on the bus on my way home from school one day. I was getting ready to alight the bus at my usual stop. The bus was full, and I was sitting next to an old man who stared out of the window all the way down the road. At one point, he gave a long, sad, sigh. His breath was so deep and heartfelt that its outward emanation touched me. I looked over at the man. His eyes were tired and watery. Staring out of the window, he was so lost in thought, he didn't notice me looking at him. I felt I needed to say something.

"Excuse me," I said, "Are you okay?"

He turned and looked at me.

"Oh," he said patting me on the arm with a sweet smile "I'm fine, thank you. I was just daydreaming about being a kid. I grew up around here and sometimes I long for those carefree days."

Thinking about him now, I fully understand his deep longing and, as I drink my tea, I find myself thinking about my own childhood, I remember…

We would play for hours on the "koppie" behind our house. Our parents would say, "You're irritating us, go out and play before we have a 'conniption fit'!" Defined in the dictionary as a fit of rage or hysterics.

And play we did. My goodness we played hard! We played war or "stingers" or "skop die blik" or "cowboys and crooks" pull down your "broeks". No, I will not explain that one to you!

We spent hours outside. We played "Tok-tokkie", knocking on someone's door and running away, we played cricket in the street using an old tomato box as wickets. The postman sometimes played wicket keeper for a few minutes as he made his rounds. He would say, "I want to play the wickedly ticket," and he'd crouch behind the tomato box for a few over's.

We played with "dingbats", "yoyo's", "woer-woer's" button on a string, "kettie's" slingshot, and "sand clods" with nary a parent in sight. Imagine kids throwing "sand clods" or "kleilat's" at each other in this modern day and age? They would have to wear helmets, protective glasses and football pads.

We played "moerball", "swingball" and "dodgeball" and used the circular washing line to swing around on.

I remember…

We got covered in "black jacks", mud, dust and "dorings" thorns. We had mulberry stains on our mouths and feet and always had a few marbles, Sugus, Licorice All Sorts, Three X mints, Jelly Tots and Lion matches, to set things on fire, in our pockets.

I remember…

We climbed trees, "koppies", fences, onto roof's and into drains and "donga's". We pegged Bicycle cards onto our choppers and played "peggy" with a knife or a screw driver. We climbed onto the roofs of the shops in the area.

We put potato's in people's exhaust pipes, whistled through a piece of grass or an acorn "doppie", caught tadpoles in the "spruit" creek, and kept them in jars in our room until they smelled to high heaven and our mom threw them out. With a disgusted look on her face.

I remember…

We played cards and Monopoly and Cluedo and most of all we played the fool.

On November 5th we made a guy and put him in a wheelbarrow and gleefully danced around him as he burned. How bizarre!

We said things like, "Inky pinky ponkey daddy bought a donkey. Donkey died daddy cried. Inky pinky ponkey." How bizarre!

We sang, "Skinny malinky long legs vrot banana feet, went to the bioscope and couldn't find a seat, he sat on a lady and out popped the baby, skinny malinky long legs vrot banana feet." How bizarre!

Back in my day we uttered things like:

"Here comes the bride, all dressed in white, she slipped on a banana skin and broke her spine."

"I'm the king of the castle and you're the dirty rascal."

"One potato, two potato, three potato, four, five potato, six potato, seven potato more."

"Finders keepers, losers weepers."

"Ask your mother for a sixpence to see the big giraffe with freckles on his nose and pimples on his…ask you mother for a sixpence."

"What's the time, half past nine, hang your broekies on the line."

I remember…

As the sun set, you would hear all the neighbourhood dad's calling for their kids to come in for dinner, and out of the veld and bushes and trees and dongas and drains came us naughty rascals, dirty, smelly, satiated, played-out and content little ruffians, ready for a bath and dinner. And then a bit of Mark Saxon and Serge or Squad Cars, or Pick a Box on the radio, and then the deepest of deep sleeps after a hard day at play.

As I sit here drinking coffee and gazing out of the window at nothing in particular, I feel a very strong, almost painful yearning for those carefree days of my youth. It seems the further I get from it, the more I long for that time in my life.

And "Foefie Slide" across the river. "Bok Bok", "I spy with my little eye", "Stingers" with a wet tennis ball, Spinning tops, Yoyos, "Arlies" marbles and goons, "Chinese bangles" twisting Wrists, Swimming "kaalgat" naked in the rivers or dams, Fishing, Shooting doves with a pellet gun, braaiing and eating them and Blowing up antheaps with crackers.

I really miss the little hooligan I once was in a country that had so much to offer, now gone forever.

Chapter 22 - ANNALS OF WARS WE DON'T KNOW ABOUT

It's rare and quite refreshing to see insight like this on the Border War from foreign Defense analysts, or even contemporary South African Defense analysts, due to political bias, but this one by an American, Robert Goldich is particularly accurate from the panel of consulting historians. The following then his words on the Border War.

The South African Border War of 1966 – 1989 : Robert Goldich

The following account submitted by Robert Goldich summarizes the poor understanding the west has on the inappropriate and cold-blooded destruction of the White Africans.

There aren't many truly unknown wars these days. Military history writing, scholarly and popular and in between, has mushroomed over the past several decades. But military events under the Southern Cross receive much less attention, because the vast majority of the developed countries are well north of the Equator.

Reading South African accounts of the 23-year long Border War between South Africa and the Angolan liberation movement UNITA on the one hand, and the Angolan government and army, supported by large Cuban forces on the other, is almost hypnotically compelling. This is not only because for most of us north of the Equator it is so distant. The names of both natural features and people involved, and the range of cultures they represent, sound exotic to our ears, and hold one's attention.

The tactical and operational lessons from the Border War are mostly variations on usual military themes solid and relevant training, doctrine, and attitudes but that the most significant lessons of this conflict for the United States are far broader, and sobering, in nature.

What happened?

South Africa came under steadily increasing foreign criticism and isolation beginning in the 1960s due to its policy of apartheid, or racially discriminatory separatism. Armed resistance by black Africans took two forms. One was isolated acts of terrorism in South Africa itself mounted by black liberation movements based in bordering countries, mostly under the direction of the African National Congress (ANC) and its military component, Umkhonto we Sizwe (MK). The MK's attacks were mere pinpricks at best.

Far more formidable was a guerrilla movement against South African rule in Southwest Africa (SWA), later independent Namibia, beginning in the late 1960s, by the South West African People's Organization (SWAPO). The latter would also have remained insignificant had not Portuguese colonial rule collapsed in Angola, directly north of SWA, in 1974-1975. This left a military vacuum from which SWAPO forces could train, equip, and debouch into northern SWA without any hindrance. Interestingly, nothing similar developed on the other side of Africa. Mozambique, where Portuguese rule had also evaporated, had close economic ties with South Africa and was not willing to see those vanish for the sake of anti-apartheid military campaigns. Furthermore, South African special operations forces, both covert and clandestine to varying degrees, severely crippled the MK's ability to build up and sustain forces capable of attacking South Africa from all of the black African states which bordered South Africa.

To make things far worse for South Africa, and potentially the West in general, the Soviet Union committed huge amounts of military hardware, and military advisers/trainers for FAPLA, the acronym for the Angolan army. Cuba made an even more massive military investment. It ultimately dispatched an expeditionary force to Angola which reached a maximum strength of about 55,000, with a total of almost 380,000 Cuban military personnel serving in the country from 1975 through 1991. If SWAPO took over, or destabilized SWA, whether or not Angolan or Cuban troops moved into SWA, the front line would shift south several hundred miles to the border with South Africa proper.

The Border War was not a directly existential conflict for South Africa, but the strategic imperatives driving it were existential indeed, due to the potential for threats to the territorial integrity of the country.

<u>What to do?</u>

In retrospect, the South African national strategy was brilliant. Like all strategies, it evolved over time in a series of incremental decisions, but in retrospect South African military and political leaders had a deep sense of balance and control which stood them in good stead. The South African Defense Force (SADF) fought SWAPO insurgents inside Southwest Africa, and sometimes in southern Angola, largely with infantry units composed of volunteer black soldiers, both Angolans and men from SWA, commanded and staffed by white South African officers and some white NCOs. There was also a paramilitary internal security force known as Koevoet, manned initially by white South Africans, but more and more with former SWAPO guerrillas. All of these forces knew the country and the terrain, and after a rocky start in the late 1970s and early 1980s, the SADF decisively defeated, and reduced to a bare minimum, the ability of SWAPO to threaten SWA. But the South Africans did not rely on just these black units, highly trained and cohesive as they were. Periodically, the South African Army "mowed the grass" against SWAPO bases and concentrations in southern Angola. Extraordinarily effective mechanized infantry and light and medium-weight armored vehicles, supported by field artillery units whose G5 and G6 155mm cannon were the most effective in the world at the time, repeatedly annihilated SWAPO units and destroyed SWAPO base camps. The counterinsurgency campaign against SWAPO was as demanding as the more glamorous mechanized warfare in southern Angola; the South Africans repeatedly have written of the dedication and willingness to fight and die of SWAPO guerrillas. The use of black units thus kept white draftee casualties to a minimum, and hence helped dampen political controversy over the Border War.

Only one of the South African incursions into southern Angola involved as many as 4,000 troops, and the other large ones were about 3,000 maximum, one brigade at best. These were all-white units, manned by two-year conscripts and junior officers doing their required National Service, as the draft was called in South Africa, with the NCOs and field-grade officers of the career force. There were some reinforcements from reservists, but most were kept in just that status. The South African government did not want to raise the profile of the war among the governing white population by calling up large numbers of white reserve units, and as reserve units almost always do, they required considerable training before being committed to a theater of operations. When SADF reserve units with insufficient training and reorientation from civilian to military attitudes were committed in larger conventional operations involving a high operational tempo and much firepower, near-disaster resulted on several occasions.

South Africa's concern was SWAPO. If SWAPO had not been operating from Angolan bases, South Africa would not have cared much about Angola being a Marxist state with Soviet advisers and equipment, and a huge Cuban contingent propping up the Angolan regime as part of Fidel Castro's profound believe in proletarian internationalism and advancing the cause of Communism wherever he could. Thus, until the late 1980s, South African ground forces in Angola were under strict orders to avoid clashes with the Angolans and, even more so, with the Cubans. However, as SADF operations in Angola became more and more successful, Castro and the Soviet Union became convinced that South Africa was not just fighting a strategic defensive, although its forces on the ground were ferociously effective in the tactical offensive but trying to topple the Angolan Marxist regime. More and more, South African troops were fighting large contingents from FAPLA, the Angolan army. FAPLA forces suffered tactical defeat after defeat. The FAPLA soldiers were largely unwilling pressed men, one South African told me that the term "conscript" implies too much legalism and formality in the process, and officers up through colonel were often incompetent and cowardly. Accounts from Soviet advisers describe their incredible frustration with the military disasters their advisees kept incurring.

But FAPLA did not go away. No matter how many times South African infantry closed with and destroyed FAPLA troops; South African armor smashed FAPLA mechanized infantry vehicles, armored cars, and tanks; and South African artillery did both things, the Soviets kept resupplying their Angolan clients with hardware. The toll of human and material casualties kept rising.

At the same time, the view from Luanda, the Angolan capital and, especially, Havana, was equally bad. In a series of battles from late 1987 through the first few months of 1988, the SADF inflicted major defeats on FAPLA. Castro felt that if Cuba did not come to the aid of Angola the Cubans had hitherto done their best to avoid fighting the South Africans as the South Africans had avoided major clashes with the Cubans his whole position in southern Africa would be imperiled. Furthermore, Gorbachev had come to power in the USSR, and Cuba could see the handwriting on the wall for Soviet military assistance to both Angola and, conceivably, to Cuba itself. But one thing Castro would not do is leave Angola with his tail between his legs. In the late spring of 1988 he moved a full Cuban division into southern Angola, threatening an invasion of SWA, although looking back it is virtually certain that this was a careful exercise of coercive diplomacy rather than a real intention to invade. South Africa responded by calling up large numbers of reserve units, deploying them to SWA to strengthen the forces already present to a full division, and, without threatening to attack the Cubans, acted along the lines of "go ahead, make our day." Nonetheless, even this mobilization was severely restricted by huge logistical deficiencies and reserve readiness issues. If the Cubans had attacked, the SADF would have beaten them but at very high cost in both men and materiel. The Cubans weren't as good as the SADF, but they were much better than the hapless FAPLA.

A much larger war seemed imminent. But neither Cuba nor South Africa wanted one. The Border War was a major drain on South African public finances, and the white public was weary of it. Furthermore, there was a rising tide of unrest among black South Africans, threatening the domestic rear area of the apartheid regime. Castro was also looking for a way out. The Cuban people were down on the massive deployments to Angola. Castro did not want to get involved in a long, drawn-out guerrilla war in southern Africa.

So, both sides, from mid through late 1988, blinked. In particular, Fidel Castro blinked, and one unspoken reason for this was his fear of South Africa's nuclear weapons. South Africa unquestionably had them and gave them up after the war was over and the apartheid regime had ended. But in fact, it had never intended to use them against the Cubans, rightly assuming that the international consequences would be catastrophic. It was, as one book states, a gigantic bluff but it was backed by real nuclear weapons and Castro could not know it was a bluff. So, in August 1988, Cuba and South Africa, with the USSR and the USA in the wings, agreed on a mutual withdrawal of their troops from Angola over a period of time. The timeline was longer for Cuba, but Castro kept his word and he was able to say that he had achieved his objectives in southern Africa true, in the sense of propping up the Angolan regime; and that military defeats FAPLA had inflicted on the SADF had forced the South Africans to come to terms absolute nonsense.

It turned out that the SADF's long commitment to the Border War had been sustained just long enough to make the collapse of the Soviet Union and Warsaw Pact ensure that even if a leftist regime came to power in SWA, which it did through free elections in 1989, becoming independent Namibia, it would no longer be able to destabilize South Africa itself. Probably more importantly, the Cuban, Soviet, and general Marxist-Leninist threat to South Africa was gone by the time that South African President F.W. De Klerk released Nelson Mandela from prison and laid the groundwork for black majority rule which would have had no truck with the apartheid regime's Border War.

White-ruled South Africa, by sustaining a long war without having a large army sustaining heavy casualties bogged down a la Vietnam, had used just enough military power to achieve its objectives and kept domestic white dissatisfaction to a sustainable level. Eventually a real rarity a win-win diplomatic situation for almost all parties concerned was reached. Cuba was able to leave Angola claiming it had won by helping black majority rule come to South Africa. SWAPO got what it wanted an independent Namibia under its control through free elections. South Africa avoided a Marxist-Leninist state on its borders and had a transition to black majority rule much less rocky than most everyone had envisioned. The United States, which had been supporting South Africa's UNITA guerrilla allies, insured that there would be no Soviet client state in southern Africa largely because the entire USSR was falling apart. The only real loser was, in fact, the soon to be defunct Soviet Union, which gained nothing from its investment in southern African warfare.

<u>How did the South Africans do it?</u>

South Africa faced formidable obstacles in fighting the Border War. The SADF was politically constrained from deploying large forces to the Border War because of the government's concern about white casualties, from what I can tell, far, far greater than that of the United States in Iraq and Afghanistan; and the cost to the white South African taxpayer. Thus, the SADF fought most of its battles against enemy forces three, four, and more times their own in numbers. Furthermore, in 1977 the United Nations had placed an international arms embargo on South Africa due to apartheid, placing the South Africans on their own for weapon system acquisition and, more significantly, maintenance and repair. Their work in these areas was ingenious, but qualitative superiority and ingenuity are never a total substitute for numbers "quantity has a quality all its own." While some have characterized the South African logistical situation as "chaotic" due to lack of an implemented logistical doctrine, my sense is that the tyranny of distance and terrain were much more important, and more damaging to the ability of the SADF to support its troops in combat.

The war posed enormous logistical problems for the South Africans. It is about 1,200 miles from Pretoria and Johannesburg to the SADF's operational area in SWA/Namibia and southern Angola. It was about 750 to 800 miles from South Africa proper through Namibia to the Angolan border. It was roughly 200 miles from the Angolan border to the places where the heaviest fighting with FAPLA took place.

Road transportation in SWA was poor. That inside Angola was almost nonexistent and those roads which did exist were mined by the Angolans, forcing the SADF's mobile columns to "bush-bash" across incredibly thick brush. All of this placed a huge burden on the South African Air Force and the one area in which the South Africans, in the last few years of the war, were clearly hampered by their enemy was airpower. The FAPLA and Cuban pilots were no match for those of the SAAF, and their skill at air-to-ground operations far less as well, but their MiG-23s were somewhat superior to the SAAF's French Mirages, and the SAAF's bases were so far from the theater of operations that they could spend very little time on station. This forced the SADF to conduct most of its air and ground logistical operations at night. By the end of hostilities in 1988, the SADF's forces inside Angola were in serious trouble due to their inability to replenish their stocks and resupply and maintain them.

But South Africa also enjoyed immense superiority in several areas. It had the advantages in operational maneuver, combined arms operations, and command and control growing out of the standard Western types of doctrinal development, military training centers, and professional military education, although there are indications that the SADF's high competence at battalion and below was not matched by its ability to conduct operations at brigade and division levels. One South African told me "thank God we never really fought at division level." Basic training for all new recruits was rigorous and demanding, and for officers even more so, even if both were eventually assigned to combat support or combat service support skills and units. All of this was adapted to unique southern African conditions, notably the largely flat terrain ideal for armored and mechanized infantry and artillery operations. One thing which comes through all of the books noted below is that white South Africans consider themselves Africans, first and foremost, and not Europeans you frequently hear whites say that they are a member of one of the two white tribes of their country, Afrikaners or English. There has been white settlement in southern Africa since 1652. The whites are not recent interlopers, any more than the roughly 320 million Americans who are not Indians/Native Americans, 408 years after the first foreign settlers arrived to stay, can be considered such.

Intangibles were important. White South African soldiers, whether volunteers or conscripts, were not fighting in a far-away land with no direct connection, and posing no direct threat, to their homeland. While the SADF had to deal with expeditionary logistics on the ground, its mindset was that it was an army fighting on its both sides of its own borders. I have little doubt this greatly contributed to the willingness of white South African conscripts to serve and minimized opposition to the Border War and to conscription.

The South African Army melded two great fighting traditions. One was that of the British Army, forged in South African participation in both World Wars. The other arguably more significant was that of the Boers during the Boer/South African War of 1899-1902. The Boers held off a much larger British expeditionary force for three years, inflicting huge defeats on the British during the initial stages of the war, and being crushed eventually by a ruthless counterinsurgency campaign which resulted in South Africa essentially being granted its independence within the British Empire, similar to Canada, Australia, and New Zealand. The Afrikaner tradition during the last two years of the Boer War of irregular warfare, emphasis on mobility, and refusal to get bogged down in positional warfare stood the SADF in good stead. Whenever it deviated from this tradition, it had problems.

Finally, I once heard then US Army Chief of Staff General Edward C. "Shy" Meyer say to an Israeli colonel that the leadership of the Israel Defense Force (IDF) had it easy compared to him. The Israeli started laughing and noted that the Israelis didn't think they had it so easy. General Meyer said that "you know exactly who you're going to fight and where you're going to fight them. I can prepare for some likely scenarios, but basically I don't know who I may have to fight and where." The same was true for the SADF. Everything the SADF did could be oriented toward fighting on their northern border against the forces of black African states and insurgencies. They had the strategic disadvantage of fighting on their own borders the farther away from your homeland you can defend it the better off a country is. But this had at least as many institutional and psychological advantages, and the South Africans were able to use those advantages to the fullest.

This latter point suggests that there is a very limited application of the successful ways in which the South African military fought the Border War and achieved the political objectives it had in doing so, for the United States. As former U.S. Secretary of Defense Robert Gates put it, the United States has a 100 percent record since 1945 at predicting where the next war will be we've always been wrong. We didn't predict Korea and Vietnam. We certainly didn't predict the 1990-1991 Persian Gulf War or the conflicts in Afghanistan and Iraq. This wasn't primarily because of strategic incompetence, or the usual mantra about intelligence failures, although they were obviously very much there. It was due, as British Prime Minister Harold Macmillan said in the late 1950s, to "events, my dear boy, events." If you're a super or hyperpower committed to fighting for your security across the oceans, all over the world, then predicting where every potential war is going to turn into a real one is almost impossible.

This also means the U.S. armed forces simply can't completely orient themselves toward one conflict in one place. We were forced to emphasize a potential conventional war with the Soviet Union and the Warsaw Pact, and various Soviet allies and surrogates around the globe that is, World War III because it was the most demanding contingency we could face. But that left us conspicuously unprepared, particularly in doctrinal and organizational terms, for the counterinsurgency wars we faced elsewhere. This melancholy military-planning situation has arguably gotten worse, not better, since the end of the Cold War. Now we don't even have a single possible conflict we can spend most of our time and thought preparing for. The alacrity with which some parts of the U.S. military, notably the U.S. Navy, have turned to preparing for a possible war with China, illustrates our desperate desire for something to focus on.

So, the biggest lesson of the South African Border War for the United States is that Americans are stuck. As General Meyer said, we don't know who we will fight or where we will fight them. And this is bound to result in U.S. armed forces, notably the Army, trying to prepare for a whole range of contingencies. We can, and have, attained extraordinarily high levels of general tactical and operational competence since the U.S. armed forces struck rock-bottom in the last days and short-term aftermath of the Vietnam War, 40 years ago. But because we just can't focus on one theater of operations and one enemy only, we can't tailor our whole military establishment to meet one threat as the South Africans could in the long Border War and we need to stop flagellating ourselves about this. A melancholy and inconvenient truth. But as that well-known military analyst Mick Jagger sang, you can't always get what you want especially in preparing for war or fighting one.

Combat Veteran

1. **NEVER QUESTION THE LOOK IN HIS EYES:**
   You really don't want to know what he's thinking.
2. **NEVER SHAKE HIM TO WAKE HIM:**
   It could be a while before you regain consciousness.
3. **NEVER SNEAK UP ON HIM FROM BEHIND:**
   See above comment.
4. **NEVER ASK HIM IF HE HAS KILLED ANYONE:**
   He may say your next.
5. **NEVER PROVOKE HIM:**
   PTSD means he has a short fuse and a long memory.
6. **NEVER DISRESPECT HIS FLAG OR COUNTRY:**
   He has lost friends defending both.
7. **NEVER RUN DOWN HIS BROTHERS IN ARMS:**
   They are closer than family.
8. **NEVER CALL HIS WAR A SIMPLE CONFLICT:**
   conflicts are for pussies, men fight wars.
9. **NEVER EXPECT HIM TO FIT INTO YOUR SOCIAL AGENDA:**
   There are never enough chairs and never enough walls.
10. **NEVER FORGET, TO HIM THREE IS A CROWD:**
    large crowds coming at him are just incoming rounds.
11. **NEVER BRING UP HIS PAST, IT'S HIS PERSONAL NIGHTMARE:**
    He already knows he's messed up, let it be.

Manufactured by Amazon.ca
Bolton, ON

12747225R00252